# MIRACLE

www.**booksattransworld**.co.uk

## Also by Danielle Steel

* Published outside the UK under the title PASSION'S PROMISE

# DANIELLE STEEL

# MIRACLE

## BANTAM PRESS

LONDON · TORONTO · SYDNEY · AUCKLAND · JOHANNESBURG

TRANSWORLD PUBLISHERS
61–63 Uxbridge Road, London W5 5SA
a division of The Random House Group Ltd

RANDOM HOUSE AUSTRALIA (PTY) LTD
20 Alfred Street, Milsons Point, Sydney,
New South Wales 2061, Australia

RANDOM HOUSE NEW ZEALAND LTD
18 Poland Road, Glenfield, Auckland 10, New Zealand

RANDOM HOUSE SOUTH AFRICA (PTY) LTD
Endulini, 5a Jubilee Road, Parktown 2193, South Africa

Published 2005 by Bantam Press
a division of Transworld Publishers

Printed in Great Britain by
Clays Ltd, Bungay, Suffolk

1 3 5 7 9 10 8 6 4 2

Papers used by Transworld Publishers are natural, recyclable products
made from wood grown in sustainable forests. The manufacturing processes
conform to the environmental regulations of the country of origin.

To miracles,
large and small,
that bring forgiveness.
And to great loves,
oh so rare,
and hard won.

with all my love,
d.s.

"... all human wisdom was contained
in these two words: Wait and Hope!"

ALEXANDRE DUMAS
*The Count of Monte Cristo*

# MIRACLE

# 1

THE SAILING YACHT *VICTORY* MADE HER WAY ELEGANTLY along the coast toward the old port in Antibes on a rainy November day. The sea was choppy, as Quinn Thompson stood silently on the deck, looking up at the sails, savoring his last few moments aboard her. He didn't mind the weather or the gray day, or even the rough seas. He was an inveterate and seasoned sailor. The *Victory* was a hundred-fifty-foot sailboat, with auxiliary engines, that he had chartered from a man he had done business with frequently in London. Her owner had had business reversals that year, and Quinn had been grateful to have use of the boat since August. He had used her well, and the time he had spent aboard had been good for him in every way. He was healthy, strong, and more peaceful than he had been when the trip began. He was a handsome, vigorous, youthful-looking man. And more than he had been in months, he was resigned to his fate.

He had boarded the yacht in Italy, and after that spent time in Spanish and French waters. He had hit a traditionally rough patch in the Gulf of Lions, and relished the excitement of a brief and unexpected storm. He had sailed on to Sweden and Norway afterward, and returned slowly through several German ports. He'd been on the boat for three months, and it had served a useful purpose. It had given him all the time away that he needed, time he had used well to think and recover from all that had occurred. He had been stalling his return to California for months. He had no reason to go home. But with winter setting in, he knew he couldn't delay his return much longer. The owner of the *Victory* wanted her in the Caribbean for his own use by Christmas, as they had discussed when they agreed to the charter. Quinn had paid a fortune for three months aboard, but he didn't regret a penny of it. The stiff price of the charter meant nothing to Quinn Thompson. He could afford that, and a great deal more. Materially and professionally, he had been a very lucky man.

The time on board had also served to remind him of how passionately he loved sailing. He didn't mind the solitude, in fact he thrived on it, and the crew were both expert and discreet. They had been impressed by his skill, and quickly realized he knew far more about the *Victory*, how to sail her hard and well, than did her owner, who knew next to nothing. Above all, for Quinn, she had provided both a means of escape and a gentle haven. He had particularly enjoyed his time in the fjords, their stern beauty seemed to suit him far more than the festive or romantic ports in the Mediterranean, which he had assiduously avoided.

His bags were packed in his cabin as he stood on deck, and,

familiar with the efficiency of the crew by then, he knew that within hours of his departure, all evidence of his time aboard would have vanished. There were six male crew members on board, and one woman, the wife of the captain, who acted as stewardess. Like the others, she had been discreet and polite, and rarely said much to him, and like the owner, the entire crew was British. And he and the captain had enjoyed a comfortable and respectful rapport.

"Sorry for the chop on the way in," the captain said with a smile as he joined Quinn on deck. But he knew by now that Quinn wouldn't mind. Quinn turned to nod at him, undisturbed by the waves breaking over the bow, and the rain beating down on them. He was wearing foul weather gear, and in fact, he liked the challenge of hard sailing, rough seas, and the occasional storm. The only thing he didn't like was leaving. Quinn and the captain had spent hours talking about sailing, and the places they'd been. And the captain couldn't help but be impressed by Quinn's extensive travels, and the depth of his knowledge. Quinn Thompson was a man of many hats and many faces, a legend in the world of international finance. The yacht's owner had told the captain before Quinn arrived that he had been a man of humble beginnings who had made a vast fortune. He had even gone so far as to call him brilliant, and after three months on the boat with him, the captain didn't disagree with that opinion. Quinn Thompson was a man whom many admired, some feared, a few hated, sometimes with good reason. Quinn Thompson was direct, sure, powerful, mysterious in some ways, and unrelenting about anything he wanted. He was a man of infinite ideas, endless imagination in his field, and few words, except when he was in one of his rare expansive moods, which the captain had enjoyed as well, usually after a few brandies. For the most part, they had kept their conversations confined to sailing, a topic that they both enjoyed, more than any other.

The captain knew Quinn had lost his wife the previous spring, and Quinn had mentioned her once or twice. There were times when a wistful look came over him, and some somber days in the beginning. But for most of the hours they stood beside each other on deck, Quinn kept his own counsel. The captain knew he had a daughter as well, because he'd mentioned her once, but Quinn seldom talked about her either. He was a man who was quick to share ideas, but rarely feelings.

"You ought to make Mr. Barclay an offer for the *Victory*," the captain said hopefully as the crew took down the sails, and he turned on the motor, glancing at Quinn over his shoulder as they headed into port. Quinn smiled in answer to the comment. His smiles were hard won, but when they came, they were well worth it. They lit up his face like summer sunshine. The rest of the time, and far more frequently, he seemed lost in winter. And when he laughed, he was a different person.

"I've thought about it," Quinn admitted, "but I don't think he'd sell her." Quinn had asked John Barclay before chartering her, if there was any chance he would, and Barclay had said only if he had to, and had admitted he would give up his wife and children before his sailboat, a point of view Quinn both understood and respected. He didn't repeat the comment to the captain. But in the past three months, Quinn had fallen in love with the idea of buying a boat. He hadn't owned one in years, and there was no one to stop him now.

"You should have a boat, sir," the captain ventured cautiously. He would have loved to work for him. Quinn was hard but fair, respectful, and exciting to sail with. He had done things with the *Victory*, and gone places, John Barclay would never have dared or dreamed of. The entire crew had loved the three months they had spent sailing for Quinn Thompson. And Quinn himself had been thinking of buying or building a boat since August, especially now that his months on the *Victory* were over. It would be the perfect answer to getting out of San Francisco. He had already decided to sell the house, and was thinking of buying an apartment somewhere in Europe. At sixty-one, he had been retired for nearly two years, and with Jane gone, he had no reason to stay in San Francisco. He realized that a boat might restore joy to his life. In fact this one already had. He hated the fact that people often disappointed each other. But boats never did.

"I've been coming to the same conclusion myself all morning," Quinn said quietly. He hated to leave the *Victory*, and he knew she was sailing in two days for Gibraltar, and after that to St. Martin, where her owner was meeting her for Christmas with his wife and children. The price Quinn had paid to charter her was helping Barclay to afford her, and had made an enormous difference. She would surely be his for at least another year as a result. "Do you know of anything comparable up for sale at the moment?" Quinn asked with interest, as the captain kept his eyes straight ahead, watching their course as they came into the channel, and he pondered the question.

"Nothing up to your standards, I suspect, not a sailboat." There were always large power boats changing hands, but fine sailboats of the caliber Quinn would want were harder to come by. In most cases, their owners loved them—and wouldn't part with them easily. He was still thinking about it when the first mate joined them, and the captain asked him the question, and Quinn was intrigued when the young man nodded.

"I heard about one two weeks ago, when we left Norway. She's not finished yet, but she's up for sale. She's still in a ship-yard in Holland. Bob Ramsay commissioned her last year, and he just decided to sell her. He wants a bigger one. I hear the one for sale's a beauty." All three men knew she would be if she had been commissioned by Bob Ramsay, he was a notable sailor with three handsome yachts he competed with in all the European races, and he generally took all the prizes. He was an American with a French wife and they lived in Paris. He was a hero in the international sailing world, and all the boats he had built were exquisite.

"Do you know which yard she's in?" Quinn asked, suddenly wondering if this was the answer to his prayers, as the young man brightened.

"I do. I'll call them for you, if you like, as soon as we dock."

Quinn was leaving on a flight to London that afternoon, spending the night at a hotel, and flying to San Francisco the next morning. He had called his daughter, Alex, in Geneva about seeing her before he flew home, and she had said she was too busy with the children. He knew the real reason for her not seeing him, and he no longer had the energy to fight it. The battles between them were too bitter and had gone on for too long. She had never forgiven him for what she perceived as his failures in her childhood. And she had told him months before that she would never, ever forgive him for calling her so late in her mother's illness. In fact, he realized now that blind hope and denial had kept him from calling her earlier than he had. Both he and Jane had refused to believe she would actually die. They kept telling themselves and each other that she would survive. And by the time Jane agreed to let him call their daughter, it was only days before the end. And even then they didn't think she would die. He wondered at times if he and Jane had wanted to be alone for her last days, and had unconsciously failed to include Alex.

When Alex had flown home to see her mother, Jane was ravaged. Alex had arrived two days before Jane died, and she was either in such extreme pain or so heavily sedated, Alex had hardly been able to speak to her mother, except in rare lucid moments when Jane continued to insist she would be fine. Alex had been numb with grief and shock, and blazed with fury at her father. All her misery and sense of loss had channeled itself into the resentment she already felt for him, and the flames of disappointment and grief and anguish were fanned into outrage. She sent Quinn one searing letter of agony as soon as she returned home, and for months after that she hadn't returned a single one of his phone calls. In spite of Jane's final pleas for them to make peace and take care of each other, Quinn had all but given up on Alex since his wife's death. He knew how distressed Jane would have been over their estrangement, and he felt badly about it, but there was nothing he could do. And in his heart, he thought Alex was right. Without meaning to, he and Jane had cheated her of enough time to say good-bye.

The phone call he had made two days before from the *Victory* had been one last futile attempt to reach out to her, and he had been met by an icy rebuff. There seemed to be no way now to bridge the chasm, and her anger over her childhood had smoldered for too long. For all the years he had been building his empire, he had spent almost no time with Jane and the children. She had forgiven him, Jane always understood what he was doing, and what it meant to him, and never reproached him for it. She had been proud of his victories, whatever they cost her personally. But Alex had come to hate him for his absences, and his seeming lack of interest in her early life. She had told him that on the day of the funeral, along with her fury at not having been warned of the severity of her mother's illness. And although she had her mother's fragile looks, she was as tough as he was—in some ways even more so. She was as unrelenting and unforgiving as he had often been in the past. And now he had no defense in the face of her ire. He knew she was right.

There was a tender side of Quinn that few knew, and Jane had always been certain of, a soft underbelly that he kept well concealed, and that she cherished, even when it was least visible. And while Alex had his strength, she had none of Jane's compassion. There was an icy side to her that even frightened Quinn. She had been angry at him for years, and it was clear she intended to stay that way, particularly now that she felt he had cheated her of her last days with her mother. That was the final blow to their relationship as father and daughter. And he realized now, in the face of Alex's accusations, that he had wanted Jane to himself for her last days, and hadn't wanted to share her with Alex. Terrified of Jane's death, he had clung to denial. There had been so much to say to each other, after all the years he'd been away, all the things he had never said to her, and never thought he had to. In the end, he had said it all to her, they both had. And it was in those last weeks that she shared all her journals and poems with him. He had always thought he knew his wife, and it was only at the very end that he discovered he hadn't.

Beneath her calm, quiet, bland exterior had lived a woman of boundless warmth and love and passion, all of which had been directed at him, and the depths of which he had never fully understood until far too late. More than anything Alex could accuse him of, he now knew that he could never forgive himself for it. He had hardly ever been there for Jane. He realized he had abandoned his wife even more than he had abandoned their daughter. Jane should have been as angry at him as Alex was, but all she had done was love him more, in his endless absences. He was deeply ashamed of it and consumed with guilt he knew he would suffer for a lifetime. It seemed an unpardonable crime even to him, and even more so now that he had read all her journals. He had brought them with him on the trip, and had been reading them for months, each night. And even more than the journals, her love poems sliced into him like scalpels and tore his heart out. She had been the most compassionate, forgiving, generous woman he had ever known, and she had been a treasure far greater than he had ever suspected. The worst of all ironies was that it was only now that she was gone that he understood it. Too late. So much, much too late. All he could do now was regret his failures and her loss for the rest of his lifetime. There was no way to repair it, or make amends, or even atone for it, although he had apologized for it before she died. Worse yet, Jane had assured him he had nothing to regret, nothing to reproach himself for. She promised him that she had been happy with him for the years they shared, which only made his guilt worse. How could she have been happy with a man who was never there, and paid almost no attention to her? He knew what he had been guilty of, and why he had done it. He had been obsessed with his empire, his achievements, and his own doings. He had rarely thought of anyone else, least of all his wife and children. Alex had every right to be angry at him, he knew, and Jane had had every reason to hate him, and didn't. Instead she had written him love poems and was fiercely devoted to him and Quinn knew better than anyone how little he deserved it. In fact, he had dreams about it almost every night now. Dreams in which she was begging him to come home, and pleading with him not to abandon her, or forget her.

Quinn had retired the year before she died, and they had spent a year traveling to all the places he wanted to explore. As usual, Jane had been a good sport about following him wherever he wanted. They went to Bali, Nepal, India, the far reaches of China. They had gone back to places they both loved, Morocco, Japan, Turkey. They hadn't stopped traveling all year, and for the first time in years, grew ever closer to each other. He had forgotten how entertaining she was, what good company, and how much he enjoyed her. They fell in love all over again, and had never been happier together than they were then.

It was in Paris that they discovered how ill she was, and the seriousness of it. She had had stomach problems for months, which they both thought were a harmless by-product of their travels. They flew home after that and had it checked out again. And it was even worse than they thought, but even then, they had both denied it. He realized now from her journals that she had understood the severity of what ailed her before he did. But she remained convinced nonetheless that she would beat it. She had been suffering in silence for months before that, not wanting to spoil the traveling he wanted so much to do, and had waited so long for. She was upset because their coming home had meant canceling a trip to Brazil and Argentina. It all seemed so pointless now, and so empty without her.

Jane was fifty-nine when she died, and they had been married for thirty-seven years. Alex was thirty-four, and her brother Doug would have been thirty-six now, if he had lived. He died in a boating accident at thirteen, and Quinn realized now that he had scarcely known him. He had much to regret and repent for. And he had the rest of his life in which to do it. Jane had died in June, and now, as they sailed into port in Old Antibes, it was November. It had been an agonizing, interminable five months without her. And Quinn knew with absolute certainty that he would never forgive himself for having failed her. His dreams and Jane's journals were a constant reminder of his failures. Alex had long since tried him and found him guilty. He didn't disagree with her.

The captain came to Quinn's cabin after they docked, to

give him the information about the sailboat that was under construction and up for sale in Holland. He had just called the boatyard. He was smiling as he crossed the threshold.

"She's a hundred and eighty feet long, and she sounds like a beauty," he beamed. "She's a ketch, and the yard says there's been some interest, but so far no one's bought her. Ramsay only just decided to sell her." The two men's eyes met, and a slow smile spread over Quinn's face. It was the happiest the captain had seen him. For most of the trip, Quinn had seemed tormented. "Are you going to go and see her, sir?" the captain asked with interest. "I'd be happy to change your flight for you. There's a flight for Amsterdam half an hour after the one you were going to take to London."

Quinn couldn't believe what he was hearing. It was more than a little crazy. A hundred-and-eighty-foot sailboat. But why not? He could sail around the world for the rest of his life. He couldn't think of anything he would have liked better. He could live on the boat, and sail around to all the places he loved, and those where he hadn't been yet. All he needed with him were Jane's poems and journals. There was nothing else in the world now that mattered to him. He had read them again and again. Their crystal clarity and open love for him were like a blow each time he read them.

"How crazy is that?" Quinn asked the captain, as he sat back in a leather chair in his cabin, and thought about the hundred-and-eighty-foot sailboat for a minute. He felt it was more than he deserved, but it was all he wanted. Living on a yacht was the perfect escape route.

"It's not crazy at all, sir. It's a shame for a sailor like you not to have a boat of your own." He wanted to tell Quinn that he would love to work for him, but he didn't want to be intrusive. But if Quinn bought the boat, he had every intention of saying it to him. There was no love lost between him and John Barclay, the *Victory*'s owner. Quinn Thompson was just exactly the kind of man he wanted to work for, he was the consummate sailor. John Barclay ran the *Victory* like a houseboat, and had no real need for a seasoned captain. Most of the time, all they did was sit in port, or at anchor while they went swimming. "She's a year away from completion, maybe less, if you push them. You could be sailing her wherever you want by the end of next summer. Or at worst, a year from now, sir."

"All right," Quinn said, looking suddenly decisive. "Let's do it. Do you mind changing my flight for me? I can fly to London after I see her." He had no schedule to meet, no timetable to follow, no one to see or be with, and the past three months had proven to him what he had suspected. He wanted a sailboat. And there was no one to stop him now. "Do you mind calling and telling the yard I'm coming?" Quinn's eyes looked hopeful and bright.

"Not at all, sir. I'll speak to the yard owner, and tell him to expect you."

"I'll need a reservation at the Amstel. Just for tonight. Tomorrow, I'll go straight from the yard to the airport, and fly to London." It was an exciting decision, and if he didn't like the boat, he didn't have to buy her. He could even commission one of his own from scratch, but that, Quinn knew, would take longer. It would take at least two years to build a boat comparable to the one Ramsay had ordered, possibly even longer.

The captain made all the arrangements for him, and half an hour later Quinn shook hands with him and the entire crew, and thanked them for their kindness to him. He had left generous tips for each of them, and had written a sizable check to the captain. He promised to let him know how things turned out in Holland. And as he sped toward the airport in Nice in a limousine, Quinn felt the same anguish he had felt for months, wishing he could tell Jane what he was about to do, and what he hoped would happen in Holland. There was always something he wanted to share with her, something that reminded him with agonizing acuteness of how empty his life was without her. He closed his eyes for a moment, thinking of her, and then forced himself to open them. There was no point allowing himself to get sucked into the black pit of grief again. It had been a constant battle since June. But the one thing he did know, and believed with every ounce of his being, was that a sailboat was at least one way to flee the places he had been and lived with her that had become too painful for him. A sailboat was something for him to live for. He could never replace Jane with a boat. But he sensed, as they reached the airport, that she would have been pleased for him. She always was. Whatever he chose to do, she always supported him, and celebrated each and every idea he had, no matter how crazy it seemed to anyone else. Jane would have understood, better than anyone. She was the one person who would. The one person, the only person he knew, who had really loved him. More than he had ever known when she was alive, he knew now without any doubt, his entire life with her had been a love poem, just like the ones she had written and left for him.

# 2

THE PLANE TOUCHED DOWN AT SCHIPHOL AIRPORT IN Amsterdam at six o'clock, and Quinn took a cab to the Amstel Hotel. It was one of his favorite hotels in Europe. Its ancient grandeur and exquisite service always reminded him some-what of the Ritz in Paris. He ordered room service shortly after he arrived and found himself torn between missing the com-forts of the *Victory* and her crew, and excitement over the boat he was planning to see in the morning. He found it nearly im-possible to sleep that night with the anticipation of it. All he hoped now was that he would love it.

He slept fitfully, and was up and dressed by seven the next morning. He had to wait another hour for a car and driver to come, and passed the time by reading the *Herald Tribune* over breakfast. It was an hour's drive from the hotel to the boat-yard, and by nine o'clock, he was in the office of the owner of the shipyard, a powerfully built older man, with an ebullient style, who had the plans on his desk, in anticipation of Quinn's visit. He had heard of him, and read of him over the years, and the night before, he had made some calls, and done some careful research. He had a very clear idea of what Quinn was about, and knew of his incisive, and allegedly ruthless reputation. To those who crossed him, or failed him in some way, Quinn could be fearsome.

Quinn eased his long, lean frame into a chair, and his blue eyes seemed to dance as he went over the plans with the owner of the shipyard. His name was Tem Hakker, and he was a few years older than Quinn. Both his sons were in the office with them, and explained the plans in detail to Quinn. Both of the younger men were in charge of the project, and took a great deal of pride in it, with good reason. The boat was going to be spectacular, and Quinn had fresh respect for Bob Ramsay's genius as he listened. The giant sailboat seemed to have almost everything he would have wanted. Quinn had a few additional ideas, and made suggestions as they talked, which in turn impressed both younger Hakkers, as well as their father. Quinn's ideas were of a technical nature, which improved on Ramsay's initial concept.

"He's crazy to give up this boat," Quinn said as he went over the plans with them again. He was anxious to see the boat now.

"We're building him an eighty-meter," Tem Hakker said with pride. Two hundred and fifty feet. But the one they were discussing seemed vast enough to Quinn. It was everything he could ever have wished for, and all he needed.

"That ought to keep him happy," Quinn quipped easily, referring to the eighty-meter, and then asked to see the boat still under construction that Ramsay was selling. And when he did, Quinn stood in awestruck silence and whistled. Even the hull looked beautiful to him. There were already large sections of the boat completed. The main mast was going to stand a hundred and ninety feet tall, and she was to carry eighteen thousand square feet of sail. She was going to be a sight to behold when she was completed. Even in her unfinished state, she was, to Quinn, a creature of exquisite beauty. It was love at first sight, and he knew looking at her that he had to have her, which was how he did things. Quinn Thompson was a man of instant and almost always infallible decisions.

They spent an hour examining her, discussing changes Quinn wanted to make now that he'd seen her, and then he and Tem Hakker walked slowly back to his office. Hakker and Bob Ramsay had agreed on a price for her, and after a few rapid calculations, keeping in mind the changes Quinn wanted made, he quoted a price that would have made most men blanch. Quinn showed no emotion as he listened, and just as rapidly countered. There was a long silent pause, as Hakker looked at him and took the full measure of the man, and nodded. And as he did, he stuck out his hand and Quinn shook it. The deal was done, at an impressive price, but there was no question in either man's mind that the yacht was worth it. Both men were delighted. And Quinn told him he wanted it completed by August, which he knew was optimistic, but now that he had seen her, he could hardly wait to set off on his travels and life of escape aboard her. The months of waiting for her would seem endless, but the anticipation thrilled him.

"I was hoping you would agree to November. Or perhaps

we could have her ready for you in October," Tem Hakker said cautiously. Quinn Thompson drove a hard bargain.

In the end, after some discussion, they compromised on September. Or at least by then Tem Hakker thought she would be ready for sea trials. And with luck, she would be ready to sail away by the end of the month, or at the latest the first of October. Quinn said he would live with that, if he had to. And he had every intention of flying over to see the work in progress as often as he could, and hold them to the date they had agreed on. It was nearly a year away, and Quinn could hardly wait to sail her.

Quinn left the yard at noon, having written a hefty check, and he called the captain of the *Victory* before he left to tell him the news and thank him.

"Good job, sir," the captain said, sounding ecstatic. "I can't wait to see her." He had every intention of writing to Quinn after that, to broach the subject of a job with him, but he didn't want to do it over the phone. Quinn was already thinking of it himself.

He had a million details and plans on his mind now. And he waved at the Hakkers as he drove away. They were every bit as pleased with the deal as he was, perhaps even more so. A boat of that scope and magnitude was not normally as easy to sell as it had been to Quinn Thompson. He hadn't hesitated for an instant, and as he drove back to the airport to catch his flight, he knew he had a new home as well as a new passion. All he wanted to do now was sell the house in San Francisco, and do whatever work he needed to do, to do so. There were a few things he knew he had to clean up before he sold it. But his mind was full now with all the details of the boat. He knew it was going to be a new life for him, for whatever years he had left. And it was going to make going back to the empty house that much easier, or at least he thought so.

He had had a small sailboat years before, and had encouraged both of his children to learn sailing. Like her mother, Alex had hated it, and after Doug's death in a boating accident at a summer camp in Maine, Jane had finally convinced him to sell the boat. He never had time to use it anyway, and had acceded to her wishes. For more than twenty years he had been content to sail on other people's yachts from time to time, always without Jane, since she didn't like boats. And now suddenly a whole new world had opened up to him. It seemed the perfect scenario for his final chapter, and just the way he wanted to spend the rest of his days, sailing around the world on a boat that was better than any he had ever dreamed of. He was still smiling to himself as he boarded the plane to London, and he spent the entire night making notes about it in his hotel room. The prospect of his new boat had changed the entire mood and tenor of Quinn's existence.

As Quinn boarded the plane to San Francisco at Heathrow the next day, he realized that soon San Francisco would no longer be home to him. All he had left there were memories of Jane, and the years they had shared, and he could take all of that with him. Wherever he went, whatever he did, she would always be with him. He had her precious journals in his briefcase, and shortly after take-off he took one of her poems out to read it. He read it again and again, as he always did, and then sat staring out the window. He didn't even hear the flight

19

attendant speak to him and ask him what he'd like to drink as she offered. He was lost in his own thoughts, until she finally caught his attention. He declined the champagne, and asked for a Bloody Mary, which she brought to him before serving anyone else. The seat next to him was empty mercifully, and he felt relieved, as he hated talking to people on planes. The flight attendant commented to the purser about him when she went back to the galley. She said he looked like someone important. But when the purser glanced at him, he said he didn't recognize him, and agreed that he was a good-looking man, but he didn't appear to be particularly friendly. In fact, he wasn't.

"Probably just another CEO, tired after a week of meetings in London." It was what he had been once upon a time, not so long ago. But now he was someone very different. He was a man with an extraordinary new sailboat. Neither of them could have imagined it as they looked at him, but more important, he knew it. It was the only thing he had in his life to be pleased about, as he flew toward San Francisco. His wife had died, his daughter hated him, or thought she did, his son had died years before. He was alone in the world with no one to love him, or care about what he did. And in a few hours, he would be walking into an empty house, the house he had shared with a woman he had thought he knew and didn't. A woman who had loved him more than he felt he deserved, and toward whom he felt both grateful and guilty. In fact, he was certain of how unworthy he was, as he read her poem again, and then slipped it back into his briefcase. He closed his eyes then, and thought of her, fighting to remember every detail of her face, her voice, the sound of her laughter. He was desperately afraid that the memories would slip away from him in time, but he knew they wouldn't as long as he had her journals. They were his last hold on her, the key to the mysteries he had never understood, nor cared to discover. The poems and journals, and his regret and love for her, were all he had left of her that mattered.

# 3

THE PLANE LANDED IN SAN FRANCISCO RIGHT ON TIME, and Quinn passed through customs quickly. Despite his long absence from the States, he had nothing to declare, and he looked somber as he picked up his valise and briefcase, and hurried outside with his head down. He wasn't looking forward to getting home to the empty house, and he had realized with a pang on the plane, that he had managed to time his return to just before Thanksgiving. It hadn't even occurred to him when he made his plans, but he had no choice anyway. His charter of the *Victory* had come to an end, and he could no longer come up with a valid reason to linger in Europe, particularly if Alex refused to see him.

She had been polite but firm. Her outbursts at him had occurred before and after the funeral. And since then, any contact he'd had with her had been distant, formal, and chilly. In her own way, she was as stubborn as he was. She had been furious with him for years anyway. She and her mother had

23

discussed it endlessly, and despite all of her mother's efforts to soften her point of view, Alex had continued to maintain her harsh, judgmental position. She claimed her father had never been there, for any of them, not even when Doug died. Quinn had come home for three days for the funeral. He'd been in Bangkok, concluding a business deal, when he got the news, and turned around and left again the morning after the funeral, leaving eleven-year-old Alex and her mother to grieve and mourn, and cling to each other in their solitary anguish.

He had been gone for a month that time, putting together an enormous deal that had made headlines in the *Wall Street Journal*, returned briefly again, and then took off to spend two months in Hong Kong, London, Paris, Beijing, Berlin, Milan, New York, and Washington, D.C. Now that she was an adult, Alex said she could hardly ever remember seeing her father, let alone talking to him. Whenever he was home, he was too busy, exhausted and jet-lagged, and sleep-deprived, to spend time with her or her mother. And in the end, he had managed to cheat her of even a decent amount of time to say good-bye to her mother. Quinn had heard it all before, during, and after the funeral, and would never forget it. There was no turning back from what she'd said and the bitter portrait of him she had painted. And the worst of it was that, as he listened to her, Quinn knew without a doubt that he couldn't deny it. The man she described was in fact the person he had been then, and was until he retired. And whatever changes had occurred since then, most of them positive, Alex was not willing to acknowledge.

Quinn had tried to make up to Jane for the long years when

24

he'd been busy and absent, and thought he had in some ways, as best he could, during the year and a half they had shared after he had retired. But there was no way he could make it up to Alex. It was also noticeable to him that she had married a man who scarcely left home, except to go to the office. She had married a Swiss banker right after college. They had gone to Yale together, and married almost minutes after they graduated, thirteen years before. They had two boys, lived in Geneva, and Quinn had commented to Jane right from the first that it was Alex who told Horst what to do, and what she wanted. They were inseparable, and seemed happy, sedate, and secure, though uninspired and unexciting. Quinn found his son-in-law painfully boring. Alex had been careful not to fall into the same trap she thought her mother had. Instead, she had married a weak man, to do her bidding, as different as possible from her father. Horst rarely, if ever, traveled, and worked in the bank his grandfather had founded. He was a responsible young man, who loved his wife and sons, and had no great ambitions. Alex had known when she married him that she would never be sacrificed to his career or accomplishments or passions. To Quinn's practiced eye, Horst had none. He simply existed, which was what Alex had wanted.

Her sons were six and nine, two beautiful little blue-eyed towheads, just like their mother, and Quinn scarcely knew them. Jane had gone to Geneva frequently to visit them, and Alex had brought the boys to San Francisco once a year to visit her mother, but Quinn had rarely been around when they came to town, and he always seemed to be in some other part of the world when Jane went to Geneva. Often, when Quinn was away, Jane took the opportunity to visit her daughter. Looking at it in retrospect, it was easy for him to see why Alex was angry. And she had no intention of letting her father make up for it, or atone for his sins, both real and perceived. As far as Alex was concerned, she had lost not one, but two parents. Quinn had died in her heart years before she had lost her mother. And the trauma of losing her brother when she was eleven years old had remained an open wound for her. It made her particularly protective of her children, despite her husband's pleas to give them just a little more freedom. Alex was convinced she knew better. And more than anything, because of her brother's accident, she hated sailboats.

Jane had never been fond of them either, but Quinn suspected she would have been happy for him, about the new boat he was building. Jane had always wanted him to be happy, to fulfill his dreams, and to achieve everything he had wanted to accomplish. Alex no longer cared what he did. As a result, Quinn was a man with no family, no ties to anyone, he was as solitary as he looked as he stepped out of the cab on Vallejo Street in a cul-de-sac filled with trees that all but obscured the house he and Jane had lived in for their entire marriage, and that Alex had grown up in. He had wanted to buy a bigger one as his fortune grew, but Jane had always insisted she loved this one. And Quinn had too while Jane was still there to come home to. Now, as he turned his key in the lock of the big rambling English-style house, he dreaded the silence.

As he stepped into the front hall and set his bags down, he could hear a clock ticking in the living room. The sound cut through him like a knife, and felt like a heartbeat. He had

never felt as alone or as empty. There were no flowers anywhere, the shades and curtains were drawn, and the dark paneling in the living room, which had once glinted and shone,
now made the room look tomblike. He couldn't remember the
house ever seeming as dark or as depressing. And without
thinking, he went to the windows, pulled back the curtains,
opened the shades, and stood staring into the garden. The
trees and hedges were still green, but there were no flowers,
and it was a dark November afternoon.

The fog had come in while they were landing, and it was
swirling through the city. The sky looked as gray as he felt, as
he picked up his bags and walked upstairs. And when he saw
their bedroom, it took his breath away. She had died in his arms
in their bed five months before, and he felt a physical pain as he
stared at the bed, and then saw her smiling in a photograph
next to it. He sat down on the edge of the bed, with tears rolling
down his cheeks. It had been a mistake to come home, he knew,
but there was no one else to sort through her things, and his
own, if he was to sell the house in the spring. And he knew
there was work to do on the house. Everything was in good order and worked well, but thirty-seven years in one house was
almost a lifetime. He felt he had to organize the work and sort
through their things himself, no matter how painful. Some of
the rooms needed a coat of paint, and he wanted to consult a realtor to find out what he had to do to sell it.

It was a long hard first night home for him, and he longed
for Jane with such loneliness and agony that at times he
wanted to run into the street in his pajamas, just to flee it. There
was no escaping. He knew he had to face it. There was no

27

reprieve. His life without her was his sentence. Life without parole. He knew his solitude was forever, and felt he deserved it. And that night, he had the same dream he had experienced frequently before he left on his travels. It was a dream in which Jane came to him, held out her arms, pleading with him, and she was crying. At first the words were indistinct, but even without them, the look on her face tore his heart out. And then the words would come clear to him, and they were always the same, with subtle variations. She would beg him not to leave her, not to abandon her again. And each time he had the dream, he promised her he wouldn't. And then like a nightmare, not a dream, he would see himself pick up a suitcase and leave anyway, and all he could see after that was her face, crying after he left her. He could still hear her sobs when he woke up, at whatever hour, and her words would echo in his head for hours afterward, "Quinn, don't leave me...Quinn, please..." her arms outstretched, her eyes devastated. And whenever he woke from that dream, he felt panicked. How could he have done that to her? Why had he left so often? Why had his own pursuits always seemed so important? Why didn't he listen?

The dream entirely dismissed the reasons for his trips, and swept away the empire he was building. And all that was left afterward, in the dream, was his own crushing sense of guilt and failure. He hated the dream, and the fact that it had returned almost immediately, as soon as he came back to San Francisco. There was something so tragic about Jane in the dream, although in real life she had been tenderly empathetic and understanding, and had never reproached or implored him the way the woman in the dream did. Quinn hated the dream, and in some ways, he knew that guilt was the chain that bound him to her, as much as love had. But the fact that the dream had returned with a vengeance the moment he got home did not cheer him. It was a burden he knew he had to live with.

The next morning, he showered, shaved, dressed, swallowed a cup of coffee, rolled up his sleeves, and began digging into closets. He was still trying to get the dream out of his head, and felt haunted by it. He began with the easy closets downstairs, where Alex had stored all the mementos of her childhood. Jane had been urging her to take them for years, but she preferred to leave them with her parents. There were ribbons and trophies from her horseback riding days, and a few for tennis tournaments she'd been in, in college. Endless photographs of her friends, most of whom Quinn didn't recognize, from kindergarten to college. There were tapes, and home movies, a few battered old dolls, and a teddy bear, and finally a box at the back that he wrestled toward him. It was sealed and he used a penknife to open it, and when he did, he found that it was full of photographs of Douglas, many with Alex. The two of them laughing and smiling and cavorting, several of them skiing, and a whole pack of letters from him, when he had gone to camp in Maine, and she had gone to one in California, closer to home. And as though directed to by angels' wings, Quinn found himself opening a brittle, yellowed old letter, and he saw with a start that the date was the one on which Doug had died. He had written to Alex only that morning, hours before the sailing accident that had ended his life at thirteen. Tears streamed down Quinn's face as he read it, and suddenly he realized what they had all felt afterward, what he hadn't allowed himself to feel. In spite of the fact that he had loved his son, he had kept him at a distance. Quinn had barely allowed himself to know him.

Doug had been a handsome boy, happy, kind, intelligent, and looked just like his father, but Quinn had always put off getting closer to him. He had always thought they'd have time "later." He had fantasized their becoming friends as men, and instead the boy had slipped right through his fingers. And even then, he hadn't properly grieved him. It had been too painful to admit that he had missed the chance to know Doug better. And once again, guilt had consumed him, and he had fled so as not to face it. Each reminder of the lost child was like a silent accusation. In fact, he had insisted Jane put Doug's things away as soon as possible, and strip his room. Quinn had thought it would be too painful for her to leave Doug's room intact and treat it as a shrine. He had left for Hong Kong and insisted that everything be packed and gone before he came home the next time, supposedly for her sake. And dutiful wife that she had been, she had done it, just to please him, at God only knew what cost to her.

Quinn found almost everything that had been in the boy's room the following afternoon, when he went through a large storeroom behind the garage. It was all there, even his clothes, his sports equipment, his trophies and other memorabilia. She had saved every single thing, right down to his underwear.

Twenty-three years later, she had saved every bit of it, and he even found three of Doug's sweaters tucked away at the back of Jane's closet, when he began taking things apart upstairs.

It was a sentimental journey that enveloped him for weeks. Again and again, he found himself confronting memories and realizations about himself, and Jane, that were excruciatingly painful and made him feel even more guilty.

Thanksgiving came and went, and he dutifully called Alex on the holiday, although she didn't celebrate it in Geneva. Her responses to him were brief and cursory. She thanked her father for calling, in a voice that was icy cold, and Quinn was so put off by her, he didn't even ask to speak to Horst or the boys. Her message was clear. Stay away. We don't need you. Leave me alone. So he did.

He didn't bother with a turkey, since he had no one to share it with, and he did not even bother to let any of their friends know he was back in the city. As painful as his mission was to weed through their belongings and sell the house, it would have been even more painful, he thought, to socialize with people. Jane had been his link to the social world. It was she who kept in touch with everyone, who loved to entertain their friends, and gently encouraged Quinn to slow down for a moment, and enjoy a quiet evening among people they knew well. And most of the time, he had done it for her. But without her softening influence and warmth, he preferred his solitude. He was alone now, and would forever stay that way. He had no interest whatsoever in seeing anyone. It would only make her absence more acute, and more painful, hard as that was to imagine.

By day, he was going through her closets, her treasures, her memories, and his own. And at night, he sat in bed, exhausted, reading her journals and poems. He felt as though he was steeped in her essence, like a marinade he was soaking in, until everything she had thought, felt, breathed, kept, loved and cherished was now a part of him, and had seeped into his skin. She had become his soul, as though he had never had one of his own before, and now theirs had joined and become one. He had never felt closer to her than in those final months before her death. And now again, as he waded through everything she'd owned, not only her papers, but her evening gowns, her gardening clothes, the faded nightgowns that she slept in, her underwear, her favorite sweaters. And as she had done with her son's sweaters hidden at the back of her closet, Quinn found himself putting things aside to save, the things that had meant the most to her. He could barely bring himself to part with any of it, and now he understood only too well what it must have done to her when he had insisted she take apart Doug's room. Life had finally turned the tables on him, and he felt that what he was experiencing now was suitable punishment for everything he had done to her. He embraced the task with reverence and humility, and accepted it as the penance he deserved.

It was mid-December before he had brought some semblance of order to what was left, and had decided what to throw away and what to keep. There were piles of things to give away, or box and store, all over the living room. And it was still too big a mess to call a realtor in. His only distractions were the calls to Tem Hakker every week to check on the progress of the boat they were finishing for him. Quinn had had a nice letter from Bob Ramsay by then, congratulating him on his new acquisition. He was also delighted to be off the hook, and free to pursue his much larger new sailboat. According to the Hakkers, things were going well, and on schedule. For the moment, taking apart the house in San Francisco seemed a much bigger job to him, but Quinn was glad he was doing it himself. It gave him some sort of final communion with Jane, a sacred ritual that he could perform that kept her close to him. And every night, he read her words, in her firm, slanting hand. More often than not he dreamed of her afterward. And two or three times a week, he had the dream where she begged him not to leave her. Even by day, he felt haunted by it.

He had come across thousands of photographs of them, from the early days when the children were small, on their travels, at important occasions, and more recent ones from their last trips. And she had kept every single newspaper article that ever mentioned him. Nearly forty years of them put away in files and boxes, some of them so frail that they fell apart when he touched them, but all of them organized chronologically. She had been meticulous in her respect and admiration of him. So much more than he had been of her. Seeing his accomplishments described in the clippings, he realized again and again how selfish he had been, how totally absorbed in his own world, while she loved him from afar, waited for him to come home, forgave him everything, and made excuses for him to the children. She was an admirable woman.

Danielle Steel

Although he was not a churchgoer, Quinn went to church on Christmas morning and lit a candle for her. He did it mostly because he knew it would have meant something to her, and she would have been pleased. She had lit thousands of candles for Doug over the years. And whenever anything worried her, or she had some special concern, she went to church and lit candles. He had teased her about it, and now he was surprised to find a strange sense of peace steal over him as he did it for her. As though the warmth and bright glow of the tiny candle would somehow make a difference in some unseen way. And then he went home, feeling slightly relieved. The things he was donating were in boxes by then. Those he was keeping were in sealed cartons piled up in the garage. He was going to put them in storage at some point before he left, along with whatever furniture he was keeping. They had had some fine antique pieces, and if nothing else, he thought he should keep them for Alex. He doubted that he would ever have a home where he would use them again. If all went according to plan, he had every intention of living on his new boat for the rest of his days, once it was ready.

On Christmas night, he finally indulged himself. It had been a hard month since his return. He drank most of a bottle of fine old red wine he had found in the wine cellar, polished it off with two brandies, and went to bed. And he felt better for it, despite the hangover he had the next day. He was glad that the holidays were almost over. He spent New Year's Eve at his desk, going over papers that his attorney was going to file in probate court after the first of the year. He worked for hours, as he listened to a driving rain battering his windows, and he could hear the wind whistling through the trees. It was midnight when he finally got up and glanced outside, and saw that the slimmer trees were being pressed almost level to the ground with the gale force of the wind. He didn't bother to turn the television on, but if he had, he would have discovered that it was the fiercest storm to hit northern California in more than a century, and there were power lines down all over Marin County and the East and South Bay.

He was in bed and sound asleep in the dark house, when he heard a tremendous crash outside, followed almost as quickly by two more. He got up and glanced out the window again, and saw that the biggest tree in his garden had fallen over. He went outside in his pajamas and a slicker to look at it in amazement, and saw instantly that it had sheared off a corner of the roof when it fell. And when he walked back into the house and stood in his living room, there was a gaping hole open to the sky, as the rain poured in. He needed a tarp to cover it, but didn't have one. All he could do for the moment was move the furniture out of the way so it wouldn't be ruined by the rain. He had been unable to determine what the other two crashes had been. The rest of the trees around the house were swaying violently in the wind, but none of the others had fallen, and the rest of the house appeared to be undamaged, until morning.

He had been unable to sleep for the rest of the night, as he listened to the storm raging around him, and it was still raining the next morning, when he got up at first light, he put on boots and his slicker again, and took a walk around the house to survey the damage. The hole in the roof was ugly, several of the shutters had been torn off, and two big windows were broken. There was glass and debris everywhere, and the garage had been severely damaged and was flooding. By sheer luck, he had put all the boxes to store on long wooden tables, so none of their papers and mementos had been destroyed. But he spent the rest of the morning moving them into his kitchen. The living room looked like a disaster area. He had moved the rugs and furniture in the middle of the night, and set down tubs and towels to catch the rainwater coming in through the hole in the ceiling. It was a part of the living room that protruded beyond the rest of the frame of the house, and there was a branch coming through it, and some of the fine old paneling had splintered from the impact. He learned from the newspaper that morning that at least a dozen people had been killed, mostly by fallen power lines, or trees, and hundreds had been injured around the state. Thousands were temporarily homeless and huddled in school gymnasiums as lowlands flooded. It was a storm of mammoth proportions.

And as he made one more trip from the garage to the kitchen, carrying a large box, he saw what must have caused the second and third crashes the night before. Two trees had fallen in his neighbor's garden. They were smaller than the one he had lost, but had nonetheless done considerable damage when they fell. There was a small woman with dark hair, looking mournful and dismayed as she assessed the destruction, and she happened to glance up at Quinn as he walked past her.

"Mine came right through the roof at four o'clock this morning," he said cautiously. "I heard two more crashes, it must have been your trees going down," he observed, and the woman nodded. And none of them were small trees, it was very impressive. "How bad is the damage?"

"I'm not sure yet. It looks pretty nasty. The house is leaking like a sieve, and I've got Niagara Falls in my kitchen." She looked frightened and worried. Quinn didn't even know her name, he knew the house had sold just after Jane died, but he had never met the family who bought it, and had never been interested in who they were, and still wasn't. But he felt sorry for her. She seemed to be dealing with it on her own, and it made him think of Jane, who had handled anything and everything, and every possible crisis and disaster on her own, in his absence. He assumed this woman's husband was of the same breed as he had been, a man with a job that took him far from home on New Year's. At least half of the New Year's Eves of their marriage Quinn had spent alone in other countries in hotel rooms. And obviously, this woman's husband was no different.

"I've got some spare buckets, if you need them," Quinn offered helpfully. There wasn't much else they could do on New Year's Day, and it was easy to figure out that every contractor in the state would have his hands full by Monday morning.

"I need a roofer. I just moved in, in August, and they said the roof was sound. I'd love to send them a picture of the kitchen. It looks like someone turned on the shower." The storm had also broken nearly half her windows. The house was even more exposed than Quinn's was, and less solidly constructed. It had changed hands several times in the past dozen years, and Quinn paid no attention to who lived there, although Jane always made some small effort to welcome new

37

neighbors. But he had never seen this one, or her husband, even in passing. She had a faintly desperate look as she tried to clear away some branches. It was still pouring rain and the wind was still ferocious, though not quite as vicious as it had been in the early hours of the morning. The damage looked like what he'd seen in the aftermath of hurricanes in the Caribbean, or typhoons in India. It was definitely not what one expected to experience in San Francisco.

"I'm going to call the fire department and get them to put a tarp on the roof. Do you want them to take a look at yours too?" he offered. It seemed to be the least he could do, and she nodded gratefully, looking wet and distracted. The damage all around them was upsetting, and all up and down the street, people were doing what they could to clear away fallen trees, pick up debris, and tie down what they could to minimize further damage, as the storm continued raging.

"I'm not sure a tarp will make much difference," she said, looking unhappy and confused. She had never had to handle a situation like this. Nor had Quinn, and he somehow felt that Jane would have been far more efficient than he was. But he had to manage on his own now.

"They'll tell you what you need. I'll ask them to bring several tarps, just in case." And as an afterthought, he remembered his manners. "Sorry," he said, reaching a wet hand over a low hedge, as he juggled a box in his left arm, "I'm Quinn Thompson."

"Maggie Dartman," she said, shaking his hand firmly. She was small, and had tiny, graceful hands, but her handshake was strong. She had long dark hair that hung down her back in a braid, and her hair was matted against her head in the driving rain. She was wearing jeans and a parka, and looked soaked to the skin, and he couldn't help feeling sorry for her. She was very pale, and had big green eyes that looked anything but happy. He couldn't blame her, he wasn't pleased with the damage to his house either.

"Bad luck your husband's not around," he said sympathetically, making an easy assumption. She looked to be in her late thirties or early forties, and there were no children afoot, which made him wonder if she was even younger, and hadn't started a family yet. These days everyone got started older. She looked at him oddly when he mentioned her husband, started to say something, and then didn't. And a moment later, Quinn left to call the fire department. They had had hundreds of calls like his, and said they would be over in an hour or two to cover the hole in his roof. He dutifully mentioned his neighbor, and told her the fire department would be over to help, when he went back to get the last box in the garage, and saw her dragging a branch out of her driveway.

"Thanks very much," she said, and nodded. She looked like a drowned rat, and he was tempted to offer her an old raincoat of Jane's he was sending to Goodwill, but didn't. There was no need to get too friendly. She seemed polite, but she was also reserved, and a moment later, she went back into her house. He wasn't sure, but as he saw her go, he thought she was crying. He wondered how many times Jane had cried when she had to cope with emergencies without him. And as Quinn went back into his own house, thinking of it, he felt guiltier than ever.

# 4

THE FIRE DEPARTMENT COVERED THE HOLE IN QUINN'S roof, and as he had promised, he directed them to check on his next-door neighbor. By late that night, the storm abated, but the damage throughout the state had been tremendous. Like everyone else in town, he called a contractor on Monday morning, and a roofer. He found their names on a list Jane kept on a bulletin board in the kitchen. The roofer just laughed when Quinn called him.

"Let's see," the man said, sounding harassed but good-natured. "You're the forty-eighth call I've had this morning. I think maybe I can get to you sometime in August."

"I hope you're joking," Quinn said drily. He was not amused. He was also not used to dealing with problems like this. Whatever happened around the house, even something of this magnitude, would have automatically been Jane's problem. Now it was his, and he had to admit he didn't enjoy it. He had dialed the roofer and the contractor more than a dozen times each before he got through to either of them. Everyone who'd suffered damage in the storm was obviously frantic to get someone to repair it as quickly as they could, and he was no different.

"I wish I were joking," the man at the roofing company responded. "There's no way we can do it." He gave Quinn four names to try, all reputable firms, he said. And the contractor did the same when Quinn called him. He gave him the name of two well-known contracting firms, and a third number that he said was a young carpenter who had gone out on his own a few months before, but did fine work, and he highly recommended him. Predictably, the two contracting firms were as busy as the first one. He still hadn't found a roofer yet, and feeling exasperated, Quinn called the young carpenter the first contractor had recommended. Quinn was beginning to realize that getting the repairs done was going to be far from easy.

There was an answering machine at the number when he called, and he left a concise description of the damage, explaining what had happened. And the last roofer he called agreed to come and take a look the following morning, but he warned Quinn when they spoke that there were a good six or eight weeks of work ahead of him by then. It looked like Quinn was going to be living with a hole in his living room ceiling and a tarp over it for a long time. This was not the way he had planned to spend his final months in San Francisco.

It was eight o'clock that night when the young carpenter finally called him. He sounded matter-of-fact and businesslike, and apologized for the hour of the call. He said he'd been out looking at storm damage since early that morning. Quinn was just grateful that the man had called him. He offered to come by at seven the next morning if it was all right with Quinn.

"I'm doing a quick job for a friend tomorrow. All their bedroom windows broke, and they have a brand-new baby. I'd like to come by and see you on the way there, if you don't mind my coming that early. I want to get his windows taken care of before I start any big jobs."

"Are you already booked by anyone else?" All day Quinn had been hearing that people had three to six months of work lined up from the storm, and he was beginning to feel desperate. He couldn't even think of selling the house until he repaired the damage the storm had done.

"Not yet. I saw eight or nine potential clients today, but I haven't signed any contracts yet. I don't like to take on more work than I can handle. And a lot of people feel more comfortable with bigger firms, where they know they can count on big crews. I have three subs I use when I need them, and whenever possible I do the work on my own. I keep better control of the job that way, and it keeps the prices down, although it's a little slower going, but not much. I don't have to correct anyone's mistakes that way. Why don't we take a look in the morning and see what I can do for you, Mr. Thompson?"

"Sounds good to me," Quinn said, feeling relieved. He would have met him at five in the morning, if he had to. He liked the way the man sounded. He sounded straightforward and sincere, honest and responsible. His name was Jack Adams. And then Quinn told him about the trouble he'd had, understandably, finding a roofer.

"I've got a good guy I work with in San Jose. I'll call him

tonight and see how booked up he is. He might be able to come in for a couple of weeks. I'll let you know what he says tomorrow."

"Perfect." Quinn thanked him and hung up. It would be wonderful if he could put the whole job in this man's hands, and trust him to take care of it for him. He might even be able to do whatever else was necessary to get the house in shape to sell it.

Quinn went to sleep that night, in the bed he had shared with Jane, and for once he didn't read her poems and journals. He went straight to sleep, after thinking about getting the house in shape again, and hoping that Jack Adams was the man to do it.

He woke at six, feeling refreshed, put on jeans and a heavy sweater, socks and boots, and went downstairs to make himself a cup of coffee. He had just finished his second cup, when Jack Adams rang the bell at seven o'clock sharp. He looked neat and clean and well organized. He had short dark hair, and big blue eyes that looked honest and friendly and kind. Quinn offered him a cup of coffee, and he declined, he wanted to get down to business as quickly as possible, and give Quinn an idea of what he felt he could do to help him. He had liked Quinn on the phone, and the two formed an instant bond, as Quinn led him from the living room to the garage, and all around the house wherever something had been broken, loosened, destroyed, or damaged. He didn't carry a pad and pen with him, which worried Quinn, but as they moved along, he seemed to remember every detail of what they had just seen, and shot his mental list back at Quinn with amazing accuracy and precision. If his work was as good as his mind was sharp, Quinn felt certain that, by sheer luck, he had found a winner.

Jack Adams was a nice-looking young man, somewhere in his mid-thirties. He was as tall as Quinn, and as lean, and there was an odd similarity between them as they walked around the house, and through it, but neither of them was aware of the physical resemblance between them. To passersby, they would have looked like father and son. Although Quinn's hair was gray now, it had once been as dark as Jack's, and they had the same frame, and the same way of moving, almost the same gestures as they discussed the problems and the repairs to be done. In fact, Jack was almost the same age as Douglas would have been. He was thirty-five years old, and Doug would have been thirty-six. And he looked very much the way Doug might have looked if he'd grown up into manhood. It didn't even occur to Quinn as the two men were talking. In his mind's eye, Doug had stayed forever thirteen.

"How long do you think it will take?" Quinn asked him pointedly as they walked back into the house again, and this time Jack accepted a cup of coffee. There was more to do than he'd anticipated, and Quinn had talked to him about additional work, if he'd take it on, so he could get the house in shape to sell it. There were a dozen other jobs he'd been offered since the storm, but he liked the idea of sticking with one job and completing it, and some of what Quinn needed him to do was challenging. His friend in San Jose had agreed to do the roof, and was scheduled to start in two days, and Quinn had been enormously relieved to hear it. What Jack did was inspire confidence and give his clients the sense that he had everything well in hand. Both the self-assurance he exuded and his obvious expertise made Quinn want to secure his services as quickly as possible, if Jack was willing.

"All of it?" Jack narrowed his eyes, thinking about it, and then took a sip of the steaming coffee Quinn handed him. "I'd say, three months, maybe two, depending on how many guys I use. There are two I'd like to have with me on this job, at least in the beginning. I can finish up the loose ends myself, depending on how much work you want me to do to help you sell it. Maybe all three of us for the first two months, and then either one or two of us for the last month. How does that sound to you?" Jack asked fairly.

"That sounds about right to me. Will you oversee the roofer too?" Quinn had no desire to become the job foreman on the project, but Jack had no intention of letting him do that, and there was no need to. He was totally competent, and the men he used liked working for him.

"I'll take care of everything, Mr. Thompson. That's my job. All you do is write the checks. And I'll keep you apprised of what we're doing." Jack was well spoken and intelligent, and there was an instant respect between the two men. Quinn needed his help, and badly, and he knew it. And from everything Jack had seen of Quinn, he liked him. Jack had a sense that Quinn would be fair with him. He was a businessman, and probably a good one, to the very tips of his fingers. You could see easily that he was used to being in command, and Jack also sensed correctly that Quinn didn't want to be bothered with the details. As far as Jack was concerned, he didn't need to be. He wondered if there was a wife he was going to be dealing with too. There were a number of photographs around of a pretty, middle-aged woman, but Quinn hadn't mentioned her. He was handling the matter himself, maybe just because it was easier for him to do it. But whatever his circumstances, Jack didn't feel they were any of his business, and didn't ask any questions of a personal nature. Quinn liked that too. Jack Adams was all about business, just as he was.

"How fast can you work up an estimate?" Quinn asked matter-of-factly. In the hands of any of the larger firms, Quinn knew it would have cost him a fortune. But this man was young and independent, and hopefully not insanely expensive. Quinn didn't think he would be. Jack wanted the work, and seemed excited about the prospect of working for him.

"I can have it to you by this afternoon," Jack responded as he set down the mug and glanced at his watch. He wanted to do the job for his friend that day so he would be free to do this one. "If it's all right with you, I'll drop it by this evening. I have a friend who does some of the paperwork for me. It leaves me free to get out in the field and do what I need to do. I'll call the numbers in to her today, and bring it to you when I finish work. Will that work for you?"

"Perfectly. You can have her fax it to me if that's easier for you." He handed Jack the fax number on a piece of paper, and Jack stuck it in his pocket, and held out a hand to Quinn.

"I hope we'll be working together, Mr. Thompson."

"I hope so too," Quinn said simply, and smiled at him. He liked everything about him, his look, his manners, how bright he was, what he had said about the work to be done. Jack Adams was the best thing that had happened to him since the storm that hit San Francisco.

Jack left a few minutes later, and drove off in his truck.

Feeling immensely relieved, Quinn went to put in a call to Tem Hakker in Holland, to check on the progress of his sailboat. And he couldn't help wondering, as strange as it may have seemed, if Jack liked sailing, or knew anything about boats.

# 5

JACK ADAMS CAME BACK, AS PROMISED, THE NEXT DAY and the work began in an orderly, efficient way. He had faxed Quinn a very reasonable estimate, as promised, the day before. The deal had been made, and a contract signed. He brought two big burly young men with him, and they kept to themselves and went straight to work. They greeted Quinn, or nodded, when he went in or out, but Jack was the only one who had contact with him. And the roofer appeared to do his work at the end of the week. The tree had done more damage than they'd thought at first, and the roofer consulted with Jack and Quinn about what needed to be done. It was an extensive job, but Quinn had no choice in the matter. The roof had to be repaired, and Quinn wasn't trying to cut corners. He wanted it done right, in the best possible way, no matter how expensive it was, even though he was selling the house. And Jack respected him for that, as he did for all else. He had already figured out in the first few days that Quinn Thompson was a pleasure to work with, as long as you were fair with him, and told him honestly what was happening, and what you thought you could do about it. What he didn't like were misrepresentations and lies, or people who shirked their responsibilities. But there was none of that with Jack Adams in charge of the job. He was completely professional, and every few days, he brought Quinn up to speed.

He was coming into the house to do just that at the end of the second week, when he found Quinn sitting at his desk and poring over some plans.

"Building a new house somewhere?" Jack asked pleasantly. He never asked questions inappropriately, but Quinn was so intent on what he was looking at that Jack couldn't help but be intrigued. And whatever the plans were for, it looked huge.

Quinn looked up with a tired smile. He had done a lot of paperwork for Jane's estate that week, and it was tedious, depressing work. His reward to himself for doing it was spending some time going over the latest plans for the boat. "Not a house, Jack. A boat. Do you know anything about boats?"

"Not a thing," Jack admitted with a grin. "I've looked at them a lot, and watched some sailboat races on the bay. But I've never been on a boat in my life."

"You're missing a great thing," Quinn said, as he turned the plans around on his desk, so Jack could see them. He knew he would appreciate the precision with which they had been done. Jack was meticulous himself. "She'll be ready in the fall. I'm going to live on her, after I sell this house." Jack nodded, looking the plans over carefully. He didn't ask questions, he was just admiring what he was seeing.

"Where are you going to sail the boat to?" Jack asked with interest.

"Everywhere. The South Pacific. Antarctica. South America. Europe. Scandinavia. Africa. I can go anywhere I want with a boat like this. I bought her in November, the day before I came home from Europe."

"She must be beautiful to see," Jack said admiringly, but without a touch of envy. He had a great deal of respect for Quinn, and thought the man deserved all he had.

"Not yet, but she will be when she's finished."

"Where is she?" Quinn was amused when he asked the question. The name of the boatyard was written boldly across the page, with the word NETHERLANDS printed out clearly, but Jack had obviously not seen it. Quinn assumed he had been too dazzled by the boat's exquisite design to notice, and he couldn't blame him. Quinn was already deeply in love with his new boat, and he was sure that anyone who would see her would be too.

"She's being built in Holland," Quinn answered.

"Do you go over often?" Jack was intrigued by him. Everything about Quinn suggested style, elegance, and power. He seemed like a real hero to him.

"I will until she's finished. I want to oversee the details myself."

"When are you putting the house on the market?" They had talked about it, and Jack was aware of it, but Quinn hadn't given him any precise dates. Now that he had seen the plans for the boat, Jack knew that Quinn's departure was not vague or simply a possibility, it was real.

"I'll put the house up for sale as soon as you're finished, or sometime in late spring. I'm assuming it will take a few months to sell. I want to be out of here by September or October. The boat should be ready by then."

"I'd love to see her. I hope you bring her here." But that was exactly what Quinn didn't want. He wanted to get as far away as he could from his relentless memories, and the world he had shared with Jane. All he wanted now was to sail away and take his memories with him. Being in the house he had shared with her, in the city where they had lived for nearly forty years, was just too hard for him. He hardly slept at night, and roamed throughout the house, aching for her. Thinking about all the things he had never done for or with her was a heavy weight to bear. What he needed now was a reprieve, and he felt certain the boat would give that to him. Jack knew that Quinn's wife had died. Quinn had mentioned it to him one day the previous week, and Jack had told him quietly how sorry he was to hear it. He sensed now some small measure of how lonely Quinn was. Quinn had also said that he had a daughter who lived in Geneva.

"Maybe you'll come to Europe and see the boat one day," Quinn suggested as he put the plans away. Jack laughed in answer, and told him a trip to Europe was as foreign to his world as a rocket ship ride to outer space, and about as likely for him.

"I think I've got enough to keep me busy here. But that certainly is a handsome boat," he said respectfully, and as he did, Quinn had an idea. He strode across the room to a bookcase where he had an entire library of sailing books, some very old and some quite rare. He took a heavy volume out and offered it to Jack. It was an introduction to sailing that Quinn had used as his bible for years in his earliest sailing days.

"This will teach you everything you'd ever want to know about sailboats, Jack. You might enjoy it sometime in your free time." Jack hesitated as Quinn held it out to him.

"I'd hate to lose it or damage it." The book looked much loved and well worn, and possibly even valuable. He was obviously uncomfortable about borrowing it.

"I'm not worried about it. See what you think, you can return it when you're finished. You never know, you might have a chance to go sailing with a friend one of these days. This book will teach you everything you need to know." Jack took it slowly from him, and flipped through some of the sketches and pictures. There were diagrams and sailing terms throughout. It was a wonderful book that Quinn had always loved. He had given it to Doug to read that fateful summer before he left for camp, and Doug had pored over it, and memorized parts of it in order to impress his father, and had. It had been one of their few great exchanges and precious moments before he died.

"You're sure you want to lend it to me?" Jack asked, looking worried. Quinn smiled and nodded, and a few minutes later, Jack left with the book under his arm. And although it was Friday night, he had mentioned that he would be back in the morning. His crew were only working for him five days a week, but he had already told Quinn he would be putting in some weekend hours on his own, and it was all part of their contracted price. He liked working alone sometimes, and getting a handle on some of the details himself. He was even more conscientious than Quinn had thought he would be, and the work was going well. He was supervising the roof work too, and Quinn was pleased with the results, although there was still a lot of work to do. Jack was going to be around for months, until the house was not only in good repair, but ready to put on the market.

On Saturday morning, Quinn looked out the window when he got up and saw Jack outside. It was raining again, and had been for most of the month. But Jack didn't seem to mind. He was used to working in the elements, and the only problem the rain represented for them was that they couldn't finish the roof until the weather was dry. The wet weather was drawing things out. But there were plenty of other projects at hand.

Quinn went outside to talk to Jack after he read the paper and had coffee, and he found him in the garage. He was checking on the repairs they'd been forced to do out there, and as the two men walked out of the garage half an hour later, chatting casually, Quinn noticed his neighbor struggling to open an enormous crate someone had delivered in front of her house. And as she had been before, after the storm, she was once again wrestling with it herself. She never seemed to have anyone to help, and as Quinn watched her, he thought of Jane once again, with a familiar pang. In all those years, he had never once thought about how difficult life must have been for her, with him gone all the time. And now he never seemed to stop thinking about it. This woman was a living reminder of the life Jane had been challenged with during all of his working life.

And as Quinn thought of it, Jack eased through the hedge

54

that separated the two houses, and went to help her. He took the tools from her hand, and within minutes he had the crate open, and offered to take its contents, a piece of furniture, inside. Before Quinn could say anything, they disappeared into the house, and a few minutes later, he was back. Jack was cautious when he mentioned her to Quinn.

"I don't know how you feel about it, Quinn." They called each other by their first names by then, and Quinn was comfortable with it. He liked everything he knew about Jack, and above all the fastidiousness and devotion with which he worked. "She asked me if I could do some work for her sometime. I told her I had a long job here, and she asked if I could do a few repairs for her on Sundays, if I have any spare time. I don't really mind, it's my day off, and I get the feeling she really needs the help. I don't think she has a man around."

"People probably used to say that about my wife too," Quinn said with a sigh. "Don't you need some time off? You can't work seven days a week, you'll wear yourself out," he said with a look of concern. He wasn't crazy about the idea of Jack working for her. He worked hard, and needed some rest, at least on Sundays, since he worked extra hours for Quinn on Saturdays.

"I think I can handle it," Jack said with an easy smile. "I feel kind of sorry for her. I was talking to the mailman the other day, he says her son died last year. Maybe she needs a break and a helping hand." Quinn nodded. He couldn't argue with that. And he made no comment, sympathetic or otherwise, about her son. He hadn't told Jack about Doug. There was no reason to, and Quinn thought it sounded maudlin. It was enough that he knew Jane had died. But he and the neighbor had something in common, not that it was something he wanted to talk about.

"I don't mind. Just don't let her take advantage of you, Jack," Quinn warned, and Jack shook his head. He was willing to help her, he wasn't being forced. And she had managed to find a roofer on her own, and gotten the work she needed done. But she said there were a number of smaller repairs she hadn't found anyone to tackle yet. And like Quinn, she had observed how diligent and competent Jack was about his work.

"She seems like a nice woman. Sometimes you just have to put out a hand, even if it costs you some time. I've got nothing else to do on weekends except watch football." It was more than Quinn had to do, but he didn't say that to Jack.

And the following day, he noticed Jack going in and out of Maggie Dartman's house. She stopped and said something to Quinn a little while later, as she was going out, and thanked him for allowing her to use Jack's services on his day off.

"He's a great guy," Quinn reassured her, not wanting to get involved in their arrangement. It was entirely up to Jack what he did in his spare time, and by midafternoon, Quinn noticed that Jack's truck was gone. He really was a decent man.

It was the end of the following week when Quinn remembered the book he'd given him, and asked Jack if he'd had time to read it yet. Jack looked slightly embarrassed and shook his head, and apologetically explained he hadn't had time.

"I can see why, between working here six days a week, and doing extra duty at my neighbor's," Quinn pressed him a little bit, good-naturedly, and Jack rapidly changed the subject.

# Miracle

Quinn sensed that he felt guilty he hadn't read the sailing book yet, and he didn't want to put pressure on him. He had just thought he might enjoy it, but the poor guy was working himself to the bone on both jobs, particularly Quinn's. He didn't know why, but he had the feeling that Jack could be a born sailor if he wanted to. He had shown such interest in the plans for the boat, and teaching him something about sailing was something Quinn could do for him. He hoped he'd read the book at some point, and not just say he had, but he forgot to mention it again.

It was late January and the work was going well, when Quinn spent an entire afternoon making a list of extra projects he had for Jack, and comments about the work in progress, and he went outside to hand it to him. It was the first really sunny day they'd had in weeks, and the roof work was finally finished, although it had taken longer than planned. He wanted Jack's comments on the list he'd made, and stood waiting for him to read it, as Jack folded it and put it in his pocket, and promised to read it that night, which irked Quinn a little bit. He hated putting things off, and wanted to discuss it with him, but Jack said he had too much going on that afternoon to concentrate on it properly. He promised to discuss it with Quinn the next day when he came in.

But that afternoon, the work having gone particularly well that day, and hating the lull that came on Friday nights when everyone left, Quinn asked him in for a glass of wine, and he mentioned the list to Jack again, and suggested he take it out of his pocket, and they go over it together. Jack hesitated, and tried to brush it off, as Quinn insisted. He was like a dog with a bone about his list, and for an odd moment, Quinn thought he saw tears shimmer in Jack's eyes, and wondered if he had offended him. Jack was generally easygoing and unflappable, even when things went wrong on the job, but he was obviously upset by Quinn's suggestion, so much so that Quinn was afraid he might quit, and that worried him acutely.

"Sorry, Jack," he said gently, "I didn't mean to press you, you must be dog tired by the end of the week. Why don't you skip tomorrow?" he suggested, trying to pacify him and back down from the pressure he had provided, apparently too much so for Jack. But Jack only looked at him and shook his head, and this time the tears in his eyes were clear. The look he gave Quinn was one of deep sorrow and immeasurable trust, and Quinn didn't understand what was happening. Just looking at Jack upset him. It was as though something in the younger man was unraveling, and could no longer be stopped. And out of nowhere came an explanation that Quinn was in no way prepared for, as Jack quietly set down his glass of wine. He looked straight at the man who had hired him, and spoke in a voice rough with emotion, as Quinn watched him, and listened with an aching heart. He had meant no harm with his questions and suggestions, but he could see that he had hurt this man whom he had come to respect and like. It was one of those moments when you can't go back, only forward. Like a pendulum swinging only forward, and never back.

"My parents left me at an orphanage when I was four years old," Jack quietly explained. "I remember my mother, I think I do anyway, I don't remember my father, except I think I was scared of him. And I know I had a brother, but I don't remember him at all. It's all kind of a blur. And they never came back. I was state-raised, as they say. They put me in a couple of foster homes at first, because I was so young, but they always sent me back. I couldn't be adopted because they knew my parents were alive somewhere, and you can't stay in foster homes forever. I got comfortable in the orphanage, and everyone was pretty good to me there. I did okay. I worked hard. I started doing carpentry when I was about seven. And by the time I was ten, I was pretty good. They let me do what I wanted, and I did whatever I could to help out. And I hated school. I figured out early on that if I did work at the orphanage, they'd let me skip classes, so I did, a lot. I liked hanging out with the grown-ups better than the kids. It made me feel independent and useful, and I liked that. And by the time I was eleven or twelve, I hardly ever went to school. I stuck around, going to school when I had to, till I was about fifteen. And by then, I knew I could make a living as a carpenter, so I took one of those high school equivalency tests. To tell you the truth, a friend helped me take it, a girl I knew. I got my diploma, and I left the orphanage and never looked back. It was in Wisconsin, and I had a little money saved up from jobs I'd done. I hopped a bus and came out here, and I've been working ever since. That was twenty years ago. I'm thirty-five now, and I make a good living at what I do. I work hard, and I like it. I like helping people, and working with someone like you. No one's ever been as nice to me as you are, not in all these twenty years." His voice cracked as he said it, and Quinn's heart ached for

him as he listened, but he still had not understood. "I'm a carpenter, Quinn, and a good one. But that's all I am. That's all I'll
ever be, all I've ever been. That's all I know how to do."

"I didn't mean to push you, Jack," Quinn said gently. "I admire what you do a lot. I couldn't do it. You have a real talent
for finding solutions and making things work." And Quinn
had noticed that he had a knack for design as well.

"Maybe not," Jack said sadly, "but you can do a lot of things
I can't, and never will."

"I've been lucky, and worked hard, like you have," Quinn
said, offering him the kind of respect that grows sometimes
between two men, no matter what their origins or how simple
or complicated their field. Quinn Thompson was a legend, and
Jack Adams was a carpenter, and a good one, as he said, and
an honest man. Quinn didn't want more than that from him.
But Jack wanted a great deal more for himself, and he knew he
would never have it. The burdens of his past were too heavy,
and he knew it, better than Quinn could imagine. Quinn had
no concept of the life Jack had led, or the path he had followed
to get there.

"You're not lucky," Jack said quietly. "You're smart. You're
educated. You're a lot better than I am, and you always will be.
All I can do is this." He said it with total self-deprecation.

"You can go to college, if you want to," Quinn said hopefully. There was a sense of despair about Jack that he had
never seen before in the month he had worked for him. He had
always been so matter-of-fact and so cheerful, but what he was
seeing now was very different. It was a glimpse into Jack's

heart and soul, and the sorrow he had concealed there for a lifetime. If nothing else, Quinn wanted to give him hope.

"I can't go to college," Jack said with a broken look, and then looked straight into Quinn's eyes. Quinn knew he had never seen such trust. "I can barely read," he said, and then dropped his face into his hands and cried quietly. The shame of a lifetime spilled over and devoured him, as Quinn watched, feeling helpless. And without a sound, he reached toward him and touched his shoulder, and when Jack looked up at him again, it brought tears to Quinn's eyes too. He was sure now that no one, in his entire life, had admitted anything as important to him. This man whom he scarcely knew, but liked almost like a son, had dared to bare his soul. It was a precious gift.

"It doesn't matter," Quinn said, still touching him, as though his hand on the young man's shoulder would keep the connection between them, and it did.

"Yes, it does. I can't read books, or letters, or your lists. I don't know what it says at the post office, or what the forms say at the bank. I can't read a contract. I took an oral test at the DMV. I can read signs, but that's about it. I can't read what it says on medicine bottles, or directions, and maps are hard for me. I can hardly read anything. And I can sign my name. That's it. I'll never be more than a carpenter who can't even read. I can't even stay with a woman for more than a few weeks, because if they figured it out, they wouldn't want me. They'd think I was stupid, or ridiculous. All I can do is what I do, the best I can. But that's all I can ever do, or ever will."

It was instantly obvious to Quinn that Jack wanted so much

more out of life, but had no idea how to achieve it. His eyes were full of sorrow and the limitations he had lived with for a lifetime as he looked at Quinn. And what he had said was so overwhelming that Quinn didn't know what to say to him at first. He wanted to put his arms around him and hold him, as he would a child. But Jack wasn't a child, he was a man, and as decent and kind and capable as any man Quinn had ever known. He wanted to help him, but he wasn't sure how. All he could do was accept him, and try to let him know that whether he could read or not, he had won Quinn's respect forever, particularly now. His grip on Jack's shoulder remained powerful and firm. And a few minutes later, Jack stood up, and said he had to leave. He looked embarrassed by the admissions of the night, and Quinn could see that Jack looked shaken.

"I have a friend who reads things to me," Jack said softly, as he picked up his jacket. "I'll know what's on your list by tomorrow," he said simply, as Quinn nodded and watched him go. It had been a moment Jack had allowed Quinn to share with him, a glimpse not only at his vulnerabilities, but into his very soul.

Quinn lay in bed thinking about him that night, until three o'clock, deeply moved by what Jack had shared. And when he woke in the morning, and saw Jack's truck outside, he pulled on a pair of pants and a sweater, slipped his feet into loafers, and walked outside to find him. The two men exchanged a long look that spoke volumes, and Quinn asked him to come inside with him. Jack looked as tired as Quinn felt. He had lain awake for hours too, wondering if he had done the right thing in telling Quinn. And in fact, he had. His greatest fear, the one that had kept him up all night, was that of losing Quinn's respect.

"I memorized the list," he said to Quinn, as they stepped into the house and Quinn closed the door. He nodded and walked into the kitchen, as Jack followed, and both men sat down.

"I need you to put in some extra hours," Quinn said quietly, and Jack couldn't read what he was seeing in Quinn's eyes. There was no mention of what had been said the night before. "I want you to stay two hours after work every night, and maybe an hour or two on Saturday too." He sounded stern as he said it, although he didn't mean to, and Jack looked worried. There had been nothing about that on the list.

"You don't think the work is going fast enough?" Jack inquired. It was going faster than he'd expected, and he had assumed Quinn thought so too.

"I think the work is going fine. But we have some additional work to do." Quinn's heart was beating faster as he said it. This was important, and he wanted Jack to agree to do it, for both their sakes. It was as important to Quinn now as it was to Jack. They had formed a partnership the night before, a silent contract, a bond that could not be broken. Jack had given him something precious when he trusted Quinn with the truth. And Quinn was going to honor it, and felt honored, to his very core.

"What kind of work?" Jack asked, looking puzzled.

There was a long pause as the two men looked at each other. There was something very naked and raw in the room. It was hope. "If you'll let me," Quinn began cautiously, "if you'll allow me the privilege of doing so, I'm going to teach you how to read." There was a deafening silence in the room, and Jack turned away from him, with tears pouring down his cheeks. And Quinn was crying too. It was a long time before Jack turned to look at him again, and longer before he could speak.

"Do you mean that? Why would you do that for me?"

"Because I want to, we both do. I've done a lot of dumb, stupid, mean, selfish things in my life, Jack. This might turn out to be the first decent thing I've ever done, and I'd appreciate it if you'd give me that chance." It was Quinn asking Jack for something, both of them had much to gain from it, not just Jack. It was a journey they were both embarking on, to an unknown destination. "Will you do it?" Quinn asked him, and slowly Jack nodded, and dried his face with his hand.

"Are you kidding?" Jack smiled slowly, and his expression of jubilation was mirrored in Quinn's eyes. Jack had wanted to attend a literacy program all his life, and had been too ashamed. But he felt nothing shameful about learning to read with Quinn now. All he felt was pride. "When do we start?" He beamed.

"Now," Quinn said quietly, pulling the newspaper toward him, and pulling his chair around so he could sit next to Jack. "By the time you finish this job, you're going to read better than anyone I know. And if it takes longer than the work you're doing here," Quinn reassured him, "that's okay too. There was a reason you told me what you did last night, for both of us. Now let's see what we can do." Jack smiled up at his teacher, and Quinn poured them each a cup of coffee and sat down again. The lessons had begun.

# 6

THE READING LESSONS WENT WELL FOR THE FIRST FEW weeks. Jack spent his days working on the repairs on the house. And for two hours afterward, and sometimes more, he and Quinn sat at the kitchen table and wended their way slowly and painfully through the newspaper. Eventually Quinn used his old sailing book as their textbook, once Jack was more comfortable. They were a full month into it, when Quinn shared with him one of Jane's simple, lovely poems. It was a victory when Jack not only got the meaning of it, but was able to read it slowly and smoothly out loud. And when he did, he looked up at Quinn in amazement.

"That's beautiful. She must have been quite a woman," he said softly, still moved by what he'd read, and thrilled that he had been able to read it at all.

"She was," Quinn said sadly. "I didn't always know that about her. I only discovered who she was in the last months we spent together. I don't think I ever really knew her before."

He had learned even more about her, through her poems and journals once she was gone. The tragedy was that for thirty-six years before that, he had barely known her, and much of the time, took her for granted or ignored her. It was an admission he had only recently come to accept about himself, and not one he was proud of.

"She looks beautiful in the photographs," Jack said quietly. She had been a delicate, almost fragile-looking woman, but there had been far more strength in her than anyone ever suspected, least of all her husband. And her spirit had been gentle and graceful to the core.

"She was beautiful," Quinn admitted. It was easy for Jack to see now how much Quinn had loved her. "She was a remarkable woman," he added with a wistful look, as they wound up the lesson.

Jack was making impressive progress, and Quinn was giving him something he had always dreamed of. In a way, it was a gift of freedom, and one by one Quinn was helping him to sever the chains that had bound him. His inability to read had been like a death sentence to him, or at the very least a lonely prison. It was Quinn who was imprisoned now, condemned to his own loneliness and bitter recriminations forever. He was still having the recurring dream, but less often ever since he'd started helping Jack with his reading. It was almost as though doing something for another human being was helping to assuage his guilt.

It was late February, when they were finishing their lesson on a Saturday, that Jack mentioned Quinn's neighbor, Maggie Dartman. He was still doing work for her on Sundays, and slowly fixing the house that had been in serious disrepair when she bought it. But each time he worked for her, he was struck by how lonely she was. Her house was full of photographs of her son who had died. She had told Jack the boy had committed suicide two days after his sixteenth birthday. She never explained why, and it was obvious to Jack by then that there was no man in her life. The work he was doing for her could have been done by any man in residence, if there had been one to help her out. She had mentioned to him once that she was a teacher, and had been on sabbatical for a year and a half, since her son died.

Quinn and Jack had fallen into an informal tradition of having dinner together on Friday nights, after they finished his reading lesson. Quinn cooked and Jack brought wine, and it was an opportunity to get to know each other better. At times the relationship was one of friendship between two men, and at others Quinn took a fatherly attitude toward him. Jack was fascinated by Quinn's accomplishments. He had grown up on a farm in the Midwest, and had gone to college with a scholarship to Harvard. And from there he had progressed rapidly into his enormous success. Jane had believed in him from the moment she met him. She had been there before he ever made a penny, and never doubted his abilities for a minute. Success had come early for him, and bred more success. He had made his first million before he was twenty-five. He had had the Midas touch, as they said in the financial world. To the uninitiated, it looked like he had never made a bad deal in his life. But the truth was that when he had, he had managed to turn it into something better. And he always knew instinctively when to cut his losses. He was, in his own way, a genius. But from all Jack could see, success hadn't brought him happiness. There were few men as unhappy and solitary as Quinn Thompson.

And all Quinn wanted now was to become even more solitary, as soon as his boat was ready. He talked to Jack about it like a woman he was in love with and waiting for. It was all he dreamed of now. After being abandoned by Jane when she died, and the torturous relationship he had with his daughter, the boat being built for him in Holland was a nonthreatening companion of sorts who couldn't torment or reproach him, and whom he in turn could not disappoint or hurt. Being alone on the boat, isolated from the world, would be an immense relief. And while he waited for her, he was helping Jack to find his dreams.

There was much about the friendship that they both treasured. And while Jack was getting to know Quinn better, at the same time, with his weekly visits, he was growing extremely fond of Maggie. There was something so kind and vulnerable about her. She usually made Jack lunch on Sundays when he worked for her. And like Quinn, perhaps for similar reasons, she seemed desperately lonely. He seldom saw her go anywhere. She was always in her house, reading or writing, or just sitting and thinking. He saw her face whenever she passed one of her son's photographs, and the look in her eyes tore Jack's heart out.

"You should invite her over sometime," Jack finally suggested to Quinn. "She's a nice woman. I think you'd like her."

Quinn looked instantly upset at the suggestion. "I'm not interested in meeting women. I had the best there was. I'm not going to date anyone. It would be disrespectful to Jane, and a travesty to her memory." Quinn already knew he would never betray her. He had hurt enough people in one lifetime and had no desire to hurt more. But Jack was quick to clarify his suggestion, and surprised by how sensitive Quinn was.

"I didn't mean like that, Quinn," Jack corrected the impression he had given him. "She's a nice person, and she's had some tough things happen to her. I don't know all the details, but losing a son would be enough to bury most people. I don't think she sees anyone. She never goes anywhere, the phone doesn't ring. I never see friends come to visit her. It might just be nice to have her to dinner on a Friday sometime. She has a nice sense of humor. It would be an act of kindness. She doesn't look like she's interested in meeting anyone either." From things she had said to him, Jack had accurately guessed her state of mind. She was living with her memories and regrets as much as Quinn.

"I thought she was married." Quinn looked surprised. "I assumed she had an absentee husband who was away on business."

"So did I at first. She just looks that way, and it's a big house for a single woman. She must have a little money. I don't know if she's widowed or divorced, but whatever she is, she's alone in that house day after day. Maybe her husband died too, and left her some money." The house was substantial, and couldn't have been inexpensive when she bought it, despite the somewhat shabby state it was in. And she seemed cautious about how much she spent to repair it. She always discussed with Jack how much things would cost her. "I don't know her story,

Quinn, but whatever it is, I don't think it's a happy one. I think you'd be a good Samaritan if you invite her over to have dinner with us some Friday after work."

"Yeah, maybe," Quinn said vaguely. But two weeks later, when he pulled an enormous veal roast out of the oven, Jack looked at him in dismay.

"Even I can't eat all that, it's a crime to waste it." Rather than shrinking, for once the roast seemed to have grown exponentially when Quinn put it in the oven. It had turned out to be a lot bigger than he expected, and was an experiment of sorts. It was the fanciest meal he had prepared since they had begun their Friday night dinners. "Do you want me to call Maggie and see what she's doing?" Quinn hesitated, looking less than enthusiastic about it, and then reluctantly relented. Jack seemed to be determined to include her, and Quinn was beginning to wonder if Jack had a romantic interest in her.

"All right, it can't do any harm, I suppose. Tell her it was your idea. I don't want her to think I'm pursuing her, or interested, or that this is some ploy to introduce us. Tell her I'm a disagreeable old recluse with an oversize veal roast to share with her." Jack laughed as he went to the phone and called her. She sounded startled, and as hesitant as Quinn had been. She asked Jack bluntly if it was some kind of a setup, and if it was, she wasn't coming. He assured her that it was nothing more than a Friday night dinner shared by three friends, two of them neighbors. Finally, she agreed to come, and rang Quinn's doorbell ten minutes later with a cautious expression.

When he opened the door to her, Quinn was startled by how much smaller she was than he had remembered. They had chatted with each other over their respective hedges. But standing on his doorstep, she looked not only fragile, but tiny. And there was something in her eyes that gave Quinn the impression she was both frightened and sad. If nothing else, it made him want to reassure her. He could see why Jack felt sorry for her. She was a woman who looked as though she needed to be protected, or at the very least needed a friend.

He stepped aside and invited her in, and she followed him quietly to the kitchen, where Jack was carving the veal roast. She brightened visibly the moment she saw him. The smile that lit her face made her seem instantly younger. And Quinn relaxed the moment they sat down, and he handed each of them a plate, and filled their glasses with wine.

"How are the lessons going?" she asked comfortably, after thanking Quinn for inviting her to join them. Jack had confessed to her what they were doing every day after work, and how grateful he was to Quinn. Maggie had said he must be a nice man.

"It's coming, slowly, but surely," Jack said as he smiled at her. But in truth, he was making good progress. He was able to read clearly now, though very slowly, and some words still stumped him. He had all the sailing terms down now, but was anxious to move on to broader concepts. Quinn was desperate to teach him about sailing as well as reading. He wanted to share that with him, as it was his passion. And Jack was growing anxious to read other books as well. Quinn had also shared many of Jane's poems with him, which touched Jack profoundly. They were lovely and obviously heartfelt.

"He's a star pupil," Quinn said proudly, and Jack looked

slightly embarrassed. "Jack tells me you're a teacher," he said to Maggie, as he served dessert and made coffee.

"I was," she said easily, enjoying their company more than she had expected. They were a motley crew, drawn together by proximity, circumstances, and good intentions. "I haven't taught in nearly two years." She looked a little wistful as she said it.

"What did you teach?" Quinn asked with interest. He could easily imagine her surrounded by very young children, maybe kindergarten.

"Physics, in high school," she said, and surprised him. "The subject everyone hated. Or actually, they didn't. Most of my students were fairly gifted. They don't take physics unless they have a knack for it. If not, they opt for biology or calculus, or integrated sciences. Most of my students went on to major in physics in college."

"That means you did a good job with them. I always liked physics in college. I never took it in high school. What made you stop?" he asked casually, and was startled and saddened by her answer.

"My son died. Everything came to a grinding halt after that," she said honestly. There was no artifice about her, and Quinn liked that. "He committed suicide nineteen months ago." She could have told them in days or weeks, but no longer did that. She hated the fact that it was months now, and soon it would be years. Time was slowly creating an ungovernable distance between them. She couldn't control it, just as she had been unable to control his actions in the end. "He suffered from severe depression. Most depressed kids don't

72

commit suicide, even if they think about doing it. Usually, it's more bipolar kids. But Andrew couldn't pull out of it. He pretty much lost his grip once he got to high school. I just didn't have the heart to go back to school once he died. They gave me compassionate leave to do some grief counseling. And after I did, I realized I wasn't ready to go back. I'm not sure I ever will be." But sooner or later, she knew she had to work, at something, if not teaching.

"What do you do now instead?" Quinn asked quietly.

Maggie sighed before she answered. "I've started counseling other parents like me. I'm not sure I'm a big help to them, but at least I've been there. And three nights a week I work for a suicide hotline for teenagers. They call-forward a line to me, and I can do it from home. I'm not sure if it's a good thing or not, but at least I feel like I'm doing something to help someone, instead of just sitting home and feeling sorry for myself."

Quinn wondered if that kept the wound open for her, but in spite of a look of sorrow in her eyes, she seemed to be a fairly well-balanced person. He wondered where her husband was, but didn't want to ask her. She volunteered the information a short time later on her own.

"I probably would have gone back to work by now, but Andrew's death kind of unsprung my marriage. I think my husband and I blamed each other for what we couldn't change or stop. Things had been shaky between us for a while, and in the year after Andrew's death, the marriage fell apart completely. He walked out two days after the anniversary of Andrew's death. Our divorce was final the week after Christmas." She said it in a strangely matter-of-fact voice, as Quinn realized that

that was when he first met her, and an instant later, she confirmed what he had thought. "I got the papers in the mail the day the storm hit on New Year's Eve. The storm seemed like a suitable end to all of it. I must have seemed like a crazy person the day I talked to you," she said apologetically. "I'm not even sure I was coherent. I was pretty upset."

"You seemed fine to me," Quinn said reassuringly, remembering her standing in the pouring rain without a raincoat or umbrella. There had been something devastated in her face when she told him she had Niagara Falls in her kitchen. And now he understood it better. She seemed to have no need to hide what she was feeling, and he suspected that she felt better now. Better enough to come to dinner at least, and he was suddenly glad that Jack had pressed him to invite her. More than anything else, this woman needed friends to distract her. They were like three souls in a lifeboat. And for the moment, Quinn was rowing. And he suddenly decided to share something with her, if only to let her know that she was not alone in her agony, and would survive it.

"My son died twenty-three years ago, in a boating accident," he confided as he set his fork down and looked at her across the table, as Jack watched them. He had never heard that from Quinn before, and was deeply touched by the admission. The only child Quinn had mentioned to him was Alex, in Geneva. "He was thirteen, and I think I only realized recently how deeply it changed both of us. I withdrew even deeper into my work, and my wife became more introverted and stayed that way. We were both grief-stricken, but when I read her journals, after her death, I understood better how profoundly it altered her. I was busy then, and probably insensitive about it. I'm sure I wasn't much help to her. It was too painful for me to talk about, so I seldom, if ever, did. She wrote some beautiful stories about him." There were tears in his eyes as he spoke, and he didn't confess to her that he had forced Jane to put away Doug's things within weeks after he died. And the little she had kept unboxed, she had concealed from Quinn in her closet. In a sense, he had forced her to do that, and now that he understood what it had meant to her, he deeply regretted what he'd said and done. He had thought he was doing the right thing for her, for himself, and even for Alex. But now he knew he'd been wrong. He had learned so much about her and himself in the months since she'd been gone.

"It's not a great thing to happen to a marriage," Maggie said, looking at Quinn. Her eyes bored into his like drills, as though asking a thousand questions. She wanted to ask him how he had survived it, or how his wife had. She still blamed herself for the end of her marriage.

She had always felt that her husband had lacked empathy for the depths of their son's depression, and that perhaps unknowingly, because of it, he had exacerbated Andrew's desperation. And because of that, she had never forgiven Charles for Andrew's death, and he knew it, whether she said it or not. He in turn felt she should have been able to stop it. Their final year together had been one of relentless silent accusation, until they could no longer stand each other. And no matter what they did to each other or themselves, nothing would bring their son back. Although she was devastated when Charles left, she felt he had made the right decision for both of them. In the end, their marriage had been as dead as their son. Charles had given her the best settlement he could, in the form of the house he had paid for her to buy, to escape the one where their son died, and he had given her enough money to live on for the next few years. Eventually, she'd have to go back to teaching. But for the moment, she was still hiding, as Quinn was. He understood that much about her. She had wrapped herself in a cocoon, to protect herself from the realities and blows of life. She needed time to heal, and was giving herself time to do it, which seemed sensible of her. But when she wasn't talking or even sometimes when she was, her eyes looked agonizingly sad to Quinn.

"You've been through a lot of trauma," Quinn said softly, and she nodded. She had no need to deny it, nor did she want to portray herself as a victim. In spite of the injuries she'd sustained, Quinn had a sense that she was both brave and strong.

"A lot of other people have been through trauma," she said sensibly, "the counseling work I do reminds me of that. Suicide is the second biggest killer of kids in this country. We have a long way to go before most people understand that. Andrew tried it twice before the last time."

"Was he on medication?" Quinn sounded sympathetic and concerned.

"Sometimes. He wasn't always willing to stay on it. He was pretty clever about pretending to take it, and then not. He didn't like the way it made him feel. It either made him feel anxious, or too lethargic. I hear a lot of that on the hotline." Quinn admired her for the volunteer work she was doing. She was a nice woman, and it was easy to see why Jack liked her. She was open and honest and not afraid to show her vulnerability. Talking to her reminded Quinn that there were others who were suffering as much as he was. He told her about Jane then. The years he had worked too hard and too much, been away most of the time, his retirement, her sudden illness, and death.

"It was all over before we knew it."

"How long has it been?" Maggie asked sympathetically.

"Nine months. She died in June. I traveled for the first five months. I've been back since November. I came back to put the house in order, and sell it this spring."

"And then what will you do?" she asked with interest. She noted that he had opted for the geographic cure, as they called it in counseling. And she didn't want to tell him that it didn't work. At some point, wherever he was, he was still going to have to face the fact that she was gone, and however he had failed her, or felt he had, whether accurate or not. Most important of all, he was going to have to forgive himself, just as she had to forgive herself, and even Charles, for Andrew's death. Unless he could, Quinn would never outrun the agony he was still feeling.

"I'm building a sailboat in Holland," Quinn explained to her, and told her about the months he had spent on the *Victory* that fall, and his decision to buy Bob Ramsay's boat and complete it. "I'm going to sail around the world for a while, maybe forever," Quinn said with a look of relief, as though he was sure that on the boat, he would no longer have to face his own demons. She could have told him different, but didn't. She knew better. But the boat he described to her sparked her imagination, and she smiled with pleasure.

"She sounds like a beauty," Maggie said with a look of admiration and nearly envy.

"Do you sail?" Quinn seemed surprised.

"I used to. I grew up in Boston, and spent my summers on the Cape. I loved to sail as a kid. I haven't in years. My husband hated boats, and Andrew never liked them much. It's been a long time."

"Jane and my daughter didn't like sailing either, especially after my son died. I had a boat years ago, when we first moved out here. But I was too busy to use it. I sold it the year after Doug died. This is going to be a rare opportunity for me to indulge my passion." He smiled at both of them. Jack was enjoying the exchange between them, glad that he had encouraged Quinn to invite Maggie to dinner. More than they knew, or even he did, they had much in common. And they were each in need of companionship and friendship. They both spent too much time alone, and had too many painful memories to dwell on. A night like this did them both good.

"A hundred and eighty feet of ketch is a lot of passion," Maggie teased him. "That must be very exciting," she said as her eyes danced.

"It is, and it will be. She'll be finished in September." He offered to show her the plans then, and they pored over them sitting at the table, as Jack cleared the dishes, and then returned to the table to join them. It was a particularly nice evening, and much to Quinn's surprise, the Friday night dinner was even more pleasant as a threesome. Maggie had definitely brought something to it, despite her heartfelt confessions. But everyone's spirits seemed to lift as Quinn described the boat in its most minute detail. Maggie asked all the right questions. She was extremely knowledgeable about sailboats, and knew of all the most important builders and naval architects and designers. Her extensive knowledge impressed Quinn considerably. And after he put the plans away, Jack suggested a game of liar's dice, which was what he and Quinn usually did at the end of their Friday evenings. Maggie laughed at the suggestion, and looked amused.

"I haven't played in years," she warned, and managed to beat them both at least once each, and then Quinn took over. He was the expert among them, and usually beat Jack as well. They had a good time nonetheless, and it was after midnight when Maggie finally left them and went home. She was scheduled to be on the teen suicide hotline at one o'clock, and she was in surprisingly good spirits.

Jack only lingered for a few minutes after she left. "She's a nice woman," he said, smiling at Quinn. "She's had a tough time. He was her only kid, and the guy who does her gardening says she found him." She hadn't told them that. "The husband doesn't sound like a great guy for leaving her after all that," Jack said, although she had described him charitably. She was a good woman, and a pretty one, and deserved to have had someone who stuck by her. It was hard for Jack to imagine the trauma they'd been through.

"People do ugly things to each other in those circumstances," Quinn said wisely. "Jane probably should have left me too. Thank God, she didn't. I wasn't very sensitive to her needs then. All I could think of was how I felt to have lost my son. I thought if I didn't talk about it, the pain would go away, instead it just went underground and ate at us both." But he had seen clearly in Jane's journals that she understood, not only her grief but his, and had allowed him to mourn in the way he needed to, on his own. She had carried the full weight of her solitary grief on her own shoulders, not unlike Maggie when she lost her son.

Jack left a few minutes later, and Quinn was in his kitchen for a long time, putting things away, and washing the dishes. And when he went upstairs finally, he saw the lights on in Maggie's kitchen, as he looked out his bedroom window. By then, he knew she was on the phone, answering the teenage hotline. Her lights were still on when he got into bed. He took out one of Jane's journals, and fell asleep holding it, but tonight for the first time, he felt more peaceful when he thought about her. However foolish and insensitive he'd been, for some reason he knew that she had truly forgiven him. Or maybe he had always known that. What he didn't know, and perhaps never would, was if he could forgive himself.

# 7

AT QUINN'S SUGGESTION, MAGGIE JOINED HIM AND JACK
for dinner on Friday night the following week, and all three of
them were in good spirits and had had a good week. They
talked about the boat, and played liar's dice again. She
brought a chocolate cake she had baked for them. And over
the next month, their Friday night threesomes became a com
fortable tradition, and an easy beginning to the weekend.

Jack's reading was going well, and he was working dili-
gently at it. Maggie had brought Quinn some books to help
him use some excellent teaching techniques that would be
helpful to Jack. And Quinn showed them both the latest plans
from Holland. The boat was moving ahead toward completion
like lightning. It was April by then, and Jack's work was nearly
finished. They had dragged it out as long as possible. Quinn
had called a realtor who came to see the house. He suggested a
few more things that Quinn could do to make it more appealing to a buyer, and Quinn decided to put it on the market in

May or June. He didn't want to sell it too soon, he needed somewhere to live until the boat was complete in September. The realtor felt certain the house would sell quickly, and was anxious to list it.

Quinn told Maggie and Jack about it on Friday night, and had already given Jack the list of further improvements suggested by the realtor. And this time he was able to read it. The two men had exchanged a smile about it. By then, Jack was reading with ease.

The following week, there was a heat wave, and the three of them had dinner on Friday night in Maggie's garden. She set up a picnic table, and covered it with a blue tablecloth. They ate fried chicken and hamburgers, and a potato salad Quinn had made and carried over. The evening had all the earmarks of a summer picnic. Maggie was wearing a white linen dress in the warm night air, and for once her long hair was down, cascading past her shoulders. The big announcement of the evening was that Jack said he had met a very nice young woman at his church, and the other two teased him about it. Maggie said she was happy for him, and Quinn accused her of being hopelessly romantic. Jack had just turned thirty-six, and she felt it was time for him to find someone to fall in love with. Now that he could read, he had nothing to hide, and nothing to be ashamed of. She said over dessert that she hoped he would get married and have children.

"What about you?" He turned the tables on her, as they each helped themselves to watermelon and fresh cherries for dessert.

"I've already done that," she said, giving little credence to the question. She had just turned forty-two, and was convinced her romantic life was behind her. She had been married for eighteen years before the divorce, and said she had no interest in another husband. Her son's death, and her husband's abandonment had cured her, or so she said. She claimed that she was content to live alone forever.

"You're only six years older than I am," Jack pointed out, and Quinn laughed.

"You two should get together," he suggested. Jack had already thought of it, but he hadn't wanted to spoil their friendship, and now fate had lured him in a different direction with the girl he'd met at church.

"I don't think so," Maggie said, laughing at Quinn's suggestion that she and Jack pair up. They were a loving and supportive, but definitely odd, threesome. And all three of them were sad that in a few months, their Friday night evenings would be disbanded. Quinn would be off on his boat by then, and now Jack was well on his way to having a woman in his life, if not this one, then undoubtedly another. The only plans Maggie had were to go back to teaching in September. She had spoken of it several times recently. She had nothing else to do, nowhere she wanted to go, and no one she wanted to be with. Her solitude had become a safe, comfortable cocoon to hide in, just as Quinn's was. But Maggie felt that she ought to go back to work.

The following Friday, Quinn surprised them. The weather was still warm, though not as warm as it had been the week before. But the days were long and sunny, and summer seemed to be on the way.

"What are you two doing tomorrow?" he asked innocently, but he already knew. He had planned it, although the idea had come to him on the spur of the moment, when he went to watch a sailboat race on Wednesday night, from the yacht club.

"Working for you," Jack said comfortably. He had a date planned for that night. He had already told the woman he was seeing that he was not available on Friday evenings. He called it a poker night, so he didn't have to explain Quinn or Maggie, or his reading lessons. She knew nothing about that, and he still would have been embarrassed to tell her. Maggie had told him weeks before that he didn't need to say anything. It was no one's business, although she saw his learning to read as a great accomplishment on his part, and told him he should be proud of himself.

"I thought I'd see if I can clean up my garden tomorrow," Maggie said easily. They were dining in Quinn's kitchen, as they did most of the time. He was the best cook of the group, and had the most equipment. Maggie hardly ever cooked, and lived on fruit and salads. She admitted once to both of them that she hadn't cooked since her son died, and didn't want to. The thought of cooking for anyone brought back too many memories of all she'd lost, and what her life had been. They all preferred Quinn's cooking, and he said he enjoyed it anyway.

"I have a better idea," Quinn said with a mysterious look. "I want you both here and dressed at nine o'clock tomorrow morning. Wear sneakers," he said cryptically, and Maggie laughed at him, and raised an eyebrow. She was a lovely-looking woman, although Quinn seemed not to notice. She had become like a little sister to him, and an older one to Jack.

The three of them had become family to each other. It was what they needed, more than anything else.

"If I didn't know better, Mr. Thompson, I'd think you were taking us sailing." She tried to guess what they were doing, and he laughed at her.

"My boat is in Holland. That's a long way to go for a sail. Just bring sneakers and don't ask too many questions."

"Are you sure you don't want me to do the finish work on the upstairs railings?" Jack asked, looking worried.

"It can wait," Quinn assured him. He looked immensely pleased with himself, and Maggie looked concerned.

"I hope we're not going hiking. I'm too lazy and too out of shape, and I threw my hiking boots away last winter. I swore I'd never do that again."

"Just trust me," Quinn said gently. She beat him at liar's dice that night, and went home victoriously with three dollars, to work on the hotline until three in the morning.

The next morning she rang his doorbell promptly at nine o'clock, wearing jeans, an old sweater, and a parka. The morning was cool and breezy, but brilliantly sunny. There wasn't a hint of fog on the bay, and he and Jack were already drinking coffee. She noticed when he answered the door that Quinn was wearing jeans, a heavy sweater, a thin shell, and deck shoes.

"You said sneakers," she said accusingly, as she pointed. She had worn bright red canvas sneakers, as he had said to, and a red sweater to match them, and her eyes were dancing with anticipation. "I want to know where we're going."

"All in good time, my dear. Don't be so nosy," Quinn admonished. They had come to treat each other as sister and brother.

"I feel like I'm being kidnapped," she said as she joined the two men in the kitchen and helped herself to a cup of coffee.

Their Friday nights together had made them supremely comfortable in each other's company. Maggie never bothered to dress up or wear makeup when she was with them. Her long dark hair was clean and shone in the braid she had worn. Quinn liked it when she wore it loose, but he had never said that to her. And now as he looked at her, he found himself wondering what she would look like with lipstick. She never bothered to wear that either. She wasn't trying to lure either of them. Seduction was not even remotely on her agenda.

They piled into Quinn's station wagon shortly afterward, and Maggie commented that it was the first time they had ever gone anywhere together. The physical boundaries of their relationship in the past several months had been limited to Quinn's kitchen. And she thought it was fun going out together, particularly under the mysterious circumstances Quinn had created. He was in a good mood, and seemed happy and playful, as he headed down Vallejo, and turned left on Divisadero. They were driving toward the water, and took a left along the shoreline on Marina Boulevard. Maggie wondered if they were going to cross the Golden Gate Bridge and go somewhere in Sausalito. But instead he took a right onto the grounds of the St. Francis Yacht Club. She wondered if they were going to have lunch on the deck at the club, and watch a regatta, which was the next best thing to sailing.

"This is fun," she said happily, and Jack grinned at her. She was in the front seat next to Quinn, and Jack was just behind her.

"I have a date at seven o'clock," he reminded Quinn. "I'd better be home by then, or she'll kill me."

"You'll be back before that, I promise," Quinn assured him. He parked the car and shepherded them toward the dock where the boats were, and then Maggie saw her, and instinctively she knew she'd been right. There was a splendid yacht tied up, much bigger than those that usually were tied up at the yacht club. She was smaller than the one he was building, but she was a hundred and twenty feet of sheer beauty.

Quinn walked confidently to the gangway and stepped aboard, and held out a hand to his two cohorts. "Come on, you two. She's ours for the day. Don't waste time just standing there gaping." Jack looked stunned, and Maggie looked ecstatic, as they followed him on board. A crew of four were waiting for them. She was a truly lovely sailboat. There were four cabins below, a handsome dining area on deck, and a short ladder up to an elegant little wheelhouse. And the main saloon was luxurious and comfortable, with a dining area they could use at night or in bad weather. She was named the *Molly B*, after the owner's daughter. The owner was an old friend of Quinn's, and had just brought the boat up from La Jolla for the summer. Quinn had chartered her for the day, as much to amuse Maggie as to introduce Jack to sailing.

They wandered all over the boat, as Jack looked at every tiny detail. He was impressed more than anything by the woodwork, and Maggie could hardly wait to get out on the bay and sail her. They were under way in ten minutes, and

Quinn looked every bit as happy as they did. He divided his time equally between his two friends, and was amused when Jack chatted with the stewardess, who was a pretty young girl from England. His attention to her left Quinn time to sit with the captain and Maggie and talk about sailing. The wind was perfect that day for their sail. They went out under the Golden Gate and headed toward the Farallones, and none of them minded when the water got a little choppy. Quinn was relieved to find that Jack didn't get seasick.

"You are a sneaky devil," Maggie teased Quinn as she sat on the deck next to him, enjoying the wind and sun on her face. And despite a slight chill to the wind, the weather was warm enough. "What a nice thing to do for us," she said gratefully. If she had dared, she would have thrown her arms around him and hugged him. But even after their many Friday nights together, there was always something a little daunting about him. Even at his warmest, Quinn always kept a slight distance from others. Her eyes told him how happy she was, and that was enough for him. The day had turned out precisely as he wanted.

By the time they got home that afternoon, all three of them were happy and tired. Quinn had been delighted to see that they both loved it, and couldn't stop talking about how wonderful it had been as they drove back to his house. They hated to leave each other, just as they had hated to leave the *Molly B.* Jack had thanked all of the crew members, and Quinn, profusely. Maggie didn't know how to begin to thank him. She offered to cook dinner for him, but he said he had work to do. He was still struggling through probate. It was taking forever.

Jack left them in time for his date, and Maggie thanked Quinn again before she went back to her own house, looking like a kid in her braid, white jeans, and red sweater and sneakers. Quinn smiled as he had all day, as he watched her. It was obvious to him that she loved sailing as much as she said she did. But who wouldn't, she said to him, on a boat as luxurious as the one he had chartered. She couldn't even imagine how fabulous the boat was going to be that he was building in Holland, and wished she could see it, although he had said he wouldn't be bringing it to San Francisco, except perhaps at some point, on his way to the South Pacific. But before that, he wanted to sail around Africa and Europe.

Quinn was sitting peacefully in his living room with a cup of tea, reading a sailing magazine, when Maggie rang his doorbell. She was still in her sailing clothes, her hair had come loose from its braid, and she looked slightly embarrassed.

"I don't mean to bother you," she apologized. "I just wanted to thank you." She was carrying a big covered bowl, with a loaf of French bread tucked under her arm. She had made him his favorite pasta. "I'll just leave this with you. I thought you might be hungry." He was, in fact, and had been thinking about dinner, but was too lazy and relaxed to do anything about it, so she had done it for him. "I haven't had a day like that since I was a kid," she said happily. "Thanks, Quinn. It was such a nice thing to do. You didn't have to take me, but I'm glad you did." They both smiled, remembering how much Jack had loved it. It was quite an introduction to sailing. And he had taken to it like a duck to water. He didn't even mind when it got choppy, or when they tacked or jibed, and the boat heeled as far as it could over the water. Maggie had just plain loved it, and it had reminded her of the best days of her childhood.

"You're a very efficient sailor," Quinn praised her, as he set the bowl of pasta down in his kitchen. There were tomatoes and basil and bits of sausage in it, and fresh mushrooms. She had made it for him once at her place, on a rare Friday night at her house, and he said that he loved it.

"I didn't get a chance to do much today," she said modestly, but he could tell from what she said to the crew that, given the opportunity, she knew what she was doing. And she had that look of pure glee and excitement that came over avid sailors whenever they were on a sailboat.

"We'll have to go out again sometime. My friends left the boat here, but they're in Europe." The boat belonged to yet another of his business connections. He could smell the pasta by then as he took the cover off, and as he glanced at her gratefully, he invited Maggie to join him.

"I wasn't trying to invite myself to dinner," she said, looking embarrassed. "I just wanted to thank you for a lovely day. I really enjoyed it."

"We all did. Why don't you share the pasta with me, and we can play liar's dice afterward? I need the money," he teased and she laughed. She hesitated for a minute, but he insisted, and she finally agreed to join him. He got out two plates, and they sat down easily at the kitchen table. And while he began eating, she made a salad. They talked about boats and sailing all through dinner. It was easy to see how much it meant to him. He came alive whenever he talked about boats, more than about anything else, business, or friends, or travel. He was always wistful when he spoke of Jane, and tense when he mentioned Alex. But when he talked about sailing, he seemed to relax and glow and become instantly expansive.

She was surprised by how fast the evening went with him. And by the time she finished dice with him, it was ten o'clock, and she felt guilty for keeping him from whatever he'd planned to do that night. She took her pasta bowl after she helped him clean up, and he walked her home.

"Thanks for a terrific day," she said happily, smiling up at him.

"Thanks for dinner. You owe me ten dollars," he reminded her. He had been impossible to beat that night, but she didn't mind losing to him. It had been the best day she'd had in years, surely since Andrew's death, and long before that. "Are you on the hotline tonight?" he asked, feeling comfortable with her. He always did, she was half sister and half friend. He had made a decision that night as he talked about sailing with her. He was going to wait and see how it turned out, and tell her about it the next time they met, probably the following week on Friday night. They rarely ran into each other on the street, as neither of them went out very much. Jack was the go-between, sending news and greetings back and forth during the week, since he saw both of them, and visited both houses while he worked.

"I'll be on the phone after twelve o'clock," she said easily. "I have a regular, who calls me every time I'm on. He's a sweet kid, he's fourteen. His mom died last year. He's been having a tough time. I think I'm really beginning to miss being with kids." She had already decided to go back to work in September, and had gotten her old job back, for three months at least. She was filling in for the teacher who had replaced her and was going on maternity leave. After that, the school had promised to find something for her, if they could. But it was a start, and Quinn agreed that going back to work would be healthy for her.

"Good luck on the phone tonight," he said gently. It was easy to imagine how skilled she was with kids. She had a warm, easy open way about her, and he had seen her begin to blossom slowly into the woman she had once been, ever since they'd met. Their Friday nights had benefitted all three of them, even him.

"Thanks again, Quinn," she said, and then turning to him, she threw caution to the winds, and gave him a hug. He looked surprised as she smiled at him, and a minute later, she was gone, her door was closed, and he was on his way home. Her hair had brushed his cheek, and he could smell the perfume she wore. It was a fresh airy scent that seemed so typical of her. She was like a breath of air, a summer breeze that had passed through his life, taking with it the sadness that had burdened him for so long. And he had done the same for her. He had become the anchor she had clung to when she was trying not to drown. And Jack was the glue that held them together. Quinn was grateful they had all met, and knew he would miss their company once he was gone. In five months, when his boat was finished, they would each go their separate ways, but hopefully they would be different and better than when they met. And richer for the experience. The storm that had happened on New Year's Eve, and brought them together, had proved to be a blessing for them all.

# 8

QUINN SHARED HIS NEWS WITH THEM THE NEXT TIME THEY dined together, as usual, on Friday night. He had chartered the *Molly B* for the entire summer, until September, when he planned to leave. And he invited them to join him on it the following weekend. This time Jack couldn't do it, he had agreed to take his new girlfriend on a picnic with some of her friends. But Maggie looked extremely enthusiastic.

"Do you mean that, Quinn? I don't want to be a nuisance or a pain in the neck, I don't want to intrude."

"I wouldn't offer it if I didn't mean it, Maggie. I'm going out on her tomorrow. Do you want to come?" Looking at him with a sheepish smile, she admitted that she did.

It was a perfect day for sailors the next day, on Saturday, when they left. She met him outside his front door, in a heavy white sweater, jeans, and her bright red sneakers, that always made her look like a kid to him. It was a cold, blustery day with a strong wind, and they took off out of the harbor at a good speed. The seas were rough that day, and he could see that Maggie loved it. The stewardess was seasick, and one of the men made lunch for them. They had sandwiches and tea, and Maggie sat smiling on the deck, next to Quinn, as they ate them. By late afternoon, the sun came out. They stayed on board for dinner, and were both happy and relaxed when they finally went home.

"You're so nice to share the boat with me. I don't know what I did to deserve all this," Maggie said gratefully as they drove home. He had changed her life with his kindness and generosity, and now with their adventures on the *Molly B*. She had no idea how to thank him, and when she said as much to him, he said he enjoyed her company. He said he was going back on the boat the next day, and invited her to come with him again. "How rude would that be?" she asked him honestly, and he laughed at her. There was something lighter and happier about his tone these days. His friendship with Jack and Maggie had lightened the load for him. He seemed happier and far less gloomy.

"Not rude at all. I can be alone on her whenever I want. I was thinking of taking her out for a couple of days this week. I don't need to be alone tomorrow. Why don't you come?" She could see in his eyes that he meant it, and she enjoyed his company too. So she went with him.

They had perfect weather and a gentle breeze. They sat in the shelter of Angel Island, and sunbathed on deck. Quinn had brought shorts with him, and she wore a bathing suit. And by the time they left the boat that night, she felt as though they had been friends forever. He started talking about Jane on the way home. He told her about the poetry Jane had written to him, most of which he hadn't seen until after her death. But when he spoke of it now, he sounded proud more than bereft. He was healthier than he had been since her death.

"It's amazing how you think you know someone, and then find out you don't," he said thoughtfully, and Maggie smiled and sighed as she looked at him as they drove home.

"I felt that way about Charles too, but not in the good way you mean. After he left, I wondered if I had ever known who he was in eighteen years of marriage. It's an odd feeling, and not a nice one, in his case. I think he hated me after Andrew died. He needed someone to blame, so he blamed me."

She had had a double trauma in losing both of them, and Quinn could only guess at what it had done to her. He had seen it in her eyes the day they met, but her divorce papers had only arrived the day before. They weren't a surprise for her, but they must have hurt anyway, and he could only guess at how much. Her husband had delivered the ultimate one-two punch, and it had decked her for a while, but she seemed to be slowly coming back to life. Quinn's friendship had been an immense source of strength and peace for her, as had Jack's. But it was Quinn who, in some ways, was the anchor of the group. Jack was the common bond they shared. And Maggie was the light and joy and fun for Quinn, far more than she guessed, or knew. He enjoyed her sunny spirit, her energy, her dry humor, and occasionally insightful wit. But more than anything, he appreciated her tenderness and compassion, which she shared with him and Jack. She was the motherly woman's touch he and Jack both needed and sometimes longed for, without even knowing it. She was Peter Pan's Wendy to the two lost boys they had both been when they all met. And now they were all getting stronger.

Maggie heard from Jack that Quinn had gone out on the boat that week, and had sailed up the coast for two days. He came home on Friday morning, and was in good spirits when they met on Friday night. He told them all about it, and reported on his own boat's progress in Holland. Everything was going according to plan, and Maggie was happy for him, although she was beginning to dread what it would be like when he was gone for good. She and Jack would still have each other, but Jack seemed to be getting serious about the woman he had met, and she knew that one day there might no longer be room, or need, in his life for her. Eventually, in their own ways, they would all have to grow up and move on. But for the moment, it was so nice the way things were.

She sailed on the *Molly B* again with Quinn that weekend, and on Sunday night when he dropped her off, he invited her to come out on the boat with him again that week. They were starting to show his house, and he didn't want to be around. It was hard to believe that it was already early May. She had nothing else to do so she agreed to go with him. She told him she was turning into a sailing bum, and loving every minute of it.

The crew left them alone most of the time, except when Quinn and Maggie wanted to chat with them. And after lunch, as they sailed peacefully down the coast, she lay on the deck near Quinn and fell asleep, and when she woke, he was sound asleep himself, lying next to her. As she looked over at him, she smiled to herself, thinking that it had been a long time since she lay next to a man, even a friend.

"What are you smiling at?" His voice was a low, gentle rumble as she lay looking at him.

"How do you know I'm smiling? Your eyes are closed," she said softly, wanting to cuddle up next to him, but she didn't want him to think she was strange. She was just hungry for human contact and affection. It had been so long since she'd had that. And the proximity to Quinn reminded her of that, and was very pleasant.

"I know everything," he said wisely, as he opened his eyes and looked at her. They were near the bow of the boat, on comfortable mattresses, lying in the sun. The crew were on the fly bridge deck, and the aft deck, and it was nice to be alone. "What were you thinking when you were smiling?" he asked, as he rolled over, and looked at her, with one arm tucked under his head. It was almost like lying in bed next to him, while wearing all their clothes.

"I was smiling because you've been so kind to me...and I love being here with you, Quinn....I'm going to miss you next winter when you're gone."

"You'll be busy by then. You'll be teaching again." He stopped for a minute, and looked at her, and then spoke very softly in their shelter from the wind, as they lay beneath the sails. It was the perfect place to be. "I'll miss you too," he said honestly, surprised himself that he meant it.

"Will you be lonely out there all alone?" she asked, as she

moved imperceptibly closer to him. She didn't realize she'd done that, nor did he. It just seemed easier to talk.

"It's what I need," he said quietly. "I don't belong here anymore. I don't belong anywhere. My roots are gone...like our trees that fell last winter....I've fallen, and I'm drifting out to sea." Just hearing that made her sad for him. She wanted to hold out a hand, but she wasn't sure it would make any difference to him. There was no holding him back, and she had no right to anyway. All she could do was watch him leave and wish him well on his travels. Their time together was limited, and destined to end soon. "I was kind of that way when I was married too. I came and went a lot, but I never really felt I belonged anywhere. I always wanted to be free. My family paid a big price for that, but I couldn't have done it otherwise. I think Jane understood it, but it must have hurt her terribly." It was what most of her poetry had been about, about letting him go, and knowing that he needed freedom more than he needed her. "I was always unhappy when I thought I was on a leash."

"And if you had no leash?" she asked quietly.

"I would sail away and probably turn up again eventually, like a bottle in the ocean, with a message in it," he said, smiling at her. He could smell her perfume again, and feel her warmth as she lay near him.

"What would the message be?" she asked gently, and without thinking, he put an arm around her and pulled her close to him, as they lay on their backs, looking up at the sky and the sails above them. There was nowhere else on earth either of them wanted to be, and no one else they would have wanted to be with. He was perfectly content lying next to her, and he hadn't felt that way in years, nor had she.

"The message would be," he said thoughtfully, pondering it, "I can't be other than I am ... even if I wanted to ... the message would be I love you, but I have to be free ... if not, I'll die ... like a fish out of the ocean, gasping for air.... I need the ocean and the sky, and the fine line of the horizon with nothing on it but the sun as it goes down.... That's all I want now, Maggie ... wide, open, empty space. Maybe it was all I ever wanted, and I wasn't that honest with myself before. Now I have to be." And then he looked down at her with her head on his shoulder, and he smiled. "Have you ever seen the green flash when the sun goes down? It just happens for an instant, and you have to be looking at just the right time. It's the most perfect moment in any sunset, and if you blink, you miss it.... That's all I want now ... that perfect instant, the green flash when the sun goes down, and night comes.... I have to follow that wherever it leads me...."

"Maybe the green flash you're looking for is within you. Maybe you don't need to run as far as you think." She knew he was still running *from*, as much as he was running *to*, but only he could discover that, as she knew.

She had had her own inner battles over Andrew, and whether or not she could have changed things, or stopped him, or saved him, or was responsible for his death, as Charles had said she was. The moment had come for her finally when she knew that there was nothing she could have done. For her, the truth had come in a thousand tiny moments, like shards that formed a window she could finally look through. It came in talking to others like him, on the phone late at night, and long nights of introspection. It came in moments of prayer, and nights of bitter tears, but in the end what she had seen, as she looked into herself, had brought peace to her. She couldn't have saved him, she couldn't have changed it. All she could do was accept the fact that he was gone now, and had chosen to be. It was about acceptance and surrender, and loving someone enough to let them go forever. That had been the green flash for her, and she hoped that one day Quinn would find that too. He was still tormented about what he hadn't done, and hadn't been, and couldn't do, and until he surrendered and accepted and knew that he couldn't have changed anything, not even himself, he would have to run. It was in standing still that one found the truth, not in running, but that was impossible to explain to anyone. He had to find the answers for himself, wherever he had to go to find them, and until then he would never be free, no matter where he went to find freedom.

She looked at him then with everything she was thinking, and felt for him, and all the gratitude for all he'd done for her, and she turned her face toward him as she looked at him. And as she did, he leaned toward her and kissed her, and they hung in space for an endless instant with their eyes closed, feeling a green flash of their own. It was a moment in which two worlds gently approached each other and melted into one, and neither of them wanted the moment to end. It was a long time before he opened his eyes and looked at her. He wanted her, but knew he had to be honest with her, or whatever they shared would damage both of them.

"I have no idea what that means," he said gently, and she nodded. In the months of their friendship, she had come to understand who he was. "I'm a man with no past and no future, all I have is the present to give you. My past is worthless, my future doesn't exist yet, and probably never will, not with you. All I can give you is this moment, right now, before I leave. Is that enough for you, Maggie?" He wanted it to be, but he was afraid it wasn't. As he looked at her, he remembered all the years when Jane had looked at him with such disappointment and pain. He knew now that however much he had loved her, she had needed more of him than he had to give, and he didn't want to do that to anyone again. But this woman was different, and maybe for an hour or a moment or these few months before he left, they could share the little he had left to give. She wanted nothing more than that from him.

"It's enough, Quinn. . . . I'm in the same boat as you." The past was too painful, the future was unsure, all they had was the present moment and whatever it brought them. They had learned their lessons separately in agonizing ways, and neither of them wanted to give or get more pain than they had already endured and encountered.

"I'm leaving in September, no matter what happens between us. Do you understand that?" His voice sounded firm, and she nodded again, looking peaceful.

"I know," she whispered, and told herself that whatever did happen, no matter how much she came to love him, if she did, she would have to let him go. It was the only way to love him. Loving him meant never holding him, as well as letting him go, and she knew that to the roots of her soul.

He seemed to relax then, as he pulled her close to him. They lay side by side together, looking up at the sails, and saying nothing. There was nothing they had to say. They each had all they wanted. All they needed was to lie beside each other, looking up together, into the open sky, above the sails.

# 9

WHEN THE THREESOME CAME TOGETHER AGAIN ON FRI-day night, Jack sensed something different between them, and he couldn't figure out what it was. Quinn seemed happier and more relaxed than he had seen him in months. And when Maggie joined them for dinner, she was wearing her long dark hair loose down her back. They had spent the night together on the *Molly B* the night before. Neither of them was encumbered, their life and time were their own. And they were beginning to spend more and more time together on the boat.

And as usual when they played dice, most of the time Quinn won. Jack stayed until nearly midnight, and Maggie made a point of leaving when he did. And the following morning, she and Quinn left for the boat. They had never spent a night in each other's house, Quinn felt very uncomfortable about sleeping with Maggie in the bed he had shared with Jane, so they didn't. But the *Molly B* provided neutral turf for them, and it had begun to feel like their own. They were each surprised by their shared passion. Quinn hadn't felt that way in years. And although he hadn't admitted it to her, with Maggie he felt as if he had regained his youth. With him, she had found something she had never known before. Above all, the passion and the love they shared had brought them both peace. It was a union that soothed both their souls. She wouldn't have been ready for it years before, and neither would he. But they had come together at a time that healed them both.

It was another month before Jack looked at them standing near each other one night cooking dinner, and finally figured it out. He couldn't imagine why he hadn't thought of it before. It was days later before he had the courage to mention it to Quinn.

"Did I miss something?" he asked, smiling shyly, not quite sure how to ask what he wanted to know. Quinn was still and always the elder statesman of the group. But Quinn was quick to catch his drift.

"What do you think you missed?" He smiled at the younger man. Jack was reading as though he had done so all his life, and Quinn was proud of him.

"You and Maggie? Is it what I think?"

"It could be." Quinn smiled at him and handed him a glass of wine. They had just finished their lesson, and all Quinn was doing now was polishing the gem Jack had become. They were reading Robert Frost and Shakespeare and all the poets Jane had loved, and Jack had hungered for. "I'm not sure what it is," Quinn said honestly. "Whatever it is, we're both happy with it, and that's enough for both of us." He loved the way she instinctively understood him, the way she let him be who he had to be, but at the same time respected herself. Letting him be himself was not the sacrifice for her it had been for Jane, so he had no need to feel guilty. And having lost so much in her life, Maggie expected less of him. She was tender and loving, and at the same time, independent and self-sufficient. She loved him, and was doing so with wide-open arms, which was exactly what he wanted from her. He never wanted to hurt or disappoint anyone again, as he had Jane.

"Are you in love with her?" Jack asked, looking excited, he wanted it to be that, for both of them. And he had noticed how happy Maggie looked these days. She was either singing in her garden, or happy in her house. She had blossomed like a flower in the sunshine in the past month.

"I'm not sure what that word means anymore," Quinn said, thinking about it as he looked at Jack. He had become almost like a son to him. "Love is a word that pierces men's hearts, like a poisoned dart, and then they turn and poison someone else. I don't want to do that to anyone anymore." He had understood fully in the year she'd been gone, just how badly he had hurt Jane. She had forgiven him for it, but he would never forgive himself. And he didn't want to do that to anyone again. "Heinous crimes are committed in the name of love, like holy wars. There's nothing worse."

"Don't be so hard on yourself," Jack said wisely. He knew that Quinn was.

"I have to be, Jack. If not, I'll be hard on someone else. I can't do that again, least of all to Maggie. She's had enough pain in her life." He loved her, but the last person he would admit it to was himself.

"Will you take her with you in September?" Jack asked with interest. He was pleased by the news. He thought they needed each other, and they both deserved happiness, more than most people he knew. And he loved them both.

"No, I won't," Quinn said without hesitating. He was sure of that, and had told her that from the first. She understood. "This is for now. Neither of us is asking for more than that. There's no future here." Jack was sad to hear it, but hoped they'd change their minds at some point. And he mentioned to Maggie discreetly the next day that he was pleased about what was happening with Quinn. She smiled, kissed Jack's cheek, and said nothing more. But she was glad that he knew. She had wanted to share it with him, but wasn't quite sure how. She didn't want to be indiscreet about her involvement with Quinn.

The following week was the anniversary date of Jane's death, which was hard for him. Maggie had already been through one with Andrew and knew how hard that day was. And Mother's Day, now that she'd lost her only son, was even worse. Maggie left Quinn alone in the morning of the anniversary, and went for a walk with him in the afternoon. And that night, he spent the night on the boat alone. He seemed better when he came back the next day.

The day after the anniversary, like the hand of destiny meddling in their life again, his house sold. He got the price he wanted for it, the new buyers were moving out from the East in the fall, and they agreed to wait for it until October 1, which worked perfectly for him. It made it more real for Maggie that he was going to leave. But she knew that anyway, and had made her peace with it, or so she said.

And in late June, he invited her to go to Holland with him, to see the boat. He had been over three or four times that spring, to check on it, but this time he wanted to show it to her. He gave her the plane ticket as a gift. She hesitated to accept it, but it was expensive for her, and Quinn knew it. He insisted that she let him invite her, and she was wildly excited when they left. They flew to London on a night flight, and from there flew to Amsterdam. He had booked a beautiful suite at the Amstel to share with her. She felt as though she had died and gone to heaven. And she could hardly wait to see the boat. After studying the plans with him for months, she wanted to see it in the flesh, and he was excited to be showing it to her. It was like taking her to his new home.

They slept for a few hours at the Amstel, and then they went to the shipyard after lunch. It was a beautiful sunny day in Amsterdam, which Quinn knew was rare. And the moment she saw the boat, Maggie caught her breath. She was speechless for a few minutes, and there were tears in her eyes. She had never seen anything as beautiful in her entire life, and it meant the world to her that he had shared it with her.

"Oh my God, Quinn, she's incredible." Seen from where she sat in dry dock, as Maggie looked up at her, she looked more like an ocean liner than a sailboat. The boat Quinn was building was huge. They rode hydraulic lifts to get on board, and Maggie was amazed at how far the interior work had gone, and it reminded her once again of how soon Quinn would leave. But she wasn't thinking of that now, she was sharing in the joy of the boat with him. He looked proud to see her so impressed. He hadn't dared to hope for a reaction as positive as this. Maggie exhibited pure, unadulterated pleasure on his behalf, and enormous admiration for him. It was a huge undertaking, and she delighted in it for him.

They spent the afternoon at the boatyard with Tem Hakker and his sons, and Quinn went over some more drawings with them. They looked forward to his visits to walk around the boat with him, and suggest improvements in the most recent plans.

Quinn and Maggie had dinner in the hotel that night, and went back to the yard at the crack of dawn the next morning. She got up early with him, and enjoyed the sights she saw on the way back to the boatyard. She was immensely grateful that Quinn had invited her to come with him. She knew that his sharing that with her was his way of demonstrating to her how much she meant to him. His excitement was tangible as he walked the boat with the Hakkers again. Maggie followed them quietly, listening to their suggestions and Quinn's. And she was amazed once again at the caliber of the work they had done.

The main saloon was wood paneled, as were all the cabins, Quinn's stateroom looked palatial to her, and all of the bathrooms were done in the finest Italian marble. And of course, the decks were teak. They were still working on the superstructure. She was going to be painted dark blue, and the superstructure was silver. He had thought of a hundred names for her, and had just settled on *Vol de Nuit,* after a book by Antoine de Saint-Exupéry, which Quinn had loved since his youth. It meant night flight, which suited the sleek look of the boat, and the purposes he intended her for. Maggie could easily imagine him sailing through the night from one exotic place to another, on his solitary adventures, much like a pilot in a night sky, beneath the stars, feeling at one with his maker. Even the color of the boat reminded her of a night sky, and the silver of the stars within it. Her name had been a long time coming. And when they left that afternoon, all of the Hakkers' most pressing questions had been answered.

They picked up their things at the hotel in the late afternoon, and got to the airport just in time to catch a plane to Paris. They had talked about spending a day in Paris but decided against it. Maggie was content with having seen the boat, which was what they had come for. They spent an hour at Charles De Gaulle, and then boarded a night flight to San Francisco. And because of the time difference, they were due to arrive in San Francisco at midnight. It had been a short trip, but a meaningful one for both of them. As they settled back in their seats, she looked at him with a long, slow smile of gratitude and kissed him.

"What was that for?" he asked, looking pleased. She had been a wonderful companion on the trip.

"For taking me to see your baby," she said, looking happy. "She's even more beautiful than I thought she'd be." She had even seen samples of his bed and table linens, flatware, crystal, and china. Everything he had chosen for the boat was exquisite. She was far more spectacular than she would have been if she'd been completed by Bob Ramsay. Quinn's taste and eye were absolutely flawless.

"Thank you for coming with me," Quinn said graciously, as he settled down in his seat, content next to Maggie. He had enjoyed sharing the boat with her. He had never known another woman with an equal passion for sailboats. And even he had to admit, this one was special. There wasn't another boat like her. It meant a lot to him that Maggie understood that. *Vol de Nuit* was going to be a yacht that no one forgot once they'd seen her. He would have loved to share her with Jane, but in his heart of hearts, he knew that she would not have appreciated or enjoyed her as much as Maggie. Sailboats had never been Jane's passion. In fact, if she'd been alive, he knew he would never have bought her. Particularly after they lost Doug, Jane had wanted nothing to do with sailboats. But she hadn't liked them even before that. It was something one was either born with or wasn't. It was rarely an acquired passion. And as it was in Quinn's, Maggie's love for boats was in her bloodstream.

They each selected movies to watch on their individual screens, and ordered dinner. They chatted quietly while they ate, about the details of the boat, and afterward, Maggie put her seat back and watched the movie till she fell asleep. Quinn looked over and saw her dozing next to him, and with a smile, he gently covered her with a blanket. It had been a whirlwind trip, and he'd accomplished a great deal, but more than that, he had come to know Maggie even better. Not just her love for boats, or understanding of the fine details of the project, what he had discovered was something far more important, and deeper. He had found the true generosity of her spirit, in being able to rejoice for him, and celebrate his accomplishment, knowing full well that the boat she'd seen was what would ultimately take him from her. She had faced her rival squarely, saluted and admired her, and was prepared to move away gracefully when he left her. It was the one thing Quinn had never found in any woman, not even Jane, and it was what made him realize now that he loved Maggie.

# 10

THE PLANE FROM PARIS ARRIVED IN SAN FRANCISCO slightly delayed, at one o'clock in the morning. Maggie had been asleep for most of the night, and was rested when Quinn woke her just before they landed. He had filled her customs card out for her, and handed it to her, as she smiled sleepily at him. She was sorry to be home again, and wished they had decided to spend a night in Paris. The trip seemed like a dream now. But she also knew that Quinn was busy. He had much to do before his move, and he wanted to close Jane's estate by September, which was no small project, and Maggie knew that. She followed Quinn's timetable, and was just glad he had taken her to see his sailboat.

They went through customs rapidly at that hour, and took a cab to the city. They were halfway there when he looked at her. They had no reason to go home that night, and suddenly he didn't want to. He liked sleeping next to her, and he was still reluctant to spend a night with her in either of their houses. His own still felt like Jane's house, and he realized it would until he left it.

"Would you like to sleep on the *Molly B* tonight?" he asked with a smile as he put an arm around her, and she nodded. She hadn't wanted to sleep alone that night either. She was growing accustomed to him, and missed him on the nights they didn't spend together. But she also knew that she would have to get used to it eventually. No matter how much she loved sleeping with him, and being with him, and making love with him, he would be gone soon.

"I'd love it," she said happily. She knew she would forever remember the months they were spending on the *Molly B* together.

"We can take a sail in the morning. I don't have to meet my attorney till four-thirty."

The boat was locked up tight when they arrived, but Quinn had the key for the doors and the alarm. The crew were on board, but they were undoubtedly sleeping. The first mate was on watch as they came in, and he carried their bags to Quinn's cabin, and offered them something to eat, but neither of them was hungry.

They both took showers and went to bed, and as soon as they did, Maggie nestled close to him, and he put an arm around her.

"Thank you for a wonderful trip," she whispered to him. "I think you and *Vol de Nuit* are going to be very happy with each other."

He wanted to tell her then how much her generosity of spirit meant to him, but for some reason, he didn't. He didn't know what to say to her. He knew now that he was in love with her, but it didn't change anything for him, and he didn't want to foster false hopes or illusions. He was afraid if he told her how he felt, she would think that he might stay, or return for her, and he knew he couldn't. He felt he owed it to Jane somehow to be alone, to venture on with his solitary travels. After all he had done, and failed to do in his life, he knew he did not deserve to spend the rest of his life with Maggie. She was young enough to find someone else, have a wholesome life, and forget him.

And he had never said it to her, but it concerned him that he was twenty years older than she was. She was young enough to be his daughter, which seemed ridiculous to him. He never felt their age difference, but he had had his life, his children, his career, his marriage, and now he felt he had to atone for his sins. Indulging himself with a woman two-thirds his age, and dragging her around the world with him seemed as selfish as what he had done to Jane, and the egocentric life he had led, for which Alex could not forgive him. He knew he was doing the right thing in setting Maggie free when he left, and promising her nothing. If anything, he was going to urge her to forget him. His mind was full of thoughts of her, his heart eased with the warmth of her next to him, but he said nothing to her.

He was already up and dressed when she awoke the next morning. They had left the dock at eight o'clock, and the *Molly B* was already sailing. It was a bright June day, and as Maggie got up, it was odd to realize that she had woken up in Amsterdam the previous morning. She smiled to herself, thinking of it, like a delicious dream, and went to join Quinn on deck in her robe and nightgown.

"Good lord, what time is it? Where am I?" she asked as she squinted at him in the sunshine. Her tousled hair cascaded down her back, just the way he liked it. She looked scarcely older than his daughter, and wasn't. There were only eight years between Maggie and Alex, but Maggie seemed an entire generation older. She had suffered a great deal in her lifetime, particularly in recent years, which made her seem far more mature, and a great deal wiser, and more compassionate certainly, than his daughter.

"It's ten o'clock. This is San Francisco Bay, you'll notice the Golden Gate straight ahead, and I'm Quinn Thompson," he teased her.

"Hello. I'm Maggie Dartman." She played the game with him. "Didn't I meet you in Amsterdam? You're the owner of that fabulous yacht, *Vol de Nuit*...or was I dreaming?" It all seemed like a dream now, but it wasn't.

"You must have been dreaming," he assured her. The stewardess asked Maggie what she'd like for breakfast, and Maggie smiled at how spoiled she was getting. She turned to Quinn with a grin. "To think, I used to eat Hostess Twinkies and left-over hot dogs for breakfast."

"Don't ever invite me over for breakfast. I'll stick to dinner." He grinned at her.

"Good decision," she said, as the stewardess handed her a cappuccino just the way she liked it. The crew of the *Molly B* were terrific. It was going to be tough getting used to real life again, when Quinn was gone. Because of the man, not the breakfast.

Quinn had already begun hiring his crew for *Vol de Nuit*. One was Italian, two were French, and the other seven crew members were British. He had hired John Barclay's captain from the *Victory*, after a letter he had received from him in April, asking if there might be a position for him. He had been following *Vol de Nuit*'s progress with interest. Quinn had offered him the job as captain by return fax, and followed it up with a phone call. The man's name was Sean Mackenzie, and he was arriving in Amsterdam with the rest of the crew just before the sea trials in September. They were on schedule so far.

Maggie sat next to Quinn at the helm of the *Molly B* for the rest of the afternoon, and they got back to the dock at three o'clock, in time for Quinn to meet with his attorney. And before they left the boat, they agreed to spend the night on her again that evening. Both the boat and the man were becoming a dangerous habit for Maggie. The more time she spent with him, the harder it would be to see him leave in the beginning of October. He was coming back to San Francisco one last time after the sea trials, and then, she knew, it would be over. But she wouldn't allow herself to think of it, she had promised him that when he left, she would let him go without a murmur, and she had every intention of keeping her promise, no matter how hard for her, or how painful his absence. He was a gift that had come into her life unexpectedly, and when the gift was taken from her, as she knew it would be, she was going to be both gracious and graceful about it. It was all Quinn had

117

ever asked of her, and she owed him that, or felt she did. It seemed to be her destiny to lose those she loved, to let them leave her life, no matter how costly to her.

"Are you all right?" Quinn asked her quietly, as one of the crew members drove them home, and she nodded. "You're very quiet." He had sensed something in her silence, and he wasn't wrong, but she had no intention of sharing her thoughts with him about his departure.

"Just jet-lagged," she said, smiling. "How about you?"

"I'm fine." He was still ecstatic over his visit to *Vol de Nuit*, and invigorated by it. "I wish I didn't have to meet with the attorney. I should be home by seven." They had left their bags on the boat, so she had nothing to unpack, and little to do until he came back to get her. Her life was very simple now, although she knew it would be busier once she went back to teaching in September. She was going back to work around the same time he left for the sea trials.

Jack was at the house when Quinn walked in, just finishing some work in the kitchen, and when he saw Quinn, he looked mournful.

"Something wrong?" Quinn asked with a worried frown, and Jack shook his head. He looked awful.

"I just finished."

"Finished what?" Quinn asked, looking for his briefcase with the legal folders in it.

"Everything," Jack said, and Quinn stopped and looked at him.

"Everything?" They had dragged it out as long as they could. He had been there for six months, and not only was the house impeccable in every detail, but he had become a proficient reader.

"It's all done," Jack confirmed. "We did it."

"No," Quinn said with a slow smile, as he looked at the man who had become his friend, and to whom he had become not only teacher, but mentor. "*You* did it. And don't you forget that." He walked across the room toward him and shook his hand. "We're going to have to celebrate." And Quinn meant it.

"Can I still come to dinner on Friday evenings?" He couldn't even imagine not seeing Quinn daily.

"I have a better idea. Let's talk about it in the morning. Why don't you come by for breakfast?" And then he remembered that he was going to be on the boat with Maggie. And he wanted to spend the day sailing. "I just realized I won't be here. Why don't you come for dinner on the boat on Friday night?" Jack knew where the boat was docked at the yacht club.

"Could I bring Michelle with me?" The girl he had been dating for a while had become a serious romance for him, and they were inseparable, but Quinn was hoping she was only a passing fancy. He had an important proposition to make him.

"Of course." And then Quinn thought of something. "Does she know about our special project?" Quinn didn't want to embarrass him in case she didn't.

"You mean my reading?" Quinn nodded. "I just told her. I was afraid she'd think less of me, but she thought it was terrific."

"I like her already." Quinn had not yet met her, but knew now that he would on Friday.

"How was Amsterdam?"

"Impeccable. Everything is going along at full speed. The boat looks splendid." And then as an afterthought, between the two men, "I took Maggie with me."

"I thought that might be where she was. She's been gone all week. I wasn't sure though." The two men exchanged a long look, and Jack's eyes held a single silent question, and Quinn understood him.

He shook his head. "No. Nothing's changed. She understands. She knows I'm leaving."

Jack sighed as he looked at him. He had learned a lot from Quinn in the past six months, but now he thought it was Quinn who needed to learn the lesson. "Someone like that doesn't come into your life every day, Quinn.... Whatever you do, don't lose her."

"I never had her," Quinn said quietly. "Just as she doesn't have me. People never 'have' each other." Jane had never had him, never, or at least not until after she died. And he had only found her after he lost her. He was fully prepared to give up what he had found with Maggie, and take the best of her with him, in the memories he would have of her. He didn't need more than that. He was convinced of it. "I'm too old to be romantic," Quinn said as though trying to convince himself, "or to be tied to the skirts of a woman. She understands that."

"I think you're throwing away something precious," Jack said doggedly, and Maggie would have been profoundly touched if she'd heard him.

"I'm going to give it back, Jack. That's different." Jack shook his head as Quinn picked up his briefcase and smiled at him. "See you on Friday." It was in two days, and Quinn was looking forward to it. He had no intention of giving up their Fridays, and wondered if Jack would want to bring Michelle with him every week, or keep it a threesome. Although Quinn was willing to welcome her into the group, he also loved the intimacy of the three friends, and was leaving it up to Jack.

"Think about what I said," Jack called after him, as Quinn ignored him and closed the door firmly behind him.

# 11

MICHELLE AND JACK APPEARED ON THE DOCK PROMPTLY at seven o'clock on Friday, and Maggie and Quinn were ready for them. The crew offered them champagne, and there were balloons and lanterns hanging on the afterdeck. It looked like a party. Quinn and Maggie had put the decorations up themselves. They had said nothing to Jack, but it was his graduation. Quinn had gotten a diploma for him and filled it out carefully with his name and the date, and had referred to him as a successful scholar. It took Jack only a moment to realize what was happening, and he was moved to tears when, at the end of dinner, Quinn handed him his diploma. Maggie had had a chance to chat with Michelle by then and was pleased to find that she liked her.

And as Quinn handed Jack the diploma he'd written out for him, the two men's eyes misted over. Quinn shook his hand, and put the other on his shoulder, and his eyes filled as he hugged him.

"Well done, my friend ... well done...." Jack was so touched he couldn't even bring himself to answer. He just nodded. No one had ever been as kind to him in his life, except Maggie. The two of them had become precious friends to him, and he knew he would never forget Quinn for the horizons he had opened. His life had been changed forever. Michelle sat watching them silently, and kissed Jack when he sat down next to her again. She was in awe of both Quinn and Maggie. She seemed very young to them. She was only twenty-four, but it was obvious that she was deeply in love with Jack, and admired him greatly.

After another round of champagne, Quinn invited Jack to walk around the deck with him, while the two women chatted. Maggie felt as though she was talking to a daughter. Michelle had just finished nursing school, and she thought Jack was her dream come true.

Jack followed Quinn up to the upper deck, and they sat looking at the stars quietly for a long moment. Quinn had been wanting to talk to Jack for some time now.

"I have an idea I wanted to share with you," Quinn began as he lit a cigar, and sat looking at the brightly lit ash for a moment. "Maybe more of a proposition, and I hope you'll accept it." It sounded important to Jack, and was, or would be, to both of them, if he agreed to do it. Quinn was counting on him, it was the greatest gift he could give him. "I've just hired the crew and the captain for the new boat. They're all coming on board in September for the sea trials, and what I was going to ask you ... or offer you ... was that I was hoping you would join us."

"For the sea trials?" In spite of himself, Jack looked startled, and Quinn laughed, it was a long, low, contented rumble.

"No, my friend. As a member of *Vol de Nuit*'s crew. You could come on board as an apprentice. And if you learn to sail as fast as you've learned everything else, you'll be the captain before it's all over."

"Are you serious? About joining the crew, I mean?" For an instant, he wanted to pack his bags and run away with his beloved mentor, and then reality hit him, and he looked disappointed.

"You can do it. I know you can." Quinn had misread what he'd seen and thought he was frightened. "It will be the experience of a lifetime."

"I know it will," Jack said quietly, "or would. But I can't, Quinn."

"Why not?" Quinn looked shocked, and more than a little disappointed. He had expected Jack to think about it, and at least be tempted to do it. He was, but Quinn had changed Jack's life in more ways than he realized. Perhaps even more than he had intended.

"I'm going to college. I just got into State. I'm in a pre-architectural program. I was going to tell you tonight. And I forgot, I got so excited by my diploma. I've got a long road ahead of me. I want to be an architect one day. I could never even have thought about it without you. And I'm starting pretty late in the day. I can't take a year off to sail around the world with you, but damn, I'd have loved it." He said it with genuine emotion.

Danielle Steel

"I knew I shouldn't have taught you to read," Quinn said vehemently with a rueful grin, torn between pride and disappointment. He had really wanted Jack to come with him. As much as he knew it wasn't right to take Maggie with him, he would have loved to take Jack under his wing and turn him into a sailor. But he was nonetheless impressed by what he was doing. Jack had never even told him he'd applied to college.

"It'll be a long time till I graduate. I may be a hundred years old by then, but I'm going to do it. I'm going to do it at night and take as many units as I can. I'll have to keep working. And"—he hesitated for a beat—"Michelle and I just got engaged. We're going to get married at Christmas."

"Good lord, you have been busy. When did that happen?" Quinn looked genuinely amazed, and was sorry to give up the dream of Jack running away with him. It would have been like having a son on board. But he respected Jack's right to pursue his own dreams.

"It happened this week, while you were in Holland."

"Well, in that case, congratulations." He stuck out a hand and shook Jack's, but he felt a loss suddenly, as though his son were leaving home and not only going off to college, but getting married. It was a double header, and he could see now that there was no hope that Jack would join him. But Quinn was gracious about it, and as the two men walked back to join the women, Quinn looked sadly at Maggie. She hadn't known what Quinn was going to ask him, but she suspected, and she could see in his eyes that it hadn't gone the way Quinn wanted.

126

"The third musketeer in our Friday night dinner club has some important announcements to share with us," he said grandly, covering the dismay he felt with a jovial demeanor, as he poured champagne for the four of them. "Jack is not only going to college," he told Maggie as she listened with affectionate interest, "he's going to State in the fall. But he and Michelle are getting married at Christmas." Jack's young fiancée blushed the moment Quinn said it, and Maggie gave an exclamation of pleasure. She kissed Jack first for his accomplishments, and then both of them for their engagement. And Quinn cheered up after another glass of champagne and a brandy. The young couple stayed until one o'clock and then left. Quinn looked sad when they went to bed that night. Maggie had already understood what was behind it.

"You wanted to take him on as crew, didn't you?" she asked gently, as Quinn came to bed in his pajamas.

"How did you know?" He looked at her in surprise, and then lay back against his pillow.

"I know you. I wondered if you might. He would have been good at it, but you've given him a life, you know. What he's doing will be wonderful for him when he's finished. You've given him what he needed to have a better life than he ever would have had before you met him. Better even than sailing." She smiled at Quinn, and had never loved him more than at that moment. She loved his vulnerability and his generosity, and his relentlessly kind spirit. In another life, it was not the way people would have described him. But this was the man she knew and had come to love, the same one who had been Jack's mentor. Not the one his former business partners

127

had known, or even the man Jane had known, or whom his daughter hated. Quinn, as he was now, was governed by his heart, and in spite of his immense power and strength, he had been humbled, and as a result, he was even bigger than he had been. "Are you very disappointed?" she asked him.

"Selfishly, I suppose I am, but I'm glad too. I think college will be good for him. What about Michelle? Do you like her?"

"She's very sweet, and she adores him." She had seemed very young to Maggie, but so was Jack in his own way. They shared a certain innocence and naïveté, and she suspected, or at least hoped, that they'd be happy.

"It takes more than that," Quinn said wisely. "It takes so much more than that to be married." He had a profound respect now for the job he felt he had done so badly as a husband. He was his own worst critic.

"Maybe it doesn't," Maggie said kindly. "Maybe in the beginning all you have to do is trust yourself, and each other."

"I know myself far too well to ever trust myself again," he said, as he rolled over on his side and looked at her. "I trust you, though, Maggie." The way he looked at her, she was deeply touched when he said it.

"You're right to trust me. And I trust you, Quinn. Completely." All he could think of as she said it was that he wanted to tell her not to.

"I'm not sure that's wise of you. What if I hurt you?" He already knew he would, when he left her. But she had entered into the relationship willingly, knowing what the ground rules were, and what the final outcome would be.

"I don't think you will hurt me," she said honestly, "not intentionally. I'll be sad when you go, very sad. I know that. But that's different than your hurting me. You haven't lied to me, you haven't misrepresented who you are, or anything else that I know of. Those are the things that hurt people. The rest are accidents of life that no one can foresee or prevent. What you do about them is what matters. There are no guarantees between two people, Quinn. You can only do the best you can." What was killing him, and eating him up inside, was that he didn't think he had. There was no changing that now, no turning back the clock. Jane had done her best. And Maggie had, he knew from all he knew of her. But he hadn't. And Maggie's husband hadn't. And all Quinn could do was live with it now. He could never erase the pain he'd caused those who loved him. And he didn't want Maggie to be another casualty to him, even if she was willing. He wanted more than that for her, even if it meant protecting her from himself. He didn't think that he deserved her love. Nor did he feel he had deserved Jane's. Her journals, and the pain he'd read in them, were ample proof of that. "Don't be so hard on yourself," Maggie said, as she cuddled up to him in the dark.

"Why not? Don't be so generous with me," he said sadly. He was sad that Jack wasn't coming with him. Sad that he was leaving her. For all the joy he knew his boat would give him, he knew that it was not a sign of victory, but of defeat, when he finally sailed off. He knew he had failed to give Jane the best he could, and in a way, he was doing it again with Maggie. She was willing to settle for the brief time they had to share. And she was doing what he had asked her to do, to love him for a time, and then out of still more love for him, to let him go. It was the ultimate act of love, and she was willing to give him that too. He knew it was a lot to ask. In all fairness, probably too much.

"I love you, Quinn," she whispered, as she looked up at him. There was a thin sliver of moonlight that had stolen into the room, and she could see his face clearly, etched against the darkness around them. He lay silently next to her for a long time, and held her close to him. He wanted to say the same words to her, because he felt them in his heart, and he wanted to give them back to her. But the words he wanted to say to her were lodged tightly in his throat, and were unable to reach his mouth. And as he held her, and felt her hair on his cheek, there was a tear in the corner of his eye that slid slowly down his cheek.

# 12

JULY AND AUGUST WERE IDYLLIC FOR THEM. QUINN HAD finished most of his work on Jane's estate. He had gone through almost everything in the house, sorted it, packed it, and sent several things to Sotheby's in New York for auction. He had called Alex in Geneva several times, and asked her which pieces of furniture she wanted. She asked for only a few favorites, and a portrait of her mother, and asked him to store the rest. She said they didn't have enough room in their house for more at the moment. Each time he called, she hung up as quickly as she could. Once their business transactions were complete, she was always in a hurry to get off the phone. Quinn hadn't seen her in more than a year, since her mother's funeral, and he talked to Maggie about it one day, when they were lying on the boat, enjoying the summer sun and a late afternoon sail. They were spending most of their time on the boat these days. And Jack still came to have dinner with them every Friday night. He didn't bring Michelle with him when he came, he liked being

131

with Quinn and Maggie on his own. But he said he was happy with her, and she was a good sport about his weekly night out with his buddies.

"What am I going to do about her?" Quinn asked Maggie about Alex. "I can't get through to her at all. She completely shut me out." He told her about the calls regarding the furniture. Once she had answered his questions, Alex thanked him for the call, and hung up as quickly as she could get off the phone.

"She'll think about it one day. Maybe when something happens to her, or something frightens her. She can't shut you out forever, Quinn, she's your daughter. She needs you, as much as you need her."

"No, she doesn't," he said, looking worried. It was yet another failure on his part, to Jane. He knew she would have been devastated to know how estranged they were especially after her death. "She has her husband and her sons. She doesn't need me."

"She's punishing you. She can't do that forever. One of these days she'll see who you really were, and even if you weren't there for her all the time, she may finally understand why you weren't."

"I'm not even sure I understand why myself. I was running all the time in those days. I thought I was building something, and I was. It was more important to me than my kids, or Jane. My priorities were all screwed up. The only thing I cared about was the empire I was building, the money I'd made, and the next deal on the table. I didn't know it then, but I entirely missed the point." As he said it, he thought of Doug and Jane, and how swiftly life changes, and opportunities are lost forever. He finally understood that, too late.

"A lot of men do that, Quinn," Maggie said compassionately, and for an odd moment, he wished he had been married to her then, and not Jane. He felt instantly guilty for the thought, but Jane had become a victim to him. After all she had suffered, Maggie had greater insight into him, and understood far more even than he did. She was a very different woman from the one he'd had. "You're not the only one who's done what you did. Wives leave men because of it sometimes, children get angry. People feel cheated by what they didn't get. What they don't see is what they did have, and that it was the best the man could do at the time. You can't do it all, or be perfect for all those you love. There are women who do the same thing these days, focus on their careers and shortchange their families. It's hard to keep that many balls in the air." But the ones he had dropped were the people he had loved. He knew that now. But he also knew that he had understood it far too late. "Why don't you invite Alex to come to the boat in Holland?"

"She hates boats," he said glumly, as he lay with his eyes closed, stroking Maggie's hair, as she lay with her head on his chest.

"What about her boys?"

"They're too young. They're seven and ten, and she'd never trust me with them. Besides, I was never around for my kids at that age. How would I know what to do with a couple of kids that age on the boat?" The idea sounded crazy to him.

"I'll bet you'd have a lot of fun with them. They're just the right age to teach them about sailing. And on a boat the size of

*Vol de Nuit,* they'd be perfectly safe. Even Alex couldn't object. The crew could help you take care of them, if you asked them to. They'd have a ball. Why don't you offer to take them on the sea trials?" He thought about it, but couldn't imagine his daughter agreeing to it, particularly after their history with Doug. Sailboats were anathema to her, but Maggie was right, of course. On a boat the size of *Vol de Nuit,* the boys would be in no danger whatsoever, unless they jumped off while the boat was under sail, which he knew they wouldn't. They were sensible and well-behaved.

"I'll think about it," he said vaguely and then turned on his side so he could kiss Maggie. "You're awfully good to me," he whispered to her, as he thought of making love to her that morning. The relationship they were developing was as smooth and warm, and spicy at times, as Maggie herself was. She was an extraordinary combination of all the things a man could want. And in the privacy of the room they shared, she inspired a passion in him that he had never known before. He was falling more and more in love with her, and yet he could never bring himself to say the words to her.

They invited Jack and Michelle on the boat for a weekend, and they sailed down the coast toward Santa Barbara. The sea was rough, and Maggie liked it that way. It seemed more exciting to her, but Michelle got seasick on the way back, and Jack apologized to Quinn for what a poor sailor she was. She still looked embarrassed when they left.

"Poor kid," Maggie said to Quinn as they sat down to dinner that night. "She's a nice girl." But she seemed very young to both of them, and Quinn was worried that she wasn't bright enough for Jack. "She'll be good for him," Maggie kept reassuring him. She could see something in her that Quinn obviously didn't. He still wished that Jack would sail on *Vol de Nuit* with him. He thought it would be the most exciting experience of his life. But Jack didn't want excitement, he wanted roots and stability and a family, and an education, all the things he'd never had, and were within his grasp now, in great part thanks to Quinn. "You've given him something much better than a cruise around the world. You've given him a shot at his dreams. No one else could have done that for him."

"All I did was teach him to read. Anyone could have done that," Quinn said modestly, but she shook her head.

"The point is, no one did." Quinn just shook his head, but he was glad that things had turned out as well as they had. It was a bond he knew they would always share. And he never forgot that it was Jack who had brought Maggie into his life. She had looked so shy and sad and scared the first time she had walked into his kitchen. And now she was flourishing, and enjoying sailing with him. He knew she was sad about her son at times, but she no longer had that look of agony in her eyes that she had had when they first met the morning after the big storm.

"That was a lucky storm for me," he said to her, when he thought about it one day. "It blew a hole in my roof, and swept you right in."

"It was even luckier for me," she said, as she kissed him.

He had had more affection from her in the past few months than he had ever dreamed of. He had had a very different relationship with Jane. Theirs had been a bond of respect and loyalty, quiet companionship when they were together, deep affection, and Jane's endless patience. What he shared with Maggie was younger and more joyful, and far more passionate, just as Maggie was herself.

The last days of August were better than ever for them. They sailed almost constantly. And they seemed to get closer to each other with each passing day, perhaps because they knew that their final days were coming. Rather than pulling away from each other, Maggie seemed to love him with greater abandon every day, and Quinn could feel himself drifting closer and closer to her, and he no longer felt any desire to resist it. He felt safer with her than he ever had with anyone in his life. It was as though he knew deep in his heart that he could trust her in every way. And in the past month or two, his recurring dream had finally, mercifully, gone away. He still missed Jane, but differently. He felt more at peace now.

He only left Maggie when the movers came to pack up his house. He was sending whatever was left to storage. He had already sent Alex's things to her, and he was taking several suitcases of clothes and papers with him when he went to Holland for the sea trials in September. And once the house was empty, he was planning to stay on the *Molly B* until he left. It was a strange feeling watching the movers empty the house. He felt a pang every time he saw some familiar favorite piece loaded onto the truck. It was as though they were taking away the landmarks of his life. And when the house was finally empty, he stood looking around, and felt a terrible ache in his heart.

"Good-bye, Jane," he said out loud and heard his voice echo in the empty room where she had died. It was as though he were leaving her there, and for the first time in fourteen months, he felt as though he were leaving her behind. He looked somber when he met Maggie back on the boat again that night.

"Are you okay?" she asked him gently, with a look of concern. He nodded, but scarcely spoke to her until after dinner that night. He was essentially living with her on the sailboat he had chartered. He would never have been as comfortable with her in his own house. He had always felt it was Jane's. And he tried to explain to her what an odd feeling it had been to watch all their belongings being taken away, and standing alone in the empty house.

"I felt that way when I moved out of the house where Andrew died. I felt as though I was leaving him there, and I hated it. I just stood there with the movers and cried. But afterward I was glad I moved to the house on Vallejo. I would never have recovered there. Charles and I had lived there. Andrew had died there. It was just too much to survive day after day. It will do you good to be on the boat," she said generously. She had still never objected to his leaving, and Quinn was impressed. She had lived up to everything she had promised. He was only sorry that he couldn't take her with him on the sea trials. He was leaving right after Labor Day, and she was going back to work the day after he left for Holland. He was coming back to San Francisco for a brief two weeks after that. And even the day before he left, he still hadn't decided what to do about Alex. Maggie kept insisting he should call her, but he hadn't. It was as though he was afraid to. It was only that night, just before they went to bed, that he sat down at his desk and called her. It was morning in Geneva.

"I got the furniture," she said matter-of-factly as soon as she heard her father's voice. "Thank you very much. It all arrived in good order. It must have cost a fortune to ship it." He had sent it air freight.

"Your mother would have wanted you to have it," he assured her. But at the mention of Jane, he could hear Alex stiffen.

"I'm happy to have her portrait," Alex mused and then she thought of something. "Where are you living?" He had just told her that everything had gone to storage. He had wanted to do it before he left for the sea trials. He wanted to spend his last two weeks in town peacefully with Maggie, without worrying about final details. And he had agreed to turn over the house to the new owners two weeks early.

"I chartered a boat for the summer. I'll stay there when I get back, I'll only be here for two weeks, before I join the boat in Holland." He had already decided to make Africa his first stop on his adventures. "Actually," he said cautiously, "that's why I called you."

"About the boat you chartered?" She sounded puzzled, but a little less icy than in their recent conversations, which seemed hopeful.

"No. I was calling about the sea trials. I'm leaving for Amsterdam tomorrow. I was wondering if you'd mind if I stop in Geneva."

"I don't own the city," she said curtly, as his heart sank.

"I'd be coming there to see you, Alex. I haven't seen the boys since last summer. They won't even know me." She was about to say that she never had, so what difference did it make, but for once, she resisted the urge to wound him. "Actually, I had an even better idea. I was wondering if...if you would like...if you'd mind...if you'd allow me to take them with me on the sea trials. You and Horst are welcome to come too, of course, but I know you're not much of a sailor. But it might be a great experience for Christian and Robert. I'd love to have them." There was an endless pause at her end. She was so taken aback, she had no idea what to answer, so for a long moment, she didn't.

"On the sea trials?" she parroted back to him. "Don't you think they're too young? You'd have to keep an eye on them every minute. And is the boat safe?" But as she asked him, the hardness seemed to drop from her voice. In spite of herself, she was touched that he wanted to take the boys. It was something she knew he would have never done before.

"I hope the boat is safe." He laughed gently in answer. "If not, I'll be in a lot of trouble when I sail on her in October. She's quite a boat, Alex. I think the boys would love her. And of course you can come too," he repeated, wanting to be sure that she knew she was welcome. But he knew just how much she hated sailboats, and for what reason. Just as Jane did, for the same reasons. She had managed to poison Alex against them. And clearly his sailing gene had not been passed on to Alex, only to Doug.

"I'll have to discuss it with Horst," she said, sounding confused about the decision. But at least she hadn't said no yet. And miraculously, he could hear something different in her voice, as she did in his.

"Why don't I call you tomorrow before I leave. I'm flying to London. It's a quick hop to Geneva, and from there to Holland." He was momentarily hopeful, although he wondered if the

139

consultation with her husband was just a stalling tactic. He still couldn't believe she would let him take the boys to Holland with him. But he had decided Maggie was right, and it was at least worth asking. He said nothing about Maggie to her. She didn't need to know. In five weeks he and Maggie would part company, and Alex need never be the wiser that he had spent the past several months with her. It seemed disrespectful to her mother's memory to tell her, so he didn't. And when he got off the phone, he looked hopefully at Maggie. She was smiling at him.

"What did she say?"

"She said she had to talk to her husband. But she didn't hang up on me or tell me I was out of my mind and she'd rather die than let me take her children. That's something."

"I hope she lets you do it," Maggie said sincerely. And for the rest of the night, he put Alex and his grandsons out of his head, and concentrated on the woman he loved. He hated to leave her. And he wished she could come to the sea trials. They were going to put *Vol de Nuit* through all her paces. He was going to be on board for three weeks, and then come back to San Francisco. He had told Maggie to use the *Molly B* as often as she wanted, and she thanked him, but said it would make her sad to be on board without him, which touched him.

They spent a long, loving night in each other's arms, and Maggie wouldn't allow herself to think that these were almost their final moments. They had two more weeks when he got back, and even then she knew she had to release him completely. It was going to be anything but easy, but it was what she had promised him in the beginning.

# Miracle

The next morning, when he got up, Quinn called Alex in Geneva. He held his breath when she answered. It was nearly dinnertime in Switzerland, and he could hear the boys in the background.

"What did Horst say?" he asked, giving her an out if she needed one. She could blame it on her husband if she refused his invitation to his grandsons.

"I...he...I asked the boys," she told him honestly in a choked voice. "They said they want to go with you," she admitted, as tears sprang to Quinn's eyes. He hadn't realized until then how much it meant to him, and how vulnerable he was to her. Although it was what he had expected from her, he knew now that it would have hurt him if she refused him. She still hadn't said yes yet, and he was almost sure she wouldn't.

"Will you let them?" he asked cautiously, praying that she would allow it. He hardly knew Christian and Robert, and this was a golden chance to do so, in a way that they would always remember.

"Yes, I will, Dad," she said quietly. It was the first gesture of trust and respect she'd shown him in her entire lifetime. All his memories of her were of anger and resentment. This was decidedly different. "Just keep an eye on them. Chris is still a baby. But Robert is very independent. Don't let him climb the masts or do anything crazy." It was the greatest gift of love she could give him, to trust him with her sons. The war between them had ended at last, or at least the first white flag had gone up.

"Do you want to come with them?" He threw caution to the winds again, by inviting her, but she was quick to decline the invitation.

141

"I can't. I'm six months pregnant." He was startled to hear it, and it reminded him again of how little she shared with him, almost nothing. But they had covered a lot of ground that morning. He hoped it would be the beginning of a new era in their lives.

"I'll take good care of them, I promise." He would guard them with his life, for her sake. He never wanted her to experience the tragedy that he and Jane had. And it had been Alex's tragedy too, when she lost her brother. It had traumatized her forever, and Quinn knew from Jane that his daughter was extremely cautious with her children, which made it all the more meaningful that she was trusting him with them. Particularly after all the hostility between them. It was an enormous gesture of forgiveness and confidence in him. "Thank you, Alex. You don't know what it means to me," he said, and she sounded gruff when she answered. She had thought about it all day, trying to decide what she should do about it. "I think Mom would have wanted me to do it." He wasn't sure he agreed, given how much Jane hated boats, but he wasn't going to argue the point with her. She would surely have been pleased at the rapprochement between them.

"I'll change my tickets at the airport, and be in Geneva tomorrow. I'll call and let you know what time my flight gets in, and what time we fly to Holland. You may have to meet me at the airport. We can visit when I bring them back to Geneva, if that's all right with you." He wasn't sure if he was welcome.

"I'd like that," she said quietly. His offering to take her sons with him had been some kind of epiphany for her, maybe for both of them. Other than her children and her husband, he was all she had now. "How long will they be with you?" She had forgotten to ask him before, and was surprised when he told her.

"The sea trials last three weeks, but I can get them back to you sooner, if they have school. I'll fly them in myself, if you like, or I can send a crew member with them. But I'd like to see you."

"Keep them as long as you like, Dad." It was a rare opportunity for her children, and they weren't old enough for school to make that big a difference. And she was sure her children would be crazy about their grandfather's sailboat. It must have been in their genes, they were always talking about sailing and loved boats.

"Thanks, Alex. I'll call you later." Quinn's flight was at six o'clock that night, and he still had a number of things to do before he left for the airport. Among other things, he had to sign some papers at the attorney's. And when he hung up, Maggie was waiting to hear about Alex's decision.

"What did she say?" She was looking anxious as she asked him. She had left the room for most of the conversation.

Tears filled Quinn's eyes as he answered. "They're coming with me." She threw her arms around him then and kissed him, and after that she let out a whoop of glee, and he laughed as she danced around the cabin. She was as pleased as he was. She knew what it meant to him to have evidence of his daughter's forgiveness. It was the greatest gift she could give him.

He packed his suitcase on the boat, and half an hour later, left for the attorney's office. He was meeting Maggie at her house at three that afternoon, and she was driving him to the airport. When he met her there, he was wearing a suit and tie, and carrying his briefcase. She had brought his suitcase from the boat, and they were both ready. She was wearing a short black dress and high heels, and she looked young and pretty. He hated to leave her, and said as much in the car, on the way to the airport.

"I wish you were coming with me."

"So do I," she said softly, remembering their brief trip to Holland three months before, when she had seen *Vol de Nuit* for the first time. His yacht was her only rival for his affections, but she was nonetheless a formidable opponent, and in the end, the boat would be the victor. Or rather, his freedom. And Maggie did nothing to resist it. It was a fact of life with him, and loving him, that she accepted.

At the airport, she went in with him as far as she could, and he kissed her before he left her. He told her he'd call as soon as he got to the boat, and hoped their communications system was in full operation. "If not, I'll call you from a pay phone," he teased. Or more likely, Tem Hakker's office.

"Have a wonderful time," she said generously, as she kissed him again. "Enjoy your grandsons!" she called after him, and he turned and smiled at her, and spoke in a clear strong voice as he looked her in the eyes, and nodded.

"I love you, Maggie," he said, as she stared at him. It was the first time he had said it. But she had given him so many gifts, among them the gift of suggesting that he call Alex. He wasn't going to make the same mistakes again, of keeping what he felt a secret. And besides, she had earned it. The words, so much deserved, had been hard won.

# 13

QUINN CALLED ALEX FROM THE FIRST-CLASS LOUNGE, and she sounded sleepy when she answered. It was one o'clock in the morning for her, and he told her quickly what time he would arrive that day, and his flight number from London. And then he told her to go back to sleep, and he hung up. He was excited to see her, and pleased for her that she was pregnant. He knew Jane would have been happy for her too. But for once, his thoughts weren't of Jane, as he sat and waited for his flight. All he could think of now was Maggie, and he was beginning to realize how hard it would be to leave her. It wasn't going to be as easy as he had thought it would be in the beginning. He was going to have to peel her from his skin like a bandage sticking to a wound. She had protected his heart for the past many months, and leaving her would expose it again. But he knew he had no choice. If he delayed his trip, it would only be worse, and he couldn't take her with him. He knew taking her would be the wrong thing to do. He had made a

vow to Jane's memory. To atone for his sins and be alone. He
was convinced that that was why the recurring dreams had
gone. He and his conscience had made a deal, and finally
made peace to honor his promise to her, or he would be devoured by guilt forever. He needed the solitude of his life on
the boat, for himself, and the freedom to leave just as he had
told Maggie he would in the beginning. Above all, he needed
his freedom. He felt he had no right to companionship forever.
He had to leave. And Maggie needed to go back to her own
life, with friends and people she knew, and her teaching. He
couldn't drag her around the world with him. He had to do
what he had said he would. No matter how painful for both
of them, he had to leave her. But for the first time in his life,
he was beginning to question just how much he wanted his
freedom.

But once he got on the flight to London, he felt better, and
told himself it was a sign of age that he was getting so attached
to her, and it would be better for both of them to end it. In a
way, he perceived his love for her as weakness. And he
couldn't allow himself to indulge it.

He slept on the flight, which was rare for him. And in London,
he changed planes with minutes to spare. He flew into Geneva at
five in the afternoon, local time, and the minute he got off the
plane, he saw Alex. She was wearing her blond hair long, as
Maggie did, and he was startled to realize that Maggie looked
nearly as young as she did. And he was touched when he saw
her pregnant. He had never seen her that way, neither with
Christian nor with Robert. She walked cautiously toward him,
as the boys walked a few steps behind her, carrying their back-

packs, and looking almost exactly like her. They were lively little towheads, and they were jostling each other and laughing.

Alex's eyes were serious when she saw her father. "How was your flight?" she asked, without touching him. She did not reach up to kiss or hug him. She kept her arms at her side, as they looked at each other. He hadn't seen her since she left after Jane's funeral, and when she had, she hadn't even said good-bye to him. This was their first meeting.

"You look beautiful," Quinn said, smiling at her. He could barely resist the urge to hold her, but he knew the invitation to do so had to come from her, or at least the gesture.

"Thank you, Dad," she said, as tears filled her eyes, and his misted over. And then she put her arms out to him, and he folded her into his, just as he had when she was a baby, which she no longer remembered. "I missed you," she said as she choked on a sob.

"So did I, baby...so did I..." And as they stood together, the boys were swarming around them, and tugging at their mother. The moment Quinn let go of her, he had one grandson pulling at each arm, asking him a thousand questions. It surprised him to realize that both of his grandsons had Swiss accents when they spoke English. Horst and Alex spoke French to them, but their English was fluent, despite their accents. He was still holding Alex's hand, as he answered the children's questions.

They had an hour before the flight to Holland, and he suggested they go to the restaurant nearest them for an ice cream, which the boys thought was an excellent decision. They were both talking at once a mile a minute, and Alex smiled as she walked along beside her father. She looked beautiful and young and very pregnant, and for an instant Quinn wished Maggie could have seen her. He was sure they would have liked each other.

"You look great, Dad," she complimented him as she ate an ice cream with her children. Quinn ordered a cup of coffee, he was beginning to feel the two flights he'd taken so far, and the jet lag. But as he looked at her, he felt as if all the anger she had felt toward him for so long had dissipated. He didn't know where it had gone, but he was grateful for its disappearance.

Half an hour later, he boarded the plane with the boys. They would be in Amsterdam at seven-thirty, and on the boat two hours later. He had already warned the crew they were coming, and the head stewardess was going to help him watch them. He didn't want anything to happen to them. He owed Alex that much, and reassured her again just before their flight left. He told her to relax and enjoy three weeks of peace with her husband. He promised that if the boys got homesick, he would bring them back to her sooner. She was waving and wiping tears from her eyes when he last saw her. He was busy with the boys for the entire flight, and grateful for the distraction the flight attendants provided. They had coloring books and crayons for them, and brought them each a glass of fruit juice. And the boys kept him laughing and amused. Although they hadn't seen him in more than a year, they seemed to be entirely at ease with him. They wanted to know all about his new sailboat. It kept him wide awake and well entertained answering all their questions.

When they arrived in Amsterdam, they were met by the

captain and first mate, and Tem Hakker. They had brought a station wagon, and the first mate kept the boys amused all the way to the boat. Once there, they were amazed by the size of the boat, and the stewardess whisked them off to the galley for dinner.

Quinn was extremely pleased by all he could see, and he asked about a thousand details, and he was happy with all of Tem's answers. He and both his sons were coming on the sea trials with them. They had their course mapped out, and a list of maneuvers Quinn had devised to put *Vol de Nuit* through all her paces. It was nearly midnight by the time Quinn settled into his cabin, sat down with a sigh, and dialed Maggie.

"How's it going?" It was nearly three in the afternoon for her, and she had been hoping he'd call. And when he did, she was thrilled to hear him. "How are the boys?"

"Terrific. They act like they saw me last week, and they love the boat." He had gone to check on them in their cabin, and they were sound asleep by the time he got there. It was as though someone had pulled the plug on them, and their energy had shut down as they recharged their batteries. He suspected they would be up at the crack of dawn the next morning.

"How's *Vol de Nuit*?" Maggie asked excitedly.

"More beautiful than ever." He wished Maggie could see her, but he knew that wasn't going to happen, as did she. She had seen her once, and he promised to bring home lots of photographs from the sea trials.

They chatted for half an hour and Quinn gave her all the details. The boat was even more splendid than he'd expected. She looked incredible now that she was in the water. They still

149

had to christen her, but they were going to do that at the yard when he came back in October. Tem Hakker was going to arrange a little ceremony, his wife was going to be her godmother. He would have asked Alex to do it, but it was too hard on her to come from Geneva.

"How was Alex?" Maggie asked, sounding concerned, and Quinn smiled as he answered.

"A different woman. Maybe the one I never knew. I think she's forgiven me. Or at least she was very loving and gracious. I don't deserve it, but I'm grateful for it." Maggie had urged him to bridge the gap and call her, and he was grateful for that too. Her gentle hand had touched his life in a thousand ways, and the one that had brought Alex closer to him again was the most important to him. He hadn't realized until then how much he'd missed her. Seeing her was a little bit like seeing Jane again. Alex looked strikingly like her mother, except that she was slightly taller.

"You *do* deserve it," Maggie reminded him, and then remembered what he had said before he left her at the airport. "Thank you for what you said to me," she said, still sounding moved by it. It had been the greatest gift he could give her, and the only one she wanted.

"What did I say?" he teased her, and lay down on his bed as he talked to her. He was looking forward to the next few weeks, and also to seeing her again afterward in San Francisco. This was the trial balloon for his freedom, and the deal he had struck with his anguished dreams. He was sacrificing the love he had found with Maggie, and himself, to pay the debt he still felt he owed Jane.

"You said you loved me," she reminded him, "and you can't take that back now."

"I wasn't intending to." It still didn't change anything. He was still going to leave her. But he knew he would love her even as he did it, and maybe it was better that she knew it. He hadn't wanted to be unkind to her and strengthen their bond before he broke it, but he knew how much it meant to her, and it was the least he could do for her, to at least say it. He did love her, and she was happy to know it.

They chatted for a few more minutes and then hung up. And he was sound asleep in his new bed ten minutes later. He was utterly exhausted, but happy in his new home on *Vol de Nuit*. This was where he belonged now.

# 14

THE SEA TRIALS WENT EXTREMELY WELL. ALL THE SYSTEMS performed even better than expected. His grandsons had fun. The crew were more efficient than he'd hoped. And the weeks flew by like minutes. Quinn couldn't believe how fast the time had gone, and he had spoken to Maggie several times in San Francisco. She said she was exhausted and harassed, she had forgotten what teaching was like, and how boisterous her students could be, but she sounded happy and busy, and said she could hardly wait to see him. He had made a point of calling her less often than he wanted. He knew he had to start to pull away now, or it would make the final break that much more painful. And the time for that was rapidly approaching. He knew he would see her again one day, he had no intention of abandoning her completely. He would call from time to time. But he was determined not to take her into his new life with him. That had been their agreement from the beginning, and he was going to hold them both to it. As much for his sake as for Maggie's. But he was still looking forward to his last two weeks with her in San Francisco. It would be their final gift to each other.

He hated to leave the boat when he did, and the boys cried when they left the crew, but Quinn promised them they could come back as often as their parents would let them. He had a sense of the continuity of life, as he left the boat with them, and realized how much Doug had looked like Robert. Only the color of their hair was different. Jane had always said he looked like Quinn, but seeing his grandson made him realize that his son had looked a great deal like Jane, except that his hair was the color of Quinn's. But he had the impression now that his features had been his mother's. And for the first time in twenty-four years, he realized how much he missed him. He had finally allowed himself to feel it. All his pores seemed to be open these days, and Quinn nearly cried again when he saw Alex waiting for them at the airport.

He spent a night with them, and the boys regaled their parents with the tales of all their adventures. There hadn't been a single dicey moment, and the boys would long remember the trip they had spent with their grandfather. They had been beautifully behaved with everyone, and were affectionate, bright, loving children. And the next morning, before he left, Alex thanked him again, and told him how much it had meant to her to see him. It was as though all the rage had gone out of her, like an illness that had been cured, a miraculous healing she'd experienced during the year he hadn't seen her. She told him she had prayed about it.

"Will you be all right on the boat, Dad?" It seemed a lonely life to her, but he had told them again the night before that it was the life he wanted.

"I'll be more than all right," he said confidently, "I'll be extremely happy." He was sure of that now. He had been thrilled with every moment he'd spent on the boat in the past three weeks. She had more than lived up to his expectations. And his decision to spend his life on her seemed the right one to him, in spite of Maggie. Or perhaps even because of her. He felt he had no right to a new life with a woman other than Jane. Maggie had been an adventure of the heart, a moment of sunshine amidst rain, and it was time for him to continue on his solitary path now. He was absolutely certain that it was what he wanted.

He promised Alex when he left that he would try to come and see her after she had the baby. He could fly from wherever he was. He planned to be in Africa by then, enjoying the winter, and all the places he was planning to visit. He and the captain had spent hours talking about it, and Sean Mackenzie had had some excellent suggestions. Quinn was focused on that now, and a part of him had already left the life he had led recently in San Francisco.

Maggie felt it when he got back. Outwardly, he seemed to be the same as he had been when he left three weeks before, but he was already ever so subtly different. She couldn't put her finger on it, but even on her first night with him, she sensed that part of him had already escaped her. She didn't say anything about it to him, but when he held her, his embrace no longer had the passion it had had just a few weeks before. The eagle was already reaching for the skies, and preparing to leave her.

She was frantically busy at school, and trying to make time for him. They had moved onto the boat again, and she hated to do it, but she had to spend part of every evening correcting papers. She planned to give her students as few assignments as possible during his final weeks with her, but she still had to do some work. And Quinn had a lot of loose ends to tie up too. It was only when they went to bed at night that she felt they found each other again and truly connected. It was when she lay next to him with his arm around her that she felt all she had for him, and knew that he felt the same way about her. The rest of the time, Quinn seemed to have put his guard up. It was a sensible thing to do, given the fact that he was leaving her, and he hoped that would make it less painful for her. He was no longer the man he had been years before, who thought only of himself. This time he was determined not to hurt anyone more than he had to. And the last person on earth he wanted to hurt now was Maggie.

They went on easy sails over the weekend, and the weather was spectacular. It was sunny and warm, and the breeze was exactly what they wanted it to be for sailing. Jack came to dinner with them on Friday night, and he said he was loving school, and Michelle was busy planning their wedding. Quinn offered to charter a boat for their honeymoon, and Jack declined regretfully. Michelle would have hated it, since she got seasick, unlike Maggie, who would have loved it.

Their first week together on the boat was easy and comfortable, Quinn and Maggie managed to make time for each other, and they spent a lot of time talking at night, as though storing memories to save for the many years ahead when they would no longer be together. Waiting for him to leave was like planning a death, or a funeral. They knew it was coming, and even when. She felt as though he were going to pull the plug on her respirator, and even though she had always known it would come to this, she had never expected it to hurt quite so acutely.

By the second week, the anticipated end began to cause both friction and tension between them. It was impossible for it not to. Maggie began dreaming of Andrew every night, and she had a nightmare about Charles, and woke up screaming. And there was very little Quinn could do to help her. All he could have done was change his plans, and decide not to leave, and Maggie would never have expected that of him. But nonetheless, as the days rolled by, she felt as though the life and air were being sucked out of her. She could hardly breathe on their last weekend, and Quinn was feeling the full weight of what it was doing to her, although she never said anything about it. He knew he had to leave her, even though for a crazed instant he almost asked her to come along. But he owed more than that to Jane. And Maggie needed a real life again, with people and friends and work. He couldn't just abscond with her on a boat. And if he took her with him, however tempting that was, he would have broken his vow to Jane. He said as much to Maggie again as they sat on the aft deck under the sails. She was looking miserably unhappy, and could no longer conceal it, nor tried.

"I can't believe she'd have expected that of you," Maggie said, looking out to sea, and feeling as though she were about to scatter her own ashes. "I read her poems to you. She loved you, Quinn. She wouldn't have wanted you to be unhappy."

And the odd thing was, he wasn't. He was sad to be leaving her, but there was a certain sense of peace to be going to solitude and freedom, almost like a monastic life he had chosen. He needed the respite he knew it would give his soul. He no longer had the energy to begin a life with anyone, and he hadn't earned it. He had made too big a botch of the last one, as far as he was concerned. And he didn't want to make a mess of it with Maggie, he didn't want to risk it. He loved her too much to hurt her. They had each suffered enough pain in their lives. He wanted to leave her knowing that he had made her happy. They had been good to each other, and he didn't want more than that from her, nor did he feel he could give her more than he had. They had done it, and loved well. And now it was time to end it. On Monday, he was leaving for Holland. All that remained to them now was one final weekend. Jack came to dinner on Friday night, and he and Quinn said good-bye with a warm hug and a powerful handshake.

On Sunday, Maggie was agonizingly silent. She could barely talk to him. There was nothing left to say. It had all been said a thousand times, a thousand ways. She wished that she had had Jane's gift with poems. But all she felt in her heart now was pain, the agony of loss she had already felt too often for one lifetime.

Quinn lay next to her on the deck, and held her hand. They lay there for a long, long time, and the crew left them alone, knowing what was coming. Quinn had ordered a sumptuous dinner for them, with caviar and champagne, and Maggie barely touched it. And shortly afterward, they went to their cabin. It was then that she began to cry, and looked at him with eyes that tore his heart out. It almost made him regret coming back after the sea trials. This was too hard for both of them, and he wondered if he had made a mistake coming back to San Francisco, if that had been even crueler to her. But however they had done it, or when, the end would have been excruciatingly painful.

Before they went to bed, she stood in her nightgown and said the words he had dreaded hearing. "Quinn, please take me with you."

"I can't, Maggie. You know that," he said sadly.

"No, I don't. It doesn't make sense to me. I don't understand why we have to do this." Tears were rolling down her cheeks in silent rivers.

"We agreed to this in the beginning," he reminded her. "You know that."

"That was then, and this is different. We didn't know we'd love each other then. I love you, Quinn."

"I love you too, Maggie. But sooner or later, I would hurt you." He wanted to add that he didn't deserve her, but he stopped himself. That was the flaw in all of it. He still felt he had to atone for his past sins. Alex had forgiven him. And Jane would have, Maggie was sure. But Quinn couldn't forgive himself. And as long as he didn't, he couldn't allow himself to be happy. He had to find solitude to atone for all that he could never change now, and he wanted Maggie to understand that. "I've hurt everyone I've ever cared about. My daughter, my son, Jane.... How can I forget all that? Can't you understand that?" In Maggie's eyes, he was like Charles, unable to forgive himself for what had happened. And he had also blamed her. Quinn blamed only himself. And whatever their reasons for leaving, whether it was Andrew, Charles, or Quinn, she was the loser.

"You can't run away forever, Quinn," she said, looking agonized.

"Yes, I can," he said sadly. "I ran away in the past, and it was the wrong thing then. But this time it's right, Maggie, I know it. You'll have a better life without me." There was no reasoning with him. He was convinced that he was doing the right thing, and it was what he wanted. Maggie couldn't sway him. He would not let her.

"I don't want a better life. I want to be with you. You don't have to marry me, or betray Jane. You can stay married to her forever. I just want to be with you. How can you throw this away, or walk away? It's totally crazy." It made no sense to her now, particularly because she knew he loved her. But to Quinn, that was all the more reason to leave her. It was what he expected of himself. He owed this final sacrifice to all the people he had hurt in the past, whether or not Maggie understood it.

In the end, she lay and sobbed in his arms for most of the night, and in the morning they both looked as though someone had died. It took every ounce of courage she had to dress and follow him upstairs to breakfast. She just sat silently with tears rolling down her cheeks, as he looked at her, as bereft as she was. She hadn't felt this awful since Andrew had died, and that had made just as little sense to her. Her beautiful child had taken his life. And now this man was leaving her because he loved her.

"This is what I believe is right," Quinn said quietly. "Please don't make it harder than it already is." And out of sheer love for him, she nodded, and at least tried to pull herself together. He had already told her that he didn't want her to take him to the airport. And she knew she couldn't. He held her for a last time, and kissed her, storing the memories for himself, and she touched his face one last time before he put her in a cab. His was coming in a few minutes.

As she pulled away, he stood on the deck watching her. Their eyes never left each other for a single moment. He raised his hand once and waved at her. She blew him a kiss as the cab pulled away, and as soon as they were out of sight of the boat, she was engulfed in sobs, and the driver watched her silently in the rearview mirror. She had him take her home, and didn't go to work that day. She couldn't. She sat in her kitchen, watching the clock. And when she knew his plane had taken off, she put her head down on the table and sobbed. She sat there for hours, crying and never moving. She had cherished the months she spent with him, and now she knew she had to do what she had promised, no matter how painful. She had to let him go, to be how and where and what he wanted, whether or not it made sense to her. If she loved him as she said she had, she had to let him have the one thing he wanted of her. His freedom.

She sat with her eyes closed for a long, long time, thinking of him, and willing him to be as free as he wanted. And as she did, his plane circled slowly over the bay, and headed north toward Europe. He was looking down at the Golden Gate Bridge as they flew over it, as tears slid silently down his cheeks.

# 15

FOR THE NEXT SEVERAL WEEKS, MAGGIE FELT AS SHE HAD when Andrew died. She moved through the days as though swimming underwater. She had no energy, she never smiled, she hardly slept at night, and when people spoke to her, she barely heard them. She felt disconnected from her entire world, as though she had fallen from another planet, and no longer spoke the language or understood the words people spoke to her. She lost her ability to decode the world around her. She went to work and was painfully distracted. She could barely manage to give assignments and correct papers. All she wanted to do was stay home, and think of the time they had shared. Each remembered moment now seemed even more precious.

The only useful thing she did was volunteer again for the teen suicide hotline. She had taken two months off from it over the summer. But since she couldn't sleep at night anyway, it

Danielle Steel

seemed like a worthwhile use of her time. But she was just as depressed as her clients, although she made an effort to sound normal when she spoke to them. But nothing about her life seemed rational or normal to her anymore. Quinn leaving had opened up the wound of loss again, and reminded her of everyone she'd ever loved and lost. She felt as though yet one more person she loved had died. At times, she felt as though she had died herself.

She had dinner with Jack on Friday night. She hadn't wanted to, but he had called her that morning and insisted. She thought seeing him might remind her of Quinn. The bond to Jack was another valuable gift he had given her. And Jack looked almost as depressed as she did. He said he really missed him. Quinn had shared so much with them, and given of himself so freely, and yet she knew he couldn't forgive himself for past sins. She had his Satcom number on the boat, for emergencies, but she had promised herself not to call him. He had a right to the freedom he so desperately wanted. And she would give it to him now, no matter what it cost her. But the rest of her life stretched ahead of her like an empty desert. Jack said he had been so upset the night before that he and Michelle had had an argument about their wedding. And now he was sorry that he hadn't gone with him.

"At least he invited you," Maggie said ruefully. They had both cried at the beginning of dinner.

"Every time I read something, I think about him." He told Maggie then that college was hard, but he loved it, and he still wanted to go to graduate school in architecture when he finished. And he was determined enough to do it. "I'm going to be the oldest architect in San Francisco," he said, and they both smiled.

It was nearly Christmas before Maggie felt halfway human. She and Jack had continued to have their Friday night dinners, although they no longer played liar's dice. It reminded them both too much of Quinn. Instead, they sat and talked about him. It was the only time when Maggie could indulge herself and do that. No one at the school where she taught knew anything about him. Jack said Michelle was sick and tired of hearing about him. Their wedding was scheduled for the week before Christmas. Maggie had promised to attend, but she wasn't in the mood for it. She hadn't bothered to buy a dress, and pulled a short black dress out of her closet the afternoon of the wedding. Jack had told her a few days before that he'd had a postcard from Quinn. He had flown back from Cape Town, to see Alex and the boys in Geneva. Jack had brought the card with him, and asked Maggie if she wanted to see it, but she didn't. It would just make her cry again, and there was no point in that. She had cried endlessly in the past two months. Her gift to him was to free him.

She went to Jack's wedding that afternoon, cried copiously during the ceremony, and felt morbidly depressed during the reception. She didn't want to dance with anyone. She just wanted to go home, to be alone, and think about Quinn. She was trying to pull out of it, but after Andrew's death, it had become increasingly difficult to lose anyone or anything. And losing Quinn was a loss of such magnitude that it had reopened all her other wounds. But no matter how painful it was for her, she knew she had to survive it. She owed Quinn that.

And as soon as it seemed respectable to her, she slipped away from the wedding. It was a relief to go home, and escape the noise and food and revelry. It had been good to see Jack happy again, and Michelle looked beautiful and ecstatic. Maggie was sure they would be very happy.

It was only on Christmas Eve that she began to find a sense of peace about what had happened. Instead of looking at the years she wouldn't share with him, she thought of the months she had, what a blessing they had been for her, and how lucky she was to have known him. Just as she had done two and a half years before with Andrew. She concentrated on gratitude instead of loss, and she thought of calling him on Christmas morning, and after wrestling with herself for two hours, she managed not to. She knew that if he wanted to talk to her, he would have called her, and he didn't. All she could do now was wish him well, and cherish the memories. And there were many of them. It was enough for her, it had to be. She had no choice but to go forward, with or without him. And when she went to church on Christmas Eve, she lit a candle for him.

# 16

ON CHRISTMAS EVE, QUINN WAS IN GENEVA WITH ALEX and her family. He went to midnight Mass with them, and in the long-forgotten tradition of his youth, he lit a candle for Maggie.

Alex had had the baby two weeks before, and as he had promised her he would, he had come to see her. It was something he knew Jane would have done, and he did it for her, since she couldn't.

Alex had had a girl this time, and the boys were fascinated by her. They were constantly holding and touching and kissing her. And Alex was remarkably relaxed when they nearly dropped her. She was happy to have some time with her father. He sat with her quietly and talked, while she nursed the baby. And being there with her reminded him of the many times when he hadn't managed to come home from some far corner of the world for Christmas. He apologized to her, and she said she understood it. It meant a lot to her that he had flown in from Cape Town just to see her. He had left the boat there, and was flying back to it on Christmas morning.

Quinn had spent a week with them, and as he sat with Alex after Mass that night, he was tempted to tell her about Maggie, but decided he shouldn't. He still felt he had done the right thing, but was surprised by how much he had missed her in the two months since he left her. Their attachment had been greater than even he had understood, and he couldn't help wondering what Alex would think about it. But he didn't have the courage to tell her. He felt sure that she would view it as a betrayal of her mother.

He still loved Jane, and thought about her, but it was Maggie who came to mind constantly, as he sat on deck at night and looked at the ocean. Jane seemed more like part of the distant past, and Maggie was integrally woven into the fabric of the present. But no longer the future. Whatever future he had would be spent alone on *Vol de Nuit*, contemplating his failures and victories, and the people he had loved and who were no longer with him.

He was grateful that Alex was no longer part of his past, but had come into his present. He kissed all of them, and left presents for everyone, when he left early on Christmas morning. He had spent a week with them, and didn't want to intrude on them. He thought they should spend Christmas together, and holidays were painful for him now anyway. In truth, he had never really liked them.

He flew back to Cape Town, and it was late that night when he joined the boat again. It was a great relief to be there. *Vol de Nuit* was home now.

They sat in port for another three days provisioning, and Quinn spent hours with the captain charting their route. They were going to sail around the Cape of Good Hope, and travel up the east side of Africa. There were places where it seemed unwise to go with a yacht the size of *Vol de Nuit*. He didn't want to enter hostile areas, or expose the crew to unnecessary danger. And by the time they set sail again, Quinn was happy to be sailing and heading for new locations.

The weather began getting worse after the holidays, and in the second week of January, it began raining. They had three days of heavy rains and rough seas, and Quinn couldn't help remembering the storm of a year before in San Francisco. It was in the aftermath of it, on New Year's Day, that he had first seen Maggie, standing in the pouring rain, with everything she was wearing soaking wet. And as he thought of it, he was tempted to call her, but resisted. Hearing her now, and talking to her, would just be painful for both of them. He was determined to let her go. He wanted her to have a better life than he felt he could give her.

They changed their course after a week of rain, and by the second week, the entire crew was tired of it, and so was Quinn. They got out their charts and began mapping a new course, hoping to find better weather, but it was worse instead. *Vol de Nuit* was pitching and rolling in heavy seas. Everyone but Quinn and the captain was sick, and Quinn jokingly said they'd have to lash the crew to their beds if the weather didn't get better. He was in his bed that night when he heard a crash. The seas were so rough that a piece of furniture had broken loose and fallen over. He looked at the gauges next to his bed, and saw that the winds had reached gale force. He put on his clothes and made his way to the bridge to talk to the captain. Their new course seemed to have taken them into the worst of the storm. Quinn was startled by the size of the waves breaking over the deck when he met the first mate, the engineer, and the captain in the wheelhouse. They were looking over the weather reports and watching the radar. There was green water sweeping over the deck, and the waves were crashing over the wheelhouse. And each time the bow dove down and came up again, it felt as though the masts would break, but Quinn was sure that they wouldn't.

"Looks like we're rock and rolling," Quinn said cheerfully, but he was shocked to see that the captain looked worried. "How're we doing?" Quinn didn't expect to have any problems. *Vol de Nuit* was sound and able to withstand almost any weather, and conditions, and rough seas had never frightened him. They just had to get through it. And Quinn was never seasick.

"There are some nasty reefs out there," the captain said, after carefully examining their radar and sonar. "And there's a tanker in trouble. The navy responded to them a while ago, but it looks like things are going to get worse before they get better."

"Looks like a hurricane, doesn't it?" Quinn said, as though it wasn't happening to them. And then a moment later, he turned to the captain. "I want the men in harnesses. Have we got the safety lines up yet?"

"We put them up an hour ago," he said reassuringly. They

wore harnesses with lights on them, and clipped the safety lines to their harnesses in case they got swept overboard, but Quinn knew that if anyone went over the side in waves like this, it would be almost impossible to retrieve them.

"Tell them to be careful," Quinn said to the first mate, and started out on deck to see how the crew were doing. Everyone had yellow foul weather gear on, including Quinn, and the captain told him sternly to put a harness on before he left the wheelhouse. "Yes, sir." Quinn smiled at him, and was glad that Sean was being careful.

Quinn put the harness on and went outside to join the other men. And as he did, there were some nasty crashing sounds in the galley. The boat was shuddering by then, and the only thing Quinn was worried about was breaking a mast. There was nothing they could do at this point, but ride through it. But it was unsettling for everyone, and as Quinn watched the waves, he was genuinely concerned for the first time. They were the roughest seas he'd ever seen. The waves were as tall as skyscrapers, towering seventy or eighty feet above them. It would have been a challenge to any ship, and was to *Vol de Nuit*, and as he stood looking into the darkness, he heard a shout a few feet away from him. One of the younger crew members had nearly gone over the side, and two of the other men had grabbed him. They were clinging to the safety lines, and all three of them looked like they were going to be swept off the boat as the sailboat dropped straight down into a giant trough. It was an eternity before they rose again and the mammoth waves crashed over them.

"Get everyone inside!" Quinn shouted and gesticulated at them through the wind, and the men began slowly crawling back up the boat, the deck was at a nearly-ninety-degree angle, and it seemed a lifetime before the crew were crowded into the wheelhouse, dripping water. It was the first time in his life that Quinn had been truly worried on a boat, but he'd never seen a storm like this one, except in movies. They had tied down everything they could, but things all over the boat were crashing and breaking. He wasn't worried about the damage now, but only their survival, and most of the men looked genuinely frightened. "Well, this will be one to talk about," Quinn said to ease the tension, and the entire boat seemed to groan and shudder as they headed down into the trough of the next wave. Quinn didn't want to let on to them that even he was frightened, and he bitterly regretted the course they'd taken. It had been a calculated guess on his part, but clearly it had been the wrong one. There was nothing they could do now but ride it out, and pray they'd make it.

Morning dawned grim and gray again, and the waves only seemed to get bigger, the wind worse. The two stewardesses had joined them in the wheelhouse by then, and reluctantly the captain told everyone to put life vests on. There seemed to be a distinct possibility that they might not make it.

They radioed to the nearest ship, and were told that the tanker had gone down, and no one had made it into the lifeboats. There would have been no point anyway. No one could have survived this. Shortly after nine o'clock there was another distress call on the emergency frequency. A fleet of fishing boats had gone down. Quinn and the captain exchanged a long look, and somewhere in the wheelhouse, a crew member was praying out loud. Quinn suspected that silently, they all were. He would have offered them something to fortify them and keep their spirits up, as they'd been up all night, but they needed to keep their wits about them.

He stood at the windows watching the waves again, and as he stared into the driving rain, he could have sworn he saw a woman's face, and it was Maggie. And as he thought of her, and the time they had spent together, he had an overwhelming urge to call her, and promised himself he would, if they survived the storm, which was beginning to seem less and less likely. *Vol de Nuit* could only stand so much abuse, and the waves seemed to be getting bigger instead of smaller. There was a deafening silence in the wheelhouse, and the only sounds were those of furniture falling below, and another series of crashes in the galley.

"Well, guys," Quinn said quietly, "we're in it this time. But I'd like to keep the boat. I spent a hell of a lot of money on her." The engineer laughed a hollow sound, and a few minutes later, the rest of the crew started talking. They were telling war stories about storms they'd been in, and Quinn did the best he could to keep the conversation going, but you could smell terror on their skins, and the sight of all of them in life vests was anything but reassuring. Some of the men had lit cigarettes, and a few were still not talking. Quinn was sure that they were praying, and through it all, as he talked to them, he kept thinking of Maggie. This seemed a hell of a way to die, but in a way this was what he had wanted, to end his life at sea one day. It was just happening sooner than he had expected. He was glad she wasn't there, the last thing he would have wanted to do was kill her. And both of the stewardesses were crying.

This time, when the boat crashed down, two of the men started singing, and the others slowly joined them. If they were going to die, they were going to go like men, with guts and style. They were a brave band as the storm raged on. It seemed like an eternity, but by noon, they were moving ever so slowly into calmer waters. The storm continued to rage on, but the waves were not quite as ominous, and the boat wasn't shaking quite as badly. It was nightfall before the rain and wind began to slow down. The damage inside the boat was considerable, but they were in reasonably manageable circumstances again by midnight. The boat was still pitching and rolling, but Quinn and the captain agreed they were no longer in grave danger, and by morning, they were both certain they were going to make it. They motored into port in Durban early that afternoon with a cheer of victory and tears rolling down their faces.

"We'll remember that one," the captain said quietly to Quinn, and he nodded, looking grim. He had spent nearly two days thinking of what he had done with his life, as they all had. More than fifty men had died the night before, and Quinn was profoundly grateful that they hadn't been among them. It was a storm that all of them would remember for a lifetime. And as they motored slowly into port, and docked the giant sailboat, Quinn turned to the captain and thanked him. They had already agreed that they would have to get *Vol de Nuit* back to

Holland for repairs. But all that mattered was that all of the crew were alive. By sheer miracle, the boat had survived and they had lost no one. Both Quinn and the captain had been certain at one point that the boat would go down. It was a real miracle that she hadn't. And for the first time in his life, Quinn knew without a doubt that nothing but a miracle could have saved them.

# 17

MAGGIE WOKE UP TO THE SOUNDS OF A DRIVING RAIN ON her windows. She had been awake most of the night, unable to sleep, thinking of things she had to do that day, and papers she had to grade by the following morning. She was beginning to enjoy her work again. And she had saved a fourteen-year-old girl two nights before on the hotline. Her life was beginning to make sense again, although she couldn't say that she was enjoying it. But her mind was clear, and her heart was not constantly as heavy. Only when she thought about him. But she knew that in time, she'd survive it. She had done it before and would again. Eventually, the heart repairs. She had learned that with Andrew. The scars and memories remained, but in time, one learned to live with the damage, and even function in spite of it. She couldn't let losing Quinn destroy her life. She had no choice but to survive it. If not, everything she said to kids on the hotline was a lie, and she couldn't allow that to happen to her. If she could give them a reason to live, she had to find one. She couldn't allow herself to mourn him forever. She couldn't afford it.

She got up and showered and dressed for school. She drank a cup of coffee, and ate a piece of toast, and half a grapefruit. She put her raincoat on and went out in the rain. And she was running toward her car, with her long braid flying out behind her, and the rain beating down, as she saw a man dart toward her. She couldn't imagine what he was doing, and she had her head down in the wind and rain, when he reached out for her and she jumped away. It was a crazy hour of the day for some-one to attack her. But all he did was wrap his arms around her as she tried to push away, and he just stood there and held her. He had knocked the wind out of her, and she tried to catch her breath as she struggled to look up at him, and then she saw him. His hair was short, his face was lean, and he was as wet as she was. He was just standing there holding her. It was Quinn, or someone who looked just like him.

"What are you doing here?" she asked with a look of amaze-ment. He was in Africa somewhere, or he was supposed to be, and now he was here with his arms around her.

"The boat almost went down in a storm off the coast of Africa. I just took her to Holland for repairs," he said, sound-ing as out of breath as she was. She pulled away from him then, and looked up at him, as the rain beat down on both of them. He looked wild-eyed and exhausted, and she guessed that he must have just gotten off a plane. He looked as though he hadn't slept in days, and he hadn't. "I saw your face in the storm when I thought we were going down. I swore that if we survived it, I'd call you." She looked suspicious of him. She had suffered the agonies of the damned since she last saw him.

"You didn't call me," she said as though that made sense. But nothing did now. She didn't know why he was here, or what he was saying. It was as though he was speaking to her in a foreign language. Her mind was racing.

"No, I didn't." There was something in his eyes she had never seen there when he was with her. Something powerful and strong and sure. It was as though he had died and been born again. He had, and was free now. "I wanted to see you. Are you all right?" She nodded, remembering how powerful his arms had just seemed around her. She had thought he was going to kill her. And losing him nearly had. But like him, she had faced the storm he'd left her in and survived it. They stood there in the rain, looking at each other, trying to see what was left, if anything. They had been washed over the side by forces stronger than they were, and had no idea if they could get back. "I had a dream about Jane, on the way back to Holland. She seemed so peaceful. She told me she was fine and that she loved me. And at the end of the dream, she just smiled and walked away." Maggie listened to him and nodded. They both knew what it meant. Forgiveness at last.

"I'm late for school," she said, for lack of something better to say, and he appeared not to hear her.

"Will you come with me?" He had come six thousand miles to ask her that question. Farther than that. He had come from the bowels of death and across his entire lifetime. But the one thing he had found in the storm was all he needed. In the jaws of death, he had found forgiveness. He knew that if he had been saved, then he deserved her. It was why he had seen her face that night, as though she had been a vision and a promise. He had found what he'd been looking for, not only forgiveness, but freedom. He had paid his dues to the utmost farthing. And the final dream of Jane had set him free at last.

"Are you serious?" She stared at him as though she didn't believe he meant it.

"I am. Are you? Do you want to come with me?" She hesitated for what seemed like an eternity to him, and then finally, she nodded.

"I do. Do you still want me?" she whispered, and he laughed this time.

"I damn near went down with the boat, and God knows why we were saved, me most of all. And I came from Africa to Holland to New York to here. Yes, Maggie, I want you. More than that, I am the biggest fool that ever lived, I used to be the biggest sonofabitch that ever breathed. And I promise you, I'll never leave you again. Oh yes, I will, but not the way I did in October. I guess I needed to damn near die to figure out what I really wanted." He got down on bended knee in the rain and she laughed at him. "Now, will you come with me?"

"Okay, okay. But I have to give them notice at school. And I have to grade papers. How soon are you leaving?"

"I'm not leaving till you come with me. The boat will be in Holland for at least two months, maybe three. Can I stay with you?" he asked, as she smiled up at him. He had never looked better to her. And she looked every bit as good to him, and just as soaking wet, as she had the day he met her. "Do you want me to drive you to school?" She smiled up at him and nodded. "How soon can you give them notice?" he asked as she handed him her car keys. This was all so wonderful and so crazy, just as he was. He had come halfway around the world to ask her to leave with him, and he had to nearly die to do it. But if that was what it took, it was worth it.

"I'll give them notice today. Will that work for you?" she asked as he started the car and backed out of the driveway. They were both wet to the bone as he stopped the car again and looked at her.

"Did I tell you I love you?"

"I can't remember. But I figured it out anyway. If you came all this way, I thought you probably did. I love you too. Now get me to school, I'm late. You scared the hell out of me. I thought you were trying to attack me."

"I was just glad to see you." He grinned at her, backed the car the rest of the way out of the driveway, and drove the car down Vallejo. She agreed with him as he told her about the storm they'd been in. It was a miracle. It had taken a miracle to bring him back to her. And she reminded him, as she leaned over and kissed him, that it had been a storm that brought them together in the first place.

He dropped her off at school, and she waved at him, as he sat and watched her run through the rain. She was the miracle that had come into his life, and brought forgiveness. And love was the miracle that had healed him.

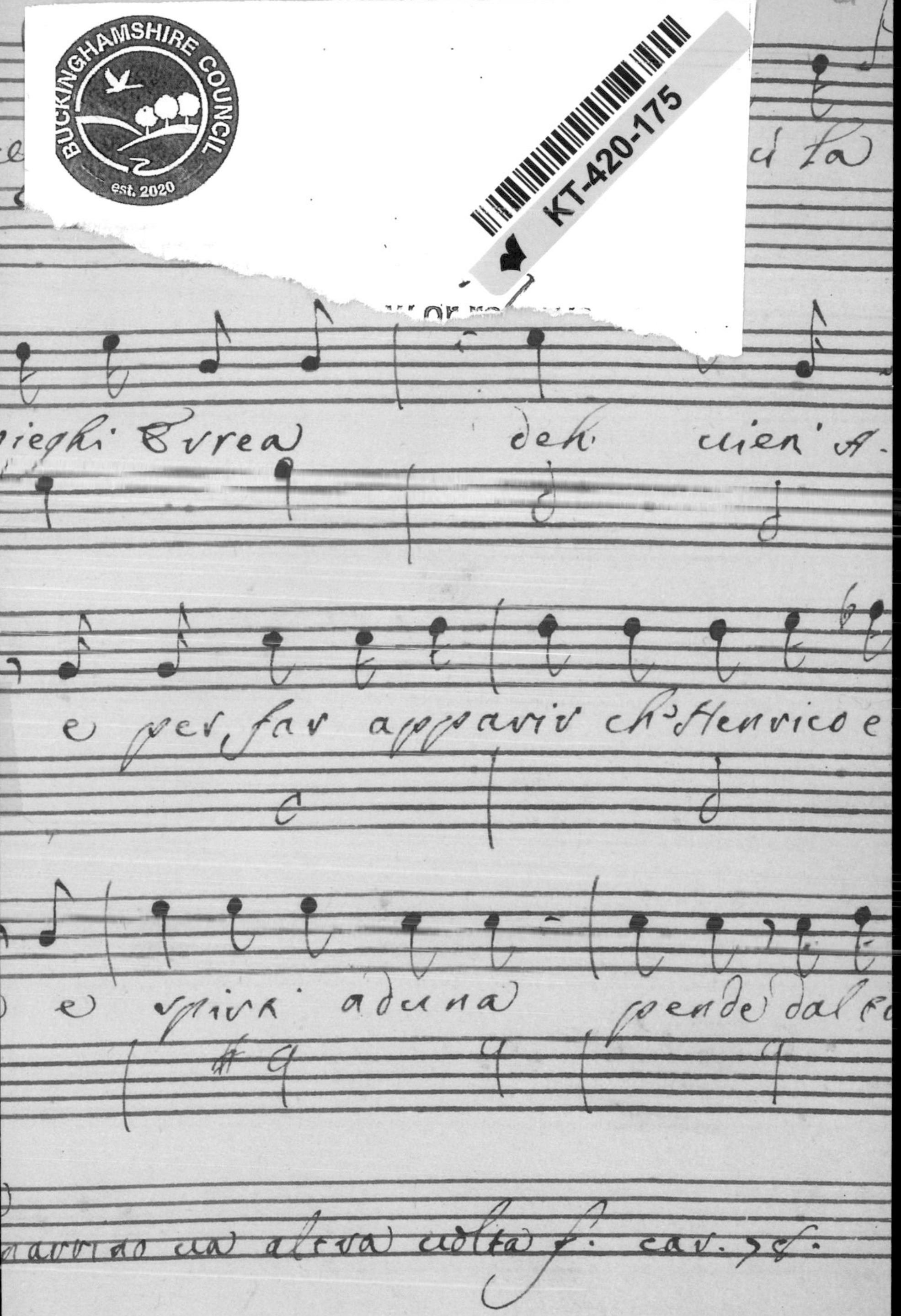
pieghi Aurea deh vien' A-
e per far apparir ch' Henrico e
e spira aduna pende dal

# The Jewels of Paradise

# Donna Leon

# The Jewels of Paradise

WILLIAM HEINEMANN: LONDON

Published by William Heinemann 2012

2 4 6 8 10 9 7 5 3 1

Copyright © Donna Leon and Diogenes Verlag AG Zurich 2012

Donna Leon has asserted her right under the Copyright, Designs and
Patents Act, 1988, to be identified as the author of this work.

First published in Great Britain in 2012 by
William Heinemann
Random House, 20 Vauxhall Bridge Road,
London SW1V 2SA

www.randomhouse.co.uk

Addresses for companies within The Random House Group Limited
can be found at: www.randomhouse.co.uk/offices.htm

The Random House Group Limited Reg. No. 954009

A CIP catalogue record for this book
is available from the British Library

ISBN 9780434022274 (Hardback)
ISBN 9780434022281 (Trade paperback)

The Random House Group Limited supports The Forest Stewardship Council
(FSC®), the leading international forest certification organisation. Our books
carrying the FSC label are printed on FSC® certified paper. FSC is the only forest
certification scheme endorsed by the leading environmental organisations,
including Greenpeace. Our paper procurement policy can be found at
www.randomhouse.co.uk/environment

Typeset in Palatino by Palimpsest Book Production Limited,
Falkirk, Stirlingshire
Printed and bound in Great Britain by
Clays Ltd, St Ives plc

For Markus Wyler

*Oh mio fiero Destin, perversa sorte!*
*Sparì mia vita e non mi dale a morte.*

*Oh, my proud Destiny, perverse Fate!*
*To destroy my life, but not give me to death.*

Agostino Steffani,
*Niobe*, Act 2, scene 5

# 1

Caterina Pellegrini closed the door behind her and leaned her back and then her head against it. First came the slight trembling of her legs as tension began to relax its hold on her muscles, then the deep breaths that helped relieve the tightness in her chest. The desire to wrap her arms around herself in an expression of wild, uncontrollable glee was almost irresistible, but she beat down that temptation, as she had beaten down many in her life, and stood with her hands at her sides, leaning against the door and telling herself to relax.

It had taken great patience, but she had done it. She had put up with a pair of fools, smiled at their manifest-ations of cupidity, treated them with the deference they so evidently did not deserve, all the while manoeuvring them into giving her the job she wanted and which they held in their gift. They had no wit, but they had the power to decide; they had no grace of spirit, but they could say yes or no; they had little understanding of her qualifications and a badly disguised contempt for her learning, but she had needed them to choose her.

And they had, both of them, and none of the other applicants she had thought of – not without a wry consciousness of how much her language had been affected by the historical period in which she had spent her academic and professional life – as her rivals. As the youngest of five sisters, Caterina was endowed with a healthy sense of rivalry. Not unlike characters in a Goldoni play, the sisters were: Claudia the Beautiful; Clara the Happy; Cristina the Religious; Cinzia the Athletic; and, last born, Caterina, the Clever. Claudia and Clara had married fresh out of school; Claudia had divorced within a year and upgraded to a lawyer she seemed not to like very much, while Clara stuck to her first husband and was happy; Cristina had taken vows and renounced the world, then gone on to take advanced degrees in the history of theology; Cinzia had won some medals in diving at the national level, but then had married, borne two children, and grown fat.

Caterina, the clever one, had studied at the *liceo* where her father taught history and had consistently won the yearly prize in Latin and Greek translation while picking up Russian from her aunt. From there she had spent an ignominious year as a vocal student at the Conservatory, then two years studying law at Padova, which disappointed, and then bored, her. The lure of music returned then, and she had chosen to study musicology in Florence and then in Vienna, where her thesis advisor, learning of her fluency in Russian, had arranged a two-year research grant for her to accompany him to St Petersburg to help with his research on Paisiello's Russian operas. That concluded, she returned to Vienna and finished a doctorate in Baroque opera, the degree and her possession of it sources of delight and pride to her family. This qualification, after only one year of trying to find a job, had earned her a sort of internal exile to the South in the form of a position as lecturer in counterpoint at the Conservatory of Music Egidio Romualdo Duni in Matera. Egidio Romualdo Duni. What scholar of Baroque opera would not recognize his name? Caterina had always thought of him as Duni Who Also Wrote, the man who had written operas with titles identical to those of more famous or more gifted composers: *Bajazet, Catone in Utica, Adriano in Siria*. Duni had left as little trace in Caterina's memory as he had on current opera production.

A doctorate from the University of Vienna, and then a job lecturing first year conservatory students in counterpoint. Duni. There were entire weeks when she thought she might as well have been lecturing in mathematics, so far did this subject seem from the magic thrill of the singing voice. This dissatisfaction did not bode well, something she had known almost as soon as she arrived. But it had taken her two years to decide to leave Italy again, this time by accepting a position at Manchester, one of the best centres in Europe for the study of Baroque music, where she had spent four years as a research fellow and assistant professor.

Manchester had appalled Caterina by its physical ugliness, but she had been content enough at the university, digging into the music – and to a lesser degree, the lives – of a handful of eighteenth-century Italian musicians whose careers had prospered in Germany. Veracini, Handel's great rival; Porpora, Farinelli's teacher; the practically forgotten Sartorio; Lotti, a Venetian who, it appeared, had been everyone's teacher. It was not long before she began to see the similarity between their destiny and her own: in search of the work and fame they had

3

failed to find in Italy, they had emigrated north. Like some of them, she had found work, and like most of them, she had suffered homesickness and longed for the air, beauty, and possibility of joy offered by a country she realized, only now, that she loved.

Salvation had come, as is so often the case, by chance. Each spring, the wife of the head of her department gave a dinner for her husband's colleagues. The Chairman always made it clear that it was a casual thing: come if you're free. Older and wiser heads knew that the invitation had the same weight as a ukase from, say, Ivan the Terrible. Not to go was to cast aside all hope of advancement, though to attend was to sacrifice one evening of life to tedium so encompassing as almost to be fatal. Heated exchange of insult and vituperation, even blows, would have been a source of delight, but the dinner conversation was rigidly governed by caution and a tight-lipped politeness that failed to camouflage decades of rancorous familiarity and professional jealousy.

Caterina, aware of her own incapacity to be bland, avoided conversation and devoted herself to the study of the personal and sartorial peculiarities of her colleagues. Most of the people at the table appeared to be wearing the unwashed clothing of their larger-sized friends. The shoes appalled her. And then there was the food. Though she sometimes discussed the other subjects with Italian colleagues, none of them had the courage to mention the food.

Her saviour was a Romanian musicologist who had spent the last three years, so far as Caterina could judge, in an alcoholic stupor: the fact that he was drunk in the morning and drunk in the evening never prevented him, however, from smiling amiably at her when they passed in the corridors or library, a smile she always gladly returned. He was possibly sober and unquestionably brilliant during his classes, where his analysis of the metaphors in the libretti of Metastasio broke new ground, and his explication of the Viennese court poet Apostolo Zeno's correspondence concerning the foundation of the Accademia degli Animosi was a source of wonder to his students. He often wore cashmere jackets that fitted him very well.

On the night of her salvation, the Romanian was seated across from her at the Chairman's dinner, and Caterina found herself smiling back into his wine-dulled eyes if only because they could speak easily in Italian. Most of the other people at the table had learned Italian to facilitate their reading of opera libretti; thus few of her colleagues could hold a conversation in that language without descending into wild declarations of love, terror, remorse and, upon occasion, bloodlust. Caterina preferred to converse with them in English. While she considered the use of the language of opera libretti as dinner conversation, Caterina studied the people at the table. Revelation occurred: how well a phrase such as, *Io muoio, io manco*, expressed her current feelings. Even *Traditore infame* would not be far off as a description of many of her colleagues. And was not the Chairman himself *Un vil scellerato*?

The Romanian set down his glass – he didn't bother with food so had no fork to set down – and broke his silence to ask, in Italian, 'You want to get out of this place?'

Caterina's answering glance was filled with curiosity, as was her voice. 'Do you mean this dinner or this university?'

He smiled, took his wine glass, and looked around for another bottle. 'This university,' he said in a completely sober voice.

'Yes.' She picked up her glass, surprised to hear her own admission and struck by its force.

5

'A friend has told me that La Fondazione Musicale Italo-Tedesca is looking for a scholar.' He sipped, smiled. She liked his smile, though perhaps not his teeth.

'La Fondazione Musicale Italo-Tedesca,' she repeated. There was something with a similar name at home, she recalled, but she knew little about it. Dilettantes, amateurs. Surely he was speaking about something in the German-speaking world.

'You know it?'

'I've heard of it,' she said in the tone she'd use if someone asked her if she'd heard about the infestation of bedbugs in New York hotels.

He finished the wine and held up his glass. Looking at it, he said, surprising her with the angry vehemence with which he spoke: 'Italy.' The glass was from Italy? The wine?

'Money,' he added in what she thought he intended to be a seductive voice. 'Some.' When he saw how little effect this had on her, his smile returned, as if she'd just agreed with him about something he had believed for a long time. 'Research. New documents.' He saw the jolt this gave her and glanced towards the head of the table, where the Chairman sat. 'You want to end up like him?'

In a voice that slipped towards possibility, she smiled and said, 'Tell me more.'

He ignored her and looked in vain at the bottles on the sideboard. Perhaps he had already reached the point where the trip back and forth was impossible for him.

He placed his empty glass next to that of the woman to his right, who had turned to her other neighbour. He switched glasses.

'Idiots,' he said in a suddenly loud voice. They were speaking Italian, so the slurring of his speech, though it did nothing to lower the volume of his voice, at least managed to disguise the hard dentals of that word. No one so much as glanced in his direction.

Taking his napkin he wiped methodically around the edge of his neighbour's glass; only then did he take a long drink from it.

Seeing that he had all but emptied what had now become his glass, Caterina leaned across the table and poured her white wine into the small quantity of red at the bottom. He nodded.

His smile faded and he muttered, 'I don't want it. Maybe you'd like it?'

'Why?' she asked, confused. Did he mean her wine?

'I told you,' he answered, giving her a sharp look. 'Aren't you listening? It's in Venice. I hate Venice.'

So it was the one at home: a job in the city. She didn't know everything, but she knew a lot: how serious could this place be if she'd never heard anything about it save the name? Italians cared little for the Baroque. No: only Verdi, Rossini, and – God help us all, she thought, as a small shudder walked a descending cadence down her spine – Puccini.

'You're talking about Venice? The job's in Venice?' His eyes had continued their retreat from focus all the time he had been talking, and she wanted to be certain that this possibility existed before she opened her heart to hope.

'Hateful place,' he said, making a sour face. 'Disgusting climate. Horrible food. Tourists. T-shirts. All those tattoos.'

'You've said no?' she asked with wide-eyed wonder that begged for explanation.

'Venice,' he repeated and swilled his wine to wash away the very sound of it. 'I'd go to Treviso, Castelfranco. Friuli. Good wine.' He looked into his glass, as if to ask the contents where they had come from. Finding no answer, he turned back to her. 'Even Germany. I like beer.'

7

Having spent many years in the academic world, Caterina did not doubt that this would sufficiently explain his acceptance of a job.

'Why me?' she asked.

'You've been nice to me.' Did that mean half a glass of white wine or the fact that she had spoken to him with respect and had smiled at him occasionally during the last years? It didn't matter. 'And you're blonde.' That at least made sense.

'Would you recommend me?' she asked.

'If you get me a bottle of red from the sideboard,' he answered.

# 2

Greater changes had resulted from stranger things, Caterina reflected, calling herself back from memory. The research job was hers, and she was back in Venice, though hired only to complete a single project. She looked around at the office where she was to wait for the Acting Director. If an office could be a small, high-ceilinged cubicle with two tiny windows, one behind the desk and one so close to the ceiling as to provide some light but no view, then this was an office. The desk and chair added to that possibility, though the absence of computer, telephone, and even paper and pen suggested more a monk's cell than anything else. The location – in what had once been a two-floor apartment at the end of Ruga Giuffa – could be used to argue either case. But it was a cold day at the beginning of April, and the room was warm: it had to be an office that was meant to be in use.

What little she had been able to learn about the Foundation before applying for the job had prepared her for this dismal little room: nothing in it – and nothing not in it – surprised her. The internet had provided some information about the Foundation: it had been established twenty-three years before by Ludovico Dardago, a Venetian banker who had made a career in Germany and was a passionate lover of Baroque opera, both Italian and German. He had left money for the creation of a foundation to 'disseminate and promote the performance of the music of composers who travelled and worked between Germany and Italy during the Baroque era'.

However modest the rooms, the location was propitious, only a ten-minute walk from the major collections of the Biblioteca Marciana, where manuscripts and scores were to be found.

When she thought about the events that had brought her to this room and viewed her situation in a certain way, Caterina concluded that she had been hired for a bit part in a bad nineteenth-century melodrama: The Rediscovered Trunks? The Rival Cousins? For more than a year, two cousins, descended from different sides of a mutual ancestor's family, had been embroiled in dispute over the ownership of two recently rediscovered trunks that had once belonged to their mutual ancestor. Both possessed archival evidence proving their descent from the former owner, a cleric and musician who had died without issue. Unable to find legal redress, and with great reluctance, they had finally consulted an arbitrator, who suggested that, in light of their refusal to divide equally the still-unknown contents of the trunks, a neutral and competent researcher be hired, at their shared expense, to examine the historical record and any documents contained in the trunks for any evidence of a preference for one side of the family over the other. In the event that such a document was found, both agreed – in a contract drawn up by the arbitrator and signed in front of a notary – that the entire contents of the trunks would become the exclusive possession of the person whose ancestor was so favoured.

When the arbitrator, who had some weeks ago invited her to Venice for an interview, had explained all of this to her, Caterina had decided that he was joking or had taken leave of his senses, possibly both. She had, however, smiled and asked him to explain a bit more fully the particular circumstances, adding that this would help her more clearly to understand the duties the position might entail. What she did not tell him was how the sight and smell and feel of Venice had so overpowered her that she knew she wanted the job, regardless of the conditions, and to hell with Manchester.

Dottor Moretti's explanation contained elements of myth, family saga, soap opera, and farce, though it contained no names. The deceased cleric, he told her, was a Baroque composer who would easily be within her competence; he had died almost three centuries before, leaving no will. His possessions had been disbursed, but two chests believed to contain papers and – perhaps – valuables had finally been found and brought to Venice. One undisputed element in all of this was the claimants' descent from the relatives of the childless musician: both had produced copies of baptismal and marriage certificates going back more than two hundred years.

Here Caterina had interrupted to ask the name of the musician, a question that obviously startled Dottor Moretti by its rash impropriety. That would be revealed only to a successful candidate, and she was not yet to be considered that, was she? It was a small snap of the whip, but it was nevertheless a snap.

Would the candidate, she asked, be told the name of

the musician before beginning to examine whatever papers might be found?

That, Dottor Moretti had explained, would depend upon the nature of what was found in the trunks. Another snap. The two heirs, he surprised her by saying, would interview all likely candidates. Separately. No longer able to contain herself, Caterina had interrupted again to ask Dottor Moretti if he were making this up. With a look as sober as his tie, the arbitrator had assured her that he was not.

Her task, he had gone on to say, would be to read through the documents that were believed to be in the trunks and that were likely to be in Italian, German, and Latin, though others might well be in French and Dutch, perhaps even English. Any passages referring to the deceased musician's testamentary wishes or to his affection for or involvement with various members of his family were to be translated in full: those papers relating to music or other areas of his life did not have to be translated. The cousins would expect frequent reports on her progress. It seemed that Dottor Moretti experienced a certain embarrassment in having to say this. 'If you send these reports to me, I will forward them.'

When Caterina expressed a certain difficulty in understanding why no one knew the contents of these trunks, Dottor Moretti told her that the seals appeared to be intact. Assuming this to be true, the chests had not been opened for centuries.

Caterina had the good sense to say that all of this sounded interesting, adding that, to a researcher, it was fascinating. As she spoke, she ran through the names of composers, but since she didn't know either his nationality or where he had died – or lived, for that matter – there was little chance of identifying him.

She must have impressed Moretti, for he told her he would like her to speak that afternoon to two men he suggested she treat as gentlemen. He asked only one thing of her, he added: once she learned their family names, she could easily trace them back to the composer. He trusted she would not do so until the decision about the position had been made, then explained, before she could ask, that this was a request from the two presumptive heirs, 'men with a certain fondness for secrecy'.

Caterina said she would begin research only if granted the job and would not pursue it in any way were she not chosen.

That same afternoon, she had met the contesting heirs, introduced to them, separately, by name. They met in 'the library', which turned out to be a room holding photocopies of the libretti and the scores of the operas and orchestral works of the dozen or so composers who had most delighted Signor Dardago. The library had a large table and bookshelves on which the photocopies no longer made the attempt to stand upright. There were just three or four books on the shelves, lying flat as though placed there in haste. She looked more closely and saw that one of them was a historical novel about a castrato.

Nothing either of the men said or did suggested that they were anything but gentlemen: the evidence that such an attribution was mistaken had come that evening from her parents, with whom she was staying and who, in the best Venetian way, told her what was common knowledge about each of them.

Franco Scapinelli was the owner of four shops selling glass in the area around San Marco. He was also – though nothing that happened during the interview would have suggested this – a convicted usurer who was forbidden from owning any business in the city. But who could forbid a man from giving his sons a hand in their shops? What sort of law would that be?

The other contender, Umberto Stievani, owned water taxis, seven of them, and declared, according to a friend of Caterina's father – a friend who happened to work in the Guardia di Finanza – a yearly income of just over eleven thousand Euros. The combined income of his two sons who worked for him as pilots did not reach that of their father.

During the interviews, both men claimed great interest in the manuscripts and documents and whatever else might be contained in the chests, but as Caterina listened to them she realized their interest was not in any historical or musicological importance the purported documents might have. Both had asked if any manuscripts would have value, meaning would anyone want to buy them. Stievani, no doubt because of his time spent among taxi drivers, had used the elegance of their language to ask, *'Valgono schei?'* Caterina wondered if money could be real to him only when named in Veneziano.

They must have approved of her, for here she was less than a month later, both her position and her apartment in Manchester abandoned, standing in an office at the Fondazione Italo-Tedesca, eager to begin work. And she was home again, her spirit salved by the sounds and smells of the city, by the enveloping familiarity.

She took a closer look around the room. Three small prints hung to the left of the window behind the desk. She moved across the room, not a difficult thing to do, and took a closer look at these bewigged men in their plastic Ikea frames. She recognized Apostolo Zeno by the length of his wig and the long white scarf popping out from his robes. Familiarity with prints of the bewigged Handel made it easy to recognize him. And farthest to the left was Porpora, looking as though he'd stolen his wig from Bach and his jacket from a naval commander. Poor old Porpora: to have been such a high flyer and then to have died in penury.

Caterina examined the window behind her. About the size of one of the prints, 15 x 20 centimetres, it had to be the smallest window she had ever seen. It might even be the smallest window in the city.

She put her face close to the glass and saw the shutters of the apartment on the other side of the *calle*: green, weather-stained, shut, as if the inhabitants were still asleep. It was ten in the morning, surely time that respectable people – hearing herself think it, *gente per bene*, she felt as though she were channelling her grandmother's voice – would be up and about, off to the office, off to school, busy, doing, working.

Caterina, a victim of the work ethic, had always thought she must be a throwback to some Northern European invader, a blond-haired Goth whose genetically fuelled lust for industry had lain dormant for generations, centuries, only to burst into bloom with the birth of the last child of Marco Pellegrini and Margherita Rossi. How else explain the atavistic desire for serious work that had driven her even when she was a child? Or her response when offered a job as city counsellor for music education by the mayor, an old friend of her father? She saw no sense in diverting money from one school to another, nor in overseeing music instruction in schools that had no books, no musical instruments, and teachers of music who, though unable to read musical notation, found perfectly legible the intentions of the politicians who offered them the jobs. She had refused.

Thus her flight to Vienna and years of study, more digging through the archives in St Petersburg, and then her galley years in Matera after the desire to return to Italy had become too strong to resist. Then renewed flight to Manchester, and now this, whatever 'this' was.

A light knock at the door pulled her from these reflections. 'Avanti,' she called. Thinking it would be a friendly gesture to be seen approaching whoever was there, Caterina started towards the door just as it opened and a woman the age of her mother entered the room. Like her mother, this woman was short and tended to roundness, as did her soft-skinned face, above which rose a structure of intertwined braids and tresses that sent Caterina's memory to a production of Cherubini's *Medea* she had seen many years ago at the Teatro Massimo in Palermo, in which the costume designer had clearly confused Medea with Medusa and had topped the head of the soprano with a loose-fitting helmet of snakes, whose twining and twisting had done a great deal to aid her performance by distracting the attention of the audience from her singing. Unlike those of the singer, this woman's serpents were motionless.

'Dottoressa Pellegrini?' the woman asked, and Caterina wondered if she had perhaps expected to find someone else in the room. The woman gave a very small smile and extended her hand. 'I'm Roseanna Salvi, Acting Director of the Foundation.' Caterina had been told that Dottor Asnaldi, the former Director, had left a year before, and his assistant was now in charge until a permanent replacement could be found.

'How very kind of you to come and find me, Dottoressa Salvi,' Caterina said, taking her hand. She addressed her both with her title and in the formal *Lei*.

The contact was fleeting, quite as if Dottoressa Salvi were fearful to entrust her right hand to this other woman for more than a second. She whipped her hand behind her back, embracing it safely with the other.

16

'Would you care to take a seat?' Caterina asked, deciding to act as though this had always been her office. She turned to her desk and only then realized that there was just the one chair in the room.

Caterina smiled, hoping for a mirror-smile on the other woman's face. Nothing, only attentive politeness. 'Dottoressa,' she said, 'perhaps you could take the chair.'

Her hands still hidden, the other woman said, 'I'm afraid I have to correct you, Dottoressa.'

Here it came, Caterina thought. Territoriality, competition, beat down the newcomer, get the pecking order established: so much for female solidarity. Saying nothing, she smiled again.

'There's been a misunderstanding. I'm not a doctor. Not of anything.' As she spoke, Not-Dottoressa Salvi's face relaxed, and her hands came out from behind her back.

'Ah,' Caterina said, impulsively placing a hand on the other woman's arm, as if to provide comfort. 'No one told me. In fact, no one's told me anything, really.' Then, to ease the situation she said, 'Call me Caterina, please. And no "Dottoressa".'

Signora Salvi smiled, and the snakes surrounding her head turned into mere curls. 'And I'm Roseanna,' she said, avoiding the informal *tu*, no doubt leaving the decision to the Dottoressa.

'Can we call one another "*tu*"?' Caterina asked. 'Since we're working together.' She didn't know if that was precisely true, but at least they did work in the same place, and that was close enough for collegiality.

As usually happens when one person suggests grammatical informality, the mood of the conversation eased with the establishment of equality. Signora Salvi turned towards the door and said, 'Let's go to my office.' Then, with a smile, she added, 'At least it has two chairs.'

In Signora Salvi's office, two doors away from her own, Caterina noticed that the second chair was almost the only difference; that and a larger window looking out to the courtyard behind the building. There was a table just as small as Caterina's. No telephone here, either, but on the table stood something Caterina had not seen for more than a decade: a typewriter. Electric, assuredly, but still a type-writer. Caterina would have been no more astonished had she seen a woman on the street in a crinoline and bloomers. She drew closer and looked at the keyboard. Yes, the letters were all there.

Signora Salvi saw where her attention rested and said, her shoulders raised in a shrug of resignation or apology, 'We don't have a computer any more, so I've been using that.' Remembering her role as hostess, she offered a chair to Caterina. She pulled her own to the side of her desk so that the typewriter was not between them, and sat down.

Each of them waited for the other to break the silence and set the mood until finally Caterina gave in to her simple curiosity – elementary school children did their homework on computers, people used them on trains. 'How is it that an institution like this doesn't have a computer?'

Signora Salvi looked at the typewriter, then at Caterina. 'It was stolen.'

'What happened?'

'Someone broke in one night – it was about three months ago – and took the computer and the printer and some money that was in the drawer,' she said, pointing towards the back of the desk.

'How did they get in?' Caterina asked, thinking of her own tiny window.

'Through there,' Signora Salvi said, indicating the considerably larger window at the back. 'It must have been easy. All they had to do was get into the courtyard, prise open the shutter and break the glass. They didn't take anything else, so far as I could tell. But that's because they couldn't get into the other offices. All of the doors were locked.'

'Were the police here?' Caterina asked.

'Of course. I called them as soon as I saw what had happened.'

'And?'

'Oh, the usual,' Signora Salvi said, as if dealing with the police were part of an annoying daily routine. 'First they acted as though they thought I'd done it, and then they said it was kids stealing things to pay for drugs.'

'Is that all?'

'They told me to get the window fixed,' Signora Salvi said with some evidence of disgust. 'They didn't bother to ask what kind of computer it was or to take fingerprints. Or to ask anything at all, for that matter.' Then, sounding even more disgruntled, she added, 'And they didn't talk to anyone else in the building or to the others that share the courtyard.' She shrugged to dismiss the police, then smiled again.

'How do you get on without it?' Caterina asked, looking at the typewriter as if it were a votive statue of the missing computer.

In a confessional tone, Roseanna said, 'There was really very little in it. I keep the records of any new documents that are added to the collection and answer the letters we receive.' She gave Caterina a very small smile and added, 'The Foundation doesn't really do much, you know. And I'm here only three hours a day. I have to be here in case anyone comes to ask for information.' Her next smile showed signs of embarrassment as she said, 'But no one ever does. Well, once in a while, but not to ask questions: just to use the library.' She gave Caterina, who was busy trying to think of how anyone could possibly use such a library, a long, appraising look and then added in a softer voice. 'They're very peculiar.'

'In what way?'

Signora Salvi shifted around in her seat, and Caterina wondered if she had been made nervous by her own impulsive confidence, or perhaps didn't want to speak badly of the people who, in a sense, helped keep the Foundation running. Caterina smiled to encourage her.

'They look like the people who go and sit in the Marciana all day. I think some of them come here only to keep warm. In the winter, that is, because we're closer to wherever they live than the Marciana is.'

'Do they ask about the music?'

'Almost never. Most of them don't know what the Foundation's for. I don't know how they hear about it, or what they hear: I suppose they tell one another that it's warm and no one will bother them for three hours. But they come, and they sit there. Sometimes they bring a newspaper, or they find one that's been left. Or they sleep.' She gave Caterina a long look, as if assessing her trustworthiness, and then said, 'Sometimes, when it's very cold, I keep it open longer.'

'What are you supposed to be doing?' Caterina asked, curious to learn anything about this place where she was to carry out her research.

'I think, at the beginning – I've worked here only three years – the Fondazione really did what Dottor Dardago wanted: it made contributions to support performances of operas, and it gave money to people who worked on scores and research.' Here she gave a smile Caterina found quite engaging. 'It's all in the files: how much they gave and who they gave it to.' She stopped. 'Then things changed.'

'What happened?'

'The first Director made some bad investments, and the endowment shrank. So the people who are interested in grants stopped asking us for help because we had none to give. Dottor Asnaldi came twelve years ago, and things just kept getting worse. Then, two years ago, they had another big loss, and Dottor Asnaldi left.'

'Leaving what behind?' Caterina asked, though she had no right to do so.

Roseanna raised a hand and scratched beneath one of her curls, then said, 'There's an accountant who looks at the books every six months, and he says the endowment's almost gone. He thinks there might be enough to keep the office open for another year, at best.'

'And then?'

'And then we close it, I suppose,' Roseanna said and gave a small, disappointed shrug. 'If there's no more money . . .' she began but did not finish the sentence.

'Who decided this? Dottor Moretti?'

'Oh, no. Another lawyer, Fanno, the one who's in charge of the endowment.' Caterina did not recognize the name and did not think it important enough to ask who he was. From the little she had learned and seen, it was evident that the Foundation was not long for this world, not with no computer and no telephone, and with that castrato novel on the shelf. Though she didn't work for the Foundation, curiosity urged her to ask, 'Are there records of the correspondence going back to the beginning?'

'Oh yes,' Signora Salvi said. 'They're upstairs.' She pointed to the ceiling, as if to remove any possible uncertainty Caterina might have had about where upstairs might be.

'Upstairs?'

'In the Director's office.'

'I thought this was the Director's office,' she said.

'Oh, no. I mean Dottor Asnaldi's office – well, his ex-office.' Then in a smaller voice, she added, 'That's where the chests are. In the storeroom. They're safe there.'

# 3

Like Lot's wife, Caterina turned to salt; unlike the other woman, she turned immediately back into flesh and said, 'But that's im . . .' before she stopped herself, realizing that she had no idea at all where the chests were or could be, just as, in all of this, she had no idea of what was possible or not. The cousins had spoken of the chests as though they belonged in a bank vault, yet here they were, being kept in an apartment with rooms on the ground floor that had windows without bars. Further, it was an apartment thieves had already entered with no difficulty.

Caterina could not understand the Foundation's involvement with the chests. What Roseanna called the endowment was almost finished, the offices could have been in Albania, the heat and access to a place to sit drew a number of not-quite-vagrants to the library, and yet the Foundation was somehow, however peripherally, involved.

Hoping that none of this was visible in her expression, she continued, as though she'd paused to consider the exact word. '. . . impressive, really impressive. To have them safe in a storeroom.' It was the best she could do, and Roseanna smiled in response so Caterina went on, 'How did that happen?'

'The previous owners had the storeroom built into the wall; I don't know why. It was here when the Foundation first rented the apartment: Dottor Asnaldi used to joke about it: sometimes he'd put his umbrella inside and close all the locks.' Then, voice lower, Roseanna asked, 'They told you some of this, didn't they?'

'Perhaps not all of it,' Caterina answered. 'There was a certain lack of background in what I was told, if I might call it that.' Short of a direct request for information, Caterina could have given no clearer message.

'Since you're going to be working on the papers, I suppose you should know where they came from.'

Caterina thanked her.

'One of the cousins called Dottor Asnaldi at home about four months ago. I don't know how he got his number, and I don't remember which one of them it was. He wanted to know if the Dottore would be interested in reading some documents and writing a report on them. All I know is that he met with the two men – the cousins – but he turned down their offer. I never knew why.' Here Roseanna gave the smile/shrug combination that Caterina was beginning to recognize.

Caterina nodded, and Roseanna continued. 'But he called me because he'd left me in charge and said it might be a good idea to keep the papers here, in the storeroom: that's why they're upstairs.'

'I'm surprised they didn't ask the Marciana or the Conservatory, even a bank. That is, if they think the papers might be valuable,' Caterina said.

Absentmindedly, Roseanna ran her hand over the

surface of her desk, as if feeling to see if it needed to be waxed. 'It's cheap,' she finally said. 'That is, cheaper.'

'Than?'

'Than the Marciana or the Conservatory or a bank. They offered to pay three hundred Euros a month, and that was in winter, when we had the heating bill to think about.' She opened her hands in a gesture replete with resignation. 'Dottor Asnaldi called me with the suggestion, and I agreed. The others would have cost much more.'

Given that the place had been broken into recently, a bank might also have been safer, though Caterina saw no reason to pass this idea on to Roseanna.

'I was in charge, you see. As Acting Director, I had to sign the contract.'

She seemed so proud of the title that Caterina said 'Complimenti', in a low voice, which caused Roseanna to blush.

Feeling that Roseanna's pause was a suggestion that she inquire, Caterina asked, 'What happened then?'

'Dottor Moretti convinced them they should find someone competent to read the papers.'

'Did he think this would settle all their problems and end their dispute?'

'Oh,' Roseanna said with a laugh, 'I don't think the person exists who could do that.'

That lightened the mood and gave Caterina the courage to try to satisfy some of her curiosity. 'Presumably, the trunks are safe up there.'

'Of course. The storeroom is really just a small closet, but it has *una porta blindata*. If you think about it, it's much more than most shops have.' Then, 'There's another, smaller cabinet: that's where the archives are kept.'

'The archives?' Caterina asked.

'The letters,' Roseanna said. 'But Dottor Asnaldi always called them the archives.'

'Where are they?'

Roseanna raised her eyes and gazed at the ceiling, reminding Caterina of the holy cards of Saint Thérèse of Lisieux so often found lying on the tables in the back of empty churches. The hair-snakes on her head, ironed flat, would have looked just like the saint's black veil. 'Upstairs.'

The unsummoned images came to Caterina of Ugolino imprisoned in the Tower, Vercingetorix in the Mamertine – quickly cancelled because that prison was underground – Casanova escaping from the Piombi. First there was the Director's office, and now there were the archives. How many other things were hidden away on the next floor?

'Upstairs?' Caterina repeated unnecessarily.

'It's in the same room, but it's only a simple wall cabinet with a key.'

'What's kept in the archives?'

'Some scores that Dottor Dardago collected,' Roseanna explained.

'Are they part of the endowment?' Caterina asked, wondering why, if they were, they had not been sold to continue with sponsorship or, at least, alleviate some of the misery around them.

'No. Dottor Dardago left them to the Marciana, to be given to them if the Foundation ever ceased to function. I suppose he didn't want things ever to be sold off, piece by piece. The Foundation merely has the use of them for as long as it's in existence. That's always been very clear.' But then, in a lower, more confidential voice, she added, 'It's only a few things, really: a printed copy of an opera by Porpora and some musical scores.' When Caterina seemed about to ask, Roseanna said, sounding sad to have to say it, as if she were confessing to some minor vulgarity on the Foundation's part, 'No, only copies, and not even from the times they were written.' Then, after a pause, she added, 'I'm afraid Dottor Dardago was an amateur.'

To Caterina, this amateur's collection hardly sounded like something that belonged under lock and key, but her work did not concern the archive, and so she asked nothing further about it.

'How do you get there?' Caterina asked.

Roseanna's glance made her confusion obvious. 'The stairs.'

'Can a person go up there?'

Roseanna made as if to push away Caterina's question. 'I don't know if you can go up there yet.'

Like most people, Caterina disliked being told she could not do something. Like most professional women who had risen in a male-dominated profession by dint of skill and tenacity and superior talent that was never acknowledged and could seldom be admitted, she had learned to stifle her instinctive desire to shout at the source of the prohibition, though she had never learned to control the pounding of the heart that resulted from unexplained opposition.

After a few moments, Caterina asked, in a voice she managed to make sound entirely normal, 'Sooner or later, I have to go up, don't I? If I'm going to be working there.' Recalling something, she added, 'You mentioned that you receive letters. Would it be possible for me to have a look at them?' When Roseanna did not respond, she continued, 'It's possible that people who contacted the Foundation in the past – with real musicological information or questions, that is – might be the sort of amateur a researcher dreams of finding.' The only dream researchers had about amateurs and their suggestions were nightmares, but Roseanna need not be told this.

'We never know what will be useful,' she added with a broad smile meant to include Roseanna in that 'we'. 'Whose rule is it, anyway?'

Roseanna thought for a moment and then said, 'It's not a rule, really. It's just that the cousins are rather . . .'

'Secretive?'

This time her smile was bigger than her shrug.

Caterina smiled in return and said, unwilling to admit to no motive higher than her own mounting curiosity about the Foundation, 'All I want to do is save time by learning if there are any people who might eventually be able to help in the research.' As if confessing uncertainty to a friend, she said, 'I don't know if it will help me with these documents, but it might be useful to know who the interested people are: they often know a lot more than the experts do, especially in a field as narrow as this one.' It was lame, and she knew it, but Roseanna might not.

Apparently sufficient good will had been restored because Roseanna got to her feet, saying, 'I suppose you can.' Then, with a smile of solidarity, she added, 'Besides, I'm the Acting Director, aren't I?'

She led the way from her office, turning towards the back of the building. The hallway ended in a door. She took a set of keys from her pocket, opened the door, and started up a set of steps. Caterina followed. At the top, another door led into a small entrance corridor with wooden doors facing one another.

Roseanna opened the door on the left and let them into an office complete with barred windows. The desk was large, and a dark wooden cabinet was fitted into the wall to the left of it. On either side of the cabinet hung etchings of bewigged men. Even from this distance, Caterina recognized round-faced Jommelli. The other might have been

Hasse. She liked him: any man who would marry Faustina Bordoni had to be a hero.

Roseanna nodded towards the wooden cabinet, saying, 'All of the correspondence is in there.' Caterina saw that the key was in the lock. Looking around for the storeroom, she noticed a pair of smooth metal doors, almost a metre high, set into the wall to the right of the desk and partly blocked from her sight by the desk and the chair.

Pointedly ignoring those doors, she asked, 'How far back does the correspondence date, Roseanna?'

'To the beginning.'

'What do people write about?' Caterina asked with genuine interest.

'Oh, all sorts of things. You'd be amazed. Some send us copies of manuscripts or scores and ask us to identify them or verify the handwriting, and some ask for biographical information about the composers. Or what we think of new CDs, or whether we think it's worth going to see a particular production. We've even been sent documents and manuscripts, but never anything of great importance. There's no telling. If you read through the files, you'll get an idea.'

'If it's no trouble,' Caterina said, interested in the letters and wanting to show Roseanna that she had come up here in good faith and not in the hope of learning the identity of the composer whose manuscripts might well be behind those thick metal doors, doors she continued to ignore.

Roseanna turned the key of the cabinet, latched her fingers expertly under the side of one door, and pulled it open. The other swung after it.

Caterina had met Roseanna only a brief time ago, but she had seen enough – the conservative clothing, the neatness with which the snakes were wrapped around one another – to know she could not have been responsible for the chaos inside the cabinet.

There were two shelves, each sized to hold Manila folders, and on each of them files lay splashed about. Some leaked papers, others appeared untouched; still others were strewn across the shelves as if flung by a heavy wind.

Roseanna's gasp was entirely involuntary. '*Maria Vergine*,' she exclaimed. No liar, Caterina thought, would say that. Then Roseanna gave her astonishment an upgrade and whispered, '*Oddio.*'

When she reached for the files, Caterina said 'No, Roseanna. Don't touch anything.'

'What?'

'Don't touch anything,' she repeated.

The other woman looked at her with open curiosity. Then, 'I don't want the police here again,' she said with sudden energy.

Caterina leaned closer to the shelves. 'But look at it. Someone's been through those papers.' Remembering no doubt what she had seen in the cinema, she asked, 'Who else has a key to this room?'

'I do. That's all.'

'Dottor Moretti gave me one to the building,' Caterina said, wondering how difficult it would be to get into this office. 'So no one else has one?' she asked. From Roseanna's expression she saw she had gone too far. She tried to modify the effect by continuing, as if naturally, 'It must be a terrible shock for you, Roseanna. To have someone come in and do this.' Her tactic of excluding Roseanna as a possible suspect was as crude as it was obvious.

Caterina ran through what she knew about the police: their first suspects would be anyone with keys to the building. Or, learning that the disturbance – she didn't even know if it had been a theft – concerned correspondence about centuries-old music and the men who wrote it, they would simply leave. That is, if they came in the first place.

In her most placatory tone, Caterina said, 'You're right, of course. This is not for the police.' That made them partners and equally complicit.

'What's missing?' Caterina moved away from the cabinet, as if to give physical evidence of her trust in Roseanna's competence. Her sister Cinzia had been involved with an anthropologist for some years and had passed on to her sisters what she had learned from him about dominance displays in simians. Caterina thought of this as she moved back from the desk, leaving access to the cabinet entirely to Roseanna.

The Acting Director gathered the files on each shelf into a stack, tapping papers back inside the folders. She put the first pile on the desk and beside them those from the shelf below. Then she opened each file and straightened the papers until she had them in an order she seemed to like.

She returned to the top file on the first stack and began to page through the letters; Caterina, to disguise her impatience, went and studied the second portrait to see if there was a name printed at the bottom. Beside her, Roseanna methodically opened one file after another, fingering through the papers in each.

Caterina returned her attention to the men with the wigs.

'Caterina,' Roseanna said.

'*Sì?*'

'I don't understand this,' she said hesitantly.

'What?'

'Nothing seems to be missing.'

# 4

'What?' Caterina asked, amazed that someone would have gone to the trouble of breaking in and then not have taken anything. What she had seen did not suggest vandalism. Nothing had spilled out of the cabinet, nothing had been destroyed. There were signs of a hasty, careless search: nothing more.

Roseanna gave her a Manila folder. Neatly typed (yes, typed) on the flap was 'Sartorio, Antonio, 1630–1680.'

'What's in it?' Caterina asked as she handed it back without opening it.

'The letters we've received over the years concerning him,' Roseanna said, hefting it in her right hand as if she could judge by the weight.

'Everything seems to be here,' Roseanna said. 'And in this one,' she added, passing another file to Caterina. 'But I can check.'

Caterina began to read the top letter in the file she held, which was in German and addressed to the Director of the Foundation by title and not by name. The writer began by saying that, the last time he had been in Venice, he had been unable to find Hasse's grave in the church of San Marcuola and asked, in a peremptory manner, why the Foundation had not seen to the placing of a memorial plaque in the church. The writer was a member of the Hasse Society in . . .

Caterina pulled her attention from the letter and asked, 'What did you just say?'

'I wanted to check if anything's missing from the Porpora file.'

'How?' Caterina asked, suddenly interested.

Roseanna turned back to the cabinet and reached inside. She placed her hand on one of the decorative knobs on the inlaid panels that ran perpendicular to the shelves. She gave it a sharp twist, and the panel tilted forward and down, revealing a vertical drawer the width of the panel, about ten centimetres. Reaching in, she pulled out a student's notebook, on its cover the bronze equestrian statue of Marcus Aurelius.

She set the notebook on the desk, opened it near the front, and pressed it flat by running her hand down the centre. She placed the file she was holding beside the notebook and removed the letters. Methodically, she paged through them, each time putting her forefinger on an entry in the notebook: it was too far from Caterina for her to read. When she had checked every letter, Roseanna turned to her and said, 'They're all here.'

'May I?' Caterina asked and picked up the notebook.

'Porpora' was written at the top of the page on the left, and below it were columns that listed the date of the arrival of the letter, the name and address of the person who sent it, and the date the letter was answered.

'Why do you keep it?' Caterina asked in a voice she made as neutral as she could.

Roseanna pursed her lips in embarrassment, carefully avoiding Caterina's gaze. 'I've always kept permanent records of things, even my gas bills. It's just a habit of mine, I suppose. This way, if anything goes missing or gets misfiled, I've got a record that it did arrive. I've kept it since I started here.' Head lowered, she added, 'I began it with all the correspondence that was already here and kept adding to it over the years.'

Caterina stopped herself from asking if the Foundation had a website or email address or any evidence that it was functioning in the current millennium.

She thought of the letter complaining about Hasse's grave: such things did not lead to burglary. 'Can you remember anyone asking a strange question or making a threat?' she asked.

'Some of the letters are strange,' Roseanna said. Then, as if hearing a playback, she slapped her hand over her mouth.

Caterina didn't bother to fight the impulse and laughed out loud. 'You should have seen some of the people I took classes with.' Swept away by memory, she added, 'Or from,' and that set her off again.

Roseanna resisted, then gave in and said, laughing, 'If you think they're strange, you should see the people who come here. Not the ones who come to sleep: the ones who come to ask questions.'

Still laughing, Caterina waved a hand in the air. She knew, she knew. She'd spent a decade of her life with them.

'The ones who write letters are usually better,' Roseanna told her. 'There's an elderly gentleman in Pavia who still listens to phonograph records. He writes and asks for suggestions about which ones to buy. Would you believe it?' Roseanna shook her head at this. This was a woman who still used a typewriter, Caterina thought.

Caterina took the notebook and, knowing that Roseanna's list would be in alphabetical order, paged back from 'Porpora' to 'Hasse'. The letters in the file dated back twelve years; for Caldara a bit more than that, though there were only two letters.

She flipped back towards the end, passed 'Sartorio' and found 'Steffani'.

'Why is it that the entries for Steffani start so recently, Roseanna?'

'Uh, he's been forgotten for a long time,' Roseanna answered.

'I see,' Caterina said. She remembered seeing his portrait in a book she had once read: round face and sagging chin, bishop's cap with white hair sneaking out on both sides, long fingers caressing the cross he wore across his chest. The man had been dead for almost three centuries. Caterina closed the notebook and set it on the table. As she did, her eyes were drawn to the photo of the statue. Marcus Aurelius. Emperor. Hero. Blamed by generations of historians for having passed the throne to his son Commodus, as if they thought he should have remained childless. Childless. Without heirs.

Illumination flashed upon her, forcing out an involuntary grunt, as though someone had punched her in the stomach. 'Marco Aurelio,' she pronounced. 'Of course, of course.'

Startled, Roseanna turned to her. 'What's wrong? What's the matter?' She dropped a file on the table and put her hand on Caterina's arm. 'What's wrong?'

'Marco Aurelio,' Caterina repeated.

Roseanna looked at the cover of the notebook. 'Yes, I know, but what's wrong with you?'

Caterina rubbed her forehead, then tapped her fingers lightly against her head a few times. 'Of course, of course,' she repeated. Then, to Roseanna, she said, 'The trunks belonged to Steffani, didn't they?'

The other woman's mouth dropped open. 'Who told you? They said no one was to say anything until the person they chose started to work on the papers. How did you find out?' When Caterina remained silent, Roseanna took her arm again, this time with greater force. 'Tell me.'

Caterina pointed to the notebook. 'That told me,' she said.

It was obvious that Roseanna had no idea what she was talking about. She picked up the notebook and paged through it, as if Caterina had seen the answer written inside. 'I don't understand,' she confessed.

'I remembered,' Caterina said. 'Things I read when I was at university. His first opera was *Marco Aurelio*.' Roseanna gave no sign of recognition, but how many people would know this? 'And I remembered reading that he had no direct heirs, and no one ever knew what happened to his possessions after his death.' The Church was mixed up in it, too, she recalled but could not remember the details.

Roseanna went and sat behind the desk. It was the Director's desk and the Director's chair, yet she looked like anything but a Director. She leaned forward and propped her chin on her hand. 'Yes. You're right. It's Steffani.' She pronounced it with the accent on the first syllable, as an Italian would. As Steffani had not.

'I don't see what difference it makes,' Roseanna went on in a voice grown suddenly brisk. 'Really. You would have known as soon as you started reading and found his name in the papers. It's those two men,' she said, her voice growing warmer. 'Everything has to be secret. No one can know anything. If one of them saw that the other one's hair was on fire, he wouldn't say anything.' Her tone was a mixture of anger and exasperation. 'They're terrible men. One's worse than the other.'

'The cousins?' Caterina asked.

Roseanna raised her head and gave an angry flip of her hand. 'What cousins? They're just two men who smell the possibility of money. That's the way they're related.' Then, after a moment's reflection, 'And in mutual suspicion.'

'Are they really his descendants?' Caterina asked. 'Steffani's?'

'Oh, they are, they are.'

'How do they know that? Or prove it?'

Here Roseanna gave a snort, either of disgust or anger. Then she gave Caterina a sudden, assessing look and said, 'It's the Mormons.'

'I beg your pardon?' Steffani, she remembered, had been a clergyman, so where'd the Mormons come from? 'He was a priest, wasn't he? And long before the Mormons.'

'Oh, I know that,' Roseanna said. 'But that's how you can find your ancestors. By asking them.'

Caterina, who took very little interest in her own ancestors, could hardly imagine asking the Mormons to look for them. 'What have the Mormons got to do with this?'

Roseanna smiled and waved her fingers before her face to suggest a lack of mental stability. 'It's what they believe, or at least what Dottor Moretti told me they believe. They can go back and baptize people in the past.' Her expression showed how much faith she put in this possibility.

Caterina stared at her for a long moment. 'You think you can marry them in the past, too, and inherit their money?'

It took Roseanna a moment to realize this was a joke, then she laughed, losing a decade as she did. She wiped her eyes and said, her voice a bit rough after laughing so hard, 'It would be convenient, wouldn't it?' She considered the possibilities and said, 'I suppose I could marry Gianni Agnelli.' Then, with a careful attention to fact that made Caterina admire her, she added, 'No, he lived too long. I'd want someone who died young.'

Caterina stopped herself from naming a candidate or two and returned to the business at hand.

Wiping away a few vagrant tears and still smiling, Roseanna said, 'Dottor Moretti told me they're very good at tracing people's ancestry, and they're generous about giving the information.'

'How do they do it? This is a Catholic country. And parts of Germany are, too.' This rang another historical bell: Steffani had been mixed up in the squabbles between the Protestants and the Catholics. How long ago it was, and how futile such things seemed now. Before his time, people died disputing how many angels could dance on the head of a pin, or whether the Host was real flesh or merely a symbol. During his lifetime, the wars still went on. She shook her head at the thought of it: how many millions had died for those angels and for that flesh/non-flesh Host? Centuries later, and the churches are empty except for old people and kids with badly tuned guitars.

'What's wrong?' Roseanna asked.

'Nothing,' Caterina said. 'I was just trying to remember what I read as a student about Steffani.'

'There are books about him in the Marciana, I'm sure,' Roseanna said. 'I haven't read about him, but some of the others are fascinating. Gesualdo killed his wife and her lover, and he was a hunchback, too. Porpora went bankrupt, and all I ever read about Cavalli said he sat around all day, writing operas.'

Caterina gave her a long look, as if seeing a different person, but said nothing.

'I like this music, so I started reading about it, and about the composers. The Conservatory has books, but they wouldn't let me use the library.' From her tone, it was difficult to tell whether she was offended. But then she smiled. 'At the Marciana, when I told them I was the Assistant Director here, they let me use them.'

'Good for you,' Caterina said with a blossoming smile.

'Thank you,' Roseanna said in a voice best suited to confession. 'And their lives were interesting. Besides, if I work here, I should know something about what we're doing, shouldn't I?'

First the woman wanted to marry the richest man in Italy, and now she struck a death blow to every political appointee in the country. What would she want next? A functioning political system? The Philosopher King?

'Tell me more about the Mormons,' Caterina said.

It looked as if Roseanna might have preferred talking about the music, but she said, 'Dottor Moretti's used them before. He said they have files going back hundreds of years: you can trace your family back all those generations.'

'So these two cousins can trace their ancestry back to Steffani?'

'To his cousins, they could: that's how they're descended. The Mormons have copies of parish registers from all over Italy, and they sent Dottor Moretti copies of all of the documents: birth certificates, death certificates, marriage contracts.'

Caterina thought of the two cousins: she doubted that they would be more computer savvy than Roseanna. 'Who did it for them?' Caterina asked. 'The online search?'

'Not them. The Mormons did it all.'

'Interesting,' Caterina said. 'There was no will, was there?'

'No one could find one, so the Church claimed everything; some things were sold to pay his debts, and the rest was lost until the trunks turned up.'

Caterina sat back in her chair and studied her feet. The cousins had no interest in the contents of the trunks, save for what price they might bring; if they were the papers of what her profession would call a major minor composer, dead almost three centuries, what was their value? The Stabat Mater was a masterpiece, and the few opera arias she knew were wonderful, though strangely short to the modern ear. She'd gone down to London to see *Niobe* a few years ago and found it a revelation. What was that heartbreaking lament, something about *'Dal mio petto'*? With a key change towards the end that had driven her wild when she heard it and then again when a musician friend had shown her the score. But her personal excitement would hardly influence the price put on a manuscript. A page of a score by Mozart was worth a fortune, or one by Bach, or Handel, but who had ever heard of Steffani? And yet the cousins were willing to hire a lawyer/arbitrator and pay her salary? For two trunks they thought were full of papers?

Some English poet she had read at school said that Fortune went up and down like a 'bucket in a well'. So did the fortune of composers as taste changed and reputations were re-evaluated. The roads to concert houses were littered with the bones of the reputations of composers like Gassmann, Tosi, Keiser. Every so often, some long-dead composer would be resurrected and hailed as the new master: she had seen it happen with Hildegard von Bingen and Josquin des Prez. For a year or so no concert hall was without at least one performance of their music.

And then they went back to being dead and written about in books, which is where Caterina thought they both belonged. But if what she had heard in London was any indication, Steffani did not belong there, not at all.

'Are you listening, Caterina?' she heard Roseanna ask.

'No, I'm sorry,' she said with an embarrassed grin. 'I was thinking about something else.'

'What?'

'That no one much values Steffani's music these days.' She said it with regret, thinking of the beauty of the arias and the mastery shown in the Stabat Mater. Maybe it was time for a return to the stage for the good Bishop?

'It's not the music those two are after,' Roseanna said.

'What is it, then?' Caterina asked, wondering what else might have lasted and come down through the centuries.

'The treasure.'

# 5

The word astonished her. 'Treasure?' she repeated. 'What treasure?'

'He didn't tell you?' Roseanna asked.

'Who?' Caterina asked. Then, 'Tell me what?'

'Dottor Moretti. He must know about it,' Roseanna said, sounding surprised. 'I thought he'd have told you when you accepted the job.'

Caterina, who had been strolling along a beach, looking idly at the shells underfoot, was swept away by an unexpected wave. The water, she realized, was deeper than she had expected. She thought of the two cousins, and there came a sudden vision of sharp fins slicing through the waters. To escape this fantasy, she put her hand on Roseanna's arm and said, 'Believe me. I don't have any idea what you're talking about.'

'*Ma, ti xe Venexiana*?' Roseanna asked, exaggerating the pronunciation of the words.

Caterina nodded: she had been away from home so long

that Italian now came more easily to her than did the language she had heard at home as a child, but still dialect was the language of her bones.

'You're Venetian and you don't know anything about those two?' she asked, leading Caterina away from the idea of treasure.

'The usurer and the man with the fleet of water taxis who has almost no income?' Caterina said, and Roseanna gave her a look that was the equivalent of a stamp in her passport. To know that much about them was to be Venetian.

'What else do you know?' she asked Caterina.

'That Stievani's sons and nephews drive the taxis. And make a fortune. All undeclared, of course.'

'And Scapinelli?'

'That he's a convicted usurer but still works in the shops of his sons. Who are not angels, either.'

Roseanna considered all of this for some time and asked, moving even further away from any mention of treasure, 'Is your mother Margherita Rossi?'

'Yes.'

'And her father played in the Fenice orchestra?'

'Yes. Violin.'

'Then I know your family,' Roseanna said and sighed. 'Your grandfather used to give my father opera tickets.' She did not sound at all pleased at the memory, or perhaps her displeasure resulted from the obligations imposed upon her by that memory.

Caterina had the sense to remain quiet and wait and allow Roseanna to decide how to tell things. 'They're very bad men,' Roseanna said and then added, by way of explication, 'They come of bad families. One side was originally from Castelfranco; the other's from Padova, I think. But they've been here in the city for generations. Greed's in their bones.'

Suddenly tired of what sounded like melodrama and overcome with impatience, Caterina said, 'And what about treasure? Where does that come from?'

'No one knows,' Roseanna said.

'Does anyone know where it is?' Caterina asked.

Roseanna shook her head and abruptly got to her feet. 'Let's go for a coffee,' she said, and headed for the door without waiting to see if Caterina followed her.

Outside, Caterina stopped in the *calle*. It had been years since she had been in this part of the city, so she had no idea which bars still served decent coffee.

Roseanna stood for a moment, moving her head from side to side, like a hunting dog testing the air for the temperature or passing prey. 'Come on,' she finally said, turning to the right and, at the first corner, right again. 'We can go to that place in Campo Santa Maria Formosa.'

There were two of them, Caterina remembered, the one with the outside benches that remained in place until the really cold weather arrived and the one opposite it, along the canal, that she had been told – and thereafter always believed – had once been the room where the bodies of the dead in the parish were kept before being taken out to the cemetery on San Michele.

They walked down Ruga Giuffa, making small talk: admiring this or that, pointing to a perfume they had once tried but got tired of. Because they were Venetian, they also commented on the shops that were gone and what had come after them: the wonderful place that sold bath-room fixtures replaced by the cheapest of fake-leather bags and belts.

After crossing the bridge, Roseanna continued straight across the *campo*, to Caterina's relief avoiding the bar alongside the canal. In front of the other bar, Roseanna stopped and asked, 'Inside or outside?' This time, it was

Caterina who tested the temperature before saying, 'Inside, I'm afraid.' But before they went in, she pointed to the near corner and asked, 'What happened to that *palazzo*?' As Caterina recalled, the building, as Steffani's chests were now, had been at the centre of a contested inheritance, but in this case rumour said it concerned first and second wives, a far more deadly game.

'A hotel,' Roseanna said, making no attempt to disguise her disgust. 'They hacked it up inside and brought in cheap imitation furniture, and now tourists can tell themselves they're staying in a real Venetian *palazzo*.' She pushed open the door and went into the bar. Caterina saw that there was nowhere to sit and delighted in the fact. She had had enough of *gemutlich* coffee houses with velvet benches and whipped cream everywhere: alongside the strudel, inside the cakes, on top of the coffee. Here a person stood, drank a coffee in one swift gulp, and went back to the business of the day.

Roseanna called the barman by name and asked for two coffees, which arrived almost instantly and were as quickly consumed. Roseanna did not speak, nor did Caterina: so much for the idea of an intimate conversation. Back outside, Caterina glanced at her watch and saw it was just after eleven, so she turned left and headed towards the bridge that would take them back to the Foundation. 'You still haven't told me about the treasure,' she said, deciding that push had come to shove.

Roseanna, walking beside her, nodded, then said, 'I know. It's so crazy I'm almost embarrassed to talk about it. And I don't know how much you're supposed to be told.'

Caterina stopped before the bridge and pulled Roseanna aside to keep her out of the way of the people passing by. 'Roseanna, I know who it's all about, and I know what type of men the cousins are, and now you've told me there's some sort of treasure: it doesn't take much imagination to understand that's why they're so interested in the trunks and the papers.' Tired of all the secrecy, she spoke before she thought. 'What do they think the applicants who didn't get the job are doing? Not telling people about all of this?'

As often happened with her, the more she thought about the situation, the more her anger grew. What in God's name do these fools think is in the trunks, the manuscript of Monteverdi's lost *Arianna*? A missing papal tiara? Saint Veronica's veil?

Roseanna started to speak, but Caterina ignored her. 'You're the one who mentioned it, who used the word "treasure". I didn't. So tell me what this is all about.' Her heart was pounding, sweat stood on her forehead, but she stopped because she realized there was no threat she could make. She needed the job: the scholar she had once been was curious to follow the paper trail that led back to Steffani.

Roseanna moved away from her but made no attempt to go back across the bridge. She looked down at her shoes, shifted her bag from one shoulder to the other. 'First, let me tell you there were no other applicants. Only you.'

'Then why did they tell me there were?' Caterina all but bleated.

'Capitalism,' Roseanna said.

'What?'

'To beat your price down.' She smiled, and Caterina saw the force of her logic. 'If you thought there were a lot of people after the job, you'd be willing to let them pay you less than you're worth.'

Caterina raised a hand to cover her face from the embarrassment of it.

46

Roseanna latched her arm into Caterina's and turned towards the bridge, pulling Caterina along beside her. 'All right,' she said. 'I'll tell you what I think is happening.'

The story she told was at times unclear, her telling of it filled with backups and turnarounds, with omissions and additions, and corrections and afterthoughts, with what she had heard at the Foundation, read, and imagined. In essence, it filled in some of the gaps left in the story Caterina had been told by Dottor Moretti and had inferred from her meetings with the cousins. Letters from Steffani existed in which he spoke of the poverty of his life. When she heard Roseanna say this, Caterina tried to recall ever having seen a letter from a Baroque composer – indeed, any composer – who complained of the excessive richness of his life. But there also existed a letter – Roseanna had indeed put in her time reading at the Marciana – written in the last year of his life in which he mentioned some of the objects in his possession, among them books and pictures and a casket and jewels. The catalogue of the more than five hundred books he owned listed first editions of Luther, which would be of enormous value today.

'Is that the treasure?'

Roseanna stopped and pulled her arm free to raise it, along with the other, in a gesture of complete exasperation. 'My God, listen to me. We don't even know if there are papers in the chests – or what's in them – and here I am, talking about treasure. The whole thing's crazy.'

Caterina took great comfort from the other woman's unconscious use of the plural. And yet Roseanna had a point in saying that they were all crazy: Caterina was swiftly approaching the same view. If the cousins had learned of the possibility of unearned wealth, Caterina had seen enough of them to know they would be driven wild by the thought of 'treasure'.

As to the chance that any papers in the trunk would lead to the discovery of a treasure, Caterina was less certain: it was unlikely that any treasure – whatever it was – would still be resting, safely undiscovered, in the place where it had been put. Realizing that her speculations led nowhere, Caterina asked, 'What else did you find out?' Producing her easiest and most relaxed smile, she coaxed, 'I had to do a lot of that sort of reading while I was in school; it's comforting to know that someone else finds it interesting.'

Roseanna, who had been spared the experience of reading back issues of *Studies in Early-Baroque Counterpoint*, gave Caterina an uncertain glance and said, 'I understood only the historical parts, not the musicological.'

'Good,' Caterina said with a smile, 'the historical part's usually more interesting.'

This earned her another puzzled glance, enough to warn her to treat her profession with greater seriousness. 'What else did you read?'

'One of the articles said that his possessions went to a Vatican organization called Propaganda Fide and disappeared, then these two trunks turned up a few years ago when an inventory was made. Somehow the cousins managed to have them sent here: I was never told how that happened.'

Caterina saw there was little to be gained from trying to penetrate the mysteries created by the cousins. Thinking out loud and returning to the question of the trunks, Caterina said, 'If they were autograph scores, then the music would have a certain value.'

'What does "certain value" mean?' Roseanna asked.

'I have no idea. That usually depends on how famous the composer is and how many of his manuscripts are on the market. But Steffani's star isn't in the ascendant, so no one's going to be paying a fortune for whatever might be there.'

Nudged by curiosity, Caterina asked, 'Did Dottor Moretti tell you when they'd come to open the chests?'

'Noon,' Roseanna said and looked at her watch. Then, sounding like a guilty schoolgirl and not at all like the Acting Director of the Fondazione Musicale Italo-Tedesca, she said, 'We better get back.'

# 6

They had been in Roseanna's office only a few minutes when they heard the front door open and close. Footsteps approached, and then Dottor Moretti was in the doorway. Just as she remembered him: dark grey suit with a faint stripe of lighter grey, dark blue tie with a stripe so discreet as to reveal itself only under torture. Caterina was certain he would be able to comb his hair in the reflection from his shoes, were it not that a man such as Dottor Moretti would never comb his hair in public. He'd give it a discreet tap, perhaps a faint stroke in the wake of a heavy wind. But a comb? Never.

He was a tidy man, not tall and not short, a few centimetres taller than she. His hair, neither dark nor light, was thick and cut short, already turning white at the temples. The oval lenses of his gold-framed glasses were so clean that she wondered if he wore a new pair every day. His nose was narrow and straight, his eyes a very pale blue, hardly the eyes of the cliché Italian, though perhaps those of the cliché Veneziano. Caterina doubted, however, that dialect ever passed those lips: in the few conversations they had had, he had used an easy elegance of language, as if he had chosen to speak as an adult from his very first words. She had no idea of what part of the country he came from, and his speech provided no clue.

A grey woollen topcoat was folded over his arm, and the other hand held the briefcase she had noticed before: smooth brown leather with twin brass locks that looked as though someone gave them a very careful buffing at least once a week. Caterina, a great admirer of men's clothing and often of the men who wore it, coveted the bag.

Dottor Moretti looked to be in his early forties, though from the faint wrinkles around his eyes his age might be greater. He seemed to smile only when a remark amused him; Caterina had found herself, when last they spoke, trying to make him smile, perhaps even to laugh. It had taken her no time to realize that he was responsive to language used well; as to his feelings about music, she had no idea.

'Signore,' he said with a small bow to both of them that, had another man made it, would have been faintly ridiculous. As made by Dottor Moretti, it was a show of respect and attention, meant perhaps to be read as a man's declaration that he lived to serve these ladies' wishes. Caterina, remembering that he was a lawyer, dismissed that idea and chose to read it as an old-fashioned gesture from that marvel of marvels, an old-fashioned man.

'Dottore,' she said, getting to her feet and extending her hand. 'A great pleasure to see you again.'

'The pleasure is once more entirely mine, Dottoressa,' he said, releasing her hand. He turned immediately and offered it to Roseanna, who rose from her desk to take it, saying only, *'Buon giorno, Dottore.'*

Dottor Moretti set his briefcase on the floor against Roseanna's desk. She gave a half-wave, half-shrug that presented the surface of her desk as the one place where he might sit in this two-chaired room. Caterina was interested to see how he would react. He did not surprise her: he folded his coat, placed it neatly on the desk, then leaned back against it and folded his arms.

'I'm glad you're both here,' he began. 'Signor Stievani and Signor Scapinelli should arrive at noon. This gives me the chance to speak to you before they get here.'

'To tell us what?' Roseanna asked. So far, Caterina noted, nothing she said to Moretti had required her to choose between the polite or the familiar form of address. Linguistically, then, they could be friends, they could be enemies, they could be lovers. Roseanna's manner with him, however, suggested equal parts of interest and deference, effectively eliminating the second possibility.

Ignoring her question, Dottor Moretti continued. 'They're very eager for Dottoressa Pellegrini to begin work.'

'Today, I hope,' Caterina said. Did he think she had stopped in to borrow a cup of sugar from Roseanna?

'Yes.'

'The sooner she reads through it all, the sooner they can stop paying her salary,' Roseanna observed in a dead level voice entirely free of irony or sarcasm. Time is money, she was Venetian: that's the way things are.

Again ignoring Roseanna's comment, Moretti asked Caterina, 'Do you have any objection to beginning so soon, Dottoressa?'

She smiled. 'Quite the opposite, Dottore. I'm very eager to begin and discover what treasures . . .' she began, giving the briefest pause, '. . . await us in those chests.'

His glance was quick, and he turned it immediately into

a smile. 'I compliment you on your energy and eagerness, Dottoressa. I'm sure we all look forward to the results of your research.'

'That can't be all those two want,' Roseanna said. Dottor Moretti gave her a long, assessing look, as if surprised at this unwonted frankness in front of the researcher who, like him, was meant to be entirely neutral. He bent down and snapped open his briefcase. He pulled out some papers and handed one to Caterina, keeping another for himself. 'I've spoken to the two . . .' and here he gave a pause even more infinitesimal than Caterina's '. . . gentlemen, about the procedure for the research.'

'Procedure?' Roseanna asked before Caterina could speak.

'If you'll take a look,' he said, raising the paper and peering over the top of his glasses at Caterina, 'you'll see written what I've already told you: that they want written reports.' He glanced back at the paper and read aloud, '". . . with a summary of the documents read and translations of any that might refer to our deceased relative's desires regarding the disposition of his worldly assets."'

Caterina enjoyed the words, which the cousins must have learned from Dottor Moretti: 'deceased relative', 'disposition of his worldly assets'. Ah, what a marvel language was, and blessed they who respected it.

'The Dottoressa is not to have private or personal contact with either of the two . . .' again that pause '. . . gentlemen. In the event that she has information to convey, or in response to any request from either of the two parties that she provide further information about the documents, it must be provided to me and the two parties at the same time. Further, all emails must go through me.' He glanced at Caterina, who nodded in understanding and acceptance, deciding to wait before asking about the computer on which she was meant to send these emails. Before leaving Manchester, she had returned to the university the laptop it provided to all researchers and had only her own desktop, which she had no intention of bringing from her apartment.

'And,' he went on, looking up and through the lenses of his glasses as he said this, 'in the event that either of them should request a meeting to explain any of the documents, they must both agree to the time and place, and I'm afraid I must be present at any such meeting.'

With a small smile, Caterina said, 'I hope your fear does not result from the thought of my presence, Dottore.'

This earned her one of his smiles. 'Only from the thought that my presence might not be as enjoyable as theirs is sure to be,' he replied.

Caterina returned her attention to the paper he had given her. Was a lawyer supposed to speak of his clients this way? The cousins might have enough money to pay a man wearing a suit like his, but they seemed to lack the price of his respect. They must be very sure of Dottor Moretti's ability to find the best person to lead them to whatever treasure there might be, but then she remembered what Roseanna had said about Caterina's being the only person interviewed, and she wondered how concerned the cousins were about anything except price. Further, was she meant to be complimented or flattered by the slighting way he spoke of them, as if to suggest he was being open and honest with her?

'I see there are other conditions,' she said, holding up her copy of the paper. 'What's this about having to read any papers in the order in which I find them?' she asked tersely. 'Of course I will.' She felt her voice growing sharp and paused a moment to try to relax. 'How else would a scholar go through papers?' Her visceral resentment told her a good deal about the way she felt about the cousins.

'Unfortunately,' Dottor Moretti began, putting on a serious face, 'I did not make the list of requirements, Dottoressa, nor is it in my competence to question them. They were given to me, and it's my task to persuade you to follow them.'

'Of course, I'll follow them,' she said, 'but these gentlemen might consider the fact that they are paying me for my expertise, and part of that is knowing how to deal with documents.' In the face of his silence – neither obstinate nor patient; just silence – she went on, 'I have only a general historical context for any documents I might find,' she said, 'I'm at home in the music of the period, but I foresee needing to do research beyond reading the actual documents.' He said nothing, and so she concluded, 'I would like to establish that as one of my conditions.'

'One?' he asked.

She held up the paper and said, 'I haven't finished reading this yet. There might be more.'

Roseanna broke in and said, 'Perhaps they're hoping that there will be a folder on the top with neat lettering on the outside, saying, "Last will and testament". And below it in a different hand, just to save time: "List of everything of value and where to find it".' If she was trying to make a joke, one glance at Dottor Moretti's face showed she had not succeeded.

'You've told me he died intestate,' Caterina said. 'I can only hope I do find a will among the papers, or something in which he makes his desires known. But I'd still have to read the rest of the papers, of course, to see that he did not subsequently contradict this.'

If she had expected surprise or disagreement from Dottor Moretti, she was mistaken. 'Naturally,' he muttered and then gestured towards the paper in her hand, as if to suggest she finish reading it.

'And this,' she said, tapping at the paper with her finger: 'that I will not write anything – article or book – about any personal information contained in the trunks and that I will not speak of it in public or private. Not until I am given permission by both of the heirs, as well as by you.' She paused briefly and then asked, feeling a flutter of anger at what she saw as petty, ignorant obstructionism, 'I assume this does not apply to my reports?' Her smile was falsity itself.

Dottor Moretti used the universal gesture of surrender and held up both hands in front of his chest. 'I don't make the rules, Dottoressa: I only transmit them.' Then, with a small smile, he added, 'If you'll continue reading, Dottoressa, you'll see that this prohibition does not extend to any musicological information that might be contained in the documents.'

'Meaning?' she asked.

'Meaning that you have the exclusive rights to edit any scores that might be found, whether of orchestral or vocal music, that you judge to be of artistic importance.' He pointed to his copy, and she found the sentence on hers.

She kept her face impassive as she read, though this hope had at least partially animated her willingness to toss over the job in Manchester: most musicologists would have traded their first born for this opportunity. Two chests possibly filled with the papers of a once-famous composer of the Baroque period. They could contain operas, many of his famous chamber duets, unpublished arias. And she would be the one to write the articles and edit the scores. Boosey & Hawkes, she knew, had begun to publish Baroque music: she also knew she could not find a better company. If anything could launch her career, this was it.

She nodded, as if this were a normal part of any job she'd ever had. Then she asked, 'And if I were to publish any of the other papers?'

He lowered his hands and said, 'I do civil law, Dottoressa: breach of contract is something my office deals with every day.'

'What does that mean, Dottore?' Caterina asked, conscious that her tone had changed.

'To do so would be a breach of contract, Dottoressa, in which event a case would surely be brought against you. It would be a very long and it would be a very expensive case.' He left it to her to assume that, though the length would concern them both equally, perhaps the cost would be more of a burden to her.

'How long would a case like this take to pass through the courts?' she asked, then explained. 'If I might ask for the sake of curiosity.'

He let the hand that still held the paper fall to his side. 'I'd imagine the least it could take is eight or nine years. That is, if the verdict were appealed.'

'I see,' Caterina said, preferring not to ask how much it might cost. 'I'm perfectly willing to agree to the conditions.'

His whole body seemed to relax, and she wondered if he had some personal interest in controlling the information in the trunks. What could he and the cousins fear would be hidden in those documents? What scandal might have survived all these generations, quietly ticking away inside two locked chests? Caterina gave herself a mental shake and dismissed the idea: to think like this was to enter into the world of paranoia in which the cousins seemed to live.

Before Dottor Moretti could thank her for agreeing, she held up a hand and said, 'I want to make something clear.' He leaned forward, the very picture of attention. 'I want to repeat that I am not a historian, so it might be necessary for me to spend time reading about the historical background in the Marciana to get some sense of what was going on when these documents were written. Is that understood?'

Dottor Moretti smiled. 'Your letters of recommendation said you were an eager student and researcher, Dottoressa. I'm happy to see signs of it now.' His smile broadened. 'Of course you can read. It will be of invaluable use, I hope, in helping you to put any events mentioned into their correct historical context.'

Roseanna broke in to say, 'I doubt that they'll like paying for historical context.' In response to Caterina's glance, she said, 'You've met them: they have blunt minds. They think in numbers and yes and no.' She looked across at Moretti.

'I think you're right, Signora, that they won't grasp the need for this,' he said. Then to Caterina: 'You're a scholar. Of course you have to do the background reading: otherwise it makes no sense for you to read anything. They won't like it, but I think I have sufficient influence with them to encourage them to allow it.' Then, after a pause, 'I think it's both essential and prudent that you do it.'

Caterina was struck by his use of that word, for Dottor Moretti, more than any other thing, was a prudent man. For Caterina, however, the term was descriptive: it could as easily be a vice as a virtue. She hoped it was a virtue in the lawyer.

Her reflections were interrupted by a loud knocking at the front door.

Dottor Moretti looked at his watch and said, looking at Roseanna, 'You were right, Signora: it's just noon. Indeed, our two guests do think in numbers.'

# 7

Roseanna got to her feet, saying, 'Dottore, might I ask you to open the door for our guests?' It was Monday, Caterina recalled, the day the library was closed to visitors, so they would have it to themselves. It was the only room she had seen with more than two chairs, and so the only place where all of them could meet. She had not seen the cousins since the interviews in that same room, when she had met with them to present her qualifications.

She and Roseanna went down the corridor to the library. The room was warmer than either her office or Roseanna's had been; the heat, unfortunately, brought out the scent of the bodies and clothing that had been present in the room during the last weeks. Roseanna went immediately to the windows and threw them wide, then returned to the door and opened it: Caterina felt the draught sweep past her and out the door. 'Keep them open as long as you can,' Roseanna said and went to receive the visitors.

Caterina, in the accidental role of major-domo, went

over to the windows and stood in the draught cutting into the room. When the footsteps approached, she shut the windows and moved back to the table. In less than a minute, Roseanna came through the door, followed by Moretti, carrying his briefcase. Caterina wondered whether the cousins would force themselves through the door side by side or stand outside to fight about who went first.

Her fantasy was wasted. Signor Stievani came in first, closely followed by his cousin, the usurer. Or would it have been better to say that the tax evader came in first, closely followed by his cousin, Signor Scapinelli? Caterina smiled with every indication of pleasure and shook hands with both men, then turned to the table and pulled out a chair for one, just as Roseanna pulled out the one opposite for his cousin. Neither of the cousins seemed surprised by her presence.

With casual authority, Dottor Moretti moved to the head of the table, waited for everyone else to sit, and then took his place. He nodded to both men and began *in medias res*. 'I've already explained the conditions of her employment to Dottoressa Pellegrini. You are both already familiar with what they are. She has no objections to any of the requirements. In fact, she was just about to sign the agreement as you arrived.' So saying, he looked at Caterina, who took the pen he handed her and signed the agreement, then passed it back to him.

Dottor Moretti opened his briefcase and pulled out a blue folder. He slipped the agreement into it and replaced it in his briefcase, which he set back on the floor, where it made a surprisingly heavy thump. 'If either of you, Signor Scapinelli or Signor Stievani, has anything to say to the Dottoressa, or to either Signora Salvi or to me, then perhaps you could do so now?'

While he spoke, Caterina studied the two men, trying

to judge whether her first opinion – negative – would find confirmation in this second encounter with them. So far, however, all they had done was sit, each carefully avoiding the sight of the other by giving their attention to Moretti.

Caterina realized that Stievani must be older than his cousin, perhaps by as much as a decade. He had the rough skin of a man who worked outside and had never thought to protect himself from the sun, skin that reminded her of the leather of Dottor Moretti's briefcase, though the lawyer had taken better care of the briefcase than Signor Stievani had of his face. Or his hands, for that matter. The knuckles of both were swollen, the fingers twisted at odd angles, perhaps from arthritis, perhaps from decades of work on boats in cold weather. She was surprised to see that his nails were neatly trimmed and filed, surely the work of a manicurist.

His nose was long and straight, his eyes clear blue under sharply arched brows. But the face was bloated and puffed up, perhaps from alcohol, perhaps from disease, removing the possibility of beauty, leaving the wreckage of a man.

When she glanced at Signor Scapinelli, her attention was drawn, as it had been the first time, to his eyes. Her memory flashed, to the vision Dante had given of the usurers. She forgot what Circle he had consigned them to – the seventh? The eighth? They sat, for all eternity, on the burning sands of Hell, flapping at falling flames the way dogs swat at flies. Around their necks hung bags, small purses that held their meaningless wealth, and Dante described the way their eyes, even in that place, feasted on the sight of those bags. Their eyes, she decided, must have been eyes like Signor Scapinelli's: deep set, never still, with dark half-moons below them.

She had watched him notice Dottor Moretti's briefcase and the gold frames of his glasses, had seen him tote up the cost of his suit, and she felt a shiver of embarrassment that she had done much the same. To save herself from her own harsh accusations, she offered the excuse that she had done it in a complimentary way, in admiration of his taste and not in envy that he had the means to permit himself that casual elegance.

Scapinelli's clothing disguised his wealth, had perhaps been chosen to achieve that end. His jacket was faintly threadbare at the cuffs, and a button had been replaced. His hands were as large as his cousin's, though much better cared for, as were, strangely enough, his teeth, where she saw evidence of a great deal of work and expense.

He was round-faced and balding and walked with the ponderous splay-footed tread of the obese, though he was not a fat man. Caterina had no clear idea how closely related the two sides of the family might once have been, but all resemblance had been worn away by the passing of time, and now the only way these men looked alike was in the possession of two eyes, a nose, and a mouth.

Scapinelli, she was reminded when he caught her glance and moved his mouth in a quick rictus, had the distracting habit of smiling at inappropriate times, as if his face were on a timer or programmed to respond to certain expressions. Strangely, the smile never came in reaction to anything funny or witty or ironic. The last time, she had attempted to figure out what the key was, but had abandoned the task as hopeless and let him smile at will.

One might dismiss him as a happy fool because of those smiles, but that would be to make a mistake, for above the vacuous smile rested those reptilian eyes.

He spoke first, in the rough voice she remembered and speaking in Veneziano. 'Good. If she's accepted all the terms, then she can go to work.' What was next? Caterina

63

wondered. They put a time clock by the front door, and she stamped in and out every day?

Dottor Moretti spoke again. 'Before she does, Signor Scapinelli, there are a few things that remain to be settled.'

'Like what?' Scapinelli asked with a pugnacity Caterina thought unnecessary.

'You gentlemen have agreed – I think very wisely – that Dottoressa Pellegrini is to have complete freedom to expand her research.'

Signor Scapinelli opened his mouth to speak, but Dottor Moretti ignored him and continued. 'She is to send me written reports of what she reads and is to pay special attention to anything that might be regarded as your ancestor's testamentary dispositions,' Dottor Moretti said. 'Which reports I will forward to both of you with great dispatch.'

There he went again, using those wonderful phrases, she thought. If only Italians could be taught to think of 'testamentary dispositions' instead of 'making a will', they'd all have one drawn up by the end of the week.

'Yes. That's right. That's what's in the paper you gave us.' Signor Stievani broke in to say. Then the clincher, 'And she signed it.'

'We want copies,' his cousin concluded.

'And how, if I might ask, is the Dottoressa supposed to write these reports?' Dottor Moretti asked.

Scapinelli turned to her and said, 'We're not buying you one.'

Caterina turned to Moretti, leaving it to him to fight her corner for her.

'Most places of employment provide their employees with a computer.'

'She's hired as "una libera professionista",' Stievani said. 'She should have her own.' He spoke of her, Caterina thought, as though she were a blacksmith who should show up with his own bag of pliers, hammers, and horseshoes. They'd provide the fire – perhaps – but the tools were up to her.

In a softer voice, Dottor Moretti said, 'I think I can take care of that.' Four faces turned to him. 'A few months ago, our office upgraded the computers we give our younger associates. The laptops they were using are still in a closet in my secretary's office. I can have someone take out whatever refers to our office. I think access to the internet is built into these things.' He waited for comment, but then added, speaking directly to Caterina, 'It's only a few years old, but it should certainly be adequate for what you have to do here.'

'That's very kind of you, Dottore,' Roseanna said, apparently delighted that a man could so casually confess to imperfect familiarity with computers. 'On behalf of the Foundation I thank you for this largesse.' Ah, yes, 'largesse', Caterina thought, charmed to hear Roseanna rise to the level of Moretti's speech. She was also impressed with the way her graciousness was likely to prevent any embarrassing questions as to why the Foundation had no computer.

'What were you going to do with them?' Signor Scapinelli interrupted.

Dottor Moretti was momentarily confused by the question but then answered, 'We usually give them to the children of our employees.'

'You give them away?' Scapinelli asked with a mixture of astonishment and disapproval.

'That way, we can deduct them from our taxes,' Dottor Moretti said, an answer that calmed Signor Scapinelli's troubled spirit, at least to the degree that a usurer's spirit can ever be calm at the revelation of an unmade profit.

'You mentioned a few things that needed to be settled,' Caterina reminded him.

'Ah, yes. Thank you, Dottoressa,' Dottor Moretti said. 'We'd like to establish some parameters for the handling of the papers.'

'Parameters,' she repeated, for the first time unimpressed by his use of language.

'Yes. We have to settle how we will go about the actual opening of the chests and decide who will be there when you remove the contents and begin to work.'

'Let me say one thing,' Caterina declared. 'I don't care who's there when the chests are opened, but I can't have anyone present while I'm working.'

'"Can't"?' Dottor Moretti inquired.

'Can't because having someone there, looking over my shoulder – even sitting at the other side of the room – would slow me down terribly. It would double the time it will take me to do the research.'

'Simply having someone in the room with you?' Dottor Moretti asked.

Before she could answer, Signor Stievani said, sounding angry or impatient, 'All right, all right. If we're there when they're opened, and we're sure there's only papers in there, then there's nothing to worry about.' Perhaps a life spent on boats led a man to believe that papers could have no value, Caterina reflected.

'We don't want her spending the rest of her life doing this, you know,' Signor Stievani went on, addressing Dottor Moretti directly; he ignored the sarcasm and heard the statement.

'Quite right,' he agreed. 'Once the trunks have been opened, we're agreed that Dottoressa Pellegrini can stay alone in the room.'

'Then I work upstairs?'

'Yes, that's the room where the work will be done,' Dottor Moretti said. 'It's got the storeroom, and there's a wireless connection.'

'Why is that?' Caterina asked Roseanna, remembering that the stolen computer had been on this floor.

Looking awkward, Roseanna said, 'Well, it doesn't exactly belong to the Foundation.'

'"Exactly"?' Caterina asked. 'Then whose is it?'

Her embarrassment grew stronger. 'I don't know.'

'Don't tell me it's someone else's Wi-Fi you're piggy-backing on?' Caterina demanded.

'Yes.'

'Do you think that's safe?' She did not bother to ask what would happen if the line were to disappear or be secured by its legal owner.

The smile was not present in Roseanna's shrug. 'I have no idea. But it's the only line we have. Dottor Asnaldi used it, and there was no trouble at all.'

Trouble came from Signor Scapinelli, who interrupted to say, 'We're not paying for any of those things. You give her a computer, you figure out how she can use it.' Then, with undisguised contempt, 'This place doesn't even have a telephone.'

'And the computer doesn't leave that room, either,' Signor Stievani added.

Caterina turned towards the men and, after allowing her anger a few seconds to dissipate, said quite pleasantly, 'I'm perfectly content to use that connection. And the computer can stay here all the time. After all, what sort of secrets can be in papers that are hundreds of years old?'

# 8

Soon after this decision was made, Caterina noticed that both cousins grew restless. First Stievani looked at his watch, and then Scapinelli did. It took her just a moment to understand: they were afraid, if this went on much longer, that they might be expected to go to lunch with these people or, worse, expected to take them to lunch. Dottor Moretti must have read the signs at the same time, for he glanced at his watch and said, speaking in general to everyone at the table, 'I hope we've made all of the major decisions that concern us.'

He looked around and saw four nodding heads. Addressing them, he said, 'Then perhaps we can remove ourselves to the upper floor and see to opening the chests.' There was no reason for Caterina to be surprised, but she was. Though everything she had done since coming back to Venice had been aimed at this goal, she was still unprepared to hear it announced. The chests would be opened, and she would see the papers – the putative papers – she would hold them in her hands, and she would be surprised, of course she would be surprised, to learn that they were the papers of Agostino Steffani, composer and bishop, musician and diplomat.

They got to their feet. At the door, the two cousins were careful to see that Dottor Moretti stood between them: Stievani went first, the lawyer next, and then Signor Scapinelli. Women and children last.

Moretti led them only as far as the door to the stairway that led to the upper floor, where he waited for Roseanna to come and unlock the door. This done, she stepped inside to allow the men to pass in front of her.

Once they were inside the Director's office Roseanna went to the metal doors of the storeroom and dealt with three separate locks. Caterina had failed to notice the third lock set almost at floor level. With no ceremony whatsoever, Roseanna pulled open the metal doors and stepped back to allow the others to see the chests that stood, one behind the other, the back one about twenty centimetres taller than the other, in the closet-sized store-room. Caterina had seen scores of similar trunks in antique shops and museums: unadorned dark wood, metal strips rimming the top and bottom and thus creating a border into which a secure locking mechanism could be anchored. The keys were missing from both keyholes.

Signor Stievani, by far the more robust of the cousins, took Dottor Moretti's arm, saying, 'Let's pull them out: you grab the other handle.' He bent over the smaller trunk and took hold of one of the handles.

Moretti was unable to hide his surprise, both at being so addressed by the other man and at the idea of being asked to help move the chest. He reacted quickly and well, however, set his briefcase down, and grabbed the second handle. From the ease with which they moved it, Caterina got an idea of the probable weight of the chest. They carried it from the storeroom and set it to the side of the desk. Then they did the same with the second chest, which seemed to Caterina to be much heavier and which they set down next to the first.

So there they were: the two chests containing the contested patrimony of the musician whose name she was not supposed to know. Both of them had what seemed to be wax-covered ropes tied around them, the first spanning front and back and the other going across the top from side to side. The first one ended in elaborate knots from which hung fragments of what must once have been a large medallion of red wax. The surface was pitted and scarred, and it was impossible to distinguish what might once have been impressed into it. Four nails held a faded rectangle of paper to the front of the smaller chest. The bottom left corner had been torn loose from the nail, taking with it a corner of the paper. Barely legible, in faded brown ink, Caterina read, in the spidery handwriting of the times, '—fani 1728.'

Before Caterina could ask how they were going to proceed, Scapinelli demanded, 'And who's going to open them?'

Dottor Moretti surprised them all by taking from his briefcase a folding knife and a large ring of what looked like antique keys. Some were rusted, some polished bright, but all ended in serrated teeth and had obviously been made by hand.

'I showed a photo of the two locks to an antiquarian friend of mine, and he sent me these,' he explained. 'He thinks some of the keys will fit.' Caterina was pleased at this very un-lawyerly behaviour on Dottor Moretti's part. Could it be that he was enjoying their trip into the past?

'Both locks?' Scapinelli asked.

'He thinks so, and I hope so,' Moretti answered.

Caterina and Roseanna exchanged approving glances, but Scapinelli made a noise. Caterina wondered if he'd expected Dottor Moretti to have arrived certain about which were the proper keys.

Hiking up the right leg of his trousers Dottor Moretti half knelt in front of the first, smaller, trunk. Methodically, holding each by the seal, he cut the ropes and left them where they lay. He cut the seal free and handed it to Caterina, who placed it carefully on the desk. Then he went through the keys one by one, inserting them and trying to turn them. A few seemed to move in the lock, but none was successful until a key quite close to the end of the ring moved to the right two times with a grinding double creak. Moretti withdrew the key and pushed at the top; after a few seconds and some shifting side to side, he managed to raise it a few centimetres but immediately set it back in place and moved to the larger trunk.

Nailed to the front was a similar piece of paper, though this one was intact and read, 'Steffani. 1728'; there was no wax wafer attached to the ropes. Again, Moretti cut through the rope and let the pieces fall to the floor. This time the key was the third or fourth he tried, though it took considerably more effort to lift this lid. When he had raised it free of the metal band, Dottor Moretti settled it back into place and got to his feet. He opened his briefcase and dropped the keys and knife inside.

'They're ours, aren't they?' Signor Scapinelli asked, pointing to the keys. It was a statement and not a question.

'I'm expecting a judgment,' Dottor Moretti said in an English only Caterina understood, but then he reverted to Italian and added, 'The keys belong to my friend, who has asked for them back.' He gave Signor Scapinelli a friendly smile and added, quite affably, 'If you and your cousin prefer, I can ask him how much he'd charge if you'd like to keep them.' He turned to Signor Stievani and said, 'Have you a preference?'

'Don't provoke me, Avvocato,' he said. 'Leave them open and send the keys back.' With a wave towards the metal doors, he added, 'Anyone who could get through those wouldn't have much trouble with these locks.' He might be a tax-evading fraud, Caterina told herself, but the man was no fool.

She looked at her watch and saw that it was almost one. 'Signori,' she began, a term in which Roseanna was included, 'I think we should make some logistical decisions. You're agreed that the trunks will stay open. But as you saw, I can hardly move them back into the storeroom myself.'

She let them consider that. She was not going to make a suggestion, knowing the greater wisdom of letting herself accede to one of theirs, so long as it was what she wanted.

She watched their reactions. Roseanna followed the same tactic by shaking her head to show she opted out of the decision and left it to the men to decide; Dottor Moretti was there in his legal capacity and so refused to express an opinion; neither cousin wanted to make a suggestion, probably fearful – or certain – that the other would block it. Finally Stievani said, 'The chests have to be locked in the storeroom at night.' He looked at all of them, not only at his cousin. When he saw consensus, he went on. 'So why don't we let her look through them to see if there's only papers? Then we put the chests back in the cupboard, and when she's done every day, she puts the papers back in the trunk and locks the cupboard, and then she locks the room.'

'And the keys?' Scapinelli asked.

'She keeps them. Otherwise we've got to figure out someone for her to give them to every day.' Just as it looked as if his cousin was going to protest, he added, 'And we'd have to pay him.' His cousin's words were left unsaid.

Dottor Moretti looked around at them all. 'It sounds sensible to me. Does anyone object?' Then, at their silence, directly to Caterina, 'Do you, Dottoressa?'

'No.'

Roseanna held up the keys and looked in turn at the three men. She then walked to the desk and placed the three keys to the storeroom, the single key to the stairs and the key to the Director's office on the reading table. Caterina nodded polite thanks.

Dottor Moretti took the opportunity of the ensuing silence to say, 'Since we have no idea what *is* inside these trunks, whether papers or objects and of what kind, and since I suppose we are all curious, to one degree or another, to have a look, I propose we ask Dottoressa Pellegrini to open them so that we can see, and then we leave her to her work.'

This time, Caterina did not wait. 'That sounds eminently sensible,' she said and approached the smaller trunk. She went down on one knee, grabbed the lid on both sides, and pulled it up until it was suspended by her left hand. Holding it upright, she looked inside and saw the reason for its lightness: it was only half full; the string-tied packets of papers on the top layer looked as though they had been shifting about for centuries, as no doubt they had. But because they were tied in the same manner as the trunks, with separate pieces of waxed string running perpendicularly and horizontally, the piles had remained intact.

She lowered the lid and heard noises of protest. '*Un momento,*' she said and went back to her bag. From it, she took a pair of white cotton gloves, slipped them on, and returned to open the trunk again.

Caterina reached in and pulled out the top packet on the left side. She carried it to the desk and placed it upside down, then returned to the trunk to take a more careful look at the remaining papers. She had heard the others move closer and now she felt their presence around her. Methodically, she began removing the papers from the left hand stack and moving them to the table, where she turned each packet upside down on top of the others. That done, she started on the other pile and repeated the process. When the trunk was empty, the cousins leaned over and peered into it to assure themselves that it was.

Signor Scapinelli gave Caterina a sideways glance, as if intending to check her sleeves, but glanced away when she looked at him.

When the cousins appeared to have seen enough, Caterina, again methodically, replaced the papers in the same order in which she had found them, leaving only the first packet she had removed, which she placed beside the keys.

Scapinelli looked at his watch, and Caterina could all but hear him thinking that it would soon be time to invite them to lunch. Hurriedly, she repeated the process of removing all of the papers in the second trunk. When it was evident that there was nothing but papers in this trunk, either, she replaced them and stepped back from the trunk. Dottor Moretti helped Stievani replace it at the back of the closet. Then they shifted the first one back into place in front of it.

Leaving the doors open, Caterina returned to the desk. She picked up the packet of papers and placed it on the other side of the desk, directly in front of the ex-Director's chair. Thus prepared for work, she turned her attention

74

to the three men in the room. She moved the three keys together on the table. 'Thank you for your help, gentlemen,' she said to Dottor Moretti and Signor Stievani.

'And now?' asked Scapinelli, looking again at his watch, no doubt driven to it by the thought of the prices on the menus of nearby restaurants.

'I'm going home to have lunch,' Roseanna said.

'I have to meet a client,' Moretti said.

Signor Scapinelli said, 'My son is waiting for me in his shop.'

And his cousin added, 'I have to get a train.'

So strong was the temptation to sing, '*Io men vado in un ritiro a finir la vita mia*' that Caterina had to press her fingernails into her palms to stop herself from doing it. When she recovered some semblance of calm, she pulled out the chair and said, 'Then I think I'll go to work.'

# 9

When they were gone, Caterina sat down. Her job was beginning now, she told herself, conscious that, even as the trunks were being opened and the first papers removed, none of the people there had seen fit to mention Steffani's name, though all of them knew it. The idea that either of the cousins could have an interest in Baroque music was absurd, and she knew nothing about Dottor Moretti beyond the elegance of his speech and dress. By her own admission, Roseanna was interested in a general sense in the music and the musicians of the period, but wisdom had kept her almost entirely silent during the meeting and the opening of the trunks. Thus, in all of this, Caterina was the only person who took a real interest in Steffani, at least as he was represented by his music. And what else mattered, really, after all this time?

He had been a priest. She recalled that he had also been mixed up in politics at the courts where he worked as a musician, but when were priests not mixed up in politics?

He might well, then, have left the whole lot to the Church. Maybe the documents would tell, but why then would Propaganda Fide have sent them back?

She tipped her chair back and latched her hands behind her head, feeling no urge to look at the papers just yet. She wanted to think about the Big Things at work here. If she did find some sort of 'testamentary disposition', it would have little legal weight, after three hundred years. Dottor Moretti must know this. '*Tanto fumo. Poco arrosto,*' she whispered aloud. There had indeed been a great deal of smoke: the suggestion that there had been other applicants for the job, the employment of a lawyer of Dottor Moretti's apparent calibre, the many restrictions surrounding the work. What, then, would the roast be? Or what did they expect it to be?

Caterina looked around the room and wondered why Roseanna had not appropriated it: after all, it was unlikely that the Foundation would ever have another Director.

'Pity you couldn't be a singer,' she told herself aloud, as if having had the courage to choose that career would have led to something more exciting than this room and the weeks of reading that no doubt lay ahead of her. Rigorous honesty intervened here and warned her that her vocal talent would have taken her, with luck, as far as the chorus of the opera house of Treviso.

She let the front legs of the chair hit the floor and pulled the packet towards her, worked at the knot in the string that held it together until it came free, wrapped it into a neat oval around her fingers, and placed it on the corner of the desk. Almost three hundred years, and it was still unbroken and strong enough to be reused. The paper on the top was a letter written in Italian in a strongly Italianate hand. It bore the date 4 January 1710 and was addressed to *Il mio fratello in Cristo Agostino*. She lifted the letter by the top corners and held it to the light. She didn't recognize the watermark, but the paper felt and looked right to justify the date.

Caterina had some trouble with the script, though none with the language or meaning. The letter made opening reference to the opera *Tassilone*, which the sender had had the immeasurable pleasure of seeing the previous year in Düsseldorf. Only now did the writer dare to break in upon the creative genius of the composer, whose time he dared not waste, by sending his humble praise of a work in which were displayed both the highest moral principles and the most sublime manifestation of musical creativity.

She glanced up from the letter and tried to dig into the musical memories lodged in her scholar's skull to get some sense of whether this was lickspittle flattery or honest praise. Steffani, she had once read, had introduced French fashions into Italian opera, a novelty imitated by that great borrower – to avoid using a different word – Handel.

The writer continued in this vein for another three paragraphs, detailing the 'countless excellencies' of the work, the 'sublime perfection' in the musical phrasing, and the 'convincing moral principles' maintained by the text.

Below this paragraph, a few bars of music were quoted: she read the first line: *'Deh, non far colle tue lagrime'*, hearing the exceptionally beautiful largo as she mouthed the words. Suddenly there appeared the voice of a solo oboe, and Caterina's voice was stilled by the enduring spell of its sound.

The page ended, and when she turned to the second, she was disappointed to see that prose had replaced beauty. Two more paragraphs carried her to the last, in which the writer, proclaiming his own unworthiness, asked the 'Most Worthy Abbé' to intercede with the Bishop of Celle in aid of the appointment of his nephew, Marco, to the post of choirmaster at the church of St Ludwig. The signature was illegible, as in the manner of signatures of those times.

Below this, in a different, backward-slanting hand, was written, 'Good man. See if this can happen.' Nothing more.

She reached into her bag and pulled out a notebook and pen. '1. Letter of request for position as choirmaster. Favourable comment in different hand on bottom. 4/1/1710.' Perhaps Marco would show up again; perhaps another letter would thank the 'Most Worthy Abbé' for his help in winning the position for the young man.

The next paper was a letter dated 21 June 1700, addressed to *Mio caro Agostino*, the familiarity of which salutation brought the scholar in her to the equivalent of a hunting dog's freezing at point. There was general talk of work and travel, mutual friends, the problem with servants. Then things turned to gossip, and the writer told his friend Agostino about Duke N. H.'s public behaviour with his brother's wife at the last ball of Carnevale. The third son of G. R. had died of bronchial trouble, to his parents' utmost grief, in which the writer joined them: he was a good boy and barely eight years old. And then the writer told his friend that he had overheard Baron (it looked like 'Bastlar' but might just as easily have been 'Botslar') speaking slightingly of Steffani and making fun of him for singing along with his operas while attending them in the audience. The writer thought his friend should know of this, should he receive compliments or promises from the Baron. Then, with affectionate wishes for Agostino's continued good health, the writer placed his illegible signature at the bottom.

Caterina made notes of the contents and made no comment, though she felt something close to outrage that a mere baron would make fun of a musician. She set the letter aside and picked up the next document. Her heart stopped. It was entirely involuntary: the shock of seeing it grabbed her heart and tightened her throat. On top of the pile now lay a sheet of music, the notes doing their visual dance across the lines from left to right. Making no sound that could be heard by anyone, she began to sing the music line by line, heard the bass line and the violins. When she turned to the second page, she saw the words and knew she was no longer giving voice to the instruments but was singing an aria.

She turned back to the first page and let her mind play through the music again. Oh, how perfect it was, that figure in the introduction, only to be repeated in the high register, right from the start of the aria. She looked at the words and saw the predictable, *'Morirò tra strazi, e scempi.'* And who had churned out that sentiment, she wondered? 'I'll die between pain and havoc.' If she could find a time machine, she'd go back and pick up most of the men who wrote libretti and bring them back to the present, though she'd drop them off in Brazil, where they could all get jobs writing the scripts for *telenovelas*.

A glance at the opening words for the second line, *'E dirassi ingiusti dei'*, confirmed her in her temporal and geographical desires. She read through to the end of the aria, concentrating on the music, not the words. 'Well, well, well,' she said out loud and then turned off the music by looking away from the paper. 'Wasn't he a clever devil?'

She wished now that she had paid more attention to his music while at university and had seen more than the single performance of the wonderful *Niobe* in London. The genius manifest in this aria proved him to be a composer with a far greater gift than she had before thought him to possess. She paused: could it be that it had been sent to him by a colleague or a musician or even a student? She re-examined the manuscript, but there was no attribution and no signature, only the same back-slanting handwriting she had seen in the note on the bottom of the first letter.

Identification could be made in the archives of the Marciana: all she had to do was go there and have a look at one of Steffani's autograph scores, even find a book with a reproduction of a few pages of a score in his hand. She had a good visual memory and could take a clear image of the aria with her. But how much easier to stay here and read on: sooner or later, she was bound to come upon a signed score. She cheated by paging ahead to the bottom of the packet: no more music.

The beauty of the music drew her eyes back to the aria. She made a note of the probable title of the aria, then turned it face down to uncover yet another document in ecclesiastical Latin, this a letter from 1719, addressed to him as Bishop and attempting to explain the delay in forwarding him his benefice from the dioceses of Spiga, wherever that might be.

After making a note of the contents of this letter, Caterina looked at her watch and saw that it was after two. Almost as if the sight of the time had released her from the spell of her own curiosity, she realized how hungry she was. She opened her bag and pulled out her wallet. She opened flaps and slots until she found her reader's card for the Biblioteca Marciana. It had expired two years before. In a normal country, in a normal city, one would go and renew the card, but that was to be certain that a clear, prompt process for doing so existed or functioned. Though Caterina had not lived in Italy for a number of years, she had no reason to believe that things had changed, and so her first thought was to find a way to get what she wanted without having to waste time with a system that, if memory served and if things had remained the same, exulted in creating ways to block people from having what they deserved or desired.

She ran her memory through the gossip and news of the last decade: who worked where, who had married, who had inserted themselves into the mechanism that kept the city going. And she recalled Ezio, dear Ezio, who had gone to school with her sister Clara and who had been in love with her for three years, from the time they were twelve until they were fifteen, and who had then fallen in love with someone else and subsequently married her, retaining Clara as best friend.

Ezio, by common agreement, was as clever as he was lazy and had never wanted success or a career: only to marry and have lots of children. He had them now, four, she thought, but he also had – and this is why Ezio came to mind – a job as librarian at the Biblioteca Marciana.

Caterina replaced the papers in the packet, but did not bother to tie it closed. She went to the storeroom and put it into the smaller trunk, then closed the door and locked it, using all three keys.

Only then did she go back to her bag and pull out her *telefonino*. The number, not used for a long time, was still in the memory. She dialled it and, after he answered, said, *'Ciao, Ezio, sono la Caterina. Volevo chiederti un favore.'*

# 10

Caterina felt no regret at so peremptorily having left Manchester, but she did regret having had to leave her books in storage, an act that made her entirely dependent upon the internet and public collections of books. Ezio had told her to come to the library at four, so after she stopped for a *panino* and a glass of water, standing at the bar as she had done as a student, she did another student-esque thing and went into an internet café. It would take her too long to go home and use her own computer to do the basic research, and all she wanted was to have the basic chronology of Steffani's life fresh in her memory when she went to the library.

Her grandmother had been famous in the family for keeping her memory all her life, and Caterina was the grandchild said most to resemble her. As she read about Steffani's life, she justified family tradition, for most of the information was coming back to her: born in Castelfranco in 1654, he was early seen to be a talented singer and musician, choirboy at the Basilica del Santo in Padova from the age of ten. A nobleman from Munich was seduced by the beauty of Steffani's voice and took him home with him, where he had tremendous success as a musician and a composer. After two decades, he moved to Hanover, where he had more of the same. He seemed to drift away from music while he devoted himself to politics, working for the Catholic cause in a country whose rulers had decided to turn it Protestant.

'Ernst August,' she said out loud as she came upon a reference to the Duke of Hanover: yes, she remembered him. Here the writer of the article opened a parenthesis (and explained that Ernst August's people built him the most sumptuous opera house in Germany, not to delight him, but to attempt to keep him from taking his yearly, and ruinously expensive, trips to the Carnevale in Venice). His son, Georg Ludwig, was to become George I of England. Like most people trained in research, Caterina willingly gave in to its intoxication and sent Google running off after Georg Ludwig: wasn't there some scandal about his wife? Soon enough, there she was, the beautiful Sophie Dorothea, the greatest beauty and most desirable marital catch of the era; married at sixteen to Georg Ludwig (another parenthesis explained that they were first cousins) before being caught in adultery, divorced, and imprisoned for more than thirty years until her death. It all made fascinating reading, but it didn't tell her much about Steffani.

She went back to the original window and continued to read about his life after his virtual abandonment of music; he shuttled about endlessly on diplomatic missions here and there. He spent six years in Düsseldorf, chiefly concerned with political and ecclesiastical matters, producing his last three operas there. He appeared to have prevented a war between the Pope and the Holy Roman Emperor, both of them embroiled in the War of the Spanish Succession, and who remembered what that was all about? He had spent a good deal of his non-musical life attempting to persuade various North German rulers to return to the arms of Holy Mother Church. Caterina looked up from the computer and let her eyes trail to the façade of the church of Santa Maria della Fava. Suddenly her soul was enwrapped by Vivaldi, an aria for *Juditha Triumphans*, what were the words? *'Transit aetas/Volant anni/Nostri damni/ Causa sumus.'* How gloriously simple the score was: mandolin and pizzicato violin, and a single voice warning us that time passes, the years fly by, and we are the cause of our own destruction. What better message to give to the leaders of those empty churches? We are the cause of our own destruction.

'Would you like another half-hour, Signora?' the young Tamil at the cash register called to her. 'Time's up in five minutes, but you can stay online for another half-hour for two Euros.'

'No, that's fine. Thank you for asking, though,' she said and resisted the urge to look for the aria on YouTube. Steffani moved back to Hanover in 1709, but there was no further mention of his music, only travel and political involvement. Almost no more music. Was genius painful? she wondered. Did it, at some point, simply cost too much for the spirit to continue to create? As she watched, the screen went blank, taking with it Steffani, his music, the Church he served, and all of his desires to restore that Church to her former power. She picked up her bag, thanked the young man at the desk, and started towards the library.

It took her no more than ten minutes to get there; to pass in front of the two caryatids and into the lobby of the Marciana was to move from the constant crowding of the Piazza into the calm tranquillity that thoughts and the books that contained them were meant to give. She stood for a moment, as if she were a diver waiting to decompress, and then she approached the guard and mentioned Ezio's name. He smiled and waved her through an apparently deactivated metal detector and into the foyer of the library.

One of the guards must have phoned him, for by the time Caterina got to the head of the stairs, Ezio was there, coming towards her with outstretched hands. There were lines around his eyes, and he seemed both thinner and shorter than he had been the last time she saw him, almost a decade ago. But the brightness and the smile were the same. He wrapped her in a tight hug, pushed her free of him, kissed her on both cheeks, and then they took turns saying all of those sweet things that old friends say after not meeting for years. All of her sisters were fine, his kids were growing, and what was it she wanted him to do?

She explained the need to find information about a Baroque composer for a research project she was doing for the Foundation, of which he had heard, though vaguely. There was no need to explain any more. He said she was welcome to use the stacks as much as she liked, then excused himself and said he'd go and organize a reading card for her as a visiting scholar.

'No,' he said, turning back to her. 'Let me take you up to the stacks. You can get an idea of what's there.' When she began to protest, he refused to listen, saying, 'You're a friend of mine, so don't worry about the rules. Once I get you the card, you have access to almost everything.' He set off to the right and led her into the long gallery she recalled from her student days. The marble floor might have served as a chessboard for two opposing tribes of giants: there were far more than sixty-four squares, and a giant could stand on each of them. The glass viewing cases displayed manuscripts, but they passed through so quickly she could distinguish nothing more than the even lines of script and the large illuminated letter on some pages. The enormous globes of the Earth appeared to be the same, as did the outrageous vaulted ceiling without an inch of empty space. Why were we Venetians so excessive? Caterina asked herself. Why did there always have to be so much of everything, and all of it beautiful? She glanced out the windows and had a momentary sensation that the Piazza was hurrying past her stationary self.

She followed him from the gallery, like Theseus on his way to slay the Minotaur, thinking that she, too, should leave a trail of string behind. Turn and turn and turn about, and soon she had no idea where they were. These were inner rooms, so she could not orient herself by looking out and seeing the Basilica or the *bacino*.

At long last, they entered a room that had a row of windows, and beyond them she could see the long expanse of windows on the Palazzo Ducale across the Piazza. 'How do you find anything?' she asked when Ezio pointed to a wall of shelves.

'Do you mean a room or a book?' he asked.

'Both. I'd never find my way out of here. And how do I know what's here?' she asked, looking around for the computer terminals.

Smiling a broad smile, Ezio led her over to a shoulder-high wooden cabinet the front of which was entirely filled with small drawers. 'Do you remember?' he asked, patting the top of the cabinet. 'I saved it,' he said, obviously boasting.

'*Oddio*,' she exclaimed, 'It's a card catalogue.' When had she last seen one? And where? She approached it as a true believer would approach a relic. She reached out and touched it, ran her hand along the top and side, slid her finger under a flange and pulled a drawer out a few centimetres, then slid it silently back into place. 'It's been a decade. More.' In a conspiratorial voice, she said, 'I love them. They're so full of information.' Then, lower still, 'What did you do?'

In the voice of an actor in a war film suffering from shell shock, he said, 'They were going to destroy all of the cards. My superior told me: it was a direct order.' He paused and took in two very melodramatic breaths. 'First I threatened to quit if they removed it.'

She covered her mouth with her hands, though it was insufficient evidence of her horror. Then she said, 'You're here, so you didn't quit. What happened?'

'I threatened to tell his wife he was having an affair with one of my colleagues.'

Instead of laughing, which would have been her normal response, she asked, 'Would you have done it?'

Ezio shook his head. 'I don't know, really. Maybe.'

'But he gave in?'

'Yes. He said we could keep them, but we weren't to let anyone use them. The bulletin he sent said that the catalogue was to be fully computerized and the only access to the collection was to be via the computer.' Ezio made a gesture that looked suspiciously like spitting on the floor. 'He told us to do it, and then he cut our funding. So there's no money.'

'And the computer catalogue?'

He paused, smiled, changed roles and became any diplomat when asked a direct question. 'It's being worked on.'

'And your superior?' she inquired.

Again, the gesture. 'He's been reassigned to a provincial

library.' Before she could ask, Ezio explained: 'It seems three of the last people he hired were relatives of his wife.'

'Where is he working now?'

'Quarto d'Altino.' He smiled. 'It's rather a small library.'

As so often happened when Caterina heard the tales told by friends or colleagues who had remained to work in Italy, she didn't know whether to laugh or cry.

She set her bag on one of the tables at the centre of the room and opened it to take out notebook and pencil. Ezio said, 'I'll get you your entrance card.' He indicated an empty carrel that stood between two of the windows. 'You can use that one if you want. Leave the books there while you're using them. When you're finished, put them on the desk near the door over there,' he said, pointing to the desk, 'and they'll be reshelved.'

She nodded her thanks. Ezio said, 'This might take some time,' and left.

Caterina went over to the window and looked down at the Piazza. People passed to and fro, few bothering to look to the sides of the Piazza: everyone was intent on the façade of the Basilica, as Caterina thought they should be, and those leaving often turned around to have another glimpse of it from a distance, as if needing to assure themselves that it was not an illusion. To her right, the flags flapped in the freshness of springtime, and she relaxed into the ridiculous beauty of the place.

Turning from this, she went to the catalogue and found the drawer that ran from Sc to St. From Scarlatti to Strozzi, which would also contain Stradella and Steffani. Under 'Steffani' she found entries in many different handwritings and just as many spellings of his name. She also found a cross-reference to 'Gregorio Piva', which a feathery note on the card explained was the pseudonym he used for the musical compositions of his later years. She retrieved her notebook and wrote down the call numbers for the books that looked like biographies of Steffani or might be more concerned with his life than with his music, then went to the shelves and began to hunt for the volumes.

By the time Ezio came back, more than an hour later, Caterina was sitting in the carrel with about forty centimetres of books lined up on the shelf in front of her. She turned when she heard him come in, keeping her finger in the book she was reading. He placed the card on the open page, bent down to give her a kiss on the cheek and, saying nothing, left the room. Caterina put the card in the pocket of her jacket and went back to reading.

The habits of the scholar had dominated Caterina's selection. First check the publisher to see how serious the book was likely to be, and then a quick check: anything that appeared to be self-published or that lacked notes or bibliography, she left on the shelves. What scholars were thanked in the acknowledgements? The culling process had taken some time, leaving her delighted that so much had been written about Steffani.

She started to take notes. Same information about the family: humble but not poor. Early gift for music. At twelve, so beautiful was his voice that while still a choir student in Padova, he had been sent to sing some opera performances in Venice. Was it success that had made him outstay his leave by several weeks? Despite his curt letter of apology, no punishment was given when he returned to Padova.

The Elector of Bavaria heard him singing in Venice and invited him to Munich, where Steffani was appointed musician to the court. To perfect his art, he was sent to Rome for a time and no doubt began his ecclesiastical training while there. His upward rise continued, all fairly normal for an ambitious young man of his era.

His career took wing with his move to Germany. Soon he was an abbé, though Caterina could find no reference to his ever having said a mass or administered any of the sacraments. Was Abbé merely a title or did it entail clerical obligation as well as status?

She pulled her thoughts from speculation and returned to Munich and to Steffani's growing fame as a composer. He was in the employ of a Catholic Elector and much in his favour, but in 1688 he chose to leave when the position of kapellmeister, which he believed he deserved, was bestowed on Giuseppe Antonio Bernabei, the son of the composer who had been his teacher in Rome.

Luckily, he had been seen and heard in Munich by Ernst August, the Protestant Duke of Hanover, who headed a court thought by some to rival that of France. Invited there as a musician, Steffani accepted and was soon moving in the highest intellectual circles, a friend of philosophers – Leibniz for one – musicians, and aristocrats.

His talent apparently flourished, his reputation grew, and he turned out yearly operas to ever-greater success. But then in the early 1690s, when it seemed he could become no more famous than he was, he suspended it all to go on a delicate ambassadorial mission which two writers attributed to the need to 'convince other German states to look with favour on the accession of Ernst August to the title of Elector of Hanover'.

After the death of Ernst August, Steffani moved for a few years to the court of the Catholic Elector Palatine at Düsseldorf, where he worked as a privy councillor to the Elector and at the same time as President of the Spiritual Council – another mystery to Caterina. His social stature must have risen, because he used a pseudonym for the operas he still continued to write, no doubt to avoid popular suspicion should a high-ranking clergyman engage in behaviour as morally and socially compromising as the writing of operas. As for writing under his own name, there were only the chamber duets and the Stabat Mater, which he wrote towards the end of his life.

Grateful for all his services, the Elector Palatine interceded on Steffani's behalf with the Vatican. The Pope finally gave in and made him a bishop. When she read that this was, unfortunately, only titular and produced almost no income, Caterina muttered, 'The wily bastards.' Then, unexplained, Steffani abandoned the Catholic duchy and returned to Protestant Hanover, where he remained until his death.

The books contained two pictures of him, the more common a lithograph made a century after his death and said to be a copy of an original, though in the ensuing century someone had added a goatee to his chin, as unflattering and unconvincing as those added to the photos of unpopular politicians. The other was the contemporary portrait of him that she recalled, wearing his bishop's cap. In the first, he looked earnest and busy, with his bishop's mitre and crozier visible behind him. In the second, he was dressed in his ecclesiastical best. He looked reserved, but chiefly he looked well-fed.

If there was no mention that he had ever said mass or performed a marriage ceremony or buried the dead or heard a confession, then why was he pictured both times in the regalia of his clerical position? He had spent the bulk of his life as a singer, composer, and diplomat, yet neither author could find a visual record of any of these, and one claimed that such images did not exist.

More importantly, for her immediate purposes, how could such a man accumulate 'treasure', and what form would it take? And if he did have it, why then did most accounts state that he had died in debt and poverty after first selling off most of his possessions? Why should he sacrifice a passion for a duty and die poor as a result?

Caterina glanced at her watch and saw that it was after seven. She felt the sudden, irrational fear of being locked inside overnight and snapped the book closed. She took out her *telefonino* and dialled Ezio's number. It rang five times before he answered, saying, 'I'm on my way to get you, Caterina. Be there in three minutes.'

Pretending, even to herself, that she had known he was there and would come for her, she put the book back on the shelf, put her pencil and notebook in her bag, and had a more careful look around the room. She went to stand in front of the card catalogue filled with the names of the people who had given music to the world, herself filled with a pride that surprised her: we have done so much; we have made so much beauty. Subtract Italy, wipe it from history, perhaps even cancel the peninsula from the Continent, and what would Western culture be? Who would have painted their portraits, or built their churches, designed their clothing, given them the concept of law? Or taught them how to sing?

Ezio's entrance broke into these reflections, which she decided to keep to herself. 'Did you find what you wanted?' he asked.

'Too much,' she said. 'I found four biographies, endless histories of the music of the period, of the politics of the times.'

'Will it be enough to answer your questions?' He sounded very interested. She remembered that Ezio had a degree in history and had more or less learned about libraries as he worked in one.

'That depends on what I find in the documents,' she

said. Then, on an impulse, she asked, 'Am I allowed to take books with me?'

'Which ones?' he asked.

Turning back to the shelf, she pulled out one book, then another, then replaced that with a different one. 'These,' she said, showing him the two books.

He studied them, examining the bindings and not the titles, as if there were some secret library code hidden in their call numbers, then said, 'No.'

'Oh, sorry,' she said, realizing she had asked too much and reaching for the books.

'But I can,' Ezio said, slipping them under his arm.

Caterina laughed, then the scholar in her said, 'But you have to log them out.'

Still smiling at his own joke, Ezio said, 'Don't worry about it. I've known you for so many years, I know you're not going to disappear with the books. Believe me, it's easier this way.' He took her arm.

'What happens when I try to bring them back?'

'You just carry them in and put them back on that table down there,' he said, turning to point towards the restacking table.

'But how can I bring them in if they haven't been checked out?'

Confusion was written across his face. 'Just keep them in your bag and show them your card.'

'Won't they register when I go through the metal detector?'

'Of course not,' he said. 'It registers only metal.'

'Ah,' she said. 'Of course, a *metal* detector.'

Then, perhaps to keep her from getting ideas she shouldn't, he said, 'The machines at the public exit register chips in the bindings, so you can't take books out.'

Of course, she thought: who'd sneak a book into a library?

She stopped. They had come again to the front of the building, and there, ahead of them and off to the left, was the façade of the Basilica. 'What an absurd building that is,' she said. 'Look at it: all those domes and the arcs and the pillars all different from one another. Who'd build a thing like that?' she asked.

'We're in Italy, *cara mia*. Anything is possible.' He handed her the books.

# 11

They went into Florian's, to the bar at the back, and each ordered a spritz. The barman recognized Ezio and, smiling at Caterina, put a dish of cashews in front of them.

Taking one, she asked, 'Is this your reward for being an habitué? The most I ever get is peanuts.'

He laughed and took a drink. 'No. He's an old friend. We went to school together, so he always gives them to me.'

'It doesn't end, does it?' she asked, a remark that confused him.

'What doesn't end?'

'The advantages of having been born here,' she explained. Then, more soberly 'I saw in the paper this morning that there are now fewer than fifty-nine thousand of us.'

Ezio shrugged. 'I don't see what we can do. Old people die. Young people get jobs in other places. There's no work here.' Tilting his glass in her direction, he said, 'You're the lucky exception. You got called home to take a job.' Before she could respond, he asked, 'Are you staying with your family?'

'No,' she said. 'An apartment came with the job.'

'What?'

'An apartment. It's not much, and it's down in Castello, but it has three rooms and it's on the top floor.'

'Are you making this up?' he asked.

'No, not at all. It's just on the other side of Via Garibaldi, so it's easy enough to get to work.'

'How'd that happen?'

Here Caterina gave him an edited version of the facts, saying that the Foundation had an apartment it offered to visiting scholars. This was not true, and the apartment belonged to Scapinelli, who had agreed that she could stay in it while she did the research. It was usually rented out to tourists and was decorated – though Caterina thought that word an exaggeration – in the style that Venetians thought tasteful.

'Lucky you,' he said. 'Job and apartment.'

'Both temporary,' she reminded him.

He ate a few cashews and asked, 'You have any idea how long it might last?'

She shook her head. 'God knows.' She reached towards the books he had set on the counter. 'May I?'

'Oh, sure, sure,' Ezio said, handing them to her.

'The more I read, the sooner it will be done.'

'And then?'

She shrugged, then slipped the books into her bag. 'No idea. I've got job applications out all over the place: in four countries.'

'Where?' he asked, interested enough to set his glass down.

She counted them out on her fingers. 'Here, though I might as well forget about that. It's only teaching; no time for research.' Seeing how real his curiosity was, she went on, 'Germany, Austria, and the United States.'

'You'd go?' he asked, astonished.

This time, she waved the question away with her hand. 'If the job is interesting, yes. I'd go.'

'Well, good for you,' he said, meaning it. 'You've got the advantage of the language, haven't you?'

If the remark had come from another person, Caterina might have heard it as criticism of the advantage she had, but from Ezio it was admiration.

It came to her to say that she had the advantage of more than one language, but it would have sounded like boasting, and she didn't want to do that, so she contented herself with nodding in agreement.

He finished his drink. Half of the cashews were still in the glass bowl, but neither of them wanted any more. Caterina finished her drink and pulled out a ten Euro note. She placed it on the bar and caught the waiter's eye.

The waiter shook his head and made no move to approach them.

To Ezio, she said, 'Please let me pay. It's the least I can do.'

'No,' he said, pulling out his wallet. 'That would be close to taking a bribe, and you know how unthinkable such a thing is in our society.' He went on, and she remembered the clowning that had so charmed them all for years, 'I could not live with myself were I to believe, even for an instant, that I had somehow profited from my professional situation or shown favouritism in any way to someone who is a member of my family or a friend.' He pulled out a note and placed it on the counter, then looked at her, raised his hands as if to push away the approach of the Devil himself, and said, 'It would shame my ancestors.'

She gave him a soft punch in the arm and said, 'I'd forgotten that about you.'

'What?'

'How ridiculous you are.'

He heard the praise in her voice and laughed.

It was almost nine when Caterina got back to the apartment. After the cashews, she wasn't very hungry, so she decided to read for a while.

She pulled the two books out of her bag and walked to the sofa: it was a pale thing covered in rough, oatmeal-coloured cloth that silently screamed 'Ikea,' as did the tables, bookcases, light fixtures, curtains, and chairs. It had the single grace of being comfortable, so long as she put herself lengthwise, propped against the equally drab cushions.

She looked at the cover of the first book for a long time, studied the portrait of Steffani in the robes of Suffragan Bishop of Münster, whatever a suffragan bishop was. Plump of face and probably of body – the robes made that hard to distinguish – Steffani had a look of almost unbearable sadness. Thick-nosed and double-chinned, this man who was no longer composing music stared directly at the viewer, his long-fingered hand suspending the bejewelled cross he wore on a thick chain. His bald pate disappeared under his cap, leaving only puffs of hair on either side. It was a badly painted thing: were she to see it in a museum, she'd walk past it without bothering to find out the name of the subject or the painter; were she to see it in a gallery or shop, she wouldn't give it a second glance. It was interesting only because she knew the subject and hoped to decipher the painting.

She opened the book and started to read. Family background nothing special, a repetition of what she'd already read about his musical beginnings in Padova and Venice. Same story about overstaying his leave in Venice, although this time she learned that he claimed the delay resulted from an invitation to sing for a very important person, perhaps in private.

Not only was Caterina considered to be the intelligent daughter; she was also deemed the hard-nosed cynic of the family, though this was not a difficult title to earn in a family of decent, optimistic people. Thus the fact that an adolescent boy had chosen to remain behind in Venice to sing at the expressed desire of an older man who might have been an aristocrat and who was, at least, *un soggetto riguardevole* opened to her a possibility that the average person perhaps might not have contemplated at the combination of a young boy and an important man. She turned back to the cover. Almost fifty years had passed between the time of Steffani's prolonged stay in Venice and the painting of the portrait. It was hard to imagine this puffy-faced cleric ever having been a young boy with a beautiful voice.

She read on. Transferred to Munich at the invitation of the Elector of Bavaria, Ferdinand Maria, who had heard him sing, the young Steffani joined the court at the age of thirteen. Caterina began to nod as she read the names and titles of the people he met there, the musicians with whom he worked. Maybe it was time for dinner, for a coffee, for a glass of wine? The list of names and places continued, and then she found a passage from a letter Steffani had written late in life, describing his meeting with the Elector, who, according to Steffani, 'was attracted by something he must have seen in me – to what end I do not know – and, having taken me immediately to Munich with him, placed me in the care of Count Tattenbach, his master of horse.'

'I beg your pardon,' Caterina heard herself say aloud in English, repeating the language of the book. She went back and read the passage again: 'was attracted by something he must have seen in me – to what end I do not know.'

She set the book down and got to her feet, went into the small kitchen and opened the refrigerator. She pulled out a bottle of white wine and poured herself a glass. She raised it in a toast, either to the air or to Steffani, or perhaps to her own perfervid imagination, and took a sip.

The kitchen had one small window that looked across the *calle* to the house on the other side, directly into the kitchen of the family that lived there. She leaned back into the living room and switched off the light, leaving herself in the darkness, glass in hand, looking out and now invisible from beyond the window.

There they were: Mamma Bear, and Papa Bear, and the two Baby Bears, a boy about eight and a younger sister. They sat around the table, still eating; they all looked relaxed and happy. Occasionally, one of them would say something, and one or two of the others would react with a change of expression or a smile, often a gesture. The boy finished whatever it was he was eating, and the mother cut him another piece of what Caterina now saw was a cake. Tall, light in colour, with darker-chunks that, this time of year, were likely to be apples or pears; perhaps both. It looked good enough to remind her of how hungry she was. But, while they were still there and still eating, she did not want to turn on the light and become as visible to them as they were to her. The boy suddenly reached his fork across the table and speared a piece of cake from his sister's portion. He held it up on the end of his fork and waved it in front of her, then brought it, in narrowing circles, towards his mouth.

Caterina heard nothing, but she saw the father lower his own fork and glance aside at his son. Instantly the circling stopped, and the boy leaned across the table and replaced the morsel on his sister's plate. The father turned towards him again. The boy bowed his head and finished his own piece of cake, then got down from his chair and left the room.

She left them to finish their meal and took her wine back to the sofa. She set the glass down and picked up the book, continued reading at the place where she had left off.

There was no record of Steffani at the court the first year he was in Munich, neither as a salaried musician nor as a member of the orchestra. When he did begin to appear in the voluminous records, he was being given organ lessons by the Kapellmeister, Johann Kerll, who received a significant sum beyond his normal salary to teach him. By 1671, Steffani was being pampered with 'a daily ration of one and a half measures of wine and two loaves of bread'. Further, he had advanced to the position of '*Hof und Cammer Musico*'.

'*Oddio,*' she said out loud and set the book aside. There it was, the thing she had only suspected while at the same time reproving herself for thinking such a thing. She picked up her glass and finished the wine; then, turning the light on and not giving a thought to the three people who were still at the table in the house across the *calle*, she went into the kitchen and poured herself another glass.

'*Musico. Musico,*' she said aloud. She remembered a patter aria from a riotously funny production of *Orlando Paladino* she had seen in Paris that spring in which the word was also used. Even after the era of their greatness was finished, Haydn had still used the code to make fun of them. She'd read the word in scores and letters: when certain Baroque singers were described by contemporary writers or listeners as *musico*, they had always been castrati.

'*Oddio*,' she repeated, thinking of the man in the portrait, with his pudgy, beardless face, and his look of patient, unbearable sadness.

# 12

She woke at nine the following morning. After finding
that word, *musico*, the previous evening, all she had been
able to do was make herself some pasta, finish the bottle
of wine, and go to bed with the second of the books she
had taken from the library. But by the time she got under
the covers, she was too tired, or too sodden, to be able to
follow much of what she read, and she fell asleep, only
to wake in the night, close the book and put it on the floor,
turn off the light, and go back to sleep.

There was no sign of the Bear family when she went
into the kitchen to make coffee the next morning, and their
kitchen looked as clean as her own did not. 'I think it's
time you started having a life, Caterina,' she said to herself
as the coffee began to bubble up in the pot.

'Or a job with a future,' her more sensible, pragmatic
self added.

She wondered if this is what happened to unemployed
musicologists: they ended up in rented apartments filled

with Ikea furniture, looking into the windows of their neighbours for reminders of human life? In order to give herself a sense of purpose, she did the dishes from the night before and put the empty wine bottle – telling herself it had been less than half full – into the plastic container meant to hold glass and plastic garbage. That was one positive change in the city since she had moved away: differentiated garbage collection. The thought depressed her, not that the city had such a thing but that she would measure progress in these terms. No new ideas, no new politics, no influx of young people with houses and jobs; only paper on Monday, Wednesday, and Friday, and plastic on Tuesday, Thursday, and Saturday. On Sunday, God and the garbage men rested. It would make a stone weep; so would the fact that most of her friends believed that it all ended up in the same place, anyway, and the whole thing was merely a scam to enable the company that did the collecting to raise the price. She abandoned these thoughts and went to take a shower.

Half an hour later, having stopped for a brioche and another coffee, she walked out on to Riva dei Sette Martiri, having decided to take advantage of the sun and bask in beauty on her way to work. The golden angel seemed to dance in the breeze from his post on top of the bell tower of San Giorgio. The sight of it lifted her spirits to such a degree that she wanted to wave at him and ask him how things were up there.

She remembered something the Romanian, in one of his rare moments of sobriety, had asked her once: how was it that angels got dressed? In response to her astonished look, he had insisted he was quite serious, and she was the only person he could ask. 'I see how their wings come out when they get undressed – that's easy: the cloth passes the right way over the feathers – but wouldn't it disturb their feathers to have to push them through their sleeves when they put them on?' It was evident that this lack of certainty troubled him. 'Do they have buttons?' he asked.

Her visual memory had summoned up Fra Angelico's *Annunciation* in Florence, the angel kneeling, star-struck, before the baffled Virgin. His multi-coloured striped wings stuck out behind him: of course the girl looked puzzled. The Romanian, she had to admit, had a point: a careful angel could probably fold them up and unbutton his side vents when he put his robe on, but slipping them through would still snag a lot of the feathers. Slipping them off would be easier, for the cloth would run along the feathers easily, as the Romanian had pointed out. Maybe they never, being angels, needed to change their clothes?

Illumination came and she had smiled at him with an all-knowing expression. 'Velcro.'

'Ah,' had escaped his parted lips, and he bent to kiss her hand. 'You people in the West know so many things.'

She turned in just before the church of the Pietà and worked her way back past the church of the Greci until she arrived at the Foundation. She let herself in, stopped in Roseanna's office, but there was no sign of her. She opened the door to the stairs and went up to the Director's office, let herself in, and set her bag on the table. She unlocked the storeroom and took out the packet of papers she had left in the smaller trunk. Leaving the doors open, she went back to the table, put down the folder, and took out her notebook. Whispering the word '*musico*', she resumed reading the papers where she had left off the day before.

There was an affectionate letter from a priest in Padova, apparently a childhood friend, who told his 'Dear friend and brother in Christ, Agostino,' that the various members of his own family were all well and, with the help of God, would so remain. He sent his wishes and prayers that the same would remain true for his friend Agostino's family. In the absence of substance, all she could do was note the date of the letter.

The next was a document from October 1723, containing a list of the candelabra, books, relics, and paintings left to the church of St Andreas in Düsseldorf by a certain Johann Grabel. The candelabra were in brass and silver, the books all on religious themes, the relics a series of desiccated extremities, including the big toe of Saint Jerome. 'Left or right?' Caterina asked aloud. The paintings were portraits of saints, with a heavy preponderance of martyrs. Below this list was written, in Italian, in that backward hand, 'To the Jesuits. Fool.' She made a note and passed the document to her left.

She continued for another two hours, finding a random sample of letters from the later part of Steffani's life and all addressed to him, that contained requests for help of one sort or another, praise, ecclesiastical news, and more than a few requests for payment for articles such as wine, books, and paper. The letters came in from all over Europe, but strangely enough none of them made any further reference to music nor to Steffani's work as a musician. For all the evidence found in these papers, he might have been a clergyman and only that for his entire life. By the time she got to the last of the papers in the packet, there had been just that single aria to give evidence of a life beyond the Church.

She pushed the papers away from her and rested her chin on her palms and found herself thinking about her family. They had been lucky in one thing: none of them had had to survive the death of a child. One of her aunts and two of her uncles had died relatively young, but not before their parents and not before having had children. Two of her sisters had children, whom they loved to distraction. And she still had time to have them. Here, her inner cynic broke in to observe that, in a decade, it would probably be normal for women in their fifties and sixties to have children, so there was no sense of urgency, was there?

What would it be like, though, to know you'd never have them and not through your own choice? Would it bother a man to the degree that it tormented women?

She had never been especially curious about the sex lives of the castrati, had not bothered to see the film about Farinelli some years ago. She had read, years ago, of the tens of thousands of boys to whom it was done, all in the hope of producing a star. The lurid novel lying on the shelf in the Foundation's library could lie there until doomsday for all she cared. She had never bothered to speculate about what they did or did not do, and knew she did not care. She wondered only what they lost in terms of the bonding that came with parenthood, and was that worse than knowing there would be no children, no one to pass things along to, no one to teach or tickle? Was that the message in that sad man's eyes?

She reached out abruptly, retrieved the string and rewrapped the packet, took it back to the closet. She placed it on the flat top of the higher trunk at the back and took another packet from the smaller one. Back at the desk, she untied the packet and pulled out the first sheet. It seemed to be more of the same, an invitation dated 1722 for 'Monsignore di Spiga' to present his written request directly to the Secretary for Appointments and Benefices of the Archbishop of Vienna. She looked beneath this letter, hoping to find a copy of Steffani's request. It was common for people of that epoch to keep copies of the letters they sent, and they often attached the copy to the letter they were answering. But, instead, she found another begging request for help in winning an appointment to office, this one dated 1711, addressed to Steffani as the 'Assistant at the Pontifical Throne'. He was back in Hanover by then, she recalled, still working to bring Catholicism back to North Germany.

The next paper was a list of what looked like titles and clerical positions. Although it was written in German, the hand was Italianate and the document bore no date. She remembered then that one of the things she had wanted – and failed – to do in the Marciana was find an autograph score and check the handwriting against what she had found in these papers. Memory did tell her, however, that it very strongly resembled the writing in a letter of his reproduced in one of the books she had at home.

Because she had sat still too long, Caterina got up and went back to the cupboard, where she retrieved the first packet of papers. She untied it, opened it, and paged through until she found the aria. She took it back to the table and placed the first page next to the list of titles. She studied the papers for some time. Both of them had unusual d's and e's, each letter with a tendency to circle over itself back towards the left, as though the writer had tried to draw a circle but had grown tired of it and stopped a quarter of the way round. She had no idea if this was enough to prove that they were written in Steffani's hand, but she decided to believe that they were and see where that led.

She returned to the list of offices and titles that were lined up neatly beneath one another: Privy Councillor and President of the Spiritual Council; General President of the Palatine government and council; Monsignore di Spiga; Apostolic Prothonotary; Rector of Heidelberg University; Provost of Seltz; Envoy of the Palatinate in Rome; Apostolic

Vicar of North Germany; Assistant to the Pontifical Throne; Temporary Suffragan of Münster; Member and President of the Academy of Ancient Music.

Below them, in what she believed was the same hand, was a row of question marks running from one side of the page to the other. She felt the hair on the back of her neck rise. Caterina was not a woman much given to reading scripture nor, for that matter, paying much attention to it, but her mother was a religious woman and was fond of quoting it. 'If I know all mysteries and all knowledge, and I have a faith that can move mountains, but have not love, I am nothing.' Provost of Seltz. What was that? Apostolic Vicar of North Germany? What was that worth to a man condemned to be childless for ever?

These reflections were interrupted by a light knocking at her door. She got to her feet and went over to open it. It was Dottor Moretti, in a dark blue suit made of the same quality fabric as the dark grey one he had worn the day before. The tie was a bit less sober: in fact, the burgundy stripes on a dark blue field, worn by a man of Dottor Moretti's sartorial sobriety, seemed to Caterina little different from a red rubber nose and yellow clown wig.

'I'm not disturbing you, am I, Dottoressa?' he asked.

'No, not at all,' she said, stepping back from the door to allow him room to enter. 'Please,' she said, waving him over towards the table.

'I brought you the computer,' he said and smiled. 'As I said, it's nothing special, but our tech person said it should be enough for simple things.'

'All I need to do is make notes on my reading and send them to you by email,' she said.

'And read *La Gazzetta dello Sport* if you please,' he said. 'If you need distraction from the eighteenth century.'

For a moment, she didn't understand, and then she did. 'Don't tell me *La Gazzetta*'s online, too?'

'Of course it is.' Seeing her expression, he added, 'You seem surprised.'

Caught, she had to admit, 'I suppose I have certain ideas about the people who buy it.'

'That they wouldn't be computer literate?' he inquired.

'That they wouldn't be literate, full stop,' she said.

It took him a moment, and then he laughed along with her. 'I'll confess I was surprised to learn it, too. My brother reads it online.'

'He likes sports?' she asked.

'Hunting and fishing and tramping around in wet fields all day with his pals,' Dottor Moretti continued, shrugged, and smiled.

'I have a sister who's a nun,' she said to suggest he was not the only one with odd siblings.

'Is she happy?' he asked.

'I think so.'

'Can you see her?'

Caterina smiled. 'She's not locked up, you know. She wears jeans and teaches at a university in Germany.'

'My brother's a surgeon,' he said, holding up his hands. 'Don't even think about asking. I don't understand anything.'

'Is he a good surgeon?'

'Yes. And your sister?'

'Head of the department.'

'In Germany,' he observed in the tone of respect Italians used when speaking of German universities. He looked down at the bag he was holding and placed it on the table. Unzipping it, he pulled out a laptop and its electric lead. He looked around to find a socket and had to carry the computer down to the other end of the table to plug it in.

He lifted the lid, pushed a button, and took a step back from it, as though not at all certain what was going to happen and perhaps fearful there would be a loud noise or an explosion. The machine hummed and clicked, although in a very small, discreet voice. When the various lights stopped blinking, he bent over the computer and opened a program, then another. He stared at the screen, turned to Caterina, and asked, 'The thing for the Wi-Fi is down at the bottom, I think.'

'The thing?' Caterina asked herself. This was the lawyer in intellectual properties speaking, and he referred to it as 'the thing for the Wi-Fi'?

He touched the pad and moved the cursor to the bottom, tapped once, waited, tapped twice, and gave her a triumphant grin when Google appeared.

'See,' he said, 'you can send emails.' Then, looking stricken, he asked her, 'You won't mind using your own address, will you?' Before she could answer, he explained. 'Our tech man,' he said, speaking with unwonted awkwardness. 'He asked if the Foundation had an email address, and when I said I didn't know, he suggested I ask you to use your own.' Then, in a much lower voice, he continued, 'He did say I could give you an address at the office, but when he told me what had to be done to arrange that, I said I'd ask you if you'd be willing to use your own.'

When Caterina did not answer, he went on hurriedly, 'It's all right. I can have him set you up with an account at the office if you like.'

She smiled, glad to be able to relieve him of this concern. 'It's fine. I can easily use my own.' She considered the work ahead of her and said, 'Besides, I don't know how much there will be to report at the beginning.'

He indicated the papers on the desk. 'Nothing?'

'So far, all I've found are documents about his career

as a musician and a bishop and one aria that I think he wrote.'

'Aria?' he asked, quite as if he knew nothing about musical notation.

'I don't know where it's from, but it's an opera aria, not one of his chamber duets.' She saw that this distinction was not one he understood and so glossed over that by adding, 'I think it's in his hand. There's a copy of one of his scores in a book I'm reading, and the handwriting looks the same.' She pointed to the paper that lay on the table.

When Dottor Moretti made no comment, she said, 'It's probably his, but I'm not qualified to authenticate it.'

'You know what the first question from the cousins will be?' he asked.

'Of course: How much is it worth?'

Moretti said, 'I imagine it's at the whim of supply and demand, though you wouldn't think it would be like that for art, would you?'

'It's not art,' she said. 'It's just pieces of paper.'

'What? I'm not sure I understand.'

'The art is in the sound: the music, the singing. The score is just the way it's passed on.'

'But if it was written down by the composer? Mozart? Handel? Bach?' He sounded astonished and made no attempt to hide it. This was her profession, after all; she should know this sort of thing.

'If you don't know how to read musical notation, what good is the paper? If you're blind but you can still hear, what good is the paper? Unless you can *hear* it, what good is it?' She saw that he was stumbling after her, trying to understand but perhaps not managing to.

'Would you try to tell someone what a painting looks like? Or say that a perfume smells like a mixture of lavender

113

and roses? Or tell the plot of a poem?' she asked. He looked at her with complete attention, and she realized he was following all of these examples. 'If you can't hear it, what is it?' she asked.

After a long time, Dottor Moretti smiled and said, 'I never thought of it like that.'

'Most people don't.'

# 13

After that, Caterina was silent for a long time, feeling strangely exposed by having so forcefully expressed her opinion. In situations like this, in which she found herself defending a position she knew that others would find extreme, she often tried to pour unguent on what she had said, but this time she didn't want to. She believed this: the art was the sound; the beauty was in the singing or the playing. To want to own the notes written down on paper, to place a greater value on the paper if it bore the signature of the composer, seemed to her an impure desire. She remembered something from her school catechism classes, about the sin of worshipping 'graven images'. Or maybe it was the sale of indulgences she was thinking of. Or perhaps she wasn't thinking at all and didn't need a comparison: it was creepy and it was wrong to think that the written music was the real music.

The lawyer smiled. 'I understand your position, really

I do. But unless someone can write it down for the singer or the musician, they don't know what to do.'

'But that's not what I'm talking about,' she said. 'I'm talking about turning a piece of paper or an object into a fetish. Like a letter by Goldoni or Garibaldi's belt buckle. Goldoni's important because he's a great writer, and Garibaldi's famous because he banged heads and made this into a country. But his belt buckle's nothing. It's not him. And a letter from Goldoni has only the value someone is willing to put on it.'

'Isn't that true for music?' he asked. 'I mean, a performance. If everyone thinks it was lousy and howls at the singer, then how good was the performance?'

She smiled. 'Unfortunately, there isn't enough howling.'

'I beg your pardon?'

Caterina smiled again, pulled out her chair and sat down, waving to Dottor Moretti to take the chair opposite her. 'I mean that audiences are too polite. I've heard playing and singing in theatres that was disgraceful, and people applauded as if they'd just heard something wonderful. I think what's gone wrong isn't that bad performances are howled at, but that performances that should be howled at, aren't.'

'And the musicians? What about their feelings?'

This was a lawyer talking? 'I thought you lawyers were supposed to be hard-nosed and coolly analytical.'

He had the grace to smile. 'When I'm working, I'm as hard-nosed as they come and coolly analytical: it's part of the package.'

'But?' she prodded.

'But now I'm expressing some fellow feeling with musicians.' When she didn't answer, he said, 'I've had bad days in court, when I haven't presented things as well as I could have.'

'And?'

'And my client suffered the consequences.'

'And your point?'

'That people have good days and bad days, and it's . . .' he sought the proper word '. . . it's unkind to cause them embarrassment for what they do.'

'You ever take a malpractice case?' she asked.

'No. Why?'

'It's the same thing, isn't it? You get hired to do one thing, and you do it so badly that someone is hurt. Most people think it's right that you should be punished for that.'

'Bad singing hurts people?' he asked.

'It hurts some people in the audience directly,' she said, smiling and pointing at her ear. 'But it hurts everyone more generally because it lets the entire audience think – at least if no one boos – that *this* is what the music is supposed to sound like, and that does everyone a disservice: the composer, the other singers, and finally the people in the audience because it might stop them from learning what good singing can sound like.' She stopped abruptly, embarrassed to hear her didactic tone.

Dottor Moretti was silent for a long time and finally began, 'I never thought of . . .' before he stopped himself with a laugh. He looked at his watch and said, 'It's almost two. Maybe we're both being so serious because we're hungry. Would you like to go to lunch?'

Without thinking, Caterina answered, 'It's strange, but after only this short time, I feel as though I've got some sort of legal obligation to invite the cousins to come along if I say yes.'

Moretti, with full legal thoughtfulness, said, 'Since they'd assume that they'd have to pay for their part of the meal, I think we can assume they wouldn't come.'

'That's a lawyer's judgement?'

'I'd stake my reputation on it,' he said, astonishing Caterina, who had come to think of him as a man who would never stake his reputation on anything and who would never, moreover, make jokes about his professional integrity. Could it be that Dottor Moretti was not the man he seemed to be?

They went to Remigio, where lunch was easy and relaxed: he even unbuttoned his jacket when they sat down at the table. Caterina didn't pay much attention to what they ate, so surprised was she by the discovery that Dottor Moretti – he asked her to call him Andrea, after which they slipped into using *tu* with one another – was a man of culture and broad reading. He said he had studied history before deciding to transfer to law but that it had remained his – he hesitated before using such an inflammatory phrase – secret passion.

Dottoressa Caterina Pellegrini was a woman in her thirties with a certain experience of life. To find herself sitting across from a man who confessed that his 'secret passion' was the reading of history was not an experience with which she was familiar.

'I didn't tell you one thing, though,' he said, glancing away as if feeling awkward. 'I never finished my degree before I decided to come back to study law.'

'Came back? From where?'

'Well, from Spain. My mother's Spanish, you see, so I was raised speaking both languages.' Caterina was so surprised to hear him sounding – was the right word 'apologetic'? – that she simply waited for him to continue his story.

'I didn't finish,' he said.

'What happened?'

He set his fork down and ran his right hand across his

118

perfectly combed hair. 'My father got sick, and someone had to come back to be here. He was a lawyer, my father, so one of us had to be ready to take over his practice. Both of my brothers are older than I, so they already had their professions.' He paused to look at her, as if to see if she were still sufficiently Italian, after all her years abroad, to understand the compelling necessity of his return.

Caterina said, 'Of course.' Then, 'But you were a historian, not a lawyer.'

He took another sip of his water, smiled, and said, 'Not a historian: a young man who had spent two years reading history. They're not the same thing.' He paused but Caterina waited for him to tell her all of this in his own way and at his own speed.

'I'd had two years of doing what I loved, so perhaps it was time to . . . to come home and grow up.' Leaning forward, and in a deeper and more sinister voice, he added, 'Slaves to their families, these Italians.'

In ordinary circumstances, she would have laughed, but something stopped her from giving more than a grin and a nod.

'Law was . . . different,' he went on.

'Easier?'

He shrugged. 'Different. Less complicated. I did the courses in three years, passed the exams, then the state exams, and here I am, two decades later and none the worse for it.'

She wondered about that but merely smiled and poured water into both their glasses. After some time had passed and she had returned to her pasta, he asked, 'What is it about music that attracts you?'

Without thinking, she said, 'It's so beautiful. It's the most beautiful thing we've done.'

'We, as in humans?' he asked.

'Yes,' she said. 'I believe that.' Surprised to hear herself sounding so uncharacteristially absolute, she added, 'Or maybe it's just that music is the one art that most thrills me. More than poetry and more than painting.'

'And why this Baroque music? Why not something closer to us in time?' he asked, sounding honestly curious.

'But it is modern,' she answered without thinking. 'It's got strong rhythms and catchy tunes, and the singers are free to invent their own music.' Seeing the question appear on his face, she went on, 'When they come close to the end of an aria, they can sing variations on what's gone before. The conductor writes them, or they find a score with variations in it, or they can write their own.' Involuntarily, she raised her hand and drew a series of arabesques in the air with one finger.

He smiled. 'No copyright infringement?' He smiled to show he was joking.

This nudged her towards confession. 'I'm a musicologist, so I shouldn't admit this sort of thing, but I love the spectacle of it, too: dragons, people and monsters flying through the air, witches, magic all over the place.'

'Sounds like fantasy movies.'

He meant it as a joke, but she gave a serious answer. 'That's what a lot of the operas were like. It was popular entertainment, and the producers put on a show. The singers were the Madonnas and Mick Jaggers of their times. They delivered the hit tunes. I think that's why the music is becoming popular again.' She saw his scepticism and added, 'All right, all right, not mass popularity. But most opera houses do a Baroque opera every season.' She thought about this for a moment, realizing that she had never been asked these questions by an attractive man, perhaps by any man. 'Or maybe it's only that singing's so close to us. We do it with our bodies.'

'Isn't dance the same?' he asked, reminding her that he was a lawyer.

She grinned. 'Yes. But I can't dance, and I once thought I could sing, or wanted to sing.'

'What happened?' he asked, setting down his fork.

'I don't have the talent,' she answered simply, as though he had asked the time. 'I had the will and the desire, and I think I have the love of it, but I didn't – and don't – have the vocal talent.' She rested her fork on the side of her plate and took a drink of water.

'That's very dispassionate,' he observed.

With something less than a smile, she said, 'It wasn't at the time.'

'Was it difficult?'

'If you've ever been in love, and the person turns and walks away from you, saying that you aren't the right one, well, that's what it's like.'

He looked down at his plate, picked up his fork, set it down again, looked back at her, and said, 'I'm sorry.'

Caterina smiled, this time a real smile. 'It was a long time ago, and at least the training helps me now. It's easier to understand the music, at least vocal music, if you think of it in terms of music you'll have to sing or want to sing.'

'Will you excuse my ignorance if I say I believe you without really understanding you?'

'Of course,' she said, and then to lighten the mood, she added, 'Besides, it gives a person the chance to see how very strange people can be.'

'Musicians?' he asked.

'And the people around them who aren't musicians.'

'Could you give me an example?'

She allowed stories to run through her memory, and then said, 'There's a story about King George the First – but before he went to England – having a conversation with Steffani and saying he wanted to change places with him. This went on until the King actually tried to run an opera company – and this is why I'm sure this story is apocryphal. After three days, he gave up and told Steffani it would be easier to command an army of fifty thousand men than to manage a group of opera singers.'

Moretti laughed and said, 'I've always admired people who can do that.'

'What?'

'Think of giving up.'

'You think the King was serious?' she asked, amazed that he could be so literal minded.

'No, of course not. But that he could think of it, want to do it.' He stopped for a moment, then added, 'I envy him.'

She didn't want to talk about this any more, so she asked, 'Did you have a century? Or a country?' Then, after a moment's thought, 'Or a person?' When he looked confused at the sudden change of subject, she added, 'As a historian?'

He smiled and the mood lifted again. 'I did.' Seeing that he had captured her attention, he added, 'And I have a confession.'

This stumped her. 'About what?'

'Monarchy.'

Caterina waved her hand in front of his face. 'Are you going to tell me you're the lost son of Anastasia, and you're really the Czar of all the Russias?'

He laughed out loud, put his head back and laughed so loud that people at other tables shot glances at them. The laugh changed to snorts, a word Caterina would never have thought usable in connection with Dottor Moretti, though perhaps it did fit with Andrea.

When these subsided, she said, 'Wrong guess, eh?'

'At least you didn't ask if I'm the son of King Zog of Albania.' That set him off again, and he ended up removing his glasses and wiping his eyes with his napkin.

Caterina waited. She uncovered a scallop from beneath her spaghetti and ate it, then a piece of courgette, and then she set her fork down and asked, 'What are you confessing about?'

'The Spanish Habsburgs,' he said.

'Is that a rock group?' she asked mildly.

This time she seemed only to confuse him. Quickly, she corrected herself. 'Sorry. It was a joke.'

He looked serious for a moment, then amused. Finally he said, 'It's because of a *fidanzata* I had there.' Then, to prevent any question she might have asked, he added, 'We took some classes together.' She said nothing, thinking silence would prod him more than a question.

So it proved to be. 'She was an aristocrat. The daughter of a duke, and distantly a Habsburg.' He shook his head, as if to ask how it was that a man who had once known the daughter of a duke could end up in a trattoria in Venice talking about her to a musicologist.

'She always went on about her father's right to the Spanish throne. After a while, I guess I got tired of listening to it.' Then, with a quick glance at her, 'Probably because I got tired of listening to her. But I didn't know that then: I was too young. I never met her father, but I disliked everything she said about him and her everlasting insistence that he was meant to be the King of Spain.' Then, as if he'd just heard himself saying all this, he added, 'And as I began to dislike more and more what she said about him, I realized I disliked her, too. But boys don't realize that when they're eighteen.' He smiled at the boy he had once been, and she joined him.

He broke off to thread tagliatelle around his fork, but

he set it on the edge of his plate, untasted, and went on. 'So I started reading about kings – not only the one her father insisted had stolen the throne from him – and their ancestors and where they came from, and how they got to be kings, and what they did while they were. And then I found myself fascinated by the way so much of their behaviour led to such misery. Wonderful art, but endless human misery.' He looked across at her and smiled. 'But I was eighteen, as I said, so what did I know?'

She raised her water glass, though she knew it was improper to do so in anything other than wine, and toasted him. A man who so deeply regretted human misery deserved at least that much.

# 14

They laughed a great deal through the rest of the lunch. The only disagreement came when Andrea insisted on paying the bill, something he persuaded her to accept when he promised he would pass the expense on to his clients. It was perfectly legitimate, he explained, because they had talked about music and manuscripts during the meal. Indeed they had, she agreed, delighted that the bill would be paid by the two cousins and not at all troubled by questions of legitimacy.

They were back at the Foundation in a matter of minutes; Caterina found herself wishing it had been further away. At the door, Andrea looked at his watch – she noticed that it was gold and thin as a coin, which would certainly have interested Signor Scapinelli. 'I've got to get back,' he said. 'I look forward to hearing from you.'

Caterina had been studying his watch when she heard these last words. As she raised her head to smile at him, he reached into his pocket to pull out his wallet. He took a white card from it and handed it to her. 'My email is there, so if you'll send me the results of your research, I'll forward it to the cousins.' Pleased as she was by his having adopted her habit of referring to Signori Stievani and Scapinelli as 'the cousins', she was disappointed – she admitted it – that his eagerness to hear from her seemed prompted by the documents.

'Yes,' she said, with what she thought was an easy, relaxed smile. 'I'll get back to it and send you a summary by the end of the day.'

'Good,' he said, extending his hand. She shook it, slipped his card into the pocket of her jacket, and let herself into the Foundation. As she started down the corridor, Roseanna came out of her office.

'Oh, there you are,' Caterina said, smiling. She was uncertain whether, now that they had almost become friends, she should greet Roseanna with a kiss, but she left it to the older woman to decide.

As Caterina got closer, she saw there was to be no kiss. In fact, Roseanna looked decidedly unfriendly.

'Where were you?' Roseanna asked by way of greeting.

'At lunch,' Caterina said, not specifying where or with whom.

'The office was open.'

'I thought I closed the door,' Caterina said without thinking.

'Yes, the door was closed, but it wasn't locked.' Roseanna waited, but Caterina's silence led her to continue. 'The documents were on your desk, and the storeroom was open.' Caterina listened to the tone: the words, as well as the facts, left her with no defence. Her delight at Andrea's suggestion had led her out of the room and she had given not a thought to the papers or her responsibility for them, a lack of attention in which Andrea had joined her.

'I'm sorry,' was the best she could say. 'I forgot.' She reached into her pocket for the keys to the door at the foot of the stairs, and her fingers found Andrea's card. 'I won't do it again.'

Roseanna unfroze a bit but still said, briskly, 'I hope not. We don't have any clear idea of the value of what's there.'

Again, Caterina heeded the tone far more than the words, for Roseanna's disguised question hinted that she had obtained information about the value of those papers, wanted to be asked about it and to be praised for having found it.

'What did you find out?' Caterina said, moving a few steps closer to her.

Roseanna went back into her office, leaving the door open, an invitation Caterina took. When they were seated on either side of her desk, Roseanna pushed a sheet of paper across the table. Caterina recognized the letterhead of an auction house in London; below it were listed three manuscripts and the sums paid.

*Qui la dea cieca* (1713?) 9,040 Euro
*Notte amica* (first page) (1714) 4,320 Euro
*Padre, se colpa in lui* (fragment) (1712) 1,250 Euro

Caterina looked up from the paper and gave a broad smile. 'Well, who's been doing her homework?' She glanced at the paper again and asked, 'How on earth did you persuade them to give you this information?' She tapped the three sums with the tip of her finger and said, *'Complimenti.'*

Roseanna smiled even more broadly and said, all anger or reproach fled from her voice, 'I sent them an email, saying I was the Acting Director of the Foundation and telling them that, in consequence of a large donation to our Acquisitions Fund, we were interested in any available manuscripts by Agostino Steffani and curious about recent purchase prices.' Nodding at the paper, she added, 'They sent me this.'

Caterina's open-mouthed admiration was entirely spontaneous. 'Acquisitions Fund?' she asked.

Roseanna waved her hand, dismissing the possibility that such a thing existed. 'I assumed they'd answer a request if it was something that might make them money.'

'Ah, Roseanna,' she said, 'you have a real call to work in the music business.'

Caterina picked up the paper. 'So this is what his work is sold for,' she mused. 'It would help if we knew when these sales took place.'

'Yes,' Roseanna agreed. 'You could call and ask, couldn't you? Or write to them.'

'What language did you use?'

'Italian,' Roseanna said. 'It's the only one I know.'

Caterina let the page drop back on to Roseanna's desk. 'It might be enough just to know this: that a presumably complete aria is worth at least nine thousand Euros.'

Both of them sat and considered this fact until finally Roseanna reached forward and put her finger on the highest sum. 'I hope the cousins don't think of doing the same thing I did and find this out.'

Caterina smiled at her. 'They'd start sleeping in front of the door, wouldn't they?'

'With a gun,' Roseanna added.

Peace restored, Caterina went back upstairs, telling herself not to be such a fool because of an invitation to lunch. 'Lock the papers up, lock the door,' she muttered to herself as she went back into the room. Even though she knew she had to be methodical and take the papers in the order in which she found them in the packet, she paged through the remaining documents – about six centimetres of them – looking for musical scores. Near the bottom, she unearthed a sheet of paper half of which was filled with bars of music, neatly written in a very small script, obviously not by the person with the back-leaning hand. Below were two paragraphs and then the signature: 'Your brother in Christ, Donato Battipaglia, Abbé di Modena.'

She set the paper down and looked across at the wall, feeling alert or alarmed but unable to tell the cause. She looked at the signature again. Battipaglia was a new name: this was the first letter from him she had seen, and she could not recall any previous reference to him. Still standing, she turned her attention back to the letter. It began with a description of a concert – not Steffani's, the writer hastened to clarify – which had sounded like 'the scraping of a badly-oiled carriage'. In the excessively complimentary style of the period, the writer praised Steffani's *Le rivali concordi*, a copy of which the writer had had the 'inestimable fortune' to see in the library of his patron, Rinaldo III, Duke of Modena. He praised the score in its entirety as well as the seriousness of the sentiments expressed in the text, and then turned his attention to an example of 'a singular mastery of musical invention'. The bars he quoted, he said, came from the duet, *'Timori ruine'*, which he found sublime. Caterina looked at the musical extract, which he provided in full, and fell into agreement with the sentiment of the Abbé. She hummed through it. Oh, he was good, this Steffani, she thought, with his fourteen operas, divertimenti, duets, and religious music and his glorious feel for what the voice wanted to do. Then she went back to staring at the wall, trying to nudge herself towards what it was in the letter that had caught her attention.

She looked again at the signature. Wasn't it said that people revealed themselves in the way they wrote their names? But the flourishes and squiggles were in no way unusual for their epoch. 'Donato Battipaglia, Abbé di Modena.'

'Abbé,' she said out loud. 'What the hell was an abbé?'

Liszt came to mind. He was an abbé, and if he had lived the life of a priest, Caterina was the heir to King Zog.

She switched to her email account and typed in Cristina's address at the university. It was a professional question she was asking, and Cristina was always sure to check that address rather than her personal one.

'*Ciao*, Tina-Lina,' she began, 'I hope this finds you overworked and happy. Look, I'm working at that job in Venice, examining the papers of the Baroque composer who worked and died in Germany and I need some information. He was an abbé. What's an abbé? Does he have to be a priest, or can he be something else and be called a priest? (a bit of deceit, of course, that your employer would never think of tolerating).' Old habits die hard, and Caterina had spent more than twenty years of her life baiting Cristina for her decision to become a nun.

'Also, I've come to think this man might have been a castrato. I have it in my memory baggage that a castrato could not be a priest. Would making him an abbé be a way to get around this? (Not that your employer would . . .) Could you let me know about these things with something other than your usual glacial pace?

'*Mamma* and *Papà* are both very well and as happy as ever. Clara and Cinzia are fine; so are their kids. Claudia looks sensational and seems to be getting on better with Giorgio, though who knows how long that will last? Why didn't she get the same happy genes the rest of us seem to have inherited? I wish there were some way to . . . you know what I mean, but I don't know what to do. I'm fine, the work looks interesting, and . . .' she paused, wondering if she should mention Avvocato Moretti, but her good sense prevailed. They had gone to lunch together, for heaven's sake, that's all. '. . . it's sure to keep me here for some time, and by then one of those other jobs might well have come in. I hope this finds you happy and busy and giving Deep Thought to the Totally Erroneous Path You Have Chosen in Life. Love, Cati.'

Cristina, who had been the only other one in the family to opt for a professional life, had always been her favourite sister. The closeness explained Caterina's shock and, yes, horror at Cristina's decision to enter a convent, but it also permitted the irreverent tone which characterized her every communication with the *Professoressa Dottoressa Suora*.

She was about to put the computer to sleep when she remembered that Cristina had no background information at all. She started another email and added, 'His dates are 1654–1728, if that helps', and sent it after the other.

She closed the computer and slid it along the table until it was out of reach, then went back to reading.

After an hour and a half of taking notes about various ecclesiastical benefices granted, requested, or refused, Caterina got up and walked over to the windows. She opened a window and wrapped her hands around the bars; she pulled at them, and when they refused to move, did the same with the bars of the other window. Was this what it was like for Steffani, she wondered, trapped inside a body that had had physical limits placed on it? That's what prison was, wasn't it? Physical limitation, a restraint on what one was free to do. But prison was usually temporary, and the prisoner had, if nothing else, at least the hope of some day being free again.

That's the hope Cristina could have, were it not that Cristina did not see it in this light. If anything, she welcomed the limitation on her freedom, said it helped her concentrate on what was important in her life. Could Steffani possibly have come to think this way? But Cristina, for good or ill, had at least made the decision for herself. All right, she had made it at nineteen, but no one had made it for her, and no one had forced her into it. Quite the opposite – and she could always, if she wanted to, walk away. And if she did decide to leave, she'd keep her doctorate and her job, wouldn't she?

But Steffani? He couldn't walk away from what Caterina now believed him to be, nor could he have walked away from the Church that gave him definition and position and importance, even though that same Church had been complicit in making him a *musico*. Surely his genius would have brought him work and fame as a composer. Yet, the thought came to her, would it have provided him the respectability that the Church could give him? And would his genius have draped him in the crimson of a bishop and thus kept him hidden and safe from the jokes and contempt of men?

Whatever the reason, he had chosen to stay. Her thoughts went back to that duet in the letter: was it meant to be a hidden message from a man who had suffered and survived? She flipped the pages over and searched for the letter from Abbé Battipaglia.

| | |
|---|---|
| *Non durano l'ire* | Angers don't last |
| *E passa il martir* | And suffering passes away |
| *Amor sa ferire,* | Love knows how to wound |
| *Ma poi sa guarir.* | But it also knows how to heal |
| | |
| *Vera fortuna severa* | Severe fortune |
| *A'i nostri contenti* | To our peace of mind |
| *D'un alma che spera* | To a spirit that hopes |
| *Consola il desir* | Please bring consolation |

Once again, Caterina found herself quoting scripture. 'Jesus wept.'

# 15

The rest of the afternoon passed without event. She read, she made notes, she transcribed a few passages, all about Steffani's relatives: aside from Agostino, only a brother and a sister, also childless, survived to maturity. 'Cousin' frequently appeared as a form of address, both in letters to him and letters about him, but she was sufficiently Italian to realize that this was a term with an extra-legal meaning. As for testamentary instruction, she might as well have been looking for advertising jingles. She had so far found nothing written by or even containing the name Stievani or Scapinelli or any of the variant spellings of these names.

Among Steffani's friends and correspondents, the person he seemed most attached to was Sophie Charlotte, the Electress of Brandenburg. Caterina found frequent reference to Sophie Charlotte in letters to Steffani from other people, in which she was referred to as, 'Your friend the Electress', 'The Electress to whom you so warmly refer', and 'Her Highness Sophie Charlotte, who so honours you with her friendship'. The letters that passed between them showed great warmth and even more openness than could be expected, given the difference in their status.

She wrote to tell him that she was studying counterpoint, the better to prepare herself to begin to compose music, hoping that her duets would be as natural and tender as the ones he wrote. He responded by joking that he hoped she would fail in her endeavour, for should she turn to composing, 'the poor Abbé will go forgotten'.

At five Caterina got up to turn on a light but resisted the desire to go out for a coffee, chiefly because she did not want to have to lock everything up and then go through the business of unlocking it and taking it all out again when she came back. At six she went to the storeroom and exchanged packets, pulling out an especially thick one that occupied most of the space on the left side of the trunk. The first letter showed promise, for it was sent by a certain Marc'Antonio Terzago and addressed Steffani as 'nephew'. He thanked Agostino for the help he had given in finding a place as a student at the seminary in Padova for a young nephew and for this proof that 'familial loyalty was not diminished by the immense distance between Hanover and Padova'.

She registered the man's name. Steffani's brother Ventura had been taken in by an uncle and had assumed his name, Terzago. So here was an entirely different family of 'cousins'. Could they have died out, or were they ancestors of Stievani or Scapinelli? Below it there was a letter in the less well formed hand of the boy himself, Paolo Terzago, thanking his 'dear cousin' for his efforts in finding him a place at the seminary, where he was 'very happy and warm'. The letter bore the date of February 1726.

February in northern Italy: no wonder the boy commented on the temperature in the seminary.

At seven-thirty, feeling she had not progressed towards any understanding of Steffani as a man, and had gained little information about his relatives, she got to her feet, put the unread papers face down on top of the packet, tied it closed, and locked it in the cupboard.

Before she left, she thought she'd have a look to see if Cristina had overcome her legendary sloth and answered. And indeed the first thing she saw in her inbox was a mail from her sister's personal address.

'Cati Dearest,' she read, 'your Abbé Steffani does leave behind him a wake of uncertainty.' Though she knew she had not used his name, Caterina opened her Sent folder and reread her original email, and indeed, she had used only his title of abbé.

'I see you checking the Sent folder, dear, only to confirm that all you gave me was his title. To spare your suffering or believing that my having crossed over to the Dark Side has endowed me with Dark Powers, I say only that you gave me his dates and the fact that he was a composer, probably Italian (he was a castrato, or so you suspect, and that's where they came from, alas), who died in Germany.

'You gave me these facts, and the training as a researcher given me at enormous expense by Holy Mother Church, which over the course of many years and countless thousands of hours has honed my mind to razor-like sharpness, gave me the sophisticated skills to put those three pieces of information into Google. Just one name comes up. Perhaps the Church could have saved all the money it spent on me and, as you so often suggest, given it to the poor?

'Indeed, "abbé" was, at the time of your composer's career, pretty much a courtesy title, and though the documentation is contradictory (I shall spare you the details) it is safe to say that to be an abbé is not necessarily to be a priest. Some were; many were not. There is a subset here of bishops who were not priests, either, and as your composer later became a bishop, I save time by telling you that wearing the mitre did not, in those times, require ordination. For more about this see his patron, Ernst August, who was also – though married, a father, and never ordained – the Prince-Bishop of Osnabrück. Of course Ernst August was a Protestant (hiss) but they seem to have had the same dodgy rules that allowed men (of course) to become bishops and even create/consecrate other bishops without themselves being ordained. It does make a person think of yoghurt, doesn't it, where all you have to do is add a little to make more.' Here, Caterina marvelled, not for the first time, at the lack of seriousness with which Cristina often spoke of the organization to which she had given her life and spirit.

'As to the injunction that a castrato could not and cannot be a priest, your memory is, as is so often the case, Cati dearest, correct. Canon Law 1041, #5 ° states clearly that anyone who has gravely and maliciously mutilated himself or another person or who has attempted suicide cannot be ordained. It is also a basic tenet that inadequacy for marriage renders a man similarly inadequate for the priesthood, no doubt an evasive way of speaking of castration or sexual dysfunction.

'Pope Sixtus V, on 27 June 1587 (you might not like us, dear, but you must admit we're very good at keeping records), made the Church's position very clear in his Breve *Cum frequenter*, by declaring that castrati are denied the right to marry.

'So there you have it, Baby Sister, and I can add no more until I have further information from two people I've asked about this, all of which will come to you in due course. Things here are fine. I'm working on another book, this one about Vatican foreign policy in the last century. It'll probably get me kicked out or sent to teach third grade in Sicily. Or maybe you could hire me as a full-time researcher? Stay well, Kitty-Cati. Keep an eye on the family for me, please, especially poor sad Claudia, who should have married that nice electrician from Castello instead of that dreadful lawyer. I miss you all terribly. There are times when I want so much to be home that I could walk out the door and head south. Yes, that makes me remember the time we hitch-hiked to France and told *Mamma* and *Papà* that we were taking the train. Driving into Paris with that man – was he an accountant? I can't remember any more – was one of the most thrilling moments in my life. Getting a doctorate or being named full professor were nothing in comparison.

'I send my love to all of you and leave it to you to spread it around in direct proportion to how much anyone needs it. Love, Tina-Lina.'

As a researcher Caterina had been trained to read between the lines of texts. This was as much a habit for her as it was for a veterinarian to see mange on the skin of a friend's dog or a voice teacher to hear the first faint signs of excessive vibrato. Her sister's email left her uncomfortable, chiefly because of what it revealed about her mood but also because of her own initial self-satisfaction at reading it. 'ET, phone home,' she said in a soft voice.

She shifted from the mood of the email to its contents. What had begun as a wild surmise on her part was now confirmed as a distinct possibility; indeed, more than that. She thought of those long fingers, that beardless, puffy face, utterly devoid of the exciting angles and lines of the male face, even at the age of sixty, which Steffani had been when that portrait was painted.

She turned off the computer, picked up her bag, and went downstairs, but not before checking that the cupboard and the door to her office were locked. Roseanna had left. As she closed the outer door to the building, Caterina noticed a sign saying that the library was closed until the end of the month. The weather was fine, so there would be no suffering on the part of the people who used the reading room as a warm place to spend their time. But it was entirely possible that they also needed a place where they could pass the day.

Thinking about this and other things, she walked home; not the apartment where she was living, but her parents' house down near La Madonna dell'Orto, the area of the city that would ever be home for her.

She could have taken a vaporetto if she had walked back to the Celestia stop, but she didn't like that part of the city much, however well lit most of it was, so she chose to walk through Santa Maria Formosa, out to Strada Nuova, and home the same way she used to return from school.

So much taken with the thought of Steffani's life was she that, at first, she paid no attention to the man who appeared beside her, as if to pass her, and then fell into step with her. She glanced at him, but as it was not anyone she knew, she ignored him and slowed her steps. But he slowed his as well and kept pace with her. They came down into the *campo*, which was dark at this hour, its paving stones covered with a thin film of humidity that dissipated and reflected the lights. A few metres beyond the bridge, where light also came from the windows of the shops on her right, she stopped. She didn't bother to pretend she wanted to take something from her bag: she simply stood still, waiting to see if the man would move off. He did not.

The vegetable stand had already closed up and gone, but a number of people were crossing the *campo*, and three or four were within hailing distance, though she didn't know why she thought of it in those terms.

'Do you want something?' she asked, surprising herself but, apparently, not the man.

He turned and looked at her, and she didn't like him. Just like that: instinctive, visceral, utterly irrational, but the feeling was strong. Her instincts told her this was a bad man, and the fact that he stood and looked at her and said nothing was bad. She wasn't in the least afraid – they were in the middle of a *campo* and there were people around them. But she was uneasy, and the longer he didn't say anything, the more uneasy she grew. He was an entirely average looking man, about her age: short hair, no beard, normal nose, light eyes, nothing to remember.

'Do you want something?' she repeated. Again he didn't answer. He looked at her, studying her face, her shoulders, the rest of her body, and then again her face, as though memorizing everything he saw.

The desire to run or to strike out at him and then run came over Caterina, but she forced her body into obedience and remained standing still. A full minute passed. To her right, a church bell began to ring eight-thirty, and she was late for dinner.

She started walking towards the bridge on the other side of the *campo*. She did not look behind her but she listened. Her mind was humming, and she could no longer remember if his footsteps had been audible before. As she reached the bridge, the desire, the need, to turn and see if he was behind her became all but overwhelming, but she resisted it and continued up and down the bridge and then into one of the narrowest *calli* in the city. As she entered it, she prayed that someone would approach from the other end, but it was empty. She shook with the desire to turn around, but she kept walking until she was out of the *calle* and at the next bridge.

Up and down and into Campo Santa Marina, where she had to decide which way to go. Turn right and save a few minutes, but pass down Calle dei Miracoli, a narrow place with little foot traffic, or continue straight on and come out by San Giovanni Crisostomo and run into the heaviest foot traffic in the city as she headed for Strada Nuova and home. She continued straight ahead.

# 16

She made no mention of the man at dinner, not wanting to alarm either her parents or herself. He had done nothing to menace her, had not even spoken to her, yet he had unsettled her and, she admitted to herself while trying to pay attention to a story her mother was telling, had frightened her. The city was a safe island in a world that seemed to be going increasingly off its axis: to read the papers was to fear that some infection was abroad. She returned her attention to her mother's story, and to her food. Home-made polenta made from grain sent to her father by an old friend who still grew corn in Friuli. The rabbit came from Bisiol, where her mother had been buying rabbit for twenty years. The artichokes were from Sant'Erasmo: her mother had recently joined a cooperative that delivered a basket of vegetables and fruit to the house twice a week. The purchaser had no choice about what was delivered: it was what was in season, and it was organic.

Her mother had complained about never having eaten so many apples in her life, but when Caterina ate one of them, cooked in red wine and covered with whipped cream, she would gladly have signed her mother up for another two months of apples. They talked of many things: her father's work, her mother's friends, her sisters' marriages, her nieces and nephews. If, one day, she had an estate to leave, Caterina wondered, would she be happy to leave it – in the event of her having no husband or children – to her nieces and nephews? They were only children now, but who knew what they would become as adults?

As she continued to half listen to her parents, she thought about Steffani. He had passed most of his life in Germany, going back to Italy only occasionally and usually for fairly short periods. How much had he seen of his relatives or their children? *Had* he seen them, known them, tossed them in the air and played with them and sung his songs to them? And the cousins, these men who descended from the children's children of his cousins, with what right did they stake a claim to his papers and estate, and where had the idea of a 'treasure' come from? No one had explained that to her. The only reference she'd found to his estate mentioned that, after his creditors had been paid, there remained '2,029 florins, some papers, some relics, medals, and music'. It was that 'and music' that hit her with force. Exclude that, and the man had lived seventy-four years: some papers, some money, some relics, and some medals. Treasure?

'Where did we all get the idea that your great-grandfather lost everything at the Casinò?' she surprised her father by asking. Both her parents stared at her, but neither asked her if she had been paying attention to what they were saying, so obvious was it that she had not.

Her father ran both hands through his still thick hair, something he did when he wanted time to think. Her mother, as she always did when things didn't go as she had planned, put more food on their plates. Everyone in the family except her mother and Cinzia ate like wolves and never changed weight by a gram. 'All I have to do is look at a carrot and I weigh a kilo more the next day,' was her mother's mantra.

'I don't know,' her father said, not about the carrot which played so frequent a role in his wife's conversation, but about the question Caterina had just asked him. 'It's family legend. People used to talk about it when we were kids, and I talked about it with your uncles Giustino and Rinaldo.'

'Did anyone ever check to see if it was true?' she asked.

Her mother gave Caterina a startled glance, but her father smiled and said, 'No, I suppose we never thought about doing that.'

'Why?' Caterina asked.

He considered her question, then smiled again. 'Probably because it sounded so romantic and so Venetian – *palazzo* lost at cards, gambling away the family fortune.'

'What do you think really happened?'

He shrugged. 'I suppose what usually happens. My great-grandfather wasn't good with money, wouldn't listen to his wife, and lost it all.'

Her mother broke in to say, 'It's how we like to think of ourselves.'

'We?' Caterina asked.

'*Veneziani. Gran signori,*' she said, quoting the tagline of a common saying that defined Venetians.

'But instead?' she asked.

'Cati,' her mother said, 'you haven't been away so long you've forgotten. We love to make a deal and beat someone else out of something.'

'But you don't and *Papà* doesn't,' she said, knowing this was true.

Neither of her parents said anything. Eventually Caterina put her spoon down and admitted, 'All right, all right. You don't, but most of us do.'

'Do you?' her mother asked, as if she had just shown some sympathy for child prostitution or the MOSE project.

'No, I don't think I do,' she answered.

Before things could grow more complicated, her mother said, 'You've got twelve minutes to get the boat at San Marcuola, Cati.' She hadn't looked at her watch, hadn't asked the time: she simply *knew*.

Hurried kisses, promises to call the next day, and every day, her mother's insistence that it made no sense for her to live all the way down in Castello when she had a perfectly good home to stay in, and then she was out of the house and on her way to the boat stop.

Her feet knew the way: out the door and right along the canal, then left over the bridge, and stop thinking about it and let your feet do it for you, and nine minutes later she walked out in front of the church of San Marcuola, where, she reminded herself, Hasse's tomb was hard to find, and straight to the boat stop. She took out her imob and pressed it against the sensor, heard the blip of acceptance, then walked into the lighted *embarcadero*.

And there he was: the man who had followed her from the Foundation. He sat on the bench to the left hand side, his legs stretched out in front of him, feet crossed at the ankles. His arms were crossed over his chest, and he looked like any person sitting and waiting for the vaporetto. He glanced up at her and, though he noticed her, there was

**145**

no sign of recognition on his part, just as there had been none when he had looked at her on the street some hours before.

She opened her bag and slipped her imob into the inside pocket, walked past him to the front of the dock, turned right, and looked up the Grand Canal. The boat was a hundred metres away, clearly visible in the brightly lit canal. Its headlight approached. What did she do if he got on the boat with her? Ignore him and get off at Arsenale and then walk home? There were sure to be people on the street, but perhaps not on the small *calle* where the apartment was. She could call the police, but what if he didn't get off the boat when she did? The boat came and she got on, went into the cabin and took an aisle seat on the left side, where she could see who got on after her. The man did not.

As the sailor flipped the rope loose, she waited for the man to make a sudden move and jump on the departing boat at the last minute, but he didn't. The boat started forward. She turned to the left and saw him still sitting there, legs comfortably stretched out in front of him, arms folded. As she moved past him, he continued to look at her, expression unchanged.

She looked forward. She felt something sting her eye, and when she placed her hand on it she found that perspiration had run down her face and soaked her hair. It took almost half an hour to get to Arsenale, and Caterina was glad of it, for she had time to talk herself into a state of calm.

The boat pulled in; the sailor tossed the rope and wrapped it around the stanchion, and five or six people lined up to disembark. She put herself in the middle of them, matching her pace to theirs. Careful to stay behind an elderly couple who were walking slowly, she off the boat and down to Via Garibaldi until she came to the street where she was living,

Calle Schiavona. She paused, but only minimally, at the corner. The key to the front door had been in her hand since the boat had begun to slow for the stop.

The house was along on the left. She reached the door, put the key in the lock and let herself in. She turned on the light, walked to the top floor, let herself into the apartment. She walked through it, turning on all of the lights one after the other. When she was sure she was alone – though she tried not to think of it in those terms – she went into the bathroom and was violently sick into the toilet. She washed her face and rinsed her mouth, then made herself a cup of chamomile tea and took it into the living room.

Sleep, she knew, was impossible. She sat on the sofa and picked up the second of the books about Steffani she had taken from the library.

The story recounted so captivated her that she soon forgot about feeling sick, drank the tea, went and made more, and returned to the book. She read a few more pages, went into the kitchen and ate a few dry crackers, drank more tea, then returned to the book.

In 1694, the movie-star handsome – she liked this anachronistic description – Count Philip Christoph Königsmarck disappeared overnight from the castle of Ernst August, Duke of Hanover and Steffani's patron. He disappeared, she read, 'into thin air'.

It was subsequently rumoured that he had been killed on someone's orders, and even though the official version always remained that he had simply gone missing, nothing could prevent it from becoming the greatest scandal of the times. There were a few candidates for the role of killer, or sender, first among whom was Duke Ernst August himself – who objected to the openness of Königsmarck's affair with his daughter-in-law, the beauty of the century, Princess Sophie Dorothea.

With the entrance of a second double-barrelled Sophie, Caterina was forced to flip back to the genealogical chart at the beginning of the book. The Sophie Charlotte whom Steffani corresponded with and of whose friendship he was so proud was the sister-in-law of this second Sophie. The betrayed husband was Georg Ludwig, the future George I of England; his adulterous wife, Sophie Dorothea, was also his first cousin. She had been a desirable catch because of her beauty and charm and, not incidentally, because of the hundred thousand thalers a year that came with her.

The nausea had passed, and Caterina found she was hungry. She went into the kitchen and put some rice on to boil. On the way back to the sofa, she paused in front of the mirror next to the front door and asked herself out loud, 'Have you been watching too much television?' Since Caterina had never owned or lived with a television and never watched it, the question was rhetorical: it was a way of commenting on the melodrama of the story she was reading.

It was not, to say the very least, a love-filled marriage. Truth to tell, Georg Ludwig and Sophie hated one another. The book recounted an incident when an argument between them had escalated until he literally had to be pulled off of her. Georg had a series of mistresses: in fact, when he subsequently went to England to become king, he packed up two of them – whom the English looked at and quickly nicknamed the Maypole and the Elephant – and took them along. Sophie Dorothea seemed to have limited herself to only one, and everything Caterina could find suggested that her error was not the affair but her failure to keep it secret.

Steffani, she reminded herself – if simply to justify her

reading of this lurid stuff, like something straight out of a scandal magazine – was involved inasmuch as the two lovers, Sophie Dorothea and Count Philip, sent each other hundreds of love letters, in many of them attempting to disguise their passion by quoting the lyrics from Steffani's operas. To show his eagarness Königsmarck mentions the swift duet, '*Volate momenti*', where the lover begs both time and the sun to quicken their pace to thus shorten the time of the lovers' separation. If the things she had read in the Marciana were to be believed, these letters were being intercepted and read by Countess von Platen, believed to be the former lover of Königsmarck and certainly the former mistress of Ernst August, who was the father-in-law of Sophie Dorothea.

Caterina stared into space. 'Let me see if I've got this straight,' she told herself aloud. 'These two fools sent love letters back and forth in opera lyrics, but a mistress Königsmarck had dumped – who just happened also to have been the mistress of the father-in-law of her ex-lover's current mistress – was reading them, and she blew the whistle on the lovers.' She resisted the urge to go over to the mirror again and check to see if she had grown a second head.

She smelled the rice and went into the kitchen to turn off the flame. She took off the top and spooned some of it into a bowl, added more salt, and took it back into the living room with her.

Things became more interesting. Almost immediately after Königsmarck's disappearance, a certain Nicolò Montalbano, a Venetian who had been hanging around the court of Hanover for almost twenty years writing the occasional opera libretto, was reported to have been paid the astonishing sum of 150,000 thalers by persons unknown, whereupon he too promptly disappeared.

Poor Sophie Dorothea was divorced by her creep of a husband, Georg Ludwig, on the trumped-up charge that she had abandoned the marriage bed, and then old Georgie sent her off to rot away in a castle for thirty years and wouldn't let her see her kids. The author quoted a lovely but unreliable legend that she delivered a deathbed curse on Georg, and sure enough, he dropped dead in less than a year. Even so, she was to have no satisfaction from her curse, for she died before Georg did and so never saw her son become King George II of England though, as Caterina remembered, he was little better than his father. Makes a person understand the current royal family, she thought.

She sat back in her chair, then got up and went over and stretched out on the sofa, the bowl on her stomach. She stirred the rice around, letting it cool. Ernst August had spent a fortune and worked diplomatic miracles to be chosen as an elector, some sort of big deal title that only a dozen or so aristocrats got to have, and they in turn elected the Holy Roman Emperor. Yes, a big deal. But he had to wait a couple of years before he could be crowned or anointed or whatever it was that happened to turn him into an elector. While he was waiting for this to happen, he'd have had to keep his nose clean, and he'd have had to see that his family didn't disgrace him and thus scotch his chance to become an elector.

'So there you are, Monsieur Poirot,' she said out loud, waving her fork at the stout figure who did not stand by the door, 'you have your first suspect.' Instantly she added, 'And his son, Georg Ludwig, is the second.' And Steffani: how much would he have known? He was court musician, diplomat; his libretti served as the language of love. The affair was an open secret. Surely he would have known of it.

Caterina ate the rice, chewing each mouthful a long time. At one point, she remembered the face of the man who had followed her, and her throat closed up for a moment. Again, out loud, she said, 'I will not allow this to happen to me.' She did not define what 'this' was, and after a time she finished the rice and went to bed and slept.

# 17

The next day dawned cloudless and bright, and the night's sleep had restored Caterina's usual energy and good spirits. She didn't think about the man who had followed her until she left the house and went into a bar for a coffee. The barman recognized her and offered her a brioche with her coffee even before she asked for it, and she recalled thinking, last night, that a possibility for safety would be to ask one of the men in this bar to walk her home. In the bright light of an April morning, the very idea seemed ludicrous.

She had slept late and had not bothered to read her emails before she left the apartment. When she got to the Foundation, she said good morning to Roseanna, who said that she hoped the sign would keep people out as long as Caterina was working on the documents.

She went upstairs and turned on the computer. When she had lived in other countries, she had read the Italian press online every morning, but she had abandoned the habit in recent years. It was all time wasted, she feared. The frequency with which certain faces appeared on the front pages changed, but none of them ever disappeared. Only death swept away the men who had devoted themselves to politics. Theft, involvement with the Mafia, payments to transsexual prostitutes, corruption, missing millions – none of this removed them. Convict them of anything, and they were still there. Turn your back and they changed political party or reinvented themselves, changed their hairline, found Jesus, or wept on television while begging their wives for forgiveness, but they were still there. Only death removed them from the scene, though sometimes not even then, for many of them came back as newly renamed streets or piazzas.

Better to read her emails. There were three. The first one she opened was the one from Cristina.

'Dear Cati, Destroyer of My Work Routine, for you've gone and done just that, and not for the first time. There I was, happily busy with my chapter on Pope Pius XII (what the likes of you would call a Nasty Bit of Goods, I fear) (an opinion I am coming to share) (which I ought not to admit) (but do) and his various evasions and prevarications, when your request, like a dog that has found a very interesting bone, drags in Clement VIII and drops him at my feet, to make no mention of the question of castrati, the title of abbé, and the various deceptions to which men in power are prone. Just as a bit of history, you might be interested to learn that Pius X banned castrati from the Sistine Chapel. In 1903. You want deception, I give you deception, my dear.

'As you can see, I've been busy in your interests. I've found – not without difficulty – a *breve* from Clement VIII, declaring that castration was sanctioned for singing in "the honour of God". And I ask you here, Cati – and I'm not joking – please not to comment on this or try to provoke me about it: its existence is sufficient provocation.

'There is also the dispensation, which a pope can give for pretty much anything he chooses. So, as that American songwriter told us, "Anything goes."

'Yes, my tone is an indication of how tired I am of my current research; not of the research itself, which is fascinating, but of what it makes me think and feel. So I welcome the chance to jump back in time and read about these long-dead people. You've sent me into the archives and created a curiosity that has put me in touch with colleagues I've not contacted for years; to my surprise, they seem as lit up by this subject as I am and have been raining down information upon me. Or perhaps we are all tired of our own research?

'One old classmate of mine, a man who is now teaching at the University of Constance, suggested I tell you to take a closer look at the Königsmarck Affair: he says he has seen a manuscript that claims your musician was involved in it. He said he would send further information if you want, although my guess is that he'll send it to me, anyway, even if you don't want it, since there doesn't exist the scholar who doesn't love gossip, even if it's a couple of hundred years old. I know of the Affair only in the most superficial manner but would love to read what he says and will do so if it's addressed to me. Ah, how proud *Mamma* would be to learn that the taboo about privacy she fed us with her milk is alive and well in Tübingen. From which city I send you my love, dear Cati, as well as my offer to continue to look into all of this for you. It keeps me from my own work, and I want that. For now. Love, Tina-Lina.'

Oh my, oh my, oh my, Caterina thought: it sounds as if Tina is coming to the end of the line. It had always puzzled her that it was Cristina who had been bitten by the religion bug, not Cinzia or Clara or Claudia, who were not given to asking questions about the world they found themselves in. All of them were lukewarm where religion was concerned: Cinzia and Clara had their kids baptized and confirmed, even went to church once in a while, and told the kids that God loved them and it was wrong to lie or to hurt people. Cristina excepted, her sisters had little respect for priests, hated the Vatican as only Italians could hate it, and thought the Church should not be allowed to comment on politics.

'Stop it,' she told herself out loud and read the other emails. One was from a classmate from Liceo, saying he'd just heard she was back in town and would she like to go to dinner? 'Not unless you bring your wife and kids, Renato,' she said and erased the mail.

The last was from Dottor Moretti, informing her that he had received phone calls from both cousins the day before, asking why she had not informed them of the progress of her researches. Nothing more.

She wrote back to him immediately, saying she was still reading through the documents in the first trunk and had not yet found anything worth reporting about the testamentary dispositions of the Abbé Steffani. She thus found it necessary to expand the focus of her research – if he could be formal in his mail, then she could be too – and would be obliged to consult other sources. She would, therefore, be absent from the office of the Foundation for the rest of the day while she pursued these researches.

'Take that, Dottor Moretti,' she said, as she punched the Send key, and off it went. Mention of the aria she had found could wait.

She flipped open her phone and saw that there was one

message. She recognized the Romanian's voice instantly, the easy Italian, the occasionally fumbled word. She saw that it had come in at three-thirty in the morning, making her grateful that she had turned the phone off before she went to bed.

The Romanian, she was surprised – and then not, when she thought about what a brilliant teacher and researcher he was – had been offered the chairmanship of a department of musicology – he did not bother to say where – and was considering the offer, both depressed and inspired by her having had the courage to leave Manchester and abandon him to the 'misery of boredom'. His voice trailed off and ended in the middle of a sentence. She closed the phone and placed it on the desk.

Caterina was suddenly overcome by an attack of conscience. The cousins were paying her to find something in these papers, and the least she could do was have a look through them to see if anything referred to this Königsmarck thing. She opened the storeroom and removed the thick packet she had been reading the day before. Back at the table, she untied the string, again pausing to marvel at its survival all these centuries, and started to read the top sheet. Realizing it was a letter she had read, she chastised herself for not having followed her usual scholarly routine by placing the already-read documents face down on top of the pile before tying it closed.

Or had she? She tried to remember, but the events of the previous evening had wiped out any recollection she had of her routine actions before leaving the office. Caterina was unsettled by this lapse of memory. She paged down until she found a document she had not read and started there. By limiting herself to date, salutation, first two paragraphs, and signature, she speeded the process of reading; this way, she moved quickly through the remaining documents, finding nothing that appeared to be related to Steffani's family, his feelings for them, or his possessions and will.

She closed the packet and took it back to the storeroom, set it upside down on the top of the taller trunk, and pulled out another packet, almost as thick as the other. Underneath there was nothing except the wooden bottom of the trunk.

Opening this packet, she left the strings on the table beside it. As quickly as she could, she went through the papers, touching them with the care that comes to anyone who has spent time reading documents that are hundreds of years old. She always held them at the centre of the page on both sides and lifted them gently from the page below. At the first sign of resistance, she moved the sheet lightly on its axis: so far every page had quickly come free.

After the first ten sheets she accepted the fact that she was wasting time: the only way to guarantee that she understood everything was to read each document carefully from beginning to end.

That decided, she put the papers back in order, closed the packet, and took it back to the storeroom. She slipped them all back inside the trunk, then closed and locked the metal doors.

She connected to the internet, put in Cristina's address and wrote: 'Dear Tina-Lina, Of course, it's all right for you to read whatever goes between me and this man in Constance, and of course I'm curious about anything he has to tell me about Steffani. I've read a bit about it myself, and it seems that they – the two lovers – used lines from his operas in their letters. You believe in the Holy Ghost, so you should have no trouble in adding that to the list of things to believe. At any rate, dear one, I have so far seen no other mention that Abbé Steffani was involved in the matter, and it's already risking exaggeration to consider this "involvement."

'Listen to me, Tina-Lina. We all love you and respect you and will love you and respect you whatever you do or whomever you do it with. I'm back to doing research, so I'm reading between the lines of texts, and that includes yours. Stay well, know that you are loved, eat your spinach and say your prayers. Love, Cati.'

She clicked Send.

She left the room, locked the doors carefully and went down to Roseanna's office, hoping that she would have heard all the noise of her industry and caution. But she had left.

She stopped in a bar for a *macchiatone*, ate a tuna *tramezzino*, and had a glass of water. Her reader's card got her into the Marciana without trouble and with no search, and she found her way – telling herself she must be using the same system as passenger pigeons, feeling the electromagnetic waves from the various places she passed near – to the second floor reading room with its view of the Palazzo Ducale. She set her bag down and took her notebook over to the card catalogue. Before pulling open the drawer marked K, she patted the cabinet on the top as though it were the dog or cat of an old friend. Not only did the catalogue have eleven books, in three different languages, for the Königsmarck Affair, but it contained a number of handwritten cards in a series of hands best described as 'spidery' that directed her to other books and collections in which further information was contained: in two cases these were held in the manuscript collection.

She jotted down the names, authors, and call numbers

of these and took them down to the main desk, where the librarian gave her the forms that would summon them from their store cupboard. When she gave the completed forms to the librarian, the woman took them with an almost total lack of interest or enthusiasm, leaving Caterina to suspect that her grandchildren might some day see the tomes from the manuscript collection, where-upon she slipped into Veneziano and said she was a friend of Ezio's.

'Ah,' the librarian said with a smile, 'in that case I'll get them and bring them to you at your carrel.' She studied the numbers on the paper. 'Take about half an hour,' she said and smiled again.

Caterina thanked her and went back to her carrel, stop-ping to collect the books about Königsmarck. One, she was surprised to see, was a nineteenth-century French novel. She shrugged and placed it unopened on the shelf in front of her.

Half an hour later, the librarian found her hunched over her desk, notebook open at her side, pages covered in pencilled notes. Caterina was as incapable of using a pen in a library as she was of punching a hole in a lifeboat. When the librarian set the two large manuscripts on the table, Caterina jumped, as if the woman had poked her with a stick. The librarian said she had logged the books out to Ezio, so Caterina could keep them there as long as she needed to.

When the woman was gone, Caterina lowered her face into her hands and rubbed at it, ran her fingers through her hair. She was suddenly hungry, ravenously, desper-ately hungry. She opened her bag and at the bottom found half a dusty Toblerone, which she'd been eating on a train to – how long ago it seemed – Manchester. She looked around guiltily and saw the backs of two men seated at the carrels at the other end of the room. She got to her feet, moved away from her carrel, and from the books and manuscripts, then tore free a dusty triangle. Slipping it into her mouth she let it melt, then chewed at the nougat, enjoying the way it clung to her teeth to prolong the sensation of eating.

Back at the carrel, she looked at her notes. Königsmarck had disappeared on the night of 1 July 1694, when he was seen to enter the palace and make his way towards Sophie Dorothea's apartment. It was generally accepted that he had been the victim of four courtiers, their names, at least according to the Danish Ambassador to Hanover, well known and spoken of at the time. His corpse was said to have been wrapped in a sack, weighted with stones, and tossed into the river Leine, never to be found.

In less than a month, the English envoy to Hanover, George Stepney, relayed to one of his colleagues that in the House of Hanover a political murder had taken place. 'Political murder,' Caterina muttered under her breath. Hearing it like that urged her to get to her feet and go over to study the façade of the Palazzo.

'Political murder', she said again, and then only 'Political'. Not a murder for honour and not a murder for love, though the second was always really the first. Political. The involvement of the Hanoverians in the murder would do more than weaken, perhaps destroy, their claim to the electorship. What of their claim to the throne of England, which they so desperately coveted? Surely even the English would baulk at inviting a murderer or the son of one to become king.

Although this was not her field, it was her century of study, and Caterina had a wealth of background information. Aristocrats were free to have lovers, so long as those women who did had already given their husband an heir and a spare and then were relatively discreet in their choice of lover. Don't endanger the bloodline; don't imperil the passing of the estate from father to son. Men could legitimize their bastards; women never.

Caterina remembered a conversation she had had with the Romanian, years ago, when she had first gone to Manchester. It was, in fact, the first time she had eaten dinner in Commons. Drunk, he had pulled out a chair beside her, asked if he could sit there, and sat down with only a glass and a bottle of red wine. He had said nothing while she ate her salad and then a piece of swordfish she remembered had been overcooked and covered with a sauce that added to the unpleasantness of the meal.

'We never know who our children are,' he said, then turned and asked, 'Do we?'

'Who's we?' she asked, the first words she ever spoke to him.

'Men.'

'You never know?'

'No,' the Romanian said sadly, shaking his head and taking a long drink from his glass. He refilled it, shook his head again, and said, 'We think we know, we believe, but we never know. Do we?'

'If it looks like you?' she asked.

'Men have brothers. Men have uncles,' he said, this time sipping from the glass.

'But?' she asked, certain that this was a point he meant to lead somewhere.

'Women *know*,' he said with heavy emphasis. 'They *know*.'

Caterina thought it incorrect to mention DNA tests to a man the first time she spoke to him; furthermore, he was a colleague and not a native speaker of English.

Instead, she said, 'More proof of our superiority,' and sipped white wine from her own glass.

The Romanian smiled, took her hand and kissed it, then gathered up his bottle and glass, got to his feet, and started to walk away. When he had gone three steps, he turned back and said, 'There's no need of proof, my dear.'

# 18

The memory faded; Caterina returned to the book she had been reading. She dipped back into Steffani's life at the time he was working as a diplomat, first in Hanover and then in Düsseldorf, where he moved in 1703. He worked to facilitate the making of treaties and to arrange princely marriages, though with little apparent success. He failed to prevent his former patron Maximilian Emanuel from getting mixed up in a war against England and Germany he had no chance of winning, and he failed to arrange a marriage between Maximilian Emanuel and Sophie Charlotte, who turned him down, got an upgrade, and ended as Queen of Prussia. Poor woman, she held the title for only a few years before dying at the age of thirty-six, though in the few years she was queen she won the friendship of Leibniz. Caterina recalled the frequent references to her in the letters found in the trunk, the queen who 'had so honoured' Steffani with her friendship. Did Andrea Moretti feel himself so honoured by the friendship of Caterina Pellegrini?

She continued to read the account of the tangled history of the times in which Steffani had lived and worked, when Protestant and Catholic monarchs fought for the souls, and taxes, of whole nations. It seemed that Steffani was in the business of propaganda: her choice of word, she admitted. Politicians often used religious enthusiasm to disguise the lust for raw power, though it was possible that Steffani sincerely wanted to win souls back to the One True Church. So many One True Churches. Yet Steffani did almost no preaching; nor, for that matter, did he administer the sacraments, whether to large or small groups. The Abbé busied himself with the titled and powerful, attempting to return them to the embrace of Catholicism or to convert to it from their born religion of Protestantism. To the best of Caterina's understanding, all this missioneering had little to do with religion: these were political moves based on the chances of alliance or marriage. If power shifted away from a king or emperor, an elector or a count, one way to ensure survival was to bail out of the religion of the loser-to-be and sign up with the other side, then wait to see if reconversion would be necessary. She thought of a classmate of hers from Alto Adige. Though his family had lived in the same house for centuries, his grandfather had been born in Italy, his father in Austria, and he in Italy, nationality changing as the border shifted back and forth according to political whim or the spoils of war.

She wondered what belief, today, held the same force for the majority of Europeans. One way to determine that would be to try to think of the things people would die for. Transubstantiation? The Trinity? Surely not. To save their family or the life of a person they loved? Yes. But beyond that, and perhaps the attempt to save their property, Caterina could think of nothing. At dinner parties, she had heard people – mostly in England and mostly men – assert that they would give their lives for the freedom to say or write what they wanted, but Caterina didn't believe that, just as she had never believed it for herself.

She thought of all those legends she had been taught in school, all those stories of heroic resistance and sacrifice: Giordano Bruno, Matteotti, Maria Goretti, the endless list of martyr saints. How long ago that was, and how different we are from them.

She had no idea what danger Steffani or his fellow Catholics might have been in during the years when he was attempting to change the course of history, but her sense of the times suggested it wasn't great. He might not have had to die for what he believed, but the more she read, the closer she came to the view that he had truly been willing to live for it. He seemed to have been conscientious about his job: he travelled tens of thousands of kilometres in Germany and Austria, Belgium and the Netherlands; went back and forth to Rome a number of times. Here she thought of the accounts she had read of what it was like to cross the Alps in the eighteenth century: carriage, horse, or foot, and the endless winding back and forth and up and down on impassable roads, through snow, avalanche, mud, never knowing when, or if, you would arrive. *That* was dedication.

If what she suspected was true, he had been castrated to prepare him to sing in a church choir. And yet, and yet, and yet he had remained faithful to the Church for his entire life, dedicated his energies to the propagation of that faith, had worked with full strength and conviction to convert or return rulers to that faith and thus bring into the flock the people they ruled, thus expanding the power of that Church.

She found some contemporary opinions of Steffani and read them eagerly, curious to know what people who had actually known him would have to say. 'The metamorphosis of a mere entertainer into a Bishop is as ludicrous as the scene in Lucian where a courtesan is changed into a philosopher.' Anger swept over her. He was far more than an entertainer, you supercilious bastard: she had heard the music and she knew. And then she read another one, commenting on Steffani's acceptance of praise for one of his operas: 'The haughty style seemed to me more to befit the theatre than ecclesiastical humility.' Why shouldn't he be proud of his music? And where'd this nonsense about 'ecclesiastical humility' come from? When had anyone ever seen any of *that*?

Caterina got up and went to the window, looked out, seeing nothing. Was that why Steffani so needed the Church: to give himself respectability and to protect himself against open affronts? These mean-spirited comments showed that he could never be free of them nor safe from them. They could criticize his vanity or make fun of his 'short black hair that is slightly mixed with grey and a satin cap, a large cross with brilliant diamonds and a large sapphire on his finger', but so long as the cross on his chest was a bishop's cross, they could never make fun of his masculinity.

She thought of what she had read of the apparent profligacy of his life: earning and spending great amounts of money, collecting books and relics and paintings, eating and drinking well, travelling often and always in style. Was all this meant to prove that he was one of the truly anointed? She thought of that round, sad face, turned back to her desk, and picked up the French novel about the Königsmarck Affair: at least lust, adultery, and jealousy made sense to her.

She opened the book, and her eye fell on an elaborate bookplate showing a nearly naked woman lying on a sofa, a book held open in one hand while the other lay on her rather-more-naked breast. Caterina's eye fell on the title of the book the woman was not reading: *La città morta*. Above the drawing appeared the name Gabriele d'Annunzio and below it *'Principe di Montenevoso'* and *'Presidente dell'Accademia Reale d'Italia'*. Left entirely without power to comment, even to herself, Caterina began to read.

'Little did the handsome and gallant Count Philip Königsmarck know what destiny held in store for him when, at the tender age of fifteen, he first set his gaze upon the beautiful Princess Sophie Dorothea. Destiny had chosen her to be his love, his joy, the star to the wandering bark of his passions, and, ultimately, the cause of the train wreck that was to carry him to death and her to a life of misery, pain, abandonment, and shame.'

The same destiny that had endowed the Count with these things had endowed Caterina with a sensitivity to truth and accuracy, and so she looked up from the opening paragraph and said, 'He was sixteen, and she wasn't a princess.' She drew a veil of unknowing between her mind and the metaphor of the train wreck and returned her eyes to the page. Although the book was written in French and she could read the language easily, she still didn't have the immediate knee-jerk response that a native speaker would have. It took a split second before the absurd vulgarity of the language caused her to giggle.

Within ten pages, Caterina was lost in a world of climactic intemperance, with 'gusts of sighs', 'floods of tears', 'tempestuous passion', and 'lightning flashes of rage'. Sophie Dorothea, she learned, was 'married to a brute', and was 'a loving mother', 'an injured wife', 'a delightful tease', and 'slow to anger'.

Königsmarck was 'a clever rake', 'ambitious and hard-working', 'one of the most brilliant swordsmen of his time', and 'unfaithful to all women until his heart was given – for life and for death – to the beautiful Sophie Dorothea'.

After forty minutes, hands still holding the book, she told herself to stop this, to stop reading. It might have been good enough for d'Annunzio, but it was not good enough for her. She realized only now what the good sisters had meant when they warned the ten-year-old Caterina and her classmates that a book could be an 'occasion of sin' though she was in some confusion as to the precise nature of the sin she was committing. What religion said it was a sin to waste other people's time or to be unwittingly ridiculous?

Again she walked to the window, where she opened her bag and took out an energy bar, the sort of thing people think is meant to be eaten during an assault on Everest. She glanced at the motionless backs of the two other researchers, who appeared not to have moved since last she looked at them, muffled the noise she made opening this wrapper, and ate it in four bites.

She had skimmed a hundred and fifty pages, and once back at the desk she flipped to the end to see the page number: there were just forty pages left. Life is never guilt-free, she reflected, and perhaps it was good enough for her, after all. 'Jealous wrath', 'violent rages', and 'unbearable torture' came at her, only to be countered by 'moments of bliss' and 'joy such as she had never known', which is not to overlook 'two spirits united as one'. The villains appeared – all wearing the requisite 'dark cloaks' – and the worst of them, Nicolò Montalbano, was the one to commit the 'vile deed'. Not from any interest in the prose or curiosity about the fate of the protagonists, but simply because she was growing progressively hungrier,

Caterina speeded the pace of her reading, and within another fifteen minutes she was done with it. She snapped it closed and tossed it – something Caterina was not in the habit of doing with books – on to the desk.

How had it happened that the historical accounts, which were more or less locked to the reported facts, had fascinated her and aroused her sympathies for these two careless fools, while the fictional telling of the tale, which was meant to bare their souls and was free to attribute to them the most tempestuous emotions while playing with the reader's, only left her feeling relieved that these two selfish little geese had been removed from the scene?

The energy bar had not been enough. Hunger attacked her, and she gave in to it. She chose three of the books and put them in her bag, left the library unquestioned, crossed the Piazzetta and started back towards Castello, walking along by the water and happy to do so. At the bottom of the first bridge she turned left and down a *calle* running back from the Bacino. Up on the right, her feet and stomach remembered, there was a ridiculously small bar that used to serve tiny pizzas topped with a single anchovy. And so it was, and the spritz was unchanged, and after three of the first and one of the second, Caterina was ready to go back to the Foundation and work her way through the remaining documents in the last packet in the trunk.

They dealt with the transfer to Steffani of a benefice and an estate in Seltz, which she learned was on the Rhine and belonged to the Palatinate. It was one of those cities that ping-ponged between Catholic and Protestant: the Reformation turned it Protestant, and the French turned it back to Catholicism. And then the Jesuits came on the scene, and Caterina, *una mangia-prete* of no indifferent conviction, had a presentiment that things would get worse for everyone involved, and there would be a lot of empty pockets. She remembered then that backward-slanting note added to the list of things that had been left to the Jesuits. 'Fool.'

The account she read was complicated, for it attempted to explain in historical and legal terms what was, to put it crassly, a case of people's fighting over money. The earnings from Steffani's appointment as Provost of Seltz were denied him because of the prior involvement and subsequent claims of the Jesuits, who insisted that the monies were theirs by right. The case rumbled through the ecclesiastical courts for years as the Pope dodged this way and that way to avoid making a decision about who was to sweep up the loot.

In 1713, Steffani, who insisted on his full right to the money, received just 713 thalers out of the total payments of 6,000. Appeals and people willing to defend Steffani's claim to the money went to and from Rome, but the matter continued to drag on without resolution. 'Jesuits,' she muttered under her breath, much as a person of lesser civility would utter an obscenity.

Some documents suggested that the missing money was a serious blow to Steffani's finances. Because the legal cases took place in the decade before his death, and since his claims repeatedly referred to his parlous financial condition, Caterina again wondered where all the money had gone. He was to retire soon after his unsuccessful attempt to collect the benefice of Seltz; some accounts claimed that he also had severe difficulty in collecting the money from his benefice in Carrara. Caterina remembered that the sale of indulgences was one of the grievances that Luther made public when he nailed up his theses on the door of the cathedral. Had the bargaining with benefices been another?

170

The dispute continued as Steffani's financial situation worsened. He repeatedly petitioned the Pope, the Jesuits, and various temporal rulers. What surprised Caterina were the names of the people to whom he felt comfortable enough to write to ask for help: the King of England, the Elector of Mainz, the English Ambassador in The Hague, even the Emperor himself: 'I have asked the Emperor if he, as an act of charity or fondness, could buy the paintings from me so that I can survive a little while longer.' 'My lamentations can be matched only by those of Jeremiah. In the end I need to plead for alms. The King of England urges me to remain in Hanover more strongly than do the people in Rome. It is the world turned upside down.' At the same time that he was addressing these people, he was writing to others to tell them he was reduced to begging for alms. 'I now have nothing more to sell with which to maintain myself.' 'I have sold all of my possessions, even my small chalice, made of silver. Because of this, I can no longer provide myself with even those things people think are necessary.' All the letters implied that at this time in his life he was reduced to selling his possessions, which rendered the cousins' belief in a family 'treasure' even more ridiculous.

Caterina went back to the computer and to the archives holding material on Steffani: in Munich, Hanover, and Rome. She logged in to the Fondo Spiga in Rome, named after Steffani's benefice, and started scrolling down the papers that were posted. And found the cousins. No, not the cousins, but the men who must have been their ancestors and thus the direct heirs to Steffani's estate. In 1724, the Abbé wrote to Giacomo Antonio Stievani and to the archpriest of Castelfranco, Antonio Scapinelli, inquiring about the deeds to some houses in the San Marcuola section of Venice which the three of them had jointly inherited but which had been somehow usurped by the Labia family. Steffani suggested that the men meet to arrive at an agreement on how the estate should be reclaimed and divided among them: the archive had no record of a response from them.

An heir writes to his cousins to ask how they might divide property they have inherited in common, and the others fail to respond to, or even acknowledge, the request, no doubt preventing any attempt to sell the property or divide and pay out the profits. Caterina remembered how much it used to annoy her, when she was younger, to hear her mother speak of her distrust of anyone who 'came of greedy people'. She had attempted to reason with her foolish mother, victim of her antiquated beliefs in heredi-tary family characteristics. Ah, those who have eyes and see not.

Reading randomly in the archives devoured the rest of Caterina's afternoon, and by the end of it, though she had found out more about the financial difficulties that afflicted Steffani near the end of his life, she had no firmer grasp of the man.

At seven, mindful of the cousins' eagerness and reluc-tant to have to listen to another admonition about having failed to do what she was being paid – they'd surely mention that if they dared – to do, she typed in Dottor Moretti's address and wrote, 'Dear Dottor Moretti, pursuant to our agreement, I am continuing with my reading of the documents: to make sense of them in the historical or personal context, I find it necessary to conduct further background research, without which many refer-ences, lacking context, will have little or no meaning. I would not like the claim of either Signor Stievani or Signor Scapinelli to be in any way weakened by my failure to understand a reference which might favour the case of either one of them, and thus it is necessary . . .' she backed up and deleted that word, replacing it with 'imperative' '. . . that I pursue my research at the Marciana, where I am currently reading through books and documents in Italian, French, German, English, and Latin' – take THAT, cousins – 'some of which make reference to the family situation and do create a context that suggests the Abbé's assumption of familial responsibility and mutual interests.'

Here she began a new paragraph to describe her archival research and transcribed Steffani's letters to his cousins, noting drily that the archives contained no response from them.

'I am optimistic that wider familiarity with this information will be of great service in my pursuit of a clear understanding and interpretation of Abbé Steffani's testamentary dispositions.' She closed with a polite salutation and signed both her first and last name, omitting her title. She was also pleased that the letter avoided the use of any form of direct address, either polite or familiar.

Send.

When she looked at the table and saw that she had, in five hours, read only four documents, she thought of the weeping Francesca's words to Dante as she explained how she and her lover Paolo, standing at her side there in Hell and mingling his tears with hers, had spent their day reading until, 'That day we read no further.' Their reading had led them to lust, to sin, and finally to death and Hell: Caterina's was going to lead her to pasta with tomatoes, olives, and capers and half a bottle of Refosco. How much she would have preferred lust and sin.

# 19

She left the Foundation and, a slave to beauty, took the longest way to the *riva*. Once in sight of the water, she turned towards the Basilica to watch the light disappear behind its pale domes. As she turned away and started walking towards Castello, she noticed how the remaining light fell on the faces of the people walking towards her and brightened them in every sense. The tourist current was high with the approach of Easter, and sudden riptides had begun to sweep past the unwary natives or slack tides becalm them, permitting large chunks of flotsam to flow around them. Things had changed in the years she had been away, and the local population now had the freedom to move swiftly against the approaching current only a few months a year. But, Caterina observed, that was better odds than the salmon got.

She had slipped her *telefonino* into the outside pocket of her bag, telling herself why it was necessary to do this. Perhaps she'd decide to call a friend and suggest dinner;

perhaps her mother would call; or another old classmate would learn she was back in town and suggest the cinema and a pizza. 'Or perhaps the heavens will catch fire, Caterina, and you'll have to call the firemen,' she told herself out loud. A short woman walking by with the aid of a cane gave Caterina a startled glance and looked around quickly, searching for a place to move away from the crazy woman.

Caterina ignored her, pulled out her phone, dropped it inside her bag, and zipped the bag shut. The phone did not ring, and so she had both the time and the sense to stop in the neighbourhood store and buy olives, capers, and tomatoes, go home, make the pasta, and drink the rest of the Refosco.

Only then did she turn on her own computer and look at her mail. Sure enough there was one from Tina.

'Dear Cati,' Cristina began, 'this is the email that my friend in Constance sent. To me. Addressed to me. So I read it. Let me send it along to you so you can read him before I say anything.'

"Dear Sister Cristina, I'm happy to give what information I can to your sister and hope it will be of help to her in her research. Even after that, I will still be in your debt for your generosity in helping me gain access to the Episcopal Library of Trent.

"Your sister is evidently familiar with the 'Affair', so I need waste no time outlining it. The manuscript, which I came upon while researching a book on Post-Reformation ecclesiastical taxation, is in the possession of the Schönborn family and appears to be the memoirs of the Countess von Platen, one of Count Philip Christoph Königsmarck's former lovers, reported by all to have been passionately jealous of him. She had also been the mistress of the Elector Ernst August, by whom she had two illegitimate children.

(I've no idea of the proper form for putting a footnote in an email and so am forced to use this parenthesis. She, Clara Elisabeth von Platen, also tried to persuade her lover, Königsmarck, to marry her own illegitimate daughter by Ernst August, which fact you are free to use should a colleague ever attribute dissolute morals to the Italians. And to prevent your going off to discover the destiny of her daughter, be pleased to hear that she was said to be the mistress of Georg Ludwig – her half-brother and soon to be King George I of England, to which country she accompanied him, later becoming the Countess Darlington and dividing his favours with the Duchess of Kendal, Melusine von der Schulenburg.)

"How the manuscript could have ended up in the archives of a family that also has an important collection of musical manuscripts, among which are many by your sister's composer, is not within my competence to determine. Letters from Countess von Platen now held in the Graf von Schönborn'sche Hauptverwaltung in Würzburg confirm the handwriting.

"In this manuscript, which begins with the explanation that it is being written in the shadow of death, she claims a desire to tell the truth in God's ears before that event. I read manuscripts, not souls, so I have no idea if this is the truth or her invention. Her desire to make her peace before God is quickly forgotten, for she does not miss a chance to speak badly of most of the people she mentions, even those who had died decades before.

"Of Königsmarck's murder, after saying only that four men were involved and one of them gave the fatal blow, from behind, she says she hopes "his spirit found peace", though she also says she is not surprised at the manner of his death, 'at the hands of those he injured', which presumably implicates the family of the Elector, although even the most cursory reading of the Count's brief history might extend that list.

"After a bit of moralizing about the 'justice meted out to this sinner and betrayer of womanhood', she writes, 'though it was the hand of God that struck him down, it was the Abbé who gained from the fatal blow that sent him to his Maker'.

"Then, as if someone had asked her for evidence, she writes, 'Did he not, Judas-like, make possible and profit from the crime? The blood money given to him bought the Jewels of Paradise, but nothing can buy him manhood and honour and beauty.'

"After that, at the beginning of the next line, as though the writer intended to continue with the text, there is the single word 'Philip', but nothing follows that word. The memoirs continue on the next page, but she has nothing further to say about Königsmarck."

There followed his hope that her sister could make use of this information, then some details of his own ongoing research, a polite closing, and an offer to facilitate access to the manuscript, should her sister so desire.

'And there you have it, my dear,' Cristina continued. 'I've no idea what the Countess means by all of this. She doesn't say she was there, she doesn't say she saw your Abbé kill him, only that he "made possible the crime". Like my friend, I don't read souls, only texts.

'Let me go back to the idea of reading souls for a minute, if I might and if you don't mind. Mine is very tired and because of that probably illegible. I keep working at the research, but the more I read, the more irrelevant it all seems. The Vatican's foreign policy during the twentieth century? What can any thinking person believe it was except manoeuvring in pursuit of power? On the wall in front of my desk, I've put an old photo of the Pope giving communion to Pinochet, and that's enough to make a person go out and join the Zoroastrians, isn't it? They, however, don't allow people to convert, and can you think of a more noble tenet for a religion to have?

'Yes, Kitty-Cati, I'm thinking of jumping ship, of telling them they can have their wimple back, not that I've ever worn one, or would. I'm deeply tired of it and of having to close an eye and then close the other one and then close a third one if I had it, so much do I read and see about what they've done and still do.

'They're drunk with power, the men at the top. Please don't tell me you told me so. It's not the basic faith that's troubling me. I still believe it all: that He lived and died so that we would be better and it – whatever "it" is – would be better. But not with these clowns in charge, these old fools who stopped thinking a hundred years ago (I'm in a generous mood and so left the other zero off that sum).

'Please don't say anything at home, and please don't be angry that I asked you that, as if I couldn't trust you to keep your mouth shut. I know they don't really believe it, but I don't want them to worry about me because they know I do and know how much it will cost me to walk away. Isn't it funny how it all shifts around at a certain age, and we start worrying about them and try to spare them from being hurt? You think that's what it means to be a grown-up?

'I'll probably wake up in the morning with a hangover for having said all this, but you're the only one I can say it to. Well, there's someone here, but he doesn't want to hear this sort of thing from me. Or, more accurately, he does; what he doesn't want is for me to go back and forth or agonize over it, just to DO it. Yes, Kitty-Cati, it's really a "he", just to put your mind at rest after all these years. No, that's to do you an injustice. You wouldn't care one way or the other, would you? And he's nice and single and uncomplicated and very smart and leaves me alone when I want to be left alone and doesn't when I don't, and where does a girl find that sort of thing these days. Eh? It's still too soon to tell you more about him, but don't worry, please: he's a good man.

'All right, go back to your research, and I won't go back to mine. I just don't care about it any more, and I know myself well enough to know I won't ever care about it again. I find your Abbé and his doings far more interesting, probably because he is so far removed in time, so if you don't mind, I'll continue to work as your research assistant. That failing, you think Uncle Rinaldo would hire me as an apprentice plumber if I came back? Love, Tina-Lina.'

For the first time in her life, Caterina was hurled into a crisis of faith. So strong was Caterina's faith in her sister's faith that she had stopped arguing with her about it years ago and confined her comments to the odd flash of sarcasm. The zest of confrontation had gone out of it for Caterina in the face of what she believed was Tina's happiness at having found the place in the world where she belonged and where she could work at what she loved while believing that to do so somehow made a difference to the god she worshipped.

And now along comes Tina and pushes down the graven image that Caterina had built. She had no idea what happened to an ex-nun, or even how a nun went about becoming an ex. Did she have to ask permission of someone, or was it enough simply to pack her bag and walk out, a clerical Nora closing the door behind her?

So certain had Caterina's faith in her sister been that she had never seriously considered the possibility that she'd bolt. A marriage couldn't just be walked away from because it was, at base, a contract between two people, and the contract had to be dissolved before they could be free of one another. With whom did a nun make a contract: the order she joined or the god she joined it to serve? And who had God's power of attorney?

Caterina felt the pull of irony and the absurd, two tidal forces she found hard to resist. Their mother was forever giving the girls the advice that they should think one year ahead before trying to assess the importance of any situation, but Caterina had always found her life trapped in the instant. Tina's pain – for it had been pain animating her email – was now, not a year from now. If you discovered the man you had been married to for more than twenty years was not the man you believed him to be, that his virtue was a show, his honour a sham, what did you do?

Caterina closed the window and created a new mail: how strange that Windows should use that verb, rather than 'Write'. 'Tina-Lina, my dearest dear, you've got a job, a family that loves you beyond reason (I'm in there, as mindless as the others), your health is good, you have intelligence, grace, and wit. And you still have the Baby Jesus, asleep in His bed. If you do jump ship, you have a safe, warm berth to come to, though I'm sure they would keep you on there: you just switch from the Catholic side to the Protestant, and how clever of you to work for a university that is religiously ambidextrous.

'If you decide to come home, no one will care why, and *Mamma* will be delirious at the possibility of cooking for you again, and she'll love it even more if you bring your friend and give her another mouth to feed. You are such a hotshot in your profession that universities will fight to have you.

'I shouldn't say this, but I will: in the end, does it matter if your God exists or not? And isn't it pretentious and self-important of us to insist that we know how to describe or define him/Him? We can't figure out the value of pi, and yet we think we know something about God? As *Nonna* said, it would make the chickens laugh.

'To put an end to your worse existential uncertainty, I promise to call Uncle Rinaldo tomorrow and ask him if he wants an apprentice. Love, Kitty-Cati.'

# 20

Instead of sitting and contemplating the collapse of her favourite sister's life, Caterina chose to work. Spurred by the email from the professor in Constance, she began looking into Countess von Platen and learned of her semi-official position as the mistress of Ernst August.

Caterina was struck by how little things changed in this world of hers. Kings were once wont to make their mistresses the duchess of this or the countess of that, and now prime ministers gave them cabinet ministries or ambassadorships. And the world chugged on and nothing changed.

She checked the dates and, sure enough, the Countess had been in Hanover at the time Königsmarck disappeared. There was a great deal of contemporary testimony stating that Königsmarck had been one of her lovers and that she was violently jealous of the younger man. Caterina also found an 1836 magazine article about Countess Platen's purported memoirs, in which the reviewer wrote that she claimed to have been a witness to the murder. The Countess was often named as the person who reported the affair between Königsmarck and Sophie Dorothea to the Elector Ernst August, though what Caterina had read made her suspect that the few people who might not have known about this affair were the deaf and the blind and perhaps the halt and lame.

'If only she'd played by the rules,' Caterina caught herself thinking. If only silly, besotted Sophie Dorothea had been a bit more discreet about her affair, things could have gone along without fuss: Georg would have his mistresses, she could have her lover, and she would have ended up Queen of England, instead of a prisoner in a castle, cut off from her children and the world and all visits save that of her mother, whom she did not particularly like.

Caterina had been reading all day and she was tired, but she told herself she didn't have to clock into the office at nine the next morning so could continue reading as late as she chose. Besides, she was intrigued by how much these people and their behaviour seemed familiar to her: change their clothing and hairstyles, teach them other languages, and they would feel completely at home in Rome or Milan or, in fact, London, where a number of the minor players had remained and prospered.

Adulterous behaviour among the Hanoverians was no news to Caterina nor to any person in Europe who knew where the Saxe-Coburg-Gothas and the Windsors came from. Not that, she reflected, their Continental relatives had distinguished themselves by the sobriety of their comportment.

She had been using the standard JSTOR site to access scholarly journals, but now, sated with the serious tone of what she had been reading, she switched to a more mainstream search. She was not troubled to find a Thai girl who was looking for a considerate husband – 'age and looks don't matter' – lurking at the side of the page, and she was so accustomed to seeing ads for cars, restaurants, mortgages, and vitamins that she no longer saw them in any real sense. On the ninth page of articles available under Steffani's name, she found a listing for *Catholic Encyclopedia* and thought she'd have a peek, much in the way one tried to see what cards another poker player might have in his hand.

It was only towards the middle of the article that Steffani's clerical endeavours were mentioned, when it was noted that the Church had made him Prothonotary Apostolic – whatever that was – for North Germany, presumably in return for 'his services for the cause of Catholicism in Hanover'. 'Services?' The wording in the article was unclear; the closest date used in conjunction with his appointment to that post was 1680, when Steffani would have been twenty-six.

That ambiguity set her grazing through another source, where she found mention that he was an apostolic protho-notary by 1695. The year after Königsmarck's murder. 'Services?'

She heard a noise, a dull buzzing, and with no conscious thought, her mind turned to the man she had seen on the street and who had been sitting at her boat stop. A bolt of panic brought her to her feet and took her to the door, but as she moved away from the table, the sound grew dimmer. When she realized it was her *telefonino* ringing in her bag, Caterina felt her knees weaken and her face flush with heat. She walked back to the table, opened her bag, and pulled out the phone.

'*Pronto?*' she said, in a voice out of which she had forced every emotion save mild interest.

'Caterina?' a man asked.

Aware of how moist the hand that held the phone was, she transferred the phone to her other ear and wiped her hand on the back of her sweater. '*Sì.*' She was every busy woman who had ever been interrupted by a phone call, every person who had been disturbed at – she looked – nine-forty in the evening – and who certainly had better things to do with her time.

'*Ciao.* It's Andrea. I'm not bothering you, am I?'

She pulled out a chair and sat 'No, of course not. I couldn't find the phone.' She laughed, then found the whole situation funny and laughed again.

'I'm glad you did,' he said. 'I wanted to tell you about the cousins.'

'Ah, yes. The cousins,' she said. 'They aren't happy?'

'They weren't happy,' he said, stressing the second word. 'In fact, Signor Scapinelli accused you of spending all of your time walking around the city and drinking coffee.'

'But?' she asked, repressing the impulse to observe that it was better than accusing her of walking around the city drinking grappa.

'But I used the same technique you did in the mail and explained that you were merely being conscientious and wanted to be sure you missed nothing that might make an attribution of the putative estate in favour of one claimant or the other.' Oh, my, she thought, how lawyerly he sounded.

'Thank you,' was the only thing she could say.

'There's nothing to thank me for. It's true. Unless you read whatever background information you can find, you won't understand the context of what you read in the documents. And then either you'll make the wrong decision, or you won't be able to make any decision at all.'

'It's possible,' she said with the mildness of the hardened

researcher, but then she considered the second possibility and asked, 'What happens if I can't make a decision?'

'Ah,' he said, drawing out the sound. 'In that case, any documents that have value would be sold, and they'd divide whatever they bring. So far, though, you haven't found anything that could be of great value, have you?'

'No, not to the best of my knowledge.'

'Then, as I said, they'll sell everything for whatever they can get and split the profits.'

'But?' she asked, responding to the underlying uncertainty in his voice.

'They've told me there's a legend, on both sides of the family, about the ancestor priest who left a hidden fortune.' The fact that Andrea could also tell this story, she thought, made it no more believable than when Roseanna had told it.

'There are lots of legends,' she said, then added drily, 'but there are few fortunes.'

'I know, I know, but the Stievani family insists he had it when he died. They have an ancestral aunt – this is in the nineteenth century – who supposedly had a paper from him where he said that he had left the Jewels of Paradise to his nephew Stievani – Giacomo Antonio – who was her great-grandfather.'

The use of the exact phrase Countess von Platen had used in her condemnation of Steffani shocked her. In a voice she tried to make dispassionate and lawyerly, she asked, 'And this paper?'

This time he laughed. 'If you ever get tired of music, you might consider the police force.'

Caterina laughed outright. 'I'm afraid I'm not cut out for that sort of thing.'

'You ask questions like a policewoman.'

'Like a researcher,' she corrected him.

'Could you explain the difference?'

Realizing how much she enjoyed sparring with him, Caterina said, 'Researchers can't arrest people and send them to jail.'

He laughed. 'That's true enough.'

Out of the blue, it came to her to ask him. 'Do you believe this story about the aunt?' He was their lawyer, for heaven's sake. What did she expect him to say?

He was silent for so long that she feared her question had offended him by its impertinence. Just as it occurred to her that he might have hung up, he said, 'It doesn't matter. It's legally worthless.'

'And if the paper had miraculously been preserved?' she asked, passing from impertinence to provocation.

'A piece of paper is a piece of paper,' he said.

'And a fragment of the True Cross is only a splinter of wood?' she asked.

There was a long pause before he asked, sounding falsely casual, 'Why do you say that?'

She thought the comparison ought to have been clear enough, but she decided to explain. 'If enough people choose to believe something is what other people say it is, then it becomes that to them.'

'Like what?' he asked amiably.

'The example I just gave you,' she said, 'Or the Book of Mormon or the Shroud of Turin, or a footprint in a stone where someone or other jumped up to Heaven. It's all the same.'

'It's interesting,' he said, not sounding persuaded.

'What is?'

'That all of your examples are religious.'

'I thought I'd use that because it's the area where they're all sure to be nonsense.'

'Sure to be?'

She had the grace to laugh. 'To the likes of me, at least.'

'And to the rest of us?'

'Then a piece of paper isn't only a piece of paper, I suppose,' she said. 'Depends on what you want to be true.'

He was silent for so long that she was sure she had gone too far and offended his beliefs or his sensibility and he was going to say good-night and hang up.

'Would you be free for dinner tomorrow evening?' he surprised her by asking.

When she and her friends had first started going out with boys, there had been general agreement that one should never accept the first offer: it was a bad tactical move, they had all decided, with the wisdom of teenagers.

Well, she was no longer a teenager, was she? 'Yes.'

# 21

When she finished the call, Caterina had the choice of
going to bed or going to work. She returned to the article
in the *Catholic Encyclopedia*. Near the end there was a
remark that, in light of everything she had discovered
about Steffani, deserved closer scrutiny. 'A delicate mission
was entrusted to him at the various German courts in
1696, and in 1698 at the court in Brussels, for which office
he was singularly fitted by his gentle and prudent
manners.'

Could this 'delicate mission' at the German courts have
been related to the Königsmarck murder? In everything
she read about it, the murder was referred to, even in the
indices, as the 'Königsmarck Affair', a triumph in
rebranding if ever she had seen one. Had that rebranding
been the office for which Steffani was singularly fitted
because of his gentle and prudent manners? Gentle and
prudent men are not often believed to be in the employ
of murderers or of men who commission murderers, are

they? She switched away from the *Encyclopedia*, determined to consult more reliable sources.

Duke Ernst August had for years longed to add the title and power of 'Elector' to his string of titles, and it was finally granted to him by the Emperor in 1692. Soon after, his daughter-in-law's attention-getting lover disappeared, leaving not a trace save in the memoirs and gossip of members of his court and of the North German aristocracy. His disappearance was referred to as an 'Affair', and the man who stood most to profit from it remained unblemished by it.

She dived into the catalogue of the library of the University of Vienna, in whose waters she had been swimming for years, and quickly discovered the precise honours and powers that came along with the title 'Elector'. Besides electing the Holy Roman Emperor, an elector got to call himself Prince. 'Big deal,' Caterina muttered to herself, having picked up the phrase from an American friend. More interestingly, the electors had the monopoly of mineral wealth in their territories, in an age when currency was based on gold and silver. They could also tax Jews and mint money. Thus 'Elector', beyond being an honour that would satisfy the urgings of vanity, would satisfy those of greed, as well. Who could resist such a combination?

But if your fool of a daughter-in-law put your reputation at risk by her public carryings-on with a noted rake, how seriously would your position be treated by the gilded and titled, or even by the common people? And how likely was it that the other electors would vote you into the club, a prerequisite her reading had revealed to her? Caterina had but to think of the death, three centuries later, of another beautiful young princess believed to have taken a lover, even though she was no longer married to the heir to the throne. When she died a very public death along with her lover, the world had exploded in an orgy of wild surmise and gossip about the 'true' cause of their deaths. Would it have been any different if the death of Königsmarck had been a public event? Official information always moves with glacial majesty, while gossip travels at the speed of light. Softly, then, softly in the night: how much better a quiet disappearance that left behind only the 'Affair' than a corpse at the side of the road.

She opened the book about Steffani and had another look at the portrait, said to have been painted in 1714. Take away twenty years of fat, remove the double chin, give him back some of his hair, and he'd look as able as any man to stick a knife into another man's back. Many accounts spoke of the sweetness and peacefulness of Steffani's character. He was in Germany as a diplomat, a class of man not best known for breaking up pubs in drunken brawls while in pursuit of their goals. But still his mission was the reconversion of Germany to Catholicism, and who better to start with than the Protestant Duke of Hanover, and how better to win his favour than by doing him an enormous favour by eliminating an inconvenient relative who would make a mockery of his claim to the electorship? As Stalin was later to observe: 'No man, no problem.'

Steffani might have failed to reconvert North Germany to the true religion, but he did win religious toleration and a new church for the Catholics of Hanover, and his Vatican masters might well have calculated this as a fair exchange for the death of a man who was, after all, only a Protestant. Caterina came upon another reference to Nicolò Montalbano and the 150,000 thalers. She might have been a bit hazy about the exact value of a thaler in 1694, but she was in no confusion about the size of 150,000.

The next year, Steffani's opera, *I trionfi del fato*, presented the idea that humans are not entirely responsible for their emotions and thus not for their actions. What more anodyne sentiment with which to calm the gossip-bestirred waters of the electoral court? Was this part of Steffani's 'delicate mission'?

It was past midnight, and she decided she had had enough of speculation and wonder and moving around to see events from a perspective that might make them look different.

In the kitchen she drank a glass of water, then went into the bathroom, washed her face and brushed her teeth. As she looked at herself in the mirror, she saw a woman in her mid-thirties with a straight nose and eyes that were green in this light. She put the toothbrush in the glass on the side of the sink, cupped some water in her hands and rinsed out her mouth. When she was upright, she looked at the woman again and told her, 'Your sister is a historian. She'd know how to find this Montalbano guy. Besides, she's living in Germany, and that's where all this happened.' Nodding at her own sagacity, she went back to the desk and turned on the computer again.

'Tina-Lina, I'm sorry to leave you in existential high water, but I want to ask you a favour. Hunt around and find me more about Nicolò Montalbano, a Venetian living at the court of Ernst August when Königsmarck was murdered and who came into a lot of money soon after his death. His name is already familiar to me, but I think it's familiar because of his involvement with music and not for murder and blackmail. I'd be very grateful if you would try to find him in other places. I also came across mention of him in a lurid novel about the euphemistically called "Affair", an exact reference to which I can send you, should you want to read it and learn. If Uncle Rinaldo can't take you on as an apprentice, perhaps you could give a thought to a literary life. Think of the use you could make of your years of historical study; think of the passionate scenes you could toss into novels about the Council of Worms or the War of the Spanish Succession, and I'm sure there's some neck-and-neck competition to be Bishop of Maienfeld that you could transform into the *Gone with the Wind* of our times.

'It's late, I'm tired, and I'm having dinner tomorrow night with a very attractive man I've met here. I almost hope nothing comes of it because he's a lawyer, and I'd hate to have to revise my opinion of them as blood-sucking opportunists.

'There's a spare room in this apartment they've given me, just in case you think about coming home and maybe don't want to stay with *Mamma* and *Papà*. Love, Cati.'

As soon as she sent the mail, she realized she should not have said that last, about coming home. That's the trouble with emails: you write them in haste and send them off, and that means there's never time to steam open the letter and read it through again to see if you should say it or not.

She turned off the computer and, leaving the open books where they were, went to bed.

The next day she awoke filled with an inordinate sense of expectation, and for the first few moments she could not locate the source of the feeling. But then she remembered her dinner date with the blood-sucking opportunist, laughed out loud, and got out of bed.

Andrea was to come by and pick her up at the Foundation at seven-thirty: this would give her the chance to stop there before going to the Marciana to spend the day in the library, and then return to the Foundation to send a report of the day's reading. She could not rid herself of conspiratorial glee at the thought that she would go to the Foundation to send her email to Dottor Moretti to send on to the cousins and then go out to dinner with him.

As soon as she stepped outside, she felt that the weather had changed and the spring had decided to become serious. She had spent time in Manchester, she reminded herself, and she had learned to mistrust the weather, but still she saw no need to go back up four flights of stairs to get a heavier jacket or a scarf. When she came out on to the *riva*, however, she was hit by the wind coming from off the water and hurried towards the Arsenale stop, deciding to take the vaporetto, even if it was only one stop. A Number One came from behind only a minute after that, but her automatic calculation told her there was no way to get it, even if she were to break into a run, which she refused to do. She watched it pass her by, and she kept on walking, cutting in at Bragora to get away from the wind.

She let herself into the building and went down to Roseanna's office. The door was open, and she looked in to see Roseanna at her desk, her *telefonino* at her ear. The other woman smiled and waved her inside, said a few polite words into the phone, then ended the conversation. She dropped the phone on her desk, and came around her desk to give Caterina two kisses. 'Any progress?' she asked, but with interest and not reproach.

'I've been doing background reading at the Marciana,' Caterina explained. Roseanna leaned back against her desk, her hands propped flat behind her, ready to listen.

'I found a letter he wrote to two men called Stievani and Scapinelli.'

'Really?' Roseanna's curiosity was splashed across her face.

194

'Yes. The original two cousins,' she said and was pleased to see Roseanna's answering smile.

'What did he tell them?'

'They – he and the two of them – were heirs to some houses near San Marcuola that had been taken over by the Labia family. He wanted to meet them to discuss what to do about getting possession of the houses and selling them. It sounds like he was short of money.'

When Roseanna didn't respond, she continued. 'They didn't answer him.'

'What happened?'

'I don't know. There was no answer from them in the archives.'

'What did he sound like?' Roseanna asked thoughtfully, as if she were speaking of a person Caterina had just met.

'Excuse me?'

'Steffani. What did he sound like in his letter?'

'Polite,' she said after a moment's reflection, not having given this conscious thought while she was reading the letter. 'And weak,' she added, surprising herself even more. 'He practically begged them to get in touch with him, and he kept insisting that his only motivation was the good of the family, almost as if he thought they'd have reason to doubt that.' She considered the letter a bit longer and added, 'It made me – I don't know – uncomfortable.'

'Why?'

'Because the tone was so humble. People then were more formal with one another than we are, and the language was more elaborate and full of all sorts of formulaic courtesies,' she conceded. 'But this was too humble, and I suppose it troubled me because it was so out of place in a man of his stature.'

'As a musician?'

'Yes. And he was a bishop, for heaven's sake. So to hear

him use this tone with two cousins from a provincial place like Castelfranco, to try to convince them that they should help him get money . . . well, it was difficult to read.' It occurred to her that, if anyone knew for certain whether Agostino was a castrato, it would be members of his family; perhaps this explained his painful deference to them.

'Does that mean you've come to like him? Steffani?' What strange questions Roseanna asked: Caterina had never thought in terms of liking him or not. His life puzzled her, but she had persuaded herself that her main interest was in trying to find out enough about him to be able to do her job.

She raised a hand and made a see-sawing gesture. 'I don't know if I like him.'

She did like his industry, the fierce pace at which he drove himself, but those were qualities, not a complete person. 'I have to keep on looking,' she heard herself say.

'Upstairs?' Roseanna asked.

'No. In the Marciana. I've still got a few things to look at.'

'Good luck.'

Caterina smiled her thanks and, spirits suddenly uplifted, started for the Marciana.

She found her carrel as she had left it the day before. She had stopped on the way to replenish her supply of chocolate and energy bars, though her researcher's conscience did not rest easy about this. Before turning her attention to the books, she stood at the window and reviewed the last few days. What she had read, both in the documents at the Foundation and in the books in her carrel, had raised as many questions as they had answered.

She opened her notebook, pressed it flat, then opened a new book. This one separated its analysis into biography and music. She had started it two days before but been waylaid by the allure of the 'Affair'. Well, enough of that. Back to work.

Carefully she read over the by now familiar details of Steffani's early life, until he went to Hanover in 1688 as court composer. As ever, she was struck by how odd that combination now seemed.

Vivaldi was a priest as well as a musician, but he had used his position in the Church as a means to further his music, the real centre of his life. He had lived and worked as a musician, and he had composed up until his death, probably in the arms of his life's companion, Anna Girò. Caterina knew precious little about his life, but she knew that things ecclesiastical, other than sacred music, played no part in it, nor did he ever aspire to any higher clerical position.

Yet benefices and titles rained upon Steffani. The shining purpose of his life, for which he apparently abandoned composing, was the return of North Germany to the Catholic Church, at which he proved a dismal failure. She found accounts of his endeavours in two histories of the Church in North Germany, written in Latin and German. Each praised his enterprise and dedication, describing his achievements in Hanover and Düsseldorf. The German text devoted a mere five pages to his work as a musician.

When she emerged from the second of these, hunger drove her from the library and to the nearest bar, where she had two sandwiches and a glass of water before returning – unquestioned and unexamined – to her place in the library.

The next book was a 1905 edition of the correspondence between Sophie Charlotte and Steffani, in French, which both of them wrote with ease and grace. One of his letters found him at a low ebb. 'The bitter grief I suffer because of the affairs of the world; the pain I suffer in seeing so many people whom I respect wishing to destroy themselves entirely.' He wrote of leading a life 'that is truly a burden' and of his 'unlimited hypochondria'. He described a life in which his only friend and source of safety was his harpsichord. It seemed to Caterina that, after saying all of this, he suddenly realized he had to try to joke his way out of the truth he had revealed, but the tone did not ring true to Caterina. What did ring true was the ease with which he addressed the recipient: she hoped the Queen had accepted this because of his musical gifts rather than his clerical position. Or was it the unspoken awareness that he was a castrato that rendered his liberties harmless?

She continued reading the letters, trying to think of them as the performance of a person whom fate had moved up the social ladder but who remained aware, no matter how high he rose, of just how precarious his position was. Seen in this light, a new tone became audible in his prose. She noted the excessive gratitude he poured upon Sophie Charlotte for the simplest favour, the flattery that sometimes became overwhelming: 'since you have power over all'; 'the graces that your Majesty deigned to bestow upon me'; 'the letter with which your Majesty honoured me'; 'Your Majesty cannot do anything that is not at the peak of perfection'; 'I have the pleasure of serving your Majesty.'

At this point, Caterina told herself to bear in mind that Steffani was corresponding with the Queen of Prussia, a woman renowned throughout Europe for the depth and breadth of her learning. Caterina remembered the palace in Berlin named for her and the enormous, passionate support she gave to countless musicians. This thought was enough to dispel her last opposition to Steffani's deference. 'Narrow-minded liberal,' she whispered in self-accusation.

But still . . . but still, she was filled with the desire to take Steffani and shake him by the dangling ends of his alb and tell him that, three hundred years later, Sophie Charlotte had been remaindered to footnotes in histories of Prussia read by a few hundred people, while his music was still performed and admired. 'Narrow-minded snob,' she whispered to herself this time.

# 22

'The troubles of this century no longer cause me much pain because they are making you again turn your hand to music. Throw yourself in headlong, I implore you. Music is a friend who will not abandon or betray you, nor will she be cruel to you. You have drawn from her all the delight and beauties of the heavens, whereas friends are tepid and cunning and mistresses are without gratitude.' This was the answer Steffani received from the Queen in response to his troubled letter. Her words rose above the usual courtly language and revealed her heart. Caterina felt her own heart warm to find that he should have had this gracious, generous support from a woman he admired so fully.

Nevertheless, within months, the correspondence was dead. Steffani, in response to a request from a Medici cardinal, implored the Queen to change her decision not to allow her favourite court musician to return to his monastery in Italy. And she, in queenly fashion, was not amused. The correspondence ended, but not before Leibniz, that most savvy of philosophers, remarked to a friend that he understood Her Majesty's anger. 'After all, if a Duke had only one hunter, and someone requested him to give it up, how else would he expect the Duke to respond than by anger?'

Well, Caterina thought, old Leibniz certainly had no illusions about describing the pecking order in a royal court, did he? And he'd certainly hung around enough of them to have learned a thing or two about the position of musicians, and let's forget all the flowery praise. Steffani's bishopric hadn't protected him one whit, not when he stepped over that invisible line. You're a genius and I am enthralled by the beauty of your music, but just remember to stay in your proper place, and don't think for an instant that you can question the decisions of the Queen of Prussia.

Looking at her watch, Caterina saw that it was after six, which gave her just barely enough time to get back to the Foundation and write a report to Dottor Moretti. Because she was going to be out to dinner that evening, she left the books where they were, planning to return the next day to continue reading the background material.

She got to the office before seven but found no sign of Roseanna. She went up to what had become her office, but did not open the storeroom. Instead, she turned on the computer. There were three emails, but before so much as glancing at the names of the senders, she opened a blank mail, addressed it to Andrea but, addressing the cousins by their surnames, gave a hurried account of the results of her research that day. Without bothering to read it over, she sent it off and returned to her inbox.

The first mail was from a bank she had never heard of and inquired if she wanted to take out a loan. Delete.

The second came from a young Russian woman, twenty-four, with a doctorate in electrical engineering, hoping to begin a meaningful correspondence with a well-educated and well-bred Italian man. Resisting the temptation to forward it to Avvocato Moretti, she deleted it.

The last was from Cristina, sent early that afternoon. 'You studied law, Cati, and it wasn't so very long ago, so surely you remember what those legal people call a statute of limitations on wills. Any unclaimed bequest Steffani might have made lapsed centuries ago: if there turns out to be something of value among those papers, it in no way belongs to the egregious cousins but, alas, to our even more egregious State.

'I don't have any idea of what sort of people you're mixed up with. The non-heirs sound unpleasant, at least to someone who has been out of the city for as long as I have. Surely their lawyer must know this basic legal fact, which makes me wonder what he's up to. I don't want to say anything unpleasant about him in case he's the lawyer you're going out to dinner with, but if it is he, he should have known.

'If you have no luck with him, and if you can tell me exactly where the trunks were in Rome – that is, what bureau or office had them – I might be able to do a bit of trekking through the muck for you and find out how they were released. I still have a number of friends there who believe that the discovery of truth begins with an accurate account of verifiable events and is not an elaborate progress towards some predetermined truth. Besides, I'm curious.

'Thanks for your offer of hospitality. If I decide to bolt, it's the first place I'd go, believe me. Love, Tina-Lina.'

The clock at the bottom of the computer told her it was seven-fifteen and so, without planning what to say, Caterina hit Respond.

'Dear Tina,

'The trunks were in the care/possession of the Propaganda Fide, as sinister a name as your lot could come up with short of KGB or CIA. I was told that someone who was doing an inventory found the trunks. His research probably found the names of the original cousins too and he looked for people with the same surnames in the area about Castelfranco and got in touch with them. That's certainly what I or any other researcher would do, but it's only a guess.

'When I opened them, it looked as though no one had done so since the time they were first sealed, but I'm sure breaking and entering and leaving no traces is the least of the Black Arts practised by the PF.

'Yes, tonight's lawyer is the cousins' lawyer. I'll ply him with wine and grappa and try to get him to explain how they got their hands on the trunks. That failing, I might be forced to tempt him with the possibility of my charms, and where's the grown man who could prove resistant to those?

'Thanks for the information about the statute of limitations, and I'm ashamed I never thought of it. Of course I knew it, but I'm afraid Avvocato Moretti quite drove all memory of the study of the law, to make no mention of good sense, out of my head. Or maybe I simply wanted to keep this job because it's interesting and lets me be at home. Love, Cati.'

Ten minutes after she sent the mail, her *telefonino* rang. Her first thought was her parents, calling to see if she was free for dinner, ever ready to feed their last-born and save her from a night of solitude.

She answered with her name.

'*Ciao*, Caterina,' Andrea said. 'I'm out in the street. Come down when you're finished.'

'Don't you have a key?' she blurted.

'Yes, but I'm off duty tonight,' he said with a laugh. 'Listen, there's a bar out on Via Garibaldi, first on the left. I'll be in there, all right?'

For a moment, she was taken aback, then said, 'I'll be two minutes. Order me a spritz, all right? With Aperol.'

'*Sarà fatto*,' he said and was gone.

The tactic of playing hard to get had never appealed to Caterina, not because it was not effective – her friends had used it with great success – but because it was so obvious. Above all, she hated being kept waiting, and few things could embarrass her as much as keeping another person waiting unnecessarily. She turned off the computer, put her *telefonino* in her bag, then locked up and went downstairs.

Andrea was there, standing at the bar, that day's *Gazzettino* spread open beside him as he sipped at a glass of white wine. A spritz of the proper orange stood on the counter to the left of the newspaper.

He heard her come in, looked up, and smiled. Closing the paper, he set it to the side of the counter. 'I didn't take you away from anything, did I?' he asked. For a moment, Caterina was puzzled by the change in him. Face and height the same, wire-rimmed glasses and carefully polished shoes. But he was wearing a light tweed jacket. A tie, of course, and a white shirt, but he was not wearing a suit. Was this an honour or an insult?

'No, not at all. I was sending an email.' She nodded towards the paper. 'Anything there? I haven't read the papers for days.'

'Same old things. Jealous husband kills wife, North Korea threatens the South, politician caught taking a bribe from a builder, woman gives birth at sixty-two.'

Andrea, obviously judging this the wrong way to begin

their evening, handed her the spritz, tapped his glass against hers, and said, '*Cin cin.*'

'Sounds like I'm wiser to stay in the eighteenth century, then,' she said and took a sip. It was perfect, sharp and sweet at the same time, and today was one of the first days of the year when a person might want to drink something cold.

'Still digging?' he asked, but idly, as if he were only being polite.

'I've stopped digging,' she said. His expression of more than mild surprise led her to add, 'That is, digging into things that don't concern me.'

He gave her a long, appraising glance, as if weighing her answer, and then said, 'That's the first time I've ever heard a woman say that.' His smile and the glance that preceded it took any sting out of the remark.

'Ha, ha,' she said in the manner of a cartoon character and then allowed herself to laugh, managing thus to disapprove of the remark while still being amused by it.

'What is it you're not digging into?' he asked and took another sip of his drink. He signalled the barman and asked for some peanuts. 'I didn't have lunch today,' he said by way of explanation.

Caterina started to ask why, but he said only, 'Meeting,' then, 'Tell me about your not digging.'

He sounded curious, so she told him the background to the Königsmarck Affair. His lawyer's mind, accustomed to hearing many names dragged into a story, seemed to keep them all straight. When she moved on to the account contained in Countess von Platen's memoirs, he stopped her to ask if this was Königsmarck's ex-mistress, impressing Caterina with both his memory and his concentration.

'She's an unreliable witness,' he said. He watched her

expression, then added, 'I mean in legal terms, theoretical terms.'

'Why?' she asked, though it was evident. She wanted to know if he had some other, lawyerly reason so to judge her.

'The obvious one is that she had reason to dislike him, especially if he ended the affair. That means she'd be unlikely to speak in his favour.'

'To say the minimum,' she agreed. 'Why else?'

'It means, as well, that she might attempt to hide the real killer.'

'For ending a love affair?' Caterina asked, unable to stifle her astonishment.

'Your surprise does you credit, Dottoressa,' he said, raising his glass to her and finishing his wine. He set it on the counter and went on, 'And, yes, for ending the affair.' Before she could protest, he said, 'I don't practise criminal law, but I have colleagues who do, and they tell me things that would make your hair stand on end.'

He saw that he had her complete attention. 'You've probably read the phrase in the paper: *motivi futili*. My friends have told me about a lot of trivial motives that cost people their lives: a car parked in someone else's space, the refusal to give a cigarette, a radio too loud, or a television, or a minor car accident.' He raised his hand to the barman, signalling for the bill.

'So keeping quiet about the murder of someone who said he wasn't in love with you any more, especially if he wasn't graceful about it . . . it makes complete sense to me. So does saying something that might protect the murderer.'

'So you doubt her account? That she saw Steffani kill him?'

'Is that what she says? That she saw him do it?'

Caterina had to think back over the precise wording in

Tina's friend's email. 'Something about his having received blood money,' she said.

'I'm not sure that's the same thing as saying she saw him commit the murder,' Andrea said and then, just as she was about to make the same suggestion, added, 'Maybe we could talk about something else?'

What a relief his suggestion was. He paid the bill and moved over to the door to hold it open for her.

He led them to a small trattoria behind the Pietà, a place that held no more than half a dozen tables, the stout-legged sort Caterina remembered from her youth, with surfaces scarred and carved and edges hollowed out by countless forgotten cigarettes. Bottles stood on mirrored shelves behind the zinc-covered bar; a rectangular space with a sliding door opened into the kitchen.

Two of the tables were already taken. The waiter recognized Moretti and showed them to a table in the far corner. He handed them menus and disappeared through a pair of swinging doors.

'I hope you don't mind eating in a simple place,' he said.

'I'd rather,' she said. 'My parents keep telling me how hard it's become to find a place where the food's good and you don't have to take out a mortgage to pay the bill.'

'That's not the case here,' he said, then laughed and said, 'I mean, the food's good, not that it's cheap.' Then he added, 'That's the reason I come – that is, because the food's good.' Hearing what a pass he had talked himself into, he shrugged and opened his menu.

Conversation was general: families, school, travel, reading, music. Much of Moretti's life was completely at one with the persona he presented: father a lawyer, mother a housewife; two brothers, the surgeon he had already mentioned and the other a notary; school, university, first job, partnership. But then came the odd bits: a case of encephalitis seven years ago that had left him in bed for six months, during which he had read the Fathers of the Church, in Latin. When these facts were spread on the picture Caterina was attempting to form of the man, everything went out of focus for a moment. A brush with death: she knew little about encephalitis save that it was bad, quite often fatal, and just as often left people gaga. Perhaps that last explained six months reading the Fathers of the Church, her cynical self remarked, but her better self limited her to asking, 'Encephalitis?'

He bit into a shrimp and said, 'I went for a hike in the mountains above Belluno. Two days later I found a tick on the back of my knee, and a week later I was in the hospital with a temperature of forty.'

'Near Belluno?' It was only two hours from Venice, a beautiful city where nothing happened.

'It's common. There are more and more cases every year,' he said, then smiled and added, 'More evidence of the wisdom of living in cities.'

She decided not to ask about the Fathers of the Church. The evening continued, and conversation remained general and friendly. The absence of reference to Steffani or Königsmarck came as a great relief to Caterina. How pleasant to spend a few hours in this century, in this city, and, she added to herself, in this company.

They shared a branzino baked in salt, drank most of a bottle of Ribolla Gialla, and both turned down dessert. When the coffee came, Andrea grew suddenly serious and said, with no preparation at all, 'I'm afraid I have to confess I haven't told you the complete truth.'

There being nothing she could think of to say, Caterina remained silent.

'About the cousins.'

Better than about himself, she thought, but said nothing to him, certainly not this. If he was confessing he had lied, she had no obligation to make it easy for him. To appear to be doing something, she poured sugar into her coffee and stirred it round.

'The story of how the trunks got here,' he said, then drew one hand into a fist and placed it on the table.

'Ah,' she permitted herself to say.

'They didn't track them down. The trunks turned up during an inventory, and the researcher did find Steffani's name on them, and he did do the research and locate the descendants.'

He paused and gave her a quizzical glance, but Caterina kept her face impassive. 'Descendants,' he had said. Not 'heirs'.

She stifled her curiosity and drank her coffee. He must have realized she was not going to be cooperatively inquisitive, so he said, his voice a mixture of the pedantic and the apologetic, 'They have no claim to ownership. You studied law, so you probably know that it reverts to the state.'

Caterina kept her eyes on her coffee cup, even lifted the spoon and ran it around the empty bottom a few times. Then she carefully spooned up the mixture of melted sugar and froth from the bottom and licked the spoon before replacing it on the saucer.

She raised her eyes and looked across the table at him, in his lovely, expensive jacket and his moderate tie. He met her eyes with his own steady glance and said, 'I apologize.'

'Why did you tell me a different story?' she asked, consciously avoiding the use of the word 'lie'.

'They asked me to.'

'Why?'

He looked down at his own empty coffee cup and said, 'They said they didn't want to have to explain how the trunks got here. The real way, I mean. Or so I presume.' Even in his explanation, she noticed, he still strove for clarity.

Making herself sound the very voice of moderation, she asked, 'Why wouldn't they want anyone to know?'

He tried to shrug but abandoned the gesture, with one shoulder higher than the other. 'My guess is that they bribed someone to have the trunks sent here.' When her gaze remained level on his, he actually blushed and said, 'In fact, it's the only way it could have happened.'

'The researcher?' she asked, knowing this was impossible. He would have no power over where the trunks went.

Andrea smiled at her question and said, 'Not likely.'

'Then who?' she asked, doing her best to look very confused.

'It would have to be someone at the Propaganda Fide, I'd guess. Or at the warehouse.'

'Then why me?'

'What do you mean?'

'Why me? Why spend money on a researcher when they could just get the trunks here, open them up, and have a look themselves?'

'They needed a researcher,' he said, holding up his thumb to count the first reason. 'He was a cleric and worked in Germany, so they needed someone who could read different languages.' He held up his forefinger. 'And that person would also have to have some understanding of the historical – perhaps even the musical – background.' Another finger shot up.

'That's absurd,' Caterina snapped, finally losing patience with the role she had decided to play. 'I just told you: all they had to do was open them, take out any musical scores that might be inside, do a minimum of research on what Steffani's autograph scores are worth, and sell them. Split the money and hire someone at the university to read through the other papers. Sooner or later, they'd know whether there was a treasure hidden somewhere or not.'

Andrea tried to smile, reached a hand halfway across the table, as if to place it on her arm, but pulled it back when he saw her expression.

He picked up his coffee cup, but it was still empty, so he set it back in the saucer. 'There was a . . . a falling out, I suppose you could say.'

'Of thieves?'

Her directness obviously distressed him. He had to think of a response before he said, 'Yes, you might describe it that way. Once they had the trunks here, they realized how little they trusted each other.'

'And I suppose they began to add up the sums,' she said angrily.

'I don't understand.' Though she thought perhaps he did.

'They'd have to pay by the page or by the hour if they hired a freelance translator, and they didn't know what was in the trunks or what the papers – if there were papers – would say. Or what they would be worth.' As she spoke, Caterina remembered an old folk tale about three thieves who discovered some sort of treasure. One went off to town to get enough food and drink to keep them going while the three of them decided what it was worth and how to divide it up. While he was gone, the two who remained behind planned his murder, and when he came back, they killed him. They ate and drank to celebrate their victory, but the dead man had poisoned the wine he brought back, so they too paid the price of the Jewels of Paradise.

She looked across at Moretti, her face neutral, waiting for him to speak.

'Neither of them trusted the other not to cheat,' he finally said. 'Even though they had no idea what was in the trunks, each still believed the other would be clever enough to cheat him out of his share. Or to see that the division wasn't equal.' He saw that he had her interest and went on. 'Nothing can shake them loose from their belief in a treasure.'

'Have you tried?'

'Yes.' He shook his head to show the hopelessness of that endeavour.

'So they agreed to pay my salary?'

This question made him visibly uncomfortable.

'What is it?' she asked.

'For the first month, yes,' he said.

'What?'

'It was in the contract.' She thought it embarrassed him to say this, and that surprised her. She suppressed her own embarrassment at not having bothered to read the contract.

'You told me my position was secure until I'd read through all of the papers,' she said in a cool, firm voice. 'I left my job to come here.'

'I know,' he said, his eyes on his plate. Could it be that he was ashamed of the part he had played? She had no doubt that he had played it.

She said nothing.

Forced to continue, Moretti finally said, 'I thought at the beginning that they'd continue to pay you until you had a definite answer to give them: yes there is a treasure or no there is not.' He made that half move with his hand across the table, but again he stopped. 'I thought they were serious. That's why I worked to convince them you could do the research in the library.' She thought it best not to tell him she'd realized the futility of that research.

'They've changed their minds, I assume?'

'Stievani called me this afternoon. One month. That's all. If they don't have an answer by the end of one month, they'll figure out a way to do it by themselves.'

'Good luck to them, the fools,' she couldn't stop herself from saying.

'I agree.' Then, in a calmer tone, he said, 'If you want, I can try to persuade them.'

She smiled. 'That's kind of you, Andrea. I'd appreciate it if you could try.' Suddenly, she opened her mouth in an enormous yawn. 'Sorry,' she said, looking at her watch.

He imitated her gesture and said, 'It's after eleven.'

From the way he said it, she wondered if he had to be home before midnight. He signalled the waiter with a writing gesture. In a very short time, he was there, with a real receipt. 'You always do that?' she asked, pointing to the bill as he set a few notes on top of it.

'Pay the bill when I invite a woman to dinner?' he asked, but with a grin.

'No. Ask for a *ricevuta fiscale* in a restaurant where you come often.'

'You mean because of the taxes they'll have to pay?' he asked.

'Yes.'

'We all have to pay taxes.'

'Does that mean you pay yours? All of them?'

'Yes,' he said simply.

She believed him.

They got to their feet. He opened the door for her and they walked together, talking of things other than Agostino Steffani and the cousins, towards the apartment where she was staying. At her door, he kissed her on both cheeks, said good-night, and turned away.

Caterina went up the stairs to her apartment, unlocked the door, and let herself in.

Again she looked at her watch: it was almost midnight. Cristina did not have a *telefonino*, so she could not leave her an SMS and ask her to call if she was awake. There was a phone in the apartment, with a meter: it would be much cheaper to call Germany on that.

She took her *telefonino* from her pocket and dialled Cristina's number. It rang six times before a groggy voice answered with '*Ja?*'

'*Ciao*, Tina,' she said. 'Sorry to wake you up.'

After a long pause, Tina said, 'It's OK, I was reading.'

'Lying's still a sin, dear.'

'Not really, if it's in a good cause.'

'You rewriting the Commandments now?'

'I'm awake, so tell me what's wrong – I can hear it in your voice – and I'll leave the rewriting of the others till tomorrow morning.'

'You know that lawyer I told you about?'

'Yes.'

'He's a cold-hearted bastard like the others.'

'Why do you say that?' Tina said, sounding sad.

'Because he's been reading my emails.'

# 23

'Which emails?' Cristina demanded, her voice fully awake.

'The ones I've been writing on the computer he so generously gave me to use in the office. He said his company wasn't using it, so he had one of his tech people work on it . . .' Here she had to stop and take a few deep breaths before going on. 'And he took it there, and I've been using it ever since.' Two more deep breaths. Her knees were shaking; she sat down on the sofa.

'How do you know he's reading them, Cati?'

'At dinner tonight, he told me I'd understand something because I'd studied law.'

'Well, you did. Two years, if I remember correctly.'

'I never told him.'

'Then maybe he read it on your CV.'

'It's not there,' Caterina said with fierce energy. 'I never talk about it, and I did not include it in the CV.'

'But how do you cover over a gap of two years?'

'I added a year to the things I did before and after. I

figured they wouldn't check: no one ever does. And if it wasn't in the CV, and I never said anything to him about it, then the only way he knows is from your mail.'

'How can you be sure?'

'I just told you, Tina,' she said. Hearing the anger in her voice, she moderated her tone. 'He knew I studied law, and the only way he could have known that was from reading your email, where you mentioned it.' How many times would the sleep-sodden Cristina have to hear this before she understood?

'But why should he say that to you?'

'He was telling me that things revert to the state after a certain period if no heir makes a claim, and I suppose he meant to be complimentary or inclusive, make me feel like one of the pack, and said I should know that because I studied law.'

'Did you react?'

'I hope not. I acted as if it didn't register with me. He probably thinks he read it in my CV. After all, who wouldn't mention something like that?'

'You, apparently,' Tina broke in to suggest. Her laugh restored the usual warmth of their conversation.

'What's he up to?' Caterina asked, aware of a vague sense that the documents in the storeroom had been moved or tampered with.

'That's not the question to ask.'

'What is, then?'

'What to do? If he didn't realize you know he's reading them, then you and I can just continue to write back and forth. We have to. If we suddenly stopped, he'd suspect something.'

'What is this – James Bond?' Caterina asked.

'Only if you want it to be, Cati,' Cristina said calmly. 'If not, then you continue to do your job, read the papers and tell the cousins what they say, let them find their treasure or not, and then you take the money and run.'

'That's very worldly advice.'

Tina said nothing, which probably meant she didn't want to begin a discussion like this, not at this hour.

Thinking out loud, Cristina said, 'I wonder if the cousins put him up to it?'

'Who else would he be doing it for?' Tina asked.

It certainly sounded like something the cousins would do to be sure she didn't try to cheat them. Her only question was whether Dottor Moretti – Andrea – would be party to such a thing. The fact that she believed he might saddened her immeasurably.

For a long time, neither of the sisters spoke. Caterina ran through the jumbled memories of her conversations with Avvocato Moretti. For a moment, she thought of encephalitis and its effect on the brain, but she dismissed that. 'He spent six months recovering from encephalitis by reading the Fathers of the Church in Latin,' she said aloud. Then she asked, 'Is your computer on?'

'Like the love of the Holy Spirit, my computer is always on.'

'Put in his name and see what comes up.'

'Should I call you back?'

'No, just do it,' Caterina said briskly.

She heard the footsteps, the sound of a chair scraping the floor, and then a long silence.

'What's his full name?' Cristina asked.

'Andrea Moretti.'

'How old?'

'About forty-five.'

'Born in Venice?'

'I think so.'

There was a long, silent pause, during which Caterina

stood first on one foot and then the other, an exercise someone had once told her would help her keep her balance in old age. '*Ach du Lieber Gott*,' she heard her sister say, speaking in German and shocking Caterina by doing so.

'What?'

'Do you want to guess where he studied?'

'I know I'm not going to like this, so you better just tell me,' Caterina said.

'The University of Navarra,' Cristina told her.

'Novara?' Caterina asked, wondering what he was doing in Piemonte.

'Navarra,' Cristina said, pronouncing it as though it had four R's.

'*Vade retro, satana*,' Caterina whispered, then added, 'Founded by that lunatic who started Opus Dei,' too late to consider that this was perhaps not the way to refer to a colleague of a woman who had taken final vows.

'They run the place. Their graduates are everywhere,' Cristina chimed in, suggesting that she might not have been offended by the remark.

'I never would have thought . . .' Caterina began but let the thought wander off, unfinished. 'That means I can't believe anything he's told me.' She'd said it.

'Probably.'

Leaving her reflections on Avvocato Moretti's motivation to some later time, Caterina asked, 'Then what's he after?'

'With them, power's always a safe guess,' Tina said, causing Caterina, who had the same suspicion, to wonder if they'd both fallen victim to paranoia of the worst sort.

Caterina couldn't stand it any more. 'If you can think that, Tina, why do you stay with it?' There was such a long silence that she finally said, 'Sorry. None of my business.'

'That's all right,' Cristina said in a very sober voice.

'Really sorry, Tina-Lina.'

Again Cristina was silent, this time for so long that Caterina began to wonder if she had gone too far. She waited and something like a prayer formed in her mind that she had not asked the wrong question of her favourite sister.

'Right,' Cristina said decisively. 'So we go on corresponding naturally, and I'll pass on any information I find or anyone sends me.'

'Good,' Caterina agreed. 'But . . .'

'I know, I know, if I learn anything that he shouldn't know about, I should send it to . . . to where?'

Caterina floundered, trying to think of someone she could trust to pass on information. She didn't want to involve her family. Her email account at the university in Manchester had been cancelled when she left. That gave her the idea. 'Look, you can send it to the address of a friend. He almost never reads his emails, and I have his password. I can go into an internet café to check.' When Cristina agreed, Caterina carefully spelled out the Romanian's email address.

After that, they both started to laugh, though neither of them knew why. Feeling better, Caterina said goodnight, hung up, and went to bed.

The first thing she did the next morning was send two emails to Dottor Moretti, just as if they had not had dinner together the previous evening. The first was formal and described in some detail Steffani's correspondence with Sophie Charlotte and explained that the ease of his connection with her would have given him added social status and, directly or indirectly, aided him in his pursuit of work as a composer. Declaring that she was sensitive to her employers' understandable desire to see her research come to a conclusion, she announced her intention to suspend her library reading for a few days and continue with the papers in the trunk.

In the second, to 'Andrea', she used the familiar form of address and thanked him for the pleasant time she had had with him the previous evening, both the conversation and the discovery of a good restaurant.

She gave considerable thought to how to close the email and decided on '*Cari saluti*, Caterina,' which, while being informal, was nothing more than that but certainly suggested continuing good will.

That done, she took a shower, stopped and had a coffee, and walked to the Foundation, arriving soon after nine. She went up to the office, unlocked the cupboard, and took the pile she had last been reading. She sat at the desk and started to do the job she was being paid to do, at least until the end of the month.

There were three documents in German, all of them reports from Catholic priests about the success of their mission in various parts of Germany governed by Protestant rulers. To one degree or another, they spoke of the deep faith of their own parishioners and the need to remain strong in the face of political opposition. All asked Steffani to intercede with Rome for more money to aid them in their labours, a phrase two of the writers used.

There were a few letters from women with German surnames, none of whom Caterina managed to find in any of the articles or records she consulted online, praising Steffani for his music. One asked if he would favour her with a copy of one of his chamber duets. There were no copies of answers to any of these letters.

Had Steffani, then, gone through his papers in the years immediately preceding his death and chosen to keep those he thought important, or had everything simply been bundled up by the people sent to sort out his possessions? Try as she might, she could find no common thread, even common threads, among these papers. Save for the musical score, nothing seemed more important than anything else.

She retied the stack and took it to the storeroom. Now there remained only one more parcel in the first trunk. Back at the desk, she untied it and began to read.

After more than an hour of close reading, she had got through only one of two tightly written pages, front and back, and had decided that this was bottom-feeding. These were accounts of the events and conversations, kept in a hand other than the one she had verified to be Steffani's, – did he have a secretary? – leading to the conversion or reconversion to Catholicism of various German aristocrats and dignitaries. Because no identification was provided beyond their names, Caterina could not measure the political importance of their religious change of stance. She was diligent with the first page, searching through the usual historical directories and sites for their names and managing to identify most of them. But what was the importance of the conversion of Henriette Christine and Countess Augusta Dorothea of Schwarzburg-Arnstadt, even if they were the daughters of Anton Ulrich of Braunschweig-Wolfenbüttel?

It was two and she was hungry and she was bored to the point of pain, something that had rarely happened during past research. It was all so futile, trying to find some indication of where Steffani might have left treasure, only so his greedy descendants could fight over it. Better to go out and find more novels like the one owned by d'Annunzio and sit reading them until the end of the month, producing inventive reports and translations of the papers she did not read: perhaps she could use the plots of the novels as sources for her summaries of the unread papers? Perhaps she could go and get something to eat?

She carefully locked the papers away and locked up as usual. Then she went down to Roseanna's office and found the door open: it had been closed when she came in and had remained so when she knocked on it. So Roseanna had been in and had not come up to check on her. Good or bad?

She left the building and locked the door. During the time she had been inside, the day had turned to glory. The sun beat down, and she was quickly warm, and then so hot she had to remove her jacket. She decided to walk to the Piazza, if only to have the chance to look across at San Giorgio and up the Grand Canal. As to lunch, God would surely provide.

She cut out to the *riva*, turned right and walked towards the Piazza, eyes always drawn to her left by the excess on display. There were more boats moored to the side of San Giorgio than she remembered, but everything else was the same. Remove the vaporetti and the other motor-driven boats, and it would look much the same as it had centuries ago. As it had in Steffani's day, she told herself and liked the thought.

At the Piazza, she stopped and looked around: Basilica, tower, Marciana, columns, flags, clock. The ridiculous beauty of it all moved her close to tears. This was normal for her; this was one of her childhood playgrounds; this was home. She crossed in front of the Basilica, thinking she'd go back towards Rialto, but the crowds coming towards her down the Merceria frightened her, and she turned right past the *leoncini* and headed back, feeling abandoned by God, towards San Zaccaria.

Halfway to the end of the Basilica, she glanced into one

of the numerous glass shops to the left and saw, sitting in a chair behind the cash register, reading a newspaper on the counter in front of him, the young man who had followed her the other night. She missed a step but kept moving forward and regained her balance. There had been no doubt about it, no hesitation before she recognized him: it was the same man. She continued walking; it was only when she was long past the window that she turned back and noted the name of the shop.

It provided scant comfort to know he was not a paid killer; seeing him had still been a shock. She might not know who he was, but finding out would not be difficult. She could ask Clara or Cinzia to help: they could take one of their kids, to make themselves even more innocent, and start talking to him in Veneziano. Clara would be better: her radiant happiness would drag secrets from anyone. Caterina's thoughts turned to Clara's husband Sergio, who weighed just short of a hundred kilos and stood almost two metres tall. He was a far better choice of visitor.

Immeasurably cheered, she continued down towards San Filippo e Giacomo and turned off to go and have three of the small pizzas, two for lunch, and one to celebrate her discovery of the man who had followed her.

# 24

She returned to the Foundation and found Roseanna in her office, sitting at her desk, reading, and looking quite the Acting Director of the Fondazione Musicale Italo-Tedesca. So fond of her had Caterina become in these days and so accustomed to seeing her that her hairstyle now seemed carefully executed and eye-catching.

'What are you reading?' Caterina asked as she came in.

Roseanna looked up and smiled in greeting. 'A book about psychoactive medicine.'

'I beg your pardon,' Caterina said. 'Why that?' Few subjects could seem farther from the business of the Foundation.

'My best friend's been diagnosed with depression, and her doctor wants her to start taking these things.' From the harsh tone Roseanna used, Caterina was left in no doubt about her thoughts on the subject.

'And you disagree?'

Roseanna set the book face down on the desk. 'It's not

my place to agree or disagree, Caterina. I don't have any medical or pharmacological training, so some of what I read I don't even understand.'

'And the book?' Caterina asked.

Shrug and smile. 'We've been friends since school, best friends, and she asked me what I thought she should do. So I decided to read about it, both sides, and see if I could make any sense of it.'

'Have you learned anything?'

'Not to trust statistics or numbers or the published results of experiments.' Roseanna said instantly, then added, 'not that I ever did; well, not much.'

'Why?'

'Because the people who make drugs don't have to publish the bad results, only the good ones, and medicines are usually tested against a placebo, not against another medicine.' She patted the back of the book affectionately. 'This writer makes the observation that it's not hard to make a medicine that is more effective than a sugar pill.' Her eyes went into half focus for a moment, and then she said, 'I've never smoked, but I've seen how my friends who are smokers seem to relax as soon as they light a cigarette. So you could run a test and show that smoking a cigarette is an excellent way to reduce stress.'

'Better than a sugar pill?' Caterina asked.

'I'd say so.' Then, as if suddenly aware of how far afield this conversation was from their common interest, she asked, 'I thought you had gone to the Marciana.'

Caterina shook the suggestion away. 'No, I'm going to read through the papers, at least those in the first trunk, before I go to the library again.' She paused and then added, 'I can't make up my mind about him.'

'Because he was a priest?'

'No, not that. It's because I don't have any idea what

he wanted. Usually we can tell that – what a person most wants – if we've been around him for a while or read about him. But, with Steffani, I just don't know. Did he so desperately need to be accepted as an equal by the people he worked for? Did he really want to save the Church? He writes about his music and the pleasure he takes in it, but there's no compelling desire to be famous for it, to be thought a great composer. It's obvious that he loved it and loved composing it, but . . . but he gave it up so easily. If it were his compelling passion, he couldn't have done that: just stop.'

Caterina saw no reason why she shouldn't tell Roseanna what she had discovered, or thought she had discovered, so she added, 'He might have been a castrato.' She tried to say it neutrally, but she wasn't sure she succeeded. It was not a remark that lent itself to neutrality.

'Oh, the poor man,' Roseanna said, pressing one hand to her face. 'The poor man.'

'I'm not absolutely sure he was,' Caterina said immediately. 'But he's described somewhere as *un musico*, and that's the word that was used for them.'

'To fill the choirs to sing the glory of God,' Roseanna said calmly, as if there did not exist sarcasm sufficient for the words.

'There's only the one reference,' Caterina said, choosing not to mention the Haydn libretto.

Neither of them found anything further to add. 'I'll go back upstairs,' Caterina said. She headed towards the door, and was almost there when Roseanna said, 'I'm glad they hired you.'

Without turning back, Caterina acknowledged the remark by raising her right hand in the air. 'Me, too,' she said and pulled her keys out of her pocket.

\* \* \*

Upstairs, she sat at the desk and pulled her *telefonino* from her purse. On the way back, she'd considered what to do about the man who had followed her. Before she made the call, she wanted to be sure what to say. She had no proof that her research was related to the fact that he followed her, and then waited for her, but no other explanation made sense of it. Any of the many odd men in the city might have followed her; in fact, it had happened to her once, years ago. But he knew which vaporetto stop she would take, which meant he knew where her parents lived and where she did. Or else blind chance had she dismissed this possibility even before it was fully formulated.

She tried to tell herself he hadn't done anything more than cause her some emotion between surprise and unease, but then she remembered kneeling in front of the toilet and vomiting, and admitted that he had terrified her. Accepting that, she punched in the number of Clara's husband, Sergio, who owned and managed a factory on the mainland in Marcon that made metal sheeting.

Sergio had been left an orphan at the age of eleven; part of his joy in marrying Clara was that she gave him back a family. She had four sisters, and two of those had children, so, with glee, he had taken on the whole lot of them, becoming the big brother none of them had had and acquiring not only a wife, but the endless set of obligations and responsibilities he had pined after for years.

'*Ciao*, Caterina,' he answered.

'Sergio,' she began, deciding to waste no time. 'I have a problem, and I thought you would be the person to help me solve it.' By presenting it this way to Sergio, she knew, she was pandering to his desire to be loved by the family and his need to believe himself a useful part of it.

'Tell me,' he said.

'A few nights ago, a man followed me from where I'm working to Campo Santa Maria Formosa. I was on the way to *Mamma* and *Papà*'s,' she said, conscious of using those names to reel him in, 'and then he was waiting at the vaporetto stop when I went home.'

'The same man?' Sergio asked.

'Yes.'

'You know him?'

'No. But I know where he works. I walked past a shop, near the Basilica, and he was sitting behind the counter.' She started to describe the man and was astonished to realize that all she remembered was light hair, cut very short.

'What do you want me to do?'

That was the essential Sergio: no time wasted asking if she was sure or if she had considered the consequences of getting him mixed up in this. Blood was thicker than water. Had he asked this question while she was being sick into the toilet, she probably would have told him to rip the man's head off, but time had passed and the menace had been let out of the situation, as air could be let out of a balloon.

'Maybe you could stop by and ask him what he wanted?'

'You want to come?'

Caterina remembered a time, decades ago, when she had come home from school after hearing the expression, 'Vengeance is a dish that is best eaten cold', and told her mother how clever she thought it was, forgetting that her generation had been brought up in a different epoch. Caterina had been surprised by her mother's failure to laugh, then more surprised when she said, 'It doesn't matter, darling, if it's hot or it's cold: vengeance still destroys your soul, either way,' and had asked her youngest daughter if she'd like a piece of chocolate cake.

For a moment, Caterina toyed with the thought of the man's expression when she walked into his shop with Sergio looming at her side. 'No, he didn't hurt me. He scared me, but it was just the one time, and I haven't seen him since. Except in his shop.'

'All right. Tell me where he is and I'll talk to him.' Then he asked, 'Is there any hurry?'

She was about to say that there was, but good sense intervened and she said, 'No, not really.'

'Then I'll go past it on my way home. Not today and not tomorrow. I'm sorry, I can't, really. But I will, I promise.'

Caterina had no doubt of that and reassured him that there was no hurry, none at all. She described the location of the shop and did not remind Sergio that he had a factory to run and shouldn't spend his time coming into the city in the middle of the day. She wanted an explanation, and if Sergio could provide it for her, all the better. To suggest that she had no sense of urgency whatsoever, she spent a few minutes asking about the children, all possessed of genius and beauty beyond that usually bestowed upon even the most gifted children. Then a voice called Sergio's name and he said he'd call her after he'd spoken to the man.

Caterina returned to the documents and read through the three remaining sides of paper listing the names of the people Steffani successfully brought to or back to the Church. She forced herself to do the basic historical research and was rewarded by identifying all but six of them. Even if the result turned up nothing meaningful about Steffani, the professors who had taught her how to do research could still be proud that they had taught her so well.

She plodded on, all but aching for anything that would save her from the tedium of these letters.

As if to wish for it were to make it materialize, the next paper was the manuscript of a *recitativo*, '*Dell' alma stanca*'. Caterina had perhaps spent too long a day reading through papers of a certain banality, and so to come upon this title pushed her, if only for an instant, beyond the limits of her scholarly patience, and she said out loud, 'This *alma* is certainly very *stanca.*'

Recovering from that moment of truth-telling, she took a closer look at the score and recognized both the music and the handwriting. She sang her way through the soprano part, remembering that it was scored for – wonder of wonders – four viole da gamba. She joined her voice to the silver shimmer of the instruments and heard how well it worked and then heard how sublime it sounded. As often happened, the quality of the music far outclassed the libretto, and she felt a moment's sympathy for Steffani for having had to use these thread-bare sentiments over and over. She remembered the performance of *Niobe* she had seen, where in the following aria, strings and flutes had joined the viols. She realized that the score must have been printed and thus the sale of this page would not condemn it to some private archive, never to be heard. Smiling, she made a note of the document, listing the packet number and counting through the sheets to get the right page number. This way, either the victorious cousin or the two of them together could easily find one of the saleable documents and do with it as they pleased.

The next paper was a letter from Ortensio Mauro, whose name she recognized as that of Steffani's best friend and librettist. Dated 1707, it must have been sent to Steffani in Düsseldorf and seemed to describe events in Hanover, which he had left four years before. She read a few paragraphs of gossip and then found this: 'Here there is singing and playing every evening . . . You are the innocent cause of this. This music has more charm than Sympathy itself, and all that are here feel the sweet ties that stir and exhilarate their souls. You might issue a blessing, confirm or consecrate, excommunicate, whatever you like; neither your blessing nor your curse will ever have such force or charm, such power or pathos, as your agreeable notes. There is no end here of admiring and listening to them.' She ran her hand across the surface of the page, as if to caress the spirit of the man who had been generous enough to write that.

Another two hours passed as she read her way through more of the documents left behind by a busy and active life. Some of them could be there only because of a random gathering up of documents. There was a series of land transfer papers from a farm in the town of Vedelago: the names Stievani and Scapinelli appeared on all of them as sellers. A quick look at a map showed her Vedelago was about ten kilometres to the east of Castelfranco, the town where Steffani was born. Then there were more about the sale of another farm in the same town, these too bearing the names of the ancestors of the cousins. A letter dated 19 August 1725, from Scapinelli, said that, of course, their cousin Agostino would be sent his share of the money received from the sale of the houses, but he must understand that these things took time. There was only the one letter. And then there were no more documents: she had read through all of the papers in the first chest and had found nothing that in any way expressed a 'testamentary disposition' on the part of Abbé Agostino Steffani, though she had found tantalizing mention of the two families.

She put the papers back in order, tied up the bundle, and took it back to the open storeroom. She put the papers, all read and tallied, back inside the trunk, closed the trunk, flirted with the idea of beginning with the papers in the other, but decided her time might be better spent considering her immediate future.

# 25

Caterina was in no way a greedy person. She had little interest in the accumulation of wealth and spent most of what she earned on leading what she considered a decent life. Part of this might have resulted from the security that comes with happiness. She had always been loved and cared for by her family, so she assumed that being loved and cared for were things that would continue throughout her life, regardless of her salary or wealth. Many people were strongly motivated by the desire to accumulate money, she knew, but she found it difficult to muster the energy for the attempt.

Caterina did, however, have a sense of fair play. She had been promised a job and had left the relative security of Manchester to return to Venice in order to begin that job, she told herself, ignoring the fact that she had been eager to leave Manchester and would have jumped at any offer, as well as the fact that she had overlooked the time limitation stated in the contract she had been so eager to sign. She had, she admitted, been told that the position was temporary, but she had chosen to believe it might last several months. Now she heard that it would last only one month, even though she had no idea how long it would take her to read the remaining documents.

She turned on the computer and checked her emails. There was an offer for unlimited local calls and high speed internet for only eighteen Euros a month, the offer of a smartphone for next to nothing, and an email from Tina. She deleted the first two and opened the third, curious to learn how their conversation of the night before and the revelations prompting it would have affected Tina's style.

'Dear Cati, As you might have expected, the interest of my friends has waned in the absence of new information or questions about Steffani. Even my friend in Constance has gone mute, so I guess you are on your own. I've been reminded of a deadline and so have to get back to my more recent events, but please understand that I'll always abandon them to help, if you give me some idea of what to look for. You don't even have to tell me why.

'Maybe the Marciana has some of those compilations of documents and letters to do with musicians from the period. It's the librarian's equivalent of what the rest of us do with oddly matched socks: just throw them all in a drawer and forget about them. I'm sure the librarians could tell you if they have such things.

'Other than that, I have no advice to pass on to you and can hope only that you will discover more dark revelations about lust, adultery, and murder, so very much more interesting than my own tedious analysis of Vatican foreign policy. Love, Tina-Lina.'

It was a very limp attempt to sound limp, so perhaps it would convince whoever else was reading her emails to believe that Caterina and her sister were both bored with the research and everything surrounding it.

Caterina opened a new mail and answered, 'Dear Tina, Yes, once we got beyond the thrills of the Königsmarck Affair, things have indeed become a bit dull. Blame it on the even tenor of Steffani's life, I fear.

'I did, however, come on papers today that have him, as well as members of the Stievani and Scapinelli families, involved in the transfer of ownership of some farms near Castelfranco, and I'm going to try to see if I can find more about it tomorrow. Right now, I'm too tired after almost an entire day of reading handwritten documents in Latin and German and Italian to see straight or even think. I'd like nothing better than to lie on the sofa and watch reruns of something uplifting like, for example, *Visitors*. Remember how we adored it? Good Lord, it must be twenty-five years ago, and I still remember those giant reptiles gobbling humans down as if they were large mice. How I'd love to watch it tonight, pretend I was a Visitor, and gobble down dozens of people.' She read over what she had written and cancelled the last sentence. Though Caterina had no idea why, she wanted Dottor Moretti to read and believe that she was tired and bored with her research.

She continued the email: 'You think they stole the idea from Dante? I've always wondered about that.

'On that note of unresolved attribution, I'll go home – to an apartment where there is no television and thus no possibility of *Visitors* – have some dinner and get in bed with *l'Espresso*, which this week promises me revelations about garbage in Naples and the dangers of breast implants. Or maybe I'll take the biography of Steffani – who had to worry about neither of those things – and finally finish reading it. Love, Cati.'

She switched to the site of Manchester University and opened the Romanian's mail, whispering a silent apology to him for invading his privacy, his life; perhaps his secrets. When she noticed that there were one hundred and twelve unread emails, she smiled and retracted the prayer. She put the senders in alphabetical order and, seeing that there was nothing from Cristina, put them back in the order of arrival and left the site without having glanced at the names of any of the senders, very proud of her own force of will.

After that, she wrote to Dottor Moretti, saying that she was following the trail of land transfers near Castelfranco that involved both Steffani and his two cousins. These papers, she told him, might display some preference for one side or the other of the family and thus be useful in her research.

She pushed the Send key, thinking that a person could get to enjoy this James Bond stuff, locked up everything, and went home.

The search for records of the land transfers took her two days. She worked in the Foundation office because she did not want to turn herself into a recluse in the apartment. She did not so much as open the door to the storage place where the trunks were kept. First she accessed the records of the Ufficio Catasto of Castelfranco, the city closest to the village where both parcels of land were located and where the titles were registered; then she searched in Treviso, the provincial capital. The online information from the first office stated that what records they had from the eighteenth century had been put online, though when she phoned to point out the impossibility of finding these records, no one she spoke to seemed able to tell her just where online they had been put. When she

236

was forced to call the office in Treviso to ask for the same explanation of their files, the woman she spoke to gave her the appropriate file numbers but could not tell her to which general file the numbers referred.

At last, doing what she should have done in the first place, she entered the three names into the records of land transfers currently online in the province of Treviso. When a flood of documents from the last few years began to arrive, she moderated her search to the last twenty years of Steffani's life, which reduced it to a trickle.

Caterina waded through these for the rest of the first day and most of the second and found that some years had not been entered into the online records but that, during the years for which there were records, the two families inherited, sold, bought, borrowed money again, and lost countless lots of property. She extrapolated some familial relationships when inheritances were left to 'my beloved son Leonardo', or 'the husband of my much loved sister Maria Grazia's second daughter'. Steffani inherited three pieces of land during this time, then two of them were sold, but from none of the documents could she infer any preference on his part for either side of his family: pieces of earth passed into and out of his ownership, and that was that.

Caterina was diligent and sent a daily email to Dottor Morelli to report on her findings and was careful to list every reference to either cousin's ancestors. His responses were always pleasant, although he explained that he was sending them from Brescia, where he was working on a complicated case, and looked forward to seeing her when he got back to the city. The first day she went to lunch with Roseanna, but the second day the other woman did not appear in the offices.

On the morning of the third day – aware that she did

it because she wanted to enjoy the long morning walk along the *riva* – Caterina returned to the Marciana and entered by means of her by-now-standard invisibility. Her carrel was just as she had left it: even the wrappers from her chocolate and power bars were still in the wastepaper basket.

Following a suggestion from Cristina, she decided to take a look at the two outsized volumes of manuscripts the librarian had delivered to her days before and which had remained there untouched. To open them on the small space, she first had to move the other books to the shelf above.

She slid the two large volumes to the centre of the desk and opened the first. She read quickly through the opening pages and discovered just what Tina had said: this was the sock drawer, and there was little matching that could be done. There was a marriage contract between a 'Marco Scarpa, *musicista*' and 'Elisabetta Pianon, *serva*'. She found a bill from a 'supplier of wood' to the 'Scuola della Pietà', though in the absence of anything other than price, Caterina had no idea if the wood was for burning or for making musical instruments.

There was a contract between someone listed as 'Giovanni of Castello, *tiorbista*' and 'Sor Lorenzo Loredan', setting a price to be paid for the playing of a series of three concerts during the wedding ceremonies of '*mia figlia*, Bianca Loredan'. The next document was a letter addressed to Abbé Nicolò Montalbano. Caterina's hands tightened into fists and she sat up straight. She looked at the name again.

In the references she had found to Montalbano, the title 'Abbé' had never been attributed to him. Though known chiefly as a librettist, Montalbano had remained, for the researchers she had read, a figure of shades and shadows.

The Countess von Platen had referred to him as the person 'who gained from the fatal blow and who had made it possible'; it was Montalbano who had received the 150,000 thalers soon after Königsmarck's disappearance.

The letter, the letter, the letter, she told herself: read the letter that is lying there under your eyes. It was dated January 1678, and was a list of criticisms of Montalbano's adaptation of the libretto of *Orontea*, the first opera to be presented in Hanover. She knew the music had been written by Cesti, the composer of *Il pomo d'oro*. The writer, whose name was indecipherable, was harsh in his criticism of Montalbano's text and said that he much preferred the original libretto of Giacinto Cicognini.

The next page in the collection was a list of the singers in the first Venice performance of Cesti's *Il Tito*. She continued reading through the documents but found no further reference to Montalbano, though she did find many more cast lists and letters from men who seemed to be impresarios and musicians trying to organize performances of operas in different cities and countries. They wrote to ask if a harpsichord would be provided by the theatre or, if not, could one be rented from a local family and, in that case, who would guarantee the quality of the instrument? Was it true that Signora Laura, the current mistress of Signor Marcello and said to be with child by him, was still going to sing the role of Alceste?

Caterina read through to the end of the first volume, filled with a sense that the real life of music and opera was contained in these papers and not in the dry things her colleagues spent their lives writing and reading.

The second volume interested, and then disappointed, her by containing the libretto of an opera entitled *Il Coraggio di Temistocle*, which, judging by what she could make out from the Prologue and the list of characters, extolled the virtues of the leaders of the Greek forces at the Battle of Marathon but was not the libretto of Metastasio. Caterina held out against the thumping and thudding of the verse for eleven pages before giving in and giving up.

The libretto took up the entire volume. She closed it and set it on top of the other, then carried them both over and stacked them where they would be taken off to be refiled. She resisted the impulse to take another look at the libretto for fear it would become worse. If this was an example of what had eventually led to the death of *opera seria*, Caterina had no uncertainty about the justice of its demise.

Now, standing at the window and looking across at the windows on the opposite side of the Piazzetta, she throbbed with uncertainties about the demise of Count Philip von Königsmarck and the identity of the Abbé whose fatal blow had sent him to his maker.

Her mind wandered from this and turned to the fate of the woman involved in the search, and then it passed involuntarily to the strange loneliness of her life. She was in her home town, with relatives and friends all over the city, yet she was living the life of a recluse, going from work to home to bed to work to home to work. Most of her school friends were married, with children, and no longer had time for their single friends or their single pursuits. She blamed her failure to contact old friends on the urgency with which she had invested her research. She might as well have been one of those miners British novelists were always writing about, who never saw the light of day save on Sunday, when they had to go to church in the rain and dark and cold, and who were probably happier in the mine, where at least they could spit on the floor. She was in the Work Pit, her link to the outer world her cyber contact with Tina, a few apparently friendly conversations with a man who was betraying her, occasional phone calls to her parents, and precious little else.

Her link to the outer world rang and she answered it gladly.

# 26

'Cati,' said a voice she recognized as Sergio's. 'I have to talk to you.'

'News?' she asked brightly before the sound of his voice registered. A second too late, she asked, 'What's wrong?'

Instead of answering her, he said, 'Tell me where you are.'

'I'm in the Marciana.'

'I'm down at the Museo Navale. I can be there in ten minutes. Where can we meet?'

'Florian's. In the back.'

'Good,' he said and broke the connection.

Sergio had sounded tense and worried, something she had never heard before, and she began to castigate herself: her rash request that giant Sergio go and menace the man in the shop had refused to factor in Sergio's sweetness of character. What was to stop the man who had been so successful in terrifying her from turning his attentions, and his menaces, on Sergio? As she walked towards Florian's, she thought about the possible consequences: it would be easy enough for this unknown man, whom she assumed was Venetian, to use the same spiderweb of connection and information to identify Sergio, and from there it would be simplicity itself to find his factory, his home, his wife, his children. His sister-in-law.

She had set it all in motion, had hidden behind a man and his muscles and his size in hopes of intimidating another man who had used the same weapons against her. And all she'd managed to do was put at risk the people she most loved. So preoccupied was she with these thoughts that she failed to notice the elaborate gilded mirrors or the silk-covered chairs and sofas when she reached the café, nor did she respond to the smiles and greetings of the waiters. She went to the bar at the back, distracted by bitter regret and self-castigation. 'Fight your own battles,' she whispered to herself as she sat on the tall stool at the bar.

'*Scusi*, Signorina?' the waiter said with a smile. '*Non ho capito.*' She gave him a startled glance. No, no one would understand what she had done and what it might lead to.

'*Un caffè*,' she said. She didn't want coffee, but the thought of adding alcohol of any sort to her fear repelled her. The coffee came quickly, one of the advantages of sitting back here. She tore open an envelope of sugar and spilled it slowly into the cup, stirred it around, set the spoon on the edge of the saucer, and turned to one side, more to avoid her reflection in the mirror than to be able to see Sergio arrive.

Waiters came to the bar and spoke their orders, carried trays to the people sitting at the tables in the café. She had noticed some courageous souls sitting at tables in the Piazza, shivering in their jackets and scarves in the thin spring sun as part of the full price of the Venetian experience.

243

She glanced at the coffee, realizing it would be cold by now and even less appealing. When she looked up again, Sergio was there: tall, thick-bodied, safe. She slid from the stool and wrapped her arms around him, put her face into his neck and said, 'I'm sorry, Sergio. I'm sorry. I'm sorry.'

When she pulled away from him, she saw surprise spread across his face, and when she glanced at the waiter, she saw it mirrored on his, mixed with open curiosity.

'What's wrong?' Sergio asked. 'What's happened?'

'That man. What did he do?'

Sergio held her by the arm and moved her back to the stool and didn't release her until she was back on it. 'What happened?' she asked, needing to know the worst.

'That man?' Sergio asked.

She felt a sudden flash of irritation. What other man could she mean? 'What did he do?' she asked.

Sergio turned to the waiter and asked for a glass of white wine, anything he had. He looked at her untouched coffee, placed the back of his fingers against the side of the cup. 'Two glasses,' he said to the waiter and turned to Caterina.

'Tell me what happened,' she said, then added, 'Please.'

Sergio managed to smile, though she suspected it was to soothe her anxiety. 'I couldn't go until yesterday evening. I had to talk to some people in a hotel about metal reinforcements.' Involuntarily, Caterina clenched her teeth at the mention of this useless detail.

The waiter set the glasses down in front of them. Sergio handed her one but did not bother to tap his glass against hers or say '*Cin cin.*' He took a long drink, then scooped up a handful of peanuts and began to put them into his mouth, one by one. How long would she have to wait before he told her what had happened?

'I went in about seven. No one else was there. The store

244

is full of crap, that stuff they get from China. Terrible, ugly things. *Robaccia*.' Was he wasting time to calm her down and prepare her for the worst?

'I went in, and he looked up and smiled, sort of waved his hand around the shop to tell me to take my time. As if any of that stuff would interest me.' Then he surprised her by saying, 'But some things did. He's got some of those butterflies the guy in Calle del Fumo makes. Really nice. Only thing in the shop – except for him – that's Venetian.'

From wanting to hold him and protect him, Caterina had passed to wanting to put her hands around his throat to choke the information out of him. But she just picked up her glass and took a sip, tasting nothing.

'So I picked up one of them and went back to where he was sitting, reading the paper.' Sergio finished the peanuts and took another sip of wine.

'I figured I'd do it like the guys in the movies: be a tough guy, start right from the beginning and frighten the little creep.' The man who had followed her was ten centimetres taller than Caterina: only Sergio would see him as 'little'.

'So what did you do?' she ventured.

'I held up the butterfly right in front of him and asked him what he was doing following my sister-in-law around and frightening her. Then I broke one of the wings off the butterfly and let it drop on the page he was reading.' Having said this, Sergio looked at his feet, then reached for his glass and took a larger sip.

He held the glass up between himself and Caterina, his thick fingers easily capable of snapping the stem with the least of efforts. He set it down and took some more peanuts.

'What did he do?' she asked, needing to know the consequences of her own rashness.

Sergio put his handful of peanuts down on the napkin beside his glass and said, 'He pushed his chair back until it hit the wall and tried to stand up.' With his index finger, Sergio pushed at the peanuts, as if he were trying to straighten them into a single line. Caterina realized then that he wanted to have something to look at other than her as he spoke.

'But he couldn't stand up. He was shaking so hard he had to put his head between his knees.' Sergio lined up a few more peanuts.

'When his head was still down there and all I could see was the back of it, he said, "Please don't hurt me, please. My father made me do it. I didn't hurt her. I didn't even talk to her."' Sergio looked at Caterina for confirmation.

She could do nothing more than nod. He hadn't hurt her. He hadn't spoken to her. He'd followed her and terrified her, but he hadn't hurt her.

'What did he do to you? What did he say?' Sergio asked.

She shook her head. 'He frightened me,' she said. Then, realizing how inadequate that sounded, she said, 'He terrified me.'

Voice much lower, Sergio said, 'He started to cry. Not like people in the movies, with tears down his face and you know it's all fake. He was almost hysterical, sobbing and wrapping his arms around his chest and keeping his head hidden like he had to protect himself.' Sergio's voice came in gusts, like the November wind on the Lido. 'He kept saying, again and again, "I didn't want to do it. My daddy made me do it. I had to frighten her. He said she doesn't work enough." It was like he was a kid again. He really couldn't stop.'

'What did you do?'

Sergio threw his arms out to his sides; they were so long that one of the waiters had to dance away from his hand. Sergio apologized to him and the waiter smiled and said it was nothing.

When Sergio looked back at her, he seemed calmer. 'If it had been one of the kids I would have told him to quiet down and given him a handkerchief and told him it would be OK. But this was the guy who followed you.'

'So?'

'So I asked him his father's name.'

'And.'

'Scapinelli,' Sergio said. 'That mean something?'

'Yes,' Caterina said, realizing she had expected it. 'Then what?'

'Then, I felt so awkward, all I could think of was to ask him how much the butterfly cost.' Seeing her raise her eyebrows, Sergio said, 'I know, I know it was a stupid thing to say, but it was the only thing I could think of.'

'What did he do?'

Sergio smiled, or came close to smiling. 'I guess he was as surprised as you were, or I was, because he looked up at me and said it cost twenty Euros but I didn't have to pay for it. He'd tell his father it got broken by a client.'

'And?'

'I did what I had to do: I reached into my pocket for my wallet,' Sergio said. He paused and gave her a pained look. 'When he saw me move, he pushed away to the side like he thought I was going to hit him. Right along the wall, still in the chair. And this time he bent down and put his arms over his head.' Then, as though the story wouldn't be complete without this last detail, he said, 'And he made a noise. Like an animal. In a trap.'

Sergio picked up his glass, looked at it, then put it back on the counter.

In a calm voice, he said, 'I took out twenty Euros and I set them on the newspaper. Beside the wing. And I told him that nothing was going to happen to him and that he could believe me.'

'And?'

'And then I left the shop and went home.'

'Did you tell Clara?'

'No. I wanted to talk to you first.'

'Good. Thank you,' Caterina said, then, 'How did it make you feel?'

'Like a shit. I've never bullied anyone in my life,' Sergio said, then knowing how impossible that would be for anyone who saw him to believe, he added, 'Not since I was a kid, that is.' He raised his hands inwards and drew them repeatedly up and down in front of his body. 'I can't very well do that, can I?'

'So it's a handicap?' Caterina asked.

'What?'

'Being so big. It's a handicap?'

Sergio smiled, as if the question had suddenly set him free. 'I never thought of it that way,' he said, voice filled with new surmise. He took another handful of peanuts and put them all into his mouth. He washed them down with the rest of the wine, turned and signalled to the waiter, and gave her an inquisitive look, but Caterina shook away the idea of a second glass.

The waiter was quickly back with another glass of wine. Perhaps, having come close to Sergio's outstretched hand, he didn't want to keep this client waiting.

Sergio took the glass and waved it in Caterina's direction. 'What should I do about Clara?'

'You tell her everything, don't you?'

Sergio nodded.

'Then you better tell her.'

'I thought so, too.'

'But tell her you were doing it for me.'

248

'You think that will change anything?' he asked. Sergio, she knew from long experience, could be as hard on himself as she was capable of being when judging her own excesses.

'You were helping someone in the family. If she wants to get angry, she can get angry with me.'

'Wouldn't be the first time, would it?' he asked, then smiled. Caterina reached for some peanuts and thought about having a second glass of wine.

# 27

Although Sergio invited her back to dinner, Caterina was reluctant to go as far as San Polo. How easily the habits of the city returned, making her reluctant to leave her own *sestiere*, viewing an invitation to San Polo or Santa Croce as little different from a forced expedition to the Himalayas. What would happen if she had to cross Il Ponte della Libertà towards *terraferma*? Take her passport? Refuse to go because of her fear of strange food and exotic diseases?

She managed to shake off these musings and persuaded Sergio that it would be easier to explain things to Clara if she were not present.

When they left the café, he said he'd walk home, which meant he'd head back towards the Accademia. He kissed her on both cheeks, told her to call him again if she needed him, and headed off towards his home and his family.

Caterina walked out to the water, noticed that the daylight was swiftly disappearing, and started along the *riva*, heading home. What a pair of failures they were. At the first sign of weakness, both she and Sergio capitulated. In her case, her dislike of confrontation was the result of size, not principle.

By the time Caterina was in university, Mina had long been a myth, and her discs could still astonish. How Caterina loved the cover of one of the old discs – it must be from three decades ago – with her head seamlessly airbrushed on to the body of a bodybuilder. A woman's head – and brain – on top of a hundred kilos of muscle and power: if Caterina had that body, she'd once believed, she'd be the head of the Music Department at the University of Vienna. Hell, she'd have been head of state.

But now, having learned that size and power could be a handicap, at least for a person as decent as Sergio, she had to dismiss even that illusion. The man had followed her because he was afraid of his father, and his fear now made him untouchable by her or Sergio. 'Mamma mia,' she whispered.

When she got to the apartment, she spent another two hours hunting for the Abbé Montalbano, chasing him through scholarly books and journals in four languages, seeking some sign of his passing in the catalogues listing the hundreds of thousands of books now available online, even though she knew he was unlikely to appear. She searched for him in historical journals and musicological theses, in the diplomatic files of minor principalities and the memoirs of forgotten noblemen and women.

Occasionally she caught a fleeting glimpse. In 1680, he accompanied Friedrich August, the son of Ernst August, as tutor on a trip to Venice and Rome. A letter from a composer for whom he wrote libretti referred to him as an intensely religious man, though in a 'superstitious way'. Montalbano was believed to be Venetian, though she found no record of his birth in the city archives. He hung around the court in Hanover for years, always ready, it seemed, to help Ernst August with the embarrassing affairs of his family. Little was written about his salary until he was paid, and royally – Caterina smiled as that word came to her – the 150,000 thalers that came to him in the year of Königsmarck's death, though some sources cut it to 10,000. The only subsequent references that Caterina found appeared in a biography of Leibniz, where he was said to have returned to his native country and become the arch-deacon of Mantova, where he died in 1695, and a reference to the account books of the court of Hanover, in which was noted a pension paid to the 'mistress of the Abbé Montalbano' for forty-seven years after his death. The money that was given to him, whatever its true quantity, might as well have evaporated for all that was ever known of it.

She switched files and found the words of Countess von Platen: it was the Abbé 'who gained from the fatal blow that sent him to his Maker . . . Did he not, Judas-like, enable the crime and profit from it? The blood money given to him bought the Jewels of Paradise, but nothing can buy him manhood and honour and beauty.'

'Pronoun reference, you fool,' she said out loud. Change the meaning of 'he' from Abbé Steffani to Abbé Montalbano, and the picture of Steffani changed focus. He ceased to be an assassin; he ceased to have been involved in a murder to curry political favour for himself or his religion. He went back to being a fine composer and a man busy advancing the interests of his church and family. 'Nothing can buy him manhood . . .' If this was not a reference to Steffani, then the writer was using 'manhood' as a synecdoche for all the manly virtues absent from a man like Montalbano and not for missing body parts.

The 'Jewels of Paradise', however, remained a mystery to her. What did Montalbano buy with his blood money and what became of it at his death?

Hunger reminded her that it was time to stop asking these questions and think of finding something to eat. She cut some courgette and put them on to fry, sliced tomatoes and added them, set it to simmer. The realization crashed in upon her that, in all this time, she had not done the obvious thing and listened to Steffani's music. She had read through it, sung through it in a soft voice, hummed a good deal of it. But she had not heard it in any real sense. She went over to the computer and connected to YouTube, typed in his name, and then selected *Niobe*, the work with which she was most familiar.

Turning down the flame under the vegetables, Caterina went back to the dining area and, glancing out the window, saw that the Bears were visible, having dinner. She switched off the light and moved back from the window, where she thought they would not see her, and studied the family. Niobe was the mother of fourteen children, and her boasting of their perfections had brought upon her the wrath of the gods, who slaughtered them all. The Bears had only two, both seated at the table with them.

Signor Bear opened the wine and poured his wife, and then himself, a glass. Caterina found that an excellent idea and went to the refrigerator and poured herself some Ribolla Gialla. The aria that came from the computer was, she thought, the lament by King Anfione, the father of the slaughtered children, sung by a countertenor whose voice she did not recognize.

Across the *calle*, Signor Bear turned to his son and slowly ruffled his hair, letting his hand linger at the base of the boy's skull for a second before returning to his fork. The singer's voice, accompanied minimally by lute and violins, sang to Caterina of the future, of his *pianti, dolor, e tormenti*. Did Signor Bear ever lie awake at night and worry about the safety of his children the way her parents, she knew, had worried about them? Did he have always at one step from him the fear of *il mio dolor*? Her father was a teacher, Anfione a king – and Signor Bear? What did he do to bring home the honey for his wife and babies? Did it matter? Grief was the great leveller.

The rhythm changed and Anfione was calling his troops *all'armi*. Almost by magic, as if the Bears had the music playing in their home, the son stabbed his fork at the food on his plate, glanced at his father for approval, waved a forkful of what looked like pieces of short pasta in the air a few times, and then, in perfect rhythm with the battle cry of the king, popped it into his mouth. Caterina laughed out loud and took another sip of her wine.

The young daughter, who sat opposite her brother, shot him a glance, the look every little sister gave to the older brother who got all of the attention. And love? Her face was a study in a child's version of tragedy, while from the computer the same voice announced '*Dell'alma stanca*', and, indeed, the little girl, in the manner of little girls, looked as though her soul were tired and dejected and abandoned. But then, just as the voice referred to '*placidi respiri*', the father leaned towards her, then leaned closer still, and kissed her cheek. Her glance as she turned towards her father was so filled with joy that Caterina looked away, telling herself it was time to check the courgette.

By the time she took her dinner and another glass of wine back to the table, the Bears had finished theirs and left the kitchen. Caterina, reluctant to read, turned her mind from the idea of children and considered, instead, the men, historical and actual, she had encountered since she came back to Venice. Her thoughts did not follow the chronological order as her speculations jumped from one to another, then leaped ahead three centuries, drawn by similarities between them: their effect on women, their loyalty to friends or causes, the seriousness of their desires.

At the end of considerable reflection, and to her great surprise, she discovered that Steffani was the man she found most interesting, although she failed utterly to form any clear sense of him or feel any emotion save pity. A priest, a proselytizer, probably a spy for the Vatican: Steffani was all of these things, and all of them were things she was historically conditioned to dislike. At the same time, she had found no evidence that Steffani had betrayed anyone, nor that he had suggested the burning of heretics. And he had written that music, the strains of which still haunted her.

As she washed and dried the dishes, she continued to think about him. He had been an insider, reared in the Vatican and familiar with the workings of Propaganda Fide. He knew what they were and worked to bring other people under their power. She stopped, a cotton towel running around the rim of her wine glass, realizing that she still had no idea whether Steffani believed it all or not. Was he a man of his era, as opportunistic as the next, using the Church as a means to accumulate power and hoping to convert people only to build up numbers? Or did he really want others to find the same salvation in faith he believed he might have found? Nothing she had read about him allowed her to decide. Was the Stabat Mater an example of glowing faith or an example of musical genius?

*       *       *

The next morning Caterina was at the Foundation at nine, bent on getting to work on the papers in the second trunk. She paused as she closed the door to the building, drawn, as if by the music of Parnassus itself, to the sound coming from Roseanna's office. Indeed, as she arrived at the open door, she found what she expected: Roseanna was typing. *Click* and *clack* and then *whir* and *slam* and *click, click click, thud, click click.*

She knocked on the side of the door, and Roseanna looked up, smiling when she saw her. 'Want to try?' she said and laughed.

Caterina shook her head as at the sight of mystery. 'No, thanks. But I would like you to give me a hand.'

Without asking what the task might be, Roseanna abandoned her task and got to her feet. 'Gladly.'

'Upstairs. The trunks,' Caterina said. 'I want to start on the papers in the second, but I don't want to have to lean over the first every time I have to get into it. Maybe you'd help me move them?'

'Good idea,' Roseanna said. 'Backs are terrible. You're sure to do something to yours if you keep leaning over like that, especially when you get to the bottom of the piles.'

Talking about bad backs and the people they knew who had them, the two women went upstairs to the Director's office. Caterina unlocked the door and let them in and was surprised to find the room warm, almost uncomfortably so. She looked around in search of the source, her mind flashing to the possibility of fire. Roseanna put her unease at rest by going over to open one of the windows and swing back the shutters, allowing the sun to flood into the room: cool spring air and birdsong entered with it. 'At last,' Roseanna said with palpable relief. She opened the other window and left them both open.

256

Caterina delighted in the fresh air and rejoiced in the sound. She unlocked the cabinet and pulled the doors open wide. For a moment, the women stood in front of the trunks, discussing the best way to move the first.

Having agreed, they each took a handle and carried the first trunk forward a metre or so, lowering it slowly to the parquet floor. They did the same with the second, which weighed more, and set it next to the other. Then they lifted the first one and replaced it in the back of the storeroom, where the other had been, and put the second trunk in front of it.

"Thanks,' Caterina said. Then, 'Curious?'

Roseanna, who had not had a clear view of the papers when the trunks were first opened, said that she was but remained at a polite distance, as if to acknowledge Caterina's right to open the trunk.

Caterina did just that, leaned over to peer inside, and saw that the papers had shifted around so as no longer to be separable into piles. A few sheets of paper had worked themselves loose and now lay vertically between the piles. Thinking as a researcher, she realized that this would create a problem of chronology among any papers that were not dated and began to plan how to remove them systematically so as to maintain the right order.

Caterina crouched next to the trunk and leaned over the edge. She slipped her left hand inside at the point where the two stacks of papers must once have met. As she slid it down, the papers rubbed against her palm. She moved her hand slowly, hoping to find a place where the stacks were still separated.

Hearing Roseanna move behind her, she shifted her own weight in surprise. Her left foot slipped on the waxed parquet, and she lost her balance, sliding forward and falling across the open top of the trunk. Her left palm landed flat on the bottom of the trunk, and her right hand on the floor just in front. She braced herself, elbows stiff.

An inglorious, awkward figure, she crouched half in and half out of the trunk, her right knee on the floor, her left leg shot out behind her. Roseanna was immediately at her side, trying to help her back to her knees. 'Are you all right?'

Caterina did not answer, perhaps did not even hear the question, as she pulled her left leg forward and put her knee on the ground. But she didn't move away from the trunk. Instead, she remained kneeling, one hand inside and one outside the trunk, both palms flat.

'What's the matter?' Roseanna asked, squeezing her shoulder to get her attention.

'The floor,' Caterina said.

'What?' Roseanna asked, looking around.

'The floor,' Caterina repeated. 'It's lower than the trunk.'

Roseanna's look became troubled but she kept her hand on Caterina's shoulder, this time trying a squeeze that would provide comfort. In a consciously soft voice, she asked, 'What do you mean, Caterina?'

Instead of answering, Caterina rose up higher, still kneeling, supporting herself on both hands. She turned and looked at Roseanna, though her hands remained where they were. 'The bottom of the trunk is higher than the floor,' she said. Seeing Roseanna's confusion, Caterina could do nothing but laugh.

'There's a fake bottom,' she said. Some seconds passed. Roseanna looked at her, saw that one shoulder was higher than the other, and started to laugh.

It took a few moments for Caterina to decide what to do. Slowly, she pulled her hand from the trunk, and got to her feet. As if a message had passed between them, both women reached to the handles and pulled the trunk forward. 'I need a stick,' Caterina said, and Roseanna understood immediately.

'The carpenter,' Roseanna said. 'Across the street. He'd have a metre stick.' Before Caterina could answer, Roseanna was out of the room.

Caterina returned her attention to the problem of getting the papers out of the trunk while keeping them in the order in which she had found them. She slid them with care to the centre of the papers, then moved her hands towards the sides of the trunk. Slowly, she lifted them upward. The papers came free and she stood, a slab of them in her hands. She walked to the desk and set the papers as far to the left as she could.

When she returned to the trunk, she could see the intermingling of small packets of papers continuing all the way to the bottom. She bent and repeated her motions, placing the next pile of papers to the right of the first. By the time Roseanna came back, there were five stacks on the table; enough had been removed to show that the rest of the papers lay in two separate stacks of neatly tied bundles.

Roseanna waved the segmented wooden stick above her head. 'I've got it,' she said, her voice as triumphant as her gesture.

Caterina smiled in acknowledgement. 'Let's get the rest of the papers out,' she said, kneeling to reach into the trunk. She picked up some bundles on the left and took them over to the table. Roseanna set the metre ruler on the table and went to the trunk. Monkey see, monkey do. Together they went back to the trunk and repeated the process until it was empty.

Only then did Caterina pick up the metre ruler and pull open its first three segments. The trunk was no deeper than that, she thought. She put the end of the stick on the floor and ran her finger down the numbers. 'Fifty-nine centimetres,' she said aloud.

She lifted it and stuck it into the empty trunk until its end hit the bottom. 'Fifty-two,' she said. Out of curiosity, she pulled out the ruler and used it to measure the thickness of the wood used in its construction: one and a half centimetres. So if the true and false bottoms of the trunk were the same, there would still be four centimetres into which to place papers or objects.

'What do we do now?' Roseanna asked.

Caterina leaned into the trunk and felt all around the bottom with her hand. Everything felt smooth. 'Do you have a flashlight?' she asked Roseanna, who was suddenly kneeling beside her.

'No,' Roseanna said, then reached into the pocket of her jacket and pulled out her iPhone. 'But I have this.' She tapped the surface a few times, and a mini-spotlight ignited. Reaching in, she beamed the light around the bottom of the trunk. As she did so, Caterina leaned forward and they bumped into each other: Roseanna dropped the phone.

She picked it up and moved to the end of the trunk. 'I'll go around it slowly this time,' she said.

Caterina nodded, wondering if it was going to be necessary to shatter the bottom to expose whatever space was underneath. She ran her hand, more slowly this time, along the bottom, closing her eyes to let her fingers have more of her attention. When she had covered all four sides, she shifted the angle of her hand and began to move her fingers along the sides of the trunk, just above the seam where they met the bottom.

Only a few centimetres from a corner she felt it, though she didn't have any idea what she was feeling. Just at the seam: the smallest of imperfections, like a small chip on the edge of a wine glass, though so smooth that, unless one were feeling for it, it would pass undetected. 'Give me a pencil,' she said, keeping her finger on the tiny opening.

Roseanna placed the phone on the bottom of the trunk, went over to Caterina's desk, and came back with a pencil. Caterina took it with her left hand and reached into the trunk to make a small mark on the bottom, just below the place where she felt the hole. Then she continued to move her finger along the remaining three sides, but the wood was like velvet.

When she was finished, she took the pencil with her right hand and prodded at the place above the pencil mark. The point of the pencil penetrated a few millimetres and stopped.

Caterina got to her feet and went to her bag and removed from it, of all unlikely things, a Swiss Army knife.

'What are you doing?' asked a shocked Roseanna.

Caterina didn't answer as she came back and knelt again beside the trunk. She turned the knife around and examined the other side, then pulled out the corkscrew. 'Maybe this will work,' she said.

Roseanna picked up the phone and shone the light on the pencil mark. Caterina manipulated the knife until the point found the hole, then pushed the point until she felt it slip inside. Gently, gently, she tried to turn it, first one way and then the other, but it refused to move. There was only one thing left to do, which was to angle her fist so that the curved point would catch in the bottom panel and, if possible, lever it upward.

She gripped the body of the knife, which had now become the handle, and pressed her fist forward as she turned it up. At first she felt the same resistance that had met her attempts to move it to the side, and then it seemed

**261**

that the point managed to penetrate something. The handle moved closer to the side of the trunk, and she had to push it with the flat of her hand.

The floor of the trunk began to move upwards. It rose steadily until the knife handle met the wall. The bottom had come loose in the corner, and she managed to slip her fingernails, and then her fingers, under it. Slowly, Caterina pulled at it until, as easily as if she were opening a box of cigars, the entire bottom panel slid up. As it reached the top of the trunk, they could both see that the board was slightly bevelled on all four sides. This allowed it to slip down easily and fit tightly into place. It could be prised up only by inserting a narrow, curved point into the hole in the side.

Caterina took the bottom, which was surprisingly thin – barely half a centimetre – from the trunk and propped it against the wall. Both women leaned into the trunk, and Roseanna shone her light into it.

They saw a piece of thick-woven cloth, perhaps a towel or small linen tablecloth. Unstained with age, it rested on the bottom. Caterina reached inside with both hands, took it at two corners, and peeled it back. Below it, resting in a thick nest of the same cloth, were six flat leather bags, the old-fashioned type with draw-string tops. Each was about the size of a human hand. A piece of paper lay atop them.

Caterina, her scholar's habits asserting themselves, picked it up with both hands and lifted it carefully from the trunk. Still kneeling, she rested it on the angle of the top of the trunk to examine it.

She recognized the back-leaning handwriting. 'Knowing my death to be near, I, Bishop Agostino Steffani, set pen to paper to make disposition of my possessions in a manner just and fitting in the eyes of God.'

She tore her own eyes from the text and looked at the foot of the page. The document was dated 1 February 1728: less than two weeks before his death.

'What is it?' Roseanna demanded.

'Steffani's will.'

# 28

'*Oddio*,' Roseanna said. 'After all this time.'

Caterina hadn't looked at the document closely, but she had noticed no witness signatures, though their presence or absence was rendered moot by the passing of three centuries. She looked across at the other woman. 'I think we have to call them.'

'Who?'

'Dottor Moretti and the cousins,' Caterina answered.

'Call Moretti first,' Roseanna said, then added, 'Unless he's here, there's no way to control them when they see those bags.'

Roseanna was right, and Caterina knew it. She had his number in her phone, and she dialled it. 'Ah, Caterina,' he said by way of salutation. 'To what do I owe this pleasure?'

She worked at keeping her voice friendly. 'I've found something I think you and the cousins should see.'

'What is that?'

'I've found a statement of testamentary dispositions,' she couldn't stop herself from saying.

'Steffani's?' he asked, voice alert and louder than it had been.

'Yes,' she said, then added, 'and something else.'

'Tell me.'

'There was a false bottom in the second trunk, and there were six leather bags hidden there. Along with the paper, signed by him.'

'Are you sure?'

'I've seen other documents he wrote, and the handwriting looks the same.'

'Have you called the cousins?'

'No, we thought that should be left to you.'

'We?'

'Signora Salvi was with me when I found them.'

'I thought you said you needed to be alone when you read the papers.' An edge had come into his voice, one she had not heard before.

'I asked her to help me move the trunks.'

'You should have asked me,' he said, and she heard how hard he had to work to keep his voice level.

'I didn't know what I was going to find,' she said calmly. 'If I had known, I surely would have called.'

She let the silence after that grow for a while before she said, 'Could you call them? And come here?'

'Certainly. I'll do it now.' He paused and then added, voice very calm, 'I'd prefer you not to look in the bags.'

'I was hired to read papers, not look in bags,' she answered. She wondered if he heard the snap.

'I'll call them and call you back,' he said.

When Caterina switched off her phone, Roseanna said, sounding surprised, 'You didn't sound very friendly.'

'Dottor Moretti is only my employer.'

'I thought the cousins were.'

'Well, he's working for them, and they've asked him to oversee my work, so in that sense he's my employer.'

Roseanna started to speak, stopped, then began again. 'I'm not so sure he is,' she finally said.

'Not sure who is what?' Caterina asked.

'That he's your employer, or even what he's up to,' Roseanna said.

'How else could he be involved?'

Roseanna shrugged. 'I have no idea, but I heard them talking in the corridor outside my office the day the trunks were delivered.'

'All three of them?'

'Excuse me?'

'Was it all three of them you heard talking?'

'No, only the cousins.'

'Talking about what?'

'They insisted on coming, the cousins. As far as I could understand, he had already persuaded them to hire a researcher.'

'Why do you say that?'

'Because that was the justification they used to be present when the trunks came. They said they wanted to see if there was enough room for the researcher to work in.' Roseanna gave an angry huff. 'As if they cared a fig about that, or would even know how much room a person would need. Or what a researcher is.' Freed of her anger at the cousins, Roseanna said more calmly, 'At any rate, that's the excuse they gave for coming. But I don't believe it for an instant.'

'Then why do you think they came?'

'To look at the trunks, maybe even to touch them, the way people do with magic things, or the way they look in the newspaper every day to see what their stocks are worth.'

266

Failing to stifle her impatience, Caterina said, 'What did you hear them say?'

Roseanna bowed her head and pulled her lips together, as if to acknowledge her own long-windedness. 'They were leaving, all three of them, but Dottor Moretti had trouble with the lock of the door to the stairs, and the two of them came past my office while he was still back there.' She waited after she said this, but Caterina did not prod.

'Stievani said something about not liking Moretti, and the other one said it wasn't every day people got a lawyer like Moretti, and they should be glad that he was sent to them.

'What does that mean?'

That shrug and smile. 'I don't know. I'm not even sure that's exactly what they said. They were walking past the door, and I wasn't really paying attention.'

Caterina wondered who would send Moretti to work for the cousins. It would be child's play to persuade the cousins to accept the services of a lawyer: if an undertaker offered them his services, they'd probably commit suicide to make use of the free offer.

Her phone rang. It was Dottor Moretti, saying he had contacted both cousins, and they would be there in an hour. She thanked him, hung up, and relayed the message to Roseanna.

'Time for a coffee, I'd say,' Roseanna declared.

'I think we can leave it,' Caterina said, waving a hand around the room and recalling the time she had failed to close up the papers and lock the room.

'*Va a remengo, questo,*' Roseanna said, consigning the trunks and the papers to hell or unimportance, or both. They went and had a coffee, and when they returned, they waited in Roseanna's office for the three men to arrive.

\*     \*     \*

It was over an hour before they got there. Caterina was surprised that the three of them came together. She had foreseen the separate arrival of one of the cousins, who she was sure would say he could be trusted to wait upstairs in the office for the others. Dottor Moretti must have imagined the same possibility and arranged to meet them somewhere else, or perhaps he had not told them why he wanted to see them, had merely said it was imperative that they meet. She found that she didn't care any longer which it was or what he had done.

Stievani looked eager; Scapinelli looked unwell, like a man who had had bad news and feared hearing worse. Perhaps his son had called him; she hoped so. Moretti looked the same as ever, even to the gloss on his shoes and the all-but-invisible striping in his dark blue suit. He nodded at Roseanna and smiled amiably at Caterina. He was indeed a prudent man.

They all shook hands, but before Caterina could say a word, Scapinelli said, 'Let's go upstairs.'

So Moretti had told them, Caterina realized. Silently, she led the way up the stairs and down the corridor to the Director's office.

They all remained by the door, though it was clear that the attention of the men was directed across the room, as if on laser beams, to the open trunk that stood to the left of the cupboard. None of them, however, moved towards it, as though each needed the support of the others to break the spell that had fallen upon them.

Caterina decided the time of politesse was ended. 'Would you like to see the document?' she asked, not bothering to direct the question at any one of them in particular.

Like men released from an enchantment, they started towards the trunk at the same instant, only to draw up short of it, as if again zapped by some magic force. Caterina walked through them, the *maga* who had the power to unravel the secret signs. She picked up the document that she had left on top of the open trunk and held it out to Dottor Moretti.

He took it eagerly, and the cousins crowded to his side, looking down at the paper. Stievani tried to move Moretti's arm higher, as if to bring the paper closer to his own eyes, and Scapinelli took out a plastic box and extracted a pair of reading glasses.

As she watched, Moretti's lips began to move, as Italians' often did when they read. After only a few seconds, he moved his right shoulder in a gesture that reminded Caterina of a chicken fluffing out a wing to win it more space. Stievani moved a half-step away, and Scapinelli used the opportunity to move even closer.

Moretti, unable to disguise his exasperation, handed the paper to Caterina and said, 'Perhaps it would be better if you read it, Dottoressa.' He had slipped back into the formal '*Lei*', which suited her just fine.

She took the paper from him, saw the way the four cousin eyes followed it hungrily. And each of these men believed that the others would abide by their agreement to let the winner take all?

'"Knowing my death to be near, I, Bishop Agostino Steffani, set pen to paper to make disposition of my possessions in a manner just and fitting in the eyes of God."' Caterina looked up at the three men to see how they'd take to the idea of God's being mixed up in this. The cousins seemed uninterested; Moretti now resembled a hunting dog that had heard the first call of his master's voice.

'"My life has been devoted to service, to both my temporal and my Divine masters, and I have tried to give them my loyalty in all my endeavours. I have also served my other master, Music, though with less attention and less loyalty.

"'I have sought, and squandered, worldly gain, and I have done things no man can be proud of. But no man can be proud of the act that set me on my path in life.

"'I leave little behind me save my music, and these treasures, which are of much greater value than any notes of music that could be written or imagined. I leave the music to the air and the treasures . . .'" here Caterina looked up from the paper and studied the faces of the men in thrall to her voice.

She did not like what she saw and returned to the page. "'. . . and the treasures I leave to my cousins, Giacomo Antonio Stievani and Antonio Scapinelli, in equal portions.

"'To eliminate all suspicions about my having accumulated such wealth as to allow me to purchase these Jewels . . .'" he wrote, and Caterina wondered if he had capitalized the word while writing in Italian because the Germanic influence on his language for all those decades meant that he automatically capitalized all nouns "'. . . I declare that the money was given to me by a friend who became a Judas, not only to me but to an innocent man. Judas-like, he regretted his betrayal and came to me to be shriven of his sin, forgetting that to forgive sins is not in my power, as it was not in his.'"

She looked at Roseanna, then at the men, and saw the same confusion on her face and on Stievani's and Scapinelli's. Moretti, however, seemed to be following everything, the bastard.

"'The money came to me on his death, and I could think of no finer, no nobler, use for it than to purchase the Jewels of Paradise, which I leave here for the edification and enrichment of my dear cousins in just return for the generosity with which they have treated me."'

There followed the signature and the date, and that was all.

'So they're ours?' Scapinelli asked when it was evident that Caterina had finished reading the document. He took a step towards the trunk and leaned over to look inside. His cousin moved quickly to stand beside him. Had the clear disposition of the will put an end to the idea that winner would take all?

To Caterina, it seemed like the moment of stupor in a Rossini opera, just before the ensemble that brought the act to a rousing finale. Would their voices join in one by one? What duets would be formed? Tercets? Would she sing a duet with Roseanna? She scorned the tenor.

'Dottoressa,' said Moretti, who had moved to the side of the trunk, 'I think it would be right for you to see to opening these bags.'

There was a long silence while the cousins considered the statement. Stievani nodded, and Scapinelli said, very reluctantly, '*Va bene.*'

Caterina walked over to the desk and set the document, face down, on the surface, then went back to the trunk. She leaned inside and, two by two, carried the bags over and placed them at the other end of the table.

'You're sure you want me to open them, Dottore?' she asked Moretti, also using the formal *Lei*. The three men had another silent conference, and when no objection was proposed, she picked up the first bag. The leather was dry and hard, unpleasant to her hand. With some difficulty Caterina untied the stiff knot that held the leather strings together and used the backs of her fingers to force open the mouth of the bag.

All at once she was overwhelmed by a reluctance to know what was in the bag and an even stronger repugnance to touch whatever it was. She handed the bag to Moretti. He reached inside, and his fingers delicately removed a slip of paper with a few words written on it in faded ink. He looked at the paper and, gasping, stood rooted to the spot.

Scapinelli, immune to presentiments or surprise, grabbed the bag from him and stuffed his fingers inside. A second later, his fingers emerged, holding a long, thin sliver that Caterina at first thought might be a decorative silver pin of some sort, tarnished with age.

Scapinelli transferred it to the palm of his other hand and studied it. 'What the hell is this?' he demanded, as if everyone else in the room had agreed to keep the information from him.

After long moments, Moretti broke the silence. 'It's the finger of Saint Cyril of Alexandria,' he said, holding the tiny scrap of paper towards Scapinelli. In a voice made low by reverence, he whispered, 'Pillar of Faith and Seal of all the Fathers.'

Scapinelli turned to him and shouted, 'What? Seal of what? It's a bone, for the love of God. Can't you *see* it? It's a piece of bone!'

Moretti reached out and took it from Scapinelli's hand. He removed his handkerchief and wrapped the tiny bone reverently, then, holding the handkerchief in his hand, he made the sign of the cross, touching his body in four places with the cloth.

Caterina thought of a time, it must have been twenty years ago, when she had been returning to Venice on an overnight train. Luckily, her compartment held only three people, she and a young couple. At about ten, Caterina had gone to use the toilet and, finding a long line of people waiting there, she had been away from the compartment for at least twenty minutes. When she got back, the door was closed and the light turned off. She slid back the door, thinking how lucky she was to have three empty seats on which she could stretch out and sleep, when the light from the corridor flashed across the naked bodies of the young people, linked in lovemaking on the seat opposite hers.

She felt the same shame when she caught a glimpse of the expression on Dottor Moretti's face, for there she read an emotion so intense that no one had the right to observe it. She looked away, allowed a moment to pass, and handed him the second bag. The paper described it as the fingernail of Saint Peter Chrysologus. And so it went until the six bags had been opened and the papers extracted. And each time Moretti handled the piece of dried flesh or nail or the bloodstained tissues with a reverence from which even the cousins were forced to avert their eyes.

When the bags were on the table, the document placed beside it, Caterina turned away from Moretti, who was leaning over them, his hands propped on either side of them, his head bowed. Addressing Scapinelli, she said, 'I don't see the sense of disputing any of this. His wishes are clear: you each get half of what's in those bags.'

A cunning look flashed across Scapinelli's eyes and he said, 'Aren't those things always surrounded by gold and jewels? What happened to them?' Suspicion seeped into his voice as he spoke, and the final words were all but an accusation of theft.

'Signora Salvi was with me when I found them.'

Roseanna nodded.

'I called Dottor Moretti, with her here, as soon as I read the first sentence.' Then, more forcefully, 'No one's stolen anything.'

'Then where did the gold and jewels go?'

'I doubt there were any,' Caterina said.

'There always was,' Scapinelli said with the insistence the ignorant always use when defending their position.

'Maybe he didn't want there to be any gold. Or diamonds. Or emeralds,' Caterina suggested.

Stievani broke in here to ask, 'What do you mean?'

'Maybe he wanted to leave only a spiritual gift to his cousins.'

'Then what did he do with the money?' Scapinelli demanded, as if he thought she knew and was refusing to tell him.

'The money went for the relics,' Caterina said. 'That's what had value.'

Waving his hand at the bags, Stievani said, 'It's only a mess of bones and rags.'

Moretti pushed himself away from the table and took a step towards Stievani. 'You fool,' he said in a tight voice. He raised his hands but lowered them slowly to his sides.

Caterina surprised herself by laughing. 'Fool,' she said, and laughed again.

Moretti turned his glance on her, and she asked herself what had happened to Andrea. 'He believed,' Moretti said. 'He knew what they were worth. More than gold. More than diamonds.'

'And if he didn't believe?' she asked Dottor Moretti. 'If he thought they were just pieces of pig's bone and dirty handkerchiefs? What better way to free himself of the blood money he was given?' The cousins seemed to begin to understand, but she didn't want them to get off free, so she asked, 'And how better to pay back the cousins who refused to help him than by giving them things that had no value except that put on them by faith?'

274

'But he must have believed,' Moretti said, almost shouting. 'He must have believed these were the Jewels of Paradise.' He turned back to the table and ran his hand over the first of the leather bags.

Caterina, who had once thought of his hand running over skin of a different type, shivered at the sight. 'But maybe he didn't believe, Dottore. You're an intelligent man, so you have to know that's possible. Maybe he bought them knowing they were trash. And maybe he wanted that. Maybe it was time to pay everyone back. He was dying, remember, and he must have known that, so he didn't need money any more. And he didn't need the habits of a lifetime of patience.' She stopped then, already ashamed of some of the things she'd said and of the desire that had animated her in saying them. But she gave in to temptation and turned to the cousins. 'You've got your Jewels.' Then to Moretti: 'And you've got your Paradise.'

She walked over and picked up her bag. She opened it and took the keys out, all of them. She put them on the table and turned towards the door.

'You can't leave,' Scapinelli said. 'Your work isn't finished. There might be other things.'

'I'm not working hard enough for you, Signor Scapinelli, remember?' From his expression, she saw he understood. 'So find yourself another researcher, why don't you?' Then, because she felt like saying it, she added, 'Ask your son to help.'

She went to the door and did not turn around. She heard Roseanna's footsteps coming after her: click, click, click, just like her typing. She waited in the corridor. They went down the steps one after the other. In the *calle*, they felt that the warmth had increased.

Caterina felt the tiny shiver of her phone as an SMS

came in. She flipped it open and read. 'Dear Caterina. It's the University of St Petersburg. They want me to be the Chairman of their Musicology Department. But I always refused to learn *Russki*, so I told them I will accept only if you come with me as my assistant, but with the rank of full professor. And they agree. So please come with me, and we will discover vodka together.' There was no signature.

Thinking that it was time the Romanian learned a bit of Russian, Caterina typed in one word, '*Da*', and she and Roseanna went off for a prosecco.

*...ra l'oro, e l si ...ff Atm.*

Per conu

morte d'Henrico conuien che i...

...rica al mio soccorso cieai

cuovto forma incant. aur inuen...

# love your library

**Buckinghamshire Libraries**

**Search, renew or reserve online 24/7**
www.buckscc.gov.uk/libraries

**24 hour renewal line**
0303 123 0035

**Enquiries**
01296 382415

follow us **twitter**
@Bucks_Libraries

KT-420-145

# DARK QUEEN RISING

# DARK QUEEN RISING

## Paul Doherty

CRÈME de la CRIME

This first world edition published 2018
in Great Britain and the USA by
Crème de la Crime, an imprint of
SEVERN HOUSE PUBLISHERS LTD of
Eardley House, 4 Uxbridge Street, London W8 7SY
Trade paperback edition first published
in Great Britain and the USA 2018 by
SEVERN HOUSE PUBLISHERS LTD

British Library Cataloguing in Publication Data
A CIP catalogue record for this title is available from the British Library.


ISBN-13: 978-1-78029-107-9 (cased)
ISBN-13: 978-1-78029-587-9 (trade paper)
ISBN-13: 978-1-78010-985-5 (e-book)

*All Severn House titles are printed on acid-free paper.*

Severn House Publishers support the Forest Stewardship Council™ [FSC™],
the leading international forest certification organisation. All our titles that
are printed on FSC certified paper carry the FSC logo.

Typeset by Palimpsest Book Production Ltd.,
Falkirk, Stirlingshire, Scotland.
Printed and bound in Great Britain by
TJ International, Padstow, Cornwall.

*'To my dear friend Eve Khan.*
*Many thanks for your help and support.'*

# HISTORICAL NOTE

By May 1471 that most ferocious struggle known as the Wars of the Roses was reaching a fresh, bloody climax. Edward of York and his two brothers, Richard of Gloucester and George of Clarence, were determined to shatter the power of Lancaster. Henry VI, the Lancastrian King, was their prisoner in the Tower and marked down for death. Edward then moved swiftly to annihilate the Lancastrian army at Barnet before turning west to search out and destroy Henry VI's Queen, Margaret of Anjou, their son, also called Edward, and their leading general, the Duke of Somerset. The year 1471 was one of Yorkist victories, yet it also gave birth to forces intent on the total destruction of the House of York. *Dark Queen Rising* chronicles the beginning of this. Of course this is a work of fiction, yet most of this dramatic story is firmly grounded on evidence, as the author's note at the end of the novel will attest.

**House of York**
Richard Duke of York and his wife Cecily, Duchess of York, 'the Rose of Raby'.
Parents of:
Edward (later King Edward IV),
George of Clarence,
Richard Duke of Gloucester (later King Richard III).

**House of Lancaster**
Henry VI,
Henry's wife Margaret of Anjou and their son Prince Edward.

**House of Tudor**
Edmund Tudor, first husband of Margaret Beaufort, Countess of Richmond, and half-brother to Henry VI of England. Edmund's father Owain had married Katherine of Valois, French princess and widow of King Henry V, father of Henry VI.
Jasper Tudor, Edmund's brother, kinsman to Henry Tudor (later Henry VII).

**House of Margaret Beaufort**
Margaret Countess of Richmond, married first to Edmund Tudor, then Sir Humphrey Stafford and finally Lord William Stanley.
Reginald Bray, Margaret's principal steward and controller of her household.
Christopher Urswicke, Margaret Beaufort's personal clerk and leading henchman.

# PROLOGUE

'On the evening the Duke of Clarence, contrary to his honour and oath, departed secretly from the Earl of Warwick to King Edward his brother.'

*Great Chronicle of London*

'And so kingdoms fall, thrones tip and crowns topple,' Melchior, a Barnabite friar from a village outside Cologne, a Rhinelander, solemnly intoned. He stared across at his two companions who had gathered with him in this small writing chamber deep within the precincts of Tewkesbury Abbey.

'Indeed it is so,' one of his companions replied, 'and we, the Three Kings as they call us, have the true knowledge to make that happen.' He placed his hands on the book of hours. 'I would swear to such as I would on that held by our brothers at St Vedast.'

'We are nearly finished,' Balthasar, the third Barnabite declared. 'We shall soon return to our friends in London.'

'Hush.' Melchior, their leader, raised a hand. 'Do you not hear it?' The chamber fell silent. The Three Kings listened intently. The great Benedictine abbey did not echo with any sound: no bells tolling, booming their invitation to prayer; no melodious plain-chant drifting on the early morning breeze, no patter of sandalled feet; nothing but an ominous, oppressive silence. Balthasar went to speak but Melchior shook his head and lifted a finger.

'There,' he whispered, 'the clash of armies. It has begun!'

His two companions strained their hearing and nodded in agreement as the clamour from the nearby battlefield rolled through the abbey. The armies of York and Lancaster were at last locked in deadly combat along the water meadows of the Severn river.

'Edward of York,' Melchior declared, 'and his brothers have brought the Lancastrians to account. Queen Margaret of Anjou hoped to escape across the Severn into Wales, but that will not happen. Instead, she will face defeat. Her general Beaufort of Somerset and all his host will be scattered as was pharaoh's army; they will be swallowed up in disaster.'

'But our master surely will remain safe even if his House is the victor?'

'Do not worry,' Melchior replied, 'George of Clarence is the King's own brother, a man who will not put himself in harm's way even if this day is vital to him and his kin.'

'He will be pleased,' Balthasar, the youngest of the Three Kings, declared, 'the secrets we have gathered . . .' He paused. 'Is it not time we shared the fruits of our work with him?'

'True, he gave us the seed for the sowing,' Melchior replied. 'But we are the ones who planted and tended the growth of this rich, bountiful harvest: a veritable treasure chest of intrigue and scandal.'

'But we have not finished yet.'

'No, we are not. I have received messages from Brother Cuthbert at St Vedast. He has discovered a porter who served Duchess Cecily and heard her scream certain words. Cuthbert has invited him to St Vedast.' Melchior grinned to himself. 'He will be rewarded, once Cuthbert has taken a verbatim account of what Duchess Cecily shouted when she discovered that her royal son, Edward of York, had married the Woodville woman.'

'Oh, rich indeed,' Caspar the third Barnabite whispered. 'And what else? What more could be done?'

'News has arrived,' Melchior turned to face Caspar, 'that Richard Neville, Earl of Warwick, has been defeated and killed at Barnet. He may once have been York's great friend and champion but, as we know, because of his hatred for the Woodvilles, he withdrew his allegiance and entered Lancaster's camp. Anyway,' Melchior continued, 'our King-maker has paid the price for such a choice and been despatched to his eternal reward. More importantly, Warwick left no male heir, only two daughters: Isobel, married to our Lord George of Clarence; the other, her sister Anne, will, in my view, be the object of affection for our master's younger brother, Richard of Gloucester. He will be in the thick of the fight today and, if he survives, if Gloucester is victorious, I am sure he will approach his brother the King and demand the hand of Anne Neville in marriage, along with half of her father's estates which are the richest in the kingdom.'

'But surely our master will oppose that?' Balthasar demanded.

'Of course.' Melchior sighed. 'And so my Lord of Clarence has asked us to provide a solution without,' he sighed again, 'without causing the death of that young lady.'

'What happens,' Caspar asked, 'if York loses the fight today? What then?'

'Oh, safe enough for us.' Melchior rubbed his hands. 'If Warwick deserted York, so did Clarence. He betrayed his brothers for a while and sheltered deep in the Lancastrian camp, and we went with him, we had to! Now,' Melchior pulled a face, 'if York loses, if my Lord of Clarence is killed, if Clarence survives and is taken prisoner, will not be the important issue. We have certain knowledge! We possess information, valuable information, precious little nuggets of scandal hidden away in a manner known only to ourselves. If Margaret of Anjou and Somerset carry the day, they will need us, and so we will still profit in so many, many ways.' He paused, listening to the growing clamour of steel against steel rolling across the abbey grounds. 'In the meantime,' Melchior murmured, 'we must act as if York will sweep the day. Remember, our master has asked us to keep another matter in mind as well as under close watch.'

'The little Beaufort bitch?' Caspar retorted.

'The same,' Melchior agreed. 'Margaret Beaufort, Countess of Richmond, late widow of Lord Edmund Tudor, mother of now possibly the sole Lancastrian claimant, Henry Tudor. If the stories are correct, the Beaufort bitch is to become a widow again: her husband Sir Humphrey Stafford is apparently not long for this vale of tears. Now the Beaufort woman also shelters here in this abbey with her leading henchmen, her steward Reginald Bray and her clerk, Christopher Urswicke. I understand she was visiting kinsmen in Wales before being caught up in this clash of armies.'

'Why doesn't my Lord of Clarence deal with her?'

'Oh, he will in time,' Melchior declared, 'and when he can!

Remember the Beaufort woman is protected by her husband Sir Humphrey Stafford, who has at his disposal all the support of his powerful kinsman the Duke of Buckingham. My master has not forgotten that. However, the woman is being closely watched. Indeed, my Lord of Clarence and his henchman Mauclerc claim to have a spy deep in the bitch's household. So,' he rose to his feet, 'let us see what is happening. The good brothers here chatter like birds on a branch: they'll have news from the battlefield as well as information about the Beaufort Bitch whom we may have to deal with.'

'And in London?' Balthasar demanded. 'Brother Cuthbert has orders on how to deal with the porter he has questioned.'

'Oh, do not worry. Cuthbert knows exactly what to do.'

Brother Cuthbert, a purported Barnabite friar, stood staring through the narrow window in the small chancery chamber on the second storey of the priest's house: this crumbling mansion adjoined the ancient, almost derelict church of St Vedast on Moorfields, that great wasteland beyond London's northern wall. The Barnabite peered through the narrow lancet, the dark was beginning to grey. He had done his duty, now it was time to bring matters to an end. Brother Cuthbert turned and walked back to Raoul Bisset, a former porter in the household of Duchess Cecily of York. The friar smiled and lightly touched the dagger hidden beneath his robe. He studied the porter carefully. Cuthbert was now satisfied that this small, greasy tub of an old man was no spy or threat; Bisset was simply desperate for money and ready to sell the priceless morsel of information he had treasured for many a year.

'So,' Cuthbert forced a smile, 'what you have told me,' the Barnabite gestured at the transcript on the table before him, 'is the truth. Duchess Cecily definitely said that?'

'Oh yes, Brother.' Bisset licked his lips and stared longingly at the wine tray on the chest in the far corner. Brother Cuthbert walked across, filled a pewter goblet, brought it back and watched as Bisset greedily drank.

'You were saying?' Cuthbert demanded.

'Brother,' Bisset licked his lips, 'the duchess had a fiery temper and a tongue which cut like a razor. She and her husband Richard of York were forever quarrelling and her tantrums only worsened with age. After her husband was killed at Wakefield fight, Duchess Cecily would lash out with both tongue and cane. The only person who could placate her was her favourite, her eldest, Edward who is now King. The duchess dreamed that her darling son would marry the princess of some great foreign house, be it France, Castile or some other kingdom. She boasted as much and would constantly lecture him and others on the need for such a marriage. Duchess Cecily detested the Woodvilles. She hated them with a passion beyond measure and would not allow them into her presence—'

'And this remark,' Brother Cuthbert interrupted, 'you were there?'

'Yes, yes, I stood outside her chamber. I was bringing up a parcel and I noticed the door was slightly open. The duchess, who was sheltering at Windsor, had just received a messenger who had been dismissed to the buttery.'

'The duchess was alone?'

'Oh no, no, no, her chamber priest was present. Well, that poor man has long since died. He fell down some steps. Anyway,' Bisset tapped the transcript before him, 'this is what I heard. Now, Brother, I was promised a reward. Good silver, freshly minted coins?'

'This chamber priest, was he hearing her confession?'

'He may have been,' again Bisset tapped the transcript, 'but this is what I heard. Now, Brother, my reward?'

'Yes, yes, of course, but it is not here. You see St Vedast,' Cuthbert waved a hand, 'is a derelict church, once the heart of a small village until the Great Plague wiped the hamlet from the face of the earth.'

'Yes, yes, we had the same outside Framlingham in Norfolk.' Bisset fell silent as the smile faded from Brother Cuthbert's face. 'I am sorry,' Bisset stammered, 'you were saying?'

'Moorfields is now the haunt of outlaws, wolfsheads and other malefactors, Master Bisset, so we hide our coin deep in the cemetery. Anyway come, come, I will take you to your reward.' He made to turn away but then came back and watched as Bisset struggled to his feet.

'What is it, Brother?'

'When you worked in the duchess's household, were you ever visited by Bishop Stillington of Bath and Wells? Did you ever hear his name being mentioned by the duchess or by any of the great ones who visited her?'

'Never.'

'And does the name Eleanor Butler mean anything to you? After all, you were a porter, you brought people and goods into the households and dwelling places where the duchess resided?'

'Brother, the name means nothing to me, nothing at all.'

'Are you sure?'

'Of course,' Bisset gabbled on, 'as in any great household, rumour and gossip were common enough. Stories about the duchess and her husband.'

'But you witnessed nothing first hand?' Cuthbert pointed back at the table. 'Only what you have just told me?'

'Brother, that's the truth, but now I am hungry and I would like to go. You promised me shelter and food as well as those coins.'

'Of course.'

Brother Cuthbert led Bisset out of the chamber, down the rickety stairs, along a passageway which swept past the small refectory and out into God's Acre; a gloomy graveyard which looked even more sombre with the river mist swirling in. Cuthbert walked briskly, gesturing at Bisset to hurry as he listened to the old porter's gasps and groans. They made their way along the pebble-strewn path which wound around the ancient headstones and decaying funeral crosses of that sombre house of the dead. They passed through a clump of yew trees and onto a stretch of wasteland, a tangle of weeds, briars and sturdy bushes. Brother Cuthbert stopped and bowed at two of his colleagues who stood resting on spades over a freshly dug grave. Cuthbert walked back to the porter, who stood sweaty and gasping, staring around.

'What is this?' Bisset exclaimed. 'Why have you brought me here? You don't keep coin . . .'

'Here's payment, my friend.' Cuthbert stepped closer and thrust his dagger deep into Bisset's belly, twisting the knife so the blade turned up, rupturing the flesh. Cuthbert dug and dug again as he watched Bisset gag on his own blood and the life light fade in the porter's eyes. The Barnabite withdrew his dagger and watched the dying man topple to the ground. Once Bisset lay silent, eyes staring, mouth gaping, the Barnabite turned to his two companions who had stood silently watching the killing.

'He has his reward,' Cuthbert snapped. 'Now bury him with the rest.'

# PART ONE

'When both armies were too exhausted and thirsty to
march any further, they joined battle near Tewkesbury.'
*Crowland Chronicle*

'Bless me, Father, for I have truly sinned. It is a month,
yes, it was on the second Sunday of Lent that I was last
shriven of my sins.'

Margaret of Beaufort, Countess of Richmond, widow of
Edmund Tudor, mother of Henry, their only son, and now wife
to a very frail Henry Stafford, paused in her prayers. Margaret
crossed herself and desperately tried to recall her examination
of conscience. She had sat in the lady chapel judging herself,
weaning out her faults, but now she could not recall them.

'My Lady?' Brother Ambrose, priest-monk of the Benedictine
community of Tewkesbury Abbey, was now quite alarmed. He
moved the shriving veil which hung between the mercy pew
where he sat and the prie-dieu against which the young countess
leaned. Ambrose scrutinised Margaret's thoughtful face. She was
not beautiful or even pretty, but she had a look of considerable
charm; her complexion was pale and clear, her eyes grey as a
morning mist beneath dark, arched brows. She was full lipped
and generous mouthed; other monks judged her to be solemn,
even severe. Brother Ambrose, however, could detect good
humour, even merriment beneath that studious face, ever ready
to smile even as the world turned against her. Ambrose realised
that was now happening as Fortune's fickle wheel was about to
be given another cruel spin.

'My Lady,' he whispered, 'I shall pray for you.'

The countess abruptly rose. She clutched a pair of doeskin
gloves and used these to smooth down her fur-trimmed red dress.
She touched her dark-auburn hair, as if to make sure it was almost
hidden by the exquisitely bejewelled and embroidered headdress.

'My Lady?' Brother Ambrose rose but then fell silent as Lady Margaret raised a hand.

'Can you hear it,' she whispered, 'the noise of battle?'

'My Lord Edward of York and his brothers, Richard of Gloucester and George of Clarence are moving swiftly,' Brother Ambrose replied. 'Abbot John receives a constant flow of intelligence from the battlefield. York intends to put Queen Margaret of Anjou, the Angevin she-wolf and her son Edward to the sword. My Lady, our prayers are with you. I understand that your kinsman, Edmund Beaufort, Duke of Somerset, also intends to end all troubles and bring this war, short and cruel, to an end.'

Lady Margaret, however, was no longer listening, but moved to the window of the guesthouse chapel deep in the enclosure of Tewkesbury Abbey. Margaret pulled back the shutters; she turned slightly. 'What date is it?' she murmured.

'Saturday the fourth of May. The feast of St Pelagia and Florian . . .'

'. . . The year of our Lord 1471.' Margaret finished the sentence. 'Truly a day of destruction,' she added.

The countess broke off as a chapel door was flung open. Reginald Bray, accompanied by Margaret's chancery clerk, Christopher Urswicke, hurried into the small chapel. They paused just within the doorway and Margaret heard the distant but chilling sound of mortal combat; the vengeful, vicious crash and clash of steel. Sharp bursts of cannon echoed above the murmur of men roaring their hate and screaming their pain on this hot, early summer's day around the village and abbey of Tewkesbury.

'What is it?' Brother Ambrose demanded.

'Madam,' Urswicke ignored the Benedictine, 'madam, you must come now. We have news from the field. Somerset has broken. He and his army are in full flight.'

Margaret swallowed hard, the pain at what she'd just heard, despite her own secret dreams and ambitions, was a blow to both body and soul.

'How can that be?' she demanded.

'Urswicke is correct,' Bray declared, his harsh voice rasping and loud. 'Madam, do not busy yourself in prayer, but come.'

'To do what?' Ambrose protested.

'What can be done?' Margaret glanced to all three men. 'What can be done when worlds collapse and chaos sweeps in?'

'Come, madam.' Urswicke grabbed his mistress's hand: he nodded at Ambrose and hurried the countess out of the guest-house chapel. They hastened along paved alleyways where stone-faced saints and angels peered down at them from corners and enclaves. On the tops of pillars, the gargoyles, with their monkey-faces and snarling mouths, seemed to mock Margaret's mood. She decided not to look but kept her gaze down on the ground as they swept around the small cloisters. Here the air was sweet and heavy with the constant tang of incense and the flow of fragrant smells from the abbey kitchens. The day was drawing on and the abbey bells would soon toll, summoning the brothers to break their hunger before returning to the church for another hour of prayer. The battle raging in the fields around the great abbey was certainly making itself felt. Black garbed monks, hoods pulled close, hurried backwards and forwards, caught up in a panic-growing fear. Margaret glimpsed Abbot John Strensham, deep in conversation with other senior monks in the small rose garden which stretched in front of the chapterhouse.

'Ignore them,' Urswicke whispered. 'Mistress, ignore them! Play the part! Play it now, for the game is about to change if York carries the day.'

Margaret stopped. She squeezed Urswicke's arms and stared into his face. He always reminded her of a choirboy, an impression heightened by his soft, precise speech. Urswicke was smooth-shaven with pale, almost ivory, feminine skin, light-blue eyes as innocent as any child's, merry-mouthed with a mop of dark-brown hair which he apparently never combed. 'A simple-faced clerk' was how someone had described Christopher Urswicke, son of Thomas Urswicke, Recorder of London. Margaret smiled faintly as she held Urswicke's innocent gaze. She looked at him from head to toe. He dressed like a clerk garbed in a dark-brown gown over a jerkin and loose-fitting hose, yet beneath the gown were dagger and sword, and the boots on his feet were spurred as if he was ready to ride at a moment's notice.

'My Lady?'

'I must remember,' she replied. 'There is more to a book than its cover, and that certainly applies to you, Master Christopher. But come . . .'

All three hastened down the cloistered walk and out into the warm sunshine. They approached the abbey church and entered through a postern gate, climbing the rough-hewn steps leading up into the great tower. Bray was insistent that they reach the top to see precisely what was happening. The steward's sallow, close face, pointed nose, thin-lipped mouth and square chin were laced with a fine, sweaty sheen. Hot and exasperated, Bray plucked at his chancery robe, running a finger around the neckline of his cambric linen shirt to clear the sweat coursing down his neck. Margaret noticed the cut marks on Bray's cheeks, a sure sign of her steward's agitation when Bray had shaved that morning. Margaret paused on the first stairwell.

'The page boy, Lambert, who brought messages from kinsman Tudor,' she whispered, 'how goes he in all of this?'

'Safely ensconced with the grooms in the abbey stables. Ignore him,' Bray hissed, 'and everyone else will. Start fussing and the world will fuss with you. Isn't that right, Christopher?'

Urswicke just pulled a face. Reginald Bray, chief receiver and principal steward in the countess's household, was regarded as most skilled in his trade, but his dark humour and blunt speech were equally well known. They continued to climb, becoming more aware of the strong breezes piercing the lancet windows. The horrid din of battle was also becoming more pressing. Lady Margaret, still praying quietly that her own boy would stay safe, listened to the gasping breath of her two companions, aware of the sweat now soaking her own clothes. She tried to distract herself by glancing at the bosses carved in the different stairwells and turnings. Most of these were heavy-winged angels, each carrying a musical instrument, be it the bagpipes, flute or trumpet.

'We need the protection of St Michael and all his heavenly cohort,' Urswicke exclaimed, following her gaze.

'I am sorry,' Lady Margaret paused, resting one hand on his shoulder. Bray stood just behind her ready to help. 'You are limping, Christopher?'

Urswicke turned and grinned. 'My ankle is slightly twisted but I am sure you have other concerns. Madam, we live in hurling times. Kingdoms are now lost and won in a day.'

They continued on till they reached the top of the tower, pushing back the heavy trapdoor, helping each other through the hatchway to stand on the gravel-strewn top. They crossed this and leaned against the moss-encrusted crenellations. All three stared out over the murderous mayhem spreading out across the abbey's great water meadow, fed by the twisting Severn glinting sharply in the early afternoon sun. The Lancastrian battle phalanx had buckled and broken; already both foot and mounted were streaming away in retreat, pursued by the fast-moving, vengeful Yorkists in full battle array. Even from where she stood, Margaret could glimpse the Beaufort standards and pennants quartered with the royal arms of both England and France. Other standards were also visible: those of Beaufort's allies such as the Courtenays of Devon and the De Veres of Oxford. The Lancastrian banner bearers, standards held high, were desperately trying to make a stand to mount a defence. The Yorkists, however, were pressing hard, breaking the Lancastrians up, filleting their battle formation like a butcher would a slab of meat. The bitter sound of the bloody conflict now carried stronger: shrill cries and screams, bellowed curses, shouts of defiance and the heart-stopping groans and moans of the wounded and dying. Margaret also glimpsed the streaming banners of Edward of York as well as those of his two brothers, Gloucester and Clarence, a host of Yorkist insignia, be they The Sunne in Splendour, the Bear of Warwick or the Boar of Gloucester. These billowed around the royal banner, which rippled in a gorgeous sea of colour: blue, scarlet and gold. The Yorkists had unfurled the sacred standard of England, usually kept behind the high altar of Westminster Abbey. Edward of York was using this to emphasise his right to the Crown, as well as his solemn assurance that he would show no mercy or pardon to the enemy fleeing before him. The course of the battle was becoming more distinct as the Lancastrians retreated even more swiftly and the Yorkists followed, spreading out to curve inwards so as to complete their encirclement.

The fresh, green grass of the great meadow was now decorated with the colours of the fallen; their tabards, pennants, shields, banners and standards. Columns of smoke smudged the horizon as other Yorkists broke off from the pursuit to pillage and burn the Lancastrian camp. Margaret shaded her eyes and prayed for

her kinsman, Beaufort. Early that day Margaret had learnt how
the Lancastrians had camped the previous evening at Guphill
Farm, in a stretch of the twisting Gloucester countryside known
as the Vineyards. The Yorkists were now pillaging this and
Margaret wondered what had happened to the Angevin queen
and her son. The roar of voices, men screaming their pain or
laughing in their victory, made her close her eyes and whisper
a further prayer. Beside her, Urswicke was threading his ave
beads whilst Bray quietly cursed. A blood-chilling roar forced
Margaret to open her eyes and stare down. The Lancastrian line
had buckled and snapped completely. Any resistance had
collapsed. Men were now retreating across the great meadow
and the thick press of the Yorkist banner bearers were surging
forward.

'They are fleeing,' Urswicke exclaimed. 'My Lady, your
kinsmen are desperate to seek sanctuary here. Come, they will
soon be below us.'

Margaret followed her two henchmen down from the top of
the tower. She tried to curb the sheer terror welling within her.
They reached the shadows of the northern transept. Lancastrian
knights and footmen were already thronging through the main
entrance, desperate to shelter in the abbey's cool darkness. Monks
came hurrying along the nave, hands fluttering in agitation at
the first sharp echoes of weaponry just outside the main door. The
Yorkists had dismounted, fully intending to continue the slaughter
even in these sacred precincts. Urswicke, quick-thinking and eager
to escape what could be a bloody massacre, pushed Margaret
towards a doorway, beckoning at Bray to follow them through
into a musty, cobwebbed chamber, with steep steps leading up
to a small choir loft. Urswicke turned the key in the lock and
placed the bar in its slats before leading the countess and Bray
up the narrow, spiral staircase. The choir loft was small and
cramped, angled into the wall so the singers and trumpeters could
clearly see what was happening just within the main doorway
below, as well as the porch beyond: here processions would
assemble before sweeping up the long, cavernous nave towards
the majestically carved rood screen which shielded the sanctuary
and choir beyond. No such procession would assemble now.
Margaret stared pitifully down at the frightened, blood-streaked men

surging through the main door, desperate to escape their furious pursuers who now edged in, shields locked, swords flickering out like the poisonous tongues of a host of vipers.

The fighting below grew more intense. Margaret glimpsed her kinsman Edmund Beaufort, helmet cast aside, as he backed further up the nave, his gloriously embroidered tabard with its glowing colours drenched in blood. On either side of the duke, his remaining household knights were desperate to mount a defence, but they broke up as the Yorkists pursued them further down the nave, hacking and hewing so blood swirled along the ancient paving stones. The struggle often became solitary, individual Lancastrians being surrounded by Yorkist knights. No mercy was shown. Margaret watched as one of Beaufort's banner knights fell to his knees in abject surrender. His tormentors simply tore his armour and weapons from him, pushed down his head and severed it with one clean blow. The Yorkists laughed as the head bounced across the paving stones, whilst the still upright torso spouted blood like a fountain before toppling over. The nave was no longer a Benedictine house of prayer, more like a butcher's yard in the Shambles.

Men shrieked in their death agonies under a hail of cutting blows from mace, sword and axe. The Lancastrians tried to hide in the chantry chapels along each transept, but the trellised screens of such small shrines proved to be no protection. Nor were the tombs of the former lords of Tewkesbury such as the Despensers and the Fitzalans. Margaret, standing in the corner of the choir loft, gripped the balustrade in sweaty fear as more and more vengeful Yorkists poured through the main entrance, as well as through the Devil and Corpse doors along the transepts either side. Abruptly trumpets shrieked, their noise braying along the nave.

'The King, the King!' a harsh voice bellowed.

Margaret peered down, twisting to see the three men who now strode into the church, all armoured and visored for battle. They stood like spectres from a nightmare; each of them had removed their war helmets, thrusting these into the hands of one of the squires milling about them. The central figure, his blond hair shimmering in the sunlight, lancing through the great windows of the nave, turned slightly. Margaret narrowed her eyes as she recognised the smooth, tawny features of Edward of York, Edward the King, the great killer of Margaret's kinsmen, the Beauforts. Beside Edward stood his two brothers: on his left George of Clarence, thinner than his brother, his wine-fat face laced with sweat. On the King's left, the small, wiry, sharp-featured youngest brother, Richard of Gloucester, his long, reddish hair framing an unusually pallid face. All three princes were armed with sword and dagger. Edward raised both hands in a sign of victory before lowering them, pointing both sword and dagger down the nave.

'Kill them all!' Clarence bellowed. 'Show no quarter, give no mercy!'

A scream answered his words as a Yorkist squire, holding a dagger to his prisoner's throat, now drove it in. More shouts of despair and cries of triumph broke the stillness, followed by a clatter of weapons. This abruptly ceased as the abbey bells began to toll, crashing out their peals as a deep-throated chanting rose from the sanctuary. The heavy curtain across the rood-screen entrance was abruptly pulled back. A hand bell rang as a line of monks, cowls pulled close, left the sanctuary and processed into the nave. A cross bearer and two acolytes together with three thurifers preceded Abbot John Strensham who, garbed in all his pontificals, walked slowly down the church. He had removed the golden pyx from its silver sanctuary chain and now held this up in both hands.

'Behold the Lamb of God,' he intoned in a hollow-sounding voice. 'Behold the Lamb of God who takes away the sins of the world.' He walked on, holding the pyx high as he gazed directly at the King. 'I hold here,' he declared, 'the body and blood of the Risen Christ. I hold it here in this terrible place which is supposed to be the House of God and the Gate of Heaven. Yet you, your Grace, have turned our abbey into a butcher's yard. Look around you, do not pollute these sacred precincts. Desist! The killing must end.'

Margaret could only agree as she murmured a prayer in reparation at the abomination which now stretched along that shadow-filled nave: wounded, tired men, broken in body and shattered in soul, clinging to the pillars and trellised screens of the different chantry chapels. Some of the wounded, terrified at the prospect of immediate slaughter, crawled across the blood-drenched floor in a vain attempt to hide amongst the long line of black-garbed Benedictines.

'Look,' Urswicke hissed, Margaret did so. George of Clarence was now walking forward, pointing his glistening, blood-wetted sword at the abbot.

'Be careful,' Strensham warned. 'These are sacred precincts, God's own sanctuary.'

'Tewkesbury,' Clarence bellowed back, 'does not possess such a right. It cannot grant sanctuary. The men who shelter here are traitors taken in arms against their rightful King, who has unfurled his sacred banner and proclaimed his peace. They have insulted that. They are blasphemous liars,' Clarence edged forward 'These miscreants have sworn, on other occasions, to be loyal and true to my brother the King. They are oath-breakers as well as traitors and so deserving of death.'

'They are also,' Richard of Gloucester stepped forward to join his brother, 'murderers. They have the blood of our House and kin on their hands, including the unlawful slaying of our beloved father and brother after Wakefield fight.'

'Deliver them!' Clarence shouted, shaking his sword. Abbot Strensham walked as close as he could to the pointed blade.

'George, Richard,' Edward the King dramatically re-sheathed his weapons, 'our quarrel is with traitors, not Abbot Strensham and his Benedictines,' a note of humour entered the King's voice, 'and certainly not with Holy Mother Church. These malefactors, double-dyed in treason and treachery, men twice as fit for Hell as any sinner, have sought sanctuary here. Let them have it.'

The King stepped forward, one hand raised. 'Abbot Strensham, you have the word of your King.' Edward turned away and, escorted by his brothers who also re-sheathed their weapons, left the abbey church. The Yorkist knights streamed after them. Abbot Strensham gave a deep sigh, raised a hand, snapping his fingers. Two monks hurried forward to close the heavy, double portals, turning the key in its lock and bringing down the great bar whilst others of the brothers did the same at both the Devil's porch and Corpse door.

'Are you ready?' Urswicke bent down and stared at his pallid-faced mistress, mouth all puckered, her tired eyes watchful and wary. 'Abbot Strensham has arranged for you, and you only, to slip through the rood screen into the nave.' He gestured at Bray. 'Reginald and I will accompany you into the sacristy but no further. Mistress,' he added, 'be careful. You know you have to be. A person claiming sanctuary cannot, according to canon law, receive any visitors who might bring weapons, purveyance or comfort, be it physical or spiritual, to a sanctuary seeker. So be vigilant and remember the risks both you and the abbot are taking, not to mention your kin.'

'Yes, yes.' Margaret sighed. She got to her feet, took a deep breath, pulled up the hood of her gown and, with Urswicke leading the way, they left the guesthouse. Urswicke paused whilst Bray locked the doors behind them; they then continued along stone-paved passageways where harsh-faced angels, sullen saints and smirking gargoyles peered down at them from the shadows. An eerie silence had crept through the abbey, as if it was part of the thick river mist now seeping in from the Severn. All sound was dulled, the echoing song of plain-chant, the ringing of bells, the slap of sandalled feet on stone and the cries and shouts of the lay brothers working in the vast abbey kitchen and buttery. All this seemed to have been cloaked by an ominous silence. Occasionally black-garbed figures, robes flapping, would flit across their path. Now and again Margaret glimpsed peaked, white faces of monks peering out at them from some window or embrasure.

Edward of York's men were also there but Abbot Strensham had issued his own orders. The sacristan of the abbey did not fire the sconce torches, light the powerful lanternhorns or lower the Catherine wheels, their rims crammed with candles. This lack of light proved to be a real obstacle to York's soldiers, who did not know the abbey with its twisting runnels, narrow winding paths, different gardens, herb plots and flower beds. They had to thread themselves through a veritable maze of stone where it was so easy to lose their way. Urswicke, however, faced no such difficulty as he followed the precise directions provided by Abbot Strensham.

At last they reached the small door to the minor sacristy of the great abbey church. Urswicke knocked and Abbot Strensham himself ushered them in. He had a hurried, whispered conversation with Urswicke and Bray ordering them to stay then, taking Margaret by the hand, he led her out of the sacristy. They crossed the darkened sanctuary, through the rood screen, down steep steps into the nave and across to the chantry chapel of St Faith. Margaret felt she was walking through the halls and chambers of the underworld, where ghosts gathered and pitiful moans and groans mingled with the whispering of desperate men. The light was very poor and this only deepened the illusion that all of this misery was part of some blood-chilling nightmare. At the entrance to the chantry chapel Margaret paused and stared at the dark shapes huddled along the nave.

'We do what we can for them,' the abbot murmured, 'but they are all doomed men. Edward of York is intent on their deaths. Both I and Somerset know that.'

The inside of the chantry chapel was opulently furnished with blue-dyed turkey rugs. The polished woodwork of both the screen and the chapel furniture gleamed in the light of the six-branched altar candelabra. Edmund Beaufort, Duke of Somerset, the leader of the Lancastrian host, sat slumped in the celebrant's chair, feet resting on a stool. On the floor around him lay his battle harness, his weapons stacked in the far corner. Margaret, aware of Abbot Strensham leaving and the door closing behind him, walked softly around and stared into the face of a great lord whom she knew faced certain death. At first Somerset did not even acknowledge her but sat cradling his head in one hand, the other tugging at the sweat-soaked tufts of his blond hair which fell down to his shoulders.

'My Lord,' she whispered, 'my Lord I am here. Margaret Beaufort, daughter of the first Duke of Somerset.'

'Margaret, Margaret, Margaret.' Somerset's hand fell away. He straightened up, removed his feet and pointed to the stool. He then abruptly leaned forward. He grasped her hands, drew her close and kissed her softly on each cheek before gesturing at the stool. 'Margaret, my little Margaret.' He sat back in the chair. 'How long has it been?'

'Four years.' She smiled through the dark. 'Four years almost to the day. You remember, the May Day celebrations?'

'Yes, yes.' Somerset gestured at his stained but still glorious tabard lying on the floor beside him. '*Sic transit gloria mundi,*' he murmured, 'thus passes the glory of the world, Margaret. My brother John was killed in today's battle, Courtenay of Devon likewise. God knows where the rest are or what the future holds for them! And as for you, the last of our line.' Somerset joined his hands in prayer. 'Little Margaret, since I heard of you visiting me, I have been reflecting. I shall give you a homily, a sermon on the times. Much of it you will already know but some of it points to the future. So Margaret, let me begin my sad story of kings. Remember the verse that all the waters of the sea cannot wash away the balm and chrism of coronation? A king is sacred! Henry VI, son of Henry V and Catherine of Valois, is God's vice-regent here in this kingdom. True,' Somerset wiped his sweaty, bewhiskered face, 'our enemies claim that Henry sits closer to the angels than any of us; that he is not of this world yet he is still our King. We Beauforts descend from John of Gaunt, son of Edward III and his mistress Katherine Swynford; we also have a claim to the throne. We are legitimate and have been declared such by both King and Parliament, yet we support the Crown. Henry VI, holy but witless, married Margaret of Anjou, the so-called Angevin she-wolf. She produced an heir, Prince Edward.' Somerset shook his head. 'A most unlikeable young man. Another killer! God knows what will happen now to Henry or his son because the House of York, also descended from Edward III, believe they have a claim to the throne, one superior to anyone else's. Richard of York was killed at Wakefield but his three remaining sons Edward, Richard and George have continued the struggle and so we are here. We have been brought to this pass. The Beauforts and the House of Lancaster are truly finished. Margaret of Anjou and her son will be captured and slain. Many of those who supported them, men such as Richard Neville, Earl of Warwick – the so-called King-maker – was killed at Barnet along with many of our comrades.' He paused and peered at Margaret. 'You will need protection. You are a Beaufort, Margaret. Your husband is Sir Humphrey Stafford?'

'Fought for York to protect us all,' Margaret replied. 'He too was at Barnet, and grievously wounded! I cannot say if he will survive. Thankfully his kinsmen the Staffords of Buckingham are well protected by Edward of York and sit high on his council.'

'And if Sir Humphrey dies, Margaret, as I too am going to die very soon. Oh yes.' Somerset held a hand up. 'I am reconciled with that. Edward and his brothers want to destroy Lancaster root and branch. You Margaret,' again he touched the back of her hand, 'you are the last sprig of our tree, or at least your son is, Edmund Tudor's golden boy. Where is he?'

'Safe.'

'Where?'

Margaret just stared back.

'Yes, yes,' Somerset whispered, 'it's best not to say . . . But to return to you. If Stafford dies, will you take a third husband?'

'God will decide.'

'Yes, *Deus vult*, Somerset replied. 'Listen Margaret, your father, my kinsman, the first Duke of Somerset, died out of sheer despair. Some even claim that he took his own life.'

'Some are liars. Why do you mention that?'

'I just wonder if we Beauforts are cursed, whether we are doomed to fail. This morning I thought we would carry the day. I really,' he paused to control the stutter which marred his speech, a legacy, or so they said, of a powerful blow to the head during a tournament at Windsor, 'I truly thought victory was within our grasp. I plotted to clear the field and destroy York.' He clenched his fist. Margaret watched and recalled how Somerset was a man of bounding ambition and fiery temper: she secretly wondered if such faults played their part in his defeat and that of Lancaster along the meadows outside.

'Pity poor Warwick killed at Barnet. Pity your brother-in-law Jasper Tudor did not reach us in time. Pity that we were unable to ford the Severn.' Margaret flinched at the self-pity which curled through Somerset's voice. 'Pity us all Margaret.' Somerset, eyes closed, rocked backwards and forwards. A loud scream echoed down the nave and Somerset broke from his reverie. 'Be on your guard against Clarence.' He hissed. 'Clarence is a killer to the very marrow, a Judas soul bound up like Lucifer with his own ambition. He intends to kill you, murder your son and anyone else of Lancastrian blood. He will do all this and then, like the rabid wolf he is, turn once again on his own kith and kin. He will prowl both court and kingdom. Murder, treachery and ravenous ambition will trail his every footstep: these hounds of

Hell will be famished, hungry for the taste of blood and for Clarence's self-preferment . . .'

Christopher Urswicke gently removed Mauclerc's hand and pushed it away.

'What is the matter, Christopher? Are you not interested in the male as you are in the female? Do you not prefer the company of men to that of women or are you . . .?'

'Hush now.' Urswicke leaned over and pressed a finger against Mauclerc's lips. 'Remember why you are here,' Urswicke hissed to this most sinister henchman of George Duke of Clarence.

'Yes, here we are.' Mauclerc's voice was mocking. He fell silent as Urswicke drew his dagger: the blade gleamed in the light of the lanternhorn set on the garden table deep in a rose-fringed arbour overlooking the kitchen garden of Tewkesbury Abbey. Urswicke placed the dagger on the table before he twirled it; the blade spun, glittering and pointed. 'Do you threaten me Urswicke?'

Mauclerc leaned closer, the lantern light casting shifting shadows. Urswicke watched intently. Mauclerc was a dagger man and Urswicke wondered if others lurked in the darkness behind. He held Mauclerc's gaze, studying him carefully. Clarence's henchman had a wolfish face with those narrow, slightly pointed eyes, the hollow cheeks, squat nose, and a mouth which seemed unable to close fully around the jutting teeth. A man who wore a perpetual sneer, as if he had judged the world and found it wanting to himself. Mauclerc scratched his black, glistening shaven pate, then abruptly snatched at the dagger, but Urswicke was swifter. He grasped the knife, twisting it in his hand so it pointed directly at Mauclerc's face. Clarence's henchman smiled thinly.

'I've heard of that Urswicke.' He murmured. 'Fast you are, swift as a pouncing cat. A born street fighter, despite your delicate frame.'

'Or because of it? So Master Mauclerc, put both hands where I can see them and do not think of even touching either the dagger in your belt or the Italian stiletto in the top of your boot. Nor must you whistle or, indeed, make any sound to draw in your escort which must not be far from here. Good? Do you understand?' Urswicke didn't even bother to wait for an answer.

He re-sheathed his blade and leaned against the table. 'So we are,' he began, 'at the witching hour on this balmy May evening in Tewkesbury Abbey. A short distance away the corpses of the Lancastrians are being stripped and collected like faggots of wood for the fire. Here in this abbey, the remaining surviving Lancastrian leaders lie bloody and besmirched: their only defence is Holy Mother Church in the person of Abbot John Strensham—'

'They'll die,' Mauclerc interrupted. 'They will all die. Clarence my master is insistent on that.'

'Even though, for a while, he turned coat and fought for Lancaster, changing back to his royal brother when Warwick and Somerset seemed weaker?'

'My master,' Mauclerc retorted, 'had no quarrel with his brothers but only with the Woodvilles. The King's marriage to Elizabeth of that name offended many of the lords. The Woodvilles are grasping, a family greedy for power, deeply ambitious without the talent to match . . .'

'Like so many of our noble lords.'

Mauclerc drew his breath sharply. 'You insult my master?'

'No Master Mauclerc, I tell the truth, but enough of this fencing, this sham swordplay.'

'You talk of my master betraying his own brother,' Mauclerc jabbed a finger at Urswicke, 'yet you are here to act the traitor to your own mistress, Margaret Beaufort.'

'My loyalty is to the King,' Christopher insisted. 'My own father is Recorder of London, an important judge and the most fervent supporter of Edward of York.'

'Though your relationship with your father is hardly cordial?'

'We have our differences.'

'You mean he has his women who, I understand, drove your mother to an early grave . . .' Mauclerc paused as Urswicke's fingers fell to brush the hilt of his dagger.

'My father is my father,' Urswicke murmured. 'I am who I am, a clerk, a lawyer well versed in politics who now accepts his hour has come. The House of Lancaster, the fortunes of the Beauforts are finished, shattered and pushed into the dark.'

'We were not talking about them but your mother?'

'Leave that, Master Mauclerc. Let us concentrate on what's going to happen.'

'Oh, that's easy enough. The King, not to mention Gloucester and Clarence, are determined to pull Lancaster up by its rotten roots and consign that stricken tree to the fires of history.'

'And my mistress, the countess?'

'You mean your former mistress?'

'True.' Urswicke half smiled. 'But her fate?'

'She is married to a Stafford who, like many of his tribe, fought for our King, in particular at Barnet. Consequently she is safe providing she behaves herself. Her son is another matter. You see, once all this is over, the English court will divide. There will be the King, his wife Elizabeth Woodville and her brood. Close to them Richard of Gloucester and George of Clarence. Then there are the Yorkist warlords, men such as William Hastings, Stanley, Buckingham and the others and, of course, Holy Mother Church. We now deal with the Lancastrians. There is Henry VI, that holy fool who lies locked up in the Tower. He can stay there, he will never come out.' Urswicke tried not to flinch at the venom in Mauclerc's voice. 'Yes, yes Christopher, Henry VI will not be making any more royal progresses through the kingdom. He can stay imprisoned, pattering his prayers and preparing for his own funeral. We, however, are going to hunt for his Queen, Margaret of Anjou, and the bastard Edward, her son. We want to capture them. In the meantime, those who have taken sanctuary here must die and my master intends to kill any other remaining Lancastrian with even the weakest claim to the throne.' Mauclerc pushed his face closer. 'And that includes your mistress's son, Henry Tudor, the offspring of her former husband Edmund who was, as you know, half-brother to that holy fool Henry. What we now want to know are the whereabouts of your mistress's son?'

'In a while,' Urswicke replied. 'We must not travel that road so swiftly. We must proceed at a canter, not at a gallop.'

'Time is passing, Urswicke. You must make choices. As I have said, Somerset and the others are for the slaughter. You want protection from my master and you shall have it, but it comes with a price . . .'

'It always does.'

'Or it can be interpreted as a token of good faith by yourself.'

'I offer you three such tokens.'

'And what are these?'

'The whereabouts of Margaret of Anjou and her son.'

Mauclerc's surprise was palpable. He half rose, gasping for breath. 'Nonsense.' He breathed. 'How can you?' Mauclerc sat down. 'Why should she . . .?'

'Margaret and her son are desperate to cross the Severn and seek the protection of my mistress's brother-in-law, Jasper Tudor, who hides behind the vast fastness of Pembroke Castle where, by the way, her own son also shelters. So,' Urswicke waved a hand, 'you have two tokens, take them or leave them.'

Mauclerc stretched out a hand, Urswicke clasped this. Mauclerc uyuuuuuu, lui yu uuu yui to his feet. 'Hold.' Urswicke peered up through the dark as he gestured with his head towards the abbey. 'The Lancastrian defeat, so swift, so crushing. What happened? And I might be able to give you another token.'

'Edward of York,' Mauclerc paused as if gathering his thoughts, 'Edward of York,' he replied, 'came on fast, passing through Southwick, aiming like an arrow for this abbey. Margaret of Anjou and her army were desperate to cross the Severn but they failed. She and Somerset had no choice but to advance to meet us. The Lancastrians divided their host into three battle groups. Prince Edward and Lord Wenlock held the centre. Somerset their right, Courtenay of Devon their left flank. They advanced swiftly through the Vineyards and reached the south of the abbey.'

'And King Edward's army?'

'Also divided into three phalanxes. King Edward held the centre, Gloucester the left, Lord Hastings the right. What the enemy didn't know was that King Edward had hidden a host of two hundred mounted spearmen on a wooded hill a little to the south of Gloucester's phalanx.'

'We heard the sound of cannon fire?'

'Yes. King Edward brought up his artillery and archers to deliver a shower of missiles on Somerset's battle line: this proved to be a sharp and deadly hail. Somerset was left with no choice but to attack, and became embroiled with Gloucester and the King's phalanxes. The Yorkists held the attack until the spearmen King Edward had hidden on that wooded hill charged out to smash into Somerset's line, forcing it back. The Yorkists then began to roll the Lancastrian line up as you would a piece of piping . . .'

'But the Lancastrian centre, surely . . .?'

'Ah.' Mauclerc tapped the side of his nose; he paused as an owl hooted hauntingly through the dark.'

'Three times!' Urswicke exclaimed.

'Three times what?'

'If an owl hoots three times through the dark, it's a prophecy for those who hear it. If there are two people in the same place, one of them will die and the other will be the cause of it. Do you believe that, Mauclerc?'

'Aye, as I believe harridans fly through the air and the Hounds of Hell prowl this abbey. I don't believe in such babble talk.'

'The battle?' Urswicke asked, quickly trying to conceal his own unease.

'Ah,' Mauclerc laughed abruptly, 'the Lancastrian centre should have come to Somerset's aid but Lord Wenlock froze, God knows why?'

'I do,' Urswicke replied. 'And here's your third token. I met Wenlock secretly on his march to the Severn. I pretended to be sending messages to the Duke of Somerset from his kinswoman, my mistress. Anyway, Wenlock who, as you know, once fought for the House of York, was open to suggestion. After all, King Edward had once appointed him to be captain of the English fortress at Calais. My couriers delivered messages informing Wenlock that if the battle went against Lancaster and he survived, my mistress would intercede for Lord John Wenlock and so would her husband, Sir Humphrey Stafford.'

'So that explains it,' Mauclerc interrupted. 'Wenlock didn't freeze, he just didn't commit his forces to confront the Yorkists who inflicted great damage along the Lancastrian battle line. Courtenay of Devon was killed in the bloody hand-to-hand fighting, as was Beaufort's brother John. Somerset was furious. He left the battle and galloped up to Wenlock to remonstrate. Wenlock argued back, so Somerset, and he has a fiery temper, smashed Wenlock's head with his battle-axe.'

'God and all his angels,' Urswicke breathed.

'The Lancastrians witnessed this savage clash: their leaders were killing each other whilst the rest were being cut down as you would lop branches in an orchard. The Lancastrians broke. They fled towards Abbot's Mill, one of the Severn tributaries, but this was swollen due to recent rains. Many were drowned, the others tried to flee across the sunken water meadow only to be cut down. A day of great slaughter. Parts of the meadow were knee-deep in gore; there was enough spilt blood to float a boat. Edward's victory was complete, a sign of God's pleasure for the House of York. Now we must go.' Mauclerc beckoned. 'Our masters await.'

Urswicke picked up his cloak lying over the table and followed Clarence's henchman out of the arbour and across the kitchen garden. He made Mauclerc, who carried the lanternhorn, walk ahead of him. Urswicke watched the moving circle of light as they made their way under the looming mass of Tewkesbury Abbey. Night had fallen but the abbey didn't sleep. Knots of well-armed household knights, sporting the blue and yellow of York as well as the personal coat of arms of the three royal brothers, guarded all entrances to and from the abbey.

Urswicke and Mauclerc eventually left the precincts by a postern gate. They hurried down a narrow trackway into Tewkesbury village, its usual silence and tranquillity broken by the mass of soldiers camped out in the streets which led into the market square, dominated by a soaring stone cross. Edward and his brothers had taken over a merchant's house overlooking the market area, a majestic three-storey mansion built out of honey-coloured Cotswold stone; both its door and windows were flung open in a blaze of candlelight. The royal brothers were gathered in the long, wood-panelled dining hall. They lounged at the top of the common table, Edward the King slouched on a throne-like chair, his brothers either side of him. Further down, clerks of the royal chancery copied and sealed letters, proclamations and indentures. The hall was perfumed with the sweet smell of scented candles and the rich odour of melting wax. Around the room stood York's leading henchmen. Urswicke recognised Lovel, Catesby, Ratcliffe and others of Gloucester's household, as well as those of the King, such as William Hastings who played such a prominent role in the Yorkist's victory. The royal standards and other banners filled one corner of the hall. Strewn on the floor beside them were those of the defeated Lancastrians, besmirched with urine, faeces and other dirt. Urswicke glimpsed the Lilies and Portcullis of Beaufort and hurriedly glanced away. Mauclerc told him to stay before handing the lantern to a retainer and hurrying up to kneel between the King and Clarence, with Gloucester leaning over to listen to what Mauclerc whispered as he pointed back towards Urswicke. The King raised a hand, snapping his fingers, gesturing at Urswicke to approach. Mauclerc brought a stool, placing it where he had knelt. Urswicke went to bend the knee.

'No need,' Edward barked. 'Not now. Time is passing.' The King's light-blue eyes creased into a smile. 'I know you, Christopher, or rather your family. Your father's loyalty provides great comfort to me and mine. Now.' Edward raised himself out of his chair, 'Hastings!' he shouted. 'Clear this room. You sirs,' Edward bellowed at the clerks further down the table, 'gather your manuscripts, get out and do so quickly.' Edward rose and clapped his hands, the hall swiftly emptied. Urswicke glanced at the royal brothers. All three had stripped themselves of their mail and armour and now wore puffed, sleeveless jerkins, displaying the blue and yellow of York, over stained cambric shirts. The royal brothers were still blood-streaked and, as they moved on their chairs, the spurs on their boots jingled like fairy bells. They had taken off their broad, studded warbelts and hung these over the back of the chairs. Waiting for the hall to be fully cleared, Urswicke studied all three brothers closely. Edward the King, he concluded, certainly deserved the title as the handsomest man in the kingdom. Despite the exertions of the day, Edward still looked serene and composed, his beautiful face seemed slightly burnished as if with gold dust: Edward's nose was thin and aquiline, his lips full and merry, his blond hair closely cropped and sheened with sweat whilst the light-blue eyes were bright with mischief and merriment. The King had retaken his seat and now sat, mouth slightly open, staring down the hall, a heavy-lidded look as he watched Hastings usher a bevy of young damsels out of a window seat towards the door. Clarence looked almost identical to his elder brother, though sharp observation would soon notice the reddish, vein-streaked drinker's face, the mouth slightly slobbery, lips twisted into a perpetual pout. Clarence, Urswicke concluded, believed the world owed him much and still had to pay. Richard of Gloucester was remarkably different from both his elder brothers. He had long, reddish hair which framed a pale, severe face with watchful eyes and tight-lipped mouth. Rather small in height, Richard sat slightly twisted as he favoured a birth injury to his back. He kept drumming his fingers on the table while staring around the hall, as if he suspected enemies still lurked nearby. A man of nervous energy, Richard of Gloucester was totally devoted to his eldest brother, as well as to the memory of their beloved father, slain at Wakefield. Over the last few months Richard had emerged as a fierce warrior skilled in battle and totally ruthless in the pursuit and destruction of the enemies of his House. Richard turned and caught Urswicke staring at him. He winked and Gloucester's severe face creased into a genuine smile which completely transformed him.

'Christopher Urswicke.' Gloucester leaned across, hand extended for the clerk to clasp. He did so, moving to the side as Edward sat back in his own chair to allow Christopher to respond. Abruptly Urswicke felt his shoulder tightly gripped. He turned. Clarence pushed his face close, lips glistening with red wine, which drenched his breath as well as the front of his doublet. 'And how's your mistress little Meg? We will deal with her and her by-blow, the imp Henry Tudor. She cannot hide behind the Staffords of Buckingham forever. We will . . .'

'George.' Edward leaned over and gently prised Clarence's hand away. 'First,' the King beamed at Urswicke, 'we must deal with troubles of the day. Yes?'

Urswicke nodded his agreement. Deep in his heart, however, he would certainly remember what the King had just said. 'First we must deal . . .' He glanced quickly at Clarence. Then what, he wondered . . .?

'I have thrown the dice in my last game of hazard.' Somerset took his hands away from his face and stared up at the cross above the chantry chapel altar. He had described the battle outside, freely confessing how he had committed one mistake after another, explaining in detail his execution of Wenlock. 'Our only hope,' he murmured, 'is that the Angevin crosses the Severn, to be welcomed and protected by Jasper Tudor. If not . . .' His voice trailed off. 'If not,' he repeated, 'you Margaret and your boy are

the last remaining hope of Lancaster. Now listen.' Somerset stared
around the chantry chapel. 'You know, Margaret, that George of
Clarence, like Neville of Warwick, clashed bitterly with the
Woodvilles. Both nobles were furious at Edward's secret marriage
to Elizabeth Woodville, an insult which has rankled deeply.
Warwick and Clarence left the Yorkist camp in open rebellion.
However, the Queen Mother, Cecily, the Rose of Raby, successfully persuaded George and Edward to be reconciled.' He paused
at the cries of some wounded man further down the nave, a shriek
of agony at the pain as well as the despair which now darkened
the souls of all those facing imminent death. 'Soon,' he whispered,
'we will be past all sorrow.'

Margaret, despite her revulsion at Beaufort's arrogance, which
had brought him and thousands of those who trusted him to this
sorry pitch, leaned over and stroked Somerset's blood-streaked
wrist. He grasped her hand and gently squeezed her fingers.

'Anyway,' he released his grip, 'you know the rest. Warwick
and Anjou invaded, only to be brutally defeated. Clarence, as
usual, survived. As I warned you, be most wary of that most
sinister prince of blood. When Clarence was with us, I heard
strange rumours, stories and whispers. Some of these concerned
you and yours . . .'

'In what way?'

'Apparently Clarence boasted how he has a spy deep in your
household: I suspect this is most probable because Clarence is
committed to the total destruction of the Beauforts and all whom
we hold dear. However, Clarence nurses a diabolic pride, a real
hubris which could bring him down. Such a weakness would
give you the power to meddle in his affairs. Trust me, Margaret.
I confess I have been guilty of following my own pride, of not
listening to more subtle counselling. However, here on my death
watch, let me assure you: Edward of York's greatest weakness
is his own family, his queen and the Woodvilles, a pack truly
hated, cursed and reviled. Clarence will not change his nature.
He is as committed to their destruction as he is to yours. The
Woodvilles will supply all the necessities for the coming
conflagration.'

'And Gloucester?'

'Loyal to his brother: "loyalty is mine" is Richard's motto.

He will stand by Edward for as long as Edward lives. What might happen if Edward died?' Somerset pulled a face. 'To return to my argument, Clarence is the real weakness in the Yorkist defences, his soul burns with ambition. He sees himself as the rightful Lord of England. When he was allied to Warwick and the House of Lancaster, he actually proclaimed himself King. He will now return to such idle boasting like a whore to her trade.' Somerset wiped the sweat from his face. 'And so we come to the Secret Chancery. Clarence's cabal of clerks, three in number, Rhinelanders in origin, former friars. Clarence depends on these for providing grist for his mischief.'

'Which is?'

'We do not know, except the clerks are called "the Three Kings", after their city of origin, Cologne where, according to tradition, the Three Kings mentioned in the Gospel lie buried. They also take the saints' names: Caspar, Melchior and Balthasar. You may well ask, Margaret, why should I, a duke, a prominent leader of the Lancastrian cause, be interested in Clarence's Three Kings . . .?' Beaufort rose and crossed to the wall recess where the cruets were placed during Mass. Beaufort picked up an earthenware jug and drank greedily before offering it to Margaret who shook her head. 'A gift from the abbot,' Beaufort whispered, coming back to his chair. He sat down cradling the jug. 'From the little we have learnt,' he continued, 'The Three Kings have drawn up a book, a manuscript, a secret document called "Titulus Regius".'

'The Title of the King,' Margaret murmured.

Beaufort stared at his young kinswoman, the last true surviving Beaufort. He wondered if she would be safe, surrounded as she was by the different wolf packs which prowled the Yorkist court. Despite the poor light, Beaufort glimpsed a shift in Margaret's clever eyes as she stared back. A knowing look, as if Margaret Beaufort had studied the Duke of Somerset and knew his true worth. A small nun-like woman, Beaufort reflected, and again he wondered how she would cope with the victorious, vicious Clarence, who would watch her and her household with his spies and paid assassins.

'The "Titulus Regius".' Margaret demanded: 'What is it?' She paused as a door was flung open further down the nave. Margaret sprang to her feet and hurried out of the chantry chapel. She feared armed Yorkists might have broken in but it was only Abbot Strensham. Apparently one of the wounded Lancastrians, realising he was in danger of death, had pleaded with one of his companions who, in turn, had begged a sympathetic Yorkist guard to fetch a priest so the dying man could be shriven. Margaret watched the shifting shapes of Abbot Strensham and his prior, who followed the lead of the bobbing light from the sacristan's lantern-horn down the nave. She froze at another fierce cry which was answered by raucous singing from the Yorkist soldiers outside. Margaret returned to the chantry chapel where Somerset was drinking from the wine jug.

'Remember this,' he continued as Margaret sat down, 'our three Yorkist warlords have a strange family history, or so rumour has it: their mother, Cecily Neville, daughter of the Earl of Westmoreland, was apparently an outstanding beauty, so much so she was called the Rose of Raby. She also has a hideous temper. Rumour has it that Clarence, using the Three Kings as searchers and scribes, is investigating his own family hunting for this and that.'

'Why?'

'God knows, but Clarence is continuing such searches. I am not too sure what he wants to prove but, to get his own way, Clarence would go down to Hell and challenge the Lord Satan. Believe me, kinswoman,' Somerset pulled his chair closer, 'if you can, strike back, meddle in his affairs. Clarence is undoubtedly doing the same to you and yours but he's even a greater threat to the House of York. Ah well,' Somerset gestured with his head, 'Abbot Strensham is still tending to that poor comrade. He might as well shrive me for by this time tomorrow; I will be brought to judgement before God's tribunal . . .'

Margaret rose, she kissed her kinsman and crept out of the chantry, silent as a shadow back up the sanctuary steps and into the sacristy where Bray was waiting. He explained how the abbot, prior and sacristan were still in the church so he would escort her back to the guesthouse. They left the abbey precincts and made their way along paved passageways, tunnels of stone lit by the occasional lantern. They crossed the cobbled courtyard stretching in front of the guesthouse, clearly lit by sconce torches fixed to the walls. Margaret heard a sound from the sloping, tiled roof of their lodgings. She glanced up and stared in amazement at the blaze of fire which came hurtling through the darkness towards her. She pushed Bray to the left even as she darted the other way. The flaming bag of oil crashed onto the cobbles, followed by another and then a third; all three bursting into spouts of flame and fiery oil. Bray raised the alarm screaming, 'Harrow! Harrow!' The door to the guesthouse was flung open and Owain Mortimer, principal squire to the Countess Margaret, darted out, followed by his twin sister Oswina. Margaret, gasping for breath, pointed up at the sloping roof. Once her trembling had subsided, she beckoned at her companions to follow her down the narrow gulley which ran along the side of the guesthouse. They turned into the backyard, a place where the refuse was piled; a stinking, slimy midden heap, home for a horde of rats which squealed and scurried away at their approach. Margaret and Bray stopped by the narrow siege ladder leaning against the back wall of the two-storey guesthouse. Bray immediately climbed this to examine the broad ledge against which the rest of the roof rested. He glanced swiftly around and clambered down.

'So easy,' he gestured at the roof, 'especially for a trained assassin. He took those satchels of oil, each primed with a slow-burning fuse. He then crouched on the ledge before climbing up the tiles. Easy enough; he could rest against them and wait. He knew we would have to return here. He hears our approach, sees us clear in the light of our sconce torches. He takes his tinder, the first is lit and . . .'

'The back of this guesthouse is blind.' Owain Mortimer pointed up the wall. 'All the chambers are to the front. No one inside would even hear or see anything amiss. No one,' he repeated wearily in his sing-song voice, 'no one at all.'

'We were abed,' his twin declared, 'though we were not sleeping, I was worried about you mistress.'

Margaret held up a hand as she stared at the ladder. 'Let us go inside,' she declared. 'It's best to be there.'

They returned to the stark parlour close to the guesthouse entrance. Oswina busied herself lighting candles whilst Owain poured a jug of breakfast ale into four stoups on a wooden tray.

'Is Christopher back, has he returned?' Margaret asked, sipping her drink.

'No he's not here,' Owain replied, 'and nor should we, so close to your enemy; the rest of the household agree, they have gone to their chambers and locked themselves in. God knows mistress, what will happen on the morrow. The Yorkists will drink deeply tonight. They will all be in a bloodlust and looking for vengeance. Have you decided, Mistress – what we should do next?'

'Not yet,' Bray retorted.

'Then when?' Oswina replied.

Margaret, still holding the tankard, sat back in her chair. 'The assassin,' she spoke, her voice sounding harsher than she had intended, 'the evil soul who tried to burn me alive, who could it be? Why now? Why now? Though I suspect,' she put down the tankard, 'that those fiery missiles were the work of York, Clarence in particular.'

'They wish to root out the Beaufort tree.' Bray lapsed into his usual homily, a whispered tirade against the House of York. Margaret sat back in the cushioned chair and let her mind drift. She had to curb the fear curdling within her. She closed her eyes and prayed for her husband Humphrey Stafford, now lying grievously wounded after Barnet. The news she had received from her manor at Woking was most disturbing. Humphrey, never the strongest of men, suffered from a life-long skin corruption, St Anthony's fire, which some leeches likened to leprosy, so much so that four years ago, she and Humphrey had joined the confraternity of Burton Lazars. Margaret had bought statues, triptychs and other paintings celebrating St Anthony's life to decorate the solar of her manor house, praying constantly beneath them, yet these supplications had not worked any miracle. Now the household leeches reported how the contagion had been grievously affected by the wounds Sir Humphrey had received: a knife cut to the thigh and a sword blow which had glanced off his shoulder. Margaret murmured another prayer and opened her eyes. She really should return to Woking but not until the present business, vital to her, was completed in London.

Margaret half listened to Bray and Mortimer's heated whispering and her mind went back to her manor house, wondering what was happening there. She loved her Woking estates; she had inherited them as part of a legacy from her grandmother, the

redoubtable Lady Holland, along with a rich collection of manuscripts and delicately inscribed psalters and other devotional
literature. Margaret tried to recall the manor in an attempt to
soothe her humours: how her residence was screened by copses
of ancient oak, beech and copper set in lush, fertile parkland.
The house itself was twice-moated; the outer one contained the
poultry runs, livestock sheds, warren, granges and a small deer
park. The inner moat, crossed by a drawbridge leading through
a fortified gateway, contained the manor itself, with its great hall,
large pantry and spacious buttery. Then there was a chapel,
chancery office and, above all, a range of private chambers overlooking the herb and flower gardens, a well-stocked stew pond
and lush orchards.

Margaret felt her eyes grow heavy and she sank into a half-
waking sleep; as she did so, the different visions which always
swept in, returned clear and precise. Margaret felt as if she was
staring at a finely etched painting or the brilliant illumination
in some psalter. She sat and watched herself struggling through
snow which had drifted heavily. There were trees, bushes and
rocky outcrops, and she was sure that she was in Pembrokeshire.
She was hastening towards a great iron wall which soared up
into the wine-coloured sky. The wall was at least sixty yards
high, entered through a fortified gateway guarded by snarling,
black-haired war dogs. Margaret was not frightened of these; she
was more anxious about what was waiting for her beyond the
wall. She turned and glanced piteously at the corpses which
sprawled against the hard-packed snow. She recognised that of
her father, stretched out as they had found him in his chancery
chamber; the goblet of wine he'd been drinking had rolled close
to her dead father's head, turning his blond hair blood-red, as if
he had been struck a grievous blow. She also recognised the other
corpses, her first true husband, the beloved Edmund Tudor. He
was lying all crouched as he had on his deathbed, consumed by
a raging fever. Other corpses littered the snow, men and women
of her family and household. She wanted to go back to them but
the snow dragged at her, its whiteness hurting her eyes. She was
sure she could hear her son crying from behind the soaring iron
wall whilst the harrowing baying of wolves somewhere around
her seemed to be drawing closer . . .

'Mistress, mistress?' Margaret opened her eyes. Bray was staring beseechingly down at her. 'Mistress, you were chattering. Father Prior is here. He is very concerned.' Margaret blinked, rubbed her face and sat up in the high-backed chair and smiled at Prior Anselm, who took the stool placed in front of her, his bony, angular face wreathed in concern.

'My Lady,' he began, 'the good brothers have had their horarium severely disturbed; the abbey is full of armed men, more blood stains our flagstones than dust. Violence stalks the cloisters, our choir stalls, even the great sanctuary itself. Now we hear reports of fiery missiles being thrown down into the courtyard outside – that's true, isn't it? I have inspected the cobbles; they reek of burning oil whilst scraps of scorched leather scatter like leaves. One of our brothers glimpsed this as he hurried to fill waterskins from the well. What is this, why now?' The prior joined his hands in prayer. 'God knows what further mischief will raise its sinister head like some deadly vicious serpent – because that is what Satan is, he and his many legions.'

'Father Prior?' Margaret grasped the old monk's right hand, raised it to her lips and kissed his thick, copper ring of office. The prior blushed.

'I am sorry,' he muttered. 'But the truth is we are all terrified. We are not men of war.'

Margaret, throwing a warning glance at Bray, Owain and Oswina, quickly described what had happened, offering the conclusion that the assailant was probably some drunkard eager to do hurt to a Beaufort or a Lancastrian fugitive furious that a Beaufort should be sheltering amongst Yorkist warlords.

'You see, Father Prior,' Margaret gently touched the back of his hand, 'I am living proof that you cannot serve two masters.'

The prior laughed and clambered to his feet. He walked to the door then paused and glanced at Margaret's three companions. 'I recognise you, Master Bray, as the Lady Margaret's steward, but these young persons? They look alike. They must be brother and sister?' The prior cocked his head sideways like some curious sparrow. 'Yes, night-black hair, smooth, sallow faces, large eyes and full-lipped mouths. You must be Welsh, yes? We have some of those from the southern tribes here in the abbey.'

'Owain and Oswina Mortimer,' Margaret replied, gesturing

at the twins to grasp the prior's proffered hand. They did so hurriedly, then stepped back as if shy at the attention now being shown them. 'They are kinsmen of the noble Mortimer family, orphans raised by my brother-in-law, Lord Jasper Tudor.'

'Ah,' the prior sighed, 'a man the Yorkists would love to seize. And he is where?'

'Pembroke Castle,' Margaret retorted, 'where he will stay until he can take ship to France.' Margaret shrugged. 'Jasper entrusted Owain and Oswina to me. They, along with Reginald Bray and Christopher Urswicke, are my privileged chamber people.'

'Urswicke, ah yes. We have heard about him. A brother saw him leave for the town where more excitement is brewing. The King has taken over Merchant Strafford's house. A party of horsemen have been despatched on urgent royal business. I understand Urswicke was one of them. Now my Lady, take care. I understand my Lord of Clarence has insisted that he visits you to present his compliments.' The prior sketched a blessing in the air and then left.

Margaret would have loved to retire. She felt sweat soaked, heavy limbed, her mind fraught with anxiety which gnawed at her peace of mind, the prospect of meeting Clarence only sharpening this. She tried to compose herself, putting on a brave face while she and her chamber people hastily prepared the parlour. Clarence arrived and Margaret wondered at the sound of heavy cartwheels across the cobbles, the clatter of sharpened hooves and the deep neigh of dray horses. Owain volunteered to go and see. Margaret shook her head saying that he should stay at table and eat the light repast the refectorian had left in the small adjoining buttery.

Clarence arrived, he almost kicked the door open, mincing in like some court lady. He'd wrapped a bottle-green cloak around him which caught on the jingling spurs of his war boots. Clarence, grasping a wine goblet in one hand, simply tore the cloak free. He snapped his fingers and pointed at a stool. One of the three shadowy figures who accompanied him hastily brought this across. Clarence sat down with a heavy sigh, his sweaty face creased into a false smile, lips glistening with wine, eyes bright with malice. He stroked his finely clipped moustache and beard, dragging at the bits of dry wine caught there.

'My Lord,' Margaret turned in her chair to face him squarely.

'My Lady.' Clarence bowed mockingly, raised his goblet in toast and drank deeply. 'Oh, by the way,' he pointed at the shadowy figures behind him, 'these are my chancery clerks who manage my Secret Seal.'

Margaret glanced up at them and tried to hide her fear at the three sinister figures garbed in hoods and blue-black robes. She recognised the colour and cut as belonging to some minor order of friars but she could not recall their name. These three were certainly not men of prayer. They stood, menacingly silent, hands up the voluminous sleeves of their robes which, Margaret suspected, concealed a dagger, stiletto, or some other such weapon. One of these leaned down to whisper in Clarence's ear and, as he did so, Margaret, with her keen sense of smell, caught the odour of oil and smoke and she wondered if one – or all – of these macabre figures had been responsible for the recent attack on her. Margaret shifted her gaze from Clarence and stared hard at his sinister companions, refusing to be cowed or frightened by them. She found it difficult to distinguish individual features but she was aware of heavy-lidded eyes and noses as sharp as quill pens. All three were thin-lipped which, with their bulging foreheads and tight-lipped grimace, gave them an odd fish-like appearance. Wolfsheads, Margaret concluded: whatever their garb or whatever Clarence said about their status, these were predators ready to strike.

'Three brothers,' Clarence whispered, as if revelling in their company. 'Excellent clerks!'

'I have heard of them.' Bray spoke up. 'Former friars, the Three Kings from Cologne.'

'Others call them that.' Clarence lifted his goblet. 'To me they are just the most faithful of retainers who accompany me here, there and everywhere. They do my bidding like the loyal lurchers they are. Now,' Clarence smacked his lips, 'I have brought you something, little Meg.'

'That is not my name. I am, sir, the Lady Margaret Beaufort, Countess of Richmond.'

'Which makes you a kinswoman to the Beaufort traitor and other vile miscreants lurking in the abbey church.' Clarence, face seething with hate, jabbed a finger. 'Where is your brother-in-law, the traitor Jasper Tudor and your dearly beloved son Henry? Little Henry?' Clarence's voice became a squeal of mockery. Bray's hands went beneath the table, close to the long, stabbing dagger in his belt. Margaret glanced up. One of the Three Kings had brought his hand from the sleeve of his gown. Margaret glimpsed the glitter of the long, thin blade.

'My brother-in-law,' Margaret retorted quickly, 'resides in Pembroke. So does my beloved son.'

'Do they now?' Clarence taunted.

'My Lord.' Margaret fought to curb the almost overwhelming desire to claw at Clarence's false, fat, glistening face. 'My Lord,' she repeated, 'I am tired and I need to retire.' She made to move 'I should do so now.'

'Oh no, no, no.' Clarence fluttered his fingers in her face. 'I must show you something before you sleep. You must say goodbye before they leave.'

'Who?'

'Come, come! You must see this.' Clarence rose to his feet and swept out of the guesthouse, Margaret felt that she had no choice but to follow. She stopped however, just before the threshold, and stared at the great war cart which stood in the centre of the small bailey. On each corner of the cart a cresset torch flared against the cold night breeze, the flames illuminating the horror displayed there. The sides of the cart were nothing more than sharp poles lashed together. Their sharp, spear-like tips provided gaps for archers inside to loose, whilst the poles would serve as a sturdy defence. Now these sharpened posts had been used to display, on all three sides of the cart, a row of severed heads thrust on the tips like so many ripe apples. The breeze shifted, rippling the hair of the decapitated heads, and Margaret caught the salty tang of dried human blood.

She walked slowly forward, fascinated by the abomination. She recognised some of the dirty, gore-stained faces, their hair pulled back and tied in a topknot so each face could be clearly seen. Margaret immediately glimpsed the once handsome face of John Beaufort, Edmund's younger brother, now contorted by a savage, bloody death. Clarence grasped Margaret by the elbow, a tight clasp as he moved her around the cart so she could clearly see the severed heads of Lancastrians killed in battle, their corpses decapitated in preparation for being tarred and poled above the gateways of different cities. As she passed the tail of the cart, she glimpsed the blood-drenched sacks of severed limbs, which would also be displayed and proclaimed to the sound of horn, trumpet and bagpipe. Margaret could take no more. She turned, gagged and retched, going down on her knees. Clarence crouched beside her. Bray protested and tried to come between them. Clarence drew his dagger.

'Enough George, enough!' Clarence clambered to his feet as Richard of Gloucester strolled out of the darkness. 'George, the King needs you. My Lady?' Gloucester pointed to Margaret resting on Bray's arm. 'I bid you goodnight and good rest.' He came closer, in the juddering light. Gloucester's harsh face seemed softer and Margaret glimpsed genuine pity in those ever-shifting eyes. 'George,' Richard lifted a gauntleted hand, holding Margaret's gaze as he spoke to his brother, 'You have no further business with this lady, the hour draws on. Judgement awaits, come.'

Clarence backed away from Margaret, fluttering his fingers in mock farewell before spinning on his heel and following his brother into the darkness, his three sinister guards close behind. Margaret watched them go as she tightly gripped Bray's arm.

'Master Reginald,' she hissed, 'I swear by the light I will kill that demon incarnate and all his ilk. How dare he threaten my beloved son?' She turned and Bray, who knew his mistress's secret soul, was frightened by the look of intense fury which had transformed her usually placid face.

'Master Bray,' she whispered hoarsely, 'this is truly *à l'Outrance, usque ad mortem* – to the death, whatever form that death takes.'

# PART TWO

'Queen Margaret was taken and securely held.'
*Crowland Chronicle*

U rswicke reined in with the rest of the Yorkist war band before the gate of Little Malvern Priory. He stared around at his companions. In the main they were Clarence's henchmen, professional killers; a few royal knight bannerets had also joined the cohort led by Sir Richard Crofts, a local magnate who knew the twisting, sunken lanes, narrow trackways and coffin paths of Gloucester as he did the veins on the back of his hands. For a while the cohort just sat, horses snorting, shaking the sweat out after such a vigorous ride, sharpened hooves scraping the ground.

'They must know we are here,' Mauclerc called out over his shoulder. He dismounted, drew his sword and pounded on the gate. '*Les Roiaux!*' he shouted, 'we are King's men, open in his name. Open, I say, or we'll force the gate.'

Lights appeared on the crenellated wall above them, moving circles of dancing torchlight. One of Mauclerc's riders primed his crossbow and loosed a bolt. Others did the same to the scrape of swords leaving their scabbards. The crossbow bolts were aimed at the pools of light which swiftly disappeared. Urswicke heard a horn bray followed by the rattle of chains and the scraping of bolts. The great gate was thrown open and Urswicke joined the charge into the entrance bailey which stretched up to the main priory buildings. Mauclerc had despatched members of his war band to search the priory's two postern gates: these must have met some resistance as the clatter and clash of arms echoed from the other side of the priory. They all dismounted. A monk carrying a cross in one hand and a lantern in the other hurried through the darkness and sank to his knees. Mauclerc and Crofts showed him no mercy. Clarence's henchmen seized the monk's head between gauntleted hands and squeezed hard, shouting questions at him. The monk, gasping with pain, dropped the lantern and pointed back to a two-storey, grey-ragstone building with lights glimmering between the shutters. Again Mauclerc shouted questions then pushed the monk away. The man stumbled to his feet and pointed at the shutters of what Urswicke believed was the guesthouse; these were flung open followed immediately by the sharp whirr of crossbow bolts cutting the air. Most of these fell short but the monk seemed almost to stumble onto one, taking the barb deep in his chest.

Mauclerc's party, weapons drawn, charged towards the building, racing across the cobbles so as to distract the aim of the bowmen sheltering in the guesthouse. More bolts whistled sharply, most missed their target. Urswicke, panting and gasping, felt one whip past his face. At last they reached the door and the bowmen above found it difficult to loose, let alone find a target. A bench was found and used as a battering ram to smash the ancient door off its leather hinges, then they were inside. Men-at-arms wearing the blue and white livery of Lancaster confronted them, thronging in the hallway, along the gallery, as well as on the stairs leading up to the solar. A savage hand-to-hand struggle ensued, sword grinding bone, dagger piercing flesh, mallet, war axe and morning star crushing heads and faces. Flesh was ripped. Blood gushed to the devilish cacophony of shouts, screams and heart-rending yells. No quarter was asked. No mercy shown, until the remaining defenders threw down their weapons and fell to their knees, hands raised in surrender. Mauclerc and Croft screamed at their own men to respect this. Urswicke, who had managed to avoid any real danger by keeping to the rear of the press, watched the surviving Lancastrians being disarmed and pushed out into the darkness. Mauclerc ordered most of his cohort to stay whilst he, Urswicke and a select few climbed the stairs to the solar. Mauclerc kicked open the door and went inside. He stood, sword drawn, staring at the group huddled before the hearth.

Urswicke immediately recognised Queen Margaret of Anjou, the Angevin, resplendent in blue and gold, surrounded by her principal ladies whom Urswicke knew by sight: Anne Neville, the Countess of Devon, Katherine Vaux, and other leading lights of the Angevin's court. Urswicke felt a pang of pity as he wondered if all these ladies knew they were now widows, their husbands being cut down at Tewkesbury. Beside the Queen stood her son Prince Edward, resplendent in silver Milanese armour, his ornate plumed helmet on the floor beside him, his warbelt lying across his mother's lap. He walked towards Mauclerc with all the arrogance of a peacock, his mouth twisted in contemptuous anger.

'What business!' He paused before Mauclerc. 'Sir, what business have you here?'

Mauclerc lurched forward and struck the prince full in the face. He then hit him again and again, ignoring the screams and cries of the Queen. The prince tried to resist but the knights who had accompanied Mauclerc seized the young man and also pummelled him with blows and kicks.

'Strip him!' Mauclerc yelled. 'Take his foolish finery as plunder.'

The knights did so, tearing off the prince's breastplate, greaves and the chainmail jerkin beneath, until the prince was reduced to standing in his linen shirt and leggings. A pathetic young man, now aware that he truly was in the hands of his enemies. Queen Margaret rose and hurried towards her son, hands out, pleading and begging. Mauclerc struck her repeatedly in the face, pushing her back, shouting at his men to strip her to her shift. He then ordered his retainers to bind the hands of both mother and son. The royal couple were hustled like Newgate felons out of the solar, down the stairs and out into the yard where a cart was waiting. Both royal prisoners were pushed into this; an archer lashed their hands and feet to the slats.

Mauclerc went back into the priory to inform the fallen Queen's ladies that they must fend for themselves, whilst their men-at-arms who survived the furious mêlée were to be stripped of all their weapons and possessions then be released. Nor did the monks escape unscathed. Mauclerc yelled how they had sheltered sworn traitors so they should look after the wounded and bury the dead. Urswicke used the confusion, the to-ing and fro-ing, to climb into the cart to sit beside Prince Edward who slouched, eyes half closed, mouth dribbling. The young prince was deep in shock like his mother. Urswicke stared piteously at them. Once these were the Golden Ones, the Mighty of the Land: they had wielded great power with legions at their beck and call. Now it was all finished. The old King Henry VI, Margaret's saintly husband, was locked in the Tower. The Yorkist warlords had put him on a sorry-looking nag and paraded him through London, showing the people that he may be holy but he was no warrior king. Henry's armies were shattered: his captains of war either killed or soon to be. The few who had escaped, such as De Vere of Oxford, were to be put to the horn and exiled for life.

The fallen Queen was muttering to herself. Now and again she would sit up, stretch across and try to stroke her son's head. Again she seemed unaware of what was really happening. For a while she sat, eyes blinking, lips moving soundlessly. She scratched her face, clawing back her greying-gold hair and peered at Urswicke.

'I know you, sir.' The Angevin's voice was surprisingly harsh. 'You're clerk to Lady Margaret Beaufort.' She laughed so abruptly behind her raised bound hand, Urswicke wondered if her wits were wandering. 'You are,' she continued, 'aren't you, little Margaret's clerk? Her son Henry is the last of us. Oh, they will hunt him down, they will pursue him like dogs would a deer through wood and thicket till they capture and kill him as they have my beloved . . .'

Prince Edward lifted his head and turned to Urswicke. 'What do you advise, sir? What do you say that I do?'

Urswicke hid his surprise at being asked about what he intended to offer. 'Defiance,' Urswicke retorted. 'Defiance! You came back to this kingdom to claim what was yours by birthright and lawful descent. You are the King's heir and they are traitors, as was their father Duke Richard, executed after Wakefield fight. So play the man,' Urswicke urged in a whisper. 'Do not ask for mercy for, I assure you, none will be shown.'

'I am a French princess,' Margaret slurred. She now sat crookedly, sifting her hair through her fingers. 'I will demand to be treated as such.' She straightened up abruptly, hands on her lap, adopting a regal pose, as if she was attending a crown-wearing ceremony at Westminster. She turned and, eyes full of hate, glared at Urswicke. 'And who are you, varlet?' She mocked. 'You are Urswicke? Your father is a Recorder of London, a fervent adherent of Edward of York. What are you doing here?' She moved her tied hands, stretching her wrists as if to snap the rough twine binding them.

'You'd best leave,' the prince whispered hoarsely. 'My mother must be left alone. Soon she will begin her rants and there will be little reasoning with her or peace for ourselves.' He half smiled at Urswicke, his handsome face now bruised and tearstained, his light-blue eyes full of fear. 'This will end in blood,' he whispered, 'certainly for me. You'd best leave.'

They reached Tewkesbury just as the greyness began to fade and the sky was scarred by fiery streaks. War had engulfed that small market town, and all the demons which trailed in its wake were making their presence felt. Huge yawning burial pits were being hurriedly dug outside the town. The dead, their dirty ghost-like flesh displaying all the gruesome wounds of battle, were piled on the ground like slabs of pork on a fleshier's stall. Some of the womenfolk of the slaughtered men desperately searched amongst the fallen for the corpse of a beloved, their grief and mourning made all the more bitter by the raucous abuse and lewd invitations from the Yorkist men-at-arms preparing the pits. Many of the Lancastrian camp followers had already been seized and ravished. As Urswicke rode by an alleyway he glimpsed one woman on her knees before a group of soldiers, their hose all unlaced and pulled down around their ankles. Plunder was rife and the royal marshals were eager to retrieve all the precious objects seized from the Lancastrian camp. The air was thick with smoke from the many campfires and the makeshift pyres where the corpses of the horses killed in the battle had been doused in cheap oil and placed on stacks of wood. These had been fired, the flames shooting up before the foulsome, black smoke billowed in filthy clouds, spreading a horrid stench across the town.

Couriers and messengers galloped along the narrow streets, bringing news of what was happening both north of the Trent and, more importantly, London. From there the news was grim. The capital was now being threatened by a fresh Lancastrian army and a flotilla of war cogs under Thomas Neville, the Bastard of Fauconberg. Urswicke overheard all of this when a chamberlain of the royal household joined their cavalcade. He also insisted that the two royal prisoners wear thick cloaks and cowls pulled over their heads so they would not be recognised. Once they reached the royal quarters, the mansion house of Merchant Stratford, the prisoners were dragged from the cart and pushed down the cellar steps to be imprisoned in a store chamber. The doors to the great hall were closed and guarded by a host of royal knights, one of whom informed Urswicke that the King, together with his brothers, Lord Hastings, Norfolk and other Yorkist leaders, were deep in discussion.

Urswicke tried to excuse himself, pleading that he should return to the abbey, but Mauclerc, jubilant at what he described as 'the best night's work ever', insisted on Urswicke accompanying him back out into the streets and across the square to The Golden Lion, a spacious, black-and-white timber tavern. The market had now been cleared of its stalls and a soaring execution platform was being constructed. The royal carpenters were feverishly working to put the finishing touches to this macabre scaffold. The rage of York was apparent. Even though this execution ground was not fully completed, it had already been used to carry out summary punishment. Lancastrian captains had been hustled up and killed just before dawn, their blood-drenched cadavers quartered, salted and tarred before being tossed into large vats beside the scaffold, their heads thrust into barrels to be pickled. Other prisoners had been hanged on the railing around the gibbet: nooses put around their necks before they were summarily pushed over to jerk and dance until they hung, swaying slightly in the breeze, wafting a host of disgusting smells around the market place. Urswicke felt as if he was in a nightmare. Hideous death pressed all around him, yet some of the carpenters were whistling and singing as they went about their business, totally oblivious to their gruesome surroundings. Tewkesbury was now possessed by the full terror of war which assailed, sight, sound and smell. Urswicke abruptly felt nervous, a spasm of fear which made him wonder if the path he was following was the correct one, a twisting, tortuous, snake-like trackway. Would this, he wondered, end in disaster, or the realisation of his mistress's dream?

'We are here!'

Urswicke broke free from his reverie. They had entered the sweet-smelling taproom, a spacious chamber; fresh green summer rushes strewn with herbs covered the floor, these exuded a spring-like fragrance to mingle with the delicious tang from the hams hanging in white nets from the rafters. The meat and other foods would dangle there until they were cured by the

smoke and steam billowing out of the great kitchen, as well as
the constant fragrances from the huge spit being slowly turned
in the majestic hearth.

Mauclerc had a word with minehost who whispered back and
pointed across to the stairs. Mauclerc and Urswicke went up
these into a well-furnished chamber where three individuals were
waiting. Urswicke suspected these were the Three Kings, the
clerks of Clarence's Secret Chancery. They lounged in chairs or
on the broad settle which served as a window seat. They rose as
Mauclerc and Urswicke entered. One of them, Melchior as he
introduced himself, hurriedly swept documents and manuscripts
from the chamber's writing table, pushing these into a chancery
coffer reinforced with steel bands and protected by three locks.
The other two pulled back their hoods. One of them gestured at
a stool close to the table before offering Urswicke some wine
and cheese from the food platter on a side dresser. Urswicke
asked for a little wine and a piece of cheese wrapped in a linen
cloth. These were handed over as introductions were made. Once
these were finished, Mauclerc talked to the Three Kings in what
Urswicke suspected was German, a spate of harsh, guttural words.
All Three Kings listened carefully, nodding and saying '*Ja! Ja!*'
in agreement. Occasionally they would glance at Urswicke and
smile thinly. He acknowledged their greeting but pretended to
be more interested in his food and drink than anything else.
Urswicke felt he had the measure of Mauclerc, a mailed clerk,
a man of war, a ruthless henchman. The Three Kings, however,
despite their pale, sharp, bony faces, seemed pleasant enough.
They were apparently skilled in tongues by their own admission,
whilst their ink-stained fingers and the spots of wax on their
robes showed they were chancery men. Once Mauclerc had
finished talking in German, all four gathered at the table.

'You must be curious?' Melchior demanded.

'Of course,' Urswicke ruefully admitted. 'You have a reputation.
A good one,' he added hastily. 'Skilled scriveners, shrewd clerks,
loyal henchmen. You are not from this kingdom, so how did you
enter my Lord Clarence's service? Three brothers, yes? Friars?'

'Former friars,' Melchior retorted. 'Members of a community,
the Barnabites, who had a small house outside Cologne. A lovely,
peaceful place until we heard our mother had been arrested and

burnt as a witch in Karlstadt, our home town, a true place of dark suspicion. Apparently she had been taken up to be interrogated, tortured, tried and executed. We received the news too late but we journeyed back to Karlstadt.' He paused, smiling slightly at Mauclerc and his two brothers.

'And?'

'As I said Meister Urswicke, we were too late. Our mother had been tried and convicted. Nobody spoke in her defence. She had been burnt alive in a market square. They didn't even give her the comfort of a swift garrotte by the executioner. Nor were pouches of gunpowder tied around her neck to hasten her end. The woman who bore us, our mother, was reduced to ashes which were then strewn on a dung heap. Nobody would talk to us. You would think we were lepers rather than friars. So what could we do? We were regarded as learned men, very skilled in tongues, proficient in the chancery, but our mother they treated as you would a piece of filth, something to be burnt, totally destroyed. So what could we do?'

'And what did you do?'

Melchior smiled a wolfish grin, his white teeth strong and pointed. 'Oh Meister Urswicke, we exacted punishment. We killed the *Ritter*, how would you say it? The lord of the town? We cut his throat in the dead of night along with those of his wife and children. We did the same to all who had sat in judgement on our mother; be they judges, jury or prosecutor. Finally we seized the executioner, a stupid burly butcher whom we drowned in his own cesspit. We then set fire to the church and city hall and fled as fast as we could to the sanctuary church of Dordrecht in Hainault. You must know it, Meister Urswicke, a busy port where, by chance, my Lord Clarence was resting during one of his many . . .'

'One of his many journeys abroad.' Mauclerc took up the story. 'My master became deeply intrigued by the story of these three brothers, warrior clerks, very skilled with the pen and the knife. He visited them in sanctuary and they talked. Indeed, my Lord spent a great deal of time in that church. A true friendship was formed, a bond made; unswerving loyalty promised. My Lord Clarence managed to settle matters. My comrades here would leave sanctuary and enter his household. They would take oaths of fealty, to serve their master body and soul, day and night, as long as they lived.'

Urswicke nodded and sipped from his goblet.

'You are shocked by what we did?' Melchior demanded.

'Oh no! Your mother was innocent?'

'Certainly not,' Melchior replied. 'She was as guilty as we are. Our mother was a self-proclaimed witch who raised three warlocks. We entered the Roman Church to gain advancement, acquire knowledge, learning, and so secure preferment. Our mother and our good selves are certainly not innocent of anything.' Urswicke nodded as Mauclerc and the others laughed, softly clapping their hands in appreciation at what had been said.

'Beyond the Rhine,' Balthasar, the youngest of the Three Kings, spoke up, 'the old religion still holds as fast as the oaks of the ancient Teuterborger forest; its roots go very deep. Much more profound than the influence of fat priests, noddle-pates and peasants who certainly don't practice what they preach.'

'Enough!' Mauclerc clapped his hands. 'Comrades, you now know the excellent service Master Urswicke performed on our behalf. The Anjou wolf and her whelp have been seized and they are for the dark. Master Christopher Urswicke is now one of us, a trusted henchman of my Lord Clarence, even though he will continue to dance attendance on the Beaufort brat. So . . .' Mauclerc rose, crossed to the door, opened it and bellowed for a servant. A short while later, minehost brought up platters of food; vegetables fried in duck fat, strips of pork covered in mustard, morsels of venison garnished with herbs and salmon from the Severn ponds. The jug of wine proved to be the best from Bordeaux. Urswicke joined his new comrades as they ate and drank until their hearts' content whilst outside echoed the ominous beat of both mallet and hammer as the execution platform was finished. Urswicke realised the meal was being used in order that he could be observed, questioned and judged, so he adopted the guise of a father confessor, listening carefully and nodding wisely.

The conversation flowed around what was to happen next and Urswicke learned more about the violent disturbances which had broken out in Kent. How some of the rebels were common robbers who, according to Balthasar, wished to dip their filthy hands into

rich men's coffers. Other rebels were farmers who had donned
their wives' smocks and wore cheesecloths on their heads to
demonstrate their resentment at the low prices Londoners were
paying for their dairy products. More ominous, however, were
the intrigues of the nobles and gentry of the surrounding shires:
these had raised the black banners of anarchy and the blood-red
standards of revolt. The rebel lords were now preparing to aid
and assist Thomas Neville, the Bastard of Fauconberg, as he
prepared to bring his fleet armed with cannon and culverin up
the Thames. Fauconberg was an ardent Lancastrian: Urswicke
listened carefully and wondered how he and his mistress could
exploit this growing chaos.

'The King has undoubtedly heard all about this,' Mauclerc
observed. 'He will be ruthless. He will crush all opposition . . .'

Urswicke drained his goblet and declared he was tired; he
added that he would rest for a while, accepting Mauclerc's offer
of using the settle as a bed. He swiftly fell asleep and was later
roughly woken by Mauclerc shaking his shoulder.

'You slept like a babe at the breast,' Mauclerc hissed, 'but our
master has summoned us, he wants us with him.'

Urswicke rose and left the chamber for the garderobe. He then
returned to splash cold water over his face and hands at the
wooden lavarium. The hour candle on its spigot in the corner
showed it to be five hours after midday. Urswicke dried himself,
making sure he was presentable. He could tell by the hurried
preparations of the Three Kings that they too had been sleeping
off the heavy effects of food and wine. They all left the tavern.
The market square had fallen strangely silent, like a mausoleum
reeking of dead things and pregnant with fresh horrors brewing.
The scaffold was draped in black and purple cloths, the entire
square being ringed by royal archers and men-at-arms.

Merchant Stratford's mansion was similarly guarded. Inside,
the great hall had been changed, its furniture swept aside. A
gleaming Arras tapestry displaying all the insignia of York and
the royal household covered the wall opposite the door; this
served as a dramatic backdrop for the canopied throne placed on
a makeshift dais. Edward now sat on this, flanked by his brothers
together with their leading henchmen, the Woodvilles, Hastings,
and others of their ilk. Banners and standards displaying the Boar

of Gloucester, the Bull of Clarence, the Bear of Warwick and the White Lion of Norfolk clustered close to the throne.

Edward sat in half-armour, his face cleanly shaven, his trimmed hair oiled, his tawny skin gleaming with perfumed nard. He wore his crown with a drawn sword across his lap, symbols that the King was prepared to deliver judgement. Urswicke joined the rest of the henchmen gathering to the left of the throne. He sensed that some bloody masque was about to unfold. A trumpet blared and the hall fell silent. A servant hurriedly placed a stool before the throne. A side door opened and Queen Margaret of Anjou and her son, still garbed in dirty, dishevelled linen shifts, were pushed into the chamber. The former Queen was ordered to sit on a stool whilst Edward beckoned the young prince forward.

'Why?' Richard of Gloucester rose to his feet. 'Why did you invade our realm and cause great hurt to the King's peace?'

'To assert my claim and that of my saintly father,' the prince retorted, stepping forward as if he wanted to shake off all traces of captivity. 'My father,' the prince yelled, following Urswicke's whispered advice, 'is the true King of England. Your father was a usurper, a mere baron of York, a rebel, justly executed after the battle of Wakefield, him and his whelp Edmund—'

He got no further. Edward the King sprang from his throne and struck the prince full on the mouth with a savage blow from his gauntleted hand. The prince staggered back, blood pouring from his split lips and bruised mouth. Margaret of Anjou struggled to her feet but the Yorkist lords closed in, knocking her half-conscious to the floor. Daggers were drawn. The prince, realising the peril he was now in, screamed at Clarence for mercy, but that lord struck with his dagger time and again at the prince's exposed chest and neck. Others, including Gloucester, joined in the blood-splattering hail of knife thrusts and dagger blows. The long blades rose and fell, glittering in the light. The prince, dying from a host of wounds, collapsed to the floor, his blood sparkling around him. Even then the Yorkist lords, led by Clarence, continued to stab, kick and punch until the King's trumpeters brayed for stillness and the heralds shouted for peace. The blood-drenched lords, chests heaving, mouths gasping for air, stepped back. The victim was no longer a man, just a sodding heap of gore; his mother, soaked in her son's blood, tried to crawl towards

him, moaning piteously, her hand going out to caress her dead
boy's face. Edward the King shouted something, waving his hand
as if he wanted to be free of the gruesome mess on the floor
before him.

'Clear the hall.' Howard of Norfolk, Earl Marshal of England,
stood on the edge of the dais, hands raised. 'Clear the hall,' he
repeated. 'His Grace wishes to be alone.'

Once outside the mansion, Urswicke leaned against the wall,
drawing deep breaths as he swiftly crossed himself.

'You are well?'

'I am well.' Urswicke patted Mauclerc's gloved hand resting
on his arm. 'I am well but I need to rest . . .' And, not waiting
for a response, Urswicke, his flushed face all sweat-soaked,
walked across the square, averting his eyes from the cadavers,
the corpses of those hanged earlier in the day, dangling on ropes
like flitches of ham in a butcher's shed.

Urswicke forced himself to think on other matters, to recall
sweet memories, to clear his mind and calm his heart. He drifted
back in time to his beloved studies in the halls of Oxford; evening
walks through the Christchurch meadows and, above all, sitting
with his mother in their high-walled garden of his father's mansion
just off Cheapside in the heart of the city. Urswicke's mother
called this 'her paradise, her garden of Eden'. It certainly was.
Urswicke's father, if he did anything well, furnished his wife and
son with the finer things of life. The garden was a true pleasance,
well stocked in length and breadth, like the great meadow of the
abbey. A sea of greenery, flowers and herbs pleased the eye and
turned the air constantly sweet. A most delightful place to wander
with its small fruit orchards, flower beds, herb plots, rose-
garlanded arbours, comfortable turf seats, stew ponds and carp
tanks with small fountains carved elegantly out of stone.

The garden was a retreat where he could escape the sly
lechery of his father and the constant pain such flirtation caused
Christopher's mother. When the weather was fine they would
go out and she would make Christopher sit and read to her. She
had a special love for the tales of Arthur and the verses of
Petrarch, which had reached England and were being avidly
translated and transcribed, along with Boccaccio's *Decameron*
and the 'Devotia Moderna' – a radical new approach to religion

coming out to the Low Countries in a number of thought-provoking treatises.

Once he had left Oxford, Urswicke had hurried home, hiring himself out as a clerk to different households. He had been greatly helped by the Countess Margaret, who was a firm, hand-fast friend to his mother. Margaret often visited the Urswickes, sometimes in the company of his mother's brother Andrew Knyvett, who served as physician to the countess's household. More often than not, Margaret's visits were by herself and, when Christopher's mother fell ill of some evil humour of the womb, the visits became more frequent. The countess even held his mother as she died quietly and peacefully in her chamber. Shortly afterwards, the countess asked to see Christopher by himself. She informed him that his mother, just before she died, had begged her to take Christopher into her household. Urswicke would never forget that meeting, standing at the foot of the four-poster bed, its curtains pulled back, the casement window thrown open to help his dead mother's soul on her journey into the light. Countess Margaret had grasped his hands and drew him close.

'Christopher,' she declared – her eyes had that fierce stare which always appeared over something deeply passionate to her – 'I loved your mother dearly and I love you as much. You are now flesh of my flesh, the very marrow of my bone and part of my heart's blood. From now on I will be your countess but I shall also be your mother, your sister, your comrade. I will stand next to you in the great shield wall of life, shoulder to shoulder, ready to confront the monsters who crawl out of the darkness and, believe me, they will . . .'

'Master Urswicke?'

He stopped, startled out of his reverie, and realised he'd entered the abbey precincts which lay silent all around him: no patter of sandalled feet, no bells or chanting, not even the usual noises from the kitchen, buttery or bakery. Nothing but an ominous, watching stillness. Abbot Strensham, fearful about what might happen, must have ordered his brothers to stay in their cells. Again Urswicke heard his name called and turned as the countess's squire Owain stepped out of the shadows.

'What is it?' Urswicke hurried towards him. 'The countess . . .?'

'She is well.' Owain drew closer, his long, dark face wreathed in concern. 'Our mistress has secretly left. She does not think it is safe here. She is journeying as swiftly as she can to London where she hopes to lodge at her husband's riverside mansion . . .'

'Yes, yes,' Urswicke snapped, 'I know where that is.'

'She also mentioned that she might visit a secret place. What is that, Master Urswicke? My mistress was insistent that you be given this message.'

'Nothing, nothing,' the clerk murmured, glancing around. 'Nothing to concern you. And what else?'

'The rest of the household are following behind. The countess, together with Master Bray and two outriders, left hurriedly. Before she departed, she asked if you would stay until the business here is completed and then join her.'

'Yes, yes I will.' Urswicke stared at the Welshman's close face, even as he prayed that the countess would exercise great caution as she entered the city. Owain pulled the gauntlets from beneath his warbelt; he put these on and stretched out a hand.

'Master Urswicke, I was instructed to wait for you. Make sure you receive the message and that you are well. I have done that. Now I must leave and join the rest before nightfall.'

Owain withdrew his hand, raised it in farewell and hurried back into the shadows along the cloister path. Urswicke made his way over to the guesthouse, now strangely quiet. The countess's retinue, together with other guests, had fled in full expectation that the bloody affray at Tewkesbury was certainly not finished. Urswicke went up into the different chambers to find them swept clean. He peered through a lancet window.

'The day is drawing on,' he whispered to himself, 'and I should be gone from here!'

He returned to his own closet chamber with its paltry sticks of furniture and narrow bed. He sat on the edge of this, lost deep in thought. He felt himself grow sleepy and shook himself awake. He glimpsed the half-full goblet of wine and drained it to the dregs before taking off his cloak; he wrapped this around him and stretched out on the bed. Darkness had fallen when he was awoken by a persistent rapping on his door. He drew his dagger and, slightly stiff, edged towards it.

'Who is it?' he called.

'Brother Norbert, remember me, sir?' the voice whined through the door. 'I am here with Brother Simeon, remember? You despatched us as messengers to Lord Wenlock whose crushed head is now poled in the market place.'

Urswicke felt a chill of apprehension. He opened the door and the two cowled figures slipped into the room. He indicated that they should sit on the edge of the cotbed whilst he drew up a stool close to them. Urswicke half suspected that these two worthies, whom he had used to convey messages, in particular to Lord Wenlock, were intent on mischief.

'You wish to speak?' Urswicke spread his hands. 'The hour is late and tomorrow beckons.'

'And it will bring more blood,' Norbert intoned lugubriously. 'Rumour has it that King Edward is determined on settling scores with all those who took sanctuary in our abbey.'

'And why should that concern me?'

'No, what should concern you, Master Urswicke, is that you are a Judas man who seemingly betrays both houses. You sent us with messages to Lord Wenlock. We now know what he did and how he died. Moreover, this abbey is clothed in darkness but we know its maze-like paths and we can thread the labyrinth. You would not even know we were there. We have watched you scurry here and scurry there. You meet the likes of Mauclerc. Even we know who he is, a man hot for devil's work. So who do you really serve, York or Lancaster?'

'I have done invaluable work for our Lord King.'

'Oh yes,' Norbert simpered, 'I was hiding in the garden when you and Mauclerc were whispering your treachery. Did you have a hand in the capture of the young prince? How will the House of Lancaster view that? Not to mention your meddling with Wenlock. And why is your mistress scurrying off so swiftly to London? What is she hiding?'

Urswicke stared hard at these two lay brothers. Abbot Strensham had chosen them because both had served as royal messengers before being granted a pension and a corrody in this abbey. Urswicke ruefully admitted he had underestimated this precious pair: they had served as royal couriers, a breed of officials with a reputation for prying and eavesdropping, ever ready to collect juicy morsels of valuable information. Both of these villains apparently hunted together and he wondered if they had used the same guile on the abbot and the other brothers.

'And so what?' Urswicke asked.

'You pay us in good pound sterling and,' Norbert rubbed his hands together, 'our little secret becomes a case of eye has not seen, nor has ear heard, nor will it enter into anyone's heart what mischief you have truly perpetrated.'

Urswicke nodded, taking a deep breath as he considered the possibilities. He did not flinch at the blackmail against himself. What worried him was any threat to his mistress. King Edward suspected her, whilst Clarence was her sworn enemy ready to believe any allegation levelled against a Beaufort. More chillingly, these two malefactors had stumbled upon the countess's great secret. She was, at this moment in time, harbouring something precious, and the lay brothers had referred to that. He did not want Mauclerc leading a swift-riding comitatus to pursue the countess and her household and thoroughly question them. Urswicke stared down at the floor and tried to recall what he knew about the abbey and its buildings. He thought hard and made a decision.

'Very well.' Urswicke pointed to the hour candle in its horned shell. 'When the flame marks the midnight hour, I will meet you out near the piggery.'

'Why there?'

'Because that's where I hid my money belt. Guesthouses lie open. Thievery is commonplace even,' he added sarcastically, 'in a house of prayer. A hundred pounds sterling, no more, for that's all I have. Take it,' he shrugged, 'or do your worst.'

Norbert glanced at Simeon who nodded his approval.

'In an hour then.' Urswicke rose, opened the door, and his visitors shuffled out into the night. Once he was sure they were gone, Urswicke hurriedly made his own preparations to leave. He packed his saddlebags with what he needed and went down to the abbey stables, where a sleepy-eyed groom promised to prepare his horse for a journey to London.

Urswicke returned to his chamber and plotted what he should do. He knew where the piggery was. Urswicke always carefully walked any place he lodged in, as a constable would his castle, looking for those places to hide, points of strength or possible weaknesses. Tewkesbury Abbey was no different. He checked the hour candle and, at the appointed time, slipped out of the guesthouse and made his way across the abbey grounds. He tried not to meet the gaze of the stone-carved gargoyles, *babewyns*, saints and angels, who glared down at him in mournful expectation, almost as if they knew what he plotted. Urswicke, however, felt composed. He had not created this situation, yet for his mistress's sake he had to resolve the challenge which confronted him.

He reached a wooden fence, climbed it, and crossed the abbey meadow, passing the cattle byres which reeked to heaven and eventually reached the hog pens where a large herd of pigs massed together, snuffling and grunting as they snouted the filthy ground. Urswicke, ignoring the stench, took up the position by the gate and waited. He half listened to the pigs, feral creatures always hungry and ever vigilant for food. The hogs sensed him, and every so often would crash against the poled fence or the iron-plated gate, stirring up the mud to thicken the cloud of filthy smells. At last Urswicke glimpsed the light of a lanternhorn bobbing through the darkness. The monks approached, almost swaggering, eager for their prize. Urswicke lifted the heavy, leather saddlebag and put his hand inside to grasp the small arbalest already primed. He moved his hand and felt the leather strap of a second crossbow.

'Well Urswicke, you have summoned us here . . .?'

The monk stopped as Urswicke abruptly brought out the crossbow and, stepping closer, released the catch so the barb sped to smash Norbert's face to a bloody, bony mess. The lay brother, still holding the lantern, crumpled to the ground. Urswicke stepped around him, dropping the first arbalest as he grasped the second. Simeon just froze, shocked to a stony stillness as Urswicke swept towards him and, with the crossbow within inches from his opponent's face, released the barbed quarrel, taking Simeon in the forehead, smashing his skull and piercing his brain. Urswicke watched his enemy slump to the ground. Certain that both men were dead, he put the arbalests back in their leather sack. He then took each of the blood-soaked corpses, dragged them to the fence and tossed them over. The second cadaver had hardly sunk into the thick, oozing mud of the piggery when the hogs, who had already smelt blood, surged in a frenzied attack to rip and tear at this unexpected, gore-smeared banquet: their squealing and grunting rose like some unholy hymn. Urswicke grasped the saddlebag and hurried into the night.

'You were correct,' he whispered over his shoulder, 'eye will not see, nor will ear hear, nor will it enter the heart of anyone about what I truly did.'

Urswicke eventually reached the stables and, as he approached the stall where his horse stood ready and waiting, a shadow slipped into the pool of light thrown by a lanternhorn on its hook close to the stable door.

'Master Urswicke,' Mauclerc stepped closer, 'I have been searching for you. You are leaving?'

'Urgent business in London.'

'Oh yes, the Lady Margaret has already left; she did so without royal permission.'

'Did she need it?'

'No but, as a courtesy, she really should have approached the royal chancery, but never mind. Everything is in a state of flux. We have received intelligence from London that the unrest there is much more serious than we first believed. We trust only a few men of power in the capital. One of them is your father. He and his comrades will have to stand like a door of steel against the rebels surging through Kent.'

For the first time in many a year, Urswicke thanked God for his father, yet he held himself tense. 'So what now?' he demanded.

'Matters move swiftly to judgement,' Mauclerc retorted. 'The King intends to force the issue here at the abbey early tomorrow. Our master also has need of you, not only here but in London as well. So, for the moment, you must stay, Master Urswicke, and see whatever the new day brings.'

Urswicke discovered that the day brought bloodshed: swift, cruel and terrible. Along with other Yorkist henchmen, he was roused roughly just before dawn, the abbey bells already tolling their dire warning, a loud protest against the King's intended actions. Edward, however, had his way. The abbey doors were forced. Yorkist soldiers flooded into the nave, searching out and seizing their enemy who sheltered in the chantry chapels, even behind the high altar. A few resisted, fighting back, but at last all the prisoners were chained and led like common felons out of the church. Abbot Strensham tried to protest but Clarence, surrounded by knights of the royal household, their swords drawn, rejected the abbot's protests. Clarence loudly declared that Tewkesbury Abbey did not enjoy the right of sanctuary. Moreover, the captured men were no ordinary felons but dyed-in-the-wool traitors who had been taken in arms against their rightful King. They were guilty of heinous treason and should answer for it.

Urswicke mingled with others of Clarence's coven and joined them as they escorted the prisoners out of the abbey precincts and down to the market place. Here the execution platform had been fully prepared. The common hangman, face all masked, stood by the execution block with a huge wicker basket beside it. A glowing brazier fanned by the morning breeze flared and smoked, the flames leaping up in bright tongues of fire. Some townspeople had also gathered to watch. A few of these, prompted by Clarence's henchmen, hurled curses and whatever refuse was at hand. In the main, however, the crowd just watched the pitiful masque unfold.

A line of broken, wounded men being herded into the square towards a great log table set up in front of Merchant Stratford's mansion. The table, now a court bench, was covered in a dark-green baize cloth. The symbols of royal justice, the royal sword and mace, rested there, along with a black, stark crucifix and a book of the Gospels. Urswicke glimpsed Edward the King standing at an upstairs window of the mansion. The King was peering down at this summary court of 'Oyer et Terminer', hastily assembled to dispense swift retribution. Behind the table sat the judges, Richard of Gloucester, who was also High Constable of England, on his left the Duke of Norfolk, the King's own marshal, and on Richard's right, Lord William Hastings, the Crown's special commissioner to the West Country and along the Welsh March. Clerks and scriveners sat ready to record a faithful account, parchment unrolled, quill pens at the ready. Gorgeously garbed heralds unfurled the royal standard as well as the banners and pennants of the three judges. These were placed behind Gloucester and his colleagues in specially prepared sockets on the three, throne-like chairs. Other heralds dragged the standards of the accused and placed these across the mud-strewn cobbles, creating a macabre carpet stretching from the table to the steps of the execution platform. A trumpeter blew a shrill blast, then, in a loud voice, proclaimed how the King's justices of Oyer et Terminer were ready for judgement.

The ceremonies and protocols eventually ended and the process began; it brooked no opposition and provided little hope for the accused. Each of the prisoners was dragged in front of the table to hear the charges read out by a clerk in a bell-like voice; every indictment was one of high treason and so worthy of death. Somerset was the first to hear this, and when asked for a reply he simply spat at his judges and cursed them now and for eternity.

'It will not be long,' he shouted, 'before you Yorkist vipers follow your father into the dark . . .'

Richard of Gloucester would have sprung to his feet but Norfolk, a cynical smile on his face, just grasped the young prince by his arm, whispering into his ear. Richard nodded as if in agreement and glanced over his shoulder up at the window where his brother the King was watching. Urswicke glimpsed Edward raise his hand. Richard turned back.

'You,' he pointed at Somerset, 'are attainted and so are worthy of death.' Gloucester then banged the table with his left hand as his right gestured at the guards to take Somerset away. The Lancastrian leader was seized and pushed up the steps onto the execution platform where he was forced to kneel before the block. Somerset's jerkin and shirt were roughly ripped and pulled down so his neck and head were fully exposed. The duke's hands were tied behind his back, even as the executioner's assistants forced Somerset to turn his head before thrusting it down onto the block. The axe man lifted his two-bladed weapon, brought it back in one glittering flash of sunlight then down, cutting the neck so sharply, Somerset's head bounced away as his torso jerked and spurted an arc of blood which drenched the entire platform. Somerset's head was then lifted, the executioner grasping it by the hair as he held it high, walking to the edge of the platform so that the judges could clearly view the half-closed eyes still blinking, the lips slightly twitching. The executioner then turned to the left and right so all could see, as a herald proclaimed, 'The fate of all such traitors.'

Urswicke was standing just behind Clarence and watched the Yorkist lord clap and jump, as if this was all some childish game put on for his pleasure and entertainment. Other prisoners, such as the Courtenays of Devon and the prior of the Hospitallers, were also tried and condemned. They too were hustled up the steps, forced to kneel, and then the great, gleaming execution axe whirled, followed by a sickening thud as it severed bone, muscle and flesh. The head would roll away before being displayed and placed in the waiting basket. The execution platform swirled in blood which seeped over the edge, into the gaps, to snake amongst the cobbles, drenching the Lancastrian banners left strewn there. After each execution, Clarence would clap his hands and chortle with glee as he performed another jig. Once the executions were over, however, Clarence became self-important, snapping his fingers for Mauclerc, the Three Kings and Urswicke to follow him across the slippery cobbles, back into The Golden Lion and up to the chamber they'd used before. Servants brought bowls of hot potage, chunks of meat and croutons in a highly spiced sauce, along with freshly baked manchet loaves and a jug of the tavern's finest Bordeaux. Clarence insisted on serving this himself, praising its richness and repeating how fitting that such blood-red wine should be drunk on the same day as the enemies of his House went under the axe.

'But now for fresh fields.' Clarence sucked on his fingers and pointed at Urswicke. 'My brother and I want you in London,' he leaned across the table, 'to keep the sharpest eye on that little bitch Meg of Richmond. You must also deliver a message to your redoubtable father, the Recorder.' Clarence shook his head. 'Thomas Neville, the Bastard of Fauconberg, intends to seize the city. You, your father and other loyal souls must prevent him. If London falls, our cause is seriously injured . . .'

Margaret Beaufort, Countess of Richmond, had left Tewkesbury on Sunday morning, reaching London late the following Tuesday to find that the news of the Yorkist victory at Tewkesbury and the summary execution of her kinsmen and others had swiftly preceded her. Margaret paused to rest and think in an ancient church just inside Aldgate. At first she busied herself lighting tapers before a statue of the Virgin, as well as paying a chantry

priest to sing three requiem masses for all those slain at
Tewkesbury. Afterwards she sat in the shadows, watching the
shifting light as the candle-flame before the different shrines and
statues flickered vigorously before guttering out. Margaret strove
to compose herself as she stared at a fresco on the pillars: this
depicted the Wheel of Fortune, how it would raise prince, priest
and prelate only to cast them down again. Margaret did not want
to be part of that wheel. Indeed her struggle was more dangerous.
The mighty Beauforts had, apart from herself, been annihilated
and wiped off the face of God's earth. She had to survive if
only for her son. If she went down, he would certainly follow.
And who would do this? The Yorkist warlords, Clarence in
particular, were her mortal enemies. In the first instance, she
would have to confront Clarence and destroy him, both root and
branch. Yet how?

A plan was forming, like a snake uncoiling, though slowly.
She had to remain cunning, prudent and patient. If she struck,
when she struck, she must not make a mistake. She heard a voice
raised further down the church and recalled the herald standing
on a cart just inside Aldgate. This city official proclaimed the
news from Tewkesbury as well as the more dangerous reports:
that the Bastard of Fauconberg's war cogs were sailing up the
Thames, whilst the men of Kent were gathering to storm through
Southwark and seize the southern gate of London Bridge. Of
course such proclamations caused deep unrest, yet Margaret was
relieved. All this upset might distract the Yorkist lords and their
ilk in the city. Margaret was determined to ensure that her beloved
son remained safe, as well as plot for the future. She wondered
about the 'Titulus Regius'. Margaret suspected that this document,
from the little that Somerset had told her, was highly injurious
to the House of York. She determined to seize such a manuscript
and use it to sow discord. Somerset was correct; Clarence may
be her avowed enemy, but he was also, albeit secretly, the implac-
able enemy of his own House and family.

Margaret threaded her ave beads through her fingers. Now and
again she would lapse into prayer as she wondered about whom
she could truly rely on and trust? Thanks to her marriage to Sir
Humphrey, she had the full protection of the Stafford family and
their leader the Duke of Buckingham. However, Sir Humphrey

was a truly sick man, made weaker by the hideous injuries sustained at Barnet. So how long would he live? Whom else could she trust? Was Somerset correct? Was there a spy deep in her household?

The countess knew she had two shield comrades, especially Christopher Urswicke. She crossed herself and prayed that her clerk would remain safe in that wolf's lair at Tewkesbury. The other stalwart was Reginald Bray, the steward and controller of her household. She glanced over her shoulder. Bray was sitting on a wall bench, legs apart, head down deep in thought. Margaret smiled to herself. Urswicke was astute but still young. He had complete loyalty for her, born out of his deep love for his mother as well as a burning resentment against his father and the heart break he had caused. Margaret also knew that Christopher was deeply grateful for what she had done to ease Urswicke's mother during the last painful months of her life.

Bray was different, a man who lived deep in the shadows. Ostensibly Reginald was her steward, a man with ink-stained fingers, well versed in matters of the chancery and the Exchequer. To all appearances, a faithful retainer, skilled in administration. Margaret, however, knew the full truth. There was a gap in Bray's service as a clerk when he, by his own confession to her, had fought in the King's array across the Narrow Seas as well as along the Scottish March. He was a veteran soldier and had risen to be one of the 'Secreti, the Secret Men' who went before the King's army to discover intelligence, spy on the enemy and, if they could, inflict damage on enemy leaders, be it through some ambush or secret attack at the dead of night. Bray was a master bowman and just as proficient in the use of the dagger and the garrotte. In truth, Bray was an assassin, a man who could become a shadow, to flit fiercely and silently where other men feared even to tread.

Margaret shifted in her seat, eyes on the dancing candle-flame even as a stratagem, subtle and complex, began to emerge in her teeming brain. She was determined to play the little maid, the court lady but, in truth, she would carry the war into the enemy's camp. She recalled her study of the classics and the writings about the Roman senate; how they would vow to wage war by land and sea, by fire and sword: that is what she would do! At times, if she could, she would cause public unrest but, in the main, her war would be secret yet just as devastating. She desperately wanted to visit her secret place, The Wyvern's Lair, but that would have to wait. At the moment the situation was too dangerous. Margaret knew she was under surveillance. As they had passed through Aldgate earlier that afternoon, Bray, sharp of mind and keen of wit, had whispered how he had glimpsed the scrutineers, informers paid by the city council, to observe and report on who entered and left the city. They must have noticed her and sent information by the street swallows, urchins who could be hired and taught to learn some message by rote. The Lords of the Soil at the Guildhall must already know that Margaret Beaufort Countess of Richmond had entered the city and would act accordingly. She crossed herself for a final time.

'Reginald,' she murmured, beckoning her steward forward. He crouched down beside her and she smoothed his cheek. 'Tell the rest of my household, now they have joined us, to go direct to Sir Humphrey's house in Queenhithe. The steward there is waiting and I am sure chambers will be ready. Tell Oswina and Owain to ensure everything is settled.'

'And you, Mistress?'

'You and I Reginald, are off to that grim house of war.'

'My Lady?'

'The Tower!'

A short while later they left St Katherine's. Dusk was falling as they made their way down Mark Lane to Thames Street. Margaret kept herself cloaked and cowled whilst Bray, sword drawn, strode beside her. The lanes and streets were narrow, a maze of arrow-thin alleyways where the upper storeys of the houses on either side leaned forward to block out both light and air. Shop signs creaked and swung precariously just above their heads, and they had to guard against the constant rain of slops from the upper windows. The stench of the refuse rotting in the lay stalls as well as the crammed open sewers running down the centre of the street was so offensive Bray had to buy pomanders from a chapman. Margaret held one of these over her nose and mouth, trying not to glance at the bloody battles being waged in and around the steaming midden heaps by cat, rat and dog. A pig which had attacked a child had been caught, tried, its throat cut, and had been hung from a three-branched gallows, the other two nooses being occupied by the corpses of housebreakers; apparently these had been caught red-handed by the bailiffs who had stripped them, placed a rope around their necks before kicking away the barrels the two wolfsheads had been forced to stand on.

Such sickening sights were common. London life in all its rawness bustled on; traders, tinkers and shop-men touted raucously for business. Hot-pot girls, sent out by the nearby taverns and cook-shops, tried to entice passers-by with what was on offer: minced chicken in pastry, beef brisket, honey-coated pork along with little beakers of ale, cider and wine. Beggars whined, clucking their dishes. Whores pouted and simpered in doorways where they stood in their garish, striped gowns and fiery-red wigs. Margaret grew accustomed to such sights and sounds, closing her ears to the raucous din, be it the wail of bagpipes, the screams of children and the constant strident cat-calling by those who thronged the streets. The countess, however, sensed something else: a palpable tension, as if the city knew that it was about to be drawn into the bloody conflict which had raged at Barnet and Tewkesbury.

Men-at-arms, hobelars and archers thronged about, all garbed in the royal livery or the blue and yellow of York. Carts crammed with weaponry were being pulled down to the different gates of the city, and Margaret even glimpsed culverins and cannon being dragged on sledges to the principal quaysides along the Thames such as Queenhithe and Dowgate. Knights in half-armour grouped at the different crossroads, where city men-at-arms were fastening chains to be dragged across the mouth of the main streets as a defence against enemy horsemen. News from Tewkesbury was being proclaimed time and again by professional chanteurs, who stood on barrels or casks to regale the passing crowd, embellishing their tale with bloodthirsty stories from that fierce battle.

They left the city, moving into Portsoken, a desolate area between the Abbey of the Minoresses and the Church of St Mary Grace's. Here the unlicensed troubadours, minstrels and actors could perform free without being troubled by city bailiffs. A travelling troupe had set up a stage and mummers, their faces hidden by hideous masks, were busy playing out the execution of the Lancastrian lords in Tewkesbury market place. They used figures fashioned out of straw, buckets of pig's blood and baskets of offal to make their account more gruesome. Margaret swiftly averted her eyes and murmured a requiem. Bray now held her arm in this squalid place of fleshers' yards and tanning sheds, which flooded the area with filth and attracted savage dogs, a real threat to the weak or unwary.

Margaret heaved a sigh of relief when they reached the great postern gate to the rear of the Tower. This was now protected and barricaded with war carts, palisades and sharpened stakes driven into the ground. Banners and pennants floated in the breeze, their gorgeous insignia besmirched by the smoke billowing from fiery braziers. Men-at-arms and mounted archers patrolled the entrance under the command of knight bannerets, and all who approached were challenged. Margaret, resting on Bray's arm, walked carefully towards the table which spanned the narrow gap between the two sides of the barricade. A royal clerk, dressed in the livery of the King's household, looked Margaret and Bray up and down from head to toe before imperiously lifting his hand, snapping his fingers at them to approach. One of the knights behind the clerk recognised Margaret as she pulled back the hood of her cloak and, leaning over, whispered heatedly into the clerk's ear. The man changed in an instant, he rose, smiling from ear to ear, beckoning her closer and tactfully refusing the warrants and licences Bray produced from his wallet.

'My Lady,' he bowed, 'you are most welcome.' He turned and spoke to one of the soldiers behind him. The man hurried off and the clerk waved Margaret and Bray through the barrier into a small enclosure. Margaret raised a hand in thanks to the young knight who had recognised her, then followed the clerk into a sparsely furnished pavilion pitched before the Tower gate.

'My Lady,' the clerk grated, 'I have sent for the constable. Lord Dudley will be here shortly.'

Margaret made herself comfortable, Bray standing behind her. She listened keenly to the conversation amongst the officers who stood close by talking about the looming threat. How the Bastard of Fauconberg intended to sweep the men of Kent into London, recalling the turbulent days of Wat Tyler and Jack Cade, when the city suffered all the horrors of attack, sack and rapine. Nevertheless, despite the impending menace, Margaret truly believed that the civil war was finished. Edward of York, that golden-haired English Alexander, would tip the scales and carry out the total destruction of his opponents. He had fought them for years: his recent victories had annihilated most of his enemies, and those who had survived would be marked down for death. Despite the sinister Clarence, she quietly prayed that the Yorkist King did not consider her to be one of these. The pavilion emptied. Bray, who stood close to the entrance, walked across and leaned over.

'Mistress,' he whispered, 'Christopher Urswicke, should he not be here?'

'He tends to urgent business in Tewkesbury,' she replied.

'His business or ours?'

'You don't trust him, Reginald?'

'My Lady I do but, if I discover that I am wrong, I shall kill him.'

'And Urswicke has said the same about you.' She grinned impishly up at him. 'Trust is trust, Reginald. You stand by it or you fall. Believe me, you and Christopher are my shield companions. If I go down, so do you. If you fall, you could very well drag me with you . . .' She broke off as Lord Dudley, Constable of the Tower, a tall, balding man with a thick bushy moustache drooping at the corners of his mouth, entered the pavilion. Margaret made to rise.

'My Lady.' Dudley raised a hand. 'Please, it's an honour to see you.'

Margaret allowed the constable to kiss the tips of her fingers; she then introduced Bray. Once the pleasantries and introductions were finished, Dudley, dressed in chain mail and half-armour, took a stool and sat down. He rested his elbows on his knees, hands joined as if in prayer. He scratched his forehead then stared long and hard at Margaret, a fierce look but Margaret held his gaze. She had met Dudley before at some court celebration and knew him to be a good soldier of some integrity. She noticed the fresh scars to his face and moved to look at those on the side of his neck. Dudley grinned in a display of broken yellow teeth. He gently tapped his bloodied skin.

'River pirates,' he declared, 'as they once were. All gone now: their souls despatched to judgement, their corpses impaled on a row of sandbanks along the Thames.' He grinned wolfishly. 'Yes, I fought with John Tiptoft, Earl of Worcester, or so he was, until he supported the wrong side. He was caught and executed. Worcester fought in Wallachia around the city of Tirgoviste, in the service of the Lord Count Drakulya. A fearsome warlord, my Lady, who took no prisoners. Tiptoft learnt about impalement and how effective it is. More striking than a corpse dangling from the end of a rope or,' he shrugged, 'heads being severed in Tewkesbury market place. Yes, we have heard the news. King Edward is preparing to leave for London and he is issuing proclamations by the day which are posted at the Conduit in Cheapside and the Great Cross in St Paul's graveyard.' He took a deep breath. 'For what it's worth, my Lady,' he crossed himself, 'the list of dead is also being posted, and again, for what it's worth, I am truly sorry for your loss. The Beaufort family,' he sighed, 'have suffered grievously.' He fell silent, tapped his boots on the ground and glanced up. 'Margaret of Richmond, I know why you are here.'

'I wish to see the old King.'

'Many, including myself, do not see him, speak to him, or even allow ourselves to be seen consulting with him.'

'I want to.' Margaret steeled herself. 'And I need to see him soon. Edward of York and his brothers march on London. Henry is a problem Edward must address. I suspect he will, sooner rather than later. Consequently, sir, I wish to have words with a dying man. You cannot refuse me that. I must add that he is a kinsman of mine. I beg you sir, I need to have words with him.'

Dudley bowed his head; when he glanced up his cheeks were tear-soaked. 'I know,' he murmured, 'but I am concerned.'

'His Grace the King, and he was crowned that,' Margaret asserted herself, 'is half-brother to my late husband Lord Tudor. You know what is going to happen. I need to speak to the old King before the clouds gather and this fortress of yours becomes shrouded in mystery, if not murder. I am no threat to you, Edward of York or any of his ilk. I am here out of sheer compassion.'

Dudley nodded and rose, barking orders at his henchmen who had gathered close by. Margaret and Bray, surrounded by men-at-arms, were led out of the pavilion and through the sombre, cavernous postern gate into the Tower. Night was falling, but that grim fortress was frenetically busy. Men-at-arms milled around. Catapults, mangonels and trebuchets and all the other hideous engines of war were being prepared. The air was riven by the screech of cordage, the clatter of armour and the cries of officers. These all mingled with strident squealing from the hog pens, where the pigs were being slaughtered, their guttered carcasses being prepared, smoked and cured in preparation for a siege. The women of the garrison were busy around the wells filling water pots. The Tower was preparing for war and the imminent attack by the Bastard of Fauconberg's forces, be it across London Bridge or from the river.

Margaret's escort marched swiftly and they were soon in the great cobbled bailey where the formidable White Tower soared up above them, stark against the early summer sky. Margaret expected to be taken there. Instead, they were led across the execution yard, past the Church St Peter Ad Vincula and into the Wakefield Tower. Here the escort left them. Lord Dudley seized a ring of keys, led them up some steps, unlocked a door and waved them into a grim, grey circular stone chamber with a small enclave which served as an oratory. A murky place, the only light being provided by lancet windows and a few tallow candles fixed on spigots. The cowled prisoner sitting at the chancery table, strewn with manuscripts and books, sighed noisily and rose to greet them. A tall, angular figure garbed in dark clothes and shabby slippers. He shuffled forward. Margaret was immediately struck by how surprisingly young he looked; a pleasing countenance with a broad forehead, well-spaced eyes and rather pallid skin which seemed to emphasise his very pointed chin and protuberant lower lip.

'Your Grace.'

Margaret and Bray sank to their knees. Henry VI, King of England, God's anointed, hastened towards them.

'Not now, not now.' He half stuttered. 'Who are you? Emissaries from my wife?'

'Your Grace, this is Margaret Beaufort, Countess of Richmond, and I am her steward Reginald Bray. We have come to pay our respects.'

'Of course, of course.' Henry gestured at Dudley to prepare the chamber, a chair for himself and stools for his visitors. At last all was ready. Margaret glanced pleadingly over her shoulder at Dudley; the constable bowed, snapped his fingers at his escort and left the chamber, closing the door behind him. Margaret sipped at the cup of posset she had been served. Bray stood close to her, fingers resting on the hilt of his dagger. 'Come, cousin.' Henry stretched forward, hands extended. 'You are so kind. You have come to visit your poor kinsman.' He smacked his brow with the heel of his hand. 'So many Beauforts, good, generous people,' he lifted his head, tears brimming in his eyes, 'all gone into the dark. Oh, the years pass and I have seen them go.'

'Your Grace,' Margaret replied, pulling her stool closer, 'time is short. You have heard the news fresh out of Tewkesbury?'

'I have.' Henry sat all slack, mouth half open, eyes fearful. Margaret stared pitifully at this poor excuse of a king. She recalled what one of her kinsmen had said, 'Poor stock breeds poor stock.' Henry's paternal grandfather had been a leper: his French grandfather had suffered fits of madness believing he was a glass vase which could crack at any time. Henry had now reigned for fifty years, a period of decline and decay. As King he had been reviled, seized, mocked and humiliated the length and breadth of his kingdom as he passed from the hands of one violent warlord to another. He certainly wasn't born to be a king, more of a monk than monarch. A saintly man who loved his book of hours, psalter and ave beads, murmuring his prayers or, if he was lucid enough, poring over ancient manuscripts.

'I have heard the news,' Henry repeated, fingers going to his lips. 'I fear for my son and beloved wife.' His hand fell away. 'You know what they say? That the prince is not truly mine but the by-blow of one of my wife's lovers?'

'It's a lie, your Grace.'

Henry peered closer at Margaret. 'Yes, yes you would say that, wouldn't you? And how is your boy, the offspring of my darling half-brother Edmund?' Margaret just stared back. Henry abruptly turned sideways, peering at her out of the corner of his eye. 'I know, I know,' he whispered, 'this is the killing time. The wheel is being turned once more.'

'Your Grace,' Margaret gestured at the chancery desk, 'you

have parchment, wax, ink, pen and signatory ring. I need a writ under your seal that it pleases you to allow the bearer of such a warrant to do as he or, in this case she . . . well, whatever I want. I need to thread my way across this city and, more importantly, find a path through the murderous maze of court politics. Your Grace, my pardon, my apologies but, as you say, the killing time is here.'

Henry sucked on his lips and nodded. 'Yes, yes, it so pleases me,' he murmured. He rose, crossed to the table, beckoning at Bray to join him. The writ was scrawled and sealed with the King's signet ring. Henry then sat down, rubbing his lips with bony fingers.

'So, sweetest cousin, what do you want?'

'The Titulus Regius?' Margaret retorted. 'The Title of the King?'

'Ah yes.' Henry smiled. 'Searchers have been busy looking for that, industrious in discovering information. Somebody told me that.' He paused. 'Everybody searches for secrets. They look for lies, sometimes the truth, which they can use against their enemies. Now.' He became all brisk. 'The Titulus Regius is the creation of George of Clarence and, if the truth be known or, so my wife hinted, it is an attack on the Yorkist claim to the Crown of England.' He licked his lips. 'It's either that or a document which shows that George of Clarence should be King of England.' Henry seemed to find that amusing and he began to laugh softly.

'How do you know that?'

Again Henry's fingertips brushed his lips and his eyes lost that knowing look; his expression grew more vacant, vacuous and slack.

'Your Grace?'

'Oh yes, oh yes.' Henry breathed out noisily, staring over his shoulder at the chancery desk. 'When my wits returned and my beloved wife held the reins of power, I learnt a great deal about George of Clarence. You see Clarence changed sides, didn't he? Flitting like a shadow, or slinking like a rat, between his own kin and the House of Lancaster. A man who blows hot and cold. He can be your firm friend on Monday and your deadly enemy on Tuesday. Anyway, during the time Clarence was in the Lancastrian camp, he insinuated that he knew great secrets. How he himself should be King. Wasn't a proclamation issued declaring that? Anyway, anyway,' Henry fluttered his fingers, 'according to my wife, Clarence later hired three clerks skilled in collecting chatter and gossip. They were making careful note of all this in a secret chronicle. I believe others helped them but I forget the details.' Henry took ave beads out of his belt pouch and began to thread them through his fingers. 'God save us, God save us. Clarence even gathered scandal about his own parents, but I forget the details. My wife could tell you more if she dare.' He glanced fearfully at Margaret. 'I shouldn't even be discussing this. If the Yorkist lords discovered . . .'

Margaret nodded understandingly; she knew all about the old King's shifting moods. How he could lapse into sudden silence, totally withdrawn from the world, or indulge in hysterical fits bordering on a frenzy. Once Henry began to change, there was little sense to be had out of him. Margaret suspected that was about to happen. She glanced at Bray, who quietly nodded, as if he'd read her thoughts and agreed with her. It was time to leave. Margaret rose and made her farewells but Henry now seemed unaware of anything and, bowing his head, he intoned the opening verse of Vespers.

'Oh Lord come to my aid. Oh Lord make haste to help me . . .'

Margaret glanced pityingly down at this broken King who'd been deprived of his crown, his kingdom, his wife, his heir, his liberty and, undoubtedly once the Yorkist lords swept into London, his very life. She left Henry to his prayers.

Dudley was waiting in the stairwell and escorted her back down through the postern gate. Margaret and Bray hastened through the bustling crowd towards the Tower quayside. They walked carefully to avoid the carts and sumpter ponies being led up to the fortress with food and munitions for the garrison. Bray wanted to hire a barge but the crowd thronging around the quay-side steps meant that they would have a long wait. Moreover, Margaret's mood changed. She believed, and Bray agreed with her whispered warning, that she had a deepening conviction of being quietly followed, watched and scrutinised. She tried to stifle the fear which coursed through her. The hunters were out, she was sure of that, but even worse, why were the dogs so close? Did they know something about what she intended? Of course she had been seen entering London through Aldgate, her presence would be noted, but this was different. She truly felt she was being closely scrutinised, her every step noted. Margaret prided herself on how her days at court had sharpened her ability to sense danger, threats as well as the means to avoid them. Of course that had been at court where she could count on powerful protection, but the power of the Beauforts had been shattered. So what did the hunters search for? Did they suspect what was hidden away in her most secret plans? Once again she recalled Somerset's warning in the chantry chapel at Tewkesbury. Did she really nurse a Judas close to her breast? Did this traitor, whoever he was, work for someone else? That must be Clarence and his coven. Was that why the King's brother hinted and baited her about her precious son?

'Mistress?'

Margaret stared fiercely at Bray who stepped back in alarm.

'Mistress,' he repeated, 'I did not mean to startle you.'

'We are being watched, Reginald, so let us play them at their own game. We must go.'

She turned, going back up Tower Street which led them into East-cheap, the great fish market around Billingsgate. The place stank of the fish, salt and offal strewn across the cobbles where cat and dog fought with the hordes of tattered beggars over the different scraps. The pillories and stocks set up in this foulsome place were being well used, especially for fishmongers who had tried to sell stale produce and were now being forced to stand, head and hands clasped, with the rotting carcasses of fish slapped across their faces. Margaret pretended to turn to look at these and slipped as if she had lost her footing. She used this to stare around, as did Bray who hastened to help her. Nevertheless, they could detect nothing amiss until they entered a narrow lane leading down to Candlewick. Bray stopped to turn back to give a beggar boy a coin when he glimpsed a sudden darting movement along the roof of a house further down the street. A small furtive shape skilfully treading the sloping, tiled roof. Bray smiled to himself and walked back to join his mistress.

'Sparrowhawks.' He murmured. 'Little street urchins who can scramble across the roofs better than any rat, cat or squirrel. They have us under watch so . . .'

He pulled Margaret into the dirty, dingy taproom of a tavern, a low-beamed room smelling of ale and fried food. Bray summoned the landlord, offered him a coin and quickly explained what he wanted. The man nodded and led both Margaret and Bray across to a door with eyelets high in the wood.

'Stay there.' The landlord tapped his barrel-like belly. 'Stay there,' he repeated, 'peer out. Let us see who comes.'

He opened the door; the small chamber was no better than a musty, cobwebbed cupboard, though it had a seat built into the wall. Margaret sat whilst Bray peered through the slats and waited. He was about to turn away when he quietly cursed, beckoning at Margaret to join him. She did so, peering through the eyelets. The noise of the taproom had stilled. No one moved but froze, staring at the men-at-arms garbed in city livery who'd slipped into the alehouse. Margaret reckoned there must be at least a dozen and she certainly recognised their leader Roger Urswicke, Recorder of London and the estranged father of her clerk Christopher. The landlord acted his part, running up to greet the visitors, fingers fluttering, face beseeching, eyes eager to help. Yes, he assured the Recorder, a man and woman had just entered his tavern but they had slipped across the kitchen garden and out through the wicket gate which fronted the alleyway beyond. Urswicke nodded, snapping his fingers at the men-at-arms to follow. Once they'd gone, the landlord busied himself around the taproom until one of the slatterns hurried in and whispered, pointing in the direction of the garden. Minehost rubbed his hands in glee and hurried across to open the door, gesturing at Bray and Margaret to come out.

'Gone.' He breathed. 'They have all left. I hate the bloody Guildhall and its nosey judges, the arrogant aldermen and clever-tongued lawyers. I say that, sir,' he peered at Bray, 'yet I apologise if you are lawyer; you look like one.'

'I am, but not of that ilk,' Bray retorted. 'However . . .' He slipped the landlord another coin and led Margaret out into the alleyway.

Margaret could glimpse no movement along the rooftops or at the mouth of the narrow runnels. They moved on, eager to hide amongst the crowd surging up from Cheapside where the long range of stalls offered everything under the sun. Trading was vigorous, as if the merchants of the city could not care which warriors fought, who was victorious, who rose and who fell. Margaret had learned a very salutary lesson in her life, something she treasured close to her heart. How the patronage of the arts, the pursuit of knowledge – be it in the cathedral schools or the halls of Cambridge – were part of the very fabric of life which any worthy prince should foster. The hideous slaughter at Tewkesbury was a grievous sin which threatened that fabric and should be curtailed at all cost. She wanted her darling son to learn the lesson, that trade not war, learning not battles were the true business of a prince. Margaret broke from her reverie as a group of bailiffs shrieked at a cutpurse and plucked him out of the crowd. Every day men were taken up and arrested, Margaret reflected, determined that would not happen to her, young Henry or any of those close to her heart. She was determined to weave the web she wanted and the most important part of this was the removal of her son from any danger.

# PART THREE

'King Henry was secretly assassinated in the Tower.'
*Milanese State Papers*

They reached the corner of St Andrew's Street. Across from this, a chanteur, his skin as dark as night, stood on a barrel, trying to entice passers by to listen to his tale about the fate of the great city of Constantinople. How swarms of Turcopoles had filled its wells with corpses and soaked the streets of the great city in blood. Margaret swiftly scrutinised him but he seemed genuine enough, hardly a spy in the employ of the Guildhall or Clarence. Nevertheless, she still had that chilling feeling of being closely watched. Bray, however, who stood staring up and around, whispered the danger was past. They continued halfway down the street, stopping at The Wyvern's Nest, a nondescript alehouse. Bray led Margaret in as he bellowed for Hempen the landlord, a fat, bustling, grey-haired tub of a man with a cruel red scar around his throat.

'Are we safe?' Bray demanded.

'Yes! Come!' Hempen led them out of the porch and across the taproom. In the corner he lifted a trapdoor, which stretched down to murky cellars. Margaret followed the taverner, a man who had nearly died of hanging until her late husband Edmund Tudor had cut him down from the gallows. Hempen was a retainer whom Margaret trusted with her life: one of the few men who would do all he could to help her and her beloved son.

The taverner, muttering to himself, led his guests along the mildewed passageway, an ancient tunnel leading from The Wyvern's Nest, across the alleyway above, and into the cellars of the house directly opposite. Margaret and Bray squeezed themselves through the narrow gap which Hempen cleared by pulling away a stack of timbers. They entered the gloomy, wet-walled cellars, a place reeking of mould and damp, a deep-cold blackness broken only by the dancing light from the lantern Hempen carried. He led them up steep steps and pushed hard at the door concealed behind a heavy dust-strewn arras: this opened and Hempen waved them into a small, shabby solar, where two individuals were sharing a bench before a meagre fire in the mantled hearth. The man, dressed in travel-stained jerkin, hose and boots, rose and warmly embraced his sister-in-law.

'Jasper,' Margaret breathed, 'thank God you reached here safely and you, light of my life,' Margaret crouched to embrace Henry, a narrow-faced, pale-skinned boy with large, pleasing eyes, smooth cheeks and a dimpled chin. She lightly touched his black hair, now nothing more than stubble, his head had been so closely shaved. 'I hardly recognised you,' Margaret smiled, 'and yet,' she lapsed into Welsh, 'I know you to be the very beat of my heart and you shall always rest at the centre of my soul.' She grasped the fourteen-year-old's arms and rubbed her hands up and down. 'He is well?' Margaret glanced sharply at Tudor.

'I am well,' Henry declared before his uncle could reply, 'and Mother, I am so pleased to be with you. I had a sickness of the belly as we have travelled far and fast. But now I feel better. I am pleased to be off the roads.' His face became more serious. 'Uncle Jasper warned that we are in great danger.'

'Yes you are,' Margaret whispered and stood up. 'But we will keep you safe.' Margaret eased herself down onto the bench, Bray standing behind her. Jasper sat on her left, her son on the other side. Margaret peered out of the corner of her eyes at him. Henry looked a little pale and thin but he seemed healthy enough. She stretched out her hands to the fire as she repressed a shiver of fear. Hempen coughed, making to leave, but Margaret gestured at him to stay, politely refusing his offer of wine and food.

'Master Hempen,' she smiled at her son, 'was not of that name when he was held over the baptismal font in his parish church at Powys. He received his new name when he was caught up in the fierce clan wars which rage along the Welsh valleys. Hempen was taken prisoner and his opponents were actually hanging him from a branch when your father, my husband, like some knight from the tales of Arthur, galloped up and cut him down.' Margaret rocked herself gently, eyes half closed, 'but that was my Edmund, a true knight. Anyway, he took my good friend here into his service. Is that not true, Master Hempen?'

The landlord nodded, rubbing the great, red weal around his neck. 'The noose did this,' he declared, 'burning like a flame from Hell. I forsook my old name and assumed a new one, Hempen, as a constant reminder of my foes and a token of remembrance for my saviour. Oh yes.' The more the landlord spoke, the more sing-song his voice became, distinctly echoing the accent of a Welsh valley-dweller. 'Lord Edmund,' he continued, 'was insistent that I leave Wales with him. He supplied me with good coin and letters of introduction to the Vintner's Guild here in London.'

'My late husband encouraged Hempen to purchase The Wyvern's Nest, and he also bought this house which stands directly opposite. Edmund knew about the secret tunnel stretching between the two, a relict of smuggling days. People can enter the The Wyvern's Nest and promptly disappear if the tavern is raided and searched.' Margaret pointed to a bell under its coping, high in the corner of the solar wall, just above the door. 'Twine is fastened to that and snakes back to the tavern: if the taproom is raided, the cord is pulled and the bell will ring its warning.' She smiled thinly. 'Edmund always had to be wary when he visited London.' She shrugged elegantly. 'And so it is now. Nothing has changed. Amongst the powerful, the Beauforts and the Tudors are regarded with disdain. However, you are here. More importantly,' she patted her son on the shoulder, 'our enemies think both of you are locked up in the fastness of Pembroke Castle. Long may they continue to believe that. I am sure Edward of York, urged on by his two brothers, will despatch troops into Wales.'

'They'll still think we are there,' Jasper broke in. 'We slipped very quietly out of the fortress and we have created the pretence that we still shelter within.' He paused. 'I did muster troops, a host of Welsh horse and foot advanced as if they intended to cross the Severn and assist the Angevin.' He waved a hand. 'Smoke in the wind. Margaret of Anjou's cause was doomed. You received my cryptic message from Lambert the page boy, my courier?'

Margaret nodded.

Jasper spread his hand. 'However, I agree with you, sister, it

is only a matter of time before Edward of York lays siege to
Pembroke and his war cogs appear off the coast.'

'Would the Yorkists,' Bray demanded, 'really besiege by land
and sea? Pembroke is a formidable fortress. It could take months
if not years before it fell.'

'Oh the Yorkist lords know that,' Jasper half laughed, 'but they
would only be too pleased to keep the fortress locked up so that
no one can get in or get out. And now we will use that to our
own advantage. Though,' Jasper rubbed his face, 'it's only a
matter of time before some traitor sells the news that we have
flown the cage.'

'And in your journey here, how did you travel?'

'Master Bray, you are looking at two pilgrims who suspect
they may suffer some affliction of the belly, their humours severely
disturbed. So, we intend to visit Becket's shrine at Canterbury
and then move north to the Blessed Virgin's house at Walsingham.
Of course now we are here, we intend to take a ship abroad. I
understand that the Breton cog, *The Galicia*, is about to berth at
Queenhithe, its master has agreed—'

'No, no, no,' Hempen intervened. 'It is not as simple as that.
We must be prudent, careful. The watchers and the scrutineers,
as thick as lice on a dog's fur, are out along the streets and
quaysides. Searchers carry the city commission and have been
appointed and despatched to watch out for any from the House
of Lancaster trying to flee the realm.'

'Yes, yes, we have already encountered the same.' And Bray
swiftly told them about the sparrowhawks and the appearance of
no lesser person than the Recorder of London, Thomas Urswicke,
eagerly searching for someone or something.

'And that could be young Henry,' Hempen retorted. 'We know
a few of the searchers and sparrowhawks. There is a rumour that
they are looking for someone important,' the landlord pointed at
Henry, 'and I suspect that is you.'

'We should move,' Bray murmured.

'No, no,' Hempen retorted. 'As I have said, the ports, quaysides
and river steps are plagued by spies. South of the river, the men
of Kent are stirring. Fauconberg threatens the city. We must not
move while such storms swirl. We could be caught up in them
and trapped.'

'We must wait.' Margaret rose and beckoned her son into her close embrace and then kissed the bristles on his shorn head. 'God keep you.' She whispered urgently. '*Pax et bonum*, my son. You must prepare yourself for sudden flight. We need Urswicke here. I am certain he is on his way.'

'Mistress,' Bray cleared his throat, 'Mistress,' he repeated, 'Urswicke's father is leading the hunt for us. It is all too close for comfort. Mistress, I beg you . . .'

Margaret lifted a hand for silence even as she winked at her son. 'Christopher,' she replied, 'I trust him with my very life. We will wait. Urswicke will help us . . .'

Christopher Urswicke made himself comfortable on the chancery stool before his father's writing desk in a gloomy chamber on the second storey of the Guildhall, its windows overlooking the great market of Cheapside. Urswicke had arrived in London the previous day but kept himself discreetly away from either The Wyvern's Nest or Sir Humphrey's riverside mansion. The clerk knew he would see his mistress in good time but that had to wait. Other pressing business demanded his attention, not least the urgent messages he carried in his courier's pouch from Edward of York and his two brothers.

The noise and smells of Cheapside seeped through the window, the perfumed fragrances mingling with the fetid stench from the slaughter sheds. He rose, crossed and opened the small door window peering down at the crowd thronging about, a sea of constantly shifting colour and noise. Urswicke, on his walk to the Guildhall, had also caught the tension, a growing fear of the impending storm gathering to the south of the city. Rumours were flooding through London that the men of Kent were now in Southwark, whilst Fauconberg's war cogs, armed with culverin and cannon, would unleash a hail of fire against the north bank of the Thames. As if to express this growing tension and mounting hysteria, a travelling chanteur, perched on his box, bellowed a warning in a powerful, carrying voice.

'The waves of death will surge about us,
The torrents of destruction shall overwhelm us,
The snares of the grave shall entangle us,
The fear of death confront us.

'Citizens of London,' the chanteur continued, 'fire and brim-stone will rain down on this city. A sea of flame sweep through your dwellings. On your knees, and prepare yourself by prayer and fasting against the day of the great slaughter.' The chanteur immediately broke off as a group of city men-at-arms surged through the crowd to arrest him, but the chanteur picked up his box and ran, still shouting his chilling warnings.

'Dire indeed.' Urswicke spun around; his father had entered the chamber, closing the door quietly behind him. Thomas Urswicke, Recorder of London, pointed down to his soft, wool-edged buskins. 'I have always been silent, soft-footed.'

'A necessary talent,' Christopher replied, 'for when you slipped down the stairs to the servant maids' quarters.'

'Now, now.' Thomas Urswicke's smooth, jovial face creased into a knowing grin, his sharp green eyes bright with life, his mouth twisted into that merry smile which Christopher knew was a mask for a mind that teemed like a box of worms and a heart full of lechery and deceit. Thomas Urswicke scratched his thin-ning blond hair and adjusted his gold-threaded guild robe. He fingered the silver chain of office around his neck, the other hand thrust through the ornamented swordbelt with its costly copper stitching and embroidered dagger scabbard. Nervous gestures! Christopher idly wondered if his father had been tumbling some wench in one of the many deserted enclaves of the Guildhall.

'Well.' The Recorder tried to assert himself, stretching out a hand. Christopher ignored this; he undid his chancery satchel, took out the sealed documents and handed them over. His father, mood all changed, snatched these, muttering to himself as he kissed and broke the seals. He read quickly, lips mouthing the words: he glanced up, staring at Christopher as if seeing him for the first time.

'Good news out of Tewkesbury.' The Recorder straightened up and preened himself. 'His Grace the King and his beloved brothers put great trust in me: these messages hint that I may be dubbed a knight.'

'For what?'

'For holding this city against rebels and traitors. I am glad to see,' his father added archly, 'that you have come to your senses. You may pretend to work for the Beaufort bitch but my Lord of

Clarence says you did great work in capturing the Angevin she-wolf and her whelp.' The Recorder sat down in his chair. 'The messages talk of a desire to impose order, to bring the violence to an end.' He tapped the documents. 'According to these, the killings at Tewkesbury included other victims. Two lay brothers were found mauled and eaten by hogs. Abbot Strensham is furious. Do you know anything about such killings?'

'How could I? The armies of both York and Lancaster contain professional killers, men of blood; mercenaries who fear neither God nor man. Father, we live in a time of war! Murder, treason and betrayal prowl the roads of this kingdom like starving, rabid dogs.'

'Aye, and talking of prowling the roads, so do traitors. We have information that Lancastrian rebels may well slip in and out of the city to foreign parts. Some of this information hints that your mistress harbours outlaws, fleeing Lancastrians—'

'Such as?'

'We don't know. Just hints that her own son, together with her traitorous kinsman, Jasper Tudor, might be amongst those she actively harbours and protects.'

'Henry Tudor!' Urswicke exclaimed. 'Never! He and his uncle shelter behind the fastness of Pembroke. Who gives you such information?'

'Anonymously,' his father replied. 'In the entrance to the Guildhall you must have seen the two lions carved out of wood, heavy statues, their mouths open in a roar. Citizens, good honest citizens, are encouraged, indeed exhorted on their allegiance to the Crown, to give any information they learn about the whereabouts and doings of traitors, malefactors, outlaws, whatever their status or station. Of course most of the intelligence is given without seal or signature. This system is valuable, especially when allegations are laid against a Beaufort: that she shelters traitors, even if these be her own son and kinsman.'

The Recorder seized the blackjack of morning ale on the table before him and drank noisily before offering it across to his son. Christopher just shook his head as he tried to school his features and curb the agitation curdling in his stomach. 'And you believe all this?'

'Yes, Christopher, I do. The Beaufort bitch certainly acts

mysteriously. I myself have ordered her to be watched most carefully and, from personal observation, since her return to this city, she acts in a highly suspicious fashion. I went hunting for her but lost my quarry. Now you are back in the city, such a pursuit should be your prime duty.' The Recorder waved a hand. 'The Beauforts are spent. Nevertheless, my Lord of Clarence wants you and me to be in at the kill, the utter destruction of that damnable family. However,' the Recorder leaned across the table, eyes all excited, 'we must also prove our loyalty and deal with other problems which beset us. The Bastard of Fauconberg has landed in Kent and sweeps towards the city. He leads seasoned troops from the garrison at Calais, men harnessed for war, well furnished with horses, weaponry and cannon. Fauconberg styles himself "captain and leader and liege lord to King Henry's people in Kent". Accordingly, Fauconberg demands to be allowed safe passage through the city so he can seek out and destroy – and these are his own treasonable words – the usurper Edward of York and his ilk.'

'And the city's response?'

'Stockton our mayor and myself have rejected Fauconberg and all his works. We have informed him that the Lancastrian generals Warwick, and his brother the Marquess of Montague, were slain at Barnet; their corpses lie exposed in St Paul's. We have also sent Fauconberg a second letter proclaiming our King's great victory at Tewkesbury. And so, my son,' Christopher caught the sarcasm in his father's voice, 'we have tasks to complete.' He rose, came round the table, placing a hand on Christopher's shoulder, leaning down so close that Christopher could smell the ale on his father's breath. 'The hurling time is here, Christopher. Stay close to me and our family will rise like the evening star. Keep the Beaufort woman under close watch and, at the appropriate time, betray her. Lancaster is finished, yes?'

Christopher nodded and rose quickly to his feet so his father had to withdraw his hand. 'I swear,' Christopher held his father's gaze, 'that at the appropriate time, I shall betray the usurper.'

'Good, good. Now to these seditious commotions . . .'

For the next week, Urswicke busied himself around London, ostensibly at his father's behest, taking messages to Earl Rivers and other Yorkist commanders. Secretly, Urswicke kept a sharp eye on the quaysides and realised that for the moment it was nigh impossible for anyone to steal out of London.

Fauconberg eventually emerged but his first assault was paltry. One of his war cogs fired against an especially fortified gate at the Southwark end of London Bridge, whilst a barge, packed with his soldiers, set fire to some houses close by. Both attacks were easily beaten off. What secretly impressed Urswicke was the work of his father and other Yorkist leaders such as Lord Dudley, Earl Rivers and Mayor Stockton. They had prepared hastily yet greatly improved the city's defences. The gates at both ends of London Bridge had been strongly reinforced with bristling bulwarks. At the same time, the entire north bank of the Thames was being fortified from the Tower right up to Castle Baynard, with a barricade of wine pipes filled with sand and gravel, on which cannon, trebuchets and culverin were positioned so as to sweep the river approaches with a veritable firestorm.

Despite the emerging crisis, being busy on this or that task proved to be Urswicke's best defence and protection. He acted the bustling retainer though he realised he was being watched. In his journeys around the city he would stop to eat and drink in a variety of taverns or alehouses and concluded that he was being followed by different people at different times in various places. A swift glance around a taproom and he would search out an individual on his own, always busy on something; be it fixing a scabbard, cleaning a boot or sharpening a knife on a whetstone. Such people always made the same mistake. Urswicke would rise and cross to the counter or jake's room and the watcher would also make to move.

For the rest, Urswicke lodged at The Sunne in Splendour in Queenhithe ward with Mauclerc and the Three Kings. They had returned with him into the city, hiring chambers at this spacious, majestic tavern. Apparently its owner Minehost Tiptree was a former member of Clarence's household. The landlord intrigued Urswicke; a bland-faced, balding man, thin as a beanpole. He seemed gushing and welcoming, but Urswicke sensed the taverner's deep unease. On the one hand he was patronised by the most powerful lord in the kingdom, yet Urswicke would catch Tiptree staring at Mauclerc with a barely concealed disdain. Urswicke was also intrigued by what the Three Kings were actually doing,

his curiosity sharpened even further by the secrecy surrounding
their chancery chamber; this was always closely guarded by
one of the Three Kings and Urswicke was rarely invited to enter.
He also noticed how the tavern was visited by strangers dressed
in the brown and blue garb of what Urswicke reckoned to be
that of an obscure order of friars. These mysterious figures,
hooded and masked, would usher the occasional visitor, similarly
cloaked and cowled, into the tavern and up to the chancery
chamber, where they might stay for hours, before being just as
quietly taken away. Urswicke was tempted to eavesdrop or even
send messages about it to the Countess Margaret: in the end
he decided not to give Mauclerc any grounds for suspicion, as
Christopher was certain that those who prowled behind him
in the city were in the pay of Clarence's devious henchman.
Mauclerc wanted to be certain of him so Urswicke decided he
would wait for the countess to approach him.

On 14 May 1471, with fresh rumours sweeping the city,
Urswicke decided that the countess must have moved to contact
him. He gave his pursuers the slip and made his way down to St
Peter's-at-the-Cross in Cheap, an ancient church, its lancet windows
so narrow the nave was cloaked in perpetual darkness. Urswicke,
silent as a ghost, crept up the transept to the statue of St Peter
where he glimpsed the small scroll pushed into a wall niche directly
behind the statue. He took this out, unrolled it and noticed the
dates, 9th, 12th, 14th. Urswicke slipped the scrap of parchment
into his belt wallet and strode out of the church. He walked swiftly,
turning and twisting along the needle-thin alleyways like a hare
in a cornfield. At last Urswicke reached the The Wyvern's Nest,
where Hempen immediately took him down the cellar steps, along
the tunnel into the house opposite. Countess Margaret, Bray, Jasper
Tudor and the young Henry were breaking their fast in the solar.
Urswicke was warmly greeted, hands clasped, and then Urswicke
sat down, staring hard at Margaret's young son.

'I know what you're thinking,' Bray followed Urswicke's gaze,
'it's difficult, nigh impossible to get out of the city.' Bray stared
challengingly at Urswicke whom he did not fully trust.

'It's made even more difficult,' Margaret declared, 'because
you Christopher, myself and Reginald are followed, inspected and
scrutinised. To be out on the streets is to be noticed. If we take

young Henry into London, we would all be seized. Yet,' Margaret tried to keep her voice from turning tremulous, 'we cannot stay here. We may have a spy, a traitor in our own household who busily searches out our secrets.' Margaret let her worry hang like a noose in the air. Young Henry glanced nervously at his uncle, who grasped him by the shoulder and pressed reassuringly, whispering in Welsh. Urswicke studied Jasper Tudor, the Welsh lord's unshaven face and worn clothing. Tudor had disguised both himself and young Henry very cleverly and, as he stared at them, an idea took root, a subtle plot which Urswicke was sure he could bring to fruition.

'You are accepted by Mauclerc and his master the Earl of Clarence.' Margaret broke into his thoughts. 'He thinks you have done good work for the House of York?'

'Yes, I informed him about the agreement we tried to reach with Wenlock. I also gave Clarence precious information about the Angevin she-wolf and her son. The messages delivered to Wenlock were in a cipher: he replied in kind about the whereabouts of Margaret of Anjou.' Urswicke ignored Jasper Tudor's sharp intake of breath.

'Do not be shocked or surprised, kinsman,' Margaret retorted. 'We had to clear the field. The Angevin has had her day in the sun: her time and that of her arrogant, bloodthirsty son are over. Now,' Margaret spread her hands, 'this war has raged for over sixteen years not only in this kingdom but in France, the Low Countries and along the Narrow Seas.' She pushed back the platters on the table before her. 'Much of the same,' she continued, 'this war could have gone on for ever and ever Amen. Margaret of Anjou could have escaped from Tewkesbury and fled abroad with her son to continue this tedious, wearisome struggle. More invasions, armies marching, days of slaughter, of blood and mayhem: this will not happen now. The Sun of York is in its ascendency. However, one day young Henry here, and those who accept him, will emerge from the shadows. We must prepare for that. We must nurse and nurture our opposition.'

'And the old King?' Jasper Tudor abruptly paused as Margaret banged the table with the flat of her hand.

'God forgive me, God forgive us,' she retorted, 'but the old

King's day is also finished. Edward of York will soon be in London and any further threat to his rule will be ruthlessly destroyed. The old King will die of some sickness or a fall, or by a cause known only to God, but Henry will certainly die. We must make sure that his one and only legitimate heir,' she pointed at her son, 'escapes to plot his return to seize what is rightfully his.'

'And how do we do that?' Jasper paused at a clatter on the stairs outside and Hempen burst into the chamber.

'The searchers!' Margaret exclaimed, springing to her feet.

'No, it's Saveraux, master of the Breton cog *The Galicia*. He's in the tavern.'

'Bring him up,' Margaret ordered.

'Do you trust him?' Bray demanded.

'With my life,' Margaret snapped, then she smiled up at Bray. 'Reginald, we need to trust the few we really trust and we must act on that trust. Saveraux's sons and two brothers were hanged on Flamborough Head by Richard of York, Edward's father. They were executed on a special gallows which soared black against the sky. York falsely accused them of piracy. They were tried but given no opportunity to reply. Sentence was imposed and immediately carried out. Now Saveraux is a blessing, a Celt like you, Jasper: he has invoked the blood feud and taken the blood oath. He is the mortal enemy of Edward of York and all his kin. So yes, I trust him, Master Hempen, show him up.'

Saveraux was a balding, bulbous-eyed, burly mariner who stank of fish, tar and oil. He was garbed in dark-brown leather jacket and leggings with thick-soled, salt-encrusted sea boots. He swaggered into the room, thumbs thrust under his warbelt which sported a sword and two daggers. He bowed to Margaret, nodded at the rest and stood scratching his chin.

'Valuable information, my Lady, you may use it as you wish. But first let me tell you. I am moving *The Galicia* further down river, close to the approaches to the estuary.'

'Why?'

Saveraux grinned. 'Ah, that's my valuable information. Fauconberg and his allies are about to launch a surprise attack on the city. The assault will be two pronged. Fauconberg is to occupy St George's Fields, that great open space between

Lambeth and Southwark. He intends to range cannon and culverin along the riverbank opposite the city. He hopes to invade the city from the south whilst another host of rebels will force the northern defences to break through into Aldgate and Bishopsgate.'

'And your source for this?' Bray demanded.

'Wars come and go,' Saveraux retorted, 'but the sea remains. We mariners are a brotherhood with loyalties which have nothing to do with York, Lancaster or anybody else. To cut to the quick, one of Fauconberg's captains, a mercenary in charge of a war barge, came to warn me to move both my ship and my crew.'

'I believe you.' Margaret snapped her fingers at Urswicke. 'Christopher, swift as you can. Hasten to the Guildhall, tell your beloved father what you have learnt here. Do not betray your source but depict yourself, yet again, as a stalwart for the House of York.'

Urswicke did so. He reached the Guildhall safely where his father gave him a warm welcome. He listened carefully to Christopher's news and almost did a jig of joy. He summoned his clerks and, with Christopher lounging in a chair, despatched messages to Clarence and the other Yorkist commanders. Urswicke decided to stay with his father and learn as much as he could. He wondered about Saveraux's warning, yet the Breton captain was soon proved correct. Fauconberg's attack on the city was swift and savage. He secretly transported a force across the Thames to capture and hold both Aldgate and Bishopsgate so he and his henchmen could use these gateways to funnel more troops into the city. The attacks were led by two of Fauconberg's principal captains, Bardolph and Quintain.

Urswicke was despatched with messages to the Yorkist captain responsible for defending both of these city gates. The clerk, armed with sword and dagger, picked his way through the streets. As he approached the once-bustling towered gateways, Urswicke smelt the burning and glimpsed black columns of smoke streaming up against the clear summer sky. Many citizens had fled. The streets were deserted, though littered with the detritus of battle. Apparently the outworks of Aldgate had been forced, the fighting so savage and bitter, they'd been forced to drop the heavy portcullis on both defender and attacker. About six of the latter had been trapped inside the walls, caught and summarily

executed, their headless cadavers impaled upside down on the
approaches to the city gate.

The area around the defences was strewn with the dead.
Corpses sprawled everywhere; faces and heads smashed, bellies
ripped open, bones shattered, dreadful wounds caused by hand-
guns and sharp arrow-storms delivered at close quarter. Smoke
billowed to obscure the view so Urswicke simply followed the
raucous din of battle. The fog of powder and fire parted and
Urswicke glimpsed his father in sallet and mailed jerkin mounting
a warhorse in preparation to lead a counter-attack. The destrier
was caparisoned for battle, eager to charge, its sharp hooves
impatiently scraping the cobbles. Around the Recorder milled
men-at-arms and archers wearing the city livery. Urswicke
glimpsed his son and pointed his sword at him, lifting the visor
which protected his mouth.

'We will drive them back!' he roared. 'Christopher, go down to
the bridge, see what is happening there. For the rest . . .'

Christopher's father lifted his sword and the soldiers around
him shouted their approval. The entrance to Aldgate was cleared
and the Recorder and his troops surged through. One of the men-
at-arms, left behind because of wounds to his arms and face,
informed Christopher that the rebels were in full retreat, falling
back on St Botolph's Church. Urswicke thanked him, turned
away, and hurried down towards the Tower, threading the streets
where makeshift barricades, bulwarks and bastions had been
hastily assembled. Stout cords and chains had been dragged
across the streets and alleyways to impede the enemy. Urswicke
was also warned to be wary of the caltrops strewn across the
cobbles; sharp, cruel traps to bring down both man and beast.

Using the warrants his father and Mauclerc had provided,
Urswicke safely negotiated his passage. He pushed his way
through the press of city militia as well as the mob, a swarm of
cutpurses and thieves who'd crawled out of their filthy dens to
see what mischief could be had. As was usual during any unrest
in the city, foreigners were singled out for punishment. Makeshift
gallows set up at street corners were decorated with the dirt-strewn,
twisting corpses of Flemish prostitutes seized from the nearby
brothels; mouldy, mildewed mansions which had been sacked
and put to the torch. More respectable foreigners had flooded

into the churches to seek sanctuary or hidden in the houses of merchant friends along Cheapside.

Urswicke eventually reached the bridge where city troops massed under their captains, a moving horde of heavily armoured men, packing the approaches to the river. Engineers pushed their bombards, culverins and cannons down towards the Thames. Dirty-faced street urchins who served as powder monkeys for the engineers, scampered around the huge war carts. Stacks of corpses killed in the furious affray which had raged across the bridge ranged two yards high, though now it was all over. The rebels had seized the first gateway on the Southwark side and burned a number of houses. Urswicke, however, soon realised that Faulconberg's troops had been severely defeated, beaten back by the bridge defenders as well as city troops who had crossed the Thames by barge and were now threatening to encircle the rebels. The attack was over and Urswicke realised it was time to rejoin the countess . . .

By 18 May, the rebels had fled the city. Yorkist forces, together with the levies raised in the city, pursued the rebels deep into Essex and Kent. Urswicke decided to act. He begged Saveraux to bring *The Galicia* to Queenhithe, berth it there and act as normally as possible. Urswicke personally checked the Breton cog, a large, deep-bellied two-masted ship with a lofty stern and prow. Once he was sure *The Galicia* was safely berthed in Queenhithe, Urswicke asked the countess to hold an urgent meeting of her small council. They all gathered in the solar of the narrow house opposite The Wyvern's Nest. Night was falling, the only light being that from candles and flickering lanterns. Once assembled, Urswicke described his plan, adding that they had to act now. Saveraux and his ship were ready, whilst Edward of York and his entire host would soon be in the city. Once he arrived, an even closer guard and watch would be imposed over the quaysides, whilst the length and breadth of the river and all its ports would be ruled by martial law, and that included the likes of Saveraux, his ship as well as other foreign cogs.

The Breton loudly agreed with Urswicke, adding that he would have to flee before any attempt was made to detain him. Bray, ever cautious, argued heatedly for doing nothing, but Urswicke, his mind and wits sharp as a razor, countered that.

He argued that the difficulties raised were nothing compared to the real danger of following any other path. If Lord Jasper and young Henry fled back to Wales, Urswicke declared, there was a strong possibility of being captured and summarily dealt with. A savage, swift death was all they could expect in some desolate spinney or lonely wood. Even if they reached Pembroke safely, what then?

Urswicke described how Edward of York was already laying siege to the castle by land and sea. How could Lord Jasper and the prince enter the castle, and would they be really safe there? If they stayed in London, the net would tighten. Sooner or later they would make a mistake, the danger being all the sharper if there truly was a traitor in the countess's household. Nor must they forget the watchers in the street, the spies swarming everywhere, the sharp and observant street swallows and sparrowhawks. True, the city was a mass of winding, stinking alleyways, but what would happen if Edward of York imposed martial law, sealing off each ward and conducting a house-by-house search?

Urswicke argued long and persuasively. He could tell by her silence that the countess was listening most intently to his suggestion and eventually she agreed, adding that, if this stratagem went awry, they could always devise some other subtle way forward. They were committed. The countess, Lord Jasper Tudor and the now fearful Henry realised there was no better plan. The Yorkist bloodlust was up. Already rumours were seeping in that royal troops were pursuing the rebels into Essex and Kent, inflicting dire punishments on all those who'd taken up arms. Individuals such as Nicholas Faunte, the Mayor of Canterbury who had decided to support Fauconberg, suffered the full penalty for treason, being hanged, drawn and quartered in the market square of his own city. The tarred, torn remnants of his corpse, along with his head poled above the city gates. Urswicke urged Jasper and Henry to prepare themselves by the evening of the following day, adding that he would counsel and advise them on what they must do so as to be ready to depart on 20 May.

Early on the chosen day, Urswicke presented himself in his father's chamber at the Guildhall. The Recorder, still brimming with glee and good humour at what he described as 'the city's great victory against the rebels', didn't realise at first the full significance of what his son was telling him. He sat, mouth gaping, and then asked Christopher to repeat what he had said. Urswicke did. He explained how downstairs in the Guildhall parlour were a man and his son, wandering beggars, scavengers along Queenhithe who had glimpsed well-garbed strangers being brought secretly aboard a Breton cog, *The Galicia*. The Recorder stared down at the tabletop, rubbing his hands, then he lifted his head and smiled at Christopher.

'We will surely profit from this, my son.' And, springing to his feet, he called a servant and told Christopher to wait until his good friend, as he described Mauclerc, came striding into the chamber. Clarence's henchman swaggered in booted and cloaked, a broad warbelt strapped around his waist.

'Master Christopher,' he exclaimed, 'what is this, what is this?' Urswicke repeated his story and Mauclerc demanded that the beggars, both father and son, be brought up for questioning. Urswicke agreed; going down to the parlour he ushered up the two informants, shaven and shorn, garbed in filthy rags, their bare feet slapping the floor. Urswicke introduced Ragwort and Henbane, father and son, who'd assumed the names of herbs. The beggars spent their lives scavenging backwards and forwards across the quaysides of London, especially Queenhithe, begging for what could be had and desperate for any opportunity to earn a coin or a platter of food. Both Ragwort and Henbane, dancing from foot to foot, filthy faces set in a manic grin which showed yellow, blackening teeth, listened intently. They both nodded vigorously as Urswicke described how they earned a living and, like others of their brotherhood, were paid by him to report anything suspicious.

'And?'

Thomas Urswicke, summoning up all his authority as Recorder, strode round the table and advanced threateningly towards the two beggars, who fell to their knees, hands joined in supplication.

'And?' the Recorder repeated. 'What?' He crouched down before the beggars. 'What did you see?'

'We were collecting pieces of coal which a barge had brought up, Your Magnificence. It was after the present troubles.' Ragwort was almost gabbling as he placed a hand on his son's bony shoulder. 'Henbane here glimpsed it – sharp he is,' Ragwort continued in a sing-song voice, 'keen as a knife, even though his hearing and tongue are not what God wants them to be. Anyway,' Ragwort scratched his son's balding skull and gently pushed him away, 'sharp-eyed, he glimpsed two men, well garbed, faces and heads hidden. They were shepherding a youth whose hood fell back, tugged by the river breeze, before he pulled it up again. Perhaps a youth no older than Henbane himself, fourteen to fifteen summers. They pushed him swiftly up onto a Breton ship. We drew closer and watched. We learnt its captain was Saveraux and the cog is called *The Galicia*. We only saw them for a few heartbeats as they disappeared up the gangplank. We set up careful watch: those strangers, hooded, visored and in a hurry, never came off that ship. Nothing more than that.' Ragwort sniffed and wiped his nose on the back of a dirty hand. 'We heard about the proclamations,' Ragwort's whining voice stumbled over the words, 'we glimpsed the watchers, the spies,' the beggar licked his lips, 'we've also heard of the great reward . . .'

He paused as Thomas Urswicke drew his dagger and pressed the tip under Ragwort's chin. 'If you are lying,' he grated, 'you will suffer the consequences.'

'Let us find out.' Mauclerc strode swiftly to the door and shouted orders to his retainers thronging outside. He turned. 'Master Thomas, you are with us?'

'As always.'

The Recorder beckoned at Christopher and ordered two men-at-arms, standing guard just within the doorway, to take Ragwort and Henbane into custody. 'You,' the Recorder pointed at the two beggars, 'will come with us.'

Mauclerc came hurrying back. 'I have sent urgent messages,' he declared, 'to the royal cog of war, *The Morning Star*, moored in port, to sail down to Queenhithe. It is to keep *The Galicia* under strict scrutiny and, if necessary, make sure it does not slip its moorings. We also have men-at-arms and hobelars assembling. Come, Come.' Mauclerc snapped his fingers. 'We will seize and search the Breton ship.'

A short while later Mauclerc led the Urswickes, the two beggars and a phalanx of armed men, both retainers and city liveries, out of the Guildhall gates. They pushed their way through the morning crowd, the soldiers clearing the path in front of them with spears, halberds and drawn swords. The air was cool, a faint river mist still curled around the stalls being set up for a new day's trading. Chapel bells clanged their summons to morning mass. Trumpets, horns and bagpipes wailed as bailiffs led the captive roisterers, night-walkers and other violaters of the King's peace down to the stocks, thews and pillories. Every one scattered at their approach. The streets, alleys and runnels leading down to the river swiftly emptied as the dark-dwellers slunk back into their dens and mumpers' castles. A deathly stillness greeted Mauclerc's war band. The Yorkist victories, as well as the abrupt and humiliating retreat of Fauconberg along with other rebels, had imposed a watchful peace over the city. The Guildhall had issued proclamation after proclamation how any disturbance would be regarded as treason against both Crown and city.

They eventually reached Queenhithe; the quayside was awash with the guts and heads of fish netted earlier in the day. These turned the ground underfoot greasy and slippery, whilst the air reeked of fire, brine and other more fetid odours. A sharp breeze tugged at their cloaks. Mauclerc shouted and pointed to the great war cog, *The Morning Star*, making its way out to mid-river before it turned and drew closer to the quayside. *The Galicia* had already cleared its berth and was ready to sail when Mauclerc ordered one of his soldiers to blow three blasts on a powerful hunting horn. Saveraux, now aware of the armed cohort on the quayside, as well as *The Morning Star* bearing down fast, immediately hove to. Sails were quickly reefed and the Breton brought his cog back along the quayside. The royal warship followed, drawing so close that *The Galicia* could only leave with its permission. A great deal of shouting ensued. The Recorder lifted his warrants to display their seals whilst a herald shouted that Saveraux's ship could only sail with permission of both Crown and city.

At last the Breton cog was fully berthed. A section of side rails were moved and a gangplank lowered. Christopher Urswicke led the charge across this, the soldiers spilling out and, following Mauclerc's orders, immediately broke into the small captain's cabin beneath the stern whilst the Recorder demanded to see the cog's licences, warrants and manifests. Screaming and gesticulating how, despite the fact that he was in an English harbour,

Saveraux protested that he was a Breton and that both he and his ship were under the direct protection of Duke Francis of Brittany. He shouted how he would, as soon as he reached Nantes or La Rochelle, lodge the most serious complaint. Saveraux gabbled on, only to fall silent as Mauclerc lifted the point of his sword to only a few inches from the Breton's face.

'We need to see your muster rolls and other documentation,' Mauclerc insisted. 'What is your cargo, what does your manifest say? And I want them now. Come on, come on.' He snapped his fingers. 'Give me the muster roll. Better still, I want the entire ship's company here on the main deck. Christopher,' Mauclerc gestured at Saveraux, 'show him the reason for our visit.'

Urswicke sheathed his sword and dragged Ragwort and Henbane across the deck, holding each by the arm. He pushed these towards the Breton who just turned and neatly spat on the deck between them. He was about to turn away.

'This precious pair,' Urswicke declared, 'could lead to your arrest whilst your cog and all it holds would be impounded.'

Saveraux walked forward.

'Tell him!' Urswicke yelled, shaking both beggars vigorously. 'Tell him what you saw.'

Ragwort repeated their story. Saveraux would have lunged at him if Christopher and one of the men-at-arms had not intervened, pushing the two beggars out of the way. Saveraux just shook his head, spitting dangerously close to Urswicke's boots.

'I know of no such visitors,' he protested. 'No well-garbed young man has been brought onto this cog.' Again he spat. 'I carry bales of English wool to Dordrecht in Hainault and more for the Staple at Calais. Now search my ship, question my crew. I tell the truth.'

Christopher shoved the beggars away and watched his father and Mauclerc organise a most thorough search of the hold, its supplies, cargo and weapon store. Nothing was found. The ship's crew was mustered. Each man declared his name and origin, which the Recorder carefully compared with what was entered on the muster roll. At last the search and questioning drew to a close. Saveraux, now protesting his innocence, and quoting the trade treaties between Duke Francis and the English Crown, shouted that he would lodge the most serious complaint. He and his ship were Bretons. If this violation of their rights continued, Duke Francis would surely retaliate against English ships and merchants. Mauclerc and the Recorder had no choice but to agree. A trumpeter blew a blast whilst the herald shouted across the water to the captain of *The Morning Star* that *The Galicia* now had permission to sail.

'And what about these,' Saveraux pointed to Ragwort and Henbane, 'the source of all this nonsense?'

'Oh yes,' Christopher retorted swiftly, drawing a leather club out of his warbelt. He strode across the deck and began to beat both beggars until they fell to their knees, hands out, crying for mercy. Christopher ended his tirade by giving both unfortunates a vigorous kick and throwing the leather club down at Saveraux's feet.

'Take these two nithings down river, as far as you can. Leave them on a sandbank. The water there is shallow enough and, if they want, they can clamber ashore and walk back to whatever midden heap they crawled from.'

Saveraux needed no second bidding. He grasped both beggars, throwing them roughly down into the black, stinking hold, shouting how they would receive further beatings before they left his ship. Both Mauclerc and Urswicke's father had now lost interest in the proceedings and led their cohort back down the gangplank. Christopher followed and, without a backward glance, strode across the cobbles and into the tangle of alleyways which ran from Queenhithe up into the city.

Later that day, when the Vesper bells clanged across the city and the beacon lights flared in the church steeples, Christopher Urswicke sat in a flower arbour at The Lamb of God, a spacious, stately tavern overlooking Cheapside. Christopher watched the shadows of the massive oak trees creep across the well-tended grass, the first fingers of darkness beginning to curl around the flower beds and herb pots. A small fountain, carved in the shape of a pelican striking its breast, tinkled and glittered. Somewhere in the tavern a casement window hung open and the soft, sweet sound of a lutist playing a lullaby drifted out into the velvet darkness. Urswicke half closed his eyes as he stared into the gathering dark. He pretended he was in his father's garden and his mother, bright faced and busy, would come out through the kitchen door, humming some soft song, hurrying to sit by him on the turf seat. She would put an arm around him and talk about the little people, magical creatures who lived in a small cave at the far end of the garden. Urswicke blinked away the tears as he let himself go gently back into the past, well away from the terrors of the day with all its ever-present dangers. Tomorrow would be different. He must sleep well tonight and prepare. The news was all over the city. Edward of York was advancing in full splendour on London.

'Christopher, Christopher?' Urswicke startled, immediately stretching out for the warbelt on the bench beside him. 'Christopher, it's me.' Urswicke peered through the gathering murk at the Countess Margaret with her constant shadow Reginald Bray.

'Christopher?'

Bray gestured towards the tavern. 'You hired a chamber?'

'Aye.' Urswicke got to his feet. 'A well-sealed room furnished with all we need.'

'Good, good.' Margaret looked up at the sky. 'Thanks to you, Christopher, my son and my kinsman Jasper are now safely on the Narrow Seas.'

Christopher mockingly bowed.

'My Lady, they will be bruised and hurt after the beating I gave them. But those who hunted your son now believe that *The Galicia* simply carried away two beggars to be punished even further. I must admit,' Urswicke grinned, 'I prepared them well, blotched and stained, clad in ragged clothes. Lord Jasper is skilled in accents whilst young Henry simply had to act the sharp-eyed mute.'

'It was a risk,' Bray countered.

'A calculated one, I agree, but neither Mauclerc nor my father has ever seen Jasper Tudor or the young Henry. No accurate description of either of them is available. I set a trap and my father walked into it without a second thought. No one doubted my story, as I have been a constant source of good intelligence. Why should I be wrong about those two?' He paused, chewing the corner of his lip. 'Ah well, now they are out of harm's way. Saveraux will see they are safely delivered. Ours was a most cunning and subtle device. I have seen it used before to hide someone or something in full view. One day, not now but in the future, when Fickle Fortune gives her wheel another spin, I would love to tell my father the full truth behind what happened.'

'In the meantime,' Margaret declared, 'Edward of York is about to enter London and we must prepare, plot and plan. We must also use the old King's writ to move around this city – soon, I suspect, such a writ will be worth nothing!'

The Yorkist lords swept into London on the morning of 24 May. Edward met the mayor and leading citizens of the city in the meadowlands between Islington and Shoreditch. He received their assurances that his leading city was completely free of all rebels whilst those captured were now no more, their severed heads and steaming quarters being despatched to hang above the city gates or along the railings of London Bridge. The Yorkist King responded to such loyalty by knighting from horseback his fervent supporters in the city, including Thomas Urswicke. Once the ceremony was completed, the royal herald proclaimed they would now advance into London, processing to St Paul's, where His Grace the King could view the naked corpses of his enemies, Warwick and the others. Trumpets and clarions blew. Standards and banners were unfurled. Shouted proclamations issued as the cortège, including three dukes and all the leading barons of the kingdom, solemnly wound their way into the city. Marshalled behind the royal party were others, including Countess Margaret, since she was a Beaufort as well as the wife of a Yorkist lord. She had been summoned to trail behind the King's cortège, along with other leading ladies of the court.

During the initial ceremonies Margaret simply sat patiently on a palfrey. She had done her best to honour the occasion, being garbed in a gown of blue and gold and wearing a wimpled head-dress of the same colour and texture. She had been informed that the procession would take hours so she wore elegant leather riding boots and grasped the reins of her gentle-eyed mount, her hands protected by the softest, doeskin gloves. All around her were others, including Bray and Urswicke, suitably apparelled and well horsed. Margaret did her best to steel herself against this show of Yorkist glory and triumph. She had to accept this was harvest time, the sowing had been bloody and so would the reaping. She had to remain impassive and act the part. As the

royal procession was organised, the countess became more
intrigued by Edward's principal captive, the fallen Queen
Margaret of Anjou. The Angevin, dressed in a simple red gown
which covered her from neck to bare, soiled feet, sat on the bench
of a prison cart pulled by two huge dray horses, their hogged
manes and plaited tails garlanded with purple ribbons. The
Angevin sat, hands on her knees, staring dully into the main
distance, her lips moving soundlessly. Margaret couldn't decide
if the fallen Queen was praying, talking to herself or humming
a tune: she looked a pathetic sight, her once-golden hair faded
and streaked with white; the former Queen seemed like some
felon being taken from Newgate to the gibbet over Tyburn Stream.
The prison cart stood alongside the royal cortège. Few gave the
former Queen a second glance, even the crowds who swirled in
a sea of colour and a mixture of smells, ignored this pathetic
relic of former glory. Margaret studied the Angevin and decided
to make good use of her presence in London.

The rest of that day Margaret played out the role assigned to
her. The royal procession swept through the city to be greeted
ecstatically. The citizens, encouraged by Edward of York's
agents and gang-leaders, welcomed the victor of Tewkesbury
back into London. White silk and linen cloths hung from the
open casement windows of the mansions along Cheapside.
Carpets, cloths of gold, sheets of Rennes linen, coverlets and
counterpanes of the richest material were draped over the various
city crosses and statues. Fountains and conduits disgorged free
wine, ale, beer and different kinds of fruit drinks. The stalls of
Cheapside groaned under great platters of food piled high. City
bailiffs, armed with clubs, stood on guard against the legion of
beggars who watched all this with glittering eyes and empty
bellies. At last the royal procession wound its way back into
the Tower, preceded by the fallen Queen who had acted stoic-
ally throughout this long and public humiliation. At the Lion
Gate, the yawning, hollowed entrance to the fortress, the procession broke up. Most of the courtiers streamed back into the city
to participate in the festivities, feasting and frivolities which
would last into the early hours.

Countess Margaret noticed how the King and his two brothers
ignored this; they seemed unwilling to leave immediately but

rode up the dark, sinister gullies which cut through that formidable fortress into the great bailey before the soaring White Tower,
freshly painted to welcome York's return. Countess Margaret
and her henchmen followed Edward and his brothers. Eventually
the royal party, together with chosen henchmen such as Mauclerc,
Hastings and others, adjourned to the King's apartments, close
to the chapel of St John on the second gallery of the White Tower.
The Angevin Queen was handed over to the constable, the
grim-faced John Dudley. He ignored her cry that once he had
fought for Lancaster, and ordered her to be taken across to
be lodged in the Wakefield, the same tower which housed her
husband

Countess Margaret decided to bide her time. The evening was
warm and balmy. The setting sun, still strong, bathed the bailey
in a welcoming light. Margaret sat down on a stone bench close
to the Chapel of St Peter in Chains, watching the Tower people
streaming backwards and forwards, though she noticed they were
kept well away from the steps of the White Tower, closely guarded
by a phalanx of archers, men-at-arms and knight bannerets.
Margaret posed, all composed, listening to the cattle lowing and
the pigs screeching as they were herded up to slaughter pens.
She caught the tang of cooking from the Tower kitchens, which
mixed with the different smells from the stables and outhouses
around the bailey. She watched a group of women busy at the
wells, washing clothes as well as pots and pans from the buttery.
Margaret glanced over her shoulder at Bray and Urswicke who
stood deep in conversation. She invited them over to sit either
side of her.

'What now, Mistress?' Bray demanded.

'What now, sir?' She mocked back. 'What were you discussing?'

'The traitor, Mistress, we have a traitor in the household,' Bray
insisted. 'As you know, I suspected Christopher, I even began to
suspect myself. Had I made some hideous mistake? But now,'
he lowered his voice, 'I have reflected and so has my friend here.
Looking back at what has happened, reflecting on past events, there
is no doubt that our enemies, although they did not know for certain,
suspected something very important, crucial to our cause, was
happening. Our visits to The Wyvern's Nest were necessary but
our secret, even furtive movements in going backwards and

forwards from there deeply agitated our opponents. Christopher and I believe that someone in our household knew that we were fervently involved in a matter vital to the Lancastrian house. Such a traitor did not know the details but they conveyed their suspicions to the Recorder and the likes of Mauclerc.' Bray paused. 'In a word, Mistress, we suspect Owain and Oswina, it must be them . . .'

'Nonsense, nonsense!' Margaret leaned forward, peering through the gathering murk. 'Surely not, surely not,' she half whispered. 'I too had my suspicions, I too have reflected, yet Owain and Oswina are like kin. We have the blood-tie between us. Surely they would not play the Judas? No, no,' she shook her head, 'no,' she whispered, 'not with me, surely?' Margaret held up her hands, forefingers entwined. 'Owain and Oswina are twins; they are like that, bound together. If the sister goes out of our house, the brother always accompanies her. Yet when I made my own enquiries, I understand the twins never left Sir Humphrey's mansion, whilst no strangers were seen approaching them or, indeed, any of my household. So . . .' She paused as Sir John Dudley came down the steps out of the White Tower. Margaret rose and walked swiftly towards him.

'Sir John, a word?' She grasped the constable by the sleeve, taking him away from his escort.

'My Lady.' The constable leaned down. 'I have heard how your husband was sorely wounded at Barnet.'

'He lies grievously ill,' she agreed, and stared pleadingly up at him. 'Another widow to be, eh Sir John?' She shrugged prettily. 'Surely you must, as a widower, recognise how lonely it can be?' Dudley grasped her right hand, raised it and kissed her fingertips.

'In such circumstances, my Lady, I would hasten to give you any help and whatever comfort you needed.'

Margaret smiled brilliantly and moved a little closer. 'Lord John,' she murmured, 'times are changing. New alliances are being formed. The past is dead. Our King is triumphant and soon I must return to my manor and poor Sir Humphrey. So, Sir John, I would like to visit the Angevin queen and my royal kinsman.' She paused. 'Is that possible?'

Dudley pursed his, lips deep in thought. Margaret gently rested a gloved hand on his wrist. 'You know what is going to happen,' she whispered hoarsely, 'I am of the court party. My loyalty to Edward of York cannot be doubted, but these two prisoners, Sir John for pity's sake, for the mercy we all ask of the Lord, let me say my farewells before I leave London.' She dabbed the tears from her eyes then struck her breast. 'Sir John, Sir John, I beg you. What harm is there in saying farewell?'

Dudley quickly agreed. Margaret was taken over to the Wakefield and ushered into the chamber allocated to the fallen Queen. Dudley then left. The Angevin was sitting in a high-backed chair, the small table beside her had a platter of bread and cheese next to a jug of wine and a deep bowled pewter goblet. Little had been done to prepare the cell, which was as gaunt and stark as any corpse chamber in a death house: a cot bed, a chest, some candles and a few stools. Cobwebs spanned the ceiling like nets. Mice scrabbled in a corner whilst the shutters across the lancet windows rattled in the strengthening night breeze. The Angevin peered at Margaret as the countess pulled up a stool in front of her.

'The little Beaufort woman,' she rasped, 'I remember you. The last of your family eh?' The Angevin put her face in her hands and sobbed quietly for a while. Margaret just watched the flame on the squat tallow candle which marked the passage of time in broad red rings. The usual noises of the Tower were now fading, but she heard the sound of revelry and she wondered if the Yorkist warlords were celebrating the annihilation of their foes, including this broken woman who had fought them for years. The Angevin took her hands away and frowned at Margaret. 'Night is gathering,' she whispered, 'and I am finished. My husband, I understand, lies imprisoned in this very tower. My son is murdered, as are all your family. The Beauforts are no more. So what do you want with me, little woman?'

'The "Titulus Regius" – what do you know?'

'I don't know anything and, if I did, why should I tell you? My cause is finished. You rode in the Yorkist triumph. I saw you watching me constantly.' The Angevin showed some of her old imperiousness, pulling herself up in the chair, shaking herself, staring around as if to summon servants. 'Why should I talk to you, Beaufort? Why should I tell you anything?'

'You should tell me,' Margaret countered, 'for a number of reasons. First, I may have ridden in the Yorkist entourage, but I had no choice. I am not their friend or ally, in fact the opposite. They wish to keep me close not because of any love but to mount careful guard over me, which they do constantly. Secondly, the Yorkist lords fear me because secretly they recognise me as a rival; and so I am – or at least my son is.'

'Where is he?'

'Safely spirited away. His existence, his survival, means our struggle goes on, the dream of winning recognition for the House of Lancaster. Our cause will not die this day; in fact, it may now move from strength to strength.'

'Edward and his siblings rejoice . . .'

'For today, but the tensions are there. Edward's wife is a Woodville, she and her family are truly hated by both of Edward's brothers. A great weakness, easy to exploit, as Scripture says, "A House divided against itself cannot stand." Oh, these halcyon days of York will end soon enough. Divisions, enmities and deep hostilities will emerge. None more powerful than the overweaning ambition of George of Clarence. We know that he works on justifying his own claim to the throne. He and his most trusted confidants have a book, a manuscript, a chronicle called the "Titulus Regius". What if such a work became public knowledge? Would it seriously weaken the claims to the throne of both Clarence's brothers? My Lady,' Margaret urged, stretching forward to touch the former Queen's knee, 'I need to discover the truth about all this. I have learnt that the "Titulus Regius" is the creation of three clerks in Clarence's Secret Chancery. They work under the supervision of Mauclerc, Clarence's principal henchman.

'And so it is.' The Angevin relaxed, slumping further down in her chair. She picked up the goblet and drank noisily. 'And what do I get if I tell you what I know . . . which,' she waved the goblet, 'is not much?'

'You are a prisoner here,' Margaret replied. 'Now I do have some influence to make things a little easier, more comfortable for you. Edward of York has to be careful. You are a princess of Anjou, a former Queen of England, a noble woman of ancient lineage. True, the Yorkists wish to parade you through London;

however, from what I know of King Edward and his brother Richard, they have no great appetite for humiliating a captured lady who has suffered so much. I could persuade them that you could be lodged with your old friend the Duchess of Suffolk in much more luxurious quarters at Wallingford Castle . . .' Margaret paused. 'I also have some influence with Duke Francis of Brittany, as well as King Louis of France. Nor must you forget your father, René of Anjou. News travels fast. Your father will not be pleased at your plight. This kingdom depends on trade, on English cogs sailing wherever they wish. The powerful merchants, the men of real power, would not want foreign ports closed to their shipping. Of course, I cannot proclaim this all in a day but like water dripping onto a stone . . .'

'You would do that?' The Angevin's eyes narrowed.

'I would try my very best, I swear that on the life of my son. So, the "Titulus Regius"?'

'As you know,' the Angevin replied, 'during the civil war, Clarence deserted his family, full of his own ambition, he joined myself and Warwick in exile. Clarence is insufferable. He often insinuated that he was the only true Yorkist claimant to the throne. At first we ignored him, being involved in our own struggle. We then heard of Mauclerc and the Three Kings. Of course you know of them?' Margaret nodded. 'Believe me,' the Angevin held up a hand, 'those four are Clarence's creatures to the very marrow of their souls. We heard they were searching for evidence for this or that, God knows truly what, but Clarence seemed cock-sure of himself. Others in my party heard about this secret work, the "Titulus Regius" but we were unable to discover the manuscript, the actual text. Warwick's people even hired the most skilled picklocks to open the chest and coffers in Clarence's chancery.' She shook her head. 'Nothing came of that. And so there's the real mystery. What is the evidence Clarence is trying to collect? How is it preserved?'

'And only Mauclerc and the Three Kings know this?'

'No, I would say only the Three Kings themselves. From what we learnt, even Clarence and his leading henchman do not know. They have not yet received the full extent of the secrets that the Three Kings are digging up. There is one other, a parchment seller. I believe he trades under the sign of "The Red Keg" on Fleet Street. I do not know his name, but Clarence once referred to him as a fellow seeker of the truth. This parchment- or book-seller is a Rhinelander; he is also involved in searching for evidence to bolster Clarence's claims: be it parchment or person, anything or anyone to assist in the mischief they are brewing.' The Angevin sipped from her goblet. 'There is,' she sighed, 'no real secret about what Clarence truly intends. The real mystery is what have his clerks actually collected and, as I have said, where is it preserved?' The Angevin now became quite heated. 'I have told you this, little Beaufort, and I say it again: no one knows anything about the details, even though Clarence passed through the House of York to that of Lancaster and then back again. As I have said, his manuscripts were carefully scru- tinised not only by the likes of your kinsmen the Beauforts but even by his own brothers. Nothing! Nothing has ever been found!' The Angevin shook her head. 'I can say no more because I know no more.' She glanced pitifully at Margaret. 'A boon, a favour, my Lady?'

'If I can.'

'My saintly husband,' the Angevin's words dripped with sarcasm, 'is lodged above in the oratory chamber. Would you please take messages to him, assure my Lord of my love and my loyalty. Tell him . . .'

The Angevin bit her lip as tears welled in her eyes. 'Never mind. Never mind,' she whispered. 'All is done, all is lost, all is dark.'

Margaret realised the Angevin would tell her no more. She searched out Dudley who had been drinking in the royal quarters, a timber and plaster mansion close to the chapel of St Peter in Chains. Full of ale and benevolence, he agreed to Margaret visiting the imprisoned Henry.

'For a short while, for a short while,' Dudley slurred, 'and then Mistress, if it so pleases you, join me and my comrades at the table.'

Margaret smiled understandingly and allowed the constable, deep in his cups, to escort her up the stone spiral staircase of the Wakefield Tower. Two soldiers stood on guard outside the half-open door to the old King's prison chamber. Dudley pushed this open and waved Margaret in, closing the door quietly behind her. The light was poor. The room full of flitting shadows. Margaret glimpsed the streaks of light from the small oratory and heard the patter of a psalm: 'Out of the depths have I cried to you, oh Lord. Lord hear my voice.'

Margaret entered the small oratory shaped in a semi-circle, a narrow window high in the wall. Henry was kneeling on a prie-dieu, arms extended, staring up at the stark crucifix at the centre of the altar. Margaret coughed. Henry, however, continued to pray until he had finished the 'Gloria'. Once completed, he blessed himself and rose, shaking the shabby blue robe which covered him from neck to sandalled feet. A wooden crucifix hung around his neck, a friar's girdle with its three knots symbolising obedience, poverty and chastity about his slender waist. Ave beads wreathed his fingers. He looked gaunt, more hollow-eyed, and blood-encrusted spots peppered his mouth.

'Sister?' Henry stretched out his hands towards her. 'Angels have visited me here. Truly they did. Now I have one in the flesh.' He stepped into the pool of light thrown by a tallow candle, ushering Margaret out of the oratory.

'I bring messages, your Grace.'

Margaret paused at the sound of growing revelry; drunken men rejoicing in their victory, shouting the war cries of the House of York. Henry stood listening to the clamour, then he turned, lips murmuring as if he was talking to someone Margaret could not see. She felt the full pathos of this encounter: a shabby, former King standing in a dingy chamber with candle-flame flickering and shadows shifting, his mocking enemies only a short distance away. Margaret tensed. The cries and shouts were growing closer. The sound of spurred boots echoing on the hard flagstones of the tower staircase. Henry half turned as if listening more acutely. He then grabbed Margaret by the shoulder.

'Someone,' he hissed, his mouth close to her face, 'someone warned me that they would come.'

Margaret caught his alarm, his wild panic. The booted steps seemed to carry their own dreadful menace. The devils were closing in! Henry abruptly pushed Margaret back into the chamber and across to the lavarium, an enclave built into the wall with a carved water bowl and a jake's hole hidden behind a heavy latticed screen, its woven wood much decayed and crumbling.

Margaret stood there holding her breath as Henry pushed the screen as close as he could before hastening back into the oratory. From where she stood, Margaret could see him once again kneel on the prie-dieu, arms extended before the crucifix. The door to the prison chamber crashed open. Three figures entered the room. The foremost, Richard of Gloucester, carried a night lantern; its glow illuminated the cold features of Mauclerc and the drunken, slobbery menace of Clarence. All three were dressed in half-armour with mailed surcoats, each carried sword and club. They swept into the oratory where Henry continued to pray, his voice growing louder as he intoned the great mercy psalm.

'Have mercy on me oh God in your great kindness . . .'

Mauclerc stepped forward and shoved him in the shoulder. Margaret watched in deepening horror as the murderous mystery play began to unfold in that ancient chamber, with its oratory lit by dancing candle-flame. All around flitted shadows, as if the ghosts were gathering to watch this bloody masque unfold. The old King, tottering on his feet, rose to meet his visitors. Gloucester stepped forward, still holding sword and club. Henry stretched out his hands in greeting. Margaret caught his words of welcoming, 'to his dear, sweet cousins'. Gloucester sheathed his sword, dropped the club and walked out of the chamber. Henry now turned to Mauclerc and Clarence.

'What do you want with me? Shouldn't you,' Henry's voice rose, 'shouldn't you now kneel in the presence of your King as I now kneel in the presence of mine?' Henry then shrugged, flailing his hands, as if his visitors were of no importance. He went back to the prie-dieu. Margaret caught her breath as Clarence steeped forward, raised his club and brought it down time and time again on the old King's head. Henry slumped onto the prie-dieu then slipped to the floor, still mouthing the words of the mercy psalm. For a while he lay, arms and legs jerking. Mauclerc, at Clarence's invitation, stepped closer and delivered a final cracking blow. Henry lay still. Clarence kicked the body, grabbed Mauclerc by the arm and both men hurried out of the chamber. Margaret waited until they had gone. She slipped from behind the screen and hurried across into the oratory.

Henry was dead. He sprawled, head to one side, eyes half open, mouth gaping, the pool of blood widening, the back of his skull shattered like a broken pot. Margaret hastily crossed herself, murmured the requiem and left. The stairwell outside and the steps leading into the Wakefield Tower were now deserted. No sound except the screech of bats winging their way above her. All guards, officials and servants of the Tower appeared to have been withdrawn so the old King's execution could be swiftly carried through. Margaret stared around but she could see no one. Again she crossed herself and hurried across to the Tower kitchens where Bray and Urswicke were waiting for her.

Christopher Urswicke lounged against a pillar in the death house, which formed part of the ancient crypt beneath Chertsey Abbey. On a trestle table close by rested an open lead coffin containing the mortal remains of Henry VI, late King of England; cleaned and skilfully embalmed in the Tower mortuary by Cedrick Longspear, Keeper of the Dead in that dismal place: he was now being questioned and tortured by Mauclerc and the Three Kings. All four had paused to refresh themselves with more deep-bowled goblets of wine. Longspear sat retching and gasping after Mauclerc had loosened the cord bound tightly around his forehead. Urswicke stared round that macabre chamber, the stout, barrel-like pillars with their eerie ornamentation at top and bottom; carved satyrs, goats, monkeys and other *babewyns* and gargoyles glared stonily out through a tangle of briers and brambles. This was the death house, screened off from the rest of the crypt by a stout fence of intertwined elm-wood. Behind this rose mounds of bones, skulls and shards of skeletons, the macabre remains of monks buried centuries ago in the ancient graveyard and, when this became full, the bones were dug up and piled here, making room for fresh burials outside. Longspear whimpered and glanced pitifully at Urswicke, who hid his own guilt and glanced away. To distract himself from the prisoner, Urswicke walked over to the lead coffin resting in its oaken casket; he stared down at the pallid, narrow face of King Henry. Death was making its mark, the skin was turning slightly yellow, the eyes becoming even more sunken, the nose more sharp, whilst the bloodless lips were beginning to turn inwards. The late King's soul had definitely left on its journey to judgement but, even in death, Henry had provoked violence. The cause of all this were the deep, broad blotches of blood staining the gold velvet cushion beneath the royal head.

Henry's corpse had been embalmed and prepared for burial in the Tower before being moved to lie in the great nave of St Paul's, its face exposed for public view. The Yorkists were determined to demonstrate that the King was certainly dead. There would be no rumours of a possible escape or the opportunity for mischief-makers and malcontents to field an imposter. Londoners were now growing accustomed to viewing the enemy dead of those in power. Nevertheless, Henry's corpse drew large crowds, which surged through the old cemetery and into the nave. The body had lain in state for a day but on the second, just before the noonday Angelus, a near riot occurred when the corpse was seen to bleed from the mouth. A sure sign, so the soothsayers who gathered there proclaimed, that the King had been foully murdered. The gushing of blood from his cold, hard corpse was a public accusation of this, as well as providing the necessary proof. The Dean of St Paul's had come down all a-fluster. A cohort of royal archers was summoned to ring the corpse but the damage been done. Henry the King had been assassinated! The news spread through London. Henry was a saint! Henry was a martyr! And his killers were from the House of York who had been drunk and revelling in the Tower on the night the King had been murdered. Such rumours swept the city and the shires beyond. Margaret Beaufort, aided by Bray and Urswicke, had spent good coin secretly encouraging such gossip, fanning the flames into a real fire. Margaret used the likes of the tavern keeper Hempen and a host of other little people in Margaret's party throughout the city. The Countess of Richmond, however, genuinely mourned the death of poor Henry VI. She had confided in Bray and Urswicke the details of his murder, as well as her steely determination to exploit its consequences for her own gain.

Urswicke had played a prominent part in that and, as Henry's corpse lay bleeding in St Paul's, he had watched in quiet amusement the public consternation of their enemies. Eventually, escorted by hobelars carrying glaives, and archers bearing lighted torches and accompanied by friars of all the major orders, the royal corpse had been moved with lavish pomp and ceremony. Psalms were chanted. Thuribles smoked. Candles fluttered as the royal cortège moved upriver to the great abbey of Chertsey, founded by St Erconwald so many centuries earlier.

The funeral procession had been welcomed by Father Abbot. Once again the corpse lay exposed to public view and, to the fury of Clarence and Mauclerc, once again the corpse began to bleed from the mouth. The news, swifter than a swallow, swept through the abbey and beyond. A procession of monks appeared with cross, candle and thurifer to salute this new martyr in the heavenly court. Father Abbot was shrewd enough to realise he might receive little love from the King about what was happening, but he and his abbey could accrue great profit from the people by proclaiming how their church now housed a saint and martyr. Visions of Chertsey becoming a rival to Becket's shrine at Canterbury lured the abbot and his community not only to proclaim the great event, but to encourage the faithful who followed the funeral cortège to seek miracles. Soon the nave of the abbey church became packed with the crippled and blind, the legion of beggars who moved in a swarm from one shrine to another in search of a cure. Clarence, urged on by the King, insisted the crisis be settled and that Henry be buried both physically and as a source of future trouble.

Mauclerc demanded such matters move as swiftly as possible and he had his way. The late King's requiem mass was celebrated in a cloud of incense, the ringing of bells and the chanting of psalms. Once these were over, Henry's corpse, hidden in its lead coffin, was then placed in its elm-wood casket, to be buried with the minimum of fuss in the quiet of the church. The monastic community had been forced to agree. The royal remains were then moved down to the crypt. The Three Kings had taken Henry's corpse out of its casing and laid it on a trestle table. All clothing, shrouds and sheets were removed and the Three Kings had searched the cadaver, affording it little dignity or respect.

In the flickering candlelight, their shadows dancing against the wall, the three clerks reminded Urswicke of grey-hooded crows pecking at a corpse. During their examination, the Three Kings had been watched by a terrified Longspear, who had been summoned to accompany them from the Tower. The Keeper of the Dead had hoped that once the requiem was finished he could leave, but Mauclerc had detained him. Longspear had been hustled

down here to be confronted with the evidence for the so-called
miracle: miniature sponges soaked in blood had been cleverly
inserted into the corpse's mouth, tightly wedged between the
dead King's peg-like teeth. The sponges were of the highest
quality and, due to the constant movement of the corpse from
here to there, the blood would eventually drip, filling the mouth
and trickling out through the lips.

Urswicke knew all about this. The plot had been concocted
by the countess and himself. Urswicke, visored and cowled, had
met Longspear in a desolate place near the Tower water-gate.
Urswicke had offered six pure, freshly minted coins if the Keeper
of the Dead agreed to take the sponges and insert them in the
mouth of the royal corpse before it was moved to St Paul's.
Longspear had agreed with alacrity, asserting it would cause no
harm and simply proclaim the truth that the old King had been
foully murdered. Longspear even offered, as official Keeper of
the Corpse, to tend to Henry's face on his journey here and there.
He would intervene to maintain the position of the royal head
whilst, at the same time, gently squeeze the flesh either side of
the mouth to help the blood seep out. He had done this successfully, but now Longspear was to pay the price for his meddling.

Henry's corpse had been sheeted and returned to its coffin.
The Three Kings and Mauclerc finished slaking their thirst and
returned to question Longspear. The suspect sat bound in a high-
backed chair, his hands tied to its arms, his ankles lashed by
coarse rope and a noose placed around his forehead with a steel
rod inserted in the knot; this could be turned so tightly, the flesh
ruptured and the pain intensified. Longspear's mouth was gagged
with a filthy rag, the prisoner could only jerk in violent spasms,
face all red, eyes bulging. Now and again the rag would be
removed. Mauclerc would crouch before the prisoner, taunting
him by slurping from a wine goblet before asking him the same
question: 'Who hired you to do this?' Urswicke felt sorry for
the Keeper of the Dead, but there was nothing he could do.
Longspear could not answer except gabble that he had been
enticed to a meeting with a shadowy figure, a man who hid in
the darkness around the water-gate at the Tower. Mauclerc seized
on this. If it was the Tower, he asked, then it must be somebody
pretending to be of the House of York.

'What was his tongue?' Mauclerc demanded.

'I believe he was Welsh,' Longspear blurted out, 'but I can tell you no more. Perhaps if you free me . . .'

Mauclerc answered with a blow to the man's face; the gag was pushed back and the questioning continued. At last Clarence, who stood lounging against a pillar, arms crossed, stamped a spurred boot, the jingle echoing through the cavernous place.

'Finish it,' he barked.

Mauclerc slid behind Longspear; he jerked back the prisoner's head by the hair and slit the prisoner's throat from ear to ear, the razor-sharp blade glinting in the torchlight. Longspear shook, gargling on his own blood. He rocked violently in the chair as his lifeblood gushed out before him, then he hung still, head down. The sudden violence was followed by a deep, oppressive silence, broken only by the screech of a night bird hunting above God's Acre outside. Bats flitted through the lancet window, many of them nested in the crypt, though Urswicke, recalling stories from his childhood, wondered if they were the souls of the damned.

'It is done.' Clarence gestured at Longspear. 'Fetch a sack, some stones, bury him in the Thames. As for this . . .'

Urswicke watched as Clarence and Mauclerc pulled back the coffin sheets over Henry's corpse. They then fetched a shabby arrow chest and placed it alongside: lifting the royal corpse, they thrust it in, pushing down the lid.

'That,' Clarence declared, face all flushed, 'can join the other bastard in the Thames. In the meantime . . .' He snapped his fingers. The Three Kings, busy with Longspear's cadaver, hastened into the shadows and brought back a second arrow chest. They put this down in the pool of light and lifted the lid. Urswicke caught the foul stench and gagged. One of the Three Kings, Melchior, handed out scented pomanders, beckoning Urswicke across. Urswicke did so and stared down at the mangled remains of some unfortunate: the back of the severed head was smashed in; the rest of the limbs nothing more than a tangled bloody midden heap of human flesh. Urswicke realised that these must be the remains of someone whose head had been severed and his limbs quartered: he had suffered the full, horrific punishment for high treason.

'Edmund Quintain,' Mauclerc declared. 'One of Fauconberg's captains out of Kent, hanged, disembowelled and quartered: his corpse will replace that of the saintly King.'

And, without further ado, Urswicke was ordered to help him and the Three Kings lift the gruesome mess across to be tossed into the empty royal coffin, as if they were tipping some filthy lay stall into a city dung cart. Urswicke hid his revulsion at this blasphemous desecration, the vicious sacrilege being carried out. He concentrated on other matters. He recalled the precious Holland cloth, the pounds of spices, the pure beeswax used for the royal funeral. The pomp and liturgy surrounding Henry's corpse, the vigil set up by knights and friars. It had all been brought down to this: squalid desecration in a desolate, dirty crypt. Henry VI had once been crowned King of England and France, the lord of a great Empire. He had assumed the personal insignia of the graceful Swan and Antelope but all of that had been pecked to death by these crows of York. Clarence, in particular, seemed to revel deeply in the degradation being heaped on the dead former King. Urswicke decided he could not sustain this blasphemy and must bring it to an end. The mortal remains of Edmund Quintain were eventually sealed for burial in the royal casket: no one would even dream of the desecration being perpetrated.

'Why?' Urswicke demanded abruptly. 'Why all this?'

'So no miracles can be performed,' Mauclerc smirked, 'no special sign from heaven. Anyone who claims to have received such a grace must be an imposter, a rebel, a traitor. Think about it, Christopher. Some cripple who visits Chertsey here and throws away his crutches, dancing about like a fly on a hot plate screaming that he is cured. We'll know the filthy remains of Edmund Quintain cannot be the cause of such a miraculous event. We will arrest the cripple, put him to the question and discover more about those who lurk in the shadows and encourage such treasonable mummery.'

Urswicke nodded solemnly. He suspected that was the case and he would certainly inform the countess that this was not a path to follow: her agents in the city must not be drawn in and trapped.

'And the old King's corpse?' he asked.

'Oh, it will be sheeted in its shroud and buried in the Thames. Why?'

'I would advise against that, just in case.'

'In case of what?' Clarence retorted.

'Think, my Lord. Once the corpse goes into the Thames, we have no further control over it. Why not compromise? Bury it quietly, secretly, in God's Acre here at Chertsey. You never know when such information might be of use. Would you commit the sin of sacrilege? Let us honour the royal corpse and, if circumstances change, we can present ourselves as defenders of the old King's dignity, when others,' Urswicke waved a hand, 'might have wished Henry VI's mortal remains be scattered to the winds.' Urswicke held Clarence's gaze. He watched those cunning eyes, the full lips ever ready to pout in protest. Mauclerc whispered in Clarence's ear, the Yorkist lord nodded, still staring at Urswicke.

'I like that,' he whispered. 'On the one hand we create a false shrine and draw in our enemies like flies to a turd. On the other, if Fortune's wheel spins, we can blame those on my brother's council, who argued for the total destruction of Henry VI and all he represented. Christopher, you are within my love.' Clarence stepped forward and embraced Urswicke in a tang of rich Bordeaux. 'I accept you as my liege man, Christopher. Be assured of that.' Clarence then stepped back; snapping his fingers, he pointed at the arrow chest. 'Have that buried in some desolate part of God's Acre. Mark the place well so, if we have to, we can return to it. Get rid of the rest, for we are finished here . . .'

# PART FOUR

'I trust to God that the two dukes of Clarence and
Gloucester shall be settled as one by the word of the King.'
*The Paston Letters*

C hristopher Urswicke sat on the cushioned stool. He
studied the gold-blue and silver tapestry from Arras which
adorned the wall above the mantled hearth in the countess's private chamber at her husband's mansion overlooking the
Thames. No fire had been lit as the weather had turned decisively
warm, although outside the light was fading as a rainstorm swept
up the Thames. Urswicke stared at the tapestry, which depicted
a pelican standing on a gilt-edged chalice, stabbing its breast to
draw blood and so feed its young nestling in the bowl beneath:
a well-known parable representing Christ giving himself under
the appearance of bread and wine in the Eucharist. The four
corners of the tapestry were decorated with silver-gold swans,
the personal insignia of the House of Stafford. Urswicke heard
Countess Margaret sigh and watched his mistress dab her eyes
with a small hand cloth, which she then folded neatly and placed
on the table beside her.

'Where is Reginald?' she asked.

'On some business or other,' Urswicke replied evasively. He
had asked Bray to take over his watch whilst he stayed with the
old King's corpse as it was moved from St Paul's to Chertsey.

'The Lord's Anointed.' Margaret pointed to the tapestry. 'Just
as sacred as that emblem, Henry VI was our King, sealed with
the holy chrism. He wore the crown of the Confessor, and yet
what degradation Clarence and Mauclerc inflicted on his royal
corpse.'

Urswicke nodded. He had reported what had happened at
Chertsey, though he refused to divulge some of the more macabre
details such as pig bones being mixed amongst the remains of

Quintain. Apparently the Kentish captain had been hanged, drawn and quartered on the great cobbled expanse before Newgate, where the slaughterers plied their trade. At the end of the execution, some of the offal lying around must have been mingled with Quintain's severed limbs.

'They will be punished for that,' Margaret murmured. 'Mauclerc, the Three Kings and, of course, that demon in human flesh, George of Clarence.' She paused. Urswicke was struck by the fierceness of her expression, which had transformed the countess's usual pale, narrow face into that of some warrior woman intent on battle. Urswicke turned at a knock at the door and Bray slipped into the chamber.

'Well?' Margaret asked. 'I know you have been busy on my behalf. You have hinted at that. You have been pursuing the traitor? Have we discovered the truth?'

'Yes, Mistress,' Bray replied. 'We have the truth and I have seen the evidence with my own eyes. You told us to hunt the Judas and we did. Mistress, you are confronted with a sea of woes, you pick your way carefully through a tangle of treason and deep deceit.' Bray pulled a face. 'All we are doing is making that less dangerous. We remove the lures, the traps and the snares primed to catch us all.'

'True, true.' Margaret crossed herself. 'We wage a secret war. Very well.' She straightened in her chair. 'Take care of what you have to. If it's to be done, then it is best done swiftly.'

Within the hour, Bray and Urswicke led Owain and Oswina out of the water-gate of Lord Humphrey's mansion. The evening was close and the threatened storm seemed imminent. The clouds hung dark and lowering whilst a stiff breeze chopped the water. They clambered into the stout, deep, well-tarred bum-boat tied to its post on the narrow jetty. They made themselves comfortable and cast off, Urswicke and Bray pulling at the oars. Owain and his sister, cloaked and cowled, sat next to each other in the stern. Urswicke glanced over his shoulder at the sack of rocks Bray had placed in the prow. They'd prepared everything before inviting both brother and sister to join what Urswicke called 'a most crucial task for their mistress, a matter of great secrecy'. Both Owain and Oswina had been only too eager to obey but now, with the boat out on the river, its swollen current swirling fast and strong, their mood changed.

'What is this task?' Oswina asked plaintively.

'Where in Southwark are we going?' her brother demanded. 'Who are we meeting at such a late hour?'

Urswicke just glanced over his shoulder and almost welcomed the rolling bank of river mist which enveloped them. 'Here,' he whispered. Both he and Bray rested on their oars. Urswicke bent down; he picked up the leather sack and placed it carefully between his feet. 'They are primed,' Bray whispered, 'all set, the bolts are ready.'

'What is this?' Owain would have sprung to his feet, but the boat rocked dangerously. The squire hurriedly sat down, staring fearfully at the arbalest, all primed, that Urswicke held ready to loose.

'What is happening?' Oswina pleaded, pulling back the hood of her gown. 'What have we done?'

'Treachery and treason towards a woman who took you in and mothered you better than any I know,' Bray retorted. 'You were granted a privileged place in her household by her late husband, Edmund Tudor of blessed memory. You were given dignity, high office and all the comforts of a good life. You rejected all that. You decided to act the Judas, crying all hail to the countess when you meant all harm. You were suborned, seduced by Clarence's henchman Mauclerc.'

'He probably informed you that Margaret of Richmond, the last of the Beauforts, would soon be for the dark.' Urswicke wiped the mist water from his face. 'He bribed you with good coin and even better prospects.' Urswicke challenged. 'He wanted to seize the countess's young son. You realised your mistress was nursing some great secret. You suspected that her boy was not hiding behind the fortress at Pembroke but probably here in London waiting to escape across the Narrow Seas. We witnessed first-hand the effects of your treachery. You worked with that wretch in Tewkesbury, the one who threw fire down into the courtyard as our mistress returned. You sheltered that assassin. You kept sharp watch on the countess's inevitable return. Who was it then? One of the Three Kings?' He stared at these two traitors who just sat, mouths gaping. 'What did you plot,' he continued, 'that our mistress might be hurt, killed? Certainly delayed in her return to London and, if she was, the hunt for her young son would be made all the easier. The attack failed but messages were despatched to the city. My father, the noble Recorder of London, pursued the countess like a hungry lurcher would a hare. You kept up your treasonable practices. One of you would slip out of Sir Humphrey's mansion, the other would stay in your chamber pretending that both of you were there.' Urswicke grasped the arbalest tighter. 'We discovered that. We also found a way of pursuing you from afar. Master Bray, here, has a number of street people in his pay. To cut to the quick, you visited a shabby tavern in Queenhithe, The Crutched Friar. Mauclerc would be there as he was early today. Yes Owain . . .?'

'The c-countess . . .' Owain stuttered.

'You betrayed her,' Urswicke replied. 'You know you did, both of you! We have seen you consort with her mortal enemies, men who would, at a spin of a coin, pay to see her die, her son murdered and those she trusts, such as ourselves, barbarously executed.'

'But the countess?' Oswina bleated.

'She bids you farewell.' Urswicke released the catch and the bolt sped out, smashing Owain's face to a bloody pulp. His sister half rose. Bray handed Urswicke the second arbalest; he released the catch even as Oswina leaned forward then fell back, hanging out of the boat as the barbed quarrel shattered her chest. Urswicke gingerly rose and pulled the two corpses together. Bray handed him the sack of rocks, then grasped the oars, holding the boat as steady as he could. Urswicke pushed the rocks amongst the clothing of his two victims then tossed both corpses into the river.

'A sad end,' Bray remarked as Urswicke took his seat on the bench.

'We did not cause their death,' Urswicke hissed. 'They did. They betrayed their loving mistress. They violated all faithfulness and fealty. They forsook their loyalty to her and to us. If they had been successful, Countess Margaret would have ended her days in some dingy cell in the Tower. Her son would be some battered corpse floating in this river whilst we would have suffered the full rigour of the punishment for treason.' Urswicke glanced at his companion. 'Reginald, my friend, we did not compose our sad world's music, yet, like everyone else, we have no choice but to dance to it.'

Three days after returning with Bray from their murderous journey across the Thames, Urswicke was roused by a servant who had been urgently despatched upstairs by the countess.

'Master,' the stable boy hissed, 'a stranger, cowled and cloaked, his face visored, waits for you in the stable yard. He claims to be sent by your father the Recorder on the most urgent business. He refuses to speak to any of us, nor will he come in. He says he will stay until you meet him.'

'In which case, I will.'

Urswicke climbed out of his cotbed, crossed to the lavarium and threw cold water over his face. He then hurriedly dressed, strapped on his warbelt, forced his feet into his boots and, throwing his cloak around his shoulders, hurried down past the countess, who simply nodded as he passed. The mysterious visitor was in the stable yard, one hand on the hilt of his sword, with the other he beckoned Urswicke closer before pulling down the visor, covering his nose and mouth. Urswicke immediately recognised Spysin, one of Clarence's squires, a sly-eyed fighting man, skilled with the dagger and garrotte, who also enjoyed the most unsavoury reputation of being a pimp for his betters. Urswicke noticed how Spysin was belted, spurred and booted, as if ready to leave on some errand.

'Master Christopher,' he murmured, 'my Lord Clarence and Mauclerc need you at The Sunne in Splendour – something has occurred.'

'What has my father got to do with that tavern?'

'Nothing at all – well, at least not yet. I simply concocted the message to stir your curiosity as well as to protect my master's business. But come,' Spysin urged, 'I am also busy. I must leave on the evening tide.'

Urswicke nodded his agreement and followed Spysin along the winding streets of Queenhithe. Morning mass at the different churches was just finishing, the lanterns in their steeples doused so the bells could toll, reminding the faithful to patter their morning prayers before the merchant horns sounded to start the business of the day. Already the crowds were thronging about, although everyone stood aside as a host of knight bannerets, their destriers caparisoned in emblazoned leather, moved down to the tiltyards and tourney grounds of Smithfield. The knights in half-armour, their jousting helmets ornate and crowned with mythical beasts, were carried along with their shields and lances by a noisy entourage of squires and pages. Urswicke was sure he glimpsed his father, who was already eager to prove his spurs during the great celebrations being planned for later in the summer.

Once the knights had passed, Spysin led him on. Although the city was celebrating, the effects of the recent fighting was still clear, with makeshift gallows standing at certain crossroads, each decorated with gibbeted corpses. Not even in death were these allowed to rest, their flesh being cut and scarred by the warlocks and wizards who regarded the grisly remains of a hanged man as possessing rich, magical properties. Urswicke recalled his execution of Owain and Oswina; he felt no guilt at their deaths. If they had had their way, his corpse and that of Bray would be gibbeted in iron cages.

At last they reached The Sunne in Splendour. Its courtyard and stable bailey were packed with men-at-arms wearing Clarence's livery, depicting the Black Bull or the Bear and Ragged Staff of Warwick. The tavern had been emptied. Minehost Master Tiptree and all his scullions and slatterns stood in a disconsolate group. Every entrance to the hostelry was closely guarded by men-at-arms with drawn swords. Urswicke and Spysin had to wait until Mauclerc came out. Urswicke stared across at Tiptree who was throwing his hands up in the air and wailing about the loss of business. Urswicke realised Tiptree was deeply agitated yet, behind all his bluster, was clearly terrified about what had happened in his opulent tavern. Urswicke wondered what had caused such a commotion and the secrecy cloaking it. Mauclerc strode out and greeted them. He told Spysin to wait and took Urswicke into the taproom, where Clarence sat crouched over a goblet of wine. He gazed drunkenly at Urswicke and flailed a hand towards the broad, open stairs leading to the upper chambers.

'All dead.' He slurred. 'Show him, Mauclerc.'

They climbed the stairs and along the narrow gallery to the chancery office Mauclerc had hired for the Three Kings. The door to it had been smashed from its hinges and now leaned against the wall. Mauclerc led Urswicke around this into the chamber. The shutters from the narrow window had been pulled back, lanterns and candles had been fired to cast light on the mayhem and bloody murder which had been perpetrated there against the Three Kings and one other, whom Mauclerc identified as the parchment-seller Oudenarde. The four corpses lay sprawled on the floor, the blood from their slit throats drenching the costly turkey rugs. The victims were grouped together, as if they had clustered close against their killer. Urswicke carefully picked his way around the murdered men. He noticed how their bodies were slightly twisted, but what was extraordinary was the lack of any sign of violence either to themselves, the chamber or any of its furnishings. He found it impossible to believe that these men had been led like lambs to the slaughter offering their throats to be cut. Apart from the gruesome death scene, everything else seemed in order: no destruction, no damage, nothing at all.

Urswicke approached the chancery table. Mauclerc edged up very close behind him, as if fearful at what Urswicke might discover. The clerk tried to ignore Mauclerc almost breathing in his ear as he sifted amongst the documents strewn there before picking up a book of hours, a bulky manuscript, freshly paged and neatly bound in gold twine held fast by a clasp. Urswicke opened this, turning the pages, admiring the miniature jewel-like paintings and the glorious decoration which marked the beginning of each prayer or psalm. He turned the pages then studied the front and back of the psalter.

'It is what it is,' Urswicke murmured, putting it down. 'A book of hours.' He gestured at the documents which covered the entire table. 'Nothing has been stolen?'

'No, no,' Mauclerc retorted.

Urswicke glanced sharply at him. For the first time since they had met at Tewkesbury, Clarence's henchman seemed genuinely puzzled, surprised as if caught off balance.

'Nothing has been stolen?' Urswicke repeated.

'No.'

'And there was nothing precious here to steal?'

'No.'

'So why did the Three Kings, together with Oudenarde, work so hard here in the chancery chamber of a splendid tavern, a room your three clerks closely guarded, so no one could spy on them? Now that's a mystery, Mauclerc! What was so valuable here to explain such secrecy or to account for their murders?'

'They were working on my claim.'

Urswicke spun round. Clarence lounged drunkenly in the doorway, arms crossed, staring fixedly at Urswicke. 'You,' Clarence pointed a finger, 'you have sharp wits and an even sharper mind, Christopher. You have proved invaluable. Find out who did this. Let me see them hang. You will receive my warrant commanding you. Act on it!'

'I will, my Lord. And so first, did you or Mauclerc visit this chamber yesterday, be it day or night? Or even earlier this morning?'

'No,' Clarence spat back. 'I should object to you, a low-born knave, questioning me so closely. But that has to be done, I suppose.'

Clarence pushed himself from the doorpost and turned drunkenly, balancing the wine goblet carefully in his hand.

'Mauclerc will take care of any questions.'

Once Clarence had gone, Mauclerc grasped Urswicke by the shoulder, his cold face hard, as if the deep malice which defined the man had returned. 'We have nothing to do with this,' he declared. 'My Lord Clarence and I were busy in the Jerusalem chambers at Westminster. Minehost Tiptree sent messages about what happened here? And as far as my Lord of Clarence's claim is concerned . . .' Mauclerc pointed at the parchments strewn across the chancery desk. 'As you know, Richard Neville, Earl of Warwick, the so-called King-maker and leader of the Lancastrian host, owned estates and manors the like of which have never been seen in this kingdom for many a day. According to those who know, Warwick was killed at Barnet by something flying.' He laughed sharply. 'A well-aimed war axe or crossbow bolt. Anyway,' he sighed, 'Warwick left no male heir and you must realise the implications?'

'Yes I do,' Urswicke agreed. 'Warwick had two daughters, Isobel and Anne. If the Warwick estates aren't seized by the King, and I doubt if they will be, they will be shared out amongst the two daughters, one of whom, Isobel, is married to our master, Lord Clarence. I heard rumours,' Urswicke lowered his voice, 'that Richard of Gloucester nourishes the most tender feelings towards Isobel's sister Anne, not to mention,' he added wryly, 'her estates. If Lord Richard marries the heiress, he will certainly demand a just division of the Neville inheritance.'

'My master,' Mauclerc interjected, 'is insistent that the entire Neville inheritance, its manors, estates and holdings, everything to be found there, are rightfully his. True, Richard of Gloucester challenges this, so our Lord builds a case to justify his God given rights based on both law and tact.'

Urswicke suspected Mauclerc was lying for Clarence, but he nodded understandingly as if fully accepting what he said. He continued to survey the different parchments spread out across the table. Sharp-eyed and the swiftest of readers, Urswicke tried to make sense of what he saw. Most of the documents were bills, indentures, licences, lists and drafts of memoranda. One already laid out and sealed by Clarence caught his eye; a licence for 'Eudo Spysin, squire of my Lord Clarence, to leave the kingdom with important messages to be delivered by word of mouth to his Grace Duke Francis of Brittany.' Urswicke recalled Spysin all booted, buckled and belted, as well as the squire's self-important remark about being busy on some task and catching the evening tide. Urswicke studied the rest of the parchments, now aware of Mauclerc's impatience to distract him.

Urswicke realised he could do no more so he walked across to the window and stared out through the lancet opening. He had no illusion about what Spysin was intent on. The courier would be carrying messages, on Clarence's behalf, with the full support of the English Crown, graciously asking Duke Francis that if Henry Tudor arrived in Brittany he was to be seized immediately and despatched back to England. Clarence would offer lavish bribes and generous trade concessions to achieve this. Similar envoys would go to other kingdoms, though this did not concern Urswicke. Countess Margaret had confided how her son would shelter in no other place but Brittany, which enjoyed the closest ties with Wales and the Tudor family. Nevertheless, the danger

was pressing. Would Duke Francis be suborned? Would members
of his council, their purses bulging with English gold, argue that
Tudor was not worth alienating the powerful Edward? And what
would Clarence offer? Treasure? Trade? Treaties? Had Countess
Margaret anticipated Clarence's next move? Somehow, perhaps
because of the last treacherous act of that precious pair Owain
and his sister, Clarence had come to realise that Henry Tudor
was no longer in Pembroke but was probably on his way to
Brittany or, perhaps, already there.

Urswicke stared down through the window; he made his decision. For a brief while he would have to stay in this chamber
and act the part. But, before the tide turned that evening, he must
kill Spysin. On that he was determined. Urswicke glanced sharply
over his shoulder at the chancery table. He could detect no
disturbance amongst the different parchments and documents.
Was there something missing? Mauclerc didn't seem to think so.
So why these murders in such mysterious circumstances?
Mauclerc was now collecting the different manuscripts and
placing them in the reinforced parchment chests.

'Why did my Lord Clarence choose me?' he asked.

Mauclerc brought the lid of the coffer sharply down. He
snapped it shut, turning the key. 'We trust you Christopher. You
have given us invaluable information and have been of great
assistance to our Lord. Our master believes all this,' he gestured
at the corpses, 'could even be the work of your redoubtable
mistress or—'

'Or who?'

'Someone who is in bitter rivalry with our master.'

'Such as?'

Mauclerc walked towards him and pushed his face close to
Urswicke's. 'Gloucester,' he whispered, 'and that little mounte-
bank's claim to the Neville inheritance.'

Urswicke stared back in surprise.

'Oh yes,' Mauclerc hissed, 'there is more to this masque than
meets the eye.'

'Yet you and our Lord,' Urswicke pointed to the corpses, 'do
not seem too perturbed by the brutal murder of four chosen
henchmen?'

'We have lost the same in battle, Urswicke. I have seen

comrades cruelly slaughtered or heard of their excruciating executions at the hands of our enemies. My Lord Clarence and I have been fighting for the last twelve years.' Mauclerc sucked on his teeth. 'Men live, men die. The Three Kings were faithful, shrewd and skilled. Oudenarde the parchment-seller equally so. They were all working on creating a book, a chronicle which would justify Clarence's claim to his inheritance.'

'What about Oudenarde's shop under the sign of "The Red Keg"?'

'Oh, don't worry about that. Our searchers will already be busy there seizing and securing whatever they find.' Mauclerc poked Urswicke in the chest. 'What you must do, like any scholar in the schools, is discover what truly happened here. Present a hypothesis which is logical and possible. If the hypothesis is probable, that would be even better.' Mauclerc's fingers fell to the hilt of his dagger. 'Once we know, then we can carry out the most bloody reprisal.'

Urswicke was left alone in the death chamber. At his request, some of Mauclerc's ruffians set up guard on the stairs to the chancery chamber and the room itself. Urswicke moved swiftly. He soon established there was no secret entrance to the chamber, only the doorway, and that had been battered, its lock twisted and the inside bolts shattered: the windows were too narrow for anyone to even try and break in. Moreover, they had been firmly shuttered because of the cold early summer night. Urswicke then scrutinised the food: scraps of chicken, pieces of fruit and a manchet loaf. The jug of Bordeaux was half full, with wine dregs in the four goblets. Urswicke sniffed at all of these but could detect nothing amiss. Moreover, the chamber, like many such tavern rooms, suffered from an infestation of mice. Urswicke discovered their droppings as well as scraps of food these rodents nibbled at. He cast about; if any of the food and drink had been poisoned, he would find the corpses of such vermin. But, there again, he could discover nothing.

Urswicke decided to be as thorough as possible. He took the deep bowl from the lavarium stand and scraped in the remnants of the food along with the wine from both the jug and the goblets. He mixed this together and ordered one of the guards to take it down to the tavern cellar and leave it for the rats. Urswicke then

turned to the four corpses and, for the first time since he had
entered that sinister death chamber, he felt a deep chill of fear.
Urswicke had viewed corpses on the battlefield, in lonely copses
of the wild, windswept north, as well as those left stabbed or
hacked along the dirty runnels and alleyways of London. He had
seen the dead piled high like stacks of wood before they were
tumbled into makeshift, common graves. This was eerily different.
The four victims sprawled as if they were asleep, except each of
them had drawn his dagger and held it in listless fingers. Four
corpses, eyes staring, mouths slightly open in shock at the savage
cut across each of their throats. Even more mysterious, there was
no sign of any struggle or violence, apart from those death wounds
and the blood floating out in great pools.

Urswicke crouched down and scrutinised the scene carefully.
'Impossible,' he whispered to himself. 'Impossible.' The clerk
hurriedly searched the pockets and wallets of the dead but he
could find nothing significant. He suspected Mauclerc had already
done this at Clarence's behest. Urswicke got to his feet and
crossed to the door, resting against its lintel, and carefully scrutinised how it had been violently broken. The bolts at top and
bottom had fractured the clasps whilst the key was still in the
now twisted lock. He asked the guards outside to move away
and stared around the stairwell, noticing the heavy yew log which
had been used as a ram against the door. Urswicke walked back
into the chamber. So far he had nothing to use, nothing he could
seize on to resolve these mysteries.

He ordered one of the guards to bring up Master Tiptree.
Minehost, sweaty-faced with a nervous twist to his mouth, came
hurrying up all a-fluster, wiping greasy hands on his thick, linen
apron. Behind him trotted two scullions and a slattern who,
Tiptree explained, 'had first raised the hue and cry ready to
shout "Harrow! Harrow!"' All four tavern people were nervous
at entering the death chamber, Tiptree in particular. He was
deeply agitated, lower lip trembling, teeth chattering. Urswicke
realised he would have no sense out of him. He ordered Tiptree
and the rest to go back downstairs into the small buttery which
adjoined the great kitchen before telling the guard to maintain
strict watch over the death chamber and allow no one in without
his permission.

Once gathered in the buttery, the landlord and his minions seemed more composed as they sat on the cushioned settle. Urswicke leaned across the table pointing at Tiptree.

'The truth,' he insisted, 'because if you lie it will be the press yard in Newgate. Now, you are a member of my Lord Clarence's household, or once were, yes?'

'I worked in his kitchen. I was a purveyor of food and his principal cook – a very good one.' Tiptree tried to hide his fear behind a blustering preening.

'I am sure you were, and my Lord Clarence used this tavern when he comes to London?' Tiptree nodded. 'And last night or this morning did you notice anything untoward?'

'No, no. Yesterday evening the four gentlemen assembled in the taproom, around a special table overlooking our garden which is well-stocked—'

'Yes, yes,' Urswicke intervened 'They dined then adjourned?'

'Yes.'

'Did they receive any visitors?'

'No.' Tiptree shook his head. 'We left them be except, sometime after the Compline bell had rung for the lanterns to be lit, they ordered food, bread and chicken in a creamy sauce, along with a jug of my best Bordeaux. I took the tray up. I entered the chancery chamber. The four gentlemen, I thought them to be so because they were always courteous.' Tiptree shrugged.

'They were kindly to you?' Urswicke asked.

'Aye. And so was Oudenarde, but he was not always with them. Sometimes he'd come by himself. On other occasions he would bring people to see the clerks.'

'Which people?' Urswicke demanded, recalling what he'd glimpsed during his visits to The Sunne in Splendour.

'I don't know, sir. Always hooded and cloaked they were, even on a fine evening. Master, I am a tavern keeper,' Tiptree tapped the side of his nose, 'discretion is my main virtue. I see nothing wrong, I hear nothing wrong, I say nothing wrong.'

'Aye, and one stay in prison is bad enough,' one of the scullions scoffed, rubbing his mouth on the sleeve of his shabby jerkin. He opened his mouth to speak again but Tiptree glared at him.

'Tell the gentleman what happened this morning,' the landlord snapped.

'And who are you?' Urswicke turned to face the dirty scullion.

'I am Snotnose, or that's what they call me.' The boy wiped his face on his sleeve again. 'My first task of the day is to invite guests down to the taproom to break their fast. I knock on the bedchamber doors.' He paused at the change on Urswicke's face as the clerk realised he had overlooked the rooms where the Three Kings slept, but then comforted himself: as with the shop under the sign of 'The Red Keg', Mauclerc would have cleared the chambers of anything he did not want Urswicke to see.

The clerk glanced over his shoulder at the window; the hours were passing and he had not forgotten Spysin. He would love to return to the countess's house to consult with Bray, but time was of the essence and he did not wish to provoke any suspicion about his commitment to Clarence. He wondered about what Mauclerc had said? How the murders here could be the work of the countess? Urswicke chewed the corner of his lip. That was too fanciful! Nevertheless, it demonstrated that if Clarence and his coven could level accusations against his mistress and threaten her with the full rigour of the law, they would hasten to do so.

'Master?' Snotnose's voice was almost a screech.

'Continue.'

'I knocked then opened the door to all three chambers. They were empty, the beds not slept in. So I thought they must have spent the night in the chancery chamber. I hurried there and knocked on the door but no one answered. I tried again. I pushed hard but it was locked and bolted. I shouted and knocked again, nothing! I ran down to the taproom, into the kitchen garden and stared up. As you know, Master, the windows to the chancery chamber are narrow, but I could see the shutters had not been opened to greet the day . . .'

'By then,' Tiptree spoke up, 'we were all upset with Snotnose running around like a mad March hare. I knocked on the chancery chamber, shouted and yelled. No answer. Of course the entire tavern knew something was wrong. I sent Snotnose here to seek Lord Clarence and Mauclerc. Some of their,' Urswicke was sure Tiptree was going to say ruffians, 'some of their retainers,' the landlord corrected himself, 'lodged nearby. I decided to break down the door and, what you have seen, so did we.'

'The door was locked and bolted on the inside, the key turned?'

'Yes, we burst in. The chamber was dark. The candles had guttered out. The shutters were still pulled closed. I almost stumbled over the corpses. I called for light,' Tiptree spread his hands, 'and glimpsed the mayhem. I decided not to touch anything but left telling the others to stay well away.'

'Is there anything else?' Urswicke demanded. They all shook their heads. Urswicke stared at Tiptree; the landlord was still deeply agitated, terrified. Was there something else? Urswicke wondered. Did Tiptree fear punishment from a lord who was notorious for his vindictiveness?

'If you do recall anything,' Urswicke demanded 'you will tell me.' He then rose, thanked them and returned to the death chamber. He sat in the principal chancery chair, trying to make sense of it. The guard returned to report that the rats had eaten the food but seemed as hale and hearty as ever. Urswicke smiled at the gentle sarcasm and asked the guard to remove the corpses to one of the outhouses. They were to be stripped and any valuables, Urswicke repeated his instruction, were to be collected, piled together and handed over to Master Mauclerc. Urswicke continued to reflect on what he'd seen and heard whilst the four corpses were sheeted, put on makeshift stretchers and taken away. Tiptree and his minions came up with mops and buckets to clear the bloody mess.

Urswicke watched them for a while and left the chamber ostensibly to view the four corpses. In truth, he was searching for Spysin, but Mauclerc's courier seemed to have completely disappeared. Urswicke recalled how Spysin had mentioned something about sailing on the evening tide. Urswicke wondered whether he should go straight down to Queenhithe quayside but decided to wait. He did not want to provoke suspicion: he knew he was being watched and it would be more logical to inspect the corpses and then return to his hunt for Spysin.

The stable outhouse had been turned into a makeshift mortuary. The four corpses, completely naked, lay stretched out on old sacking rolled across on the shit-strewn, soggy floor. A lanternhorn glowed beside each cadaver. One of the soldiers had inveigled a wandering Friar of the Sack to come into this filthy death house and administer extreme unction, a pattering of prayer above the dead with a cross of wet wax etched on each forehead. Urswicke waited until the friar had finished, taken his coin and left.

'Did you find anything untoward?' he asked the soldier, who'd organised the removal of the corpses and was now going through belts, purses and pockets.

'Nothing.' The soldier pointed across to an upturned barrel. 'Some coins, daggers which they'd drawn, rings and a bracelet. See for yourself.'

Urswicke walked over and began to sift through the tawdry items. He pushed aside the four blood-encrusted daggers, pulling across the belts and purses the soldier brought; they were now empty. Urswicke could see no coins but he didn't care if the soldiers had helped themselves. He recalled the Three Kings gleefully participating in the blasphemous desecration of the old King's corpse; in death they had been given more respect than they'd shown the Lord's Anointed.

Urswicke picked up one wallet, he shook this and a piece of parchment fell out. It was only a plain strip of writing, though Urswicke noticed the vellum was of the highest quality, used solely in the chanceries of the Crown and the great lords. The strip was quite long, its edges even, and Urswicke suspected that it had been expertly cut by a parchment knife from a page which had measured too long in comparison with the other pages in some folio or book. The writing was that of some very skilled calligrapher, the verse it bore was written in Latin.

'And the captain of archers,' Urswicke whispered the translation to himself, 'lay with the wife of Duke Uriah the Hittite and she conceived a son.' Urswicke noticed how certain words were written in a different-coloured ink. He was about to peer closer when he heard shouts outside and hastily hid the strip of parchment in his own wallet. The door to the outhouse was thrown open and Mauclerc stormed in.

'Master Urswicke, come, come now.'

Urswicke followed Mauclerc and a group of his ruffians out across the stable yard and into the narrow runnels of Queenhithe. Clarence's henchmen swept through the streets like a violent windstorm. Pedlars, tinkers and traders fled. Women grabbed their children and retreated back into the shelter of shabby door-ways. Dogs and cats scurried away. Carts and barrows were hastily pulled aside. Here and there, protests and raucous shouts echoed about the 'power of the great ones of the land'. A window was thrown open and a chamber pot emptied, the slop narrowly missing members of Mauclerc's retinue. This was followed by shrieks of laughter. Clarence's retinue drew their swords. The shutters slammed shut and silence descended. They entered the quayside where the fish markets were closing down, the cobbles littered with all the rubbish of a day's trading. The heads and innards of the morning catch turned the cobbles slippery, though the legion of beggars, hunting for scraps, moved nimbly enough, filling their sacks with what they found. The air reeked of salt and brine and other harsh smells.

Mauclerc's arrival brought everything to a standstill. People became statues, frightened even to move or speak. Urswicke glanced to his left; the tide was turning. The river moving more swiftly. Mauclerc led them away from the quayside into a large, shabby tavern, The Prospect of Grimsby. This had now been emptied of all its customers. More of Mauclerc's men gathered in the gloomy taproom, a dingy place with its floor rushes turned to a mushy mess and its tawdry tables strewn with the remains of food and drink. Mauclerc told his compan-ions to wait and led Urswicke down a narrow, stone-paved passageway which led out into the yard and its jakes, an enclave built into the tavern wall and screened by a heavy door. Mauclerc opened this and waved Urswicke forward. The murdered Spysin, hose down around his ankles, lay back against the filthy wall, eyes popping, mouth gaping. The front of his jerkin was drenched by the blood which had poured from his cut throat, a deep slice running from ear to ear.

'Sweet heaven.' Urswicke crouched down, desperate to hide his own relief that at least this problem had been resolved. 'Robbery?' he asked, turning to Mauclerc.

'His money belt, wallet and weapons have been taken.'

'You do realise,' Urswicke got to his feet, 'Spysin's throat has been cut; the wound is very similar to that of the four victims at The Sunne in Splendour. I strongly suspect Spysin's murderer was the same person except,' he held a hand up, 'nothing appears to have been taken from the chancery chamber, whilst Spysin's possessions have been filched.' He turned to confront Mauclerc, and did not relish the look on that sinister man's face.

'Nothing was taken from the chancery room or any of the Three Kings' chambers?'

Mauclerc, still holding Urswicke's gaze, eyes and face as hard as stone, just shook his head.

'And here's a further problem,' Urswicke fought to remain calm, 'Spysin was a street fighter, a man of war, expert in dagger play, used to the cut and thrust, yes?' Again that cold, hard stare followed by a nod. 'So it would appear that Spysin left the tavern to relieve himself, comes in here, lowers his hose and squats on the jake stool. Now for someone to cut his throat like that, the assassin would have to be standing behind him, but,' Urswicke continued, 'that's impossible. It cannot be done. The killer must have struck from the front, yet Spysin offered no resistance. There is no evidence that any form of struggle took place. Now . . .' Urswicke broke off.

Mauclerc, resting his hand on his dagger hilt, leaned slightly forward. 'What is the matter Christopher?' he whispered.

'You know full well, you look accusingly at me. For God's sake, Mauclerc, your own henchmen will go on oath. I have been nowhere near this tavern or Spysin but busy elsewhere. You are not implying . . .'

'No, no.' Mauclerc relaxed and shrugged, as if his former mood was nothing at all. He pulled a face. 'As I have said, I did – we did – wonder if Margaret Countess of Richmond had a hand in the murders at The Sunne in Splendour. If my Lord of Clarence hates her, she certainly detests us.' Mauclerc poked Urswicke gently in the chest. 'Christopher, you talk about street fighters and you can brawl with the best of them. You are her dagger man but, of course, I concede that today you have been busy on our affairs. My own henchmen, as you say, will attest to that. Yet who, Christopher? Who is responsible?'

'Think, my friend,' Urswicke replied, 'who has the money, the power and the means to hire expert assassins?'

Urswicke gestured at Spysin's corpse. 'We are not dealing with footpads and felons but men of power and, of course,' he glanced swiftly at Mauclerc, 'you have not told me what Spysin was involved in. He did mention that he was about to take ship to foreign parts, sail on the evening tide.'

'He was taking messages abroad, our master's courier here and there.' Mauclerc scratched his stubbled cheek. 'He should have been more prudent. But I return to my question, Christopher, who is responsible for all this?'

Urswicke shook his head to hide his own relief. Mauclerc seemed genuinely mystified, his former hostility just a passing mood. Now he called him Christopher, almost suppliant in his search for answers that Clarence would certainly demand.

'So Spysin was to be despatched to foreign parts, but what was he doing here?'

'Spysin was a toper, a wine lover. He made a mistake and paid for it with his life. So never mind him. Let's return to The Sunne in Splendour.'

'No, no,' Urswicke pulled at Mauclerc's sleeve, 'Minchost here at The Prospect of Grimsby? Now is the moment to question him before time passes and memories grow dim.'

Mauclerc agreed and they gathered the landlord and his serv-ants in the taproom. They could say little about Spysin, except that he'd swaggered into the tavern, ordered a goblet of the best Bordeaux and had gone and sat in the furthest window seat. He was cloaked and booted and they suspected he was waiting to board a ship at the nearby quayside. One of the scullions reported how he'd glimpsed someone approach Spysin; it could have been a Friar of the Sack begging for alms, as these good brothers were accustomed to moving from one riverside tavern to another. The same scullion, a sharp-eyed urchin, glimpsed Spysin leave rather hastily carrying his fardel, and guessed the courier had an urgent call to the jake's stool. Spysin hurried out into the yard and, as far as the scullion was concerned, that was the end of the matter. Urswicke repeated his questions, watching faces intently, but he could detect nothing suspicious and whispered the same to Mauclerc. They left The Prospect of Grimsby and returned to the closely guarded chancery chamber at The Sunne in Splendour.

Mauclerc ordered a jug of wine, two goblets and a platter of diced meat coated with a spicy sauce. Urswicke refused the food and only sipped at his wine. Mauclerc, looking deeply agitated, slurped his goblet, only pausing to ask Urswicke to describe his conclusions about the murder of the Three Kings and Oudenarde.

'Very little,' Urswicke replied. 'We have a chamber locked and bolted within. As for the windows, if the shutters were pulled back, they are still too narrow even for a cat to climb through. No secret passageway or enclave exists except for the narrow jake's room. But this is nothing much and useful for one thing only. The food and drink the victims consumed was untainted. I have established that as a fact beyond any doubt. Even more mysterious, the four victims were able-bodied men, used to violence on the battlefield, or elsewhere,' he added drily. 'They were armed, indeed all four had drawn their daggers, which is puzzling because the bodies were lying on the floor as if they were sleeping and there is not even a trace of a minor disturbance. Mystery twists the mystery even deeper. Four men, armed, giving up their throats to be cut without protest or cry, resistance or defence? And how can that happen in a room where the door was locked and bolted from inside? So how did the Angel of Death enter? How did the assassins cut the throats of four vigorous men so silently, so softly, and how many assassins were there? One? Two, or even more? Let us say there were five or six, yet no one in that tavern saw, heard or suspected anything amiss until a scullion knocked on that chancery door.'

Urswicke fell silent; the full effect of this murderous mystery was making itself felt and, as Urswicke conceded to himself, he could find little way forward.

'Who?' Mauclerc demanded. 'Who was responsible?'

'In God's name,' Urswicke snapped, 'I do not know.'

Margaret, Countess of Richmond, together with her steward Reginald Bray, sat in the Exchequer chamber of her husband's house in Queenhithe. The mansion lay silent, its servants and retainers resting after a day's work, eating and drinking in the well-furnished buttery. A time of peace and harmony. Once the noise and the clamour of the house subsided, all the servants would gather to taste the latest offerings of the countess's cooks, who had an enviable reputation for baking the juiciest venison pie and roasting the most succulent chicken and duck.

Margaret had dined alone in her own chamber. Once the meal

was over, she had adjourned to the Exchequer, eager to go through her household accounts and reports from her bailiffs. Bray had laid out all the necessary documentation on the long chancery table and was advising her on anomalies: these proved to be legion after the chaos of the last year when the quarterly returns to her Exchequer, as well as hers to the Crown, had been so severely disrupted. Margaret hoped to raise monies for the establishment of chantries where priests could sing requiems for the repose of all her kinsmen who had died during the recent wars. She was also fiercely determined to implement her plan to fund a new college or hall in Cambridge. Once she had secured a suitable building, the adjoining lands and outhouses, she would strive to attract the leading scholars of the day from both England and abroad. Margaret was particularly fascinated by the new scholarship emerging in Europe. She was also deeply intrigued by the developments in theology and was more than prepared to support direct study of the Scripture: indeed, one of her great dreams was to have the Bible translated into English.

Margaret was still engrossed in such details when her chamberlain knocked on the door and burst in, all flustered, to announce that Richard, Duke of Gloucester, together with his henchman Francis Lovel had arrived determined to speak to her. Margaret raised her eyes heavenwards at Bray but agreed. They found Gloucester and Lovel ensconced in high-back chairs before the solar's sculptured hearth. Both men had taken off their cloaks and bonnets; a servant was laying these out across a table whilst another served white wine and sweetmeats. Gloucester rose to greet Margaret with all the courtesy of a court gallant, Lovel likewise. Margaret remained wary. Both men were dressed in the dark brown-green leather jerkins of a royal verderer, and Gloucester explained how they had been hare coursing north of the city walls.

Margaret sat down on a chair, moving it to face both men, using the fussing of the servants to study this precious pair. Richard of Gloucester's narrow, long face looked paler than usual, his sharp, green eyes bright with excitement, his lower lip jutting out as if he was quietly rehearsing some speech. He carried gauntlets which he kept slapping against his thigh as he greeted Bray, turning to the blond-haired, bland-faced Lovel to confirm a certain

point about the recent hunt. At last the courtly courtesies ran their
course. Margaret could tell from Gloucester's peaked, pale face
and the way he kept playing with the silver medallion around his
neck, displaying the Fetlock and Portcullis of York, that he was
impatient to begin. Gloucester glanced at Bray, who had ushered
the servants out and came to stand beside the countess.

'Where's Urswicke?' Lovel, his bright blue eyes devoid of any
kindness, leaned forward, jabbing a finger at the countess. 'Where
is your dagger man?'

'Standing beside me,' Margaret retorted.

'No,' Lovel smirked, 'the one with the angel's face, even
though he crawls through the shadows.'

'Is that where he met you?' Margaret retorted.

'Come now,' Gloucester intervened. 'Let us be honest, Mistress,
Urswicke lurks in the twilight. I believe he is a man who serves
more than one master.'

'My Lord, who doesn't?'

Gloucester took a deep breath as if to calm himself. 'Let us
cut to the quick,' he snapped. 'I know, we know, you know.
Indeed, we all know that George of Clarence is involved, and
has been ever since he could think, in some devilish mischief.
We also know he fears and hates you and your son.' Gloucester
paused, eyes blinking. 'I have dreams,' he murmured, 'about your
boy. My brother, the King, believes young Henry is a real threat
to the House of York. What say you, Mistress?'

'His Grace has nothing to fear from either me or mine.'
Margaret quietly wondered where this conversation was leading.
Gloucester fell silent, rocking himself gently in his chair.

'Clarence certainly fears you,' he declared abruptly. 'My
beloved brother had spies in your household: two Welsh brats,
Owain and Oswina.' He paused. 'I have their corpses outside.'

Margaret felt Bray stiffen beside her. She held up a hand.
'Corpses?'

'Yes, Mistress, corpses drawn from the Thames by the
Harrower, a city official paid to pluck corpses out of the Thames
and give them Christian burial.' Gloucester's face was now
wreathed in mock concern. 'I mourn your loss, Mistress, but the
matter deeply puzzles me. Oh . . .' He rose to his feet, Lovel
also. 'You must want to view their corpses?'

And, without waiting, both he and Lovel left the solar. Margaret stared at Bray, lifting a finger to her lips as she followed the Yorkists out. She was tempted to protest heatedly against being summoned in such a fashion here in her own house, but decided that discretion was the better path to follow.

Gloucester swept down the stairs to the hallway where more of his henchmen gathered, gesturing at the door to be opened, leading Margaret and Bray onto the broad sweep of Fetter Lane. A cart pulled by two dray horses stood there. Gloucester clambered onto the side of the cart and pulled back the canvas sheeting. He then stepped down, gesturing at Margaret to stand on the footrest. Helped by Bray, she did so, grasping the side of the cart as she stared at the two corpses. Margaret tried to remain calm at this gruesome sight. The two cadavers displayed savage death wounds; their flesh was all puffy, bloated and discoloured from the river, the soft flesh pecked by the carrion birds. Margaret crossed herself and climbed down, Bray taking her place. He glanced at the corpses, cursed and stepped off the footrest.

'Mistress,' Bray totally ignored Gloucester and Lovel as he grasped Margaret by the arm, 'Mistress, it's best if you return.' And he gently led Margaret, who acted as if she was about to faint, back up into the solar. Once there, Margaret acted the lady in distress. Bray scurried about, ordering the servants to bring a hot posset for their mistress and a footstool for her feet, warm mittens for her hands which, she claimed, had become so cold. During these ministrations, Margaret kept a sharp, sly eye on Gloucester and Lovel. Her two unwelcome visitors had sauntered back into the solar and now slouched in their chairs, legs crossed, coolly picking at spots on their hose.

'Well, Mistress?' Lovel preened himself, his high-pitched voice harsh on the ear.

'I do not think,' Margaret retorted, 'that was at all necessary.'

'Oh, we think it is,' Lovel sniffed. 'My master here also has spies, and of course the corpses were searched by the Harrower. He found copies of your wax seal on both cadavers. Anyway, the Harrower was visited by one of my master's men, a skilled searcher – so experienced, he's called "The Lurcher". Now he recognised both the seals and the gruesome remains. You see, The Lurcher had been watching; he'd set up post close to the water-gate of this splendid mansion. He saw you, Master Bray, together with Urswicke, row these two unfortunates across the Thames. He watched you return but, of course, not with Oswina and Owain. They were gone; they'd disappeared until the Harrower found them. Apparently the rocks used to weigh the dead bodies fell out and, of course, the Thames always gives up its dead, including two corpses with crossbow quarrels which had been loosed so close they were embedded deep in the flesh. So . . .'

'All your spy saw, my Lord,' Margaret measured her words carefully, 'is this. Oswina and Owain left here in a boat rowed by my two principal henchmen.' She turned slightly in her chair. 'Yes, Reginald?'

'We took them on a special errand to Minehost at The Golden Hoop. You should know it, a splendid tavern close to the priory of St Mary Ovary in Southwark. On my mistress's instruction, the taverner was to give both Oswina and Owain good purvey-ance, food, horses and other necessities for their long journey to Woking and then on into Wales.'

'Yes, yes,' Gloucester murmured. 'And I am sure Minehost of The Golden Hoop, along with a packed choir of witnesses, will swear that Oswina and Owain were seen in his tavern, hale and hearty, very much alive and busy on their mistress's business. How they left but then disappeared until their corpses were found. Those unfortunate young things were attacked by wolfsheads who murdered them, plundered their possessions and then threw their corpses into the Thames.'

'You are very perceptive,' Margaret retorted, 'I think you have described what truly happened. I shall mourn for them, I shall pray for them, and I will petition your brother the King to take more rigorous steps to clear his highways and byways of such malefactors.' She held Gloucester's gaze. In truth, she didn't really care what he knew. 'Wouldn't you agree?' she demanded archly.

'I certainly do.' Gloucester's pale, narrow face broke into an infectious grin, making him more youth-like, the sinister threat he conveyed being replaced with a gentle, merry mockery. 'Margaret, Margaret Beaufort.' Gloucester dropped his gauntlets to the floor and leaned forward, hands outstretched. 'Margaret, let us ignore all this nonsense. The corpses outside will be swiftly and quietly buried in God's Acre at St Botolph's. Let us concern ourselves with the living. You know and I know this. Brother George has a manuscript, the "Titulus Regius", the work of the Three Kings and Oudenarde who now lie slaughtered in some Godforsaken death house.' Gloucester smiled again. 'Brother George is furious at their deaths, even more so because he does not know where the the "Titulus Regius" is.'

'What?' Margaret exclaimed. 'But all four worked for Lord Clarence, that is common knowledge. They were—'

'Not stupid.' Gloucester finished the sentence. 'Seemingly, they composed the manuscript, but kept its actual whereabouts a close secret amongst themselves, a guarantee for my good brother's faith – if he has any. Clarence is a turncoat. He betrayed his own family, joined the Lancastrians and, when they failed to show him what he considered to be his due, turned coat again to be welcomed back into the bosom of his loving family. The Three Kings wanted to finish the manuscript, then hand it over and be suitably rewarded, not just to be dismissed, or worse, at my perjured brother's whim.'

Margaret shifted in her chair, staring up at the pink-plastered ceiling. What Gloucester had told her was logical, given Clarence's talent for treachery. In the beginning the Three Kings would have been given the outline of what Clarence wanted and they, together with Oudenarde, had searched for the proof, creating a chronicle which they would only hand over when finished. By then they would know all the scandalous secrets about the House of York. Clarence would be in their debt and dare not move against them. Margaret wondered if the Three Kings had also created a copy. But where were these manuscripts which could do so much damage to Edward and his brothers? She herself would love to seize such evidence. Was Urswicke making any headway in discovering the true whereabouts of the 'Titulus Regius'?

'My Lady?'

Margaret smiled across at Gloucester. 'Just reflecting, my Lord, on what a tangled web is being spun here.'

'Even more tangled,' Lovel declared, 'are the murders at The Sunne in Splendour: the Three Kings and Oudenarde the book-seller?'

'Oh yes,' she replied, 'in the city, news flies faster than swallows. I do wonder,' she added, 'who could carry out such savage executions?'

'Perhaps someone else,' Gloucester declared, 'who is hunting for the "Titulus Regius".'

'Such as who?'

'My brother my King.'

'And what has this to do with us?' Bray demanded.

'Because everyone, especially my brother George, searches for the "Titulus Regius", and its authors the Three Kings, along with their fellow conspirator Oudenarde, have been murdered. It would seem they took their secrets to the grave. Let us be frank and honest. We all search for that document, as do you my Lady.' Gloucester swallowed hard and licked his lips. 'So here's my offer. If you find the "Titulus Regius" and hand it over to me, I shall personally guarantee that your son, who must now be sheltering in Brittany, will remain untroubled.' Gloucester paused.

'And secondly?' Margaret asked. 'There is always a second.'

'Your husband Sir Humphrey, Lady Margaret, is a very sickly man, greatly weakened by wounds inflicted at Barnet. I am not being malicious but, God bless him, Sir Humphrey might not survive the summer.' He held up a be-ringed hand. 'As I said, there's no malice intended. No insult being offered. I am speaking the truth, being as practical as possible. If Sir Humphrey dies, Lady Margaret, you become a widow, but you are also a Beaufort. The last of that name. You will be alone,' Gloucester waved a hand at Bray, 'except for your faithful henchman. In time you will become vulnerable to your enemies. Entire families like the Woodvilles detest your name and, if they can, will inflict great damage on you.'

'And we must not forget your brother, George of Clarence?'

'No my Lady, we must not.'

'So you are offering me protection?'

'I have already mentioned your son and, as for you, marriage to Lord William Stanley, a powerful baron, a bachelor, well-favoured by the King, with extensive estates and power in the north. A member of the royal council; in his own way a man of integrity, shrewd and redoubtable.'

'I have met and know of Sir William Stanley.'

'A good match, my Lady. He would prove a strong protector against the malice of your enemies. Anyway,' Gloucester rose to his feet. Margaret remained seated and stretched out her hand so Gloucester and Lovel had to bow to kiss it.

'We have an agreement?' Lovel demanded.

'We shall reflect,' Margaret replied. 'Now sirs,' she stood up, 'we have other matters to attend to. Master Bray will see you out.' She bowed and turned away, though listening intently as Bray deferentially led Gloucester and Lovel out of the solar and down the stairs to their waiting escort. Once they'd gone Bray returned, slamming the door shut behind him.

'Dangerous,' he murmured, as he poured both himself and his mistress goblets of chilled wine, 'a very dangerous man.'

'He offers some protection, Reginald and, at this moment of time, we need all we can get. As the poet says, peril presses on every side. Urswicke informed me about the slaughter at The Sunne in Splendour, as well as the execution of Spysin in the jakes of a riverside tavern. All a great mystery, eh Reginald?' She laughed, fingers fluttering to her lips. 'The work of a skilled craftsman, eh Master Bray? Do you not agree?'

'Talking of skill, I am thinking about those two corpses! We made a hideous mistake, we hurried their deaths. We should have taken more care. But, at the end of the day, we could not allow those two to live as daggers pointed at our hearts. They deserved to die.' He added morosely: 'They all deserved to die, didn't they?'

He broke off at a knock at the door and Urswicke slipped into the chamber. He crossed the room, bowed and kissed hands with Lady Margaret, who studied him from head to toe as he turned to greet Bray. She caught her breath and tried to remain composed. Christopher looked weary to the point of exhaustion. He had not shaved, whilst his doublet and hose were greatly stained, his boots scuffed and his cloak laced with mud from the streets. At her bidding, Urswicke took off his cloak and warbelt. Margaret made him sit down, serving him wine and a platter of honey-coated comfits a servant brought in. Urswicke just sat, watching the retainer gather the empty goblets and platters and, once the door closed behind him, Urswicke toasted both the countess and Bray with his cup.

'Let me tell you,' he began, 'how it is. First,' Urswicke held up a hand, 'no one really knows what the the "Titulus Regius" truly is, where it's hidden, or what form it takes. Such secrets died with the four men in that chancery chamber. Secondly, how the Three Kings and Oudenarde were murdered remains a complete mystery.' Urswicke sipped gratefully from the goblet. 'Four strong men, their throats slashed yet, apart from the blood and the fact they had drawn their weapons, no other sign of violence. Spysin died the same way, murdered while sitting on a jake's pot in a tavern garderobe. An almost impossible feat. A street-fighting man, Spysin's throat was cut from the front yet with no shred of evidence that the victim, who must have seen his attacker, resisted or retaliated.'

'Mauclerc and his master must be furious?' Bray could hardly conceal his glee as he glanced slyly at Margaret.

'Oh, and deeply apprehensive. From the little I have gathered, the "Titulus Regius" may never be found.'

'But,' Bray interrupted, 'Clarence and Mauclerc must have been apprised about what the Three Kings and Oudenarde were collecting? Be it a newsletter, a chronicle, or that's what we should think. However, we must remember that the "Titulus Regius" is not Clarence's work but the creation of those Three Kings, brothers, friars from the Rhineland. I believe they brought something to Clarence which he seized upon. A poisonous plant which they could nourish and nurse to full bloom. Mauclerc patronised those brothers and their assistant, Oudenarde. They insisted on working secretly in that chancery room at The Sunne in Splendour.'

'Yes, yes I see,' Margaret murmured, shaking her head. She reflected on what she had learnt about the 'Titulus Regius'. Clarence had saved those three brothers from the law. They must have responded by discovering something which Clarence seized on as a weapon to carve his own name in pride and so advance his ambitious schemes. In the end, Clarence didn't care about whom he hurt. On this issue the House of York and that of Lancaster were no different: they were simply obstacles Clarence had to remove. Margaret closed her eyes.

'Mistress?'

She glanced swiftly at Bray before turning back to Urswicke.

'But surely,' Margaret measured her words, 'once the Three Kings were dead, Mauclerc must have seized all the manuscripts in that chancery?'

'Of course, my Lady. But I don't think they found the "Titulus Regius". If they had, I am sure I would not be investigating that murderous mystery on their behalf. I play the part as I have told you, an ambitious clerk who will serve any master for profit. But on this, my service is not too good, for I am mystified about what really happened in that tavern. As God is my witness, I have made no progress at all.'

'Are you sure, none at all?' Margaret held her breath as she glanced quickly at Bray.

'None,' Urswicke agreed, 'except,' he lifted his head and grinned impishly at both the countess and Bray, 'the Barnabites.'

'Who?' Bray asked.

'Oh, I know about the Barnabites,' Margaret declared 'I now recall them, a group of rather eccentric friars. A minor order with very few members. Their friary, if you can call it that, is a rather gloomy, shabby priest's house close to the ancient church of St Vedast; it stands between Hounds Ditch and the Moor. In fact, if I remember correctly, the Barnabites do not enjoy the most savoury reputation.' Margaret paused, staring at Urswicke.

'Mistress?'

'They have been in London for about two years. They come from the Rhineland, Germany, not far from Cologne.'

'The same place as the Three Kings?'

'Precisely,' Margaret agreed. 'I know about them because they petitioned Sir Humphrey and myself for a grant of monies. If you scrutinise the records . . .'

She went across to the chancery table and tapped the main household book, a heavy tome with the finest parchment pages all bound tight between silver-embossed calfskin covers. 'Anyway,' Margaret moved back to her chair, 'the Barnabites?'

'I made enquiries amongst the scullions and slatterns at The Sunne in Splendour. One of them told me a little more about the mysterious visitors to the Three Kings. I glimpsed the same being brought into the tavern, men and women, not many, five or six individuals in all. They were always hidden, shrouded in the distinctive blue and brown garb of the Barnabites who escorted them there.' Urswicke paused and walked across to the chancery table. He undid the clasps of the household book and began to leaf through its parchment pages, looking for the heading '*Expensae et Dona* – Expenses and Gifts'. He sifted through the different pages looking for the entry on the Barnabites when one item caught his eye. So surprised he glanced up. Countess Margaret and Bray were staring at him, so he returned to the household account, murmuring about the Barnabites. In fact he was making sure that he had read certain entries correctly.

'Christopher?'

'My Lady,' Urswicke kept studying the manuscript, 'I intend to refresh myself then pay these Barnabites a visit.'

Later that day, as the sun began to set and the shadows both deepened and lengthened, Christopher Urswicke crossed the stout wooden bridge over Hounds Ditch, that great wound in the land north of the city wall where the sewage of London was tipped by the huge gong carts. 'Hell's Pit', as some people called it, was a long line of steamy slime stretching across the heathland either side of the bridge. Here and there, bonfires flickered and burned, but even their acrid, pungent smoke could not disguise the rancid, foulsome odours. Like everyone who crossed the bridge, Urswicke brought a pomander heavily drenched in lavender to cover his mouth and nose whilst he averted his gaze from the swollen corpses of dogs, horses, cats and pigs, their bellies bloated to rupture and rip.

At last Urswicke was across, striding through the wild heathland, a blighted, neglected place with its scrawny bushes, copses of dark, stunted trees and a moving sea of coarse grass. The place was the haunt of felons and wolfsheads. Urswicke did not care; he walked with his cloak thrown back to display his warbelt furnished with sword, dagger and a squat leather case containing bolts for the hand-held arbalest he carried. Meagre light blinked and glowed through the gathering dark; Urswicke, however, knew his way. At last he breasted a small rise and St Vedast lay before him.

Once it must have been a bustling hamlet or village which had grown up around the ancient church with its rather majestic-looking priest's house built out of wood and plaster on a stone base. In the dying light, both church and house looked eerily deserted and much decayed. However, even from where he stood, Urswicke could glimpse the glow of candlelight which indicated habitation. Urswicke stared around and studied this isolated, ruined hamlet. He could make out the lines of former cottages and other buildings and concluded that this must have been one of those communities wiped out by the Angel of Death, the Great Plague which had swept the kingdom a hundred years earlier. A devastating onslaught which annihilated entire towns. This community must have died and the parish became nothing more than a lonely church and house.

Both buildings were circled by a high curtain wall. There were outhouses, storage sheds and stables, but most of the church estate was a sprawling cemetery, God's Acre, a truly desolate stretch of land to the north of the church. Urswicke took a deep breath, crossed himself and walked down the hill, along the wet, pebble-strewn path towards a main gate which looked as if it had been recently refurbished and strengthened. Urswicke glimpsed the bell rope to the side and pulled hard. The bell, under its coping, clanged noisily. Urswicke pulled again and heard the patter of sandalled feet. A voice demanded who he was and Urswicke shouted his name and how he was here on the specific orders of Lord Clarence and his most loyal henchman, Master Mauclerc. A small postern door in the main gate swung open and a cowled figure beckoned.

Urswicke stepped inside. Four figures awaited, their faces almost hidden by the deep capuchons pulled over their heads. One of these held a lantern, the rest were well-armed with swords and ugly-looking maces, morning stars, their cruel, sharp studs gleaming in the light. The lantern holder asked for proof and Urswicke handed over a copy of Clarence's seal. Mauclerc had given him a number of these to use on the duke's business.

'Come.'

The evident leader of the group who held the lantern and examined the seal, gave it back and beckoned Urswicke to follow him across the deserted cobbled bailey into the priest's house. Urswicke was immediately struck by how sinister and dingy this was: narrow with paved corridors, the ceiling and walls flaking, cobwebs spanned the corners whilst the squeak and squeal of scurrying vermin seemed constant. Urswicke was led into what he supposed to be the refectory, with a long board table down the middle. The smell of cooking fish and burnt oil hung heavy. The table top was littered with platters and goblets. Urswicke sat on a stool on one side of the table with the four Barnabites sitting opposite him. They pulled back their capuchons to reveal harsh, unshaven faces, heads shorn to a stubble, faces cruelly scarred. They reminded Urswicke of mercenaries rather than friars. Their leader introduced himself as Brother Cuthbert; he offered food and drink. Urswicke refused, pleading he'd taken his fill. The other three Barnabites introduced themselves as Brothers Alcuin, John and Luke.

Urswicke smiled and nodded as he tried to disguise his own growing apprehension. Were these four really friars or were they rifflers, dagger-men, street fighters masquerading as men of God? Such a practice was rife throughout the kingdom and Western Christendom, to the deepening fury and dismay of the Pope and other ecclesiastical and secular authorities. Time and again, the Papacy had fulminated against the practice of outlaws who joined some obscure, decaying order to hide both themselves and their villainy. Some of these malefactors simply donned the garb; others were admitted on the full understanding that they had no more interest in matters spiritual than a pig in its sty. Urswicke loved the poet Chaucer and recalled a phrase from one of his tales: *'Cucullus non facit monachum* – the cowl doesn't make the monk.' The Barnabites facing him more than justified such a description. All four studied Urswicke before chattering amongst themselves. Urswicke did not understand what they said though he guessed that all of them, like the Three Kings, were from Germany, some city or province in the Rhineland.

'We know who you are – or think we do. We have studied the seal you carry.' Cuthbert's voice was harsh and grating. 'What do you want with us?'

'The Three Kings are dead,' Brother John spoke up, 'as is Oudenarde the parchment-seller, whilst another of my Lord Clarence's retainers, the courier Spysin,' Brother John grinned in a display of jagged, yellow teeth, 'was slain sitting on a tavern jake's.'

'And I am investigating their deaths.'

'So why are you here?' Cuthbert demanded.

'I understand from tavern chatter that you,' Urswicke gestured at them, 'or persons garbed like you, brought visitors, men and women, up to the Three Kings in their chancery chamber. Who were these and where are they now?'

All four Barnabites stared at Urswicke. Cuthbert, eyes narrowing, got to his feet, indicating that his comrades follow him to the far end of the refectory. Urswicke stared around as if curious about where he was. He noticed how truly filthy the refectory was: its walls were stained, the plaster flaking, the rushes on the floor a mushy mess. He also realised there were no triptychs, crucifixes, statues, or anything to reflect matters spiritual. Indeed, the only painting was a half finished, faded wall fresco about the fall of Lucifer and his angels. A sombre painting, in which hideous-looking creatures roamed a gloomy landscape lit by flames from unseen fires. Urswicke glanced away, trying to soothe his own nervousness. He strove to keep calm despite the deepening fear that he may have made a mistake in coming to this evil place to meet such sinister men. He bent down, picked up the hand-held arbalest and slipped it onto the hook on his warbelt, covering it with his cloak. Cuthbert walked back, Brother John trailing behind him.

'We can answer your questions,' he declared, 'and show you the people we brought. Come.'

Urswicke followed Cuthbert out of the refectory, down a dank, smelly passageway which led out into God's Acre. Brother John, gasping about his sore leg, stumbled along behind him. The ancient cemetery was a forlorn wasteland; its crosses, headstones and plinths had long since crumbled. Cuthbert led him through this house of the dead, pushing aside trailing bramble and sharp gorse, which caught at Urswicke's cloak and boots. Darkness had fallen. The eerie silence was broken only by Brother John's gasping and the occasional screech of a night bird which set Urswicke's teeth on edge. He felt a creeping sense of danger, as he would threading through the treacherous runnels and dark alleys of London.

'We will soon be there,' Brother Cuthbert shouted over his shoulder as he walked on. 'Well, here we are.' Cuthbert raised the lantern, gesturing at the freshly dug graves. Urswicke abruptly stopped. Something was wrong. Brother John had fallen strangely silent. Urswicke whirled round as the Barnabite, no longer complaining about his leg, was ready to swing a morning star to shatter the back of Urswicke's head. The clerk, his dagger now drawn, danced swiftly to the left and drove his long Welsh stabbing blade deep into his opponent's belly. The Barnabite sank to his knees, choking on his own blood. Urswicke turned just in time, his weapon knocking down the sword Brother Cuthbert had concealed beneath his cloak. Urswicke backed away, drawing his sword, balancing both that and the dagger. Cuthbert, a poor swordsman, lunged forward, but he was nervous and stumbled, the point of his sword narrowly missing Urswicke's face. The Barnabite paid the penalty for such a mistake. Urswicke's sword cut deep into Cuthbert's exposed throat. He withdrew the blade. Cuthbert collapsed to his knees, eyes fluttering, his mouth gaping, his lifeblood drenching the front of his robe. The Barnabite gave a deep sigh and toppled lifelessly over.

Urswicke searched both men, removing their fat money purses yet, apart from the coins, there was nothing else. Urswicke then prepared himself. He charged the arbalest, slipping the ugly, barbed bolt into the groove, pulling back the twine over the lever so it was ready to loose. Sword and dagger sheathed, Urswicke crept back across the desolate cemetery and in through the postern door.

'Is it done?'

One of the Barnabites stepped out of the refectory, a clear target against the dim light, so Urswicke's bolt took him deep in the chest. The Barnabite staggered back and collapsed.

'It is done,' Urswicke breathed as he hurried round him into the refectory. The fourth Barnabite, Luke, was frantically trying to draw a sword from its sheath on a bench. Again Urswicke loosed, but this time his hand slipped and the bolt caught his opponent high in the shoulder, sending him crashing against the wall. Urswicke hurried across. The Barnabite had managed to draw a dagger from the pouch on his rope belt. Urswicke knocked this aside and crouched down. He studied his opponent; the man was moaning quietly, eyes half closed.

'Who are you really?' Urswicke demanded. The Barnabite just shook his head.

'Some wine,' he gasped. 'Something for the pain.'

Urswicke got to his feet and left the refectory. He searched the corpse of the Barnabite sprawled there. He found nothing except a well-filled purse. Ignoring the groans of the wounded Luke, Urswicke then ransacked both the house and church but he could find nothing significant. He returned to the refectory. The wounded Barnabite was still moaning so Urswicke took across a goblet of wine and helped him drink. The man gulped greedily. Urswicke left the pewter goblet with him and moved across to the table. He opened the small chancery coffer and emptied out the different pieces of parchment.

'Clever, clever,' he murmured, 'no manuscript. Nothing but licences for a group of Barnabites to travel through Dover, backwards and forwards across the Narrow Seas.' Urswicke was about to push these aside when he realised what he'd missed. He grabbed the licences and unrolled them. There were at least a dozen but they had one thing in common: they were all signed and sealed by no lesser person than Robert Stillington, Bishop of Bath and Wells, who'd been recently appointed as Chancellor of the Kingdom. Urswicke snatched these up, walked back and crouched before the wounded man who lay moaning, cradling the cup which he tried to pass to Urswicke.

'In a short while,' the clerk murmured, 'you will be beyond all pain.' He held up the licences. 'Why do you have these?'

'So we can travel.'

'Yes, yes I can see that. You have the Crown's permission to travel backwards and forwards to Dover. All royal officials are instructed to assist you in any way they can.'

'And?' the man gasped.

'All of them are signed and sealed by the most important man in the kingdom, the King's own chancellor, the Crown's chief clerk. Why was Robert Stillington, Bishop of Bath and Wells, interested in a group of ragged Barnabites travelling to and from this kingdom? Every one of these licences bears his name and seal, but I have worked in the royal chancery, this could have been done by some common clerk . . .'

'Wine,' the man moaned, 'give me wine.'

Urswicke could tell the man was weakening fast. He filled the goblet to the brim and helped the man drink.

'The licences?' Urswicke demanded.

'Where's Cuthbert?'

'He's dead, his throat cut, as yours will be soon. I will give you the mercy wound.'

The man tried to laugh. 'I know nothing,' he said. 'I followed orders. We would travel here and there, both in this kingdom and beyond, to take and bring certain individuals into London. I simply acted as a guard. Who these people were, what they knew and what they told the Three Kings . . .?' The man stopped, coughing violently, and Urswicke noticed the bloody froth seeping between the dried, cracked lips. 'I know nothing,' he gasped, 'Brother Cuthbert did. He once said Stillington was in his debt, that the bishop had promised to look after Brother Joachim.'

'Brother Joachim, who is he?'

'Once he belonged to our brotherhood, but then he fell sick, some evil humour of the mind. Cuthbert told me that Stillington had found comfortable quarters for Joachim at the hospital of St Mary Bethlehem here in London. Its inmates suffer from delusions, weakened wits, all forms of insanity. I will tell you something else,' the man spluttered, 'if you promise to give me the mercy cut and vow, on your own soul, that you'll hire a chantry priest to sing a requiem for mine.'

Urswicke nodded. 'I promise, what is it?'

'Oh, it's very simple. According to Cuthbert, he held Stillington in the palm of his hand. But how, why and what for, I do not know. I have spoken the truth.'

'Tell me,' Urswicke insisted, 'why did Cuthbert turn on me? After all, I carry Clarence's seal. I work for Mauclerc. Why?'

'You did not follow the protocol Cuthbert agreed with Mauclerc: you carried no specific letter. We knew about the killings at The Sunne in Splendour; you asked questions you shouldn't have. Cuthbert, who was a law unto himself, decided you were too dangerous to let go . . .'

Urswicke studied the man. He believed the Barnabite had told him all he could. He leaned forward, took the goblet, and forced the wine between the man's lips. The Barnabite drank greedily and lifted back his head so Urswicke could cut his throat from ear to ear. Urswicke crossed himself, returned to the table and

sifted amongst the other scraps of parchment. Apart from
the licences, there was nothing significant, and he realised the
Barnabites had simply lived at St Vedast. In the main, all four
men and any visitors had supped and dined in city taverns. They
bought basic purveyance for the priest's house, a little food, some
wine, candles and kindling, but nothing else.

Intrigued, Urswicke continued his searches. He recalled how
the four Barnabites had been sitting in the refectory when he
met them: a room where, he suspected, there'd been a constant
presence, so he decided to concentrate on that gloomy chamber.
His scrutiny proved successful. Urswicke noticed how one flag-
stone beneath the table was so loose it moved. Urswicke prised
this open, thrust his hand into what he suspected was the old
parish arca – a stronghold, a sealed pit where treasures could be
stored. He searched around and felt a leather sack: he pulled this
up, opened it and took out a book of hours; its calfskin cover
held finely scrubbed parchment pages. Urswicke put this down,
returned to the arca and drew out an elaborate chancery tray with
quills, sheets of costly vellum, pots of coloured ink, pumice
stones and parchment knives. He searched the pit again but there
was nothing else.

He made himself comfortable, opened the book of hours and
leafed through its pages. Some of these had small, jewel-like
paintings which emphasised the first word or letter of a psalm
or prayer. The writing was clerkly, in a range of red, blue and
black inks. The book was almost full, only a few blank pages
at the back. Urswicke closed the book of hours and wondered
why it was so precious? He recalled a similar psalter he'd found
in the chancery chamber at The Sunne in Splendour. Urswicke
had now secreted this away with a goldsmith in Cheapside.
'The Barnabites feared neither God nor man,' he whispered to
himself. 'I doubt very much whether they sang the Divine
Office, pattered a prayer or even crossed themselves. So,'
Urswicke stared down at the book of hours resting on his lap,
'why did they treasure you?'

Urswicke put the book on the table and stared at it. He carried
the purses of the dead Barnabites in the deep pocket of his
cloak. They certainly had good coin and the wherewithal to live
high on the hog, though they seemed to own few possessions,

nothing of value. So why did they treasure this psalter so much? Stored in the arca, kept well away from prying eyes? Did they intend to sell it?

Urswicke drew a deep breath and got to his feet. Taking a lantern, he combed both the priest's house and tiny church, but discovered nothing of interest. At last, with the chimes of midnight echoing faintly from the city, Urswicke declared himself satisfied. He dragged in the corpses from God's Acre and laid them alongside the other two killed in the priest's house. He then fetched the oil and kindling he'd glimpsed in his earlier searches. He piled wood over the corpses, drenched that and the rest of the furniture in oil. Once satisfied, he took a tinder, lit a torch and threw it into the refectory which, as he left the priest's house, burst into flames. Urswicke stood outside and watched the conflagration spread through that ancient mansion with its dust-dry woodwork and crumbling plaster.

Urswicke stood staring as the night wind fanned the flames even further, wafting them towards the nearby church. It was time to go. Urswicke picked up the leather sack containing the book of hours and the small pick and shovel he'd taken from an outhouse. He put these carefully in the leather sack, gripped the still flaming lanternhorn, and made his way back across God's Acre following the same path Brother Cuthbert had taken. At last he reached the place where the attack had occurred.

# PART FIVE

'A quarrel rose between the King's two brothers which proved difficult to settle.'

*Crowland Chronicle*

Urswicke picked his way carefully through the trailing bramble and gorse. Immediately freezing as an owl, soft and swift as a ghost, floated just above him. Urswicke quickly crossed himself, watching the night-bird glide down until it was skimming just above the gorse: it then disappeared and Urswicke heard the screech of some creature caught in the hunter's talons. The clerk put the lanternhorn down near one of the freshly dug graves. He took off his cloak, draping it across the sack, from which he took the pick and shovel.

'I need to disturb the dead,' he whispered. 'Eternal rest grant to them, oh Lord, but not just for now.' Urswicke began to dig. He soon realised the grave was very shallow, the corpse thrust there treated with little dignity, bound up in tight, coarse sacking. Urswicke cleared the dirt away, cut the sacking and stared in disgust at the gruesome sight. The cadaver was that of an old man with wispy-white hair, the face showing decay and corruption. The eyes had long sunk. The lips mere fragments of flesh cut back to expose sharp, dog-like teeth. The head was slightly tilted back to expose the great gash in the man's flesh. 'Brought here for some purpose,' Urswicke whispered, 'and when that was finished, so were you.'

Urswicke sketched a blessing over the corpse, kicked back the dirt, grabbed his cloak and sack and strode off into the darkness.

The following morning Urswicke, who had stayed at The Sunne in Splendour to see if the destruction of the Barnabites was reported, rose early, shaved, washed and changed his linen. He then went down to the taproom and, bearing in mind what

he'd seen in the countess's household ledger, he decided to watch
Minehost Tiptree, along with his family and servants, prepare
for the day. The bakers had already filled a basket with soft,
white manchet loaves, small rolls of bread with butter in the
middle. Lamb chops had been roasted on a grill in the kitchen
yard, and now Minehost, assisted by a bevy of sweaty spit-boys,
was preparing a full side of hog to be roasted on the great spit
in the taproom's majestic hearth. Urswicke savoured the delicious
smells as he sipped his morning ale and slowly ate the porridge
laced with honey prepared by Mistress Tiptree. Watching carefully, he asked questions of the different servants so he could
clearly identify all members of the Tiptree family.

Once he was satisfied, Urswicke put on his boots, took his
cloak and warbelt and left the tavern. So far he'd seen none of
Clarence's household or any of Mauclerc's bully boys, nor had
he even heard a rumour about the fire at St Vedast. Urswicke
clasped his cloak more tightly and followed the twisting lanes
up into Cheapside. The morning masses had finished with the
tolling of the Jesus bell and the host of traders, tinkers and stall
holders moved like a shoal of colourful fish into taverns, alehouses
and cook-shops to break their fast. Market horns sounded above
the crashing wheels of the dung carts. Half-naked children
shrieked and yelled as they clambered over the slimy midden
heaps.

The weather had changed, growing decidedly warmer, and the
battles and storms of yesterday were now a fading memory. Merry
Maytime had arrived! The season for welcoming the sun and
rejoicing in a golden glow of summer. Maypoles, adorned with
streamers, had been erected at crossroads and in every available
free space. Minstrels, troubadours, travelling troupes of clowns
and merrymen flooded into the city, hoping to be hired for this
festivity or that masque. The days were growing longer and the
light turning stronger. The great ones of the city would hold their
lavish evening banquets, either in their gardens or on the paving
in front of their fine mansions, so they were eager to hire whatever entertainment was available. May was also Mary's month,
so decades of the Rosary, the aves ringing through the air, were
recited on the steps of every church next to a statue of the Virgin
wreathed in May-time flowers. All of this merriment, of course,

was watched by the footpads, cunning men and felons who slunk like dogs, hungry for easy prey, even though the well-used stocks, pillories and gallows proclaimed stark warnings about where such villainy might end.

The criers and heralds were also busy: they proclaimed the news from the court and from the shires, as well as reminding the good citizens of the names of rebels who had taken up arms against the Crown during the recent troubles and had not been apprehended. Urswicke also noticed with grim amusement how other street criers, darting swiftly about to escape capture, spread news that the Lancastrian cause was not finished, for there was unrest here and disturbance there. Urswicke recognised most of this as the work of the fertile imaginations of the Countess Margaret and Reginald Bray.

Urswicke eventually reached the Guildhall, forcing his way through a highly excited baptismal party processing up to St Mary Magdalene Church in Milk Street. The beloved infant who was to be held over the font was bawling raucously, setting nerves on edge. Urswicke was glad to be away. He showed his warrants to the guards and was halfway across the cobbled bailey when he heard his name called. Urswicke turned as his father hurried across, his smooth face wreathed in a smile, two young women, garbed in the tightest of gowns, trailing behind.

'Christopher, Christopher, you have heard the news? I have been dubbed a knight, but now there's going to be a royal cere-mony where my knighthood will be confirmed by no lesser person than his Grace the King. He will formally bestow the honour then kiss hands with me.'

'And when will this most magnificent ceremony take place?'

'On the feast of St John the Baptist in the Guildhall chapel. You will come?'

'Of course, and will they?'

Urswicke pointed to the two willowy figures standing so close behind his father.

'I can't answer that.' The Recorder patted his son on the shoulder. 'And why are you here?'

'To study the records, I am busy on my Lord Clarence's affairs.'

'And I am off to break my fast with my maids here before meeting with the sheriffs. You have heard about the fire at St

Vedast out on the moor?' Urswicke pulled a face and shook his
head. 'The priest's house and the church were burnt to the ground.
The fire started in the former but there was a powerful night
breeze and the flames spread into the church. Nothing more than
a charred ruin now.'

'And the perpetrators?'

'We found no coins, nothing of value, just four blackened,
crumbling corpses. We believe it's the work of wolfsheads.
Anyway,' the Recorder smiled falsely and gestured back at the
Guildhall, 'the chancery chambers are over there. You will be
given all the help you need.'

Within the hour Urswicke, using his name and warrants,
ensconced himself in a small enclave on the gallery leading down
to the great chancery office in the Guildhall. Urswicke was well
served by two spindly shanked scriveners who, with their pointed
noses, wispy hair and sunken cheeks, looked like gargoyles
who'd clambered down from the stout, wooden pillars which
ranged along the gallery. Both officials, however, were very
skilled, and soon brought Urswicke all he needed: coroners' rolls,
licences issued, a list of debtors, a schedule of committal to the
prisons at Newgate and the Fleet, fines and penalties imposed,
a fair reflection of the work at the Guildhall in keeping the money
market of the city healthy and vigorous.

Urswicke, who was as skilled in chancery matters as any royal
clerk, swiftly sifted through the different manuscripts. Now and
again he would rise and stretch and sip from the jug of wine
one of the scriveners kindly brought up. Time passed, marked
by the tolling of city bells. When the Angelus rang, Urswicke
went out to a nearby cook-shop for a soft, freshly baked pastry
filled with spiced meat and mint. At last, late in the afternoon,
Urswicke had finished his work; he found it difficult to accept
the conclusions he'd reached. Nevertheless, those same conclusions rested on sound logic and hard evidence. For a while,
Urswicke just sat staring at a carving on the wall as he plotted
a possible resolution of the mysteries confronting him. He dearly
wanted to return to the countess and question her but he dared
not: his investigation was not complete because he was still
deeply confused by the sequence of events over which he needed
to impose order.

Urswicke eventually realised that he could do no more in the chancery office so he returned through the busy streets to The Sunne in Splendour. He passed an alehouse full of flickering lights and raucous noise. He paused, went in and stared round as he recalled The Wyvern's Nest and Master Hempen. An ale taster came up to him with an offer of drinks. Urswicke shook his head, deep in thought, as a possible solution emerged, an idea which took root in his mind, a possibility which could be turned into a reality. He left the tavern and, hand on sword, hurried through the darkening streets, avoiding the low-hung tavern signs, keeping a wary eye on the midden heaps and the piles of night soil. He reached The Wyvern's Nest and immediately demanded to meet Hempen. The landlord agreed, providing a secure chamber above the taproom. Once settled, Urswicke described the outlines of his plan. Hempen listened intently. When Urswicke was finished he shook his head.

'Master Christopher,' he whispered, 'to kidnap a fellow taverner and his entire family, I mean . . .'

'It is necessary,' Urswicke insisted. 'No violence, no theft. Tiptree and his family can take any moveables they wish. But they must all be removed from there and brought to comfortable but close confinement here before they are taken far away from the city. In the end, all will be well. This is for their own safety and for the enhancement of the countess's future plans, as well as protection against Clarence discovering the truth behind what happened to his henchmen in that murder chamber.' Urswicke undid his heavy money wallet and poured out the gold and silver coins taken from the Barnabites the previous evening. He pushed some of these across. 'That is for your troubles. So, to quote our mistress, if it's to be done, it's best done quickly. In the meantime . . .' Urswicke got to his feet.

'Where are you going, Christopher?'

'I deposited a book of hours with a goldsmith in Cheapside. I think it's best if I brought it here. You have a secure place?'

'Of course. An arca deep in the cellars.' Hempen grinned and ran a finger along the red rope mark which scorched his throat. 'Not even a rat could find it.'

'Good. I will not be long. Hire six veterans. Have them here, visored, cowled and armed with arbalests. However,' Urswicke went and stood over the landlord, 'no violence! They must act as if they are the masked retainers of Richard Duke of Gloucester. Two of them must also make loud reference to being involved in the destruction of the Barnabites out at St Vedast.'

'Oh yes, I've heard of that.'

'Never mind the details, gather your men. I must meet them cowled and visored here in this chamber.'

By the time Urswicke had returned to The Wyvern's Nest and placed the precious book of hours in the arca, Hempen had assembled six former soldiers skilled in dagger play and the use of both bow and arbalest. They gathered with head and faces hidden, dark shadows in the flickering light of the lanternhorn that Hempen placed at the centre of the table. Urswicke, his face also hidden, laid out some of the coins he had shown Hempen. He could tell from their sharp gasps that these men had never seen such wealth. Urswicke made them pledge their loyalty. After this was completed, he delivered his instructions, ensuring that they all understood.

Once the curfew bell had sounded and the belfry lights glowed from the city steeples, they would move to The Sunne in Splendour. Clarence had withdrawn his henchmen but Urswicke warned his coven they might have to deal with any guard or spy left to watch the tavern. Their first task was to assemble Tiptree and his entire household. They must also give the impression that they were Richard of Gloucester's men and let slip that they may have also been responsible for the destruction of St Vedast. On no account must they harm anyone, unless to defend themselves.

Once he had the confirmation of their agreement, Urswicke assured them they would be paid immediately on their return. The clerk left them in the chamber and went down to the arca; he wanted to make sure that the book of hours would remain safe and he'd glimpsed an entry on the inside of the front cover which had intrigued him. He was surprised that Mauclerc had left the book of hours in the chancery chamber but, there again, other items had been left and Mauclerc, hardly a man of prayer, would find nothing interesting in a psalter. Urswicke returned to Hempen and his party. They declared they were ready so Urswicke led them out into the street.

The night was dark, an ideal time for any ambuscade, the thin sliver of moon hidden by thick clouds. The city watch tramped the streets but they would have no quarrel with a group of well-armed men slipping through the dark. London was now occupied by the court and the city was accustomed to the great lords sending out their retainers to perform all sorts of tasks. Urswicke was confident that they would not be interfered with and they weren't. They reached The Sunne in Splendour and swiftly scaled the tavern wall, dropping down onto the cobbles. Of course the kennel dogs were aroused but, being fed juicy scraps of meat, were soon soothed and quietened. The men then hurried across to a narrow postern door leading to the kitchen and scraped on this. Urswicke held his breath as he heard stumbling footsteps. Again he scratched on the wood as if one of the kennel dogs had broken free and was clawing at the door. Bolts were drawn and a sleepy, heavy-eyed spit-boy who slept beneath the kitchen table, opened the door and peered out.

Urswicke grabbed him, stifling his mouth and whispering that he would be safe as long as he kept quiet. The spit-boy nodded his agreement. Urswicke pushed him back into the kitchen, the others gathering around him. Urswicke swiftly established that there were no guests or any of Clarence's retainers present. He urged his followers, 'for the sake of their Lord Richard to be careful, as he did not wish a repetition of what had happened at St Vedast's'. At Urswicke's urging, Hempen and his men spread out through the tavern, securing the doors and bringing Minehost Tiptree, his family and servants down into the taproom. They huddled in a cowed, frightened group. Urswicke separated Tiptree and his family from the rest, who were taken to be held in the buttery. Once they had gone, Urswicke crouched before Tiptree, keeping both visor and hood covering his head and face.

'Listen Master Tiptree,' he urged, 'and heed my advice. If you do, you and your beloved,' he pointed at the landlord's wife who sat terrified beside her husband, 'I assure you,' Urswicke continued, 'will be taken to a place of safety. So first you must collect all your moveables, items you can easily carry: monies, precious objects. Go, do this now. We will look after your family until you return.'

Urswicke stretched out a hand and patted one of Tiptree's four children on his greasy head.

'Why?' Tiptree blurted out. 'Why all this? Who sent you?'

'I am your saviour, Master Tiptree,' Urswicke replied. 'You owe me your life and the lives of your family. You must accept that as God's own truth because, if my Lord of Clarence and his henchman Mauclerc discovered what you really did, you and your entire household would suffer the most excruciating deaths.'

Tiptree grew suitably frightened, very subdued. Urswicke realised he'd hit his mark. Tiptree did not bemoan his situation as he and his family were swiftly hustled out along the streets to The Wyvern's Nest. Indeed, over the next few days, the taverner fully reconciled himself to his fate. He soothed and comforted his family and fully cooperated with Urswicke and Hempen, even though he, his wife and children were confined to two chambers on the first gallery of The Wyvern's Nest. Urswicke suspected that Tiptree would become very aware that his captors knew the full truth about what had happened at The Sunne in Splendour. Tiptree would never plot to escape so Urswicke decided to leave Hempen in charge, instructing the landlord that Tiptree and his family must still be kept in close confinement; they must never see the faces of their captors or discover who was their principal abductor.

Satisfied and reassured, Urswicke returned to The Sunne in Splendour to find everything in confusion. The disappearance of Tiptree had caused the tavern to be closed, the servants being unable even to buy purveyance or, because of the rules of the guild, serve ales and wine. The tavern was barricaded up except for the side door through which Urswicke had entered on the night of the abduction. He went in along to the taproom. Mauclerc was there, his face mottled with fury.

'St Vedast has been razed to the ground,' he raged. 'The Barnabites who sheltered there are dead. God knows what happened to their possessions or what they hid away. The Three Kings lie murdered along with Oudenarde. Now Tiptree and his family have been abducted. I talked to the other servants and they claim my beloved brother, Richard of Gloucester's retainers were responsible,' he gestured around, 'for all this, as well as the destruction at St Vedast.'

'And the murders here.' Urswicke schooled his features into a frown, though in truth he was hiding his jubilation. The game had changed: this most sinister of henchmen was no longer its master, and neither was the dark-souled Clarence.

'I am sorry.' Mauclerc, one hand on the belt of his sword, the other on Urswicke's shoulder, almost dragged the clerk deeper into the taproom, away from the doorway and any eavesdropper, 'You have a suspect?' Mauclerc demanded.

'Of course, my Lord of Clarence's younger brother, it's obvious.'

Mauclerc let his hand fall away. 'Are you saying that Gloucester is behind everything?'

'Possibly.' Urswicke restrained the laughter bubbling within him, the sheer jubilation, so reminiscent of the excitement at his keenest games of hazard or his sharp debating as a scholar in the halls of Oxford.

'And you have proof of all this?' Mauclerc asked.

'Possibly, but I am gathering more as swiftly as I can.'

'Good, good.' Mauclerc patted Urswicke on the shoulder like some absent-minded magister would a not-so-bright scholar. 'My Lord of Clarence,' he continued, 'has moved to the King's palace at Sheen to discuss certain matters. Above all, the mischief being brewed by that holy dog the Lancastrian Archbishop Neville. There are also rumours of another traitor, De Vere of Oxford, leading a fleet of war cogs off the coast of Cornwall. So I must go there. To Sheen,' he joked, 'not Cornwall.' His smile faded. 'And you Christopher, you will resolve these mysteries?'

'You have my word.'

'Excellent. Well, until we meet again.'

Mauclerc was now in a better mood. He patted Urswicke on the shoulder and left the tavern, shouting for his retainers. Urswicke stood and heard them go. He felt pleased, confident that Clarence's henchman suspected nothing. He waited for a while then returned to The Wyvern's Nest. Hempen assured him that Tiptree and his family were isolated, safe and seemingly contented enough. Urswicke went up to his own garret where he took out that strip of parchment he'd found in one of the Three Kings' wallets. He sat down and studied this time and again. 'And the captain of archers,' Urswicke whispered to himself, 'lay with the wife of Duke Uriah the Hittite and she conceived a son.' Urswicke, who had studied the scriptures, recognised the reference was from the Old Testament. A story about King David wishing to seduce Bathsheba, the wife of one of his principal commanders, Uriah the Hittite. David became obsessed with the woman. She became pregnant so David decided to remove Uriah, instructing his general Joab to leave the Hittite exposed on the field of battle. 'I know the story,' Urswicke murmured, 'but why has it now changed? What could it mean?'

Urswicke returned to his scrutiny. He had graduated as a master of the chancery, being closely instructed by the Dominican Albric in secret ciphers and hidden writing. Albric had always insisted on two principles. First, conceal what you want in public view so clearly and precisely that people will never guess that what they are looking at contains a whole wealth of hidden treasures. Secondly, search for the pattern which should not really be a pattern. For example, sentences will always begin with a certain letter; their use is random depending on what's being written. However, if certain letters are used to begin sentences time and again, ask yourself why? 'So,' Urswicke whispered, studying the script, 'what is being concealed here in public view and what pattern can I detect?' He took out the book of hours and opened it, turning the pages until his eyes grew heavy. He fell asleep for at least an hour according to the flame on the red-ringed time candle.

Urswicke roused himself and went downstairs to ensure all was well. He took some food and drink and returned to his studies. He examined once again the script containing the quotation about Uriah. Holding it up to the light, the clerk noticed how the beginning of certain passages in the book of hours, be it psalms or prayers, had a different-coloured ink. For example, 'Pater Noster – Our Father' was written in red but the rest of the script was in black. It was the same on the strip of parchment where blue ink replaced black. Urswicke read the verse again but, this time, moving from words written in black to the next section written in black, so it read, 'And the captain of the archers lay with the wife of the duke and she conceived a son.' That made sense! Urswicke then applied the same technique to other passages in both copies of the book of hours. Urswicke eventually decided to write these out in his own abbreviated cipher. The more he transcribed, the more it made sense, and the secrets the Three Kings had disguised began to emerge. In a sense, it was very simple: the secrets were concealed in public view beneath a pattern of different-coloured inks. If certain sections were linked together, then the book of hours was no longer a psalter, a prayer book, but a treasury of scandalous stories about the House of York, King Edward in particular.

Urswicke felt deeply elated that he had stumbled onto such valuable findings. He now knew what Clarence was plotting. How that sinister prince had collected all the gossip, scandal and whispered secrets about his own house and handed those over to the Three Kings, who investigated them and discovered the evidence for a range of scurrilous allegations. 'Master Clarence,' Urswicke murmured, 'you have proven to be a foul son, a foul brother and a foul lord. A truly foulsome human being who will surely meet your death in a most violent way.'

Urswicke returned to the book of hours and re-read what he had glimpsed on the inside of the front cover of each psalter: the same inscription. Simple enough. '*Teste me*, Roberto Episcopo Bathoniense – witnessed by me Robert, Bishop of Bath and Wells.' Many psalters, prayer books and other devotional literature often contained such an inscription by the local bishop, which confirmed that the work in question contained no heresy or deviation from the liturgy of the church.

'But why,' Urswicke whispered, 'why is the name of Robert Stillington, Bishop of Bath and Wells, used here? According to canon law, such a declaration should be by the Ordinary, the bishop of the place where the book was created? In this case, the Bishop of London?'

Urswicke sat back in his chair. He was sure that the Three Kings and Oudenarde had no intention of handing the book of hours over to any bishop. So why use Stillington's name? Moreover, and Urswicke was sure of this, Stillington's name had been used without his permission. No, Urswicke concluded, the reason for Stillington's inclusion was that this bishop was connected to this mystery, Urswicke was certain of that. First, because of the location of Stillington's diocese, which was close to Shrewsbury, the ancestral home of the Talbots, whose kinswoman, Eleanor Butler, played – according to the secrets contained in the book of hours – such a prominent role in all these mysteries. Urswicke shook his head, marvelling at how the twisting path of life could be dictated by a dead woman. How a former lover of the great Edward of York could stretch from beyond the grave to cause deep dissent and the most dangerous rent in the body politic. If the secrets Urswicke had just read in the book of hours were proclaimed to the world, it would rock the throne and nullify Edward of York's recent triumph.

Secondly, Urswicke returned to the question of Stillington. He had allowed the Barnabites to travel in and out of the country on their own whim. Why? What did the Barnabites know about Stillington? And this business of Brother Joachim, the Barnabite sheltering in St Mary's Bethlehem? Why did Stillington agree to that, being prepared to pay all the expenses for such comfortable lodgings? Cuthbert must have threatened the good bishop. Urswicke wondered if he should use both his name and warrants to seek an interview with Stillington, but he concluded that would be too dangerous. God knows where Stillington's true loyalty lay and, for his own secret purposes, the good bishop would only lie, deceive and mislead. Moreover, Stillington must be aware of the destruction and deaths at St Vedast. Brother Cuthbert was now dead. Would Stillington continue to pay for Brother Joachim to be lodged at St Mary's? Stillington surely must have some idea, proof or evidence, that what Urswicke had discovered in the book of hours was true, hence the phrase '*Teste me* – witnessed by me.' What form that evidence took would be difficult to establish. Urswicke made his decision. He must visit St Mary's Bethlehem, and the sooner the better.

Urswicke arrived before the main gate of St Mary's Bethlehem late in the afternoon, when the bells of its church were ringing out the summons to early evening prayer. A lay brother, garbed in a cream-coloured robe and black mantle, the hospital colours, scrutinised Urswicke's warrants and seals before admitting him through the postern gate. He led the clerk through the gardens and into the prior's parlour, which stood within the entrance to the main building. A comfortable, well-furnished chamber with its polished oak work, turkey rugs and vivid wall frescoes depicting scenes of healing from the Scriptures.

Urswicke sat down, savouring the pleasant smells after the stench of the busy city streets, where the air hung heavy with human sweat, ordure and all the reek of the middens. This was such a contrast, a veritable paradise; sweet cooking smells mingling with the fragrance of incense and beeswax. Urswicke closed his eyes and relaxed, only to be abruptly startled as the parlour door opened and closed with a slam. Urswicke rose to greet Prior Augustine; a tall, forbidding figure garbed in cream and black robes, his long, thin neck and sharp, bony face gave the impression of a bird; a likeness enhanced by his rather jerky movements as he allowed Urswicke to kiss his ring of office before sketching a hasty benediction above Urswicke's bowed head. He waved the clerk back to his chair as he sat down in the one opposite. Urswicke handed over his warrants and seals. The prior studied these, gave a half-smile and handed them back.

'Well, well, well,' the prior raised his head, 'no lesser person than the son of the great Recorder of London, the hero of the hour, a veritable Horatius who stood in the breach and defended the city against hordes of rebels.' Urswicke smiled at the gentle sarcasm in the prior's voice. 'You are also, apparently, a favoured henchman of my Lord of Clarence. Well,' the prior rubbed his hands together, 'you want my help and I am willing to assist. So what is your business, sir?'

'Joachim the Barnabite lodged here at the request, and probable expense, of Robert Stillington, Bishop of Bath and Wells and our present Lord Chancellor . . .'

The change in Prior Augustine's demeanour was startling. He leaned forward, mouth gaping, face full of fear. 'How do you know . . .?' He paused. 'That fire, those deaths out at St Vedast on the moor. You . . .'

'I know of them,' Urswicke retorted, 'but I was not involved. I was informed about Joachim from another source which will remain nameless. After all, as you say,' he bluffed, 'my redoubtable father is a Lord High Recorder of the city, whilst I am the Duke of Clarence's most trusted henchman.'

'And that of the Countess Margaret Beaufort?' Prior Augustine quickly recovered his poise, staring curiously at Urswicke. 'I have heard of you, and about you, Master Christopher. You live in a very dangerous world.'

'Oh yes,' Urswicke quipped, 'as the poet says, in the midst of life we are in death.'

'True, true,' Prior Augustine agreed.

'Joachim?' Urswicke pointed to the hour candle under its cap on a stand in the corner of the chamber. 'The hours are passing, darkness will soon be here.'

'If it's not already,' the prior murmured. He took a deep breath. 'Joachim was lodged here some time ago at the personal request and expense of Bishop Robert, who demanded that I keep the lodging confidential. He even asked me to take a vow promising I would.' The prior sniffed noisily. 'I refused. We lodge many unfortunates who suffer a collapse of the humours in both mind and soul. Men and women who are deeply disturbed. I informed the bishop that St Mary's was not a prison or a hiding place but a hospice for the sick. I accepted Brother Joachim because he was religious, a sick man and, I will be honest, the full expense of his stay here was to be met by Bishop Robert.'

'I need to meet Brother Joachim. I must speak to him. My visit here and my conversation must be kept confidential under the seal, yes?' Urswicke stretched out his hand, Prior Augustine clasped it and nodded. 'Is he lucid?'

'At times, but at others he becomes witless. He rambles, mumbling one nonsense after another. On a few occasions he claims to know great secrets, about the King and his court. He chatters about furtive alliances and illicit affiances. But,' Prior Augustine shrugged, 'we have patients who declare they really are the Holy Father or the great Cham of Tartary. Some of our inmates maintain that every night they fly to the far side of the moon and see the Hosts of Hell gather for a feast. Others confess to have seen battle fleets of demons cluster to the north of Bishopsgate. Indeed, Brother Joachim is, perhaps, one of the more lucid amongst our congregation.'

'Do you know why Bishop Stillington should care for a poor Barnabite?'

'Of course not, but I can speculate. Stillington is a shepherd who cares more for the fleece than his flock. A man of power, of wealth and status. He claimed that Brother Joachim was a very distant relative, I doubt that. So, to answer your question, Master Christopher, logic dictates that our poor Barnabite knows something highly embarrassing and possibly very dangerous to our good bishop. He has been lodged here not because of any compassion but due to the insistence of Joachim's superior, or so he calls himself, Brother Cuthbert. Master Christopher,' Prior Augustine pulled a face, 'I haven't the faintest idea what is behind all this and, to be honest, I don't really care. Such knowledge can be highly perilous. I do not wish to become involved in the filthy politics of the court or the city.'

'Does Joachim have many visitors?'

'Very few. Bishop Stillington rarely, a fleeting visit to ensure all is well.'

'Anyone else?'

'Brother Cuthbert, of course, the self-styled leader of the Barnabites.' Prior Augustine swallowed hard. 'Cuthbert was a Rhinelander. I suspect that he was a former mercenary who served on the Eastern March, the antechamber of Hell. He would come here with his hard-faced companions. He would leave these in our guesthouse so he could converse in confidence with his old friend and comrade Brother Joachim. I did not like Cuthbert at all. He had an aura of fear about him, a midnight soul; dark, sinister and secretive. All a great mystery then?'

'Aye and at the heart of it, Prior, is this question. Why should Bishop Stillington dance attendance on a poor Barnabite? After all, our good bishop has the power and the means to arrange some sort of mishap, an accident. Prior Augustine, this is London. Corpses float in the Thames, cadavers are to be found in lay stalls or at the mouth of some stinking alleyway. I would wager at least a dozen have been killed today in some sort of accident.'

'The answer to your question is simple,' Prior Augustine retorted. 'Joachim may hold secrets but he undoubtedly shared these with Brother Cuthbert who, in turn, has made it very clear to Bishop Stillington that he is also privy to highly contentious information which will remain secret as long as our bishop cares for Brother Joachim, Cuthbert and his ilk.'

Urswicke nodded in agreement. He had to be more prudent: he had almost stumbled into mentioning the licences and bulging purses he'd found out at St Vedast. He now knew the source of these: Cuthbert was a blackmailer and Stillington was his victim.

'As I said, Master Christopher,' the prior spoke up, 'it's a dangerous world. The psalmist is correct, nothing lasts under the sun. Life changes. The great fire at St Vedast is well known throughout the city and Fickle Fortune has given her wheel another spin. Yesterday evening the bishop's courier arrived to announce that tomorrow the bishop intends to return to his diocese. He has decided to take Brother Joachim with him to what he called "even more comfortable lodgings". In a sense, the courier was speaking the truth. You and I, Master Christopher, know that Joachim is being taken away to be silenced and swiftly despatched to the mansions of eternity.' The prior rose to his feet. 'I doubt very much whether our poor Barnabite will live to welcome midsummer.' The prior stared down at Urswicke. 'You may talk to him. Oh, by the way, Joachim has a passion for the creamiest cheese. Remember that.' He extended his hand for Christopher to kiss his ring. Again the prior blessed him. 'Brother Joachim,' he murmured, 'will also need all the prayers we can say for him. Two lay brothers will bring him here and stand on guard outside. Speak, have your words and then be gone.'

Urswicke was surprised at the appearance of Brother Joachim, who strode manfully into the parlour and jerked a bow at Urswicke before thanking the two lay brothers who had escorted him in. Once they'd left, Joachim, all bustling and friendly, sat down on the chair that Prior Augustine had vacated and beamed at Urswicke.

'Very rare to have visitors,' the Barnabite whispered. 'Prior Augustine told me who you are.' He extended a hand for Urswicke to clasp. The clerk did so, feeling the calluses on the Barnabite's coarse skin. 'I was a ploughboy once,' Joachim exclaimed, 'I could dig the straightest furrow and harrow the coarsest ground.' He withdrew his hand and stared at it. 'Came from south Yorkshire I did. A village close to Pontefract. Served as a soldier beyond the Narrow Seas where I met Cuthbert and the rest. We grew tired of fighting, so we followed Cuthbert into the Barnabite order.' Joachim tapped the cream robe and black mantle. 'These are the colours of St Mary's. I really should be wearing brown and blue.'

Urswicke nodded smilingly, studying Joachim, his thin, greying hair neatly tonsured, his ploughboy features, round and red-cheeked, his pointed chin unshaven. The Barnabite seemed clear-eyed enough, though Urswicke noticed how Joachim's face grew momentarily slack, mouth gaping, eyes fluttering, as if he was confused by where he was. He sat, hands on knees, smiling at Urswicke before glancing around the parlour. He pointed to a triptych celebrating the life of St Martin. 'That's beautiful!' he exclaimed. He was about to point at another painting but paused and turned to Urswicke. 'You want to see me, sir?'

'Yes, yes I do.' Urswicke dug into his wallet and took out a silver coin, pleased at Joachim's reaction. The Barnabite leaned forward, hands extended, but Urswicke shook his head. 'Not yet, but I could leave this with Prior Augustine. I could ask him to buy you the creamiest cheese, freshly baked manchet thickly buttered and a deep-bowled goblet of Bordeaux.' Joachim licked his lips, one hand going out towards the coin which Urswicke placed on the table beside him.

'Why do you offer that?'

'For what you know. Why are you here, Joachim? Why does the Bishop of Bath and Wells protect and cherish you here in such comfortable quarters?'

'Aye, and he has promised to take me to more suitable accommodation.'

'But why should he do that?'

The Barnabite's head went down.

'Cheese,' Urswicke whispered, 'the richest you have ever eaten?'

The Barnabite swiftly crossed himself and glanced up.

'Because I saw it.' Joachim was almost gabbling. 'I was there, about five summers ago in the chapel of Shrewsbury Castle. Bishop Stillington summoned me. At the time I was a wandering friar, a hedge priest begging for alms on behalf of my brothers, despatched by Cuthbert, our Father Guardian. I sheltered in the castle. Bishop Stillington got to know I was there. Oh yes, I was sitting in the refectory. The cook had cut me some cheese. The bishop's retainers arrived. They had made enquiries amongst those flocking into the castle. Anyway, they called my name and I was taken up to the chapel.'

'In Shrewsbury Castle?'

'That's what I said. I will be given the cheese?'

'Of course, but you must fulfil your part of the bargain.'

'I was taken to the castle chapel, the King was there.'

'Henry of Lancaster?'

'No, no not him. The young blond-haired sprig of York. I've seen him as he has passed through the city.'

'King Edward?'

'The same. He was in the chapel with the young woman, standing at the foot of the steps leading up into the sanctuary.'

'And who else was there?'

'King Edward and Bishop Stillington and, of course, the young woman. Fair she was, fresh and wholesome, like the dawn. Edward pledged his troth to her and she to him.'

'Surely,' Urswicke urged, though he already suspected the truth, 'that must have been Elizabeth Woodville: there are stories that Edward of York met her secretly?'

'No, no. This was Eleanor Butler. You see, I had to ask her name. Bishop Stillington made me officiate at the troth pledge. Oh yes he did. Can I have the cheese?'

'Soon.' Urswicke picked up the coin and twirled it through his fingers. 'You blessed both the King and this woman, then sanctified the troth pledge? Were there any records kept? Did you have to sign a document?'

'Yes, yes there was, on a green baize-coloured table to the right of the King. I am not too sure what it said but I scrawled my mark. Bishop Stillington wrote in the rest.'

'And?' Urswicke insisted.

'I was dismissed.' Joachim's face went slack, lips gaping, eyelids fluttering.

'And what happened then?'

'I returned to my wandering. I fell sick and Cuthbert looked after me. Strange, you see, I felt guilty about the troth pledge.'

'Did the King say anything to you?'

'No, both he and the lady acted as if they could not even see me. Master, I am one of the little ones. To the great lords I am nothing but a speck of dust, yet I know what I witnessed. I later realised that Edward of York did not honour his vow, becoming hand-fast with the Woodville woman, as Cuthbert calls her.' Joachim paused, eyes half closed. 'I wonder when Cuthbert will visit me again. I am not too sure whether he will be pleased at me being taken to fresh lodgings.'

'Ah yes, Cuthbert – does he often visit you here?'

'Of course. I confessed to Cuthbert all that I had seen in Shrewsbury Castle. Cuthbert is a good father to me. True, he could be violent, but he was the only person who cared for me. He was astonished at what I told him. He insisted that we travel to Bishop Stillington's manor outside Wells. Cuthbert told him what I had witnessed. The bishop was angry and surprised but Cuthbert said he would lodge this mystery elsewhere in case anything happened to him or to me. He insisted that the bishop look after me. He repeated that if any harm befell him or me, he would publish what he knew. The good bishop agreed. I was sent here and Cuthbert rejoined his other brothers, Rhinelanders like himself. I was the only English-born amongst them. I later learnt that Cuthbert was assisting others in some great enterprise. He talked of clerks and a book-seller.'

'The Three Kings and their associate Oudenarde?'

'Yes, yes that's it but,' Joachim's voice turned to a whine, 'I know nothing of their business.' He held out a hand. 'Master, the coin . . .'

Urswicke rose and went across. 'You can tell me nothing else?'

'No, Master, and I am becoming confused.' Joachim stared fearfully around. 'I would like to buy some cheese, I need wine.'

Urswicke pressed the coin into Joachim's hand. He then leaned down and gently kissed the Barnabite on the brow. 'God save you,' he whispered, 'God bless you on your journey.'

'And you be safe on yours. Be wary of the Watchers.'

Urswicke spun round and came back. Joachim held up the coin. 'You are so kind,' he murmured, 'you gave poor Joachim this for creamy cheese . . .'

'The Watchers?' Urswicke declared.

'Two brothers,' Joachim half smiled, 'fellow Barnabites, Rhinelanders, Odo and Bruno. Two of Cuthbert's most trusted henchmen. He informed me how they would keep close guard on St Mary's Bethlehem. They would keep sharp watch over those who came to see me, if anyone did. They are what they appear to be, begging friars, well known to those who live here. They do occasional work as lay brothers, gardeners, cleaning latrines and other such tasks.' Joachim pulled a face and stared greedily at the coin which he balanced in the palm of his hand. 'So God keep you safe, Master.'

Urswicke left St Mary's to make his way back to The Sunne in Splendour. He moved purposefully through the gathering dark, aware of the shadow-dwellers and night-walkers who clustered in the narrow doorways either side. Urswicke drew his sword and the sinister figures melted away. Now and again Urswicke would pause and stare back. He would linger in the entrances of shadowy alehouses. At first he could detect nothing amiss but, on one occasion, he glimpsed a darting figure, a shape of a man who moved swiftly back into the darkness. Urswicke walked on. He paused at the mouth of an alleyway, a thin ribbon of blackness with only one lanternhorn further down, glinting through the murk. Urswicke turned into this and ran as fast as he could before darting into a narrow enclave where he stood, sword and dagger at the ready. He heard footsteps, muttered curses. He tensed, sword and dagger at the ready. Two shadows passed the enclave. Urswicke slipped out, tapping his sword against the ground.

'Good evening, gentlemen, can I help you?'

His pursuers turned; one carried a club, the other a sword and dagger. One assailant didn't wait but lunged forward. Urswicke sidestepped, his assailant was no skilled street fighter but a lumbering oaf who paid for his mistake as Urswicke pierced his throat. The man fell to his knees, gargling. Urswicke kicked him over as he turned, dancing towards his second attacker, moving sword and dagger which caught the light of the distant lanternhorn, a shimmer of glittering steel in the darkness. Urswicke drove his opponent back. The man stumbled, dropped his club and held up his hands.

'Mercy,' he whispered hoarsely. 'Mercy indeed. I do not know who you are. Odo and I,' he gestured at the man who now lay sprawled in a pool of his own heart's blood, 'we worked at St Mary's as labourers, gardeners, we earned a penny and were given a crust. No one was interested in us. We heard you had visited Joachim, so we followed: that's what Cuthbert ordered us to do.' Again he flapped his hands. 'I ask for mercy; we were only following orders, even though Cuthbert is dead. Were you involved in that?'

Urswicke lowered both sword and dagger then sheathed his weapons. 'Your name is Bruno?'

'It is. I am a Barnabite. Will you not show me mercy, sir?'

Urswicke stepped closer, peering through the murk. 'I will grant you mercy,' he said, 'on two conditions. First, you return to St Mary's. Tell Prior Augustine I sent you.' Urswicke felt in his purse, took out two coins and handed them over. 'Take this and whatever you can find on your fallen comrade here. Fetch Joachim out of St Mary's and flee the kingdom. I am certain you are skilled enough in that already.'

'We have monies hidden away.'

'I am sure you have. However, for your sake and that of Joachim, put as much distance as you can between yourselves and this city. Be especially wary of anyone sent by the Bishop of Bath and Wells. Repeat that title.' The Barnabite did so. 'If you linger,' Urswicke warned, 'both you and Joachim will surely die. Now be gone. So,' Urswicke gestured at the fallen man, 'take what you need.'

The Barnabite hastily complied and, muttering his thanks, fled back down the runnel. Urswicke watched him go. He knew Prior Augustine would help both Barnabites. Bruno would take Joachim into his care and immediately secure passage on some cog across the Narrow Seas. Sooner or later, he reasoned, Joachim, in a period of lucidity, would tell Bruno the same he learnt earlier that day. Urswicke didn't care. He hadn't the heart to kill such an unfortunate, whilst Bruno and Joachim would eventually sell what they knew to someone abroad and, if scandal about the House of York began to seep through the courts of Europe, then all to the good.

Urswicke returned to The Wyvern's Nest, making sure he wasn't followed. He ate and drank, washed, shaved and changed into fresh linen, constantly reflecting on what he should do. He had scrutinised both copies of the book of hours so he decided he would carry out a thorough transcription of the secret chronicle concealed within its lines. In the end, it took him four days, during which Countess Margaret and Bray sent him cryptic messages. Urswicke ignored these until he had finished completely; he then replied, inviting the countess and Bray to the solar in the house opposite The Wyvern's Nest. He also issued instructions that Hempen make ready to bring Minehost Tiptree across when Urswicke asked for him. Hempen was mystified by what was happening; however he was also very aware of Urswicke's standing with the countess, not to mention the clerk's largesse with the few remaining coins taken from the Barnabites, so he heartily agreed.

Once Countess Margaret and Bray arrived and were ensconced in comfortable chairs, Urswicke poured pots of light ale and joined them around the table. For a while the conversation was desultory, until there was a knock on the door and Hempen, who'd received Urswicke's instruction, brought Tiptree into the chamber. The former landlord, pale-faced and trembling, took the other chair; he sat down, hands on knees, staring at the floor. He then looked beseechingly up at Urswicke.

'Master Hempen,' he murmured, 'told me all about the abduction at my tavern . . .'

'Yes, yes. I asked him to.'

Urswicke glanced swiftly at Countess Margaret; she continued to act composed, a slight smile on her face, her eyes holding that mischievous look which made her seem so much younger. Bray, however, was clearly discomforted, staring into his tankard as he tried to avoid Urswicke's gaze. The silence deepened until Urswicke believed he had the full attention of everyone sitting around that table.

'Master Thomas Tiptree,' Urswicke began, 'taverner, landlord, mine generous host, formerly of Lord Clarence's household, a man of deep and wide experience in the bakery, brewery, buttery and kitchen of that so-called nobleman. Master Tiptree, you eventually left Clarence's service and, with the monies you'd earned and lodged with a Cheapside merchant, you bought The Sunne in Splendour. The tavern sign is a sop to the House of York which has the sun amongst its many family emblems and insignia. You began with high expectations but times were very hard. The unrest in the shires spread into London. Foreigners decided to stay away. Domestic merchants did not regard lodgings in the city as safe. In brief, you did not make the profits you hoped for and you swiftly sank into a quagmire of debt. Your creditors, the powerful city merchants, forced closure and you were placed into the debtors' side of the Fleet Prison. Your tavern was sealed shut, no Tiptree, no servants, nothing. God knows what happened to your poor family.'

'Relations,' Tiptree murmured, 'my wife has kin in the shires.'

'Wretched people,' Urswicke continued, 'certainly no one to help debt-stricken Tiptree languishing along the filthy corridors and cells of the Fleet. A place of deep darkness, brutality and the most hideous conditions. Imprisoned there, you spent precious pennies writing letters begging for help, redress to the Guildhall. I have seen such documentation. You pleaded for your petition to be forwarded to your former lord and master, George of Clarence. No one replied, at least nobody I could discover. Clarence certainly didn't. He never came to your help; he ignored you, didn't he? Didn't he?' Urswicke repeated. 'True or false?'

'True.'

'Hapless Tiptree, deserted by all, forsaken by your former lord. You then petitioned Sir Humphrey Stafford, my Lady's husband, a man noted for his dedication to the poor, the leader of a group of city notables committed to helping those in debt – yes, my Lady?' Margaret just smiled, a look of pride, as if Urswicke was proving the trust and confidence she had placed in him. 'You, Mistress, took up Tiptree's cause. You saw him as a possible path into the councils of your sworn enemy Clarence. Tiptree's debts were paid and cancelled. More followed. Grants of money to reopen, refurbish and replenish The Sunne in Splendour, all quietly done. I have personally seen the evidence for this in your accounts, Master Bray, and you know the reason why. Due to our mistress's help, Tiptree emerged as a prosperous landlord, the owner of a magnificent hostelry at the very heart of the city. He offered its services to you, my Lady, but you quietly insisted that Tiptree show such generosity to his former master Clarence.'

Urswicke sipped at his ale. 'Now that lord is as arrogant as Lucifer. He would forget his former neglect of you and take such an offer as if it was his birthright, his God-given due. He would use such a place as yours as his own personal hostelry. Of course, he would never offer even a farthing in return. Yes?' Tiptree nodded mournfully. 'But you, my Lady,' Urswicke turned to Margaret, 'continued to secretly subsidise The Sunne in Splendour. You saw it as a squint-hold, a gap in the defences of your mortal enemy. Tiptree here would pour the wine and ale, have the tables groaning under platters of delicious food. Of course, when the drink flows, so does the conversation. Hence the well-known saying *"in vino veritas* – wine always brings out the truth". Tiptree, of course, would faithfully report whatever he saw or heard. He would have to do it discreetly. Clarence may be arrogant, but Mauclerc is as cunning and as vicious as a weasel.'

'I didn't learn very much,' Tiptree broke in. He gestured at Lady Margaret. 'You know, indeed we all do, how secretive Mauclerc is, whilst those other demons the Three Kings were no better. I tried to discover why they were so close, so mysterious in all their comings and goings. Those strangers who visited them wrapped like friars in cloaks and cowls. I wanted to eavesdrop but, Master Christopher, you have seen my tavern, the doors are thick wedges of wood. One time I did listen when the door was off the latch but, of course, they were speaking in their native tongue which, I suspect, they did all the time.'

'I agree,' Urswicke declared. 'You made little progress, which is why you were drawn into a much more devious and dangerous plot. The complete destruction of the Three Kings and Oudenarde, their associate. You were partial to that weren't you? You took up the drugged wine and you set the stage for the bloody masque which followed. You carefully plotted so that the chancery chamber become a murder room – not that you were actively involved in their deaths, only in their preparation. You see,' Urswicke shifted in his chair and held Tiptree's gaze, ignoring Lady Margaret's smile, 'the chief perpetrator was no less a person than my good friend and colleague, Master Reginald Bray: a man who acts as a clerk, a steward, a quiet household man. However, appearances can be deceptive. I began to recall Master Bray's history, snatches of gossip and comments by himself and others. A true dagger man Master Bray.' Urswicke paused.

'Christopher, Christopher,' Countess Margaret stretched out a hand, 'you are sharp and swift. I wagered you would plumb this mystery.' She glanced at Bray who wanted to speak. 'No, Reginald, let Christopher tell us how he reached his conclusions. We must know what they are and so judge if Clarence and Mauclerc, who also possess considerable cunning, have not reached a similar solution. I pray to God they have not. Christopher, continue.'

'From the very start,' Urswicke returned to his account, 'I did wonder. The destruction of the Three Kings and Oudenarde was a most deadly body blow to Clarence and his schemes: his Secret Chancery was annihilated; it would take months, if not years, for him to reassemble it. If we regard Clarence as a wheel, the Three Kings were the hub. Consequently, I am also certain that the murder of the Three Kings at The Sunne in Splendour proved to be a source of great comfort to his brothers and, indeed, many members of the court who hate or resent Clarence. I doubt very much if anyone, apart from their master, will mourn their passing.' Urswicke lifted his tankard and silently toasted Tiptree.

'And so I turn to the actual circumstances of their deaths. First, I thought it was singular that the evening chosen for their execution was also the evening they were visited by the parchment-seller Oudenarde. Few people would know about such a guest, only Mauclerc, the Three Kings, and of course the tavern master, who would be informed as a matter of routine. In addition, Clarence and Mauclerc's absence from the city meant there was no danger of their involvement, though I am certain that you would have ensured that any unexpected change could be managed. Nevertheless, while the cat's away, the mice do play and, as I will demonstrate, there was a considerable gap in time between the fate of the Three Kings being known and that news being communicated to Clarence and Mauclerc, dancing attendance on their King at Westminster. So, we have the Three Kings and Oudenarde in one place at the one time. Clarence's Secret Chancery was to be totally annihilated. No survivors, just bloody mayhem to create complete chaos, deepen the confusion, and so prevent Clarence from continuing to plot silently and smoothly. Secondly, the deaths themselves in that sealed chamber? Its door, the only possible entrance, was locked and bolted from the inside with no sign of disturbance, even though the four victims had drawn their daggers, nothing else.' Urswicke gave a sharp bark of laughter. 'Think of it, four men with their throats neatly slit in such a place in such a way? No, no, the only conclusion I could reach was that the truth behind this mystery play had been cleverly concealed. I don't believe that the door's locks and bolts were all ruptured when the chamber was broken into. Nor did those four men willingly offer their throats to be cut.'

Urswicke paused. 'This is what really happened. Master Bray and you, Tiptree, plotted to kill all four. You chose an evening when Oudenarde would be with the Three Kings, and their masters some distance away. Minehost, here, took up a jug of his best claret and four goblets. He wanted to give his guests something special to drink, the finest Bordeaux, albeit heavily laced with a powerful sleeping potion.'

'And how was that done?' the countess demanded.

'Master Bray entered the tavern kitchens and buttery in disguise, dressed as a scullion, hired cheaply to perform menial tasks around the hostelry. A common enough occurrence. In your busy kitchens and buttery, Master Tiptree, Bray would hardly be given a second thought or glance. Anyway, to return to the chancery chamber. You poured the claret and invited all four to sip and taste. Hungry and thirsty, they do so, looking forward to the delicacies you promised to bring up. You leave and your victims sup deeply on the rich, red wine. You hurry down to the kitchen and fill a platter with the remains of bread and chicken, a jug of ordinary Bordeaux and four fresh goblets into which you pour some of the wine from the jug. You and the disguised Master Bray now return to the chancery chamber. All four men have fallen into a deep, drugged sleep. You exchange both the goblets and jug, leaving the fresh wine and scraps of food so it would appear that the Three Kings and their visitor had eaten and drank but nothing to provoke any suspicion. Am I not correct, Master Tiptree?'

'Oh you are so right,' the taverner blurted back; anger had now replaced his mournful look. 'Believe me, Master Christopher, I rejoiced in their deaths. I served Clarence for a year and many a day. I was a faithful retainer. I created delicacies for his table and did my very best to ensure all was good. I saved my monies, lodged them with a goldsmith. I left Clarence's household with high hopes. But, as you said, times were hard.' Tiptree shook off Bray's restraining hand. 'No, it's important. I want to tell the truth because they deserved to die. I did petition Clarence for help and assistance. He did not reply. He did not help. Later I found out that the Three Kings used to mock my letters as if they were mummery, the stories of a jester.' He shook his head. 'Rest assured, Master Christopher, it was no mummery. I was lodged in the debtors' side of the Fleet where you daren't even sleep. The rats are as large as cats, filthy food, rancid meat, brackish water. Violence and terror stalk you on every side. Master Urswicke, I am a cook not a felon. But there was worse. My wife and children were terrified, forced to beg for help from flint-hearted relatives. My wife was big with child. We lost it. The fear and hardship tipped her wits for a while.' He crossed himself and gestured at Countess Margaret. 'She saved me. In fact she redeemed us all. I tried to perform good service for her but the Three Kings proved to be a quarry impossible to pursue. Do you know, now and again, they would rub salt in the wounds, make sarcastic references about my letters begging for help from their master? So when Master Bray asked to meet me in some lonely tavern down by the quayside, I accepted. And, when he told me what he plotted, I heartily agreed. It was I who discovered the best day for our vengeance. Mauclerc and Clarence were at Westminster and Oudenarde was about to visit The Sunne in Splendour. I served the food and the drink as you say.' Tiptree paused, lips still moving, as if still talking to himself.

'You served the drugged wine,' Urswicke agreed. 'Master Bray then carried out what you,' he pointed at the steward, 'and our mistress,' Urswicke emphasised the last words, 'regarded as lawful execution. To deepen the mystery and widen the confusion, you, Master Bray, drew the daggers of all four men and slit their throats as swiftly and as soundlessly as Master Tiptree would a chicken breast. Once completed, you surveyed the room. You are looking for anything suspicious. You hoped to find the "Titulus Regius", but of course you didn't. You scrutinised the documents on the chancery table. You did not discover anything of real importance, except for that licence issued to Spysin, authorising him on behalf of Clarence to travel to Duke Francis of Brittany. You realise what mischief was brewing. Clarence was determined to suborn Duke Francis and arrange for the forced return of Henry Tudor, the claimant to the Crown. You, Master Reginald, realised what was being plotted. You and Tiptree then left that chamber, but not before buckling and rupturing the lock as well as the bolts at the top and bottom of the door so it would look as if they had been forced. Any further work on them could take place on the morrow when you, Master Tiptree, returned ostensibly to discover what was wrong. On that evening, however, you simply locked the door from the outside and went down to the taproom. During the night, you'd keep a sharp eye on those stairs, as well as tell your porter to alert you if any unexpected visitors arrive. Nothing alarming occurred. The next morning – well, you know what happened. The doorway was forced, the key slipped back into the lock, the corpses were viewed and urgent messages despatched to Clarence and Mauclerc. Of course, you'd realise it would take time for such news to reach them and for them to return.' Urswicke smiled. 'Very clever. You were given fresh opportunity to deepen the mystery and cloud the truth. True?'

'True,' Tiptree agreed. 'I advised Master Bray to stay well away from the tavern. When we did force the chamber, I ushered those who had helped me out and studied the room most carefully. There was nothing amiss; nothing which would point the finger of suspicion at either me or mine. Before Master Bray left, he asked about Spysin and I provided him with a clear description of Clarence's courier.'

'Of course you did,' Urswicke exclaimed. 'Master Bray, you had Spysin marked down for death. He was a bully boy, puffed up with arrogance, walking about all buckled and prepared for his so-called important mission. Reginald, you followed Spysin down to that dingy tavern on the quayside. You approached him and poured a potion into his drink. God knows how you did, but you are skilled enough, right? Spysin felt unwell. He hurried out to the jake's cupboard and slumped on the latrine. He was weak, perhaps even asleep, but he could offer no defence when you opened the latrine door, cut his throat and took whatever he carried in his wallet. Spysin would not be boarding any ship to carry out a Yorkist enterprise against Henry Tudor. In a sense, a good day's work. Clarence's Secret Chancery utterly destroyed and the mischief he intended in Brittany brought to nothing. Am I correct, Mistress?'

'Christopher, you are. You have spoken the truth but it must be put within the context of my world. First.' Margaret folded back the cuffs of her gown, a mannerism she always adopted when describing something important. 'First, I, we, are dedicated to opposing this usurpation of the Crown by the House of York and, in particular, the personal malice of Clarence. We will weaken them by each and every way possible. There are no exceptions. You personally witnessed the bloodshed after Tewkesbury. Edward of York intends to annihilate all opposition and we must defend ourselves as well as weaken our opponents by any means. This is not just a matter of a cause. Edward and his brothers are a direct threat to me as well as the life and legitimate ambitions of my darling son.' Margaret's face grew tight with anger. 'We all know Clarence, if given the slightest opportunity, will kill my Henry.' Margaret's head went down. She drew out a set of ave beads from her belt purse, lacing them around her fingers. 'Secondly, I was horrified to hear how the so-called Three Kings treated the sacred corpse of a truly anointed, saintly monarch, as if he was nothing more than offal on a flesher's stall outside Newgate. They committed the most heinous treason and abominable sacrilege. They deserved to die, as do Clarence and Mauclerc. Judgement against them has only been postponed, not cancelled. They perpetrated the most sordid sacrilege.' Margaret paused and used the small napkin Bray offered to wipe the spittle from the corner of her mouth.

'You are correct, my friend.' Bray had now broken from his reverie; he got to his feet and extended his hand. Urswicke rose to clasp it. Bray beat his breast in mock contrition. 'I was responsible. Spysin entered that tavern. I managed to slip a potion into his wine. He felt unwell and stumbled out to the jakes. I followed and pulled open the door. Spysin was fast asleep. He hardly moved as I slit his throat. I took his warrants, licences, money, and left. Clarence will be wary of sending further messages to Brittany.'

'The cracks in the Yorkist supremacy are beginning to widen.' Margaret spoke up. 'I have news for you, Christopher, on this very issue. Gloucester has promised that if we help him with the "Titulus Regius", he will use his influence with Edward so that my beloved son will be allowed to reside safely in exile in Brittany. Now,' Margaret crossed herself, 'my poor husband, Sir Humphrey, lies ill. I must leave soon to visit him as the messages

I have received indicate he will not recover.' She shook her head. 'I know it sounds cold and unloving, but that is the truth. I have tried to be a good, faithful and supportive wife to Sir Humphrey. I have tended to all his ailments and done my very best to make him as comfortable as possible.' Margaret shook her head. 'God bless him and me, but I married Sir Humphrey not just because of any feeling for him but because of the world I live in. To put it bluntly, I married Sir Humphrey Stafford for protection. When he dies, I will be bereft of that protection. I shall be regarded as the widowed Beaufort woman. I have to defend myself,' she gestured around, 'and those I love, especially my son.' She took a deep breath. 'And so I come to the second part of Gloucester's proposal. If we succeed in handing over the "Titulus Regius" to him, after Sir Humphrey dies, Gloucester will press his brother the King that I be allowed to marry Lord William Stanley, a powerful northern lord who would certainly provide protection against Clarence's malice.' She paused as Urswicke whistled softly.

'That fits well,' he murmured, 'with the tapestry we weave.'

'Now, back to the present matters. What else, Christopher?'

'You,' Urswicke pointed at Tiptree, 'will have to disappear, along with your family.'

'I will help.' Margaret stretched out and grasped Tiptree's hand. 'I shall, through merchant friends in the city, arrange for The Sunne in Splendour to be sold back to the Guild of Vintners.'

'Wouldn't the Yorkist lords discover that?' Bray demanded.

'No, no. Sir Humphrey Stafford's people will make all the arrangements. It's well known that Sir Humphrey helped Master Tiptree here.'

'And if he's questioned on this?'

'Why Reginald, Sir Humphrey is a member of the Vintners' Guild, it's not the first time he has bought property in the city. The Guild will take the deeds of the tavern and offer that hostelry on the open market. Clarence may well suspect that Tiptree was involved in the destruction of the Three Kings and Oudenarde, but he can't really prove it and he knows that Tiptree will flee well beyond his reach. You, my friend,' Margaret pointed at the taverner, 'and your family will change your name and, with my help, buy a hostelry on my estates at Woking.'

'But, but . . .' Tiptree stammered. 'Clarence will see my disappearance as complicity in the murder of his henchmen. He will send Mauclerc and his ruffians to hunt me down.'

'No, no,' Urswicke intervened. 'Remember the night you were abducted, my men made it very clear that they were the retainers of Richard of Gloucester. I peddle the same nonsense to Clarence and Mauclerc. How I believe, Master Tiptree, that you're part of Gloucester's plot, and assisted those assassins to enter that chancery chamber. I will explain my reasoning as I have done here, except I will blame assassins, their names unknown, despatched by Duke Richard. You helped them and I shall hint that you, together with your family, have been despatched, God knows where! To some desolate part of the north, perhaps abroad – or even,' he grinned, 'to life eternal. Clarence has a large pot to stir. He will not waste time, energy and good coin hunting you down. Nor will he, at this moment in time, having seen the destruction of his Secret Chancery, be willing to deepen the rift with his powerful younger brother. Master Tiptree, do not worry. Clarence will be busy enough.'

'You will leave in a covered cart tonight,' Margaret declared. 'You have brought from The Sunne in Splendour all your moveables?' Tiptree nodded in agreement. Bray then left and fetched Hempen, who promised to keep strict watch over his fellow taverner until nightfall. Under the cover of dark and, furnished with letters from the countess, Hempen would take Tiptree, his household and all his treasure out of the city.

Once the taverners had left, Margaret beckoned her two henchmen to draw their seats close.

'Before you continue, Christopher.'

'You can read my mind, my Lady. I have a question.'

'And I know what it is,' Margaret exclaimed. 'Yes, Reginald?' Bray just nodded, fingers tapping the table. 'Why did we not tell you from the start?'

'Of course, but now I suspect the truth.'

'Of course you do.' Margaret rose and gently kissed Urswicke on each cheek before sitting down again. 'You are, Christopher,' she continued, 'a most cunning clerk who, on my behalf, can perpetrate the most subtle deceits. If you had been brought into this game from the start, you might have been exposed to great

danger. Mauclerc is no fool. If you made a mistake, a slip of
the tongue, of knowing something you really should not, that
would have placed you, indeed all of us, in the greatest danger.
Keeping you in the dark preserved you. At the same time, we
realised that with your keen wit and sharp mind you would
eventually discover the truth. Even though you might not find
any evidence to corroborate it. Of course you proved us wrong.
You reached the only logical conclusion possible and produced
the evidence for it. The assassins, whoever they were, must have
had some inside help, and the only real source for that was
Master Tiptree. You very successfully proved that he was
involved and why. You discovered the evidence in my accounts
as well as documents at the Guildhall. Once you'd pieced that
together, you realised that Master Bray and I were the true
architects of the devious plot carried out in that chancery
chamber. You then established my motives, clear enough in the
circumstances. I wanted them to die. I believed they should. The
Three Kings committed the most appalling sacrilege against
Henry's corpse and you realised the full extent of Clarence's
malice towards me. And now,' she stretched out a hand to caress
Urswicke's cheek, 'you have not only discovered the truth but
refashioned it so cleverly that the blame for all of it can be
placed at Gloucester's door.'

'On another matter,' Urswicke responded, conscious of Bray
staring curiously at him, 'you claim that Mauclerc is deserving
of judgement; now that is a twist in the game I must deal with
piece by piece, moving the figures across the board so that
Mauclerc's day of retribution, and that of his master, crawls like
some monster out of the dark to devour them. Mistress, that is
what you wish, isn't it?'

'Of course,' she whispered. 'I want the total destruction of
Clarence and his creature Mauclerc. Seek a path forward on this
and we will follow it.'

'And so we come to "Titulus Regius"?' Bray demanded. 'When
I was in that chancery chamber, I searched, albeit hastily, and
could find nothing of interest except Spysin's letter giving him
licence to go abroad.'

'Oh it was there Reginald, before your very eyes – and mine,'
Urswicke added hastily. 'How true,' he exclaimed, 'is the saying

of a certain cunning man who argued that the best concealment is most effective when it is conspicuous.'

'Meaning?' Bray snapped. 'Christopher, we are not involved in some Twelfth Night game, merry dancing around the maypole, or bobbing the apple on the village green or tethering the donkey against the door of the village church.'

Urswicke spread his hands. 'Reginald, I apologise, but let me show you what I mean. The Three Kings were very, very cunning.'

The clerk placed his chancery bag on the table, opened it and took out the two copies of the book of hours he had picked up in the chancery room and from the arca at St Vedast. He opened the pages of one of the psalters and gently rapped them.

'This, my Lady, is the "Titulus Regius", the Title of the King – what Clarence dreams of. It's a creation of the Three Kings and Oudenarde. All four searched out stories about Clarence's parents as well as the emergence of the Woodvilles. They wanted to create a chronicle or indictment which Clarence could use to bolster his claim to be the legitimate King of England. The Titulus lies here and can be divided into two parts. The first is about the origins of his eldest brother Edward the King, the first begotten son of Richard Duke of York and his wife the Duchess Cecily Neville, the so-called Rose of Raby. So let us begin there. Edward was born in Rouen on 28 April 1442. To cut to the quick, rumour has it that Duke Richard was not his true father but a certain captain of archers called Blackburn, Blackybourne or some such name. The rumours are persistent, pointing out that Edward's appearance, his extraordinary hand-some looks and height, being well over two yards high, are very different from the physical appearance of both his father and his brothers, especially Gloucester. Now, of course, rela-tions between the arrogant Duke of York and the passionate, vain, hot-tempered Rose of Raby could be extremely tempes-tuous. They clashed in the bedchamber and were quite happy to continue their arguments in the hall in full view of everyone. Moreover, Duke Richard was often absent from court, whilst his wife was very fond of dalliance with attractive young men, aping the tales of Arthur, Lancelot and Guinevere, of Tristan and Isolde. My Lady, you've seen this often enough, some great lady of the court playing cat's cradle with a handsome young fop or arrogant knight, be it in a window embrasure or flower-shrouded arbour.'

'Yes, yes I have, and I've also heard rumours about York and his proud, vain wife. She was a woman I stayed well clear of, her tempers were notorious. She could lash with her tongue as well as with a cane, or anything else she could lay her hands on.'

'The passionate arguments between Duke Richard and his wife,' Bray agreed, 'were well known. They say Clarence inherited his mother's vile temper and arrogance. Again, Edward of York is markedly different in character from both his parents and Clarence. Richard of Gloucester is a much more difficult character to read. Yet I must be honest. Edward, free of the malicious advice and the evil counsel of his henchmen, can be merciful, humorous and, on occasion, even magnanimous. Qualities,' Bray added bitterly, 'neither of his parents possessed.'

'Now I admit,' Urswicke tapped the book of hours, 'rumour often walks hand in hand with the most lurid scandal when it comes to the great ones of the land, be it bishop, lord or prince. The House of York is no different from that of Lancaster, where similar scandals lurk. Indeed the gossipers claim the late Prince Edward was not the son of the saintly Henry, God rest them both, but the offspring of De La Pole or some other favourite of the Angevin queen. Such stories of illegitimacy did nothing to enhance that prince or his mother. As you know, she was dismissed as a French whore and her only son a bastard. Indeed, when the late King Henry heard how his wife had conceived, he openly mocked the news, saying it was the work of the Holy Spirit, for he had certainly not lain with her.'

'I agree,' Margaret declared. 'The Beauforts also have their dark corners, and the gossipers have made great play of this affair and that. But chatter is one thing, proof is another.'

'True. And so we come to the second part of the "Titulus Regius" – the marriage of Edward of York to Elizabeth Woodville. Now, as you know, at the time of their secret marriage, Neville Earl of Warwick was King Edward's chief minister and plenipotentiary. Warwick wanted our Yorkist King to marry some foreign princess such as Bona of Savoy. Edward thought differently. He met and fell in love with the widow Elizabeth Woodville, a passionate, secret affair which, because of its passion, did not remain secret for long. The Woodvilles were, and still are, regarded as upstarts: petty-shire nobility with no right to be at court. They are grasping, avaricious and ruthless. Elizabeth looks as if butter wouldn't melt in her mouth, but many at court regard her as officious, a vindictive vixen who has ensnared Edward of York with her coy ways and bedchamber skills. Edward was, and still is, besotted with her. He may frequent the likes of Jane Shore and others, but Elizabeth always draws him back. Now, when Edward's mother, the Duchess of York, learnt that her son had secretly married "The Woodville widow", as she was then called, Duchess Cecily fell into such a frenzy. She ranted and raved. She even offered to submit in open court how her son Edward was not the offspring of Richard Duke of York but was conceived in adultery: illegitimate and therefore not worthy of the honour of kingship.'

'In God's name,' Margaret interrupted, 'and she said that?'

'Ah,' Christopher smiled, 'worse is to come. Duchess Cecily's hatred for the Woodvilles is public and very well known. However, a greater secret lurks beneath the surface, a rumour which is much more dangerous . . .'

'Which is?' Bray demanded.

'That Edward of York's marriage to Elizabeth Woodville is invalid.'

'*What?*' Margaret and Bray chorused.

'Edward's lust for older women is clear to everyone. He has from his early youth always had a penchant for the more mature ladies of his court. Now the Three Kings investigated this and uncovered a great secret: namely, that at the time of his marriage to Woodville, Edward was secretly committed by troth-plight to the Lady Eleanor Butler, widow of Sir Thomas Butler. Eleanor was the daughter of the redoubtable warrior, Talbot Earl of Shrewsbury. Eleanor died some years ago but she was very much alive when Edward married Elizabeth Woodville.'

'And the source of all this?' Margaret's voice was hoarse.

'Well, it is not mere gossip. This is a secret cherished by our present Lord Chancellor, appointed so by Edward himself.'

'In God's name, Robert Stillington, Bishop of Bath and Wells?'

'The same,' Urswicke agreed, and quickly gave both the

countess and Bray all he had learnt from Brother Joachim, the last remaining Barnabite. He explained how Stillington's name on the inside of the front cover of each copy of the book of hours was a clue to this, though in the text both he and Joachim were simply described as '*Presbyteri* – Priests.' Urswicke also described how he himself had stumbled on this when he'd studied the different licences given by Stillington time and again to Brother Cuthbert and his companions.

'Now.' Urswicke took a deep drink from the tankard of ale. 'There is no doubt that the Three Kings and Oudenarde acquired this knowledge. I doubt if they handed it over to Clarence but they certainly intended to. What we do know is that Stillington and that hedge priest Joachim witnessed the betrothal between Edward of York and Eleanor Butler. Such a holy vow is, according to canon law, valid and supported with the full force of church law. Edward of York was already affianced to someone else when he exchanged vows at the church door with the Woodville widow. Consequently such an exchange was not legal, and can never be so.'

'Saints be my witness,' Margaret breathed, 'the heirs of such a union are illegitimate and cannot succeed to the throne. If Clarence fully grasps this, he will argue that his nephews are bastards and therefore, by the law of succession, he is the next rightful King of England.' Margaret fell silent, staring down at the table top. She lifted her head. 'Do you think Clarence knows the full revelation?'

'No, Mistress, I do not. The Three Kings were extremely diligent and very cunning. Their discoveries and their secret writing were their preserve. They kept the full content of the "Titulus Regius" to themselves. They probably promised Clarence and Mauclerc a finished document, something which would delight them. They might make allusions, hint and whet their master's appetites, but not provide full disclosure. Eventually they would lead Clarence to the glorious conclusion of their work, which would win the Three Kings and Oudenarde even greater favours for the lord they served.' Urswicke paused. 'They collected the evidence. They searched out and brought into that chancery room individuals who might attest to what they wrote.'

'Such as?' Bray asked.

'Oh, former minions of the different Yorkist households; those who had served Duke Richard, his wife Cecily and their children, men and women, mere scullions who might provide juicy scandal. All servants like to gossip about their masters.'

'Yes, yes, I know what you are going to say,' Margaret interrupted. 'Richard and Cecily of York would not be the easiest lords to serve. Cecily in particular would make her presence felt; she'd cruelly punish those who disobeyed or failed her. The Three Kings would have a great deal to harvest.'

'And that's why the Barnabites were brought in. They would sift the wheat from the chaff. They would look for individuals who could substantiate their story and reject those who indulged in fanciful tales. They would do this quietly, secretly, and fear no reprisals.'

'Yes, yes. To cast aspersions on the King's legitimacy could be construed as treason!'

'Of course,' Urswicke agreed, 'Brother Cuthbert and his ruffians would tell all those they questioned not to repeat their conversation or they might find themselves indicted. He and his fellow mercenaries would select those they wanted and bring them to The Sunne in Splendour. They probably came from far afield as well as the shires: Normandy, Hainault and Flanders; countries where Richard and Cecily of York stayed during their different sojourns abroad. Others, such as Stillington, would be warned to cooperate or face the consequences. After all, what could Stillington do? If he confessed, then both Church and Crown would turn on him, so he remained silent.'

'And what happened to the others?'

Urswicke crossed himself. 'My Lady, I went out to St Vedast where the Barnabites sheltered. They were nothing more than a group of ruthless, foreign mercenaries who hid beneath the guise of being members of some obscure order of friars. They were murderers, assassins. I visited the Godforsaken, dismal cemetery near that church. I believe that the lesser people, mere minions to the likes of Mauclerc, were silenced for good. Once they had given their evidence, these unfortunates were deceived into going to receive their reward, only to be brutally murdered and their corpses hurriedly buried in that desolate graveyard.'

'Of course,' Bray declared, 'lest they take their story or their meeting with the Three Kings to any other interested party.'

'Precisely,' Urswicke retorted. Urswicke crossed his arms and stared up at the ceiling.

'Christopher?'

'Further mischief, Mistress. The Three Kings were unable to finish their task but they were very close to it. I believe they were to propose one final masque which, if Clarence was arrogant and stupid enough to implement, and I think he is, would have caused a grievous rift between himself and his two brothers. Indeed I do wonder if the Three Kings and Oudenarde were intent on serving two masters?'

'Who?'

'Well, if they had revealed what they had found and written up in the "Titulus Regius" to someone like Richard of Gloucester, they could expect even greater reward. I just wonder why they kept two copies, one in the Secret Chancery chamber, the other at St Vedast?' Urswicke shrugged. 'Of course two copies meant they had a guarantee that their work would never be lost. The Three Kings certainly brewed a pot of mischief. Anyway, I came across a final proposal hidden deep in the text. As you know, Richard Neville, Earl of Warwick – the self-styled King-maker – was killed at Barnet. He left no male heir, only two daughters, Isobel and Anne. Clarence, like a hog at its trough, married Isobel so as to seize the Neville inheritance. Richard of Gloucester, or so rumour has it, intends to marry Anne and, of course, demand that half the Neville patrimony be given to him . . .'

'Clarence would fight.'

'Of course, Reginald. So the Three Kings recommended that Anne Neville should disappear.'

'Disappear?'

'Yes, my Lady. Be abducted by Clarence's retainers, hidden away in some nunnery or even a tavern here in London. It might take months, even years to find out where she was, and who would really search for her? Richard of Gloucester? Clarence would hamper that. It would be like searching for a needle in a haystack. People would whisper that Anne Neville had been abducted, murdered or, out of sheer grief, killed herself. If she cannot present herself in court to claim her rights, then those rights must go to the last surviving member of her family, namely Isobel, Clarence's wife.'

'A witch's brew indeed,' Margaret declared. 'The stuff of civil war, the long, encroaching shadow of Cain against Abel, brother fighting brother.' She glanced at Urswicke. 'And so hangs your tale.'

'And so hangs my tale, Mistress.'

'You did well.' She leaned over and stroked Urswicke's face. 'You did so well against truly deadly adversaries.'

'And the "Titulus Regius"?' Bray demanded, pointing at the richly embroidered calfskin tomes.

'Oh very clever.' Urswicke took one of the book of hours, placed it on the table before him and opened it. He pointed to the inside of the front cover and the 'Teste Me' of Stillington. 'You know the reason for that; I will not share such knowledge with anyone else. Anyway, look at this tome. See how it is made up of different chapters or sections, all self-contained. The spine of the book is tough, hard leather, the best you can buy, reinforced with strips which will keep it firm. Observe.' He turned the book so they could clearly see the spine and he tapped it. 'This contains the chapters which are expertly sewn together with twine; these are placed within the spine which is broad enough to accept them. We are all skilled in matters of the chancery: this is the work of experienced craftsmen, the Three Kings and their fellow countryman, Oudenarde the parchment-seller. He fashioned this tome, its pages and the spine. He would then seal them using suitable twine and carefully binding. I suspect each of the Three Kings took responsibility for one of the secret scandals involving the House of York which I have already described to you. Now I have done so in brief, summarising what is written here, but the Three Kings carefully copied out their hidden narrative. Ostensibly they were transcribing the contents of an ordinary book of hours, yet they used this to hide their secret chronicle. Every so often they would change the colour of ink from black to red or from green to blue and so on. By themselves these verses mean nothing, but start running them together according to colour and they tell a tale to catch the heart and startle the mind. For example, all they had to do regarding the incident involving Stillington and Brother Joachim was to find the words 'priests', 'marriage oath', 'betrothal', 'witness', and so on. These, along with other phrases, when put together describe, in detail, the stories of Eleanor Butler and Elizabeth Woodville.'

'But they are not named?' Margaret asked.

'Of course not. Like Stillington's, their identity is hidden beneath the phrases "first betrothed" and "second betrothed". Edward of York is simply described as a "Prince of the White Rose". Again, such a phrase is broken up and scattered throughout the manuscript.' Urswicke paused and leafed through the book of hours. 'A most significant example is the story about David lusting after Bathsheba and arranging for that woman's husband to be killed in battle. The verse I found, when it's assembled together according to colour, reads as follows: "And the captain of archers lay with the duke's wife and she conceived a son, their eldest." This verse is made up of phrases all written in black on a page where the rest of the writing is in blue, and so it goes on: a secret chronicle describing the scandals of the House of York lies hidden away in this book of hours. Now,' Urswicke shrugged, 'I concede many of the witnesses to such an account are dead, but the four most powerful are not.'

'Four?' Bray queried.

'Stillington, the two Barnabites, especially Brother Joachim.'

'And the fourth is Edward of York,' Margaret declared.

'In truth he is,' Urswicke agreed. 'And that is something we should concentrate on. Edward of York knows exactly what happened. He must be fearful for himself, his wife and any possible heir. If Clarence seizes this information and uses it, I doubt if his royal brother will show any mercy. Anyway, Brother Joachim is now wandering the countryside; indeed, he may probably be abroad. Stories about scandals in the House of York will begin to seep through, the usual whispers and chatter, but the seed has been sown. God knows what harvest it will bring.' Urswicke paused and sat staring at the countess, who was lost in her own deep thoughts.

'Mistress?' Bray demanded.

'Time passes on,' she replied in a half-whisper. 'Margaret of Anjou and her son had to go into the dark.' She glanced sharply at Urswicke. 'Your intervention at Tewkesbury was crucial. Somerset's suspicions about Wenlock and his execution of that lord may have turned the tide against the Angevin. Poor woman!

Jasper Tudor, I know, would not have been waiting for her across the Severn; she could expect little help from him. At my request, he had dismissed his levies and been given one task and one task only, to spirit his nephew out of this kingdom. The Angevin and her son could have fled abroad but that would have meant more war, more agitation and yet, I know here,' Margaret struck her breast, 'how the Angevin and her son would never have been accepted in this kingdom. Our saintly King Henry, as expected, did not survive a month after Tewkesbury. Poor man, he has gone to his rightful place amongst the saints.' Margaret paused. 'Only my son,' she added fiercely, 'now sheltering under the protection of Duke Francis, will become the standard around which the rest will rally. Nobles such as De Vere of Oxford.' She smiled thinly, 'I have also been busy elsewhere. John Morton, a leading figure at Westminster, is one of us, and he will draw others in. We must not fritter away our time or wealth on feckless uprisings or surprise landings along some neglected stretch of coastline. Time will pass. Henry will grow older: come the moment, come the prince, and we must prepare for that. Now Christopher,' she leaned across and grasped his hand, 'what are your sharp wits plotting? Moving like the swiftest greyhound to keep its quarry under eye? In a word, how will you present all of this to that demon-incarnate Clarence?'

'Mistress, I hear what you say.' Urswicke gripped the countess's hands and kissed her fingertips.

'And yet what, Christopher?'

'The game is stacked strongly against us. Edward of York is triumphant. He has a fertile wife who will provide a brood of children and present him with an heir. Edward also has two brothers who would fight to the death for their inheritance. What real chance do we have?' He let go of the countess's hand. 'Please don't doubt my fealty or my passion, but what chance do we really have?'

'We have Christ's own words, Christopher, and I believe them. A house divided against itself cannot stand. A house built on sand will not survive the coming storms and tempests. Such prophecies accurately describe the House of York, and I intend to prove such predictions are correct in all their details. Now, as for Clarence . . .?'

# PART SIX

'The Duke of Clarence caused the girl Anne to be
concealed so his brother would not know where she was.'
*Crowland Chronicle*

Christopher Urswicke gently dug in his heels and his horse,
snorting at the pungent smell of burning, picked its way
across the blackened, crumbling remains of the priest's
house at St Vedast, on that stretch of desolate moorlands north
of the city wall. Urswicke stared around. From the information
he had learnt in his father's chancery at the Guildhall, the fire
which started here had been devastating. Wafted by a stiff breeze,
the flames had moved to catch and consume the church, reducing
it to a tangle of scorched stone and timber. Urswicke peered
through the dark. Somewhere nearby lay the blackened remains
of the Barnabites he had killed. Urswicke crossed himself, even
as he promised the spirits, who must be crowding around him,
that he would have a chantry priest sing three requiems for the
repose of their souls – wherever they might be.

He gently urged his horse out of the ruined house and across
through a huge rent in the crumbling walls of the ancient church
of St Vedast. He guided his mount up along the remains of the
gloomy, ghostly nave. Wisps of smoke still swirled. Tendrils of
river mist gathered and mingled before drifting apart. Urswicke's
horse made its way up into the fire-blighted sanctuary where the
clerk dismounted and stood listening. Outside the sun was setting,
a burst of dying light still strong against the gathering night.
Urswicke hobbled his horse and went into the apse behind the
ruined high altar. He sat in the alcove reserved for servers and
listened keenly. He heard a sound, the clip of high-heeled boots
and the jingle of spurs. A figure emerged out of the murk and
Urswicke rose to clasp hands with George of Clarence before

leading him into the enclave, gesturing that he sit on the ledge opposite. Clarence, ever watchful, sat down.

Urswicke opened the saddlebag he had brought across, took out four squat candles and, using his tinder, lit them, watching their flame leap fiercely. He then drew out the book of hours he had brought and laid this on the floor beside the candles. Clarence watched carefully before he rose, unstrapping his warbelt, placing it on the ledge beside him as he retook his seat.

'You are well, my Lord?'

'I am.'

'You came alone?'

'As you asked and as I promised.'

Urswicke nodded understandingly. It had been a week since his conversation with the countess, when they had discussed the secrets contained in the 'Titulus Regius'. Since then, he and Bray had been busy plotting, doing what they could to agitate the city fathers by demonstrating that the Lancastrian cause was not dead. Notices proclaiming this as a truth had been pinned to the cross in St Paul's churchyard and the Standard at Cheapside. All such declarations had warned about a coming time of deep distress and agitation. How fresh storms were brewing and how the House of York would not survive them. In the main, this had been Bray's work on behalf of Countess Margaret, who had urged them to stir the pot even if it was just for the sake of the stink.

'Well, Master Urswicke,' Clarence made himself more comfortable, flicking at the ash on his cloak, 'as you asked, I came alone.'

'Though you have men hidden away who could be with you if you wanted?'

'Of course, but your message was stark and clear. I was to come alone to this devastated church.' Clarence tapped his cloak. 'Of course, beneath this I carry a hunting horn.' He leaned forward, smiling through the gloom, so close Urswicke could smell his wine-drenched breath.

'And you carry that, my Lord, just in case matters do not proceed as smoothly as they should?'

'Master Urswicke, you are an enigma. I wonder, as do the whisperers, whom you really serve? Do you know, Master Christopher, we have a lot in common, don't we? You serve yourself and what do you hope to gain?'

'My Lord, I don't know, but when I find it I shall tell you.'

'And so matters will run smoothly?'

'Oh they will, they will,' Urswicke soothed, picking up the book of hours and handing it to Clarence. 'For you, my Lord, a gift, a pledge of my commitment to the way things should be. Now listen,' Urswicke, tapping the book of hours Clarence now held, repeated what he had told Countess Margaret and Master Bray. How the Three Kings and Oudenarde had written and concealed a chronicle narrating a series of devastating scandals about the House of York. How they had used the Barnabites who had sheltered here, to bring witnesses and other evidence to their chamber at The Sunne in Splendour. Urswicke, however, was careful. He made no reference to either Stillington or Joachim's involvement in the secret betrothal ceremony between Edward of York and Eleanor Butler. He also explained how he had found the identity of this woman. Amongst other things, her first name had been included in a prayer for former queens of England, whilst the surname Butler had also had been mentioned in a prayer for officials of the royal household. As for the Woodville woman, Urswicke explained how that was easy to guess, pointing out the references including a prayer for the royal family and, here again, Elizabeth Woodville's name had been cleverly delineated in a different-coloured ink.

Urswicke secretly congratulated himself for discovering further information over the last week, and he still believed he had not fully unearthed all the evidence that the 'Titulus' contained. Clarence, who had sat with that constant cynical smirk on his face, changed dramatically. He leaned forward, mouth slack, eyes blinking, lips moving soundlessly as he listened to Urswicke's revelations and the precise details he described. Urswicke, who had rehearsed his speech time and again during the preceding day, was almost word perfect, explaining how the Three Kings used their ink and styles of writing both to communicate as well as conceal their secret chronicle. Once he had finished, Clarence sat shaking his head, his face a mask of disbelief.

'By all the saints,' he breathed, 'of course I know some of this rumour, hearsay, tittle-tattle. I asked the Three Kings to investigate and they became as busy as ferrets searching out this person or that. They assured Mauclerc that they were gathering evidence, but nothing like this, the detail, the precision. According to this,' Clarence opened the book of hours Urswicke had handed him, 'my brother Edward has no claim to the throne, whilst his marriage to the Woodville bitch is nothing more than a pretence. The chronicle gives dates and times for this and that.'

'My Lord, I agree. In fact,' Urswicke decided to tell the truth, 'I suspect there is more hidden away here which I haven't found. Perhaps some other secret pattern but, for the moment, you have enough.'

'But why didn't the Three Kings inform me? Surely Mauclerc must have suspected?'

'My Lord, I shall come to that by and by. You do recognise what the "Titulus Regius" contains? It is called that,' Urswicke pressed on, 'because the secret chronicles, as I shall call them, mount a serious challenge about who in the House of York should wear the Confessor's crown.'

'Which is myself,' Clarence snapped.

'Of course, my Lord. Perhaps the Three Kings and Oudenarde were simply waiting for the correct moment to present you with the finished task. I think they were close to that, although,' Urswicke held up a hand, 'for all I know, there may have been fresh revelations about the duchess, your esteemed mother, or the true status of Elizabeth Woodville.' Urswicke pulled a face trying to conceal his elation at leading a man the countess hated along the path to judgement.

'What?' Clarence demanded.

'My Lord, I just wonder . . .' Urswicke, now thoroughly enjoying himself, pointed at the psalter. 'Your brother Edward, if he gave his troth plight to Eleanor Butler, did he do so to another woman? Think, my Lord, how the King has laid siege to many a noble lady who acted like the damsel in the tower, refusing to open their door until certain promises and assurances were made. Think, my Lord, reflect and remember. Refurbish your Secret Chancery. Use your trusted clerks to dig out fresh nuggets of gold, priceless information. My Lord you know the hymn,' Urswicke waved a hand, 'and I am sure you can sing it better than I.' Urswicke let his words trail away.

Clarence sat, licking his lips. He opened the book of hours

and hungrily leafed through its pages. Urswicke watched even as he strained his ears for any strange sound. The evening was drawing on. Urswicke felt satisfied with the way matters were progressing. He had prepared his lure, set his snare and he was confident that this arrogant lord would blunder deeper into the traps awaiting him.

'So.' Clarence put the book of hours down, though he continued to stare at it. 'We have the evidence about what happened in that chancery chamber but not the names of those responsible for killing my faithful retainers.'

'Faithful?'

'What do you mean?'

'As I have said, let's leave that for a while. However, my Lord, you know who is responsible for those deaths? From what I have learnt, it must be the work of your own brother, Richard of Gloucester, assisted by the taverner Tiptree. As for him, I suspect he's either dead or been spirited away to some remote part of this kingdom. Gloucester's name was certainly mentioned during the pretended abduction of Tiptree and his kin. I say "pretended", because Gloucester wanted to save that taverner from falling into your hands.'

Clarence nodded, rocking himself backwards and forwards. 'Little Dickon,' Clarence rasped. 'I shall deal with him soon enough. The Three Kings were correct: Anne Neville must disappear and that can be arranged.' He edged forward on the stone seat of the enclave, jabbing his finger in Urswicke's face. 'But come now. You talked of matters that you'd return to by and by. Well?' Clarence jibed. 'We have reached by and by. What is it? What do you have to tell me?'

'The Three Kings.' Urswicke chose his words carefully. 'They may have seriously considered that the chronicles they had collected could be passed on to others who would pay lavishly to be given such invaluable information.'

'Such as?'

'As I have said, Richard of Gloucester, the King himself, the Woodvilles, foreign powers hostile to this kingdom. After all,' Urswicke shrugged, 'successive kings of England have made great play of how the inheritance to the Crown of France, by due law and process, rightfully belongs to the Plantagenets, kings of this realm and their successors. Can you imagine the damage such opponents could inflict upon your house and its claims with this information? They would argue that the House of York has little or no right to the Confessor's crown, let alone that of France kept in its tabernacle at St Denis.'

'Do you think Gloucester's men seized a copy of the "Titulus Regius" when they murdered the Three Kings?'

'No. They may have hastily searched but they had little time and, as you can now see, the "Titulus Regius" is cleverly concealed.'

'And Mauclerc? You begged me to come alone and not inform him. Why?'

'I am very wary.' Urswicke pulled a face and shook his head to show he was uncertain about what he was about to say.

'Master Urswicke, tell me what you think.'

'Well, shouldn't the Three Kings have been better guarded? After all, Mauclerc – perhaps more than you and me – realised the importance of what the Three Kings were doing and yet, on reflection, your Secret Chancery had very little protection. Shouldn't Mauclerc have been more aware of Tiptree's treacherous nature? Didn't Mauclerc notice anything untoward in the days before those murders at The Sunne in Splendour? Or even afterwards? And the Barnabites who sheltered here or poor Spysin? Couldn't they have all been better guided and guarded? I concede that this is just petty suspicion, yet how many times, my Lord?' Urswicke fought to keep his face solemn, his voice low and sombre like that of any prophet of doom. 'How often do men play the Judas even to a most gracious lord such as yourself?' Clarence, who drank praise as if it was part of his birthright, nodded in agreement, his face so serious and knowing that Urswicke had to curb the laughter bubbling inside him.

'I am not,' Urswicke spoke slowly, 'saying Mauclerc cannot be trusted. However, my Lord, you asked me to investigate these mysteries. I simply put forward possible solutions as well as further questions which must be answered, sooner or later, now or in the future.'

Clarence, however, was lost in his own thoughts. He seized the book of hours and rose, pulling his cloak about him before imperiously extending his ring hand. Urswicke knelt and kissed the sharp diamonds which Clarence pushed against his lips.

'You,' Clarence whispered, 'have done me great service, Master Urswicke. Continue to keep a sharp eye on Mauclerc and, as for that little Beaufort bitch, the one you pretend to serve so faithfully, our enmity is to the death. You agree, Christopher?'

Urswicke clasped the proffered hand. 'My Lord,' he declared loudly, 'you have my solemn word on that.'

'You will be rewarded.' Clarence waggled his fingers. 'Until then.' And, spinning on his heel, Clarence left the sanctuary. Urswicke watched him go, listening intently. Once he was certain Clarence had left, he crossed to his hobbled horse, took the small wineskin and linen food parcel out of his saddlebags and returned to the enclave. Urswicke made himself comfortable and stared at the sack he'd also taken from his panniers containing the second copy of the 'Titulus Regius'. He and Bray had begged Countess Margaret to let them use this as bait, adding that on no account could it be found in their possession as it might prove to be their death warrants. Moreover, Urswicke had insisted, he had copied his own memoranda in a special cipher which summarised the secrets of the 'Titulus Regius'. Urswicke chewed his food, comforting himself that, when this business was done, he would dine on freshly caught salmon, grilled and sweetened with herbs, whilst both he and Bray would drink deep well past the chimes of midnight.

Urswicke reflected on what was happening in London. Bray continued to disseminate stories about the sanctity of the murdered martyr King Henry. Lancastrian sympathisers were still active in the city, spreading stories of unrest, fictitious or otherwise; about risings in Wales, landings on this coast or that, disturbances in the north under this rebel leader or another. Countess Margaret was determined on brewing this mischief. However, she was also determined to leave London to tend to her sick husband, adding that her two henchmen should continue their work before joining her in Woking.

Urswicke took a mouthful of wine, wondering what would happen to Sir Humphrey and whether Margaret would truly accept the hand and protection of Lord Stanley. Urswicke took another gulp of wine, heard a sound and stiffened. He put both food and wineskin away, got to his feet and walked to the edge of the sanctuary. A figure had appeared at the far end of the nave, carrying a shuttered lantern. Urswicke watched the three darts of light, one after the other. He returned, picked up one of the candles and turned, swaying it so the new arrival could clearly see the dancing flame. Again, the shuttered lantern replied with three sharp bursts of light. Satisfied, Urswicke walked back into the sanctuary. He placed the candle down and waited for the dark, shadowy figure to cross the sanctuary and join him.

'Good evening, my Lord.'

'And good evening to you, Master Urswicke.' Richard of Gloucester pulled down his visor and pushed back the hood of his cloak. He and Urswicke clasped hands, Gloucester taking the seat in the enclave, Urswicke sitting opposite, as he had with Clarence. Urswicke picked up the sack, took out the book of hours, cradling it as Gloucester made himself comfortable.

'I saw my brother Clarence leave. He had horsemen close by, hidden in a copse, you do know that?'

'As your men wait?'

Gloucester laughed softly. 'Whom do you really serve, Urswicke?' Gloucester beat his gauntlets against his thigh. 'Whom do you really serve?' He repeated. 'Me? Clarence? The King? Your father? The Beaufort woman?'

'All of them, because I serve myself, as do you.'

Again Gloucester laughed softly.

'You are wary, aren't you?' Urswicke pressed on. 'You are suspicious and rightfully so. Clarence is dangerous, but you fear other demons, don't you? Not your brother the King, but the Woodvilles who shelter behind Elizabeth the Queen, a greedy and ambitious horde of relatives led by the cunning Earl Rivers.'

'True, true,' Gloucester murmured. 'But as long as my brother the King lives and thrives, I am safely protected.' He laughed sharply. 'Which is more than can be said for my brother George. The King, Hastings and others are determined on that. I betray no secret as it must be obvious to everyone except George, that if he returns to his perjuring, his Judas ways, like a dog to its vomit, he will not be spared. So?'

Urswicke stared down at the ground. He was aware of the shadows of those who haunted this derelict place, those dark clouds of souls, gathering to watch. Something about Gloucester's words started an idea, like a hare that abruptly bursts out of a field of long grass. Something he must follow and pursue to its logical conclusion.

'Well, Master Urswicke? You have brought me to the ring, so dance we shall.'

'My Lord, we certainly shall.' Urswicke picked up the second copy of the book of hours and pressed it into Gloucester's hands. The prince glanced sharply at him. 'My Lord, hold that and let me tell you the tale it contains. For this is the "Titulus Regius", as well as evidence of your brother Clarence's malevolent mischief towards you, your brother, indeed his entire family. Now listen and listen well.'

Urswicke then described what he had already told to the countess, though, as with Clarence, he omitted any reference to Bishop Stillington and Brother Joachim. The Barnabites were simply described as couriers and messengers of the Three Kings and their accomplice Oudenarde. More starkly, he described the murders at The Sunne in Splendour as the work of Clarence, who was also responsible for the killing of Spysin. At that Gloucester held up a hand.

'Master Urswicke, I understand why Brother George should use my name to conceal his wickedness. But why would he kill five trusted henchmen?'

'Very easy,' Urswicke retorted. 'Your brother George is like a cock on a weather vane. He turns, he changes, according to whatever favourable wind is blowing. Yes?' Gloucester just nodded. 'I suspect,' Urswicke spread his hands, 'though I have very little evidence for this, that Clarence decided that the creators of this chronicle, the Three Kings and Oudenarde, as well as their courier Spysin, were no longer needed. Your brother George simply decided to remove them.' Gloucester, still holding Urswicke's gaze, nodded; the clerk noticed how the duke's fingers had fallen to the hilt of his dagger. 'No need, no need my Lord,' Urswicke soothed. 'I speak the truth, you know I do. Clarence has acted the Judas before and he will do so again. The "Titulus Regius" is complete, or almost so. Study it yourself. The Three Kings, Oudenarde and, I suspect, Spysin had served both their time and purpose, so Clarence's paid assassins, aided and abetted by his former retainer Tiptree, despatched them into the dark.

For all I know, Tiptree followed them. Who else could be responsible for their deaths? You certainly weren't. And who would use your name to conceal their act? Only Clarence, no one else.'

'This,' Gloucester lifted the book of hours, 'is cleverly and intricately done.' He paused. 'I will not indulge in any outburst but, believe me, Master Urswicke, I seethe at what you have told me. My brother George has impugned my father's blessed memory as well as my brother the King, not to mention my beloved mother. And yet, at the same time, if these revelations are true, then my brother should not be King and any male heir of his has no right to succeed.' He took a deep breath. 'Ah well, I agree. Clarence is as treacherous as a viper.'

'My Lord, if you are shocked, can you imagine what others would think? The Three Kings knew that. They could sell such information to any lord both within this realm and beyond.' Urswicke paused; for a brief flicker of time he noticed a shift in Gloucester's eyes, a tightening of the mouth, as if concealing a smile. 'Tell me, my Lord,' Urswicke decided to gamble, 'did the Three Kings make an approach to you?' Gloucester glanced away. 'My Lord?'

'Recently,' he replied. 'They began to show great friendliness to my henchman Francis Lovel. Chance meetings, or so they appeared to be, before and after Tewkesbury. Of course, I did wonder. Never mind.' Gloucester tapped the book of hours. 'Clarence thinks he has the only copy, yes?'

'Of course.'

'So where did you get this?'

'Hidden away at St Vedast where the Barnabites sheltered.'

'Were you responsible for the destruction of this church and the old priest's house?'

'Yes, along with others of Clarence's household. Mauclerc had decided that they too had outlived their usefulness. They all had to die; that's when I finally concluded that the deaths at The Sunne in Splendour were also their work. That's logical isn't it?'

'Yes, yes,' Gloucester replied testily. 'But I still find it difficult to accept that my brother should silence so many faithful retainers.'

'My Lord,' Urswicke silently prayed that his nimble wits would protect him from stumbling into a mistake, 'think about what has happened. Tewkesbury was a great victory. Your brother is now King triumphant. The Lancastrians are in utter disarray . . .'

'Even though their proclamations appear all over the city, whilst treasonable chatter and gossip are rife throughout London and the shires? Weeds grow faster than the grass.'

'That will pass,' Urswicke retorted. 'George of Clarence couldn't care about such nonsense. He realises Tewkesbury was a decisive victory. He would like to shut the door on the past. Seal off all memories about his days with the House of Lancaster. Above all, he has the "Titulus Regius". You know Clarence, my Lord? Once he has no need of you, then God help you. Think of all those mouths silenced. Think of the Three Kings. they nurtured scandal about your family, did this also include Clarence?'

'I agree,' Gloucester scratched the side of his face, 'the Three Kings, Oudenarde and the Barnabites were all involved in the creation of the "Titulus Regius". But why Spysin?'

'A household courier, my Lord, sent here and there by Clarence with this message or that. Words committed to memory which Spysin would never forget.' Urswicke schooled his features to conceal his enjoyment at this dangerous game of hazard. 'Rumour has it that Spysin was to be despatched abroad. Was he being sent out of the way? Did Clarence change his mind and decide on a more lasting solution? Remember, Spysin was a messenger, he would know a great deal, perhaps too much for comfort. Moreover, we must not only think of Clarence but also his henchman Mauclerc. He too joined his master in deserting the House of York and entering the Lancastrian camp. Mauclerc is a killer. He would not tolerate a clacking tongue or, indeed, anyone who might prove to be a threat.' Gloucester nodded his head in silent agreement. Urswicke decided to change the flow of conversation.

'And the other matter, my Lord? The possible disappearance of Anne Neville. I saw your grimace as I described what the Three Kings recommended. It could prove a great blow to your ambitions.'

'Yes, and I must deal with that, though it's difficult. The Lady Anne lives with her sister Isobel who, of course, is Clarence's wife. Since the death of her father, Anne clings very close to Isobel. Consequently it would be easy for Clarence to arrange matters against her and very difficult for me to offer protection.'

'True, that is a matter for you, my Lord. I have told you what I have learnt. You know how to unlock the cipher within the book of hours and read its contents.' Gloucester weighed the book in his hands, staring quizzically at Urswicke.

'What you say is logical,' he declared, 'and yet . . .?'

'Yet what, my Lord?'

Gloucester, head back, peered under half-closed eyes at Urswicke. 'Something is not right,' he whispered. 'Something is very wrong. Never mind. Not for now.' Gloucester chewed the corner of his lip. 'I shall ask my most trusted clerk to translate and transcribe,' he touched the book of hours, 'what is hidden here. Once that is completed, I shall reflect.' He turned and spat into the darkness. 'I shall certainly teach George a lesson. How dare he dishonour my parents!'

'And what about my mistress, the countess? I have loyalties to her and she must see me working on her behalf?'

'I will protect her interests from both within and without,' Gloucester replied. 'I shall use my influence to advance her affairs with my brother the King. You have my word on that, Urswicke.' Gloucester, gripping the book of hours, rose and walked out of the sanctuary, through the ruined church wall to where his horse stood hobbled in the cemetery.

Urswicke listened until he was sure his visitor had truly left. He then returned to his place, picked up the lighted candle, and went to stand in the gap in the church wall. He stood holding the candle, its flame fluttering vigorously in the night breeze. He waited until he heard the three harsh calls of a night bird echoing across the desolate cemetery. He smiled in satisfaction and strode back to the apse, where he waited for Bray, all cloaked and hooded, to join him.

'So the fish rose to the bait?'

'Faster than I thought,' Urswicke replied. 'I personally took messages to Clarence and Gloucester inviting them here. Clarence now thinks he has the only copy of the "Titulus Regius" but, of course, Gloucester and ourselves know different. All we can do is wait and see what happens. Both brothers are fired with bounding ambition. Gloucester at least has honour and talent but Clarence truly is a midnight soul absorbed with himself. But listen, my friend,' Urswicke gripped Bray's shoulder, 'to a possible future.' Urswicke sat down in the enclave, Bray opposite.

'Your story, Master Christopher?' Bray demanded, pushing back his hood and loosening the chain on his cloak.

'Oh, so many threads to pull. What if we abduct the Lady Anne Neville, hide her away but make it known that Clarence is responsible? We'd send Gloucester on a wild hunt through the taverns and nunneries of both this city and the kingdom. He would be furious. The rift between him and Clarence would deepen and, of course,' Urswicke paused to laugh softly, 'we could also be the ones who secretly find her and so enhance our relationship with my Lord of Gloucester.'

Bray rubbed his face and grinned at Urswicke. 'The countess is correct about you, Christopher. Your mind constantly teems with mischief, most of it on her behalf – why?'

'You know why. The debt I owe her cannot be measured. I shall never forget her kindness to my darling mother or to me. Such a memory burns like a flame within me.'

'And where does that flame lead you now?'

'Why, Master Reginald, to Edward of York, our warrior King. He is the vital piece in this never-ending game of chess. Clarence is dangerous but he is also a fool. He'll make his move and he will fail. This time Edward of York will not prevaricate. Brother or not, Clarence's head will roll, and so the stage will be cleared.' Urswicke turned and stared into the dark. 'Only Edward and his younger brother Gloucester will remain.'

'They are very close. Richard adores his elder brother.'

'Aye and so he does, but he hates the Woodvilles and they respond in kind. Now Master Reginald,' Urswicke plucked at Bray's sleeve, 'imagine you are Gloucester: as long as your crowned brother lives, you are safe from the deadly malice of the Woodvilles. But what if Edward suddenly dies, what would happen then?'

'Edward's heirs?'

'If he has a male issue which survives and, even if the boy does, at this moment in time, it would be a further fifteen or sixteen years before he becomes an heir in his own right.'

'A regency?'

'Of course, but who? As I suggested, if you were Richard of Gloucester, would you tolerate a Woodville regency, men like Earl Rivers and his host of greedy kinsmen? If cornered, if he was threatened and isolated, would Duke Richard reflect on what

I have handed him today? Why should he wait for the Woodvilles
to strike? Why should he accept his brother's heirs, who,
according to the "Titulus Regius", are the offspring of an invalid
marriage in the eyes of Holy Mother Church? Such children
would be illegitimate bastards, as perhaps his elder brother may
have been, not the offspring of Richard of York but the by-blow
of some lowborn captain of archers. If that is the case, and
Clarence is gone, Richard is the legitimate heir. Master Reginald,
it's just a theory like those you propose in the schools of Oxford.
What if this happens . . .? What if that happens . . .?'

'Our mistress is correct,' Bray whispered, 'a pot of mischief
is being brewed, thickened and boiled in the heat of deadly
rivalries; that pot will bubble over and all this will end in blood.'

'Aye,' Urswicke agreed. He rose, tightening his warbelt, 'this
will end in another Tewkesbury, the horrid clash of battle.' He
stood up. 'Pray God we have victory that day because this truly
is *à l'Outrance* – to the death.'

# AUTHOR'S NOTE

*Dark Queen Rising* is of course a work of fiction, but it is based on historical evidence.

- The Battle of Tewkesbury is as described in the narrative. Somerset did kill Wenlock for refusing to commit his forces. The fighting in the abbey and the summary trials and bloody executions which followed did take place, Edward of England watching the proceedings from an upstairs window of the house he was sheltering in. If you visit Tewkesbury today you can still see marks of violence in the abbey and, according to local tradition, even the faded bloodstains where the Lancastrian Prince Edward was stabbed to death.
- Margaret of Anjou and her son were captured. Edward, of course, was immediately killed. Margaret was imprisoned in the Tower and eventually released, returning home due to the good offices of the French King.
- I believe the personalities of King Edward and his two brothers Clarence and Richard have been accurately conveyed. Richard was completely loyal to both his brother and House but Clarence seemed to be constantly attracted to treachery and betrayal.
- My description of the flight of Jasper Tudor and Henry to Brittany is a work of fiction but I have never really understood the published version, that somehow or other, young Henry was allowed to slip out of Pembroke and safely journey across the Narrow Seas.
- The 'Titulus Regius' is not a work of fiction. The scandalous stories mentioned in the narrative did eventually emerge into the public forum due to Clarence's treacherous meddling as well as Richard of Gloucester's attempts to protect himself in the hurling days following the sudden death of his brother, King Edward IV. Eleanor Butler, Bishop Stillington, the stories about Duchess Cecily and the disappearance of Warwick's daughter, Anne, are mentioned by the chronicles of the time.

- I have tried to faithfully convey the personality and attitude of Margaret Countess of Richmond: her three marriages, her love of her manor at Woking and her constant patronage of the arts. Cambridge University, in particular, owes a great debt to Countess Margaret. Reginald Bray and Christopher Urswicke were principal members of her household. Some people even regard Urswicke as the founder of the British Secret Service.

- Finally, the murder of Henry VI, is I believe based on the evidence available. As regards the possible desecration of his corpse, I refer you to 'The Discovery of the Remains of King Henry VI in St George's Chapel at Windsor Castle', a report drawn up by W. H. St John Hope and published in Volume 62 of the learned journal, *Archaeologia* (London, 1911). A most interesting passage from a report by a leading physician at the time reads as follows:

*5 November 1910.*
*The following report contains all the information gathered from the skeleton which I examined yesterday.*

*The bones are those of a fairly strong man, aged between forty-five and fifty-five, who was at least 5ft. 9in. in height (he may have been an inch taller, but I give the minor limit).*

*The bones of the Head were unfortunately much broken, but as far as they could be pieced together they were thin and light, and belonged to a skull well-formed but small in proportion to the stature. Some of the roof bones (occipital and temporal, frontal and parietal) had become ossified together at the sutures. The few teeth found (second molar upper right, and first molar upper left, second bicuspid lower right) had their crowns very much worn down. The portion of the one side of the lower jaw found had lost its teeth some time before death.*

*There were nearly all the bones of the trunk, of both legs, and of the left arm; but I found no part of the right arm.*

*From the relative positions occupied by the bones, as they lay in the leaden casket when opened, it was certain that the body had been dismembered when it was put in. If the body had been buried in the earth for some time and then exhumed, it would account for their being in the condition in which we found them. It might also account for the absence of the bones of the right arm, as well as for the accidental enclosure of the left humerus of a small pig within the casket.*

*I am sorry that I can add nothing more. The state of the bones was so unsatisfactory that I could not make any trustworthy measurements.*

© Paul Doherty OBE November 2017